1

Brothers of Texas Trilogy

Romantic Suspense

Who Killed Brigitt Holcomb?

Rosie Won't Stay Dead

Deception at Fairfield Ranch

Tamara G. Cooper

Table of Contents

Dedicated with love
to my mother,
June Parsons Gallagher,
for her unwavering love and encouragement.

A Navy WAVE in World War II;
a hiker with my father, Edgar Louis Gallagher, over
thousands of miles of wilderness trails;
an avid reader who encouraged her five children
to read, study hard, and work hard;
the sixth of ten children, six of whom
served our country in the military;
a woman who never gave up, a shining light
to the many people who knew and loved her.

She was the most remarkable person
I have ever known.
Now, she is with Daddy in Heaven—united again
with the love of her life—and with her
Lord and Savior, Jesus Christ.

.

Who Killed Brigitt Holcomb?

ONE

A breeze whispered a welcome to Marianne.

Standing on the bottom rail of the ranch gate, she looked out over her inheritance. *Freedom. Escape. Independence.* She imagined the words as tumbleweeds rolling playfully across the open land. With a quick smile, she thought she could add two more words: *anticipation* and *hope.* She'd dreamed of running away so many times. She couldn't believe this was real, a new home and a new life just handed to her, far from the ugliness waiting for her back in Abilene.

She was sure not many people would consider this flat landscape with few trees or vegetation as a boon, but Marianne did. In this part of the Texas panhandle, no houses or buildings or mountains or hills blocked her view in any direction. It was all beautiful, and two thousand acres of it were now hers.

As an artist, she could live anywhere. But here, in ranching country, the breeze seemed to whisper, "This is it. You belong here." And the best part? Her parents were three hours away. She had dreamed of living far, far away from them but never actually thought she would.

All of this seemed too good to be true.

Not a soul was around. Far off in the distance, cattle standing among oil rigs bobbing to the rhythm of the wind were her only company. Feeling a little silly, she waved at them and laughed, and then breathed in the Texas heat as her head fell back. Nothing but the peaceful silence of nature surrounded her. What could be more welcoming?

"You plannin' on jumpin' that gate, ma'am?"

The man's voice startled her. She tried to turn toward it, but her right sandal slid off the rail. She shrieked as she fell and threw out her hand to stop from landing face first in the gravel. The impact jarred her, and she rolled onto her shoulder, then her back, gasping for her next breath.

A door slammed. Crunching steps—running steps—were getting closer. "Ma'am, are you okay?"

The man's arm slid under her shoulders as he grabbed her hand and tugged her to her feet. When he released her, her foot slid out of her sandal, and her ankle twisted. "Oh! This gravel!"

"Yes, ma'am." The tall cowboy gripped her shoulders and held her while she put her shoe back on. She looked up at him and found him staring at her feet. Somehow, she was embarrassed that her toenails were painted bright pink with purple polka dots.

"Are you hurt?"

"I'm fine." She pulled away from him and brushed *stuff* off her hands and clothes. "Do you always sneak up behind women and scare the living daylights out of them?" When he said nothing, she looked up at him.

He was trying to hide a grin behind his huge fist, but he wasn't doing a very good job of it. "I've never known a truck that could sneak anywhere, ma'am. I'm sure sorry I scared you."

"Well. I-I was so caught up in the beauty of the land that I didn't hear you. Thank you for your help."

"No problem. I stopped because of your shoes."

My shoes? "What's wrong with my shoes?" She'd paid several hundred dollars for these Jimmy Choo strappy sandals. They were perfect with her cropped linen trousers.

"If you're plannin' on jumpin' that gate or walkin' anywhere on Tucker Spring Ranch, you might consider the rattlers." He pointed at something behind her.

She turned around. A yellow traffic sign standing about five feet down from the gate post had "Watch for Rattlesnakes" written on it in big, black letters.

"With October pourin' on the heat like this, rattlers and other venomous creatures are out and about in droves. Those shoes are no protection against them." The man raised his thick black brows in an expression that said 'tenderfoot' as much as if he'd spoken the words.

"I didn't come up here planning to jump a gate. I thought I'd be *civilized* and *drive* up to my house."

"You're the new owner, Marianne Glaze?"

"I am. And you are?" His eyes were the color of the water around Maui—exactly the same blue. His black hair, thick black brows, and curly eyelashes made them even more alluring.

He stretched out his hand. "Mac McKenzie, owner of the ranch surrounding your two thousand acres." His warm hand engulfed hers, then he tightened his grip and let go.

"How do you know my name, Mr. McKenzie?"

"From your Uncle Cecil's attorney. We've been friends for years." He nodded at her feet. "Boots 'll protect your feet, ankles, and legs. Those

10

shoes are just about worthless in this terrain."

His gaze was so intense, she looked down at her feet. "I appreciate the advice."

"My pleasure."

"Excuse me." She needed to get her purse and the gun inside it. A woman could never be too careful, especially one out in God only knew where with a man she didn't know. As she walked quickly to her car, she glanced back at him. Mac McKenzie didn't seem tensed and ready to hurt her. Actually, he didn't seem threatening at all.

"A Jaguar XJ." He nodded approvingly at her car. "First time I've ever seen one. They're fast and sleek. Is it a V8?"

She plucked her purse out of her car and shut the door. "Yes, it is. Did you know my Uncle Cecil, Mr. McKenzie? I didn't even know he existed until today."

The attorney's letter arrived at noon, announcing her inheritance. At twelve-fifteen, she called her uncle's lawyer and spoke with his assistant. Marianne was told that papers needed to be signed and keys picked up. By one o'clock, she'd sufficiently put her excessively regimented nature on hold enough to let simple curiosity rule the rest of her day. She wanted to see her property, so she packed and left.

"Yes, I knew Cecil Tucker, and so did you." Mac McKenzie smiled, slow and easy. "I remember the day you told him you wanted his land. You were about four or five. You stood on the old bridge, pointed your finger at him, and told him in no uncertain terms that he needed to get rid of the cows because they were stinky and made too much noise."

What was this man talking about? She'd never been to this ranch. "I'm afraid you've mistaken me for someone else."

"Not at all. You told your uncle that someday, when this place was yours, you were going to take that bridge apart"—here, he lifted his hands and made quote marks in the air—"piece by piece." He looked funny throwing his head side to side with each word. She could imagine a little girl, a little *bossy* girl, making those same moves. He laughed then. "You were a cute, freckle-faced, pigtailed little girl. You knew what you wanted and weren't afraid to tell your Uncle Cecil all about it."

"Well." She wasn't quite sure how she should respond to him. He was, of course, teasing her by telling such a silly story. She wasn't above playful banter, but she didn't know this man. So, she said nothing more.

"You called your uncle's house a place for wishes."

"Did I?" The man's story had a certain ring of truth to it except, maybe, for the twinkle in his eye when he told it. "And what did you call it?"

"My second home. I was clobbered over here more times than I care to remember. I'm the youngest of eight sons."

"Eight boys? Your poor mother."

"Yeah." He grinned at her. "She's one tough lady. Back in the day, your brother Patrick and my brother Tim were pretty tight. How is Patrick?"

"He's doing well, thank you."

"Are you aware the locals say your house is haunted?"

Haunted? "No. I haven't spoken with any locals." *But a place for wishes shouldn't be haunted.*

"Your Uncle Cecil moved to Florida seventeen years ago." Mac McKenzie leaned against her car. "He returned once, seven years back, and then disappeared. Someone found his body recently in a deep ravine with a single bullet hole right between his eyes. But I'm sure you know all this."

Shock washed over her, and she stepped back. She knew nothing about a *murder!* "He was killed?" Her words were barely above a whisper.

"I'm sorry, Marianne. I thought you'd know by now."

She slowly shook her head. Her throat was so tight, she could hardly breathe. Her first thought was that she needed to leave. To go. To run. *Now!*

Her second thought was that she couldn't run away, not when she was so close to escaping. "Who killed him?"

"No one knows."

A slow-crawling shiver moved across her neck as if the fingers of a ghost caressed her. "The attorney's letter didn't mention killings or haunted houses."

"I don't expect a legal letter would mention those particulars. That house has a wounded past. Do you remember being there on your uncle's property?"

Being there? Of course not. "I've never been to this area."

Mac stared at her for a moment. "Tuckers have owned this land for over a hundred years. Your family stopped coming here after the murder of your cousin seventeen years ago."

A headache stabbed at her right temple. *Two family members were murdered up here?*

Her stomach clenched. She patted her pants pocket for the antacids she always kept available. If she popped two, the discomfort sometimes abated. But she wouldn't do it in front of a stranger. She would not show him weakness.

The last thing she ever wanted, in any shape or form, was dealing with conflict or emotional issues. She'd learned to keep her feelings hidden, releasing them only in private, away from the critical eyes of her parents—or anyone else, for that matter. Give her a strict schedule and complete control over it, and she flourished.

So, how did she fit two family murders into her well-ordered world?

"I see I've thrown you a curve, Marianne. If you don't have plans for supper, you're welcome to join me at my ranch. Maybe we can fill in some of the gaps in your history." He pointed west. "The entrance to the main house is down the road about a half a mile. Say, in an hour? You can clean up at the ranch if you'd like."

We? So, he's married, although he wasn't wearing a ring.

She sighed deeply. She didn't want to spend time with anyone right now. When she glanced around, she didn't see the beautiful world she'd loved when she first arrived. She saw only a setting for murder.

The white tip of her dog's tail wagged above the tall grass as her little beagle made a path through it, a reminder that there was still so much to explore, so much to see. Maybe tonight, the McKenzies could give her answers to the questions she'd had since receiving the inheritance letter today: who was her Uncle Cecil and why had her mother kept his existence a secret? Three more obvious questions needed answers now. Who killed her cousin and her uncle? Why? And were their murders connected somehow?

"Marianne?"

"Oh. Yes. Sorry, wool gathering. I'll be there, Mr. McKenzie."

"Mac. Everyone calls me Mac."

He drove off. She stared at his truck, knowing now was a point of decision for her. Should she drive away or should she jump the gate? Both appealed to her, but one was weakness; the other, strength. At the very least, she should check out the house and the land before she decided anything. "Nuggets! Come on. Let's go!"

Her dog ran through the tall grass, through the gate, and danced around her legs.

"Well, sweetie, I don't know what to think about our inheritance trip so far. Two relatives are dead, at least one murderer is still out there, and our house is haunted. So, first on our list is finding out who's haunting our house. Have I ever told you that I've always wanted to paint a haunted house?"

Nuggets barked at the big, black padlock.

"Yes, I see it's locked. But we didn't drive three hours up here to be defeated by an inhospitable gate." She retrieved her gun and placed it in the fanny pack holster, tossed her purse in the car, and locked it. After she'd slipped on the pack, she said, "It can't be too far, sugar bug. Just down this old lane and over that rise. Come on. Let's go."

Mac McKenzie was right.

Her sandals didn't protect her tender feet from the heavy gravel hiding beneath the scraggly weeds. Her ankle hurt, and her feet throbbed in pain. She eyed the treetops that seemed to sit on the rise in front of her. "Just another fifty feet or so, Nuggets. It appears there's quite a drop in elevation after we reach the top."

She considered stepping into the knee-level brush at the side of the path to give her feet some relief. But she imagined all kinds of ticks and crawling creatures clinging to the blades, waiting for their supper to walk by. Not to mention all those rattlers and venomous creatures out and about in droves.

She decided against it.

At the top of the rise, she caught her first glimpse of the house below and gasped. "I know this place, Nuggets."

She quickly scanned the house, the yards, the broken-down fence, the trees surrounding the property. "There was a tire rope behind the house." She hurried around back and found a frayed cord hanging from a branch. It was swift, the memory. Hugging herself, laughter bubbled up inside her.

She was a little girl again, swinging on the tire.

Summer heat. Cicadas and crickets buzzing and chirping. Gentle hands against her back, pushing her to fly higher. "Grab aholt, sweetheart." A deep voice. "Hang on tight."

My father?

She doubted it. Franklin Donovan Glaze had never taken the time or energy to push her on a swing, and he'd certainly never been inclined to call his only daughter an endearing name like 'sweetheart.'

Uncle Cecil, then?

She turned toward the house and studied it. The roof was damaged. The top of an immense oak lay across it as if the afternoon heat had coaxed it into a nap. Green shutters on the two-story farmhouse were faded now, some hanging by a thread, it seemed, from the crushed window frames under the oak. Peeling, dull-white paint exposed bare gray wood underneath. Several windowpanes were broken or missing. A ragged curtain fluttered through one window in a frantic dance as if it struggled to escape the house, but something kept pulling it back inside.

"Come look at these cricket frogs, Mari!"

With a big smile, Marianne spun toward the child's long-ago voice.

In her mind's eye, a creek ran below the fence. Large healthy post oaks hovered protectively on both sides. She closed her eyes as she felt the little girl run in answer to the command, careful to shut the gate when someone hollered for her to do it.

Where had these memories been hiding? Marianne had never felt as if she belonged anywhere. But here, on this property, she'd had friends to play with and a place where she was accepted.

She turned back to the house. She saw herself as a little girl, sitting on the concrete steps, eating watermelon and laughing with someone. Then she was alone and suddenly afraid. Her dress was wet and sticky with melon juice. "Can't you do anything right?" Her mother's voice behind her, hot with anger. Strong fingers gripped her shoulder. When she pulled away, her dress ripped. She ran toward the creek, crying. Her mother yelled, "You get back here right now, you little snot!"

But she didn't. She ran and ran until she reached the old bridge. "Nobody uses it anymore," a man had told her. When she started to dance across the bridge, he motioned her back. "That's McKenzie land, sugar bug. Tuckers stay on this side of the creek."

The little girl stood in the almost dark by the bridge, hidden by trees, so afraid of the coming night. Just enough light was left that she could make out the McKenzie's big log house in the wide valley in the distance. While she stared at it, outside lights came on. She wanted to sit on the big wrap-around porch and smell the pretty flowers clustered around the edge of the house.

But she knew she couldn't.

She slid down the bank, crawled under the bridge, and closed her eyes. Dark came quickly, and then she was too afraid to leave. Something rustled behind her. She shuddered and started crying again, quietly, so her mother wouldn't find her.

"You're all right now, sweetheart." The same voice at the swing. Large hands picked her up, and hard arms held her tightly. "I've got you. No one's going to hurt you. Uncle Cecil's going to see to that."

Oh! She remembered him! He was big. He wore overalls at the ranch. Every time he greeted her, he'd say, "Wuh, hello there, sugar bug." He'd growl and tickle her, and she'd laugh and giggle so hard.

Her heart felt so full. Uncle Cecil had loved her. He knew this place would be a safety net if she needed it. Even now, he was protecting her from her parents.

Why would anyone kill this gentle, kind man?

"We're keeping this place, Nuggets. We'll fix it up and live here. Out with the old and in with the new, huh? We're losing light so let's check out the house while we can still see."

Nuggets joined her as she walked to the front of the house. Many of the gray, swaybacked wood slats on the porch were broken or missing. A full-sized porch swing no longer hung by two steel threads but rested upside-down amidst beer cans, trash, and leaves hugging the porch wall as if to escape a looming garbage truck.

Marianne looked through the dusty windows. The inheritance letter had mentioned that Uncle Cecil left the house as he'd lived in it, but it was trashed now. Furniture was overturned, books pulled from shelves, papers strewn everywhere, drawers pulled out as if someone was looking for something.

Carefully, she walked across the porch and headed toward a towering oak at the corner. She fingertipped it as she walked around it, breathing in the scents of wood, dirt, and dried-up grass. She closed her eyes and remembered swinging on the porch, summer days, playing, laughing.

She stopped.

Something dark.

Something very bad.

Bone-chilling grief all around her. Crying, confusion, people rushing about, some shouting, wailing, screaming. She was afraid. Was it her fault? Why were they looking at her like that?

Marianne lowered her head and pressed shaking fingertips to her forehead, trying hard to see more. Her chest ached from the rush of painful memories.

Nuggets nudged her. Marianne sank to her knees and hugged her. "I'm all right, sweetie. Just so much heartache here. Did I cause it? Am I responsible for this hole in my mother's family?"

Nuggets glanced warily at the house. Marianne nodded. "I agree. We'll see it tomorrow."

She tugged out her phone, checked the time, and slipped it back into her pocket. "We need to leave if we're going to get to the McKenzie's home on time. C'mon." She headed up the drive and motioned for Nuggets to follow.

Typical of a beagle, she scurried up the rise, sniffing and exploring. Just as she reached the top, she whipped around with a worried expression and froze, staring at something below them. And then she growled, low and steady.

"What is it?" Marianne picked up her pace. When she reached Nuggets, she glanced down at the house. Evening's murky colors had settled around it, painting it with deepening hues of gray. A shadow moved past a window.

Marianne gasped. "Someone's in the house!"

Nuggets whined.

A car backfired, twice.

No! *Oh, God. Oh, God.* Someone was shooting at them!

"Nuggets!" Marianne ducked, started running, and tried to wriggle her phone out of her pocket, but it slipped to the ground as she darted down the other side of the rise.

Frantic, she searched for cover.

But there was no place to hide.

Mac rested his shoulder on the window frame near his desk, grateful for the turn of events that might land him what he wanted.

His family had waited years to buy the land they'd lost. A natural canyon bordered most of McKenzie Lake, making it impossible to get cattle to it any other way but across Tucker land. Cecil Tucker's great-great-grandfather won those two thousand McKenzie acres in a poker game. He had allowed passage, as had the two generations following him.

But not Cecil Tucker. When he inherited, he fenced the property and refused every inflated offer Dad made for his land or for crossing it. Even after he moved to Florida seventeen years ago, Cecil wouldn't change his mind.

Tanks were drying up. Mac needed water without the expense of more drilling. He needed the underground spring that fed into his lake. He needed his lake.

When Dad gave him the ranch two years ago, Mac vowed to prove that his trust in him was deserved. But Dad didn't live to see it. He was murdered eight months ago.

A hot, seething anger rushed over Mac, the swiftness and intensity of it shaking him to his core. Deep breaths no longer helped; he had to concentrate—hard—on making it stop. Sometimes, he was successful. Other times, he wanted to crush something before he let the anger go.

He hated the power the killer had over him. At a moment's notice, despair could overwhelm Mac. At other times, helplessness. But most of the time, anger ruled because there were no answers to the one question he asked every day: why?

"A squeaky-clean crime scene doesn't give us anything to go on," the sheriff, Nate Hanover, had told him. "And the bullet's not in the database."

It gnawed at Mac, night and day. Who had killed his dad, and why?

"Did your father have any enemies?" Nate had asked him.

Enemies? Of course not. Gerald McKenzie was a kind, giving man who would shuck the shirt off his back for anyone—even an enemy, if he'd had one. It hurt so much, the injustice of knowing his father lay cold in the ground while his killer was still free.

Frustrated, Mac turned from the window. He knew the anger would subside if he could get his attention on something else. Right now, he needed to concentrate on making Marianne Glaze an offer she couldn't refuse. Then he could tear down that eye-sore of a house and open up the land for his cattle.

He hadn't planned on personally meeting the new owner of Tucker's place or inviting her to supper. He preferred working through attorneys to keep negotiations on a professional level, especially if things got messy. But he'd stumbled upon her, standing on that gate rail in worthless shoes that just begged a snake to strike. He'd felt obliged to stop, to give her advice that might save her life.

A corner of his mouth slowly lifted.

Marianne Glaze might not know much about living in ranch country, but one thing he could say about her? She was sure easy on the eyes. Tall and shapely with her reddish-copper hair pulled back in a long ponytail. Pretty green eyes. A soft mouth that hesitated a moment or two before it stretched into a cautious smile. That cultured voice with just a touch of 'feisty' in it.

He couldn't help but admit that he liked what he'd seen. But a vision of beauty or not, he needed her land. He'd gladly pay more than top dollar for it.

He walked into Helen's office and placed some papers on her desk. "When Marianne sells, we'll have a fighting chance of outlasting this blasted drought."

"When? Aren't you counting those chickens a little early, boss?"

"Maybe. But what would a city girl do out here in the middle of cattle country? I've invited her for supper to talk about selling. I hope you'll join us."

"I will. I've been looking forward to this day longer than you have, Mac. You know that."

Marianne had never been so afraid in her life. Shudders racked her body. Her heart raced, and she could hardly breathe. When she tugged Nuggets closer, her arms shook so violently, she thought she'd drop her.

They were nowhere near her car. They couldn't make a run for it; her ankle hurt, and the gunman was probably watching for them to move. "We'll have to stay here until dark, sweetie. Shouldn't be too long now."

Nuggets whimpered.

"Wh-what is it, girl? Is he coming?" Marianne didn't think it was possible, but her heart beat harder, faster. Her dog sniffed the air, squirmed out of her arms, darted through the weeds, and hit the gravel path at a run, turning left toward the rise.

"Nuggets, come back here!" Marianne crawled after her, swatting at the tall brush. Her knees and hands scraped against rocks and prickly plants. Grasshoppers jumped. Bugs flew at her. "Lord, help me." She had to get to Nuggets. "Please, please don't let him shoot her."

Near the gravel path now, she could hear her dog's frantic barking in the distance. She'd cornered something or someone. "Nuggets!" Sweat dropped into her eyes, and she swiped—

"Marianne?"

She shrieked and turned around. Mac McKenzie was walking toward her. "Mac, get down! Someone's shooting at us. He's in my house, and Nuggets just ran in his direction!"

He squatted and scanned the area. "Did you call 9-1-1?"

"I dropped my phone and had to leave it. Why are you here?"

"You didn't show for supper." He shook his head, looking around. "This makes no sense. As far as I know, no one's been on this property in years. Come on." He took her hand and tugged her up. "Let's get you to your car. I'll call 9-1-1."

They ran to the gate. Mac jumped over it; Marianne crawled through the rails. He headed for his truck while she opened her car door. When the inside light came on, she gasped and tried to make sense of the papers strewn all over her two front seats and on the floorboard. The glove compartment was open as was the console. Glass pebbles were everywhere. She looked at the passenger window. Someone had broken it, but a good portion of the shattered glass still hung from the window frame. Why was someone in her car, and what was he looking for?

She quickly glanced around outside as she took off her fanny pack holster. She'd watched enough crime shows to know that she shouldn't touch anything. She brushed off the seat and sat very still, racking her brain for why anyone would be in her car. Or, for that matter, why anyone would shoot at her.

Mac returned with a rifle and a camouflage vest with lots of pockets. "Sheriff was in our area. He said he could be here in a couple minutes." He bent over and looked at the passenger window and the papers. "Is anything missing?"

"I don't know. I had nothing but car-related papers in here."

"I need to go, Marianne. Do you have a gun?"

She held up the holster. "I'll be okay."

"Good. Stay low and stay alert." Mac left, jumped the gate, and hurried toward the rise.

In the last light of evening, she retrieved her gun. Her stomach fluttered as she held the weapon against her chest and lowered her seat to a sleeping position. She hoped she wouldn't have to use it. Easing up enough to see, she watched Mac use an outcropping of rock for cover and disappear behind it.

Her pulse beat hard against her temples as she waited for something to happen. Graveyard quiet surrounded her. Lying back in her seat, the large frame of the car window showcased the light gray sky. It was all she could see. She imagined a monster suddenly appearing in one of her windows or a man telling her to "get out of the car" with a gun pointed at her head.

She felt the fear crouching, ready to pounce, and it did. Trembling started in her stomach. Then her hands began to shake. Her whole body shivered. The longer she sat in the car with her imagination running wild, the more her body shook. A quivering hand on her stomach didn't help, nor did her attempts at taking a deep breath. She simply couldn't breathe deeply. The stifling heat felt like a hot blanket wrapped around her, with sweat rolling down her arms, legs, and back. She tugged up the hem of her blouse and wiped her face.

Her heart was beating too fast. She needed to get outside and run. Too much adrenalin. She needed to *run!* A littler desperately, she reached for the handle.

Then she heard something. The sound of an engine on the road! She tensed as it drew nearer. *Oh, God.* Gravel crunched. *He's here! The shooter's here!*

Breathing too quickly, she gripped the gun with shaking hands. Slowly, she sat up enough to see above the dashboard. A white truck door opened, and a starred emblem swung toward her. *Oh! The sheriff!* She let out the breath she held, so relieved.

A slim man got out, toting a rifle and wearing a beige uniform and cowboy hat. A similarly dressed but stouter man joined him in front of the truck. As they approached her car, she opened the console, placed the gun inside, shut it, and moved her seat up.

"Marianne Glaze?" His nametag said 'Nate Hanover.' He leaned over, his gaze roaming around the mess inside her car.

"Yes, sir."

The deputy, Lloyd Mercier, covered his left ear with his hand. "Yeah, Mac. We're here. She's fine. We're headed toward you. You see anything?" The deputy turned away and walked a few paces from them.

"Do you have any place to go, Miss Glaze?" the sheriff asked quietly.

"My dog's still out there. I can't leave her."

"Then stay down. Even with your window broken, locking your doors might slow someone down if he's bent on getting you. When he spots these trucks parked here, he'll probably leave you alone. You have a legal means of protection with you?"

"I do." She touched the console.

"Then we'll be back." They crawled over the gate and jogged toward the rise with their heads moving side to side like Marines scouting out enemy territory.

Being left alone in the Twilight Zone didn't appeal to Marianne. Something crawled on her arm. She screeched and then cringed at the loudness of it. With her arm out the window, she brushed the bug off.

A vehicle's wheels crunched on the gravel behind her. An engine revved. And then something exploded, the power of it slamming her body into the steering wheel!

Disoriented, she turned around and gasped. The grill of a truck covered her back window! She stared at it, trying to make sense of it being there. She frantically opened the console, grabbed her gun, and gripped it tightly as she watched the truck.

It backed up. Skidded to a stop. Sat like an angry bull, panting, staring at her. Then the engine revved. The tires began to spin. And it charged! She screamed and hunkered down against the console. It rammed her car—steel snarling against steel. It shoved her driver's door into the large gate post, shattering her window. She shrieked and covered her head as bits of glass pelted her.

The truck slowly backed up, circled around, and stopped. Its nose was aimed right at her passenger door. The engine roared. Tires spun. And then it raced toward her like a shark after blood. She screamed again and again as the truck rammed her door, shoved her car into the gate, bulldozed it open, and forced her car down the lane.

Suddenly, the truck stopped. It backed up.

Gasping for air, Marianne tensed for another strike, but it spun off, spitting gravel at her car.

Then silence surrounded her. Long, throbbing silence.

Oh, God. She whimpered and hugged herself. Every part of her body hurt. With ragged breaths, she tried to open her door. It wouldn't budge. She shouldered it and pushed, desperate to get out, but the door wouldn't open. All the windows were broken and crushed.

There was no way out.

Sobbing, shivering, she curled into a ball and wept. She tried to think of a prayer, but her brain was fuzzy. *So sleepy.* She closed her eyes and muttered a few words to God as the quiet night settled around her.

"Marianne?"

Wha—? She gasped and sat up quickly. A light came on and then shined in her eyes. She put her hand over her eyes to block it.

"Marianne?"

"Mac?" She must have fallen into a deep sleep because she hadn't heard anyone approach her car. It was black dark now. She heard men's voices; a truck's engine turned over; someone said, "Here, Mac." She wanted to cry, she was so relieved to see Mac.

"Are you okay?" He stood right beside her. It terrified her that people had walked around her car and she had slept through it. What if that man—?

"Marianne?"

"Yes, I'm okay. But I can't get out. My doors are stuck."

"I know. We tried all of them. I'm going to fold this blanket twice, place it on the door frame, and pull you out. Are you all right with that?"

"I am if I can fit through."

"You're slim. You'll fit." Mac cleared glass from the frame and covered it with the blanket. "Okay. Turn around, on your back. Head first. Be careful of glass in the frame. I tried to get all of it, but I might have missed a piece or two."

"Wait. There's my gun." She swiped it off the floorboard and handed it to Mac. "Okay. I'm ready."

With a gentleness that surprised her for such a large man, Mac touched her head, then her shoulders, and tugged her toward him. He lifted her upper body out the window. When she was sitting on the door frame, he placed an arm behind her back, moved her a little bit more out of the window, slipped his other hand under her knees, and picked her up.

Several lights were shining on them.

Mac stared at her face as if he searched for treasure. "Are you really okay?" How could a man's deep voice sound so gentle?

"Everything hurts, but I'm fine. Did you get the shooter?"

"No. We searched the outer perimeter, too, but he was gone. The house was ransacked." He headed toward a truck.

"It was that way when we looked in the windows earlier."

"Do you have any idea what he was looking for?"

"No. But I'm wondering how the shooter got away without anyone seeing him."

"There are two other entrances to your land."

He held her tight against his chest as if she weighed nothing. It felt so good to just let go and rest in his strong arms. As he turned around, she saw her car. Bright truck lights cut through the darkness, focused right on it. "What is happening here, Mac? Why did this man—? I can't, I don't—" Tears clogged her throat, and she couldn't speak.

"Open my truck door," he said to one of the men. "She's riding with me." He set her on the passenger side. "Make sure her dog gets to the ranch."

Swallowing down the tears, she managed to say, "My luggage is in my trunk."

"Jumbo, see if you can get her suitcases out of the trunk. We'll meet y'all at the ranch."

The sheriff walked up to Mac's truck. "I need to speak to her."

Mac turned to Marianne. "Can you answer some questions?"

"Yes, I'd like to get this over with."

A feeling of *déjà vu* passed over Marianne as Mac drove under bold black letters announcing MCKENZIE RANCH in a wide, solid-wood archway. Full-leafed trees lined the driveway on both sides. Something familiar about the long tunnel of trees. The paved lane. The big barn in the distance.

"Do you need to go to the hospital in Brennan?"

"I'm okay." She massaged the back of her neck. She squirmed against the ache in her shoulder and the stinging wounds on her hands, knees, and elbows. "Just banged up a little bit."

The air had thickened. The wind had picked up. A distant rumble caused her to look west where a serrated tongue of lightning licked the land and disappeared. "Looks like rain."

"None in the forecast. Just another lightning storm." Frowning, he glanced at her. "Describe the truck to me again."

"Black, with giant tires. A huge grill on the front. Do you think he's the shooter? Did he have time to drive from the Tucker house to where my car was parked?"

"There are three entrances to your property. One from our land and two off the highway. Yes, he had time to get to your car."

"But why shoot at me and smash my car?"

Mac's jaw clenched. "Seems to me he's trying to scare you away. Somehow, you're a threat to him. Or whatever he thought he'd find in your house or car is a threat." Mac shook his head. "I don't have any answers, but I know none of us want to see someone else hurt over there."

She shivered. "But wasn't Uncle Cecil killed in a ravine?"

When ominous white bolts streaked across dark clouds already rumbling with thunder, Mac's profile made her think of a Roman soldier, all angles and points. He glanced at her, his eyes dark as they reflected the steel gray of the stormy night. "Do you recall the last day your family was here?"

A flash of people crying, screaming, wailing crossed her mind. "I'm not sure."

"Do you remember your Aunt Helen?"

"Is she Uncle Cecil's wife?"

"His sister. Your mother's sister. She's lived at McKenzie Ranch for thirty-eight years. Her daughter Brigitt's body was found on your uncle's property—your property now—seventeen years ago. She was beaten to death."

TWO

Oh, God. Oh, God. Too much. Too much chaos. Nausea swirled. Marianne slapped a hand over her mouth and moaned. Mac had the presence of mind to stop, lean over, and push her door open. She lurched for the created space and threw up twice.

Sprawled across the seat, she hung her head, spit, and blinked tightly. *It was my fault. Her death was my fault.* "You were with her! What did you *do?*" Her mother's voice, so angry, so scary. Her flat hand rose, arched above her gritting teeth, her squinting eyes. She swung and hit the little girl hard on the face, the contact like stinging shards of ice.

In the truck, Marianne sat up. Her head literally throbbed.

She couldn't face Mac. The stench was horrible, the taste bitter. She was throwing up because somewhere deep in her subconscious mind, she thought she was responsible for her cousin's murder. But how could a five-year-old cause another person's death?

Still unable to look at Mac, she said, "I'm so sorry. I don't think I—" Perusing the door and the truck step affirmed what she'd thought. "I didn't get anything on it."

"I'm the one who's sorry. I shouldn't have been so blunt. But your reaction might explain why you forgot your uncle. The trauma of that last day probably caused you to block out everything up here."

"Seeing his property today stirred up a lot of memories for me. I remember him now." She shut the truck door, humiliated by the odor, and rolled down the window.

Mac looked in the back seat, and then ripped off his T-shirt. "Here. It's all I have. And your cell phone." He eased it out of his pocket and handed it to her.

Even though she had a brother and a father, she'd never sat in a vehicle with a man without a shirt on. "No, no. I'm fine, thanks." But she'd seen plenty. Good gracious, but ranch work looked good on Mac McKenzie.

Embarrassed, she averted her gaze to the spotlighted two-story log cabin—no, it was too huge to be called a cabin—a spotlighted log *mansion* not far in front of them.

"Take it." Mac placed the shirt on her lap, and then put the truck in gear. "I showered and changed for supper. It's relatively clean."

The truck crept toward the huge house. Even though it was made of logs, the house was beautiful, a lovely oasis in a land of not much green. Hanging flowerpots lined the porch. Deep red geraniums sat in several window boxes. Huge pots on the porch held beautiful, multicolored blossoms.

Mac stopped beside a shiny, black two-door Jeep. "Don't move. I'll get your door."

When she wiped her mouth, she caught his scent on the shirt, a touch of a somewhat outdoorsy sweet smell. She held the shirt to her nose and allowed her mind to slip back to the gravel road, to the warmth of his body seeping into hers and comforting her as much as the strength in his arms. She couldn't remember a time she'd felt so protected or anchored, even with all the turmoil around her.

She folded his shirt while she continued to admire the sprawling, two-story log mansion that he called home. Welcoming white wicker chairs sat on the wide wrap-around porch next to a large swing moving in the breeze.

Her door opened. As Mac offered her a hand, an older woman opened the main house door. She glanced at Mac's bare chest and then smiled broadly at Marianne.

Mac swept a hand in her direction. "Marianne, my secretary and your aunt, Helen Holcomb."

The wind tossed Helen's short, curly gray hair as she made an "Oh!" sound and hurried down the steps toward Marianne with her arms spread wide, as if a hug between them was natural and expected and wanted.

Marianne's eyes widened.

Under *no* circumstances did her family touch. *Ever.*

Her look didn't stop Helen Holcomb.

As tall as Marianne, her aunt engulfed her in a tight embrace and stepped back. "My, you've grown into a beautiful woman, Mari. And your red hair, so pretty and long. But—" She examined her nose. "No more freckles. The boys used to tease you unmercifully about them. Remember when Luke and Mac tried to get their dog, Trapper, to lick the spreckles off your face? That's what the boys called them. Oh! You were so angry, you ran to me and ordered me to hog tie them." She chuckled. "As if I could, even then."

Marianne stared at her aunt and turned slightly to put some distance between them. Aunt Helen didn't act like someone bent on getting back at the person responsible for her daughter's death. She must not know. It made no sense, though, that her mother hadn't told her sister about it. Any chance Barbara Glaze stumbled upon to crush her only daughter, she did, with relish.

But if Helen didn't know, then why this disconnect in her mother's family?

Smiling warmly, her aunt touched her arm. "You don't remember me, do you?"

Marianne slowly shook her head.

"I'm your Uncle Cecil's sister, and your mother's sister."

Marianne studied her face. She favored Barbara except for the gray hair. Barbara Glaze wouldn't be caught dead with gray hair. Or in jeans and boots. Or facing the world without a stitch of make-up on. "I'm sorry. I-I don't remember."

"Excuse me." Mac took the folded shirt out of Marianne's hand and headed up the steps. "We had an incident at the Tucker place, Helen. I'll tell you about it over supper."

Her aunt turned to Marianne. "Are you all right?"

"Yes. I'm fine now, thank you. I'd like to wash up, if I could."

"Of course." Helen led her up the stairs to the porch. "The last time you were here, Mari, you had just turned five. My daughter, your cousin Brigitt, loved playing dress up with you and Lindsey, my sister Gloria's daughter."

Another aunt and cousin?

Helen laughed. "I see I've surprised you, dear. May I ask how Barbara is doing?"

"Yes." Good grief. "Uh, Mother's fine." She shrugged. "You know." Lying with any conviction at all had never been one of Marianne's strong points. She couldn't possibly tell her newly found aunt about her reclusive, vitriolic, drunken mother with a mouth that would make a hardened sailor glow with pride. She hoped those character traits didn't run in her mother's family. "She's okay. I guess."

Helen apparently guessed not because she nodded, pressed her lips together, and then turned toward a pickup rolling to a stop beside Mac's truck.

One of the doors opened. Nuggets bounded out and up the steps and nudged Marianne's leg as she danced around it. Marianne was just as happy to see her. She kissed her and snuggled her, so grateful she was okay. "Are you okay? Did you have a fine adventure, sweetie? Hmm?" Nuggets licked her, and then scooted under one of the porch chairs, sniffed the air, and put her head on her paws. It had been a long day for both of them.

Marianne was relieved to see the driver pluck her two suitcases, overnight bag, and briefcase out of the bed of his truck and place them on the porch. She waved at him and said, "Thank you so much." He nodded once at her and walked around to the back of the house.

Thunder boomed directly above them, and she jumped, laughing at herself. Nuggets lifted her head. "Will you be okay out here, sweetie?" Just as Marianne stopped speaking, two dogs ran up the steps and greeted a dancing and sniffing Nuggets. Then all three raced toward the back of the house. "I guess that's a yes."

Helen laughed, opened the front door, and picked up two of her bags. "You can shower in one of the guest rooms, if you'd like. Then, we'll get you something to eat."

Clean and refreshed, Marianne walked into the large living room, impressed that it was homey and welcoming despite its size. The cross-beamed cathedral ceiling flowed to the double row of floor-to-ceiling windows overlooking the well-lit, working side of the ranch. She headed for them. In a nook, two pool tables invited play. One wall was filled with books. No television or computer was in sight.

Passing under a wagon wheel chandelier holding amber glass lights, she stroked one leather chair in a grouping of sofas, oversized chairs, and recliners facing a huge rock fireplace. In one corner, a tall waterfall carried the soothing sounds of running water into the room. Beside it, an overstuffed chair sat, inviting her to rest, so she did and closed her eyes. She was bone tired after this exhausting day.

"You've discovered Joan McKenzie's favorite spot in this house."

Marianne smiled at her aunt as she rose. "I love this room."

Helen nodded as she looked around. "Joan's touch is everywhere. She brings warmth to a very male home. How was your shower?"

"It was wonderful. Thank you."

"Sit back down, Mari, and I'll take a seat over here."

Marianne sank into the leather chair and then leaned forward. She felt compelled to say something about her cousin's death and her uncle's passing, but it wasn't easy. As an introvert with a reserved nature, she had learned that meeting strangers didn't always have to be stressful if she could stay in control of the conversation. The weather, traffic, and travels were safe subjects. Murder was not.

But this had to be said. "Aunt Helen, I know I was here when your daughter died, but I wanted to say how very sorry I am for your loss."

"Thank you, Mari." Said without a twitch of blame or accusation. "And I'm sorry about your brother."

Tears clouded her aunt's eyes as she nodded quickly.

Marianne studied her hands, needing to continue but not wanting to hurt her aunt. "Did they ever catch the person responsible for either death?"

Helen shook her head and swiped at tears. "We just found out last week that Cecil was murdered. We suspected it, of course, but didn't know for sure what had happened to him the last seven years."

At that moment, a man dressed in chef whites, including a tall chef's hat, stood before them. "Madam, dinner is served."

"Thank you, James." Helen rose and motioned for Marianne to follow along. "He's so formal," she whispered as she leaned over. "But it's his style, and we accept it."

"Who is 'we'?"

"Mac and I. We eat breakfast, lunch, and dinner together when we can. As you can imagine, there's a lot of shop talk during meals."

So, he's not married. "I thought you had already eaten since I was so late."

"Mac asked James to keep everything warm until we could all eat together."

"That was very kind of him."

They walked into a large dining room. A country table with ten chairs on each side sat under another great but simpler chandelier. Helen took a seat at one end. Marianne settled in the chair opposite her.

"I couldn't help but notice your bruises and scratches, Mari. What happened at Tucker Spring?"

Marianne told her. "Do you have any idea who's trying to frighten me or why, Aunt Helen?"

"No, but since it's my brother's property, it might be connected to his work. He was sheriff of this county for many years. Maybe the person inside was looking for evidence or something, and you spooked him. A couple years ago, I was in there, and everything was in order."

"I wonder why he didn't search Uncle Cecil's home after he disappeared seven years ago. Why ransack it now? And why shoot at me and ram my car?"

"I have no idea, Mari."

The chef entered the room carrying a platter with an ornately carved antique bowl sitting on top. He set the dish in between them. Without a word, he bowed slightly at Helen and left.

"Also, my car was broken into, my papers strewn about."

"Talk to Bonnie Milhouse, your uncle's attorney. Maybe it has something to do with your inheritance."

"I'm seeing him sometime tomorrow."

Helen lifted the soup lid. "Umm. James' gumbo. You're in for a treat tonight. So, what do you do in Abilene, Mari?"

"I'm an artist. I paint portraits, sometimes landscapes, mostly in oils."

"Your mother loved to paint when she was young. She was very good."

"Some of her paintings are in their home."

"Barbara was working on a portrait of Brigitt that last visit. And then, of course, she never finished it. Oh, Mac."

He entered the room wearing a collared shirt tucked into the waistband of belted jeans. There were no words for how utterly handsome this man was. What surprised her was that he didn't seem to know it. Maybe there weren't enough women in cattle country to fawn over him, causing his head to swell. But if anyone had the right to a little arrogance, it was Mac McKenzie. She could lose herself in his eyes alone.

He sat at the head of the table, completing the triangle between her and Helen. "Marianne, we're glad you could join us tonight. Are you feeling better?"

"I am. Thank you for the shower and the dinner." She quickly looked down at her plate. She'd never been easy around men, although several had pursued her in college. Her father had always shown her the darker side of a man's character. She wasn't sure enough of herself and her judgment, nor did she have the experience, to distinguish between a man with good character and one *acting* as if he had good character. She'd seen her father present himself as a completely charming and caring man. She'd also witnessed his ugly side—abusive words, a quick and terrible temper, oppressively cynical, arrogant and abrasive, cruel and domineering.

Clasping her hands in her lap, Marianne decided to ignore the strong pull of Mac McKenzie for now. She placed her attention back on her aunt.

Helen pointed to a covered dish. "Those are homemade dinner rolls, Mari. Hand me your bowl, and I'll serve you some of James' gumbo. Marianne is an artist, Mac. She paints portraits."

"An artist? There's a wonderful gallery in Amarillo."

30

"Yes, I've seen it."

"Do you have a website? I'd like to see some of your work."

Since he seemed genuinely interested, she gave it to him. Then she turned to her aunt and took the bowl of gumbo. It smelled wonderful. "Aunt Helen, if—I mean—I'd like to do what my mother couldn't and paint Brigitt's portrait. But only if this is something you'd like for me to do."

"Oh." Her aunt smiled, reached for Marianne's hand, and squeezed it tightly. "Mari, thank you. That would mean so much to me."

Helen glanced at Mac for a moment, and then focused on Marianne again. "You asked me if Brigitt's killer was ever found. He wasn't but not for lack of trying." She stirred the soup and held her hand out for Mac's bowl.

"Any idea why someone would hurt her?"

"None." Helen filled Mac's bowl and her own, then set the ladle down and sighed. "Of course, everyone thought your Uncle Cecil was somehow involved since her body was found on his land, but he had an air-tight alibi. And he loved Brigitt."

Helen smiled at her. "But you were his favorite. Through the years, he had several opportunities to sell his land, but he kept it for you. You called it your place for wishes, and with no children of his own, he wanted your wish to—"

Mac coughed into his fist and pulled his chair closer to the table, effectively closing down the conversation. "Ladies, let's enjoy our soup. Would you like to say grace, Helen?" He held out a hand to her and to Marianne.

Marianne hesitated. She usually prayed quietly over her food. As the only Christian in her family, she tried not to draw attention to herself. Her parents sneered at spiritual 'posturing.' Frank considered her especially pathetic for relying on prayer, telling her many times, "You're praying to air, nothing more." Or, "Air, Marianne. It's just air."

But she wasn't at home.

Calmly, she placed her fingertips on Mac's palm. He gripped them lightly and bowed his head. Helen prayed, and when she finished, Marianne quickly withdrew her hand from Mac's and straightened the cloth napkin on her lap.

They ate in silence for a couple of bites.

Then Mac glanced at Helen.

Her aunt raised her brows, pressed her lips into a thin line, and settled her gaze on her soup. Was that disapproval on her face?

Mac laid his spoon in his bowl. "You've had a rough day, Mari."

Oh, yes. The knots in her stomach tightened. He was obviously leading up to something.

"I'm not sure this is the best time to discuss this with you."

Then, don't.

When he leaned back in his chair, her heart almost jumped out of her chest, even in the face of his nonchalance.

"I'll get right to the point. I'd like to buy your property."

Buy my—? She glanced at Aunt Helen, who kept her gaze on her soup bowl.

"With all the trouble today, it might be a good idea for you to let the property go."

All the trouble? Let the property go?

Confrontations were Marianne's forte. She'd lived through more than she cared to count. Three things her father had unintentionally taught her: show no emotion, reaction, or weakness; use silence to your advantage; and say what you mean.

She calmly placed her dinner roll on the side of her plate and sat back, waiting for more from Mac. But he apparently knew the same 'Silence is power' rule because he didn't say another word. Chef James entered the room, glanced at their still-full bowls, and frowned.

"It's delicious, James. We're taking our time tonight."

The chef angled his head at Mac and left.

Marianne wanted a private word with Aunt Helen. But Mac was the one in charge here, the one making the offer to buy. "Is this what you want, Aunt Helen? For me to sell Uncle Cecil's land?"

"It's not my decision, Mari. Maybe I should leave you two—"

"No!" Marianne and Mac said the word at the same time.

"Okay." Mac shook his head. "This doesn't have to be difficult. It's an honest business proposition. I'm sure you can understand my predicament, Mari, when I tell you I desperately need access across the back portion of your property to get my cattle to McKenzie Lake. I'm willing to pay you top dollar for your land."

"Did you offer to buy the land when Uncle Cecil owned it?"

"I did. He refused."

"Do you know why?"

"I don't."

"Because he wanted me to have it."

"Maybe. But he got what he wanted. You own it now." He tugged a square piece of paper from his front pocket, unfolded it, and handed it to her. "Here's the current value of the house and land. As you can see, I'm offering double its worth."

Marianne didn't care about the money. She didn't want to lose her uncle's gift—her new beginning. Aware that both Mac and Aunt Helen were waiting for her response, she eased forward to say something.

But Mac beat her to it. "Look, Marianne. This part of Texas is experiencing one of the worst droughts in our history. I need my lake. The only way to get my cattle to my lake is across your land."

"How did you get separated from your lake?"

"Triple aces against two pair. Your great-great-grandfather, Herman Tucker, won against my great-great-grandfather, Jedediah McKenzie, over a hundred years ago."

"How many acres do you own?"

"Sixty-five thousand, give or take."

"And how many of my acres would you need to get your cattle to your lake?"

"Four hundred."

"A fifth of my property."

"I see what you're thinking. You're suggesting that I'm greedy—"

"I'm not—"

"—that I have enough acreage already. I *am* greedy for your land. I own the lake; it's not on your two thousand acres. I just can't get to it without the use of your land. If I can't buy them, I'd like to lease the four hundred acres from you. I just need access."

So, he wanted her land. The difference between Mac and her father was the mode of operation. Mac had been deceptive; her father was a master of it. But instead of yelling and name calling and slicing a person off at the knees, Mac had been kind and caring. The reason he'd helped her tonight was because he wanted something from her.

She folded the paper and pushed back her chair. "I appreciate your hospitality and the meal, but if you don't mind, I'd like to think on this. I booked a room at the Brennan Inn for the next few nights. If it's at all possible, I'd appreciate it if someone could give me a ride into town."

Her aunt jumped up as if a bee had stung her rear. "I'd be happy to drive you. We could go by your cousin Lindsey Chamber's home. I called her while you were showering, and she'd love to see you again. You two were very close when you were young."

"Both of you, sit down. Let's finish our supper. Then we can make arrangements for Marianne." Mac picked up his spoon and turned back to her. "You're welcome to stay here at the ranch. But you'll get to wherever you decide to go in one of my Jeeps. Use it as long as you need it. You might consider leaving Nuggets here, though, if you go by Lindsey's. She has cats."

Add *generous* to the list of tools Mac used to get what he wanted.

Helen sat. "I'll give you Lindsey's address and directions to her house. She insisted you come stay with her tonight."

Insisted? "It's late, and I don't want to intrude." *And I don't even know her.* "I'll stop by her home, though, and see how it goes." She sat and turned to Mac. "I appreciate the use of your Jeep. Also, I'll contact my insurance agent and see if someone can determine if my car is totaled. I'm sure it is."

"There's a very reliable repair shop in this area. I'll call Milt after we eat. He can pick it up for you in the morning, keep it at his shop until you decide what you want to do."

"Where is his shop?"

"Mole's Bench. Just down the road a bit. It's our address as well."

Marianne couldn't resist chuckling. "Mole's Bench?"

"Yes. A cowpoke apparently saw a mole sitting on the bench outside a saloon, the only building in this area. He started calling the saloon 'Mole's Bench' and the name stuck."

THREE

Marianne parked one house down from Lindsey's home, a square blue box of a house that looked as if it had just landed in a wildly blooming garden. Leafy trees lined the quaint street bordered with homes built decades ago. Cozy streetlamps along the sidewalk illuminated the yards. Most homes left on porch lights showing off thick wood swings, wicker chairs, or rocking chairs. Some porches had children's toys scattered across them or strewn down the steps into deep yards of lackluster grass.

She checked the time. Almost eight. A little late for a visit, but Aunt Helen had insisted that Lindsey didn't want to wait until morning to see her.

She touched the door handle to get out just as a loud engine revved twice behind her. She gasped and turned around. *The same truck!* It crept alongside her Jeep and stopped not three inches from her driver's door!

She panicked and tried to scoot away from it, but her seatbelt locked. *No!* She struggled to get it unlatched, but her hands were shaking too much. Her heart raced as she patted the passenger seat for her purse and her gun. Her purse wasn't there or on the floorboard.

The oily smell of the engine almost choked her. She glanced up at black windows that looked like unblinking alien eyes. The truck driver gunned the engine and held the pedal down. White clouds of exhaust fumes drifted over the Jeep.

Marianne's eyes burned; she covered them with both hands and coughed. She finally unlatched the seatbelt as the truck peeled out, leaving two snaking black marks on the pavement as it sped toward a stop sign, made a U-turn, and headed straight for Marianne.

"Dear God!" she gasped, her heart pounding. She only had time to cover her head and duck before it hit her.

But the truck zoomed past. Shaking, she popped up in time to see the vehicle run a stop sign, swerve to miss a minivan, and disappear around a curve. There was a license plate, but it was caked in mud.

"Okay, okay, I get it. You want me gone." She gulped in several breaths and steadied her heart by patting her chest. A dog was barking. She followed the sound. A little dachshund was standing on his back legs with his front paws on a chain-link fence at the home next to Lindsey's house. "Well, aren't you the cutest thing?" Marianne muttered and heard what sounded like a screen door squawking open.

She turned toward that sound.

A thin, petite woman wearing a frown, ragged jean shorts, and a skimpy summer top cautiously stepped onto the lighted porch of the Chambers' home. Spikes of short blonde hair sprouted from the woman's scalp. Shoeless, she walked to the edge of the street and stared at the skid marks.

Marianne got out of the Jeep and stepped toward her. "Excuse me. Are you Lindsey Chambers? Did Aunt Helen call you?"

Lindsey cried "Oh!" and ran on tiptoes toward her, flapping her hands and grinning. "Mari! After all these years! How *are* you?" She giggled and reached for a hug. Then she pulled back and studied Marianne. "You're so tall. Still have those pretty green eyes. And you're slim like your daddy, with his height. What are you? Five six?"

"Yes. I feel huge against your petite size."

Lindsey shrugged. "My dad's shorter than my mother was. You've lost your freckles." When she laughed, her eyes closed like half moons. "And would you look at all that red hair. It's so full and beautiful." Lindsey brushed a strand of Marianne's hair over her shoulder.

All this touching unnerved Marianne so she stepped away from it. "Thank you. It's good to see you again, Lindsey."

"Me, too. I always wondered why you never came back to the ranch. And then the years just drifted by." She indicated the freshly made tire marks on the pavement. "Did you see what made those?"

"A wannabe monster truck, showing off." She glanced behind her and tried to wrap her mind around the fact that he'd followed her here. He knew where she was at this exact moment. "Do you mind if I park in your driveway?"

"Of course not."

Marianne hurried back to Mac's Jeep, maneuvered it onto the one-lane drive, and parked behind an older two-door compact car.

Lindsey grabbed the metal frame of the open Jeep. "Is this Mac's? He has several just like it."

"It is. My car isn't working right now, and he offered this to me earlier this evening." No sense in burdening Lindsey with the details of this horrible day. Hopefully, it would end on a better note with her cousin, catching up on old times—maybe happy old times—and feeling a sense of family here, too. Lindsey might have answers for why Barbara and Frank had chopped off this part of the family tree.

"You and I lost a lot of years, Mari. Come in, come in. Can you believe it's the end of October with all this warm weather?"

"I'm sure ready for cooler weather." Marianne lifted out her suitcase and then reached for her overnight bag.

"Is this work?" Lindsey picked up her briefcase and turned it over. "Oh, surely you didn't bring work with you on vacation."

"Those are my sketching tools. I'm painting our cousin Brigitt while I'm here. Aunt Helen gave me several pictures of her." She set her overnight bag on the sidewalk. "Do you remember Brigitt or that horrible day she was killed? You were eight then, right?"

Lindsey dropped the briefcase as if it had stung her. "Please don't tell me you're here to talk about her murder."

Marianne sidestepped a sweet-faced golden retriever dancing around her legs and studied her cousin. The change in her had been instantaneous. How did one learn to do that? Marianne was much more cautious and rarely showed her emotions to anyone. Obviously, her cousin didn't share the same reserved nature. "I just learned about her today. Some strange things have happened to me since I arrived this afternoon, and I think they might have something to do with my being at the Tucker place where Brigitt was killed."

Lindsey crossed her arms. "You were at Uncle Cecil's property today?"

"Yes. Earlier. Then I went to Mac's and had supper with him and Aunt Helen."

"So, why aren't you at the ranch tonight? I'm surprised Mac didn't invite you to stay."

"He did, but I didn't want to just yet."

"Why not?"

Oh, brother. "Because he wants me to sell my land and I'm not ready to do that."

"What land?"

"Uncle Cecil left me his estate."

"He *what?*" Lindsey threw out her arms and slapped her fists on her hips. "I don't believe this. I do *not* believe this. That house was promised to me. *And* the land. Mac told me last year that when they found Cecil, he'd see to it that I'd get the property, if I'd sell him the back four hundred. How did *you* end up with it?"

Marianne hadn't expected to face this kind of hostility. She chose her words carefully. "I have no clue what was promised to you or not promised to you, Lindsey. I received a letter from an attorney and—"

"Who? What's his name?"

"Jethro Bonstrone Milhouse."

"Oh, yeah. I know Bonnie. The jerk."

Marianne hastily added, "I have his letter in my luggage." Wait, wait. What was she doing? She didn't know if Mac had made any promises to Lindsey. She needed to exit gracefully from this awkward situation and get—

"May I?" Lindsey smirked and held out a stiff hand.

"Look, Lindsey, I don't know what's going on here, but I'm tired. I've had an exhausting day. I think I'll head to the Brennan Inn, and you and I can get together in the next day or two."

"You're joking, right? You're here. Stay."

So much for gracefully exiting.

"We have an extra bedroom. You can paint all you want here. Although, I'd think you could find a better subject than Brigitt Holcomb."

Marianne didn't need this stress, not after this horrible day. "Okay." Her lips tightened as she tried to figure out what to do or say next. Some form of escape was vital now. She opened her mouth to—

"You know, people still talk about her death as if it happened yesterday. She's a shadow that just lingers and lingers, like a bad headache." Lindsey's hands were shaking. Her fierce expression told Marianne she was seething with anger. It made Marianne so uncomfortable, she wanted to grab her luggage and leave without an explanation.

"I, for one," Lindsey jabbed a finger three times at her own chest, "don't want to hear another word about our cousin, her death, who killed her, where he is, and why the police never found any evidence in her case. And I certainly don't want to see a portrait of her."

With her chin jutted out and her eyes narrowed, she silently dared Marianne to say another word about it.

So she didn't. She put her overnight bag in the Jeep and kept her voice even. "Before today, I knew nothing about any of my family up here. I've now met Aunt Helen and you, found out about two murders, and inherited my uncle's property. I want to paint the best portrait I can for Aunt Helen, and I'm interested in getting to know my family again. That's why I'm staying for now."

"You're interested?" Lindsey frowned and opened her mouth as if she intended to scream at Marianne, then closed it and pursed her lips. "You're *interested*. So, let me see if I've got this right. Now that you've stolen Uncle Cecil's property from me, you're interested in getting to know me. Where have you been all these years? Where was your interest *then*?"

Whoa. This was not a picture of 'emotions well contained' that her father had preached many times to her and Patrick. They had never been allowed to express like this. On some level, Marianne admired her cousin's outrageous behavior; on another, she was reluctant to be the target of it. "I'll say it again, Lindsey. I didn't know about you or Brigitt until today. I didn't know about Uncle Cecil or his property or Aunt Helen until today."

When Lindsey took a breath to speak, Marianne held up a hand. "I experienced some trouble earlier on Uncle Cecil's land. It might be related to Brigitt's murder or his death. If it is, then I need to find out why I'm being targeted if I'm going to live out there."

"Live out there? You're kidding. Surely."

"I'm not."

"What could possibly interest you about her death?"

"I'm not interested in her death, only in the person after me."

"After you? What do you mean?"

"Someone shot at me at Tucker Spring Ranch."

"And you're thinking this person killed Brigitt?"

Marianne shrugged. "Or Uncle Cecil. Or both."

"But their deaths are ten years apart." Lindsey shook her head, looked away for a moment, then turned back to Marianne. "You're not thinking—oh, surely, you're not thinking you can solve either murder?"

Marianne lifted her chin. "I'm detail oriented. I enjoy a good mystery. And I'm too stubborn for my own good. If someone wants me gone, I dig in my heels and stay and find out why."

"Well, that's just great. An artist trying to solve a murder mystery. All you'll do is stir things up and maybe get yourself and the rest of your family killed."

Lindsey huffed out a breath and stood quietly for a moment. Then her eyes flared. The temper appeared to be returning. "We wanted to find her killer." She pointed east. "Was it my next-door neighbor? A student at the high school? A police officer? Your brother Patrick? A drifter?"

Marianne pursed her lips as Lindsey's voice rose.

"And why Brigitt? Was it random or planned? Why beat her like that? Was I next? Was her mother, Helen? Was *my* mother, Gloria?"

Lindsey shook her head, her eyes suddenly sad. She brushed a hand over her spikes, and they all sprang back to attention. "Since I was eight, the fact that her killer was never found has consumed our lives.

He ruined everything for my family."

Marianne patted her pants pocket containing the antacid packets and tried to ignore the migraine pecking away at her right temple. "I'm so, so sorry for all of you, Lindsey." A change of perspective might help calm her cousin. "I really love painting. When I paint someone, it helps to get to know him or her from someone else's viewpoint. Maybe if I can see Brigitt through your eyes and not talk about her mur—"

"I don't *want* to talk about her. I don't *want* to remember! I'm sick of Brigitt. I'm sick of her death *and* her extended after-life. Why can't you understand that?" She turned away from Marianne and marched over grass toward her front porch.

She spun around. "I'm going to get this mess with Cecil's property straightened out tomorrow." She bounded up her steps and opened the screen door. "But in the meantime, stay in your hotel and stay off his land!" She stepped inside.

The screen door slammed, followed by the front door, like a two-handed slap.

Good, good grief.

Marianne stared at the closed doors, her heart stammering, her stomach twisting. *"Now look what you've done! You are so weak. Can't you do anything right?"*

She squeezed her eyes shut against the weight of her father's words. Even when he wasn't near her, he badgered her. No matter the project, the action, the result, she expected disapproval from him; his disdain was a constant.

But not here, Father. You have no power over me here.

Turning slowly, she placed her luggage and briefcase in the back seat, slid behind the wheel, and took several deep breaths to calm her stomach. She popped two more antacids and gulped in another breath of Texas heat as she considered Lindsey's completely over-the-top reaction.

Something didn't ring true.

It wasn't so much the anger in her words that caught Marianne's attention.

It was the fear. "What are you afraid I'll find, cousin?"

She started the Jeep and backed into the street. A quick check in her rearview mirror revealed the street was clear of black monster trucks. She cocked her ear for the sound of an engine starting up, but all was quiet. She was sure some of the neighbors stood by darkened windows, watching to see if the show was really over.

She maneuvered the gear into first and sent one last glance at Lindsey's house as she drove away, toward her original destination—the Brennan Inn.

Marianne rested on the bed, slipped a hand under her cheek, and closed her eyes. Every part of her ached. Bruises appeared on her left shoulder, her legs, her knees. Scratches and bites dotted her ankles and arms. A long soak in a hot bath had helped, as had the lotion.

What a day. What a gut-wrenching, awful, stressful day. She needed to relax enough to fall asleep, but the pain reliever she'd taken earlier hadn't kicked in yet.

Her cell phone rang. She glanced at it and groaned. She was so not in the mood for any whining from her older brother tonight. But she punched the button anyway. "Patrick."

"Where are you? Sonja said she went in to clean your room, and you were gone."

"I left you a voicemail. You didn't get it?" Marianne rolled to her back and crossed her legs. She knew her older brother didn't care if she was in Brennan or at home. He wanted something from her.

"No, I didn't see it. Look, sis. I was way out of line the other night."

"Is that an apology?"

"It's the best I can do."

"You used poor judgment getting drunk at my party, Paddy." *And embarrassing me at a celebration of my first public showing in Abilene.* She knew the party was more about her father than it was about her accomplishments. Franklin Glaze needed the constant stroking of the rich and powerful in Texas and usually received it through business deals. He'd never approved of her being an artist. *"You sit around and paint what the world does, and you don't contribute anything to it? That's weakness, not the definition of success."*

But what could she have done? Not shown up at the very lavish party thrown by her adoring and obviously very proud father—the impression he gave to others?

"Just living up to the old man's expectations."

What? *Oh, getting drunk at my party.* "Then why do you stay, Paddy? Why do you keep yourself in his line of fire?"

"And you don't? You're an up-and-coming artist with one successful showing in your pocket, and you still live here with them." He grunted. "You'll be back again and soon."

"I hope not."

"Hope? Now we're dealing in hope?"

Marianne didn't have the energy to fight with him tonight.

"I'd rather deal with what's real—the old man's money. I'm not willing to do anything different if it means living by my own wits."

He wouldn't. "But I am."

"Meaning?"

She stared at the red light of the smoke alarm on her ceiling. "I can't live at home anymore."

"Where *are* you?"

"Mole's Bench. McKenzie Ranch."

Silence hummed between them.

"Cecil Tucker, our mother's brother, left me his land and house adjacent to McKenzie Ranch." She expected her brother to jump right in and start yelling at her, but he didn't. His silence told her he knew about the existence of Uncle Cecil and probably about Brigitt being killed on his property.

The seconds ticked by without a word between them. Just like his father, Patrick used silence to his advantage.

"I need to borrow your SUV. Mine's in the shop."

"I was five the last time we were at Uncle Cecil's place. You were ten, Paddy. Do you remember that last day?" When he didn't answer her, she marched right on. "What happened to Mother's family? Why the rift? Why weren't we told about the existence of her family?"

"Do they know?"

"Oh, yes. Mother wilted into a pile of tears on the library floor when I told her I was coming up here. Father pitched a martini glass in the fireplace, yelled something about closed doors staying shut, and stormed off. The usual." She sat up. "So why and when did Mother's entire family blacklist us?"

"Where are your keys?"

"Patrick. Do you know anything about it?"

"Your keys?"

"In my dresser, top left drawer."

"I need to run." He paused. "Be careful, Mari. Murder can be a messy business."

"Which murder? Uncle Cecil's or Brigitt's?"

"Well, well. So he got it, too."

A chill raced across Marianne's heart at the coldness of his words. "Paddy, talk to me."

"Gotta go. Be careful." The line disconnected.

Her head hurt. Just too much information to digest in one day.

She slipped out of bed and walked to the large window. Below, a family of four struggled to get their luggage onto a cart. One little boy discovered a spot of green grass and rolled over and over on it, laughing. A man—his father?—tickled the squirming, squealing boy and landed on the grass beside him, their faces laughing up at the moon outside Marianne's window.

She sighed as she remembered Uncle Cecil and his tickles and wondered why he never contacted her after Brigitt died.

The nightmare pulled her into utter darkness.

Ghostly apparitions darted around her as she sprinted down a midnight path. Branches grabbed at her. One snagged her hair. She jerked to a stop, yanked hard against the branch's hold, and ripped out the roots of her hair as she broke free.

Her heartbeat pounded all around her. Thump-thump. Thump-thump.

She gasped when a sneering specter raced up the trail and stopped mere inches from her face. Screaming, shaking, she fell hard on the graveled trail. On all fours, she backed up, scrambling to get away from the apparition.

Thump-thump. Thump-thump.

The ground trembled.

Leaves shifted near her feet and rose into a mound.

A decomposing hand, oozing with pus, shoved through the heap of dirt. It stretched its red-tipped fingers as if it gasped for air. It fisted and opened again. Then, like a living, breathing thing, it slowly turned toward Marianne.

Thump-thump. Thump-thump.

She opened her mouth to scream, but no sound came out. The hand stretched out of the hole and grabbed her ankle. She clawed the ground, trying to find purchase. But nothing could stop her from being dragged toward the break in the ground. Knife-like nails dug into her skin. Streams of blood trickled across her ankle. "Help me! *PLEASE!* Somebody!" But no one came.

She silently screamed until she could scream no more and then woke up, gasping for air.

Marianne groped with a trembling hand for the bedside lamp and turned it on. Shadows raced from the room. Shivering, she slid completely under the covers, but her breathing was still too ragged and too hot. She uncovered her face and breathed deeply until her heart rate slowed and her nerves settled.

"What was *that?*" she said and quickly sat up. It was so vivid, the colors, the sounds, the pain, her quiet screams. Heat coursed through her as she struggled to even her breathing again.

It was no wonder she'd had such a nightmare, with men shooting at her and ramming her car. She reached for a glass of water on her nightstand and drank all of it. Then she picked up the letter the attorney had sent her and fanned herself for a few moments. She stopped and read one part of it again: *"This property is in disrepair and needs much attention. In the event you do not want the house..."*

Marianne grunted. What was there not to want?

A haunted house, secluded, run down, in the panhandle of Texas where a drought had sucked every morsel of moisture out of the land, with a neighboring rancher who wanted her land enough to—what? Enough to—?

Marianne's eyes widened, and her jaw dropped. The letter slipped out of her hand. "Enough to hurt me?"

No, no, of course not. He wasn't the type of man to do that. Was he?

When the shooter and the rammer intruded yesterday afternoon, she hadn't even spoken to Mac about the land. It was later at the ranch that she'd refused his offer. So why try to scare her off before he even knew her intentions? That made no sense.

She tossed off the covers and sat on the edge of the bed. She still hoped she could build a life for herself and Nuggets, especially after meeting her aunt. But if Helen *knew* about Mac's plans, then why did she so warmly greet her long-lost niece and make her feel so welcome?

She didn't know, that's why.

Marianne's head pounded with the unanswered questions. She needed to get the Jeep back to Mac this morning so she wouldn't be any more indebted to him than she already was.

I'm no good at this. I'm an artist, not a detective. Evil-behind-every-tree just doesn't work for me. So, what am I supposed to think?

She glanced at her clock. Five-fifty. It was as good a time as any to start her day. She usually made a list of things to do in her daytimer, but it was in her purse, and her purse must have been left in her car. She turned the attorney's letter over, grabbed a hotel pen, and started her list.

1. *Why did Mother's family drift apart?*
2. *Why did Uncle Cecil end up dead in a ravine?*
3. *Who is haunting my house?*
4. *Who tried to scare me off?*

And Brigitt. Where to start with answering all the questions about her cousin? Her aunt, of course.

5. *Speak privately with Aunt Helen.*
6. *Who killed Brigitt Holcomb?*
7. *Why was Lindsey so afraid?*

"A good start to this day," she muttered and headed for the shower.

An hour later, dressed and ready to go, she opened the hotel door and stepped into cool air. Across the parking lot, a breakfast place, JoeMoe's, already bustled with customers. As she shut the door, she stopped and gasped. All four tires on her Jeep were flat!

She spun in search of the culprit responsible for this, but no one was around. Shaking her head, she stared at the tires. Surely, Mac McKenzie wouldn't slit his own tires, even if he thought it was a perfect way to misdirect her. But if he wasn't involved, then she had a bigger problem: someone had followed her to the hotel.

Probably watching me right now.

Behind her, a door opened. She turned toward a burly man with a full mustache dressed in a western shirt, jeans, and boots. He held a white cowboy hat, slipped it onto his head, and shut his door. Strolling past her, he bobbed his head once at her. "Ma'am," he said, and then headed toward JoeMoe's. She watched him until he opened the restaurant's door and disappeared inside.

On a sigh, she took out her list and added, "Call Mac about tires" and "Get my purse."

But the call would have to wait. She was just too hungry to make sense of all of this. She headed for "The Best Breakfast in the Panhandle," grateful when she saw a sign that read, "As a courtesy to our customers, your meal may be added to your hotel room." Good. She could eat without having to pay for it right now.

She just hoped the man following her wasn't inside JoeMoe's, waiting for her.

FOUR

Mac checked his watch as he headed to the barn. Seven-ten. The Laredo Oil conference call was scheduled for eleven this morning, so he had enough time to saddle Pal and take a nice long ride before holing up in his office.

He didn't sleep well last night. One too many dreams filled with frightened women, gun-toting idiots, and coffins. He woke up earlier than his usual four o'clock, ready to write off the worthless night and get up.

He didn't want to admit that Marianne Glaze had filled his dreams in another way—strange yearning dreams that evolved into cat-and-mouse scenarios, ending in his gasping and sweating and throwing off the covers, wondering if she was safe in Brennan.

The nightmares had nothing to do with Marianne, however.

His grief therapist had tried to help him see that he wasn't responsible for Dad's death, but Mac knew better. If he'd gone with his father to the cattle auction, Dad wouldn't have been alone on the trip back home, and he wouldn't have been killed. When his brother Kyle called to tell him about his radio interview as the "Texas Businessman of the Month," there would have been no need for Dad to pull over to search for the station, giving the assailant an up-close opportunity to kill him. Mac would have found the station, and they would have made it home safely.

One good thing about his brother calling his father was that Kyle had heard every word the killer said just before he pulled the trigger. His memory of the man's voice was the only piece of evidence in existence, other than the bullet, which proved worthless to the police.

"Good morning, Nuggets." Mac patted the ecstatically-happy-to-see-you dog and slipped on his work gloves. "You like having the run of the place last night, girl? Hmm? You enjoying your new friends?"

They walked together through the open barn doors, until something caught the beagle's attention, and she raced off.

The lights were off. He preferred letting the light of a new day ease into the barn on its own terms. Pal whinnied a greeting. Mac smiled at the eagerness in his bobbing head, his stomping feet, his swishing tail. He loved this animal; Dad had given Pal to Mac three years ago, in appreciation for his hard work on the ranch. "Hey, buddy."

Just as he reached Pal's stall, Mac stopped and tugged his ringing phone out of its holster.

Couldn't be good news this early in the morning.

Every booth and table were taken.

One bar stool was empty, next to an old codger with a frayed cap, a scruffy beard, overalls and a red T-shirt, slurping his coffee with his nose in a folded newspaper.

Marianne weaved her way past Formica tables and yellow padded chairs toward the bar stool. But before she could reach it, a man sat next to Old Codger and patted him on the back. "'Mornin,' Tank."

Marianne stood in the middle of the restaurant, completely embarrassed. She searched for some place to sit and tried not to make eye contact with any of these strangers. Her heart raced; her breathing shortened. How could such a simple thing like finding a table be so stressful?

"Hon?" Someone touched her arm.

Marianne jerked around and stepped back from the server wearing a yellow puffy-sleeved dress with a black apron at her waist. "Oh, I'm sorry. You startled me." She was so relieved to be talking to someone rather than standing alone in the crowded place.

"Why don't you come on over here and sit with Mrs. Porter?" The server—Tess, according to her nametag—put a flat hand next to her mouth and leaned toward Marianne. "She's a sweet old lady, but she can sure talk up a storm." Tess lowered her voice on the last words, but it didn't keep the patrons near them from hearing. They winked and laughed at her.

"If you need information on anybody in this town, she's your ticket. She's past eighty and was born in that house," Tess pointed outside, "on the hill. See it? Walks over here every morning for coffee and breakfast and her paper." She turned then to the old woman. "Mrs. P., hon?"

Tess filled Mrs. Porter's coffee cup, then set the pot on the table and slipped into the chair next to the woman. Mrs. Porter held a magnifying glass above a newspaper. She wore a lightweight pink sweater with pearl-like buttons over an orange blouse.

Mrs. Porter moved the magnifier to Tess's face. One giant eye squinted at the server.

Marianne stifled a chuckle.

Then the older woman lowered the glass and frowned. "You sidling

47

up to me for somethin', missy? I'm not in the mood for talking. Haven't read my paper yet. It's like a freezer in here. Should have worn a heavier sweater."

"Yes, ma'am. Mrs. P., this lady here needs a place to rest her rear. Could she sit with you a bit until a table vacates?"

Up went the magnifying glass. Marianne received a good looking-over, and then the woman reached across the table and tapped the place in front of her. "Sit over here, so I can get a better look at you. You're too far away for me to see."

Marianne thanked Tess and pulled out the chair, relieved to have a place to sit. "I appreciate this, Mrs. Porter."

"Don't go to thanking me yet, missy. I haven't decided if you're staying. Sit it down. Sit it down. What are you doing here in Brennan? I've lived in this town since Moby Dick was a minnow, and you ain't in our town."

"No, ma'am." Marianne placed her book on the seat next to her. She tugged the wrapper off her paper napkin and placed the napkin on her lap, then fiddled with the knife and fork on the table.

Mrs. Porter stared at her with the magnifying glass for several moments. "Where are you from, child?"

The elderly woman spoke so loudly that Marianne wanted to melt into her chair from embarrassment. Marianne never wanted attention. Her ideal eating out experience involved sitting in a corner, away from other humans, observing the comings and goings, the people, the food offerings, trying to figure out relationships at a table, their history, why they were angry or resentful or happy. She might be a latent writer; she could come up with all sorts of stories involving the people in a public place. Or she could tell their story through painting, which she did.

She leaned over the table and said quietly, "I live in Abilene."

Mrs. Porter frowned at her. "You live *where?*"

Maybe this wasn't a good idea. Marianne's face heated as she looked around for her server, but Tess was nowhere in sight. "Abilene," she said a little louder.

"Abilene? I know people in Abilene. What's your name?"

Good grief. This was like an interrogation.

Tess came out of a back room. Marianne lifted her hand, but Tess headed to the other side of the room. *Now what?*

Marianne looked at Mrs. Porter, who lowered her chin in an expression that said, "I'm waiting."

"Marianne Glaze is my name, Mrs. Porter." She hoped that the noise of people talking and greeting one another and laughing would cover up the fact that she was practically yelling at the old woman.

"Glaze?" Mrs. Porter's voice was booming compared to Marianne's quiet attempts. "I knew a Barbie Glaze once. You any kin to her?"

Barbie? She couldn't imagine anyone calling her mother Barbara by such a fanciful name. "She's my mother."

"And since your mama doesn't live in these parts, I'm assuming you're here to see your aunt or your cousin Lindsey?"

Small towns. "Yes, ma'am, my aunt."

"Are you the new owner out at the Tucker place?"

Marianne looked around the restaurant to see if anyone was overly interested in her response—say, oh, a man with a gun stashed under his armpit—but no one seemed to be holding a breath, waiting for her answer. "I am."

"Well." Mrs. Porter straightened, dropped the magnifier in the big black purse on her lap, picked up her fork, and slid it under a pile of cheesy eggs.

Tess appeared at the table, ready to write on a small pad. "You know what you want this morning, hon?"

"I'm sorry. I haven't looked at the menu." Marianne picked it up and tried to figure out as quickly as possible what appealed to her.

"Try the pancakes." This, from Mrs. Porter, without even a glance in her direction.

Marianne looked at the old woman. For some reason unknown to Marianne, she knew she'd passed muster with her. She closed the menu and handed it to Tess. "That sounds perfect."

"Coffee with those cakes?"

"No, thank you. Do you have green tea?"

"We do."

A gurgling sound came from Mrs. Porter's side of the table. "Unnatural to drink that stuff," she muttered. When Tess finished the order, Mrs. P. waved her away. "You haven't been in these parts in over seventeen years. I would've heard if you had. Am I right?"

"Yes, ma'am." Marianne sipped water from a small glass.

Piercing gray eyes regarded her. "Your mama was a pretty little thing; ornery as all get-out. A body couldn't put nothing past Barbie Tucker, except maybe Franklin Glaze, and look where it got her. Nowheresville, Texas, in an unhappy marriage. Yep, I know where you come from, missy. And your people."

"Barbara was raised in these parts?"

"Right there on your new property. Don't you know nothing, girl?"

A flash of heat raced across Marianne's neck and face. The old woman sounded just like her mother. She would not be talked to like that!

Another server brushed crumbs off a nearby table, and Marianne pushed back her chair. "I appreciate your kindness, Mrs. Porter, but a table just opened up and I'm—"

Gnarled fingers flapped at her, like a toddler's good-bye. "Oh, where's your backbone, child? Stay and visit with me a spell. You obviously don't know much about your own family, and I do. Don't you think it's time somebody filled your ear about your parents?"

Marianne hesitated. Yes, she'd like the answers. Her entire life, the questions had haunted her, and here was a woman full of history and facts. *Her* history and her facts.

She eased back into the chair and scooted it closer to the table.

"Here's your tea." Tess set a well-used, bulky white mug in front of Marianne with a tea label hanging over the side. "And honey and milk. You enjoy now. Mrs. P., would you like some more coffee?"

"I'll float away if I do, Theldra Anne."

Theldra Anne? Marianne glanced up at Tess and smiled.

Tess leaned over, close to her ear. "Can you imagine a dear sweet mother naming her little baby Theldra Anne? Well, mine was as sweet as they come, and she did. Don't you listen to Mrs. Por—"

"I heard that, missy."

"—ter. Just call me Tess." And with that, a quick laugh and a pat on her shoulder, she left.

"You look like your mama."

Wonderful.

"I hope you don't act like her."

She was being sized up again. Mrs. Porter's steely gaze never left Marianne's face. A little twitch in the right corner of her mouth told her she was waiting for Marianne's temper to surface again. But it wouldn't. Not where Barbara Glaze's 'good name' was concerned. Marianne couldn't care less what was said about a woman she disliked. No, no, she hadn't stepped into dislike yet, but the fence between dislike and disapproval was getting weaker.

She deliberately took her time squeezing out the green tea bag and placing it on the purple paper placemat under her cup. She doused the tea with milk and honey and sipped.

"I like you, girl. You're nothing like her after all."

"Thank you."

"Getting knocked up at sixteen sure didn't help your mama's disposition any."

Marianne's eyes widened.

"You didn't know that either? They haven't told you much about your history, have they?" She shook her head slowly. "Barbie had to marry your daddy lickety-split, and then she lost the baby two months after they married. Gave up everything to save face. You know she used to paint? Beautiful work, she did. They lived out there on the Tucker place with your grandparents for a while. Then she got pregnant again; lost that one, too. Third time's a charm, they say, and it was for her. When she was carrying your brother Patrick, they moved into Abilene, to make sure this one stayed in the oven long enough to be born. It did and it was."

Marianne listened, fascinated.

"They came back to visit several times a year, out there on the Tucker place. Then your granddaddy and grandma died, and your uncle inherited. You come along and I swear, I'd never seen such a pretty, happy baby. But that changed soon enough, didn't it?"

"Why are you telling me all this?"

"Because you don't know any of it. A body needs to know about her family."

"And my father?"

The old woman lifted her shoulders, shook her head. "Oh, Frank Glaze was a pistol of the first order. A bully, if you'll allow me. Everybody thought he'd go far in the business world, because he knew how to step on toes and keep on running. And he did, didn't he? Owner of I Spy Surveillance International, a great success, a multi-millionaire. But I doubt he has any close friends. Men like him usually don't. They see people as a means to an end. Can't imagine being married to such a man. I pity your mother."

Pity for her mother had never entered Marianne's mind. She stared at Mrs. Porter, then looked away, determined not to show the woman more than she wanted her to see.

That's when she saw the man with the simple mustache, not four tables over, looking at her above his spread-out newspaper. Their gazes locked for a moment, then the paper lifted, shutting off access to his eyes.

"And now your morning is complete, girl." Tess cheerfully set the plate of three pancakes in front of Marianne, placed the syrup next to her plate, and asked if she needed anything else. She completely shielded the man from Marianne's view.

Hurry, hurry! Move! "No, uh, this looks great, Tess. Thanks."

When Tess left, the man was gone. His newspaper was folded on the table, and three bills rested against his coffee cup. Marianne looked outside but didn't see him anywhere.

"I'll let you eat in peace, Marianne." Mrs. Porter's voice pulled her back to her table. "I reckon I've given you more information than you wanted, but there it is." She stood, grabbed her purse, and leaned over. "I come in here every morning. I'd welcome you sittin' with me again even if the place isn't full."

"Thank you for everything, Mrs. Porter."

The old woman chuckled, picked up her bill, and headed toward the cash register. Marianne watched her leave and decided she'd made a friend today with very little effort on her part.

Sweat rolled down the neck of the man sitting in the white truck by the side of the road. He sniffed twice and blew his nose, then punched a number on his cell phone. "She's about to leave the restaurant."

A passing eighteen-wheeler slapped the pickup with a blast of pulsating hot air.

"Follow her. We have to find out what she knows. I sent you a package. Get that surveillance on her."

"Yeah." The man sneezed, started the truck, and wiped his nose on the sleeve of his shirt.

FIVE

Mac squatted beside one of the flat tires. It didn't take much to figure out what had happened. The tires had deep cuts in them. Slashes, with a knife. *So, it's personal.*

He didn't care one flip about the tires. What irritated him was that someone was trying to scare an innocent woman again.

A red pickup rolled up. Adam Milton and his son got out and greeted Mac. "Yep, you sure need new tires there, Mac. My boy here 'll load up yer Jeep and take it to the shop. We'll git ya fixed up in no time."

"By noon?"

"Before that. Pro'ly an hour at the most."

"Could you bring it back here?"

"Sure thing. Any idea who did this?"

Mac shook his head. "Maybe some kids who had too much to drink last night." It might have nothing at all to do with Marianne and her inheritance. Or it could have everything to do with it.

"I'll keep my ears to the ground, see if I hear anything. And the Jaguar we picked up at the Tucker place this mornin'? Man, that was a nice car. Tell her we'll keep it until she decides what she wants to do. I bet it'll be totaled by the insurance company. Son, would ya get her purse?"

After a few moments, Milt's son ran up to them and gave Marianne's purse to Mac.

"Were the keys in her car, Milt?"

"Yep. In the ignition."

"Great. We're all set then." Mac handed him a key to the Jeep. "When you bring the Jeep back, just take this key to the front desk. Thanks, Milt."

Right now, Mac needed to check on Marianne. When the owner of the Brennan Inn called to tell him about the tires, he told Mac her room number was 112. Just as he turned toward it, he spotted her coming out of JoeMoe's.

He sauntered to the back of his truck, crossed his arms, and assumed his battle stance. Yesterday, her loveliness had knocked the breath out of him. Her red hair, sea-green mermaid eyes, and full lips had presented a stunning picture.

It was the same today.

Her long legs glided across the parking lot with equal strength and grace, her hair swaying in sync with her stride. She was beautiful. Model-like in her movements. Any other day, he'd make a move on such a woman in a heartbeat, because he'd rarely seen one that caused him to take a second, steady look.

But not today. He needed her land more than he needed to open himself up to another woman.

So why then, a wise man might ask, was he standing here admiring her beautiful face, her wind-blown hair dancing around those stunning eyes, and her long legs in modest shorts? Another sage might suggest that below the surface of such beauty could be a woman worth getting to know, and he'd probably be right.

Mac chuckled at his thoughts. So, okay. He was interested—maybe a step or two past interested.

"Good morning, Mr. McKenzie."

"Miss Glaze. Were you comfortable here last night?"

"I was. Thank you for the use of your Jeep. I'm sorry the tires were slashed. I didn't see anyone this morning when I discovered them."

"It'll be repaired and delivered back here in about an hour. You can get the key at the front desk. Milt also picked up your car, said it was probably totaled but that he'll keep it for you until you decide what you're going to do with it." He reached inside his truck and tugged out her purse. "Milt found this in your car."

"Thank you." She took it, opened it, looked inside. "I want to apologize for implying you were greedy last night. When you took that call just as I was leaving, Helen told me about the problems the drought has caused you. I'm really sorry about all of it."

"No need for an apology. How about a truce?" He stretched out his hand. The instant she touched it, his stomach clutched. He looked down at her long slender fingers with short, practical nails. Delicate fingers that might brandish an artist's brush or play a harp lullaby for a sleepy child or stroke a man's back.

His gaze shifted to her eyes, and he fell into a sparkling pool of mermaid water.

Staring back at him, her mouth slowly opened. He could see his confusion mirrored in her eyes, and his hand flexed tighter around hers. His thumb touched her knuckles once, and she shivered.

Then a car honked.

She jerked her hand free and nervously looked around. "With both of us humble, we shouldn't make any more mistakes."

"You'd think." His hand tingled. He shook it out and then reached for the envelope in his back pocket. "I stopped by Lindsey's this morning. She gave me this." He handed it to her. "It's addressed to you."

"From Lindsey?"

"No, it came in her mail today."

"Who even knew I was in the area?" She handed him her purse, ripped open the envelope, read. And gasped.

"What is it?" He looked over her shoulder and mumbled the words:
"Georgie Porgie, no pudding or pie,
Kissed a girl and watched her die.
He saw the blood
Become a flood
And laughed when he stepped in it."
Mac frowned at her. "What *is* this?"

"I have no idea. Who is Georgie Porgie? Or the girl?"

Mac glanced around the parking lot. "The only girl I know that was murdered anywhere around here was Brigitt."

"So yesterday was about Brigitt's murder, not Uncle Cecil's?"

Mac shook his head as he took the poem and studied it. "He didn't rhyme the last line."

"I noticed that. But why send this to *me*?"

"May I have the envelope?"

She handed it to him, her gaze darting from room to room, but no one at the hotel was interested in what they were doing. "Someone's watching me, Mac. I think he might've even known about my plans. He didn't just *happen* by the Tucker place yesterday. Someone told him I was there."

"Maybe he was staying there. A vagrant. Did you tell anyone you were coming up here?"

"I mentioned it to my parents." She shrugged. "And the assistant at the attorney's office in Brennan."

"Elaine Brown. I know her. She works Tuesdays and Thursdays for Bonnie. She wouldn't do anything like this."

Marianne glanced over her shoulder. "Well, I'm not going out to my place again anytime soon. Not alone, at any rate."

"That's smart." Mac folded the note and handed it to her. "Before I forget, Lindsey wanted me to convey an invitation to you for lunch."

"For today?"

"At noon."

"Are you invited?"

"I am. A referee of sorts, I understand."

Her spurt of laughter was followed by a shrug. "So, she told you about last night."

"Touchy subject, murder."

"Hmm." She looked around the parking lot again. "Okay. I'll see you at Lindsey's then." She spun around, stopped, turned back, and tugged her purse out of his hand. "Thank you."

"It was a sacrifice. I don't usually, y'know, do purses."

"You handled it very well, Mr. McKenzie. See you at noon."

He watched her walk inside her room. A cowboy stepped out of a room three doors down, but when he spotted Mac, he ducked his head and scooted back inside.

Mac called Marianne, grateful Helen had given him her number. "Hello?"

"Now you have my number. A man three doors down walked out of his room just now, saw me, and instantly retreated. I don't know if it means anything, but I thought you should know."

"Thanks, Mac."

"Any time. I'll see you at Lindsey's."

Marianne wasn't looking forward to seeing her cousin again, but she knew she had to go, to try to make amends.

In those short ten minutes last night, she'd learned a couple of things about Lindsey. She had a temper, and she was afraid. But something else was going on. Seventeen years had passed since Brigitt's death. Most people got over a cousin's death after that length of time. So why had she simply *exploded* when Brigitt's name came up?

Marianne parked in front of Lindsey's home, got out, and started up the path to her home. Something moved behind the potted plant on the ledge of Lindsey's porch. Up popped Mac's head. He was smiling broadly at her. She didn't like the little flutter in her stomach or the fact that her heart beat a little faster at the sight of him. But what woman wouldn't be flattered that that beautiful smile was aimed at her?

She was definitely flattered and a little intimidated by it.

Without his cowboy hat on, Mac's eyes seemed bluer. His black hair was cropped short and neat. Marianne admired a man who cared about his appearance, and Mac was no slouch. His boots were polished, his short-sleeved shirt pressed and tucked in with a large belt buckle featuring a white outline of a Longhorn with 'Texas Pride' written across it.

She couldn't gauge his mood as he stood on the porch and watched her walk up the steps.

"You're late."

"I am?" She lowered her voice. "Is Lindsey upset?" The last thing she wanted was to anger her cousin again.

He chuckled. "I'm just teasing."

"You have a mean streak in you, Mac." This morning, when he brought her purse and an offer of a truce, she decided he couldn't be behind the shooting, the ramming, or the Jeep's flat tires. She just couldn't round up enough suspicion toward him to make it stick.

He smiled at her, as if he could hear her thought processes. "Lindsey wondered if you would show." As Marianne walked by him, he leaned in. "So did I."

His breath on her cheek felt like a passing kiss. She squirmed and lifted her chin. "I'm an honest person. I said I'd be here, and I am." His shoulder brushed hers when he reached around her to open the screen door. "Thanks for the warning call about the man three doors down."

"Have you seen him again?"

"No." She held the door shut and lowered her voice. "Can I ask you something, Mac? Did you promise Lindsey Uncle Cecil's land if she'd sell you the four hundred acres?"

"It wasn't mine to promise. I mentioned I wanted to buy or lease the land from whoever inherited. Lindsey thought the land would be hers and said I could have access if she inherited."

"I see." Not exactly the way Lindsey told it. "Thanks." Marianne opened the door and stepped inside.

Dressed in jeans and sandals, her cousin stood in the kitchen doorway, her hair brushed forward with spikes at the crown, and they were spray-painted green. Holding a kitchen towel, she offered no greeting to Marianne and simply glanced at Mac. Maybe getting past the hurt feelings and scooting into learning how to be a family wasn't going to be easy after all.

Lindsey's lips tightened. "I'm sorry for last night. I'm willing to start over." Said like a little girl with worry in her eyes, as if she anticipated a slap for her efforts.

Marianne hadn't expected a heart-felt apology. "I didn't mean to hurt you." *Or frighten you.* "I came up here to see my uncle's property. I ended up finding an aunt, two murdered relatives, a cousin, and a pushy neighbor."

"A-hem." Mac playfully dipped his chin at her and raised his brows.

Lindsey draped the towel over her shoulder and settled her gaze somewhere around Marianne's stomach. "I called Bonnie, and it is your land. I hadn't talked to Aunt Helen since Cecil's memorial service. I didn't know about the living trust or that his estate could be settled this quickly. So. That's that." She couldn't seem to bring her gaze up to Marianne's eyes. "Mac said it's good to have you here, that you'll bring fresh perspective to a very old problem. He's wrong. You'll bring nothing but trouble. Do you like ham and cheese sandwiches?"

Uh. "Love them. Can I help you with anything?"

"I got it." Lindsey tossed the towel onto the counter near a row of small plants sitting between a bread machine and a juicer. A hint of mint filled the air. "Mac says I need to see this poem you got."

Marianne retrieved her purse, slipped the note out of the envelope, and handed it to her.

Lindsey frowned as she read, then backhanded the page, her lips tightened in obvious disapproval. "Didn't I *tell* you not to stick your nose into this?"

Ah, so there's the temper and the shrill words again.

Lindsey sniffed. "Someone's trying to scare you away." She reached for a Kleenex. "One can only hope." She blew her nose. "Who knew you were in Brennan?"

"My parents, Patrick, you, Aunt Helen, the man in the black truck, the shooter, the rammer. The sheriff and the men who helped out last night. James, the chef. And, of course—" She crossed her arms and tossed her head at Mac. "—him."

"Him flunked poetry." And then he winked at her.

Oh! Marianne's heart rolled into a foolish little dance. A flash of heat covered her neck and face. She tried to stop the smile easing across her lips but couldn't, so she turned away. The envelope slipped out of her hand, and she swiped at it, mid-air, accidentally shoving it in Mac's direction.

He stepped forward, grabbed it, and handed it to her with a laugh.

Oh! Another blush! What silliness to come out of her at such a simple gesture.

"Here." Lindsey handed the poem to her. "Someone might have overheard you talking to Helen or Mac. The person who mailed this may very well live at the ranch." She opened the backscreen door, and her cat waltzed in. "We don't know that the girl mentioned in the rhyme is actually Brigitt."

Marianne shook her head. "The poet knew I'd find out about Brigitt dying at Cecil's place. It's probably the man who shot at me." She studied each word of the poem. "The last line isn't supposed to rhyme." She raised her brows at Mac. "It's for poetic effect, to make the reader unsettled, edgy."

"Irritable," Mac added, smug. He grinned, crossed his arms, and leaned his hip against the counter.

"*And.*" Marianne puckered her mouth so she wouldn't laugh. She needed to concentrate on the matter at hand and not on the gorgeous man flirting with her. "Whoever killed her was named Georgie, George. He had a thing for her—it says he kissed her. Was it forced on her? She wouldn't have anything to do with him, so he killed her and laughed about it."

"The last laugh," Mac interjected, more seriously.

"The envelope." Marianne turned it over and held it up. "Has no stamp. It's looking more and more as if someone placed it in your mailbox, Lindsey." *To let me know he knew where I was.* She brushed a fingertip over the stamp area. "Do you know anyone named George, Mac?"

"George Radke, your uncle."

"My uncle?"

"My father." Lindsey looked down at her hands, then finally met Marianne's gaze for a millisecond before her gaze drifted to the tabletop. "He wouldn't hurt a fly."

Not what your body language just told me. But if Lindsey knew her father was somehow involved, that would explain her cousin's anger and extreme reaction last night.

Marianne folded the note, slipped it inside the envelope, and dropped it into her purse. "Did Brigitt know anyone else named Georgie or George?"

"Helen might know." Mac tugged out one of the chairs. "Or my older brother, Bobby. He and Brigitt were getting married sometime that summer or fall."

"We'll start with Helen, then Bobby."

"We?" Mac stood half-way and pulled out her chair. "Is that the Divine We, Miss Glaze?"

"It is, Mr. McKenzie. I'm hoping for a little of your help." She sat, as did he.

"Helen said she invited you to stay a couple days at the ranch. You're welcome, but I don't have a lot of time to help you. Neither does she. If you come to the ranch, you're pretty much on your own. You need to show that poem to Nate. It's a new piece of evidence."

"I will, and I promise to be on my best behavior and stay out of your way." As she placed her napkin on her lap, she paused. "But what if our poet is at your ranch?"

"We'll take precautions. I'll work up some ground rules when we get there, and then we'll get you settled into one of the upstairs rooms."

"That sounds great. I have to check out of the Brennan Inn and sign some papers at my uncle's attorney's office. I'll meet you at your ranch later."

Sitting in the rather sparse law office of Bonnie Milhouse, Marianne studied the *Cecil M. Tucker Living Trust*, dated seven years ago. It was very simple: she'd inherited everything he owned. That Uncle Cecil remembered a bossy little girl's wish and acted on it humbled her.

She lowered the document and looked at the attorney. Jethro Bonstrone Milhouse was a large man who literally overflowed his chair. The arms of the chair disappeared into his sides. He had a strong, kind face. He was typing on the only computer in the room. His desk was next to two filing cabinets and a bookshelf stuffed with thick legal books and several murder mysteries.

"Excuse me, Mr. Milhouse?"

He looked over at her. "Yes, ma'am."

"Two things are mentioned here that I don't understand. One is that my uncle hid something for me near a place he showed me as a child. Do you have any idea what he's talking about or where it is?"

"I don't, Miss Glaze. I suspect he thought you'd remember the location."

"Also, it mentions a letter would be given to me at the time of my inheritance. Do you have the letter?"

"He never gave it to me." He indicated the manila folder on the table. "There is an email from your uncle in that file. He said the letter included detailed information about the murder of your cousin. It also included directions to the location of other pertinent information and evidence in that case."

"Did he know who killed Brigitt Holcomb, Mr. Milhouse?"

"He never said anything to me about the case."

The letter would certainly be reason enough for Brigitt's murderer to ransack Uncle Cecil's house and her car. But since his living trust was never published, how would the killer have known about the letter?

Who would have told him? "I don't understand why Uncle Cecil gave *me* this information."

"He died shortly after I drew up the revised document you're holding. He called me the day before he left to return to Florida—and the day before he died, apparently—and said that he was giving this letter to someone named Bubbles. This Bubbles, he said, would take care of the letter until you inherited."

"Who is Bubbles?"

Bonnie Milhouse shrugged. "I have no idea. Because of confidentiality, I wasn't allowed to discuss this with anyone but you and Mr. Tucker." He pulled out a drawer and withdrew a set of keys with a tag on it. "These are to your property." He pushed papers toward her. "And these, you need to sign. I marked the signature lines for you. After you finish, you're all set to go."

The man in the white truck dialed a number.

"What?" His boss sucked on a cigarette and blew out a breath.

"She's back at the ranch."

"Wired?"

"No. What do you expect me to do? Waltz up and hand it to her?"

"Get it on her. We have to find the letter. But until we do, let's have some more fun with her."

Pure pleasure washed over Marianne's face as Mac ushered her into his mother's room.

"Oh, how lovely, Mac." When she made her way to the sitting room, making little sounds of delight, Mac leaned against the wall.

So many memories rested in here. His mother sewing or quilting, asking about his day at school. His racing in to tell her he had caught more fish than his brothers. His mother reading him a favorite childhood book. Tragic memories were here as well, but no one mentioned them anymore.

As Marianne wandered around the room, Mac remembered walking past this door when he was nine, soon after Joey's death. His brother was barely sixteen. Hearing his mother's racking sobs, he opened the door because he didn't know what else to do. The sight that had met his gaze made him pause then, as now, for he'd never seen his mother cry so miserably. Inching toward her, he stopped a couple feet from where she sat on the floor, her upper body angled across the edge of her bed, her head in her arms, her shoulders jumping with each sob.

No one else was around. His father and older brothers were working a fence line, and Helen was downstairs in her office. It was up to him to comfort her, and he simply didn't know how.

"Mom?" He spoke softly, not knowing if he should touch her or leave her alone. It tore at his heart to hear her moans and muffled words, to know she was crying over Joey. He glanced around the room, looking for something but he had no idea what. "Mom?"

"Noooo! Noooo!"

The agony in her voice caused him to step back and look over his shoulder at the door. Maybe he should go get Helen. No, he couldn't leave his mother. He inched closer. "Mom?" he said. "It's me. Mac."

Her head snapped up. Her hands quickly brushed across her cheeks as she struggled to her knees. "Oh, honey. I'm s-sorry." She sniffed, blinking rapidly against the tears. "I thought I was alone. I thought you were—" Her face crumbled and landed in her hands when the sobbing began again.

She thought he was Joey. Mac touched her shoulder and before he knew it, she was wrapped around him and he was holding her and his shoulder was getting wet.

"Oh, Mac, I heard your voice. I thought you were Joey. Oh, *Joey*."

She sobbed again and wept bitterly. Then the crying slowed down and eventually stopped. She pulled back and smiled her mother's smile and patted his shoulder, her bottom lip still quivering, her eyes still wet with tears. "I'm fine now, honey. I was just having a mother's moment." She wiped her face with a Kleenex.

He could tell she was fighting tears and despite the fact that they made him miserably uncomfortable, he said, "It's okay to cry, Mom. I miss him, too." He humiliated himself when tears stung his eyes. He quickly brushed a hand across them. "We all do."

Her smile wobbled as she touched a hand to his face. "I know." She hugged him tight, a long hug that made him want to cry again.

But he didn't. And neither did she.

"Your father left you behind today?"

"He asked me to watch out for you."

"Well." She stood. "You're doing a fine job of it." She leaned over conspiratorially. "Since it's just the two of us, let's raid the pantry and see what goodies we can find."

They had left then, arm in arm, a kind of contentment between them, the tears not quite forgotten as they talked over pecan pie and ice cream about catching fish and rounding up cattle.

Mac had vowed that day to protect his family against anything. His nine-year-old heart promised to make sure no one else was hurt or died.

Then, two months later when Brigitt was murdered, he felt like such a failure. "You've kicked that can of responsibility much too far down the road, son," Dad told him just before they'd entered the chapel where Brigitt's funeral was held.

He'd heard the words, but they couldn't change his resolve. When his father was killed, despair enveloped him, and he didn't know how to change it.

Mac forced himself to concentrate on Marianne as she glided over the thick white carpet. She stopped at the door to the huge balcony hot tub surrounded by black tinted windows. Mac enjoyed seeing her face flushed with delight when she turned to him.

"It's wonderful, Mac. I'm going to enjoy it here. Whose room is this?"

"My mother designed this as her own private sanctum. My father never cared for frills and female stuff, and heaven knows the rest of the house was overrun with testosterone. Mom carved out this spot to have all her ruffles and bows. After Dad died, she moved into a home she inherited from her parents in Granston, Texas. She's closer to grandchildren that belong to my brother Kevin."

He indicated the hot tub. "You can see out the tinted glass, but no one can see in."

"When did your father die?"

"Eight months ago. He was murdered."

Another murder? *Three* murders? Over seventeen years. Were any of them connected? "Mac, I'm so sorry. Did they catch the person who killed him?"

"No. It's not something I want to get into right now. The intercom works. My extension is two."

He walked to the door and turned around, holding the doorknob. "Take your time. Enjoy the hot tub—it'll help with any bruising or pain you're having from last night. When you're ready, give me a call. I'll meet you in my office and we'll work up those ground rules I mentioned earlier."

"Thank you."

"You're welcome." He stepped into the hall and pulled the door shut behind him.

Impatient for him to leave, Marianne headed for the balcony overlooking the small lake and the chapel beyond it on the right. The glass door slid soundlessly open. She stepped out and into the afternoon sun that would hopefully be chased away by the coming storm.

Despite the hovering heat, the air smelled fragrant and soft. Flower boxes filled with red, yellow, and blue blossoms surrounded the balcony. Dipping her head, she breathed in their sweet offerings.

She caught the glint of the sun off something in the scattered trees behind the chapel. A shadowed form moved through the foliage. The movement stopped. Another flash of light.

Binoculars? Was someone watching her?

She casually looked to the right, to the left, and then stepped inside and shut the doors. Rubbing her arms, she searched the trees for any movement, but there was none. Ten minutes crept by. She hoped whoever had been in the woods would step out and walk toward the house or one of the barns. But no one did.

She sat on the edge of the bed and glanced toward the sliding glass doors. Was coming to McKenzie Ranch a mistake? It was one thing to check out her inheritance and decide to live on her property. It was another to be harassed by a man who obviously wanted to frighten her away.

She would let it all play out and hoped she would know when the time was right to either give up and leave—or dig in her heels.

The huge hot tub seemed to invite her in. Moments later, she eased into its bubbling warmth and closed her eyes. The water soothed her aching muscles and the headache that had plagued her since yesterday. She sank deeper into the sweet-smelling oils until they nudged her chin.

It was all like a dream—a different kind of world, a simpler way of life. The air hinted of flying dirt, hay, and horses. Handsome cowboys lived in huge rustic cabins. Sparse trees, dry grass, and slithering creatures that could kill surrounded them.

And into this stark and rugged world, a beautiful daughter, a beloved father, and a gentle uncle were viciously murdered. Were their murders connected? Did the killers still live in the area?

And more importantly for Marianne, was she the next target?

SIX

Mac opened the glass door, tossed his hat on a rack, and headed for his office restroom. The cool water he splashed on his hot sweaty face made him feel almost human again.

Heat blanketed the panhandle. He was more than ready for the storm to come and stay awhile. Hopefully, there would be enough rain to not only cool things off but wet the land and put water in his tanks.

He dried his face and hands and strode to the refreshment center. It pleased him to see Marianne sitting in one of his office chairs. She was so engrossed in the open file on her lap that she hadn't moved.

He took a moment to study her.

The green shorts, modest blouse, and thin shoulder straps complemented her slim frame. Her hair was pulled up in a ponytail, and she looked refreshed and downright beautiful.

He twisted off the cap of a bottled water and guzzled. "Would you like some water?"

She looked up and smiled. "I'm fine, thanks. And thank you for allowing Nuggets to stay here. I can pay you for her food—"

"No need. We have several dogs, and she's no extra expense." He chuckled. "She's sure enjoying herself. A beagle needs room to explore."

"I appreciate it so much. Do you know anyone named Bubbles?"

"Bubbles? No. Why?"

"Bonnie Milhouse said Uncle Cecil wrote me a letter with directions to the location of evidence in Brigitt's case."

Evidence? "But there isn't any evidence."

"Apparently, there is. He gave this letter to someone named Bubbles, to be kept safe until I inherited. His living trust indicated that Cecil wrote me the letter and hid something for me in a special place he'd shown me as a child. It might be the evidence."

"Do you remember that special place?"

"Not at all."

"Helen might know about Bubbles and your special place."

"I'll ask her. I think this man ransacked the house and my car because he wants that letter. He somehow found out that I would receive it upon inheriting, even though the living trust wasn't published."

"Did the trust mention the contents of the letter?"

"No. An email to Bonnie mentioned the contents."

"Then to anyone reading the trust, it could have been a letter about anything."

"Maybe the killer knew about the letter seven years ago, shot Uncle Cecil because of it, couldn't find it, and now thinks I have it."

"Could be."

"So, the big question is: why didn't Uncle Cecil place this evidence in Brigitt's case file? Why give it to me?"

Mac thought about it. "Maybe the evidence points to someone he cared about."

Marianne nodded as she wrote quickly. "Oh, my insurance agent is sending someone out today to look at my car."

"Good. So where are you going to start with Brigitt?"

"Aunt Helen gave me these two boxes from private investigators. They also include Brigitt's case file. Her brother was the sheriff, and he gave her a copy. Hundreds of people were interviewed." She flipped one page over. "I called you because one note piqued my interest." She looked up with a question in her eyes.

"Go ahead. I'm finished with outside ranch work for the day."

"Okay." She read: "'On March 15th, Brigitt Holcomb died from wounds inflicted on her way home from school. No witnesses. No suspects. No warrants. No nothing.'" She shrugged. "Maybe I've watched too many mysteries on TV, but it seems a little too settled. Too clean. Nothing's-here-so-let's-move-on sort of thing."

"Same with my father. Nothing to work with." Mac looked out the window. "I remember when we found out about Brigitt. My mother was past hysterical. She had lost my brother Joey a couple months before and then Helen's daughter. Everyone was on edge for a long time, afraid the killer would strike again." He turned back around. "I was nine at the time. Helen could fill you in on any gaps."

"He killed your brother, too?"

"No. Joey died in a car wreck just after he turned sixteen."

"I'm so sorry, Mac. What a tragedy for all of you."

He yanked himself away from the encroaching memories and focused on Marianne. One problem with Marianne being at the ranch, asking questions, was that it dredged up a lot of memories that had been carefully buried with time. He was glad his mother wasn't around to hear all this. "What else have you discovered?"

She lowered her gaze to the notes. "One strong suspect, Charlie Blake, was cleared. Had a thing for her, was jealous of your brother

Bobby, and made threats against him."

"I know Charlie. He's a private investigator with his father, a former cop in Fort Worth. My dad used their firm from time to time for business purposes. Not anything recently. The family's good, solid."

"His alibi checks. No history of prior offenses or prior violence. He usually walked home from school but not the same route as Brigitt. Got home at his usual time. Suggests he didn't have time to kill her."

"Would you like to see where she was found? It's near the spring your ranch is named for, back a ways from your house. We kids used to play there. We'll test the old bridge, see if it's still crossable, and maybe beat this storm if we hurry."

"You bet." She closed the file and put it on top of a box. "You said *found?*"

"The coroner believes she died on your property but was beaten somewhere else." He plucked his hat off the rack. "Helen has a couple pair of work boots in the mudroom you can wear. Then we'll head out."

Like a cathedral, filled with silence and old memories.

Marianne stood with Mac in the warm breeze murmuring through full, thick post oaks. She listened to the hushed, steady murmur of rustling leaves and the forgotten voices of long-ago children playing in these woods. She strained to hear the guttural moans of a dying young woman and discovered she could not.

Mac glanced at her. "You feel it?" he whispered. "Woodland magic. We always talked about the feel of this place. It's still here, despite Brigitt's body being found right over there."

He motioned for her to follow him around an old peeling sign whose once-black letters could scarcely be read now: "Tucker Spring." They picked their way down an overgrown path, fighting the branches and vines dangling over the old trail and came to the bridge.

"No one's been on this thing in years."

Marianne touched the peeling wooden rail. "I remember my Uncle Cecil showed it to me one time. He said we could never walk over it, or we'd be trespassing on McKenzie land."

"A link between our property and yours. We never considered it a dividing line like Cecil did."

"Although, in reality, it was."

"Maybe." They continued over the bridge. Mac stopped at a turn in the path and looked back.

"What is it?"

He shook his head. "I remember walking through here from a fishing tank on our land. We younger kids tagged along with my older brothers, Brigitt, and friends who came over." He pursed his lips. "The laughter and teasing, the air pumping through me as I ran and scuffled with the boys. The strong sense of belonging." He looked up at the tops of the trees. "I haven't been in these woods in a long time."

"I'm surprised to see so many post oaks."

"My great-great-grandfather planted them in the 1880s. This creek is actually part of the property line between McKenzie land and Tucker land. We boys loved playing in here. There was a gravel walking path, but it's overgrown now. Right over there were three picnic tables and a stone barbecue pit. When your family came to visit, we'd all come here for a big cookout. Lots of good memories."

"Until Brigitt died."

Mac shrugged and nodded.

"Were you two close?"

"Oh, yeah. She was absolutely enchanting."

"She must have been, for a nine-year-old boy to notice."

"She was like our own special angel." He stared at something down the path for a long moment. "She was gentle and kind to the younger kids. Never a harsh word. Everyone loved Brigitt."

"Somebody didn't."

The words settled between them as Marianne stood in the quiet, feeling and listening. She flapped a hand near her face, trying to stir the warm air, but it didn't help. Sweat drops rolled down her back and chest and legs. "Do I hear running water?"

"Tucker Spring, right over there." He led her to a large flat rock that looked out over the land. Below their feet, a thin waterfall spilled from the rocks and poured into a deep, wide, clear pool.

"I would never have expected to find a place like this around here. It's incredible. Does the pool go under the rock we're standing on?"

"Yes. At least ten or fifteen feet. Would you like to go down?"

"Oh, yes. I think this will become a favorite place of mine."

"Good. We need better memories here."

"This is where she was found?"

"Yes, right there." Mac pointed to a large slanting rock, flat on one side and rising into a sharp backbone like the side of an arrowhead. "A cryptic call from an unknown number told police where to find her."

Marianne could see it and feel it. If she allowed herself, she could imagine the slap of flesh and skull against the knife-like edge. The lethal moan of a dying woman. The muted slide of her body across the huge boulder.

Did the killer laugh? She thought of the note: "And laughed when he stepped in it"—the blood. Did he enjoy watching her die? She shook her head and closed her eyes against the vividness of it.

"Come on. Let's head down."

They reached the pool and stood near the water's edge. Marianne looked up. It was as if a giant had scooped out this miraculous little oasis. She turned a complete circle, marveling at how green the plants were and how clear the water. The rock she'd stood on up above was actually a gargantuan boulder.

"Your great-great-grandfather named this Tucker Spring. You can drink this water right out of the pool." Mac squatted at the water's edge, scooped up a mouthful, and drank it. Shaking out his hand, he said, "Now that's good water, and it's on your property."

She sipped some. "Mmm. That *is* good. It's so beautiful here." She relished the sounds of the spring hitting the pool.

"Tuckers have owned this land much longer than McKenzies ever did. The underground spring feeds my lake, this pool, and the creek on our two properties. We kids loved playing down here. But none of us wanted to come to the spring after Brigitt died."

"What about your brother, Bobby?"

"He was devastated. After they found Brigitt, he couldn't function for months. Actually, years." Mac took his hat off. "Brigitt died just two months after Joey passed away. Bobby was with him." Mac slipped his hat on, stood, and grabbed a branch near his head. "Dad had given Joey a new car for his sixteenth birthday. His maiden voyage. Hugged a tree. Died instantly. Bobby didn't have a scratch on him."

"Bobby had *two* people die in two months? Maybe there's a connection."

"He didn't have anything to do with either death."

Surprised at his angry tone, Marianne lifted her gaze to his. "I'm not suggesting he did. I mentioned it because there might be a link between the two deaths."

"The first one was an accident. The second, murder. Bobby was at home at three-ten. He'd taken off work to meet Brigitt at three-fifteen. He talked to Helen, got a phone call at three-twenty. You saw the file. He couldn't have done it."

"You remember more than you thought."

"Yeah, well, *this* part I remember. Bobby didn't kill *any*body."

She lifted both hands. "I didn't say he did."

He picked up a rock and sent it sailing across the water with, Marianne thought, a bit of temper in his hands. "You hooked me into some really bad memories. Joey was a cut-up. He was tall, about six-three, and he didn't look his age. He loved Brigitt like a sister. They were very close." He blew out a long breath and squatted again at the edge of the pool. "The speculation was rampant that Bobby had reached some sort of meltdown, that he had killed his brother out of jealousy, and his future wife because of her disloyalty. Nothing could have been further from the truth. Their deaths just about killed him."

"I believe you." She crouched beside Mac and dipped her fingers in the water. "Does Bobby ever come here?"

"He rarely comes home. Has never married. Seldom dates. Brigitt was everything to him. When he goes out with a woman, he compares her to Brigitt."

"And no one ever measures up."

"You'd think—I mean, it's been seventeen years. That's a long time to hold onto her."

In the distance, thunder rumbled. A warm breeze swirled around them. Marianne twisted her ponytail into a bun. "I can't imagine loving someone that much." When Mac said nothing, she looked over at him.

"Can't you?" Whispered, gently, like the air against her neck.

Her hair fell slowly out of her hands as she looked into his eyes. *Believe,* they said to her. *Believe in the possibilities*. But she knew better than to be sucked into that lie. Hadn't she been a daily witness to her parents' miserable marriage? Beauty turned to ashes. She wanted no part of it.

She stood and tucked a strand of hair behind her ear. "Love doesn't survive."

Mac rose. Out of her peripheral vision, she saw his head turn toward her. He stared at her for a moment. Then he looked up at the sky. "We have to get back before this storm hits. But I think there's enough time to show you one more thing. Let's climb back up."

They did. As Mac led her over a felled tree, he said, "Watch out for snakes."

She froze. "Snakes?"

"I think we're making enough noise to scare them off before we can get close. Look over here." He pointed to a tree across the creek on McKenzie land. "See those boards up there? Way up there?" He touched her shoulders, moved her in front of him, and pointed to the treetops thick with leaves. In order to see, he bent over and eased to his left. His cheek ended up a mere inch or two from hers. It happened so quickly, she didn't have time to panic. But her heart began to race as she sucked in a shallow breath and tried to concentrate on what he was saying.

"There." He pointed up, and then rested both hands on her shoulders.

He was too close. She held her breath. *It's such a simple gesture. He means nothing by it.* She exhaled a bit but sounded like a sputtering chainsaw. His hands, so hot. She needed to breathe, and she was afraid her body would start shaking, exposing her anxiety.

She stepped away from him, blew out the rest of the breath, and grabbed another one. "Yes," she managed. "I see it."

If Mac noticed her panic at his touch, he didn't show it. "That platform was my brother Tim's favorite spot. Joey, Tim, Luke, and I built it when I was around seven, with Dad's help, of course. All the boys liked to play up there. We could see onto Tucker property and watch the kids play. And here." He touched the tree. "Tim's initials."

In silence, they stood side by side.

Marianne listened to the wind whispering in the trees.

Nothing moved but the leaves and those, gently and quietly, as if in deference to Brigitt's memory.

Then thunder cracked.

Mac looked down at Marianne and smiled. Unsure of herself, she tentatively smiled back.

He held out his hand.

Staring at it, she found hers in it.

Then together, they walked back to where the magic began.

Marianne stood at the open French doors in the den and lifted her chin to the breeze ushering in the rainstorm. She closed her eyes and savored the sounds and sweet scents of the rain, the coolness in the air. After a few moments, she walked back into the room, toward the empty fireplace and the oil painting above it that few could examine and not ponder its meaning. For several minutes, she studied the painting and tried to make out the signature.

"Interesting, isn't it?" Mac stopped beside her, close enough for the sleeve of his shirt to touch her arm.

She eased away from him and gestured toward the painting. "What is that guy doing?"

Mac crossed his arms. "It's called *The Stalking Horse* by Smithson Wellington. Long years ago in Britain, when a hunter spotted prey, he would sometimes slip off his horse and hide behind him. The horse and the hunter would then creep closer to the prey, and when the hunter thought he could get off a good shot, he'd step out from behind the horse and shoot."

"It's so deceptive. The animals don't stand a chance."

"Which is the idea. A sneak attack." Mac tucked his hands under his armpits. "Pretty ingenious."

"Pretty manipulative. At least give the animal a chance."

"To what? Run off? It's hard enough to get a deer. Give the guy some credit for coming up with a clever way to get his prey and his food."

She silently studied the picture for a long time.

"Mari?"

"Hmm? Oh." She shook her head. "I was just—" She shrugged. It was always difficult to share from her heart with someone—anyone, actually—and here she was, thinking of telling Mac something very personal.

"You were just—?"

"Yes. I-I was just thinking about this picture and me. I'm the one hiding behind that horse." Her head tilted as she stared at the animal, the hunter, the startled prey.

"Who's the horse?"

"My father. I've hidden behind him my entire life. Gone where he wanted me to go. Aimed at what he wanted me to shoot. Wanting so much to please a man who can't be pleased. It's not an enviable spot facing life behind a horse's rear."

"Then step out. You can't see where you're supposed to go until you do."

"That's easier said than done. Although, in coming here, deciding to keep my property, wanting to build a new life, giving up my old life, I've taken the first steps in stepping out."

"We all have our stalking horses. Different kinds. Different uses. Different reasons. This painting reminds me to step out, send the horse on its way without me, and get going."

"A faith thing."

"Yeah. It's not necessarily seeing where to go as much as trusting Who will take you there when you step out."

"Definitely a faith thing. And maybe, just maybe, aim at the horse instead of the prey?"

"Only if you aim with a riding crop to send him on his way."

At the sound of an approaching horse, Marianne walked to the open doors. Cooler wet air greeted her. The rain had already stopped, and the clouds were breaking up. Water dripped from the eaves while she noted the spitting image of Mac lazily sliding off a horse.

The man tethered the animal and was wildly greeted by a golden retriever. He seemed just as excited to see her and squatted to love on her and give her a hug. "Hello, Molly girl. How's my girl? Yuck, you're all wet. Run on, now." She did, just as he sauntered up the steps toward Marianne. Frowning blue eyes dominated his lean tanned face. Black hair teased the collar of a work shirt as a piece of straw dangled comfortably from his mouth.

A pirate. She would paint him as a pirate.

Or a swashbuckling buccaneer.

The man stopped in the doorway, rested a shoulder against the doorjamb, and crossed his arms. "I'd recognize that mop of carrots anywhere." The straw bounced when he talked. "But no spreckles. Can't say it's an improvement."

He tossed the straw, pulled the front of his hat down, and frowned at Marianne.

She lifted her chin. "As I live and breathe. Luke McKenzie." The boy with Mac and the basset hound that tried to lick off her freckles. She wouldn't have known his name except for Helen's help with fishing pictures in another room.

"You remember." A lopsided, foolishly endearing smile softened his expression. "That does my heart good."

Marianne crossed her arms and tried to look gruff. "Some things are better left forgotten. Unfortunately, you, I could never forget."

"And here, all these years, I thought you didn't like me."

She didn't bother to muffle the grunt. "I had reason enough not to, didn't I?" She tried not to smile when he took a step back.

"Easy, now."

"What?" She looked around him. "No dog with you to assail unsuspecting females?"

"Assail?" Luke sent his brother a quizzical look. "You got a dictionary in your back pocket, little brother?"

Mac's mouth puckered. "Means assault."

"Ah." Luke nodded slowly. "But it was fun, wasn't it?"

"That dog slobbering all over my face? Not at all."

Marianne and Luke solemnly faced each other. A smile eased across Luke's mouth. "Marianne Glaze." He extended his hand. "It's been a long time."

She looked down at Luke's offer, and then up into his eyes. "Luke McKenzie." She returned his smile and took his hand. "Not long enough."

"Still prissy, I see."

"Prissy? I wasn't—" But the look between Mac and Luke said it all. "Was I prissy?"

Both brothers snickered.

Her chin rose. "Little girls are supposed to be prissy and bossy. It's in our nature."

Luke playfully held up both hands. "Whatever you say, Marianne." His expression sobered. He glanced at Mac, eyes squinting, mouth in a firm line. The mood had definitely changed. "Margot's pregnant."

Mac frowned deeply. "Well, great," he muttered, shaking his head. "That's just great."

"Who's Margot?"

Luke took off his hat. "Our brother Kyle's wife of three months."

"You don't like her?"

Again, the quick glance between the brothers.

Luke slapped his hat against his leg. "You could say Kyle could have chosen better."

"Is she going to keep it?"

"I don't know, Mac. No word yet. Hey, Helen."

"Boys. Mari." Helen walked up the steps with a spring in her step until she looked at Mac, then Luke. "Something's wrong. What is it, Luke?"

"Margot's pregnant."

"Oh, no." Helen shook her head as if to clear it. "You're sure?" At Luke's look, she said, "Of course you are. Well." She touched Luke's arm. "It's in God's hands now, isn't it?" She looked at Marianne. "I wanted to show you something, Mari, if you have a few minutes."

"All right."

"I'll meet you at the top of the stairs, the first door on the left, in about ten minutes." Helen went inside.

Mac turned to Marianne. "I mentioned establishing ground rules earlier. Whatever you find out, tell me. Don't wander off without someone with you. Use one of our vehicles if you need to take a trip into town, but I'd appreciate it if you wouldn't go alone, and you'd let me know when you're leaving the ranch. While we're gone, you'll have the run of the place. Interview people. Snoop around. Or paint to your heart's content. We'll be back soon." He scooted down the steps and headed toward the barn.

"Interview people for what?" Luke asked, and then quickly joined his brother.

Marianne hurried upstairs. She was late and didn't want to keep Aunt Helen waiting. She glanced down the long hallway to her right. A young maid walked to the room next to hers and knocked. No one answered. She knocked again, listened at the door, and then entered.

"Marianne."

To her left, Helen was unlocking a door and motioned her over.

"Sorry I'm late."

"No problem. I just got here myself. I thought you might get to know Brigitt a little better in here. This was her bedroom." Just inside the room, Helen touched a frame near the door and straightened it. Then she rested her finger on the tall blonde in the picture. "This is my favorite picture of her."

Marianne leaned closer. "She's beautiful."

Looking around, Marianne took in the room. Brigitt was everywhere. Pictures on the walls. A yearbook on a lamp table. An open closet door with clothes hanging neatly and shoes placed side-by-side. Remarkable, that the room still held her belongings. Maybe just as she'd left them that day?

With her lips pressed together, Helen walked a couple steps away. "Most of these things were hers. The curtains and carpets have been changed, of course. But the quilt was Brigitt's. No one's had the heart to take out her stuff. They know how much it means to me to come up here and be with her. The maid cleans it every week."

"Does anyone use this room?"

"When I stay in the main house, I sleep in this bed. Not often, though. Not anymore."

Marianne strolled to the foot of the four-poster bed and wrapped her hand around a post. It was easy to imagine Brigitt lying here with her ankles crossed in the air, bobbing her head to music, talking on the phone. *Maybe that's how I'll paint her.*

"I feel her each time I come up here."

"Yes." *Like the woods.* "She was happy, wasn't she?"

"Bobby filled her world." Helen indicated the bulletin board on the wall. A red heart-shaped Valentine's Day card sat in the middle of it, surrounded by pictures, notes, ribbons, and test scores. The inscription on the card revealed her love of life and her love for Bobby McKenzie.

Helen sighed. "It's odd, I suppose, to have all this as it once was. But Mac's never asked me for this room, and I've never wanted to give it up." Her fingers glided over a yearbook sitting on the nightstand. "Look."

She sat on the bed and flipped through it until she found a snapshot of Brigitt laughing with friends. "That's Brigitt, on the right."

"She's so pretty." Marianne knew she had to tread lightly here and cleared her throat. "Through the years, Aunt Helen, did you come to any conclusions about who could have hurt Brigitt?"

Helen drew in a deep breath and blew it out. "It was so long ago." She shook her head, closed the vinyl-covered yearbook, and hugged it. When she glanced at Brigitt's dresser mirror, her eyes softened.

Marianne stepped toward the card with "Brigitt loves Bobby" written inside a pink lipstick heart with a pair of puckered lips beneath it. A grinning young man with black hair snuggled with a grinning Brigitt in a picture wedged into the frame of the mirror.

"Bobby?"

"Yes." Helen spoke softly behind her. "She loved him so much. Both of them, so beautiful, and so in love."

"Where is Bobby now?"

"Fort Worth." Helen continued holding the yearbook against her heart. "That day, she was alive and happy. A cheerleader, Homecoming Queen, voted Most Likely to Succeed." She glanced at Marianne, her eyes sad. "She never had a chance to prove them right."

Marianne sat beside her and touched her arm. "I'm so sorry, Aunt Helen."

She sniffed. "Can't be undone now, even if you find the men who did that to her."

Men? Not *man?*

Helen placed the yearbook on the bedside table. She stood and walked to the door, her gaze sweeping every part of the room. "I need to see to some things, Mari."

"Do you know anyone named Bubbles, Aunt Helen?"

"No, I don't. Should I?"

"Not necessarily." Marianne took a step toward her aunt. "Would you mind if I painted Brigitt's portrait in here? Not sleep in here, just paint. I think it would—"

"Of course, you can. It makes perfect sense. Here." She handed her a key. "I have another copy. Stay as long as you'd like." She turned then and left.

Marianne walked to the bed. Her fingertips slid across Brigitt's quilt, back and forth, tracing the grooves, the patterns, the stitches, the warmth of yesterday's memories, the chill of empty years. "Who killed you, Brigitt?" she murmured. "And why?"

SEVEN

The next morning, with coffee cup in hand, Mac stood on the porch of the main house, admiring the deep blue, pink and violet colors brushing the eastern sky in soft, satin strokes. He savored the silence covering his land, the cool freshness, the muted glimmer of a new day.

Glancing at the lake, he relaxed against a post as the stillness and quiet enveloped him. He never tired of this. He always looked forward to a new day. Nothing made him happier than being up early, readying himself for the decisions he had to make. He thrived on growing the ranch. "Hard work is for your children, not you. Never give up or give in when it counts." One piece of wisdom among many from his father.

And, Mac had to admit, he was looking forward to seeing Marianne this morning. He wouldn't think about why, for now. He'd just enjoy the first sight of her and let the day have the day.

Daisy clambered up the steps and nipped at his hand. Nuggets followed close behind her. "Good girl," he said, pulling Daisy to his leg and patting her side. Nuggets nudged in for some attention. Then both dogs raced down the steps, barking at the men headed for the mess hall on the other side of the house.

Mac walked around to the front and spotted Luke with Molly beside him. She ran off with Daisy and Nuggets toward an open field.

His brother pulled up, waited for him. "Hey, buddy. You 'n Spreckles have a full day planned?"

The scent of a breakfast buffet drifted through the screen door, and Mac's stomach growled. "Better not let her hear you say that. She's one tough lady. You know anyone named Bubbles, Luke?"

"Bubbles?" His brother chuckled. "Not in this lifetime." He opened the mess hall door, and they both headed for the buffet line.

Mac picked up the bacon tongs and placed several extra crispy pieces on his plate. He plopped a healthy mound of pancakes beside the bacon. Juggling his coffee mug and plate, he sat beside Luke.

"She sure grew up."

"Marianne?" Mac sent Luke a sidelong glance and continued buttering his pancakes. His big brother was on a fishing expedition this morning, and Mac didn't plan to be baited. "Yep."

"Kinda takes the breath away."

"Yep."

"Shame her freckles are gone. They added character."

"Character's still there."

Luke grinned again. "And a whole lot more." He leaned his chair back and happily patted his stomach. If Mom could see him, she'd yell something like, "Luke Aaron McKenzie! Put that chair down!" Just the thought of it made Mac smile.

"Marianne's sure—"

Someone bumped his chair. "Move, McKenzie."

Luke frowned and didn't budge. "Go around."

Mac set his fork down. Jim Calhoun was a pain to work with, but he was a hard worker, and the ranch needed his degree in animal husbandry. Since he'd returned to the area six months ago, he never let an opportunity go by that he didn't needle Luke about something. "Settle down, Cal. I need Luke to finish up here and get out to Section 32."

Luke glared at Mac, but he set his chair down and stood. "At least somebody knows how to work around here."

Cal shoved his considerable weight into Luke's path. "You got somethin' to say, McKenzie?"

"I said it. You ain't as dumb as you look, are you, Calhoun?"

Cal reared back with a tight fist. Curly grabbed it and twisted it behind Cal's back. "Git ahold o' yerself, man." He let go of his arm. "We got work to do. No time for this crap."

Mac continued to sit. These boys needed to work out their differences without interference from him, or they'd never learn to get along. "Get outside with your fight."

The screen door squawked opened. Heads turned toward it.

Jumbo, an old-timer who'd lived at the ranch as long as his brother Curly—little over thirty-five years—leaned inside. "Curly, Cal, let's go. Crew's waitin' on us."

Cal sneered at Luke. "Too bad. I was lookin' forward to kickin' your ugliness into Dallas today."

Luke's slim frame hovered a good three or four inches over the well-built man in front of him. "I got the time, Calhoun. You lookin' for excuses?"

With a glare at him and then Mac, Calhoun stuck out his chest like a rooster, shoved past Luke, and stalked out of the room. The screen door slammed behind him, and the hushed room came to life with forks stabbing metal plates, chairs scooting on hardwood floors, and mumbling voices.

Luke grabbed his hat and scowled at Mac. "Why did he have to come back? Life was a pure pleasure without that troublemaker here."

"I guess he missed you. Y'all used to be friends. What happened?"

"He came back with a burr in his saddle, that's what happened." He plopped his hat on and shoved through chairs toward the door.

At the table behind Mac, Curly leaned back, toward him. Mac depended on Curly to keep the ranch hands herded in the right direction. The men respected him.

"You know it ain't gonna end well with those two."

Mac had known Curly and Jumbo his entire life. They were like beloved uncles to him. Dad had loved and trusted them like family. "I know fighting's not going to change anything. Might even make it worse. What's the story with Cal? I'd hate to have to let him go if he's pickin' a fight with everyone."

"Not everyone. Just Luke." Curly lifted one side of his mouth. "He's such a sweetie with the rest of us."

"I doubt that."

"Then you'd be right." Curly scooted his chair back. "Come on, Abe," he backhanded the man's shoulder as he rose.

Abe took one last slurp of coffee. "Have a good 'un, boss man."

"Yeah." Mac finished his breakfast and headed for the main house. He stopped in front of Helen's desk and waited for her to get off the phone.

She did and opened a drawer. "I got your text." She handed him the book. "There's only one picture on page twenty-nine. I'll fill your ear about him over coffee. Meet you in your office in five minutes?"

"Sure. You and Marianne have breakfast yet?"

"Yes. She left about thirty minutes ago, said she wanted to take a walk about the barns and talk to Geezer in the tack room. I told her he'd been here longer than anyone."

"Born and raised." Mac chuckled. "Dad told us so many hare-brained stories about those two growing up on the ranch."

"Oh, I've heard them. They were a hoot."

Despite his resolve not to be too involved with any of Marianne's snooping around, Mac wished he could join her on her walk and point out every nook that meant something to him. He looked forward to showing her his discovery in the yearbook.

When he did, he just might invite her on one of his famous long hikes.

Marianne poked her head inside the tack room. It took a few heartbeats for her eyes to adjust. Light from a single large window at the back revealed a small worktable, hanging things on the wall, a concrete floor, a long row of saddles on the right. Hugging a wall, she walked along it until she turned a corner into a larger room.

"Hep ya, ma'am?"

She jumped at the deep gravelly voice to her left and laughed at herself. "I'm sorry. I didn't see you there."

"No ma'am, don't expect ya did. It's not too bright in here, but I like it that way. Easy on these old eyes."

She heard the hint of laughter in his voice, the spit and thud of a wad of chewing tobacco hitting a can, the tug on a small chain just before a swinging lamp spilled its light onto his cluttered worktable.

Deep brown eyes in a handsome, thin, finely-wrinkled face watched her over reading glasses perched at the end of a straight, slender nose. He reminded her of her Grandpa Roy, distinguished and reserved, albeit not in a fine Italian suit but in work-worn cowboy clothes.

"Mr. Geezer?"

His eyes crinkled as he swiped a thick hand across his mouth. "Jus' Geezer, ma'am. No mister to it."

"Yes, sir. I hope I'm not interrupting." She sideswiped a saddle draped over a wooden contraption, righted it, muttered, "Sorry," and stood before the man with her hands behind her back.

"Nothin' that won't keep." Steady, unblinking eyes regarded her. His gaze never wavered as his fingers burrowed in a small box and, before she could blink, slipped a toothpick between his teeth.

"My name is Marianne Glaze." She frowned and lifted a shoulder. "I, uh, don't quite know how to start."

"You wanna know some'in' 'bout Miss Brigitt."

"My aunt tells me you and Brigitt were close."

"Not close 'nuf," he muttered. The toothpick jumped into the corner of his mouth, making room for the exiting wad of tobacco bulleting toward the can at his feet. The toothpick bounced to the front of his mouth. He tilted his head back to see through his glasses as he picked up a long, thin piece of leather and turned it over. "Not near close 'nuf."

"Do you blame yourself for—?"

"Naw, didn't say that. Just wudn't there when she needed me." He picked up a flat-edged tool and skimmed it down the leather strap. "Nobody wuz."

He stopped and looked at her. If Helen hadn't told her that he was a gentle soul, she would have been intimidated by the frowning, intense expression facing her right now. "Any one of a hundert men wuda took them blows and cuts fer her. Don't think we wudn'ta."

"No, sir." When he frowned up at her, Marianne added, "Yes, sir."

"And we wuda kilt that son of a snake," he threw his tool down, "if we cuda found 'im." He stood then, a tall wiry man. He straightened his back as he walked around his worktable. "There," he pointed up at the ceiling, "that one yonder."

She followed his finger. A dusty saddle sat as if it was glued to the wall above their heads.

"I made that fer her, fer graduation."

"It's beautiful."

"Yep, wuz. She never saw it."

"I'm so sorry, Mr. Geezer."

Staring at the saddle, he appeared tired for just a moment, then shook his head. "Jus' Geezer, ma'am."

"Yes, sir. Did Brigitt ever tell you she was afraid?"

Frowning gray brows almost covered his eyes when his gaze snapped at her. "Afraid?" He walked toward his spitting can, didn't take the time to aim, and didn't miss. "Nothin' to be afraid of out here. Too many of us watchin' out fer that girl. It was them da-gone town folks like as not that got her. No one out here wuda hurt her."

"Do you have any idea who did it?"

He grunted. "Had my thoughts, long time ago. Still do." He sat on his stool. "That Schroeder boy, the oldest one, George. Nothin' but trouble. Used to pester the living soup outta that girl. A little over the top, we all figured. Nobody thought he'd hurt her."

"Did he act alone?"

"Don't know." He pursed his lips in a ghost of a smile, his gaze fixed on a spot just past Marianne's feet. "She used ta come in here 'n talk ta me for a spell, every day, standin' right there where you're standin'. That girl was happy as a hog in mud."

He frowned as he solemnly shook his head, his mouth drooping. "'Til near the end." His words were just above a whisper. "She wouldn't come in here. Somethin' scared her off. Never knew whut. And 'fore long. she was gone."

He looked into Marianne's eyes. "I know whut yer about, young lady, and ya better watch out. It ain't over." He shook his head and picked up the leather strip. "It ain't over jus' yet."

"What do you mean? What isn't over?"

He stared at her. The intensity in his eyes was frightening. "In here, ma'am." His fist pounded his chest. "I got me a feeling. You best be careful, like I said." He stood. "I got nothin' else to say."

"Before you leave, Mr. Geezer, could you tell me if you know anyone named Bubbles?"

"I don't. Good day to ya." He turned his back on her, walked into another dark room, and shut the door quietly.

She felt her way down the long hallway and opened the door to bright sunlight. With one last glance over her shoulder, she heard Geezer's words again. *It ain't over.*

What could he have meant by that? *What* wasn't over?

Time at McKenzie Ranch was short—Helen had invited her for only 'a couple of days'—and Marianne wanted to sketch out Brigitt's portrait. Now was a good time to move her art supplies into Brigitt's bedroom and get her mind off Geezer's cryptic warning.

Sketching soothed her. It took time to study pictures of clients, the different poses, the different 'looks', to figure out which angle complimented best. Some clients didn't particularly want a realistic portrait as much as they wanted a portrait that made them look beautiful or handsome, even if they weren't.

She picked up her box of supplies and headed down the hall. Aiming the key at the lock, she pushed, but the door was already open. She was sure she had left it locked. A quick glance down the hall in both directions revealed she was alone. She listened intently for a moment, but no movement or sound interrupted the silence.

With the tip of the key, Marianne pushed the door all the way open and set the box on a small table. Nothing seemed out of place. Of course, she didn't know this room well enough to spot many differences, but from what she remembered earlier, everything—wait.

The lipstick tube was missing from the porcelain bowl on the dresser.

She searched around the bowl, beside the dresser, under it. The lipstick was gone. Why would anyone take Brigitt's lipstick tube after all this time?

It ain't over.

A little panicked, she quietly pushed the door shut and quickly locked it. She backed up, stood in the center of the room, and closed her eyes, to concentrate on her work and not on anything else. After several breaths, she opened her eyes, slowly turned a three-sixty, and searched out pieces of Brigitt she hadn't noticed with Helen. It always helped to stand in a client's bedroom—a strange request at times, for sure—to better understand the person.

Brigitt would be thirty-five today, but Marianne had decided to paint her at eighteen. In the closet, two side shelves were full of school books and notebooks. *Studious. Serious.* Above the desk, a seventeen-year-old calendar hung on the wall with markings all over the month of March. *Engaged with life. Well liked.* Pairs of shoes were neatly aligned on the floor. *Efficient. Tidy.* Pictures of her snuggling with Bobby. *Loved. Loving.*

Marianne closed her eyes to see if the "I always feel her when I come up here" phenomenon happened again. It didn't. She unpacked her art supplies and started on sketching the ideas she—

Behind her, a soft grinding sound came from across the room. She turned around. The doorknob was moving! Someone shoved on the door. She stared at the knob, waiting for a key to be inserted, but nothing more happened.

She unlocked the door and looked out. The hall was empty. She rushed along the wall to the stairs. Empty.

Probably a maid wanting to clean. She must have interrupted her straightening the room earlier. The same person who'd taken Brigitt's lipstick?

It ain't over.

"Okay, Glaze. Time to get to work and stop this nonsense." She walked back to the room and locked the door. Sitting on the bed with her box of supplies, she selected her favorite wood pencil and began.

Mac had missed her at supper last night. By the time he got home, Marianne was already in bed. It was a little before six this morning, and he hoped she was awake. His day had started two hours ago, and he needed to be in his Jeep checking out Section 32 in about an hour. He figured he had time to start his day off right by seeing Marianne before he left.

With one finger, he tapped on her door. It opened. "Good morning, Mari," he whispered as he stood in the doorway.

A groan—or a growl—sounded near her pillow pile. Her long, slender fingers gripped the lightweight quilt and tugged it over her head.

"Sorry to wake you, but I have to get to work this morning and wanted to let you know that Helen's been sleuthing on the side for you. I think you'll be interested in what she discovered."

Marianne's hand flopped in the air, and then fluttered in a circle. "Turn around and let me get my robe on."

Mac pivoted to put his back to her. "Sleeping in?"

"In?" Her voice was husky and enticing, and his heart stumbled. "It's not even six yet."

He leaned against the doorjamb and wondered what he wanted from her. He'd lain awake last night, aware of his growing feelings for her. Everything about Marianne enticed him. She'd awakened in him thoughts of *more,* a certainty that her being here was no accident. But if there was ever a colt that needed to find her feet, it was Marianne. "That's late here on the ranch. Most of us are up before five. Some, before that."

"Five?" A long pause ensued. "Uhhh." Covers rustled, and then stopped.

"Are you decent?"

"I've got my robe on. Let me brush my teeth, and I'll be right out. You can come on in."

He turned on the light and waited for her by the door. It took her maybe two minutes to return.

"Good morning, officially." She covered her mouth when she yawned. "I'm surprised I'm coherent this early in the morning."

"You're doing great. First, this." He handed her the yearbook and turned to page twenty-nine.

"What is it?"

Her red hair lay like a broad strand of taffy over her right shoulder. Resisting the urge to touch it, he moved closer to her and pointed to a picture. "George Schroeder. Everyone called him Georgie."

Her eyes widened. "Georgie Porgie?" She eagerly reached for the book. As she did, their fingers touched, and she fumbled it. She blushed and lowered her head toward the picture of a grim young man with shaggy hair and unmistakable arrogance in his expression. Her hair fell forward and almost covered the book.

"Helen said she never cared for Georgie Schroeder. He was older than the other seniors because he'd been held back a year. Came from a bad family—a drinking father, a verbally abusive mother. He was apparently a punching bag for them. They appeared one day, rented the house on Kimball land, and rarely came into town. Shopped in Evanson instead of Mole's Bench. Helen said she might have seen Mrs.

Schroeder once in the entire time they lived around here."

Her head lifted. "She thinks this George Schroeder might have been involved?"

"She said he had his eye on Brigitt for over a year. He was always pestering her, asking her out, teasing her, watching her. He hated Bobby and threatened him when they were alone. After Brigitt was killed, George was at the top of the sheriff's list of suspects, but the family suddenly moved away. Sheriff said their names never popped up anywhere."

"We could be on to something."

"When Helen found his picture, she called her attorney to do a search on Georgie Schroeder. Here is his report." He handed the papers to her.

"Thanks," she mumbled, backed up to the love seat, sat, layered her long robe around her knees, and read.

He enjoyed watching her. She looked the best he'd seen her since she'd arrived at the ranch. All mussed and female and soft. Not a sign of prissy anywhere.

"I don't believe this."

"What?" Mac sat beside her and tried not to think about the fresh-awake fragrance of her, or her hair teasing his arm, or her leg just an inch from his.

"He's dead, Mac. Georgie Schroeder's dead. He has been for fifteen years." She shoved her hair out of her face, and then handed the papers to him.

"It appears he had no criminal record." He frowned. "Wait a minute. This is interesting. Until he was sixteen, his family lived in a religious commune in Montana. He apparently got a girl pregnant. Wouldn't marry her. Family moved to Mole's Bench. He graduated at nineteen. Was dead at twenty-one. A car wreck."

"He could have killed her. He died after Brigitt died."

"But, Mac, if someone knew Georgie killed Brigitt, why not say so? Why didn't our poet come forward a long time ago? Why make such a production of it through a rhyme seventeen years later, with him dead?"

"Maybe the poet was in on it, and he's taunting the police."

"And now he's writing limericks about it?" She bit her bottom lip and shook her head. "Geezer told me yesterday he thought George Schroeder had something to do with hurting Brigitt. He also said, 'It ain't over.' What do you think he meant by that?"

"No clue. Did you ask him?"

"I tried. He just repeated it and told me to watch my back. Maybe he knows something he's not telling. Who else was at the ranch when Brigitt died?"

"Just about every man here. The younger ones, of course not, but the older ones. McKenzie Ranch is like a small village and the people come here to stay."

"What do you know about Jim Calhoun?"

He casually stretched his arm across the back of the sofa. "Lived here awhile back, got his degree from A&M. Came back a few months ago. Why?"

"I saw him today and just wondered if he might know something. He certainly has the physique to hurt a woman. Did Brigitt have a best friend in high school? Someone she told her secrets to?"

"Helen would know." He indicated the phone. "Call her. Extension five."

She dialed, snapped her fingers at her purse. He handed it to her, and she dug for a pen, grabbed Brigitt's file, opened it, and wrote. Then she thanked Helen and hung up. "Brigitt's best friend was Debbie Miller now Engels." Marianne circled her name. "She lives in Brennan."

Wasn't she something? A slow smile of admiration eased across his mouth. "I know Deb Engels."

"Yeah? Well, I'm going to visit her today."

"Are you coming back here?"

She turned so quickly, her hair fell over her eyes. "Am I still welcome?"

"Of course, you are. 'The run of the place,' remember? Is anyone going with you?"

"I don't know anyone but you and Aunt Helen, and I'm sure y'all will be busy today. I'll be okay, Mac. Also, I've asked several people if they know a Bubbles, but no one does."

"You'll find her."

"What if Uncle Cecil gave the letter to someone who's died in the last seven years? We'll never find the evidence."

"I think we can assume Bubbles was someone relatively young and not someone's great-Uncle Stu who's ninety-two."

She laughed. "Nice rhyme."

On a grin, he rose. "Breakfast is ready. How long before you come down to eat?"

"Ten minutes."

"I have to make a phone call, then I'll join you." He walked backwards to the open door. Her belt loosened around her waist, which drew his gaze. Her brows shot up as she grabbed the belt ends and tightened the knot.

"You might try changing your present attire, though. We're not used to seeing—"

"Bossy, bossy," she muttered as she shut the door in his grinning face.

Standing beside his truck, Mac heard the front door shut. He turned around and watched Marianne walk down the front steps. It amazed him that this woman was able to tug him out of his comfort zone with just walking or smiling or waving at him. Or just standing still. It didn't take much.

Everything about her was easy to like.

And there it was again. That yearning for something intangible. This time, it wasn't in a dream. It was real, here, in broad daylight, and it was encased in the woman coming toward him.

Pale green was a nice color on her. A sleeveless blouse and matching shorts accentuated her long slender legs ending in green sandals. She'd pulled her ponytail through the back of a baseball cap. When she stopped beside him, he noticed for the first time a very light sprinkling of freckles across her nose. In the bright sunlight, her green eyes seemed translucent. He wanted to tug her close and send her on her way with a long lazy kiss, but it was too soon for that. He'd have to settle for a pat on her back. "All set?"

"I think so. By the way, where does Nuggets sleep at night?"

"Anywhere she wants. Some of the dogs bed down in a barn or out in a field. She's made a lot of friends, so she's happy." He opened his truck door for her. "The Engels live about thirty-five minutes from here on the other side of Brennan."

"I've got directions on my trusty GPS."

"Good. Call me when you get there. You have your cell phone?"

She opened a pocket on her purse, pulled out her phone, and held it up to him.

"Fully charged?"

"It is. Sure you won't need this Jeep today?"

"It's yours while you need it. Be careful, Mari."

She got in and started it. Backing up, she wiggled her fingers in a good-bye wave.

Mac headed for the barn. He never tired of the routine, the smells of hay, horse and leather, raw earth and dust. When he walked inside, ten-year-old Emma was mucking out a stall. Zach Grimes had hired his daughter a few months back to help tend the saddle horses, so she could earn money for singing lessons.

"'Morning, Emma." Reaching into a bucket, he grabbed a handful of sugar cubes.

"'Morning, Mr. Mac."

Mac held a fisted hand out to Pal as he walked to the stall gate. "How's my boy this morning?" Pal nudged his hand and bobbed his head. Mac's fingers slowly uncurled. Huge lips scarfed up the sugar cubes, and Mac laughed.

"He sure likes his sweets."

Mac glanced at Emma. "Always has had a hankering for them." His cell phone rang. He punched his Bluetooth. "McKenzie."

"Mac, someone's following me."

His stomach coiled at the panicked sound in her voice. For an instant, his brain froze. "What do you mean, 'following you'?"

"He's been behind me since I left the ranch, and he won't pass."

Mac sucked in air, blew it out. "What makes you think—?"

"He pulls up close to me like he's going to pass but he doesn't. And he could. The road's open."

"Okay. What's he driving?"

"A truck. New, white. I picked him up as I left the ranch."

"Describe him."

"Black cowboy hat. I can't see his hair. He's too far away for eye color. Mustache or something. Fifties, I think."

No help at all. "You'll be getting into Mole's Bench soon. Stay on the line until you get—"

"He's coming up on me again!"

"Speed up!"

"I *am*! He's right on my tail!"

"Spee—"

She screamed. "He rammed me!"

Mac ran for one of his pickups. "Mari?"

The line spit at him. "He—he's backing off."

"Get out of there! Go!" His fingertips dug in his pocket for keys.

"I'm trying!"

He jammed the keys into the ignition.

"Oh, no!"

Mac froze and listened. Another scream.

"Mari? Mari!"

"He—he—"

Mac roared down the driveway.

"He's toying with me." Her voice wobbled. "He's backed off—"

"Go! You can't be far from Mole's Bench."

"Oh, no." She gasped. "He's coming, Mac! He's coming!"

Mac heard the ram. "Mari!" A scream. Metal on metal, scraping, crashing. "Mari!" The line was still open. "Mari!" And then it went silent.

"Oh, God, oh God, stay with her. Please." He punched in 9-1-1.

"9-1-1. Do you have an emergency?"

"Yes. An accident out 256, east of Mole's Bench. A Jeep and a white truck. A woman's in the Jeep and not responding."

"Is the female hurt?"

"I don't know. I'm not there. Her phone went dead, but she might need an ambulance." When he reached the road, his eyes scanned both directions and then he peeled out.

"What is your name, sir?"

"Mac McKenzie, McKenzie Ranch."

"Is the truck at the scene of the accident?"

He soared to one hundred. "I don't know." One hundred twenty.

"Did the female contact you?"

One thirty. "I was talking to her on a cell phone when a white truck rammed her from the rear. She was trying to get away from him, so they were going fast."

"I'm putting you on hold. Please stay with me."

He gripped the steering wheel, his heart hammering, his hands sweating, his eyes squinting into the sunlight, searching for her. "Come on. Come *on,*" he muttered as he passed one car, then another. Where was the dispatcher? Why was she taking so long?

His heart took one fierce dive and stopped beating. "No."

"Mr. McKenzie?"

"No. No." Breathless, he slammed on his brakes and pulled over. The Jeep was on its right side, the rear up against a fence. He pulled into a dirt driveway and parked at a gate. "I-I'm here. At the accident. It—oh, man—get that ambulance here!" Frantic to get to her, he tossed his phone and jumped out. *God? God?* He ran, his gaze on the windshield. "Mari."

She was draped over her seatbelt like a ragdoll. Blood was everywhere. "Oh, God." His stomach clutched as he watched for her breath. It was low and slow. "Mari? I smell gas. I need to get you out of here." When he opened the door, it rested against his back. He unlatched her seatbelt and held onto her arm to keep her from falling toward the passenger seat. Ever so gently, he tugged her upper body into his arms. Her head fell back. *Please, Lord. Please.*

The smell of gas was strong. It wasn't safe to wait for the ambulance. "Okay, Mari. I'm picking you up now." He slid a hand under her knees. "Easy, easy." As gently as possible, he lifted her up and out of the Jeep. He shifted her until her head fell against his shoulder. Blood covered her face and blouse. Drops were on her legs, her shoes.

He carefully walked to his truck, managed to lower the tailgate, sat, and eased her onto his lap. "You're okay now, Mari. Hang on. An ambulance is on the way."

A silver pickup slowed down and pulled over. He thought he recognized an old friend of Dad's but wasn't sure until Grady got out.

"Need any help, son?"

Mac tightened his hold on Marianne. "Ambulance is on its way."

"I'll stay with you then, if you'd like."

"I'm obliged, Grady."

"Need anything out of her ride?"

"Her purse. She'll want her purse. But be careful, Grady. I smelled gas."

Mac held her close, afraid to move her any more. He shouldn't have let her go by herself. He should have insisted on going with her. And now, blood covered her. *Her blood.* Angry at himself, he gritted his teeth against the thought of hunting down the man in the white truck and giving him what he'd given Marianne.

Grady brought her purse and set it beside him. "What happened here, Mac?"

"Hit and run," he answered, searching the highway and straining to hear the first wail of a screaming ambulance.

EIGHT

"I want to know what's going on, and I want to know *now!*"

The angry words caused Marianne to open her eyes, but swirling pain clouded her vision, and it hurt to keep her eyes open. She squeezed them shut for a couple seconds, and then opened them again. *Why is Father here? What is happening?*

In profile in front of a window, Mac and Frank faced each other. Even though Mac was a good four inches taller than Frank, her father stood nose-to-nose with him. Red hair against black, green eyes glaring at blue, square jaw to square jaw.

"Mr. Glaze, you'll have to wait until—"

Frank scowled and pointed a finger at Mac. "Don't you use that tone with me, young man! I took time off work to fly up here, and I expect an explanation *now!*"

Oh, Father. Please. Not here.

Mac's eyes narrowed as if he considered punching her father. But he leaned over instead, next to his ear. "Sir, Marianne needs all of us to remain calm." He stood back. "I've told you what I know. She had a wreck." *Oh. Yes. The truck rammed me.* "I found her. The ambulance brought her here. The doctor says she has a concussion."

So that explains why my head is pounding like old water pipes.

Patrick's face appeared in her line of vision. When he smiled, his green gaze flicked to Frank and back to her, vestiges of fear and uncertainty in his eyes. "Mari? It's me, Pat."

"I can see that." She winced. "What happened?" She licked her lips. She couldn't tell if she still had lips, so she tried again to wet them. A thin film of crust covered them, and she wished she had cream to keep them from cracking.

"You had an accident."

Lindsey came out of the restroom, set her purse on an empty chair, and placed her fisted hands on her skinny hips. "You're awake." Her cousin crossed her arms. "You're banged up just like Mac's Jeep."

Marianne couldn't claim to know Lindsey very well, but it sure seemed she enjoyed giving her injured cousin a veiled I-told-you-so.

Patrick took Marianne's hand. "I drove your SUV up here, so you'll have a vehicle to drive. I'm flying back with Frank." The look he sent her said, *And won't that be a happy trip?*

She moved her head and flinched. "Thank you, Paddy. Mac?"

"I'm here." He leaned over her, took her hand. The concern in his eyes was like a salve. "You're okay, Mari. Everything's going to be fine."

Liking him was so unexpected. She knew the pitfalls of the relationship cycle that started with like, slid into love, and ended with disinterest. Her parents' grating existence together had been anything but an encouragement for her to attempt the same. But she couldn't stop the feelings growing for Mac. She met his gaze and fell headlong into his comfort.

He stroked her cheek once with his knuckle and smiled at her. *Oh, this man. This man.* She closed her eyes and gave herself permission to enjoy his caresses. Then he kissed her forehead. It felt natural between them, not embarrassing or awkward or contrived. It just felt right. She opened her eyes as he loosely threaded his fingers with hers. So this was how 'sliding into love' started. She'd never considered herself a 'touchy' person, but Mac's touch thrilled her. And made her head hurt worse.

Because she could see that he needed it, she smiled up at him. "How badly am I hurt?"

"You're mostly bruised. Some cuts, scrapes. You banged your head, your nose, but nothing's broken. You have a concussion and a small cut on your left thumb. Just four stitches. How are you feeling?"

"My head really hurts. How long have I been here?"

"Over three hours. You've been asleep most of the time."

She smacked her lips and licked them again. "May I have some water, please?"

Mac reached for the ice bucket, but Lindsey took the lid off, scooped out a spoonful, and slipped the spoon into her mouth.

Marianne crunched, moaned, frowned.

"She's in too much pain." Frank stood at the foot of her bed, waving his arms like a street cop directing ten-year-old boys on skateboards. "Everybody out! I want to talk to my daughter."

No. No more yelling. I want silence. Just this once.

Patrick and Lindsey quietly left, leaving her alone with Mac and Frank. Mac searched her eyes, and then turned to her father. "I'm sorry, Mr. Glaze. That's not possible."

Frank's teeth gritted, his eyes flared. "Get out of here, mister, or I'll call security. I'm her father!"

Mac's jaw tensed as he leaned over him again. "Then act like one, Mr. Glaze. She doesn't need this stress."

Glaring, Frank spun on his heel and stormed out.

That, she had never witnessed: someone setting her father in his place. She couldn't explain why tears rushed into her eyes at the thought. Someone had stood up to him—for her.

"Are you okay, Mari?"

She squeezed back the tears and managed to say, "I'm fine. Is my mother here?"

Mac took her hand and squeezed it. "I haven't seen her. I don't think she came."

She wouldn't. Marianne closed her eyes against more tears stinging them. It shouldn't matter, really. Her mother hadn't been there for her in a long, long time.

"Mari?" Lindsey walked tentatively toward her. "I'm leaving now. Get better." She touched Marianne's foot and headed out the door.

"We need to let your nurse know you're awake." Mac pressed the HELP button, scooped up another spoonful of ice, and slipped it into her mouth. "The doctor said he'd check on you before he left for the day. When you get out, what will you do?"

Home to Abilene or back to the ranch. Years of goal setting and working diligently toward those goals had taught her not to give up. *I can't stop now.* "Would you get Frank, please? And Patrick?"

Mac's jaw tightened as did his grip on her hand. "Are you sure?"

A champion. A sweet feeling of peace washed over her as she searched Mac's eyes. She mouthed, "Yes." This was a turning point of sorts for her. She had never summoned her father anywhere.

With a blank expression on his face, Patrick came in, sat down, and took her hand. He probably wanted to be anywhere but here, between Marianne and their father.

Frank rounded her bed and regarded her as if he were holding court. "What, Marianne?"

Oh, for a moment's peace with you. "I'm going back to the ranch. I have to finish what I started." She hoped to find the support she desperately needed in his gaze, but it wasn't there. "Father."

Behind him, Mac turned toward the window. Patrick remained beside her bed. And suddenly, she felt awake, as if she'd just come out of a deep fog.

"Thank you for coming. You can't know how much it means to me." Her voice wobbled. *Not now. Don't appear weak now.* Patrick squeezed her hand. She glanced at him and smiled.

"Are you saying you want us to go now?"

It surprised her to hear the hurt in Frank's voice. She studied his face. How sad he seemed. She could see past the aloofness, the severity, the coldness. Where had he been hiding this sadness? "I was hoping to talk to you for a minute about what's happened since I arrived here." She was grateful when Mac motioned for Patrick to join him outside. She squeezed her brother's hand and then smiled at him as he left.

"All right," Father answered, somewhat stiffly. He glanced at a nurse walking cheerfully into the room.

"Awake now, Marianne?" She swiftly and quietly checked her vitals. "Is your pain being controlled?" Marianne said, "Yes." The nurse eyed her father. "Keep her quiet," she ordered and patted her arm. "I'll send the doctor in."

He arrived a few minutes later, examined her, gave instructions, and said she could leave after a couple more hours of observation.

Marianne thanked him, glanced at Frank, and closed her eyes. It was safer. "Where's mother?" The long silence that followed had her opening her eyes.

Deep sorrow was etched into her father's face, his dazed gaze resting on her shoulder as he cleared his throat. "She figured Patrick and I could handle this."

A tear trickled down the side of Marianne's cheek. Her father's hand covered hers and squeezed while his other hand stroked the back of her wrist. Smooth hands, gentle hands.

"But I came." He sounded weary. "And Patrick."

It should have been enough, but it wasn't.

Taking a small breath, she opened her mouth to ask what she had wondered a thousand times over the years. "What happened to you and mother?"

He abruptly released her hands. "I don't think that's—"

Marianne grabbed his arm before he could retreat and winced at the pain jabbing against her skull. "Daddy, don't." She hadn't called him 'daddy' in years.

He sat back down, stone-faced. He appeared like a defeated warrior staring out over his bloodied lands. His weary sigh filled the quiet room as he glanced at her. "I'm no good at this."

Nor was she. Sharing honest feelings and working through problems had never been embraced in her family. Cold shoulders, quietly closed and sometimes slammed doors, and distance had. "Try, Father. Please."

He stared at the ring on her pinkie. "It was a long time ago." He spoke slowly, thoughtfully, and shook his head. He frowned as if it hurt him physically to speak the words. "It doesn't matter anymore."

Oh, but it does. "I always wondered why y'all stayed together," she prompted.

When he glanced out the window and exhaled again, she couldn't remember a time when her father appeared so crushed. "Did you ever love her?"

His thumb and finger rubbed his eyes back and forth as he rested his elbow on the wooden arm of the chair. "I loved your mother." He stood and walked to the window.

She allowed him the distance, allowed him to turn his back to her.

"I was working late. One of the secretaries came into my office." He shrugged. "It was stupid." As he looked outside, he shook his head. "The funny thing of it is, nothing much happened. She was standing beside me, and suddenly, we were kissing."

An airplane caught his attention. He followed it until it disappeared into clouds. "Your mother walked in on us. Beginning and end of story. She never forgave me."

That's it? One kiss? "Were there other women?" *Surely.*

"Never. Not another one. But she wouldn't accept that. Every time I was late, there were questions. Every business trip, insinuations. Every dinner meeting, accusations. After a time, she stopped asking. We drifted into not caring anymore."

"Did you try to woo her back?"

He turned to her. "Woo her? As in date her?"

"Yes."

"Not in those terms." He turned back to the window. "I've tried to reach her, tried to gain her trust. She wouldn't have it. *Won't* have it."

"Like a stalking horse."

He turned around again. "What?"

"She's used that incident like a stalking horse." At his confused expression, she said, "Years ago, English hunters would slide off their horses—"

"I know what a stalking horse is, Marianne."

"Mother's used that incident to hide from life, unsure of the next move and afraid to make it. Most of my life, she's walked behind a horse's backside."

"And acted like one."

"She's had good company."

"Are you implying I've walked behind it with her?"

96

"Haven't you?"

"I'd like nothing more than to get on with our lives."

"Then step out. Pull her with you when you do."

He shrugged, glanced out the window.

"You're my stalking horse, Father."

He frowned as he turned and met her gaze. A slight flush stained his face. So, he knew. *He knew.*

"Well." He lifted a shoulder. "When you step out from behind me, aim at something other than *me.*"

She laughed out loud. Her father had made a joke. "I'll keep that in mind." In a subtle way, he had just given his permission for her to back away from him.

Abruptly, he pulled the chair back a few inches and sat. All sadness was gone. The self-assured man was back. A window had been opened for a time, and then slammed shut.

She lifted her hand toward the pitcher of water.

"Wait, wait." He gently brushed it away, reached across her, poured some water, and handed her the cup.

She was almost too shocked to drink.

"Now." He settled back in the chair and crossed his arms, clearly oblivious to the importance of what he'd just done. "I called the sheriff. He's on his way over here to question you. Before he arrives, you need to tell me what kind of a mess you're in and why."

'Mess' was an understatement. She told him about the confrontations she'd had with this man or men on her property, at Lindsey's, and on the road to Mole's Bench.

"Who's behind this?" he asked. "Do you have any idea?"

"I have ideas but nothing concrete. I believe it has to do with my inheritance. How? I don't know."

"Then you need to come home. It's not safe for you up here."

She closed her eyes. Her headache was getting much worse. "I have to stay, at least for a little while. I have to know that I can do this."

He stood. "And I have to get back to Abilene." This take-charge Frank she knew, and it was somehow comfortingly familiar. "I'll stay while the sheriff's here, if you'd like."

"It's on her. Lucky she had her purse with her when I ran her off the road."

"Idiot! She'll see it. She'll know what it is. She's been around surveillance equipment all her life!"

"It's hidden in the lining of a small zippered compartment. She won't find it."

"I want a constant watch on her." The man sucked on a cigarette. "Keep me informed."

The moon cast a soft haze over the buildings and trees. Mac sat back in the porch swing and enjoyed the quiet as he pushed the swing into gentle arcs. Barking laughter came from the bunkhouse. A welcome breeze shooed most of the heat of the day away and made it cool enough to enjoy being outside.

He heard her coming and turned around. "Hello, Daisy."

She jumped up on his legs and licked his hand. "Ready for our walk?" Nuggets joined them. "You, too, girl." Near one of the bunkhouses, a small red dot swirled in the darkness. Someone else was enjoying the pleasant night.

As he and the dogs headed for the lake, Mac thought of his mother and wondered where she and Aurora were. The last phone call placed her and her best friend in Italy, gushing over a little cafe where they had enjoyed rich sauces, red wine, and the romantic sounds of a gifted violinist.

Mac sat in the middle of the bench that faced the lake and thought about the last year. It had flown by.

He could still feel that sweltering day he had stood with his father at the back corral, the heat soaking his skin like a hot shower. His father's sweat-stained hat slapped against the side of his dusty jeans, his gaze squinting over the land as the summer sun jitterbugged across empty fields in waves of pure hot.

"Don't have to wait 'til I'm dead," his father said as Mac clutched his hat and wiped his forehead with the back of his wrist. *"The ranch is yours now, if you want it, son."*

If? It was the only dream he'd ever had. "Yes, sir, I sure do, more than anything." Being the manager for the last four years had prepared him for this day, and he was thrilled it had finally come.

Dad's large hand slapped his shoulder and squeezed. "You'll work it hard. You always have. Papers are ready to be signed, so come on up to the main house when you're ready."

Mac grabbed his father's outstretched hand and pulled him into a tight hug. "You won't regret this."

"Never thought I would, son. You'll leave your mark, and it'll be a good one."

Mac remembered racing to his fiancée's cottage to tell her the good news. A city girl, he'd thought time at the ranch would help Susan love it. But it hadn't.

He'd raced down the hall to her bedroom door. It was open. And she wasn't alone.

It was almost comical the way both of them had sprung up in the bed like jack-in-the-boxes, grabbing for a sheet to cover up what they'd been doing. The cowboy growled and stumbled to the bathroom while Susan glared, stomped, yelled.

And left, spewing vicious words of condemnation and fault at Mac.

Daisy whined, pulling him back from a year ago. She nudged his hand and sat at his feet as the moon tiptoed across the lake.

He missed Dad. Missed his love and encouragement, his quiet contentment, his companionship. The many times they rode together over the ranch, needing time together to visit. Dad had been a huge presence in his life.

Mac took off his hat, set it beside him, and stretched both arms out along the back of the bench to allow the night breeze better access to his body. Nuggets ran off. Daisy rolled over on her back, inviting Mac to slide his boot up and down her stomach.

"We've come a long way, Miss D."

He turned around. Marianne's light was out. She'd left the hospital today and stayed in bed, just as the doctor ordered. Tomorrow, she said, she'd be raring to go again.

He tugged Daisy up to his lap. "She's something, isn't she, girl?" Daisy licked his chin, and Mac chuckled. "Whatever that something is, it sure throws me off. I didn't expect to have these feelings for her. I wish Dad could have met her as a grown woman."

Marianne was beautiful and sleek, feisty and afraid, determined and bossy. Somehow, the whole package appealed to him. He couldn't say why or what particular component drew him. Most of the time, fear was in her eyes, laced with a conflicting trait like strength or stubbornness.

He'd picked up on all the clues she sent that she wasn't interested in a deeper relationship with him, but he'd seen weakening of her resolve today. When he teased, she usually deflected or changed the subject. But he'd seen some sort of acceptance in her eyes at the hospital, and that was encouraging.

It was a matter of her trusting him. It was that simple and that complex. Her heart had been badly bruised by her parents' unhappy marriage, according to Helen. It was no wonder she was skittish about love. He would have to change her heart, little by little. Get her to trust him.

The thought made him chuckle. Changing Marianne Glaze's heart or mind wouldn't be an easy task. He would have to be patient.

"Not my strong suit," he mumbled as he stood. "Let's walk, girl. It's a night made for walking." He glanced at Marianne's darkened window again.

He wanted her. If he decided on something, he went after it. But he'd have to take this thing nice and slow. Again, not exactly his style.

His father's sanctuary had become his own, so Mac headed for the chapel to reflect on this woman, the powerful pull of her, and to figure out how in the world he could slow down this longing for her.

NINE

Bright sunlight shined through the three tall windows behind the dining room table. Mac sipped his coffee as he glanced outside at blue skies. The weather forecast indicated a fifteen-degree drop in the temperature when clouds moved in this afternoon. Finally, late October acting like it belonged in autumn.

Helen stood. "The Laredo Oil contracts are waiting on me, boss. I'll be in my office if you need me. Oh, good morning, Mari. Did you have a restful day yesterday?"

She walked into the room like a breath of fresh air and smiled at Mac and then Helen. Was that a blush? Was she remembering yesterday in the hospital with him just after she woke up? Mac couldn't stop thinking about her response to him. In fact, all night, he couldn't stop thinking about it.

"I did, Aunt Helen. I especially liked James pampering me with two meals in bed. But I'm tired of being prone. Did you sleep well?"

She shrugged. "Like a pebble." Chuckling, she stacked her silverware on her plate. A maid entered from the kitchen and took it. "Thank you, Dena. I'll see you later, boss man."

When Helen left, Marianne pulled out a chair. "Good morning, Mac."

Another blush. And she wasn't looking him in the eyes. So, yes, she was probably thinking about yesterday with him, even though nothing else happened on the way home. "How are you feeling today?"

She lifted a shoulder and sat. "A little overwhelmed. I had a lot of time yesterday and last night to think about what I'm doing here."

"And?"

"The wreck made me angry." Finally, she looked at him. "I came here to start a new life on my uncle's property. Such a simple thing, but he's made it into something I fear. I'm angry that this man is trying to scare me and hurt me. I've decided to keep going, so this morning, I called Deb Engels, Brigitt's friend." Steam rose from the mug of coffee he handed her. "Thank you." She rested her bandaged left hand on the table. "She said Brigitt wasn't at school that last day."

"Then she's mistaken. Brigitt was on her way home from school when she was killed."

Marianne blew on her hot drink and sipped. "The file says Uncle Cecil spoke to teachers, asked about any problems Brigitt had had with other students, boys liking her, fights, anyone with a motive. But isn't it interesting that there's no indication whether or not she attended school that day?"

"She was at school. There's never even been a suggestion that she wasn't."

She wrapped her hand around her mug. "I called the coroner, Kirk Romer. He lives in east Texas now. Says he stands by his report, wishes he could help me find her killer. Nothing new there. I think I'll go stay with Lindsey for a few days and try to mend fences."

A tug of disappointment had his gaze slicing to her. He'd get to practice patience right off the bat this morning. He picked up the coffeepot and topped off his mug.

"A silver coffeepot on a working Texas ranch. It's beautiful."

"My mother's. She likes pretty things. After she left the ranch, Helen insisted we continue using the nice stuff every day. How's your head today?"

"Dull ache, nothing more."

"Your thumb?"

She looked at it. "It hurts a little. I can tolerate it. So why are your feathers ruffled?"

She'd pegged him, first thing. "You're a pill, you know that?"

A smile burst across her face. "Really? Oh, that's great. Usually, I'm quiet, reserved, and I keep my mouth shut, but you bring out the pill in me. That's so great." With an impish grin, she opened her cloth napkin and placed it on her lap. "So, why are your feathers ruffled this morning?"

He smiled at the playful way she lifted her brows. What more could he hope for than to grab her and kiss that grin off her face? If he wasn't careful, he'd be plunging off the head-over-heels-in-love edge any day now. Maybe he'd already fallen off it. "I didn't think you'd be leaving so soon." He nudged the butter toward her.

She slathered a biscuit and dropped a spoonful of strawberry jam on top. "I only opted for a couple days, and this is day four. I'd think you'd be glad to be rid of me."

"Three. Part of yesterday, you were in the hospital. And Helen used those words, not me. You're welcome to stay as long as you'd like."

"Thank you, Mac. I really appreciate that." She bit into her biscuit. "Strawberry jam's great."

"Helen made it." He struggled to throw off the frustration her announcement brought on. "I'll take you into Brennan. With your hand and the concussion, you don't need to be driving."

"I'll need my SUV while I'm there. But thanks for the offer."

"Why did you decide to leave?"

"I'd really like to get to know Lindsey better."

"The feeling's not mutual."

"I know. I just want to keep trying with her." Marianne rested her arm against the table. "You're upset."

You bet I am. "Here." *A patient man, remember?* "Have another biscuit."

She did, split it open, and draped it with jam. "The biscuit won't work."

"You just want to hear me say it."

Her eyes leveled with his as her chin lifted. "Do I?"

He crossed his arms on the table and shrugged. "Don't go."

"Why?"

You're alone, Mac, because you don't know the first thing about including a woman in your life. Susan's last words haunted him.

"I'm enjoying your company." *Patience. Don't scare her away.* He pushed his chair back and stood. "And you'd be safer out here. I'd really like you to stay." He glanced outside. "The mail should be here by now. I'll be right back."

Five minutes later, he strode in. "Looks like your poet again." He tossed a pink-flowered envelope matching the first note on the table and gritted his teeth while she stared at it.

Then she held up her bandaged left hand. "Would you open it for me?"

He did, unfolded the single sheet, and handed it to her. The paper shook as she read it. She lowered her hand to her lap, a shocked expression on her face.

Mac took the note and muttered the words:

"Little boy blue, come state your case:
With trembling hands, I touched her face!
She lay so still
Beneath the hill
'Tis now a sacred place!"

Mac read it again, bursting with indignation and temper. "Touched *her* face?" The hushed words flared to life between them. "So now he's writing poems about *you?*" He mumbled a curse and threw the note as hard as he could. Then he saw Marianne hug herself and bend over as her right hand raced up and down her left arm. He needed to touch her, to comfort her.

She jumped when he patted her back.

Gently, he tugged her into his arms, pleased when she didn't resist. She nestled against him, and he pulled her closer. Holding her, he rocked and soothed her with whispered words.

When she gently pulled away, he wanted to yank her back into his arms. A patient man would let her go, so he did.

"Thank you, Mac. Now would be a good time to call the sheriff."

Marianne stood in the doorway of the den, drained from all the emotions overwhelming her. She'd trained herself to find a quiet spot, pray, get her mind on her art, or read a book that she couldn't put down—anything to distance herself from emotional turmoil. But she couldn't here. Everywhere she looked, she wondered if someone was standing behind a building or a tree or a vehicle or a door, ready to pounce if she got too close. Was it time to leave? Was she ready to give up her uncle's gift? If she left now and returned a year from now, the man after her would just start up where he left off.

At the far end of the room, near the sliding glass doors, the sheriff stood with Mac, holding a piece of paper in each hand. He glanced from one note to the other. His blonde crew cut appeared almost white, his blonde brows furrowed when he nodded toward each page.

Mac stood seven or eight inches taller than the slim sheriff. "Our poet crawled out of his hole the day after Marianne arrived in this area to check out her inheritance."

Nate frowned. "The question is why? George Schroeder's been dead for several years. *This* note," he shook the paper in his left hand, "identifies Georgie and Brigitt. *This* note," he lifted his right hand, "refers to Marianne. Why stir this up again? If the poet was an accomplice, it would eventually point the finger at him and him alone. Does Marianne have any idea who this rhymer is?"

"No. He could be a hired gun, for all we know."

"For whom?"

"Just guessing here, Nate. I have no clue."

"I'll put out some feelers, see if I can discover—"

"Pardon me." Marianne didn't want to hear anymore and stepped into the room.

Mac spun around. He glanced at the overnight bag dangling from her hand, and then focused on her eyes. She wanted to drown in the comfort he offered, but she needed to leave and find her balance again.

"Nate, would you excuse us for a few minutes?" Mac didn't wait for his answer.

Marianne turned and walked into the living room. Her bag slipped to the floor on her way to the large glass windows.

Rootless. That's how she felt. She didn't know where she belonged anymore. Back in Abilene, where life was ordered and her career as an artist was finally taking off but where her parents and the ugliness in their home pulled her down. Or here, where the roots of the past had withered and in their place were newly-planted seeds barely stretching their legs. She knew it was time to find her own place. She thought she had when she received the inheritance letter.

Cradling her left hand, she breathed in a shaky breath. "I thought coming here would be easy."

The warmth of the sun radiated through the window and took a bit of the chill out of her heart. "I thought I could find a new home, a new life, and paint. But with all the problems I've encountered, I don't know what to do. I'm afraid to stay, but I don't want to leave. I really don't want to leave."

Mac gently wrapped her in his arms, and she snuggled close. Against his shoulder, she said, "I hate to even say this out loud, but I'm so afraid of that man."

Mac's arms tightened. "He's a sick little man who hides behind limericks and big trucks and enjoys pawing unconscious women. Go to Lindsey's, if you need to, but for the right reason."

"And the right reason would be—?"

"You want to see Lindsey. Not because you're afraid."

"But I *am* afraid."

"Then don't go." He moved his hands to her shoulders and pushed her gently away. "Change the way things are. The way things could be."

She searched his eyes, not wanting to see the deeper meaning of his words there. So, she sidestepped them: "I've overstayed my welcome."

"Says who?"

"No one has to say. I just met you a few days ago—"

"Re-met."

"Same thing. I've practically moved in. I need to spend some time with Lindsey."

"Why?"

"Because I-I remember being friends with her as a child. I'd like to find out why she's so hostile to me, why she's so afraid of me." She moved into his arms and tightened her hold. "Mac? Can we agree that I'm trying to do the right thing here and that it may not be what you want me to do? I want to stay with you because you make me feel safe. But I need to know that I can leave and go where I want to go without *that man* keeping me from it."

"When you put it like that, then leave. But be safe, Mari. Be consciously safe."

He let her go then and brushed her hand away from her bag. "I'll follow you to Lindsey's, but first, let's visit with Nate. He was there that day, seventeen years ago. Let's ask him about it."

In the dining room, Mac pulled out a chair for Marianne and sat next to her. Nate straddled his chair. Dena set a silver coffee set in front of Mac. "Thank you, Dena," he said, poured three cups and handed one to Marianne, one to Nate.

"We were all still reeling from Joey's death," Nate said and set his cup on the table. "Joey and I were really tight. He had just turned sixteen and my birthday was a month later. I haven't had a friend like Joey since." Nate flushed and scooted his chair closer. "Seeing my best friend in that coffin totally freaked me out."

Mac remembered his mother said Mac didn't have to go to the funeral, because he'd had a bad dream the night before about Joey being trapped in a coffin. But he went anyway, cocooned by the strength of Dad and his older brothers.

He'd never forget what he saw that day: his big brother laid out in a casket, dead, cold. He'd always heard that big tough McKenzies didn't cry. But they did that day. All the men in his family wept the day they buried Joey, including his father. That had rocked Mac's foundation.

When Brigitt passed away two months later, he remembered thinking that every member of his family was going to die, one at a time, and there was nothing he could do about it, no matter how hard he tried to protect them.

Shaking off the thought, he made an effort to listen to Nate.

"Cecil Tucker was the sheriff, and I always stopped by the station after school to see if there was any action. He was very indulgent of my interest in becoming a law enforcement officer." A half grin eased across Nate's mouth. "I wanted his job, and he knew it."

His grin faded as he shook his head. "The call." He winced. "The *hysterical* call from Gloria Radke came in right after I arrived, so I rode out with Cecil. We sure didn't expect anyone to be *dead*. Brigitt was lying there, by this big rock at Tucker Spring. She looked like she was sleeping, except she was badly bruised, cut, and so bloody."

He shook his head slowly. "Cecil just stood there, staring at her. He said, 'Brigitt? Honey?' I fully expected her to stand up and say, 'Gotcha!' and laugh at us as she scrubbed off all that stage paint. But she didn't. Cecil sank to his knees and checked her neck for a pulse. Tears ran down his face as the back of his fingers touched her cheek. He said, 'Oh, God in heaven, sweet Jesus, help her.'"

Nate shook his head. "Helen and Eddie—Brigitt's daddy—arrived. They were past hysterical. Cecil shooed me away, told me to get across the creek. At first, I couldn't move. I remember my stomach hurt, and I was afraid I was gonna embarrass myself by throwing up. Gloria Radke put her arms around me and hugged me and walked me to the other side. Frank, Marianne's daddy, just stood back in a daze. Cecil waved some kids away who were trying to cross the creek. Then he called the coroner to come to the scene.

"The police went through your property to get to the crime scene, Mac. The whole town was across the creek, back of Cecil's house. Cars were lined up along the highway, all across his front yard and driveway. People were crying and hugging each other. All of us wanted to see what was happening, but we couldn't get close."

He looked at Mac. "Your daddy's men kept everyone back. We stared at Brigitt, waiting, just waiting for something to happen. It seemed like hours before the coroner arrived."

Nate cleared his throat. "He was so gentle with her. He pronounced her dead. Then she was taken away. No one wanted to leave. People hung out for a couple hours or so, talking, crying, wondering who could have done this to her. Cecil interviewed some people. And then everybody went home."

In the ensuing silence, a grandfather clock chimed the half-hour.

"That about how you remember it, Mac?"

He sat up. "Actually, none of the McKenzie kids were there. We were picked up at school. Did you see Brigitt at school that day, Nate?"

The sheriff pursed his lips. "That was a long time ago. I was in tenth grade. She was a senior. What does her file say?"

"That she was. Rather, it didn't indicate she wasn't."

They sat in silence for a few heartbeats.

"Well." Nate rose, as did Mac and Marianne. "If you don't have any more questions, I'll be on my way. I'll keep you posted on anything I find out. Appreciate it if you'd do the same."

"We will. Thanks, Nate."

The sheriff plucked his hat off the rack and left.

Marianne picked up her purse. "I guess it's time for me to leave, too, Mac." They walked outside.

Reluctantly, he loaded her luggage into her SUV. "You should stay at the ranch. You'll be safer with me. I can't protect you in Brennan."

"I'll be okay. I need to visit with Lindsey."

"Are you giving up, then?"

"No. I've no intentions of letting that man win. You mentioned you kids being picked up at school when Brigitt died. Was that unusual?"

"We always walked to your Aunt Gloria's house—Lindsey's house now—after school and stayed until four, when Buck picked us up. He was young, and we thought he was pretty cool."

"Is he still at the ranch?"

"No. He left a few years back."

"Did he pick you up that day?"

"My dad did. He told us about Brigitt."

She climbed into her SUV and lowered the window. "Let's talk on the phone while we drive to Lindsey's house."

"Sure. Look, Mari, I'm coming into Brennan in a few days. I'd like to take you to lunch."

"I'd like that. It'll give me something to look forward to."

TEN

Marianne opened the Chambers' back door and stepped inside the kitchen. Logan was pouring a cup of coffee. It was the same routine the past five days: she got up early to run; Logan got ready for work; Lindsey slept in.

She pinched the front of her short-sleeved cotton shirt and fluttered it, trying to cool herself off. "November showed some muscle this morning, didn't it, Logan?" She washed her hands, dried them, and poured herself a large glass of water.

"Yep. Shoved what was left of that heat spell right outta here. Enjoy your run? Your thumb bothering you any?"

"Hmm." The cool water slid down her throat. "Not much." She stretched her hand. The bandage had come off a couple days ago, and a thin scar was all that was left now. "It is definitely better. Is Lindsey up yet?"

He closed his lunch box, opened the fridge, and plucked out the iced tea pitcher. "She slept in again. Told me last night she wasn't feeling too good."

"I'll check on her before I head out." While she finished her drink, he poured tea into his thermos and screwed the lid on. There was something immensely pleasing about seeing a man fixing his own lunch. Logan was a good man. Her cousin had chosen well. "Where's the cemetery here, Logan?"

"Anybody I know?"

"Brigitt Holcomb."

"Lindsey's cousin."

"And mine."

He gestured with his thermos. "Out Willison Road, there on the south side. Just before you get to Mole's Bench. Can't miss it."

He checked his watch, tucked the thermos under his arm, and picked up his lunch box. "I gotta get my shop open. Cars lined up two deep in all three bays. Be safe driving out there, Mari. Leave Lindsey a note, so she won't wonder where you are."

An hour later, Marianne swatted at an ant crawling up her leg and watched two men dig a grave. One, an older man, worked a backhoe. The other, much younger, stood on the side of the grave with his gloved hands resting on a shovel as he seemed to admire the workings of the equipment in the hole.

The younger man thrust an arm out. "Ho, Daddy!"

The backhoe ground to a stop. The younger man jumped into the hole and completely disappeared. His head popped up a few seconds later, a grin stretching across his face and his hand holding up a small skull. "Looka here, Daddy! Somebody beat us here."

Despite the cooler weather, sweat drops dripped from the nose of the older man. "Git the rest of them bones outta there. We'll give 'im a decent burial after this."

"Excuse me." Marianne waved and fast walked to the older man. "Hello."

When the man doffed his sweaty cap, curly gray hair sprang up as if gasping for air. "Ma'am." He shut off the engine, climbed down, and blinked at her.

"I—well—would you mind, sir, if I asked you a few questions about a grave?"

Deep ruts lined the man's face when he presented a toothless grin. He slapped his cap back on and propped both gloved hands on his hips. "Well, reckon I could take a break. How 'bout you, Ornery?"

Ornery? Surely, he was joking.

Clouds opened up, letting the sunshine out. Ornery bent over, picked up the tiny bones, laid them gently on the side of the grave, and hoisted himself out of the hole.

"I appreciate your time, Mr.—?"

"Jamison." He tugged off a glove and clasped her extended hand. "Eldridge Jamison, ma'am. And that there's my boy, Ornery." The back of his hand brushed his mouth. "His name's Bertrand," he squinted one eye at Marianne, "after his mama's granddaddy." He nodded mischievously. "Ornery's more a fit, wouldn't ya say there, boy?"

The boy had to have been thirty-five at least. He grunted a knowing half-smile at his father. "'At's right, Daddy."

Mr. Jamison cackled and led Marianne to a bench under a tree where a cooler sat. He threw his well-worn gloves on the bench. "Can I tempt you with a soda, ma'am?"

"Marianne, Mr. Jamison. And, yes, thank you."

He handed her a can, took out another one, and tossed it to Ornery, who muttered a "Thank ya" and wandered off to sit under a tree.

Mr. Jamison rolled his cold can over his face. "Wheweee. Cooled off a little bit after that heat spell run off."

Marianne swatted at a gnat. "Mr. Jamison, how long have you been a caretaker?"

When he laughed, his face appeared comfortable overcome with wrinkles. He yanked on the tab of the can. "Pert' near all my life, ma'am. And my daddy 'fore me."

He saluted her with his soda. "And his daddy 'fore him."

"Do you remember Brigitt Holcomb?"

With his head back, he guzzled, then wiped his mouth. "Oh, yes, ma'am." He gestured toward her grave. "Yonder there, under that tree."

A swatch of a breeze swirled the smell of dirt around them.

"Seventeen years ago now." He shook his head. "She was an angel."

"So I've heard."

"It's the God's-honest truth. You didn't know her?"

"No, sir."

"Well, they didn't come no finer'n Brigitt Holcomb. Nice to everybody she met. Such a sweet smile." He shook his head. "Dern shame what happened to that girl." He took another swallow and set the can on the bench. Then he opened the cooler, pulled out another can, and gestured with it. "Here, ma'am. I'll show ya."

He walked around the graves, not over them. A thriving weed didn't stand a chance against his yanking fingers.

Marianne saw Brigitt's name, next to EDWARD ALLEN HOLCOMB.

"Her daddy." Mr. Jamison indicated the grave and glanced at the gray stone next to it. "And there lies our angel."

The morning was still and cool, waiting, it seemed, for another breeze. "Who dug the grave with you, Mr. Jamison?"

"My daddy. He retired a few years back, but I carry on his work and my son, Ornery, will carry on fer me." He chuckled, and then quickly sobered as he looked around the cemetery. "Reckon I can tell ya 'bout most all these people, how lonely they was in life by the number of visitors they git."

Perfect segue. "Did Brigitt have many visitors?"

Bulky, work-worn fingers touched her tombstone and lingered. "Oh, yes, ma'am. The first months anyway. Three or four young men. A woman or two. But after 'bout six months or so, only one 'r two. Her mama mostly." He took a long swig. "Now it's once 'r twice a year fer her, too."

"Mr. Jamison, if I showed you a yearbook of Brigitt's, do you think you'd be able to point out the people who came to visit her?"

"That I could, ma'am, but I know the names of most of 'em. Small school, small graduating class, small town. Ya got somethin' to write with?"

She rooted in her purse for her note pad and pen and wrote quickly as the names spilled out of his mouth.

Mr. Jamison scratched his chin and pursed his lips. "And, o' course, Bobby McKenzie. Now." He yanked on his ear lobe. "Bobby didn't come right away. Took him a couple months to fin'ly make it out here and when he come, he just cried and cried. One time I went over and put my hand on his back. He didn't even notice, I don't think. Came a couple more times after that."

"And now?"

"No, ma'am. Not at all. Hasn't for many a year."

When Ornery picked up his shovel and jumped in the hole, they ambled back to the cooler. Mr. Jamison flexed his hands a couple times before he slipped them into his worn gloves. "Shame about that girl."

"Yes, sir. Thank you for your time." Marianne waved as she walked off. The whole thing was a shame. Brigitt's death, and someone getting away with it.

Lindsey was sitting on her porch when Marianne parked and waved. Her cousin looked a little pale this morning. She placed her iced tea glass on the small table and rose when Marianne started up the steps to the porch.

"Are you okay?"

Lindsey shrugged. "Still queasy. That Mexican food last night didn't set well with me. Would you like some tea?"

"I'll get it. You just stay put." Marianne smiled at her cousin, but Lindsey didn't return it.

Even after five days, tension existed between them that no amount of talking or laughing or remembering their past together could erase. Lindsey held back from her, always leaving something unsaid, no matter the subject. She made sure that Marianne knew she was an intrusion, that her presence in Lindsey's home grated on her cousin.

Marianne poured herself a glass of tea and thought about going to her room and reading a book. Instead, she headed outside to try again to *gently* have a conversation with her cousin. On her way, she stopped at the one picture in Lindsey's home of her extended family: her mother, her father, her grandparents, and Lindsey as a baby. It was the only picture in the house of her father or mother.

112

The screen door screeched when she opened it, and then slammed shut. She sat next to Lindsey in the old rocking chair with the rattan bottom that was falling apart. She didn't expect any meaningful conversation from her cousin. Every word had to be dragged out of her, so Marianne sat back, enjoyed her tea for several minutes, and then tried again to open the doors that Lindsey had locked tight. "Does your dad live in Mole's Bench?"

Her cousin squinted at Marianne. "Where did that come from?"

"Well, you haven't mentioned him, and I just wondered."

"He lives in Dallas. He moved away after my mother died." Her head settled against the back of the chair, and she closed her eyes.

Her cousin in action again, shutting a door. "I'm sorry, Lindsey, about your mother."

She lifted a shoulder, shook her head.

"Are you and your daddy close?"

One eye opened. "Why the interrogation?" And closed again as her head eased back.

"Because I don't know you or him."

"Sounds like an inquisition to me."

"It's no different than all the other nosy questions I've asked."

Lindsey didn't answer, which told her volumes. She and her father weren't close, apparently. Interesting, that he moved away from his only child after his wife's death. Or maybe it was Lindsey who pushed him away. "Why did he leave Mole's Bench?"

"You'll have to ask him, Marianne." She stood. "I'm going to start lunch. You can stay out here if you want. I don't need any help."

"Sure." Marianne toasted her as she sauntered by and caught the screen with her foot before her cousin could let it slam.

No opening doors today. They were shut, locked, and the keys had probably been thrown away years ago.

Another beautiful morning. Marianne opened the screen door. It pleased her that it didn't squawk at her. She'd found some oil and sprayed it last night. She let it shut quietly as she stepped out onto the porch.

The sky was beautiful. Peach and lavender colors playfully scooted across it. The quiet and peace of the morning enveloped her, and she sighed deeply, so full of the beauty before her. She walked to the edge of the porch and crossed her arms as she stood there and just enjoyed.

Then she looked up and down the street, expecting someone to intrude on her morning, but no one was about yet. She took in a breath and relished the smell of the dewy grass and the freshness of the new day.

She headed for the newspaper that sat on the street curb. Two birds flew toward the beckoning sunrise as Lindsey's next-door neighbor's television suddenly blared a weather report of rain. Poor Mrs. Cleary. She was so deaf, it was difficult to carry on a conversation with her, but Marianne tried. Every day, she went over to see her and listen to the stories of her past.

Three houses down, another early bird after his newspaper waved at Marianne. She waved back and worked the plastic cover off her paper. The breeze picked it up, and she grabbed it at the same instant her bare feet hit the concrete steps.

She opened the paper. A small white note slipped out and floated to the concrete walkway. Hand-printed, childlike letters stared up at her. "Oh, no."

"What is it?" Lindsey opened the screen door with a hairbrush in one hand.

Marianne picked up the note, glanced around the neighborhood, turned it right-side up, and read:

"Wee Willie Winkle stood on a mound
And looked across The Departed's ground.
He dug a hole
For some dead soul
Then slipped in the pit and drowned."

She tossed the rhyme at Lindsey and rushed to get the paper open. "Mr. Jamison." Her voice wobbled. She scanned the front page for the story. "He hurt Mr. Jamison. And, of course, he's letting me know he's watching every move I make. Oh, here it is. Listen."

'Eldridge Jamison, caretaker of Heavenly Acres Cemetery, was found yesterday in a grave that he and his son, Bertrand, had dug that morning. Authorities report that Bertrand Jamison found his father around three o'clock after he'd missed a two o'clock doctor's appointment. Eldridge Jamison was allegedly struck with a blunt object and thrown into the grave. His condition is critical.'

"Oh, Lindsey! What have I done?"

Her cousin jabbed the air with her brush. "You couldn't pay me enough to continue this. Someone's trying to stop you, and if I were you, I'd let him." She glanced at the picture of Eldridge Jamison. "He must know something, or else why would your poet try to kill him?"

Marianne scanned the neighborhood again and walked inside. "He's trying to scare me off and doing a fine job of it." She paced a few seconds and stopped. "Lindsey, I *have* to find out how Mr. Jamison is doing."

"Okay. But call, don't go."

"Nate needs to see this note." She reached for the home phone but stopped. "Lindsey, have you considered that if our killer hurt this man because I asked him a few questions, that he might harm you and Logan because I'm here?"

Her cell phone rang in her bedroom, and she raced to answer it. Mac! Oh, how she'd missed him. "Hey."

"Hey, stranger. How's your hand?"

She told him about it and the note.

"Is Jamison still alive?"

"I don't know. I'm about to call the hospital."

"I'm coming into Brennan to take you out to a late lunch, so don't eat. You can tell me everything then."

Mac reached for his hat and ducked his head as he got out of his truck.

He'd been thinking of seeing Marianne again for days. These feelings for her were new for him. He and Susan had dated a long time, had felt comfortable with one another, and the obvious next step was marriage. But there was no *knowing* in his heart. There was no *love*. There was no giddiness at just the thought of seeing her again.

What he felt for Marianne went way beyond feeling comfortable. It felt right.

He walked up to the porch, wondering if she had missed him. He punched the doorbell and fought the grin sliding across his face as he anticipated that first glimpse of her. But no one came to the door. He rang it again. Silence answered him again. Frowning, he looked in the window, didn't see anyone.

He spun around. Lindsey's car was in the drive. A full glass of iced tea sat on the small table on the porch as if someone had just now left it there.

He opened the screen door. The front door was ajar, so he pushed on it. "Marianne? Lindsey?" He strode through the house. No one was inside. He made his way to the back door, opened it, and peered outside. Seeing no one, he headed down the steps and checked out both sides of the house.

"Oh. Hey, Mac. What are you doing here?"

He turned around. Lindsey closed and locked the door to the shed at the back of their property that housed Logan's riding lawn mower and his tools.

"I'm here to take Marianne to lunch. Where is she?"

"She's not in the house?"

"Just came from there."

"In the bathroom maybe?"

"I'll check." He tried not to panic as he bounded up the back stairs and quick-stepped toward the guest bedroom. "Marianne?" He entered the room. Her purse was on the bed. "Mari? Are you in there?" She didn't answer, so he opened the bathroom door and looked inside.

"Nope," he mumbled to Lindsey who was standing in the doorway.

Nudging past her, he headed for the front door, threw it open, and jogged down the steps. Standing still, he glanced up and down the street. Panic raced through him as he spun toward Lindsey.

"She isn't here, Linz." *Oh, God, she isn't here.* His heart tangled up in his throat. *Come on, man. Think!* "Did you see a white truck drive by here today? Or a black souped-up pickup?"

"Look, Mac. You know she likes to get out and run or walk. Maybe she—"

A screen door slammed next door.

Mac turned toward the sound.

There stood Marianne with a little white-haired lady anchored by a cane. The woman said something funny because they both laughed heartily. Marianne hugged her, walked down the steps, and waved at the lady before she headed his way.

She's okay. Mac took a deep breath. *She's okay.*

When she spotted him, her mouth dropped open, and she laughed. Her pace picked up. Man, he couldn't get to her quickly enough.

He scooped her into his arms and held her there until Marianne pulled back. His heart rate was still unsteady, but he managed a mirroring smile.

"Hey, McKenzie."

"Hey, Glaze. Are you hungry?"

"Absolutely starving. Give me five minutes, and I'll be ready to go. Would you like to go with us, Lindsey?"

Her cousin shook her head. "Y'all go on. I'm still too queasy to eat right now."

"All right." Marianne turned to Mac. "I'm craving steak. Does that sound good to you?"

The ranch-style steakhouse blended in with the rest of the western-themed downtown area. Rustic, with hardwood floors, cowboy paraphernalia on the walls, waitresses in cowgirl boots and hats and wrangler skirts. Marianne felt as if she'd walked into a very stylish barn.

"We'd like a recessed booth, please," Mac said to the hostess, whose nametag said *Stacy*, as he took off his cowboy hat.

Small private booths lined one wall, each with louvered saloon doors. "This way," Stacy said and headed for one of them. It surprised Marianne that the booth was actually quite deep and roomy.

The hostess placed their menus on the table, said, "Your server will be right with you," and left through the swinging doors.

A beautiful candle sat in the middle of their table, the dancing light shining through the intricate pattern on the globe as it cast shadows on the walls. "Oh, Mac, this is lovely."

"That's why I come here. For the food and the privacy." Mac placed his hat on a hook and slid into the booth. "So, how's your visit going with Lindsey?"

Marianne scooted into the brown vinyl booth for two that faced the swinging doors. Walls the color of cranberries surrounded them. She opened her cloth napkin and placed it on her lap. "No progress if that's what you're asking. I can't seem to reach her. Everything we talk about is a closed subject. She was so happy to see me when I first arrived, but it's been downhill since I asked her about the day Brigitt died. Why, after seventeen years, would it still bother her so much?"

"In all the years I've known Lindsey, we've never once talked about Brigitt. What about Mr. Jamison?"

"Unconscious and in critical condition."

"You think he was almost killed because you talked to him?"

"I do. It's just another show of strength. The poet wants me scared, Mac. He wants me to know that he knows where I am every second. Someone probably followed us here." She reached for her purse. "Here's the note." She handed it to him.

Mac read it and muttered something under his breath. "It's not safe here. Come to the ranch for a while."

"I'm ready to go back with you. I'll need to get my things from Lindsey's and thank her. Then I'd like you to take me to the funeral home here in Brennan. Keith Longman worked on Brigitt. He's the funeral director now."

"I can do that. Afterwards, we'll stop by Jimmy Ray's Authentic Western Wear and get you some digs for the ranch."

"You mean my tennies and flats won't cut it?"

He grunted. "Hardly. I intend to put you to work." He raised his brows and scanned his menu. "Earn your keep. You need work clothes."

"Oh?" She picked up her menu.

"Everyone at the ranch makes his, or her, way. Law of the land."

Her laugh was quick. "And just what do you have in mind for me to do, boss man?"

"Muck the stalls, feed the horses, walk a fence or two." He shook his head once, frowning. "Always a fence down."

She glowered at him. "You're dreaming, now, McKenzie. I don't do fences or any of the other things you mentioned."

"The main house, then. It'll need to be kept in tip-top shape. Our housekeeper, Mrs. Rook, can always use good help." He dodged the backhand headed his way and laughed. "And the kitchen—"

Her next attempt connected. He grabbed his arm and grimaced. "Ow! With strength like *that*—"

"Don't even think it!" She popped his shoulder with her menu just as the server walked through their swinging doors.

"Hey. Y'all ready to ord—?"

Nate walked out of his office and stopped at his secretary's desk. "I'm headed to the steakhouse, Wanda. If you want something, go ahead and call it in and I'll bring it to you."

"Thanks, but I brought a salad today. Need to watch my weight, according to Clyde. He says he can't tell me from his pig in the dark."

"What's he doing with his pig in the dark?"

She snickered. "That's what I asked him. He didn't have anything to say. Just stared at me like I'm the crazy one. Like *I'm* the crazy one."

"Back in about an hour." Nate definitely didn't want to get in the middle of those two. He opened the office door and stepped out into another sunshiny day. He glanced at the steakhouse down the street. Only one truck in front, so he'd timed it perfectly. Maybe he'd actually get through his meal without anyone bothering him.

Later, he'd say it was the strangest thing he'd ever seen. One minute, he was looking at that truck in front; the next minute, it exploded into flames like a magic trick. But the explosion shot forward, not up, a fist of fire punching through the window into the steakhouse. The ground rumbled with another explosion. *Son of a gun!*

Nate spun around, opened the door, yelled, "Wanda, call an ambulance and the fire station! The steakhouse just got bombed!" His two deputies ran toward the door. "Lloyd, Brock! Call for backup!"

"Terrorists?" With shaking hands, Lloyd opened the rifle cabinet, quickly took one out and handed it to Nate, then grabbed two more. "We're not ready for a terrorist attack, Sheriff." He pulled out his cell phone and made the call.

"Let's go! I sure hope there's somebody left alive in there." Nate ran down the sidewalk, followed by Lloyd and Brock, crossed the street, waved and yelled at some people to get out of the way, and then lifted his rifle to a shooting stance as he approached the giant hole in the wall. He motioned Lloyd and Brock around back.

Leading with his weapon, Nate stepped through the open space. "Anybody in here?" No answer. Flames consumed tables, chairs, and crawled up a wall, all to Nate's left. He walked past pockets of fire, parts of the truck, the chandelier on the floor, burning overturned tables and chairs—all made of wood. "Stacy?"

An eerie silence had fallen over the restaurant. "Stacy?" Popping sounds. Swooshing, as the fire breathed and consumed. Nate walked around the bulk of the flames and headed toward the booths. "Stacy? You in here?" Stepping around a burning table, he found her slumped on the floor. He felt for a pulse and found it strong. "Stacy, the ambulance is on the way. Lloyd! Get in here and help Stacy!"

Lloyd raced into the room and headed for her.

Nate stepped toward the private booths. Then he heard a moan. The three booths right in line with the explosion were open. Walls were crumbled. Debris was everywhere. A server sprawled on top of one of the booths, a saloon door on top of her.

Nate reached for her neck to check for a pulse. It was weak. The new girl. What was her name? Janetta. She'd been in town a week. "Brock! Need another ambulance! Anyone in here?"

Brock ran into the room as Nate heard another moan. Nate pointed to Janetta and then started digging through debris and found Marianne Glaze's face lifted toward him. "Marianne?"

She opened her eyes and frowned at him. A look of shock was in her eyes. "Nate? Nate?"

He tossed rubble to his left, away from her. He found a hand not belonging to a woman. He shoved away debris and lifted a slatted door off Mac's face. "Can you hear me, Mac?"

"Janetta?"

Nate turned toward Brock's voice as his deputy touched Janetta's back. "Janetta?" Brock felt her neck, waited, and then nodded at Nate. "Should I get her to some place safe, Sheriff?"

"Leave her. The paramedics will be here in a minute or so. Just talk to her. Let her know we're here and that she's okay."

Nate noticed Stacy sitting up and holding her head with both hands, then he turned back to Mac. "You okay, buddy?"

"Yeah. What happened? Marianne?"

"I'm here. Oh, no. Look outside!"

Mac sat up enough that he could see. "My truck. What happened to my truck?"

"Someone set a bomb in it, Mac. Let's get both of you out of here. Does anything hurt, Marianne?"

She closed her eyes. "I—no, not that I can tell."

Sirens sounded. Doors slammed. Police officers cautiously walked inside.

Nate took her hand and pulled her to her feet. Debris was in her hair, on her clothes.

"I'm okay. Mac?"

Nate reached over the mound of trash on the table and secured Mac's hand. "Can you stand? Are you okay, other than the cut on your forehead?"

"Oh, I know it's there. It hurts like the dickens." He tightened his hold on Nate's hand as he tugged him up. Debris fell off him as he stood. "Is that our waitress?"

Marianne gasped and turned toward the woman covered with rubble. "Bless her heart. The last thing I remember is her asking us for our order. Is she alive?"

Emergency medical personnel entered the room and Nate waved them over. One headed to Stacy; the other, to Janetta. Nate nodded at two police officers as they walked through to the kitchen.

"Yes. She probably saved your lives, taking the brunt of the explosion. Let's go through the kitchen and get y'all outside. You're both lucky to be alive."

Two hours later, firefighters and police still worked the scene. People stood outside the yellow tape belting the crime scene. Some spoke on cell phones, took pictures, videoed anyone involved. Bystanders overflowed the sidewalks into the street, gawking, frowning, talking. A news van from Childress was there, with a reporter interviewing people.

Just outside the cordoned-off area, Mac stood with Marianne and several Brennan police officers. Nate, Lloyd, and Brock huddled with the police chief down the sidewalk. Mac wanted to scratch his forehead, but the nurse had been specific: don't touch the wound for any reason; change the bandage daily; leave it alone.

Tiny lacerations on Marianne's forehead were surrounded by two significant bruises. She told the nurse her shoulder hurt, but she could move it.

"Are you okay, Mari?" Mac rested his hand on her back. She turned to him with a lost look on her face. Something had to be done about this idiot after her! Mac didn't want "leaving the area" to be one of her options. For her to stay here, he had to figure out a way to keep her safe.

"I'm fine. Just—" She shrugged and then shook her head as tears fell onto her cheeks.

"We'll get to the bottom of this," he whispered. "You'll be safe at the ranch. I'll see to it."

The smoking restaurant with the skeleton of Mac's truck in front was the backdrop as Nate walked over to them. "You better get out of Dodge, Marianne. This man is out to get you. I wouldn't give him the chance to finish what he started here today."

She pulled out of Mac's hug. "You think *I* caused this?"

"Absolutely not. This isn't your fault. But someone is definitely after you. Maybe Mac, too. You should consider getting to Abilene where you might be safe. Right now, you're both free to go. Let me know if I can help you." He spun around and headed inside the restaurant.

"I'll drive," Mac announced as he quickly opened the passenger door of Marianne's SUV. Lindsey had driven it to them. He helped Marianne get in and said, "I'll be right back." He headed over to where Lindsey was talking with friends.

"You need a ride somewhere, Linz?"

She shook her head. "Logan just got here. Thanks."

He hugged her, headed for his truck, and got in. "That was good advice."

"From Nate? I know, but I'm not willing to quit, are you? Your truck was blown up, Mac. It could be totally unrelated to me."

"No, he just hoped he'd get both of us at the same time. Nate said it was probably a remote-controlled bomb. But when did this man put it on my truck?"

"Someone at the ranch could have done it. Maybe at night when you were asleep."

"Yeah." How could he protect her at the ranch if this idiot could so easily gain access to his truck? Mac couldn't guard the entire perimeter. Maybe he'd have to hire security, at least for the main house. He started the SUV. "Where to now?"

She closed her eyes and shook her head as if to clear it. "It's been over two hours since it happened, and I'm still having trouble wrapping my mind around this. What if we'd been in the truck when the bomb exploded? Am I just being stupid by staying up here? You could have been killed! I'm not sure I could live with myself if something happened to you—or anyone else."

"You're rattled. So am I. I don't have any answers, but I think it's time to call in security professionals. Let them figure out what we need to do to keep you safe."

"And you, Mac."

"Maybe hire a bodyguard or two."

"And how long would you hire them for? A month? Six weeks? He seems to know everything we do. He'd just lie low until the bodyguards are gone, and then strike again."

"You may be right. I'll talk to them tomorrow and see what they suggest. Where do you want to go now?"

"Lindsey's. I need to shower and get dressed and pay that visit to the funeral director." She tugged her phone from her purse. "We have an hour and a half before he leaves his office. That should be plenty of time to ask him some questions."

Mac slowly turned toward her. "Are you serious? He'll be there tomorrow. Why don't you wait? Go to the ranch and get some rest."

"I want to, but then we'd have to drive all the way back here to Brennan. We're here. Let's make good use of our time." She closed her eyes. "All of this hurts. To some degree, everything that's happened to me is my fault."

"Wait a minute. Wait just a—"

She held up her hand. "Mac. I'm not taking all the blame—"

"You shouldn't be taking any of it!"

"I know. But I have to think that if I wasn't so unyielding about continuing this, those people at the restaurant wouldn't have been hurt.

I had no idea something like this would happen. No idea at all."

She reached for his hand and squeezed it. "For my sanity, I need to see this man. It won't take long. Then tonight, I'll fall apart when we get back to the ranch. You can fall apart with me." She looked out the window for a few moments. "Talk about lingering shadows."

"What?"

"Oh, something Lindsey said. She told me Brigitt's like a shadow that just lingers and lingers. I've thought a lot about that, and she's right. The past has lingering shadows. Even though Brigitt's gone, her shadow is still here. And this man who hurt her? He has a long shadow, too." She sighed. "I think if I work hard enough, I can shine the light on all these shadows, and they'll disappear for good."

"Work smart, Mari, so you don't disappear with them."

Marianne chided herself for being squeamish as she walked up to the funeral home. She'd witnessed two innocent people—really, three, counting Mac—being hurt today at the restaurant through no fault of their own. This was certainly not the time for her to show weakness.

No one who knew her would ever consider her to be adventurous or nosy. An artist spent most of her time alone, introspectively creating a vision. Interaction with others was not necessary, for the most part. She thrived on solitary time, staying in her mind, in her cocoon, and closing her eyes to everything and everyone around her but her work.

And here she was, going against everything she'd ever thought she was.

She was stepping out, and she was taking aim.

Glancing over her shoulder, she waved at Mac. He drove off as she walked down the sidewalk, past a shiny black BMW, toward the front door.

A gentleman wearing an expensive suit stood just inside the entrance. "May I help you, miss?" His hand slowly extended toward her as if he intended to touch her arm. She stopped before he could, and he offered her a weak smile.

"I'm here to see Mr. Longman."

"Of course. Follow me, please."

Everything was quiet. Muttered words. Thick carpet swallowing up impertinent footsteps. The unobtrusive air conditioning system that kept the rooms as cold as death.

The man indicated the director's door with the wave of his hand and left her alone in the subdued hallway. The place absolutely gave her the heebies.

She walked into the office. No one sat behind the single desk in the room. On the wall beside another door, a gold plaque stated, "Funeral Director." Marianne knocked on the door.

A thin, graying man of average height wearing an impeccable pin-striped suit bowed his head as he opened the door. "Miss Glaze?" The corners of his mouth lifted but his pointed, gaunt features and gray eyes remained placidly uninvolved in the smile.

"Thank you for seeing me, Mr. Longman."

"Yes, yes." A slender hand with a shimmering diamond ring flanked by a gold Rolex indicated she was to sit in an overstuffed white leather chair. She sat on the edge of the cushion next to a lovely green plant.

His arms folded onto the shiny, spotless desk as he sat. Black-framed glasses with thick lenses shrank his eyes to tiny dots. *Like cartoon eyes.*

"How may I help you today?"

She crossed her ankles. "I was wondering if you could help me with some facts about Brigitt Holcomb."

Not even a twitch. His cartoon eyes focused on her as a smile flirted with his mouth. It seemed awkward on his bony face. "Facts?"

"About the autopsy results. Did you see anything unusual about them?"

His head tilted toward her as if he were having trouble hearing her. "Unusual?"

"Anything you witnessed that wasn't in the autopsy report?"

He took his time settling back in his chair, resting an elbow on one hand as he pinched thin lips thoughtfully with his thumb and finger. The little dots squinted at her, appearing more hawk-like now.

"Why this interest in Brigitt Holcomb after what? Sixteen, seventeen years?"

Marianne straightened her back. "She was my cousin."

"And I was her uncle. Great-uncle, actually, by marriage." He eased forward. "You and I are possibly related. Who is your mother?"

"Barbara Tucker Glaze. My father is Franklin Glaze."

His bushy gray brows floated up as that almost-smile appeared again. "Ah, Frank and Barbara. Of course, I should have remembered their daughter was Marianne. We *are* distantly related. My wife, Esther, was your grandmother's sister. Barbara's mother's sister."

"Well, it's certainly a small world. That would make us—?"

"I believe I'm also your great-uncle by marriage."

"Yes, sir." *Pace it.* "I—"

"Just exactly what are you hoping to find, Marianne?"

"Evidence, Mr., uh, Uncle—"

"Keith."

"Yes." She tried to match his tone. "Pieces of a puzzle. Anything that might lead you to think something wasn't as it appeared."

Gotcha. A twitch. He knows something.

He glanced at her, his gaze intense. And then he laughed. An almost-warm laugh usually shared between friends. "Her gloves didn't match her dress."

Her *gloves?* Did dead people wear gloves? "It was a closed casket, right?"

"Oh, yes." He grunted, wistfully, as if he was telling a tired family tale. "But your aunt Helen didn't like the fact that the white gloves Brigitt had picked out for her Easter outfit didn't match her dress. But then, as you say, she decided to have a closed casket."

He was serious. The man was patronizingly serious. Her gaze leveled with his. "Did you find anything about Brigitt's body that didn't line up with the police report or autopsy? Anything suspicious that tweaked your professional curiosity?"

The somber wolf studied her for a long moment. "No."

"You must have an excellent memory. It's been seventeen years."

"I pride myself on my memory. It is uncommonly accurate. We worked on that case for months."

"We?"

"Cecil Tucker, the sheriff at the time."

"Any red flags?"

He shook his head. "Not in the paperwork or the coroner's report. Or my report."

"And you're satisfied, from a professional viewpoint, with the corroborating evidence?"

"Quite, Marianne." He stood.

She didn't like being dismissed in such an obvious manner and wanted to stay seated. But she didn't like being looked down upon even more and rose. "I know it's been a long time, Uncle Keith, but did you suspect anyone in particular of murdering Brigitt?"

He edged around his desk. The wolf again, slinking toward his prey. "No."

She extended her hand. "You're a busy man. Apparently, no stones unturned here." She didn't know what she'd expected or hoped for from this encounter, but she'd gleaned absolutely nothing from it, other than the fact that the man was her grandmother's brother-in-law.

"It was a pleasure, Marianne." He took her hand. "Please give your parents my warmest regards."

"I will, Uncle Keith. Thank you for your time." What she felt as he let go of her hand was a sense of catching her breath after a long absence of air. Relief, too, and the need to get outside.

She felt his gaze on her back as she walked calmly to the front entrance. She touched the door handle just as someone gunned an engine right outside the door. Through a tall thin specialty window, she spotted the black truck that had rammed her car!

Her first thought was to panic, so she did.

Her second thought was to head for the back exit. She turned around. Her uncle was gone. With her heart racing, she dashed down a long hallway, made a left turn, ran down a short corridor, and took a right.

A man opened a door and frowned at her. "What are you doing back here?"

Marianne muttered, "Sorry," and sprinted toward the EMERGENCY EXIT sign above a gray metal door. She punched the handle on the door, and an alarm sounded.

Great! The man in the black truck will know I'm making a run for it.

Outside, she looked both ways and raced down a small alley. Why had she worn sandals today?

She hit the sidewalk running. A couple of startled shoppers dodged her. An elderly woman yelped and patted her chest. A group of teens came out of a restaurant. "Move! Move!" she shouted, and they did.

Dashing around a corner, she heard the black truck before she saw it. She tried to stop as its nose headed out of the alley, but she couldn't. She slammed into it, hit her forehead on the window frame, stepped back, shook her head, and tried to retrieve her gun.

But the driver jerked the truck into park and opened his door. She spun around, kicked off her shoes, and ran away from him, into the street.

Dodging two cars in the intersection, she sprinted across. She looked over her shoulder. The man was running toward her! *Oh, God, help me!*

She ran down an alley and started across another road.

A vehicle drove alongside her. "Marianne?"

She kept running.

"Marianne! Where are you going?"

Mac! She slowed to a stop and bent over, gasping for air. Blood covered her right big toe. Good gracious, but was anything *else* going to happen to her today?

A door slammed. Mac's strong hands gripped her shoulders. "What is it? What's wrong? What happened to your head?"

She checked out the alley behind her. The man was nowhere in sight, nor was his pickup. "The black truck—the same man—chased me."

"Did you see his plate?"

She shook her head. "Still covered in mud."

"Can you describe him?"

"Caucasian. Mustache." She gulped in two breaths, blew them out, and squeezed her eyes shut. "Okay. Okay. Black cowboy hat. Wiry. Forties. If I'm not mistaken, I saw this man at JoeMoe's the morning your Jeep's tires were slashed, although he had a white cowboy hat then."

Her body was shaking so hard, she could hardly think. A loud engine started up. She spun toward the sound. *No, it isn't him.* "His eyes are more grayish brown. A scar covers the right side of his face, like a burn scar. Why haven't the police found this man?"

"Probably hides that truck in a barn until he needs it to scare you."

"Running me off the road wasn't enough for th-this *jerk?* And today, blowing up half the town of Brennan? Now, *this?* Why won't he leave me *alone?*" She burst into tears. She felt so utterly helpless and so very afraid.

Mac eased his arms around her. "You're okay. Come on. I'll call Nate. And then let's get to the ranch where you can relax."

She shook her head. "I need to do a composite for Nate. I got a good look at this man's face." She pulled out of Mac's arms and dried her tears. "When I knew he was outside the funeral home, I should have called 9-1-1, but I wasn't thinking straight. I wanted to run. I just wanted to get away from him."

"Of course you did." Mac gritted his teeth. "I should have stayed with you. That's on me." He took her arm and guided her to the passenger side of her SUV. "I'm taking you home."

Oh, she liked the sound of that. She got in. When Mac opened the driver's door, she said, "Would you make a U-turn? I tossed my sandals to make it easier for me to run. Just a couple blocks away. I have a hunch Longman knows something. I could see it in his eyes."

Mac waited for a truck to pass so he could turn around. "He's a funeral director. Brigitt had already died, had already been autopsied by the time he worked on her."

"What could he possibly be hiding?"

"Did you find out anything?"

"Yes. I have an overactive imagination where wolves are concerned. Right here."

"I'll call Nate while you get your shoes."

"All right." She got out, turned in a circle, and searched for her sandals. "He took them, Mac. That bully took my shoes!"

"She's back where we want her."

"The ranch? Good. We can't let up now. We have to get that letter or scare her out of here."

The man hung up, laughing.

ELEVEN

It was that time just before night when the fading light of the sunset enticed a few stars to appear in the darkening sky. Behind Mac, the front door opened.

"Is this a private party?"

Now this was the way to spend an evening, with the woman he was falling in love with. "Was. But you're welcome." He scooted over and caught the scent of roses as Marianne walked toward him and lounged against a porch post.

The quiet night settled around them. A full moon occasionally peeked from behind dark clouds.

"It's beautiful."

"My favorite time of the day is when the sun's coming or going. Doesn't matter which. Are you okay after today?"

She smiled. "Another rhyme. You're better at poetry than you thought." Her head eased against the post as she wrapped her slender fingers around it and sighed. She seemed to be focused on Daisy and Nuggets, playfully snarling at each other. "I'm fine, Mac. I hurt for those women at the restaurant today." She lifted a shoulder. "All of us in the wrong place at the wrong time."

She looked out, toward the lake. "Two innocent people, Mac. What am I supposed to do with that? Are other people going to be hurt because I won't let go?"

"Other people may be hurt, but don't add the 'because.' None of it was your fault. It's good that you're here. I don't know how we're going to stop him, but we will."

"He's holding all the aces."

For a long time, she said nothing more, and he wondered where she had gone.

"Have you always lived here?"

Mac crossed his arms. "I was born here. My father inherited the ranch when he was a young man, too. He didn't want it, felt too much the burden of it." He grunted. "I never understood that. It's all I've ever wanted."

"Why didn't your brothers?"

"Want it?" He shook his head. "They had their own dreams, I guess. But my father was very generous with all my brothers when I inherited. My oldest brother, Greg, and his wife and four kids live in Brownsville.

He's a leather artist and very good at it. He calls about once a month to find out news about Dad's case."

"*Is* there any news?"

"No."

"Was Greg close to your brother, Joey?"

"Everybody was close to him. He never met a stranger. Always laughing, cutting up, and just plain fun." He ran his hands through his hair and scratched the hat line at the back of his head.

"Who's next in line?"

"Bobby. He's a Christian band promoter in Fort Worth. He never married, just lost too much in too short a time. He was twenty when Brigitt died."

"How old was Greg?"

"Twenty-one."

The moon shone bright as the clouds moved east. Marianne reached for his hand and tugged. "Let's walk, McKenzie. We have enough light to see now."

When they'd walked a couple of steps, she moved to let go of his hand, but his fingers braided with hers. She glanced up at him with a question in her eyes.

He smiled.

A little shyly, she smiled back and then looked down. "Who's after Bobby?"

"Joey. Then Tim." Daisy ran over with Nuggets to greet them, then both dogs darted off as if a rabbit had called out to them. "Tim and Joey were pretty thick, just two years apart. It probably hit Tim the hardest when Joey died. I always had Luke. Tim had Joey. Tim floundered for a long time—years—after Joey died."

"Tim was fourteen at the time? There's no mention of him in the police report. Did they question him?"

"They talked to everyone in the family. Maybe Tim didn't have anything to say."

"Where does he live now?"

"Abilene. North side. Has a small ranch east of the lake. He married a couple years ago, has a new baby girl. First girl in our family since my great-grandfather had seven."

"She'll be spoiled rotten."

"I certainly intend to do my part." He directed them toward the bench near the lake. Sitting beside her would be a nice ending to a difficult day.

"Then Luke is after Tim?"

"No, the twins are, Kyle and Kevin. They were thirteen when Joey and Brigitt died, four years older than me, three years younger than Joey. They live in Granston, northwest of Houston. Kevin's married, has three kids. Kyle is married to Margot. Met her the week after Dad died. Engaged three months later. Married five months later."

"Can I ask you a somewhat personal question?"

"Margot and the baby."

"Do y'all have something against babies?"

He shook his head. "Hardly. The more the merrier."

"Then it's Margot."

"Let's just say we all think Kyle made a mistake."

"Does he?"

"Not that he's said. Last year, he inherited my mother's father's large, very prosperous ranch. Cattle. Oil."

"You're all concerned Margot's digging for gold."

He waited a heartbeat to answer her. "Yes. But she's keeping the baby, and that's good news."

"Is Luke after the twins?"

"He's a year older than me, foreman of the ranch, and perfectly content to be foreman. He just bought a couple thousand acres from me and will start building his own home next spring."

"You didn't like it."

"Why do you think that?"

"Your lip tightened on the right side. It means you were on edge, not comfortable."

He chuckled. "Your artist's eye. You're very detail oriented." He shook his head. "It felt strange breaking up what my dad worked so hard to build. Like a betrayal of his trust in me. But then, I wanted to help Luke out, too."

"I like him."

"He's easy enough to like. Struggling with our dad's death. Having trouble sleeping. Restless. Panic attacks. He needs to find a good woman and settle down, have a family."

Marianne laughed. "I'm not interested, thank you very much."

"Best news I've heard all day." In a flash, he scooped up a yellow weed and handed it to her.

She took it, sniffed it, and made a face. "Ew! That's awful!" She giggled. "What is it?"

"Texas ragwort. I was hoping you'd just admire it and not smell it."

"It is a pretty yellow." She kept her gaze on the flower. "Are all your brothers as tall as you?"

"Just about. Luke's the smallest at six-three. I'm the tallest at a little over six-five." He motioned her around the bench.

"And you're the baby?" With an impish grin, she sat and crossed her legs.

He sat, relishing the feel of her nestled up against him. "Few have muttered those words and lived to tell it."

"Oh, I'm shakin' now, McKenzie."

Daisy bounded over and sprawled at Mac's feet. He rubbed her belly with his boot.

"Where's your little friend, Daisy? Hmm?" Mac stretched an arm over the back of the bench behind Marianne. His fingers rested lightly against her shoulder.

It was more comfortable with his arm around her. The bench had definitely been made for either a large person or a snuggling couple. If Marianne turned just a fraction and leaned back against him, it would be cozier and afford them more room. But he was sure she wouldn't. He could tug her closer, but that would be too obvious and, besides, they were relatively comfortable. Well, not exactly comfortable.

Comfortable would only come if she would turn just a little and lean—

Well, strike up the band! She did it.

Mac lowered his arm and snuggled her closer to him.

They sat on the bench beneath a star-draped sky. A path of moonbeams glistened across the lake like a kiss-blown wish.

Mac's arm tightened around her.

She shifted to get a little closer.

And when Mac smiled, he noticed she was smiling, too.

Dawn crept through the sheer curtains in Marianne's room and nuzzled her awake. She looked at the clock. Five-fifty-five.

She groaned and made herself throw the warm covers off. She honestly couldn't imagine making a habit of getting up at five o'clock—or before—like the others living at the ranch. Almost six was good enough for her. Just so she didn't miss breakfast.

She took her time showering and dressed in her new cowgirl clothes. She wasn't a jeans person, but she was getting used to the material. If her plans worked out today, she'd make use of the cowboy boots. The clock said 7:05 when she left her room. She opened her door to an absolutely quiet house.

Leaning out the doorway, she searched up and down the hallway and listened. She could easily imagine she was totally alone. Where was everybody?

Cool gray light filtered in through the curtained windows, coloring the foyer below her a murky gray as she slowly walked down the stairs. At the bottom, she stopped to listen. No wonderful smells of breakfast. No maids scurrying about. No Mac coming from the kitchen with a steaming cup of coffee for her.

A little spooked, she hurried down the hall and found an unlit kitchen, lifeless in dull neutral tones. She lifted a curtain on the back door and glanced outside. Sunny skies, and no one about.

A picture of Rod Serling in a black suit, one hand at his waist, saying, "Welcome to the Twilight Zone," flashed through her mind. Her heart quickened its pace. She chided herself for being weak and headed back down the hallway toward the front door.

Her skin tingled with warning. She felt, rather than saw, someone near the front door. Foolish, that she had left her gun upstairs where it wouldn't do her any good.

Taking catlike steps, she edged around the wall and gasped. "What are you doing here?"

A tall cowboy stood just inside the foyer. He hadn't been there a few seconds ago. Had he just walked inside? Her gaze flicked to the locked door and back to brown eyes crinkling in a smile.

He clutched his hat and took it off. "Didn't mean to spook ya, ma'am."

"You didn't." With her hand on her chest, Marianne tried to even her breathing. "And Mac isn't here," she announced and winced. *Brilliant. Tell the man you're all alone.*

"Oh." His hat slapped against his jeans, and she expected an "Aw, shucks, ma'am" to tumble out. "I wudn't lookin' for him, ma'am. I was jus' checkin' up on you."

She couldn't have been more surprised. "On me?"

"Mac asked me to keep an eye out for you. A discreet eye, he said, so he's not gonna like it that you caught me." His large beefy hand stretched toward her. "Name's Hank, ma'am. Hank LeTran."

"Marianne Glaze, Mr. LeTran. My friends call me Mari."

His unease was apparent as he stared at the hat between his hands. "Well, ma'am, hope to be included in that group someday. If you need anything, you just holler."

Holler? She couldn't ever remember hollering in her life. "Thank you, Mr. LeTran."

"Hank."

"Hank. And this will be our secret."

He slipped his hat back on. "'Preciate it." Just before he left, he tipped his hat. "My eyes 'll be glued to this house until someone gets back. You holler, ma'am, if you need me."

When he was gone, she let out a long breath and closed her eyes as she backed into the wall. Utter quiet throbbed around her. She touched her heart, took two steadying breaths, and spotted a note tacked to her door. Had it been there when she left earlier? How could she have missed it? Had Hank—? No, he wouldn't have had time to get up there and back down by the time she'd returned from the kitchen.

She held her breath and listened for any sound that would indicate someone else was in the house with her. A grandfather clock ticked. The air conditioning system kicked on. Something hummed. Otherwise, all was quiet.

Despite the urge to run, she walked calmly up the stairs, glancing several times over her shoulder until she reached the top. A sewing pin stabbed the note to the hinge of a black knocker on her door. Her fingers shook as she touched it.

All of us have gone into town to see Stella's baby. Back in a bit. Helen.

Marianne's head fell forward as she heaved a sigh and tried to shake off the residual fear. Who was Stella? Did that mean Mac, too? Had he left with Helen and the other staff?

She opened her door and gasped. Her room had been cleaned! The clothes she'd just draped over the quilt rack were gone. Toiletries were straightened on the dresser. Her luggage had disappeared.

Just a maid. She chafed her arms. A very quiet maid, and one that was still in the house. Had she left the note?

Marianne jumped when her phone rang and raced to pick it up. "Hello?"

"Hello, yourself. Are you up and at 'em?"

"Yes, Mr. McKenzie," she answered a little desperately and made herself calm down. "I was up at five-fifty-five, I'll have you know." She watched the hallway, half expecting to see someone slither by. "I'm showered, dressed, and raring to go." *So come and get me.*

"I'm impressed. What's on your agenda today?"

Anything you want. "Being nosy, asking questions, taking a look

134

around. What's on yours?"

"I'm out with the fence crew right now and they're leaving me behind. Gotta run."

"But—"

The line went dead. As she hung up, she heard boots thudding on the floor below her. Had Hank come back? Her heart beat heavily as she crossed the room and crept to the railing.

A young girl with long blonde braids looked up at Marianne. She wore dusty jeans, a well-worn cowboy hat, and a short-sleeved red shirt.

"Hey." The girl took off her hat and looked so expectantly toward Marianne, she had to smile.

"Hey, yourself."

Big brown eyes watched Marianne descend the stairs.

"I'm Emma."

"I'm Mari." She couldn't resist touching Emma's braid. "Do you live here, Emma?"

She bobbed her head. "My daddy's in charge of the horses."

"Is he? And what are you in charge of?"

A delightful giggle revealed two deep dimples. "Nothing. I just hang out, do some chores. I love horses, don't you?"

"I haven't been around them much."

"You haven't?"

Amused at her gaping expression, Marianne gravely shook her head. If it was up to her, she wouldn't ever be near a horse.

"Well, come on, Miss Mari." Emma grabbed her hand and tugged. "I'll show you around."

A tall, slim, older woman with aluminum-gray hair appeared like a sentry in the middle of the hall. Her lips pursed into a thin straight line. *The mysterious maid.*

Emma ground to a stop and ducked her head. Marianne thought she heard her groan.

"Emma." Eyebrows arched, the maid looked at Marianne and her face softened. "Miss Glaze."

"Yes. And you are?"

"I'm Mrs. Rook, the housekeeper. A pleasure, miss." She turned then to Emma, noted her dirty clothes and boots, and sniffed. "Come here, child." Mrs. Rook lifted one arm and Emma walked into her hug. "You know you're not to be in this house in those clothes. They're filthy," she whispered. "Mr. Mac's orders, child."

"Yes, ma'am. Sorry."

"It's all right. Just this once." She gently nudged Emma toward the door. Then she turned back to Marianne. "I apologize for correcting her in front of a guest, Miss Glaze. I didn't want her to get into trouble with Mr. Mac. She's a good girl." She smiled. "If I can assist you in any matter, miss, please let me know." And with that, she walked down another hallway.

Marianne quickly walked outside to find her little friend. "Emma, wait up."

She turned and offered Marianne a roll of her eyes. "I just wanted to meet you."

Tethered horses stood outside the huge red barn, nodding and prancing as they walked toward them.

"I'm glad you did. Do you know someone named Stella?"

"Yes, ma'am. She's Jackson's wife. They just had a baby. That's where everyone's gone right now." Emma reached out to a brown horse, patted its cheek, and hugged its head.

Cautiously, Marianne lifted her hand to touch the horse's silky neck, but his head swung around, and she quickly dropped her hand and jumped back. She hoped Emma hadn't seen her reaction. She hated to admit she was terrified of horses. One had thrown her when she was four, and she'd never attempted to get near another horse. She considered herself particularly brave today to be standing within arm's reach of one.

"Hey, beautiful." The horse nuzzled Emma's hand. "Nothing for you right now, Sunset. Maybe later." Emma squinted up at Marianne. "She was born at sunset."

"How old is she?"

"Two." Emma rested her forehead on the horse's slick cheek and Marianne almost choked. "She thinks I'm going to be just like my mama."

"What?"

"Mrs. Rook. She thinks I'm going to be just like my mama."

"What's your mother like?" A beautiful brown eye blinked at Marianne. She eased away from the horse and wondered how much horses weighed and if they ever attacked people. Although, Emma seemed perfectly at ease around this one.

"I don't know. She left when I was a baby. Didn't like it here." Emma lifted one shoulder. "Or me either, I guess."

Marianne understood rejection. Her hand gently cruised down Emma's back. "I'm sorry, honey. It's her loss."

"That's what my daddy says. Still, I wish she'd come back and get to know me, y'know? Give me a chance." She flipped a blonde braid over her shoulder and tugged Marianne forward. "C'mon, I'll show you the barn."

The smell of hay, horses, and dirt hung in the air when she and Emma walked inside. A flat shovel lay against a stall door.

"We keep the saddle horses in here."

Which meant they were probably gentle horses, right? Marianne tried to ignore her thumping heart and asked, "How long have you lived here?"

"My whole life. Some of the men have been here longer than me and knew my mama. I'm ten. My birthday's in March."

As they walked past the stalls, Emma had a kind word, nuzzle or pat for each horse. "Mucked out every one of these," she offered as they walked down the long, wide center aisle that ended at another set of huge doors.

Marianne remembered the list of chores Mac had in store for her. Mucking was at the top of that list. "I may need lessons."

"It's not hard."

"I'm curious, Emma. Do horses really sleep standing up?"

She giggled as if Marianne had purposely asked a silly question. "Sure. It's hard for them to get up once they're down, so they don't, y'know, get down very often, except for deep sleep. That's Mr. Luke's office."

They passed a glassed-in office with a messy desk and four rows of file cabinets under a curtainless window.

Emma pushed open one of the great doors, and they walked outside. Corrals, outbuildings, two other barns, and white fences covered the land. Several men hugged the bars of one corral as they watched a man and a horse in the center of it.

"C'mon, let's go watch my daddy." Emma ran toward the corral with the lone horse and man inside.

A cowboy hailed Marianne and tipped his hat at her. "Ma'am. Hep you with something?"

Marianne lifted a hand to shield her eyes from the glaring sun and looked at the man. *Crusty* came to mind. Late forties. Gray scraggly beard. Chewing tobacco in his bottom lip. His dusty work clothes seemed to wilt on his skeletal frame. Gray eyes twinkled under his battered work hat.

She felt an instant liking for him. "Oh, we're just looking around."

He grinned. "You're the boss's girlfriend, ain't cha?"

"No, just a friend." She extended her hand. "Marianne Glaze."

Strong wiry fingers gripped it. "Jay McDougal. Soon to be McKenzie?"

She frowned. It was hard to keep up with these people. "Oh, *my* name. No, no, not at all. Nothing like that."

He laughed and shook his head as if he'd just caught her in a fib. "Come on over and watch ol' Zach. He'll teach you a thing or two about training a horse. Or a husband."

Good grief.

Marianne couldn't come up with a response to that, so she said nothing. Next to her, Emma sat on the top bar of the fence and wedged her boot heels over the second bar. Next to her, Geezer reclined on the fence. He nodded grimly at Marianne and turned toward the ring.

Inside the corral, a stocky, well-built man in his mid-fifties squinted at Marianne, his mouth set, his eyes frowning as if he intended to charge her. Dark sweat rings hung under his arms. His round, red face glistened in the cool day under a beige work hat.

She couldn't help but notice the bulk of his arms, the flatness of his stomach, the pulsing muscles straining against the leg of his jeans. It would have been easy for such a man to kill a young teenager with his bare hands. She swallowed hard when Zach's fierce gaze deepened as if he'd heard her thoughts.

"He's a stubborn one, ornery as all gitout," Jay offered.

"The horse or the man?" Marianne muttered as Zach turned away.

Jay shouted with laughter and slapped his knee. "Both, I reckon, ma'am. Jus' watch the master there, ol' Zach. He'll straighten that renegade out."

The horse's eyes bulged and his nostrils flared as Zach talked to him in soothing tones. Dust flew as the horse pranced around him.

"What's he doing?"

"At this point, just trying to show 'im he's safe. He was abused."

Marianne lifted her chin when thunderous eyes cut back to her from the center of the ring.

"Seems to like *you*." Jay grinned as he tipped his hat at her. "A horse don't never need to be beat with a whip. This one here was mistreated, so Zach's working with him, trying to undo some of the damage, teach him no one's gonna hurt 'im here. Well, it's almost noon time, and I could eat a bear whole. You have yerself a good day, ma'am." He chuckled as he walked away.

Almost noon. Time for lunch.

TWELVE

Marianne had never seen such a large kitchen. A huge butler's pantry, a couple of nooks with tables and chairs, two large islands, two cooking areas, one entire wall of nothing but cabinets and drawers—all in white. One tinted glass wall flanked the kitchen, letting in the yards and trees in the distance. None of the working side of the ranch could be seen. No log walls on the inside, either. Outside, several cozy tables and chairs sat on a long and wide covered patio the length of the tinted wall. The edge of the patio was bordered with huge pots of colorful flowers.

Marianne walked to the windows. A deer stood in the trees, its head raised and turned toward her. "I've never seen a kitchen as large as this, Aunt Helen."

"Joan tried to teach her sons to cook and needed room to spread out. Sometimes, it was really hectic and comical."

"It's beautiful, in every direction."

Helen opened a refrigerator and picked up an iced tea container. "If you'd like to help, Mari, I put the tea glasses on the island nearest you. That's an ice dispenser on the corner."

"All right." She filled the glasses with ice and tea. "I met Emma today. She's such a sweetheart."

"Our little Emma." Helen stopped to glance out the window. "She's had a tough life, living here with a bunch of cowboys and very little female influence. Still, it could have been worse, I suppose, had her mama stayed."

Helen tilted her head at Marianne, studying her. "She favored you, Mari. Green eyes, red hair, but she was petite, not tall."

That might explain why Zach had taken an instant dislike to her. "Why did she leave?"

The top of the tuna can popped up. Helen scooped out a glob of mayonnaise and placed it into the bowl. "She passed her favors around, so to speak. Zach told her to leave if she couldn't keep her belt buckled. Emma was four months old when she left. A hard woman, that one. Cut this up for me, Mari." She handed her an apple. "In bite-size chunks. Knives are in the drawer behind you. And open that box of raisins for me, please."

"Did Zach ever hear from her again?"

"No, and didn't want to, from what I saw." Helen opened a bag of chopped pecans and sprinkled them into the tuna bowl, followed by raisins, chopped celery, and chopped onions.

Marianne dumped the apple chunks on top. "Can you tell me about Mrs. Rook?"

Head down, Helen stirred the tuna salad. "She's the head housekeeper here." Helen took four pieces of bread out of a bag and placed them in a toaster oven.

Marianne leaned over and lowered her voice. "There's more."

"Yes, there is. Mac's former fiancée, Susan, stayed in one of our cottages. Mrs. Rook is her widowed aunt and lived in Brownsville her entire married life. Her husband gambled and drank away every dime they'd ever made. When she showed up the day after his breakup with Susan a year ago, needing a job, Mac hired her."

"And?"

Helen took out the toast and spread tuna salad on each piece. "I was surprised she got the job. Mac was more generous than I would have been. She's very efficient. Maybe it's because she lost her husband and had no children that she's so territorial. You'd think it was her house, and the rest of us were her servants. She expects everything just so-so, but only *her* so-so counts."

Helen cut the sandwiches in half. "She tries to make things perfect around here to compensate for her grief, her unhappiness. Behind you, Mari. The folded napkins."

Her aunt placed potato chips on each plate. "She keeps to herself and seems to be a very lonely woman. Sometimes, I forget she's even here."

"Where does she stay?"

"See that door next to the basement door?" Helen pointed with the knife. "It opens to a hallway with four bedrooms for the serving staff. At the end of the hallway, there's another staircase that leads directly to the living quarters upstairs, so they don't have to come through the kitchen. James lives in a house built just for him, about a quarter mile east of here, on McKenzie land. Joan needed help with the boys growing up. He's been here for almost thirty years."

"I see." Marianne picked up the napkins and glasses and placed them on the table closest to the wall of glass. "How big is this house, Aunt Helen?"

Helen brought the plates and joined her. "Nine thousand square feet. Pretty remarkable for a log cabin, isn't it? Mac's great-grandfather had seven girls. His grandfather had six children, and Gerald and Joan had eight sons. You can imagine how much room they needed." She laughed and then said, "Let's pray."

When they'd finished blessing the food, they sat at the table and ate for a few moments in silence.

"What was Mac like when he was younger?"

Helen swallowed a bite and sipped her iced tea. "Well, now, there's a mouthful." She chuckled. "I've been with this family for thirty-eight years and I've seen all the boys grow up. In my opinion, that one—" She pointed toward his office. "—is the finest of the bunch."

"Why?"

"Oh, so many things. One is his mind. The man is brilliant. Another is his energy. He never seems to tire. Willful, bull-headed but always honest. He was the hardest to get to bed. That's how I started with this family, you know, as a nanny for Greg and Bobby."

"No, I didn't know."

"When Mac was nine, Joey died, then two months later, Brigitt. Mac and Brigitt were very close. I've watched him struggle through the years. He loves deeply. But he lost so much so quickly that it's difficult for him to trust that someone will stay for the long haul. Trust doesn't come easy for him. Once it does, though, it's a forever kind of thing."

Marianne knew about not trusting people, but not for the same reasons. "When did you come to the ranch?"

"I was eighteen. I married Eddie at nineteen. Had Brigitt at twenty. It seemed appropriate somehow that my baby would fall in love with Bobby. He was two when she was born, and he loved her from the moment he met her. Never saw the like before or since. That little boy adored Brigitt."

Marianne pushed her plate away. "Is this a good time for you to finish telling me about Brigitt, maybe her last three months of life?"

"I will. But let's clean up and get to the chapel. I need a private place to tell her story."

The chilly breeze announced it was time for sweaters, but Marianne had left the one she'd borrowed from Helen in her room. When she opened the chapel door, she rushed inside and chafed her arms. "Brrr! Where did that wind come from?"

"It's November third. Typical November weather." Helen scooted onto a bench. "Let's sit, honey. But what I tell you in here must remain in here."

"I understand." Marianne sat in front of her and turned around, draping her arm over the back of the pew. "Is this a church for meeting on Sundays or just a place to come and pray?"

"It's held Sunday church services since it was built in the 1880s. Our pastor is John Matthews from Mole's Bench. Been here for the past twenty-three years. People from ranches all over the area come, so it's pretty packed on Sunday mornings."

"Does Mac join in?"

"Oh, yes. Just like his father, he supports the pastor financially and otherwise. Mac's a strong man of faith. He's dedicated to making sure everyone here has a place to worship."

Marianne studied the simple but beautiful altar, podium, and windows. "It's lovely and invites worship."

"It does." Helen sighed. "You asked about the last three months of Brigitt's life." She shook her head. "They were horrible."

Her aunt eased her head back, as if she were pulling strength out of the air in order to tell her story. "She turned eighteen in January of that year. And not long after, she became agitated, depressed, difficult to get along with. I asked her what was wrong. She'd just stare at me, as if she were trying to, I don't know, say something without using words. Sometimes tears welled up. Other times, her eyes were empty. I could see how miserable she was, and one night, I was particularly persistent."

She shifted her gaze to Marianne. "We had never kept anything from each other. I wanted to help her, so I was insistent that she talk to me."

Marianne's fingers grazed Helen's knee. Her aunt took her hand and squeezed hard. When tears welled up and fell down her face, she released Marianne's hand, tugged out some tissues from her front pocket, and dried her eyes.

"She started crying, Mari. I don't mean a little weeping. I mean all-out, hysterical wailing. I cradled her and rocked her and tried my best to soothe her. But she wouldn't talk. Not a single word. At one point, she shouted, 'If I tell you, they'll kill you!'"

Marianne gasped. "They?" *Men, not man.* "Who would want to kill you, Aunt Helen?"

"I don't know. She wouldn't say another word. Two weeks later, she was gone." She closed her eyes and sighed. "Then my husband died of a heart attack three months after Brigitt."

"Oh, Aunt Helen. I'm so, so sorry. I don't remember any of this. I had no idea."

"Your mother never told you?"

"My mother and I don't discuss anything. We haven't for years."

"When my sister shuts a door, it's barred with steel."

"What happened to y'all, Aunt Helen? Why did we stop coming to see you?"

Helen shook her head. "Maybe someday I'll tell you, Mari, but not today."

"Fair enough. Who do you think Brigitt meant by 'they'?"

"That one has plagued me every day since she said it. I don't have the foggiest idea what she meant. Did they do something to her? Were they threatening to? Did they want her to do something and were threatening to hurt me if she didn't? Too many possibilities. Too many questions."

She looked down at her hands and swallowed hard. "I wasn't going to tell you this, but I think I should. Brigitt was pregnant the night she was beaten. Rape was part of what they did to her."

"Rape! But that's not in the police report. Or the pregnancy."

"She lost the baby that night before she died. My cousin, Kirk Romer, was the coroner and he falsified the death certificate."

A falsified death certificate and autopsy report. "Why?"

"I asked him to. I didn't want Bobby to find out."

"Then he doesn't know?

"No. She was possibly even gang raped. Maybe that's the 'they.' Her death is something I deal with every day, Mari. Your coming here has given me a small measure of hope that you'll find something that will lead the authorities to the men who hurt her. I always suspected George Schroeder, but I saw in my attorney's report that he's been dead for a long time."

"Geezer feels the same way."

"Geezer?" Helen lowered her eyes as her face flushed.

Now wasn't that interesting? Unrequited love, perhaps? "I think he loved Brigitt very much."

"He was like a second father to her. Called her his little missy. He made her a saddle just before she died—no, I don't think he'd finished it." Her head bobbed. "Yes, I remember him working on it the day of the funeral, almost in a frenzy. He'd lost his wife and little girl in a freak river accident, and Brigitt became his little girl after that. I know he's missed her something terrible."

"He doesn't seem to think it's over."

"What's not over?"

"I don't know. He said that to me, that he doesn't think it's over yet."
Helen's face went completely white.

"Are you all right, Aunt Helen?"

"Yes." She patted Marianne's arm. "Oh, yes, I'm fine. Just all this talk about Brigitt brings up some horrible memories."

"Aunt Helen, how involved do you want to be in what I find out?"

"As much as possible. I kept vital information from the police once before and I won't do it again."

"Good. Someone is trying very hard to frighten me away, but I'm digging my heels in." She stood, as did Helen. "Something's been bothering me. In Brigitt's case file, the presumption is that she was beaten after school on her way home. But her best friend, Deb Engels, said she wasn't at school that day."

Helen pursed her lips and shook her head. "She wasn't." Her aunt walked to the foyer, and Marianne followed.

"Where was she?"

"At a friend's house."

"There's no mention of that in the file." Another pertinent piece of information left out of the police report.

The door opened just as they reached it. Mac stood with the sun behind him and even with the bright light in her eyes, Marianne could make out the anger on his face. He virtually pulsed with it.

"Why didn't you let someone know where you were?" Mac's heart pounded as he clenched his fists.

"I didn't think to do that. I was with Helen and we—"

"I don't care who you're with! You scared the living daylights out of me. Nobody knew where you were!" He'd never been so afraid in his life. He was already frantic by the time he thought to look in the chapel. But she was here, safe and sound. He made himself take a deep breath and let it out. It didn't help.

"I have work to do," Helen said quietly and left.

Marianne huffed. "We agreed—"

"We agreed you'd tell me where you were going when you left the main house!"

"Don't bellow at me."

"I am not bellowing!" Mac threw his hat on the table. *She's all right. She's all right.* "Okay. Maybe you could construe that to be bellowing. The point is, Marianne, no one knew where you were." *And I was going crazy.* "I thought you were hurt."

"We went out the side door toward the lake."

"That's a blind alley. No one on the working side of the house can see you over there."

"I'm sorry, Mac—"

"Sorry doesn't cut it! You could have been hurt or killed." He blew out a frustrated breath and purposely tried to lower his voice. "But you weren't." His gaze cut to hers. "*Next* time—"

"I will, Mac." She placed her hand on his arm. "I didn't mean to worry you."

He promptly covered her hand with his own and pulled her into his arms, right where he needed her to be. "I was so scared you were hurt."

"I'm not." She tightened her arms. "I'm all right. Besides, what could happen in a chapel?" Pulling out of his arms, she turned toward the front of the sanctuary. "It's probably the safest place on this ranch."

"Why aren't the lights on in here?"

She took his hand and tugged him around. "We didn't need them."

As he turned toward the small sanctuary, the sun tossed bright rays into the stained-glass window, casting multicolored designs on the walls. It took long moments of trying to control the panic before he could relax enough to enjoy it.

He squeezed her hand and pulled it around the back of his waist. Her face was soft with wonder as they stood in the arched doorway and basked in the mellow glory of the colored lights.

"It's beautiful, isn't it?"

"It is. Marianne—"

"I will." She touched his mouth with two fingers. "Next time I come out here, I'll let you know. I promise."

"I'll hold you to it," he muttered.

That night, Marianne watched from her bedroom window what she thought was the fence crew coming in. She searched for Mac but didn't see him. He'd missed supper, and Helen didn't know where he was or why he'd missed eating with them.

Worrying about another person was new to her. Every member of her family was so independent of the others that no one knew the others' schedules, nor did they care to. Meal times were usually alone or with Patrick, if their paths crossed. If her father happened to be home at dinner time, they ate together. It was understood that no one spoke. If she ventured a question, he ignored her.

The word "family" meant that they shared blood and not much else.

Marianne was exhausted and needed a good night's rest, so she'd come upstairs and gotten ready for bed early. And then Patrick called.

"Mother in a drunken stupor isn't news, Paddy."

"It's different this time. She's saying things that don't make any sense. Things like, 'He killed her, sure as anything,' and, 'She was always his favorite'."

"Who is she talking about?"

"Got me. She was too far gone at the time to make sense."

"Paddy, we're going to have to confront her again with the drinking."

"She's perfectly content being a drunk."

"You know she's not. She quit once and stayed sober for a long time. It's just gotten out of hand the last few months." He didn't say anything, so she said, "Are you? Are you content, too?"

"Don't put me in her category."

She didn't push it. "How's everything else?"

"Fine, as long as they stay at opposite ends of the house."

Opposite ends of the ring. "Do you have any memories of them being different? Loving each other?"

"That's long since dead and gone. I called to tell you about Mother and see how you are. I have no desire to walk down memory lane tonight. Especially *their* memory lane. So," he sniffed, "how are you?"

She lay back against her pillows and closed her eyes. "Strange things are happening here."

"You mean besides being run off the road?" She said nothing. "So, stop already."

"I'm in too deep to quit now."

"You can always quit. Especially when a killer is stalking you."

She thought of the picture in Mac's den. "If I have a stalking horse, I can shoot first."

"A what horse?"

She laughed and explained it to him. "Want to be my stalking horse, Patrick?"

"You already have one."

Father. "I came to the same conclusion. Want to trade places with him?"

"Not on your life."

She hoped it didn't come to that.

"Instead of trading places, sis, why don't you just shoot your so-

146

called stalking horse?"

"I've been thinking the same thing. Figuratively speaking, of course. In the hospital, Frank and I had a moment. I think he gave me permission to be on my own."

"Permission? You still need his permission?"

This, from Paddy. "I'm coming into Abilene tomorrow to get clothes for cooler weather."

"And get rid of your stalking horse?"

"I thought about talking to him."

"Will I see you?"

"I'll come by your office when I'm all packed. Oh, do you know someone called Bubbles?"

He snickered. "I wouldn't own up to it, if I did."

"Paddy, do you?"

"No, I don't. Why?"

"Good morning." Marianne stood in the doorway and smiled at Mac.

Now this was a nice way to start his day. He finished his orange juice and perused the yellow business suit she wore. Her hair was pulled back and up with curly wisps of red framing her porcelain face. She was so stunningly beautiful, she took his breath away. "Good morning, Mari. You look lovely today."

"Thank you." She sat opposite him, poured herself a cup of coffee, and leaned over to top off his cup.

"What's the special occasion?"

"I'm going to Abilene to get some clothes. It's been cooler and I didn't come prepared for it." Two pancakes plopped on her plate. "And I might talk to my father. I'm thinking of taking a riding crop with me."

"Good for you."

She nodded and poured syrup over her pancakes. "I'd like to say something to you, Mac. I've really enjoyed my time here at the ranch and—"

"You *are* coming back, right?"

"If I'm still welcome."

"Of course, you are."

"Thank you, Mac. I wanted to say that I've grown as a person here. I've faced some terrible things, and I'm stronger. I'm grateful to you for your support and friendship."

"Both will always be there, Mari. What about some company? I'd rather you didn't go by yourself after everything that's happened."

She shook her head. "I need to go alone." She smiled. "I'll be fine, Mac. I'm determined to be fine."

THIRTEEN

Marianne rode the elevator up to her father's office, thinking about their time in the hospital and the change she'd seen in him. She hoped her stopping by would be seen for what it was: a gesture of respect and courtesy. She didn't want him to find out she'd been in Abilene and hadn't stopped by to see him. She hoped the 'new' Frank she'd seen in the hospital would meet her today in his office.

As she opened the door to his immense, plush office, an alarm screeched. Frank's fierce gaze snapped at her as he looked over his reading glasses, yanked out a concealed panel in his oak desk, and punched in a code. The alarm stopped as he strode toward her with a wand. "What's on you, Marianne?"

A woman sitting in a leather chair in front of his desk stood and turned toward them. Her eyes caught Marianne's and a soft smile touched the woman's mouth. Something passed between them, something almost tangible. *Understanding?*

Frank's finger made a circle, and Marianne lifted her arms and turned around. "Nothing's on me, Father."

"Well, you have *some*thing or the alarm wouldn't have gone off." He shook his head and frowned. "Let me look inside your purse." He held out his hand.

When she hesitated, Frank nudged his hand toward her again. She slipped it off her shoulder and gave it to him.

In seconds, he'd located something. He pulled a small knife from his pants pocket and slit the inside fabric. The bug fell into his hand, and he disabled it. "One of ours." He looked over his glasses at her. "Did you misplace your purse recently or notice it was missing?"

"Not recently, no." Then she remembered the poem and the man pawing her on the side of the road when she was unconscious. He could have planted it then.

"Why would someone want a bug on you? What are you talking about that would interest *any*one?"

"I don't know." She glanced at the woman, not wanting to discuss anything in front of her.

Frank indicated her with a flap of his hand. "Cheryl Mallory, my daughter, Marianne Glaze."

Marianne walked over to her and extended her hand.

"Very nice to meet you, Miss Glaze. I've heard wonderful things

149

about you."

She doubted it but said "Thank you" anyway. She gripped Cheryl's small hand and then let it go. Pixie-cut, bottle-blonde hair, arched black brows, gray bedroom eyes, and pouty red lips accented the bright red tailored suit on her small frame. Cheryl Mallory was a pretty, stylish, business-like woman. Marianne wondered what she did for Frank.

Quietly, Cheryl sat in the same chair, crossed her legs, and faced her father. *An audience. Wonderful.*

Like Mac, her father was muscled in a slender way, his gait graceful as his long legs quickly covered the distance to the mirrored refreshment center. He poured a cup of coffee and didn't bother to ask either woman if she would like a cup.

"Father, I'd like a word with you when it's convenient."

His cup paused at his mouth as he stared at her for a few moments. Then he turned toward the window and continued sipping as if no one had spoken, as if no one was in the room with him.

All the old feelings of dealing with him bombarded her. She felt her stomach churning, her heart pounding, her hands trembling as she tensed with anticipation, waiting for his response.

She didn't expect him to completely ignore her.

He set his cup down, walked to his desk, and punched a button. "Come to my office." His steel-gray gaze landed on Marianne as he sat, steepled his fingers, and waited.

It was understood she was to say nothing until the summoned one arrived.

Cheryl simply stared out the window, her features soft and composed like a cat sitting on the carpet in a spot of warm sunshine. It seemed she had nothing better to do than to witness a dysfunctional family in action.

Patrick walked in. His face lit up when he spotted Marianne, then he jumped when his father threw the disabled bug at him. Of course, he fumbled it and dropped it. Cheryl arched a brow at him.

"It was in your sister's purse." Frank leaned back in his chair. "Find out who, when, and why."

In the waiting tension, Patrick examined it, glanced at his father, and then took a step back. "Yes, sir."

"Too late, Patrick. I can smell your stench from here."

Patrick's nostrils flared as his fierce gaze slinked to Frank, then down to his hands.

"It's what? Eleven in the morning? What are you working for? To be drunk by noon like your mother?"

"Leave her out of this." Patrick's voice sounded small.

"Leave her *out?*" Frank flung his arms up as he stood and marched toward his son. "And just how am I supposed to do that? She's in everything you do. I'm sandwiched between two *lushes—*"

Marianne stepped between them. "Stop it, Father."

Gritting his teeth, Frank jabbed a finger at her. "Don't you start on me, Marianne. *I'm* the one holding this family together!"

With her gaze on her father, she said, "Patrick, leave."

"Yeah, Patrick, run. Leave." Frank pivoted toward his desk. "Crawl back into your bottle. Just like your mother." He turned to Cheryl, his expression more civil. "We're done here." And then he sat and picked up a file.

Meekly, Cheryl reached for her briefcase and followed Patrick out of the office.

The air sizzled with anger. Marianne's own resentment added to the tension. She resisted the urge to cross her arms and tried to reel in her temper. She wanted to make sure her words were well chosen and precise.

Her father continued to study the file on his desk, ignoring her again.

"What about the hospital? Where's the man I saw in the hospital?"

"He doesn't exist."

"Yes, he does. I saw him. I *talked* to him. I got to know him a little."

She knew that what her father didn't want to face, he simply ignored. He stood and turned toward the large glass windows again.

She allowed him space, but not separation. "He meant something to me."

Frank didn't move or acknowledge that she'd spoken. She made a determined effort to set aside the fear nipping at her confidence and stepped toward him. "Father."

Frank shook his head. "That day, that man was scared, afraid he might lose something that meant everyth—" Hands in his pants pockets, he sighed.

"Finish it. Say what you mean."

Silence had always been his weapon. She'd figured a long time ago that he used it to cause people to question themselves. But today, she wouldn't play along.

"Father." Nor would she talk to his back. She stood beside him. "Why do you think Patrick works for you?"

Eyes at half-mast, he sent her a sidelong glance. "Spare me the dramatics."

"Why do you think I got a double major in criminal justice *and* art?"

"Because both of you saw the wisdom in what I suggested."

"Suggested? You've held the threat of disinheritance over us since we were little. But it won't work with me anymore. I don't want or need your money." She edged in front of him. A flicker of annoyance appeared when he looked down his nose at her. She lifted her chin, met his gaze.

"Don't get all high and mighty with me, little girl. We both know you wouldn't be anywhere in this world if it weren't for me."

"I graduated with honors, Father, all by myself."

"And who paid for it?" His finger poked at her shoulder. "Whose recommendations got you on the inside track?"

She nudged his hand aside. In a flash, he grabbed her wrist.

Shocked, she tugged against his hold. "Let go." He didn't. "Stop it!"

Gritting his teeth, he tightened his grip. His breath came quickly as he leaned closer to her.

Nose to nose, she shouted, "Let go of me!"

He jerked as if he'd just come out of a trance. He dropped her hand and stepped back. "I-I'm sorry. I'm sorry." He surprised her by slumping into his chair and covering his eyes with his hand. "Your mother—I have a lot of stress on me right now. Again, I'm sorry."

She wanted to cry. Her father had never hurt her physically. Not even once.

Quiet moments ticked by. Trying hard to remember the man in the hospital, Marianne stood still and waited for his next move. She held her wrist and closed her eyes. His actions today only confused her more: one moment, kind; the next, yelling at Patrick; the next, a bully. Had nothing changed for him since her accident?

At least before that day, she'd known what to expect from him. But his behavior in the hospital had given her hope that—

Abruptly, her father stood, adjusted his tie, tugged open a drawer, and pulled out what looked like a credit card. With it between two fingers, he handed it to her. "I got this for you right after I returned from visiting you in the hospital. I'm sorry I didn't get it to you sooner."

So many apologies in less than five minutes. The world must be coming to an end. "I don't need your money."

"I know. But it's a gift. Three hundred thousand. Maybe you can fix up Cecil's house with it or whatever." He slid both hands into his pants pockets. "I want you to have it."

"Then thank you." She slipped it inside her purse and headed for the door. After taking a few steps, she turned around. "If this is in any way a bribe or meant to manipulate me, it won't work. I'm stepping out from behind my stalking horse, Father. Right now."

"I know." He sighed, deeply. Then he walked toward her. "I really am sorry. May I give you a hug?"

A hug? He'd never once—

She couldn't think. This was radically off course for him. It actually embarrassed her. Did other fathers *ask* their children for hugs? Or did hugs come naturally between them? A sudden wave of grief washed over her, but at the same time, a little flicker of hope came up against it. She was so confused.

Then she looked up at him, and his expression was almost pleading. As awkward as this situation was, she stepped forward and said, "Of course."

Tentatively, he reached out, and she walked into his unfamiliar arms. She couldn't remember the last time her father had hugged her. Tears gathered, but she blinked them away. A quick but firm squeeze, and he stepped back, rubbing his hands on his pants.

"Anything up your sleeve?" An awkward smile touched his lips.

"Oh, I thought of using a riding crop," she answered quietly, "but there's no need now."

"I'm glad. Are you staying in town for a little bit?"

"No. I'm headed back to the ranch." She touched his arm. "It's important to me that you know that I love you, I respect you, and I'm no longer indebted to you, even for my education. I'm grateful for everything you've done for me, but there is nothing you can hold over me anymore."

He nodded quickly. "Understood."

"Good." She didn't know what to do now. It was obvious her father was extremely uneasy, as was she. "Do you know anyone named Bubbles, by any chance?"

"Bubbles?" He frowned as if he was really trying to think of someone. "No. I've never known anyone with that name. Why?"

"It's not important. I'm headed out now. I'll talk to you soon."

"I'd like that."

Her fingers wiggled a good-bye as she walked away from him. She opened the door and turned around. Her father was in the same spot, his hands in his pants pockets, his gaze on her.

She left then and gently shut the door behind her. When she

reached the elevator, tears stung her eyes. Alone in the elevator, she punched the down button. She couldn't wait to get back to the ranch.

Patrick grabbed the knob to his suite of offices and flung the door open. Cheryl preceded him. "I'm going home," he spat as he yanked on his tie. His father didn't know about the luxury apartment he'd leased a year ago. Frank's edict that he live at home had more to do with control than a desire for his company. They rarely spoke three words together there.

As he turned to leave, Patrick grabbed the gold nameplate boasting 'Patrick Donovan Glaze, Vice President' on his desk. A gift from dear ol' dad. He sent it flying. Then he turned his back on it as it crashed into the wall.

"Meet me there. Wear something red, hot, and sexy."

Mac couldn't believe it had only been a few hours since he'd seen Marianne. He'd acted like a besotted schoolboy all day, waiting for that first glimpse of a pigtailed little girl returning.

He glanced outside. Finally! He spotted her SUV through the trees as she drove up to the main house. She parked, reached for her purse, and got out. Nuggets ran up and greeted her.

Marianne squatted and wrapped her dog in a long hug. "Oh, you're just what I needed right now. How's my little sugar bug?" Nuggets gave her a few more kisses and ran off to join two dogs coming out of the barn.

"You're positively glowing. Things must have gone well."

She headed up the steps. "*Well* is a relative term. It didn't go as I'd planned."

"What happened?"

"Honestly?" She stopped on the porch and hugged him. "It was a strange encounter, but I said what I intended to say. My father was like a changeling, switching back and forth from the old Frank to the man I met in the hospital. It was difficult to follow him. Would you mind coming upstairs with me? I have some questions. Oh. Do you know George Radke?"

"Lindsey's father." He followed her inside and up the stairs. "A little. It's been probably six or so years since I've seen him. Why?"

"Why didn't you tell me you knew him?"

"You didn't ask."

"Well, McKenzie, I am learning to ask." She opened her bedroom door. "When I was visiting Lindsey, she wouldn't talk to me about her father. That's the why of my question to you about George Radke. Maybe you'll tell me something I can use to find out more." She found a blank page in her notebook, sat in the sitting area, and glanced expectantly at Mac, her leg shaking violently.

She was wound up like a top.

"Come here." He gently took the notebook and set it on a table, then grabbed her hand and tugged her to her feet. "I need another hug. I missed you today."

She settled into his arms, rested her head against his chest, and sighed. "I missed you, too." It pleased him when her arms went around him. "And your hugs."

"Good. Now relax." He swayed with her for a few minutes. He was aware of every curve, every part of her body. He widened his steps, hugged her tighter, and then moved into a slow dance. His fingers laced with hers, and he curled their joined hands against his heart as she followed his lead.

Quietly, they moved across the carpet. No words were spoken. No words were needed. They danced to the song whispering in his heart.

It felt so good to have her in his arms.

He slowed to a stop and just held her, pleased that she let him.

Then she gently pulled away and smiled at him. "I needed that, Mac."

"So did I, Marianne."

Settling into the chair, she looked up expectantly. "Is this a good time to tell me about George Radke?"

He nodded. "Thrifty, abrasive—"

"Must run in my family."

"Known for his underhanded business dealings."

"Underhanded in what way?"

"Ruthless, cutthroat, lies, anything for the almighty dollar."

"The kind of man who might hurt a young woman." She tapped her pen against her chin. Then her lip quivered. Tears filled her eyes.

"What is it?" Mac sat beside her.

She held out her right wrist. "My father grabbed my arm and squeezed it. He's never hurt me physically."

Mac gently took her wrist and kissed it. "I'm so sorry." Too much sadness in her eyes.

"He apologized, which helped a little. Oh." She wiped the tears off her face. "My father also found a bug in my purse."

"What kind of bug?"

"The listening kind. You should have your house and truck checked. Someone's interested in what I'm saying, where I'm going."

"Then maybe we should give him a ride. Been thinking we ought to pay my brother, Bobby, a visit." He kissed her hand again. "How about a trip to Fort Worth in the morning? I'll call him and see if he's home."

"I'd love to meet Bobby. Maybe he can fill in some of the information holes I keep falling in. What time do you want to leave?"

Tall weeds hugged the white picket fence surrounding Bobby's white frame house. Well, the fence *used* to be white, Marianne noted, but now chipped beige paint sparsely dotted the gray wood. She climbed out of Mac's truck and waited as he walked around the cab to join her.

Scraggly bushes around the house barely hid the peeling paint peeking out around the base. Overgrown grass almost covered the sidewalk.

"Needs work," she muttered as she pushed on the gate. It didn't budge. She leaned over it as Mac fingered the catch dangling from the column. Old, rusted wire connected the gate to the bottom of the rotted post. "I guess Bobby doesn't get in this way."

"Unless he gets a good running start and jumps over it."

She chuckled. "Oh, look. There's a break in the fence over there." They shimmied through it and sidestepped a wooden swing dangling by a single frayed rope from a large tree branch.

"I don't know why Bobby lives like this. He's got more than enough money for three lifetimes. I know he's rarely here, but this is absurd." He searched for a doorbell and didn't find one. He knocked. After a few seconds, the knob groaned as it slowly turned.

A fuller version of Mac stuck his head around the door, his eyes surprised and laughing. "Mac, buddy, it's so good to see you!" They quickly hugged and pounded each other on the back. "Is everybody okay?"

"Everybody's fine."

"Man, it's been a while, hadn't it?"

"Too long. Bobby, this is Marianne Glaze. Marianne, my brother, Bobby McKenzie."

"Nice to meet you, Marianne. Come in, come in." He waved them inside and grabbed newspapers off a tired brown sofa, looked around for a place to set them, and then placed them on the floor beside the sofa. "Sit, sit. Would y'all like something to drink? Iced tea? Water?"

"No. We're fine, buddy."

They sat on the sofa. Marianne glanced about the room. Mac had mentioned that Bobby traveled a lot. So, it wasn't a total surprise that there were no pictures, no plants, no trinkets in the house. Nothing that would say to the visiting world that Bobby McKenzie actually lived here. Only a sofa, a recliner, a small lamp and table at the end of the sofa, and a dinette set in the corner with two chairs. Not even a television.

Glancing from Marianne to Mac, Bobby eased into a yellow recliner, crossed an ankle over his knee, and fidgeted with the frayed edges of his jeans. "You wouldn't tell me anything on the phone, buddy. Everything okay? Mom still traveling?"

Mac fiddled with his hat. "Last we heard, she and Aurora were in Venice. Hard to imagine her doing that, isn't it?"

"Dad always wanted to travel." His foot shook as he looked from Marianne to Mac again. "So, what's going on?"

"Do you know anyone named Bubbles, Bob?"

He tilted his head at Mac and frowned. "No. Bubbles would be a nickname, I think. But I've never known anyone with that name."

A little nervous, Marianne scooted to the edge of the sofa. "Bobby, in the last few weeks, I've discovered my mother's side of my family. Helen is my aunt. She and my mother had a falling out years ago. Cecil Tucker was my uncle. His body was recently found, and he willed his estate to me. When I checked out his property, strange things began happening to me. Someone shot at me, rammed my car, ran me off the road, and other things. I believe they all have something to do with my cousin Brigitt's death."

A living, breathing shadow of pain eased across Bobby's face. He stared at her a moment, eased his head back, and closed his eyes. "Whoa."

Marianne glanced at Mac with an I-don't-know-what-to-do-now look. He sent her a just-go-ahead nod.

She waited a moment and said, "I know this is difficult for you, Bobby."

"It is, but not for the reasons you're thinking. What do you want from me?"

"Mostly fill-in-the-gap information."

"Why?"

"I want to find out who's after me. Any information you give me might help me find this man."

"But why you? Why do you think *you* can find him when the police couldn't, when private investigators couldn't?"

"I'm not sure I can, but I want to try. I want to have a life at Tucker Spring Ranch and not worry that someone will come after me in the middle of the night."

"Are you thinking this man is the killer?"

"Maybe. But I don't really know."

"Are you police?"

"No. I'm an artist by profession."

"An artist?" His head fell back again, and he closed his eyes. He didn't move for several moments. "Did Helen give you her boxes?"

Her foot nudged her briefcase. "Yes."

"Have you talked to Helen?"

"Yes."

"Did she tell you?"

She glanced at Mac with an I'm-sorry-I-didn't-tell-you look. "Yes."

Mac scooted forward. "Tell you what?"

Bobby and Marianne looked at each other. The air pulsed with the question. Bobby turned toward his brother. "Brigitt was pregnant when she died."

"Okay."

"It wasn't mine."

"What do you mean?"

Bobby took a deep breath, held it, blew it out. "She was raped—"

"Raped!" Mac jumped to his feet.

"Three months before she died. She told me the week she died. She swore me to secrecy, said they'd kill Helen and me if it ever got out."

"What is *'it'?*"

"The fact that they'd raped her."

"They who, Bob?"

"Brigitt didn't know." Bobby took a deep breath, a miserable expression on his face. "I've had to live with not knowing if they killed her because they found out she'd talked to me. Sit back down, Mac. You're making me nervous."

Mac turned to Marianne as he sat. "You knew about this?"

"Helen told me day before yesterday that Brigitt had miscarried the night she died. She mentioned the rape."

"And you didn't *tell* me?"

"She asked me not to. She doesn't know you know, Bobby. She said she kept it out of the official documents so you wouldn't find out." Marianne opened her briefcase, pulled out a file, and opened it. "What happened to Brigitt? I'm not talking about the cover-up. I want to know what really happened to her."

Bobby waited a couple of moments before he told her a horrific story of rape and beatings and murder. "Another girl was there. Brigitt heard her muffled screams but never saw her. When it was over, they dropped Brigitt off near Cecil's home and left."

Bobby jumped up and walked to the window.

Marianne knew he was distancing himself from what he'd just told her, and she couldn't blame him. She wanted to throw up or punch something or run as far away from this room as she could go. But she didn't want to appear weak. She tried listening impassively, but it didn't work—she was anything but emotionless. "Why didn't Brigitt tell someone? Why haven't you?"

"I had to protect Helen. Brigitt said they had pictures of two mothers who were killed because their daughters told. Gory, bloody pictures, several copies of each hanging on a clothesline, corner to corner and crossing in the middle of the room. They took her blindfold off so she could see the pictures. She had nightmares about it, about everything. They had a picture of Helen as a threat, a reminder not to tell. Apparently, that's how they kept the young women they kidnapped in line. Those men knew where we all lived. We couldn't watch each other twenty-four hours a day."

"Brigitt never said a word to her mother?"

"Only that something had happened, that she couldn't say anything."

"Did she know any of the men?"

"George Schroeder. When they released her, they told her she'd better keep her mouth shut if she wanted her mother and me to stay alive. They also said they'd come for her again when the mood hit them. They did, and they killed her."

"Does anyone else know this?"

"Helen and I have never talked about it."

"Did any of them use first names?"

"George."

George Schroeder. Or maybe Radke?

"Buddy and K.J. She didn't see their faces, of course. They were behind her when they removed her blindfold."

Marianne wrote down the names. "Did she mention anything about an unusual voice?"

"No, nothing."

"A sound? A machine running? Outside noises? A train? Traffic? Airport sounds?"

"Creaking in the floors in a couple places. Nothing else."

"Any slip-ups from the men? Did any of them mention business names, wives' names, children, anything like that?"

"No."

"Any idea where she was?"

"She didn't have a clue, Marianne. Just took about an hour to get there. Could have been in a circle, for all she knew. The last bit was a bumpy ride on a dirt path. Inside, a musty smell."

"Musty? As in old?"

"Dirty and old."

"Could be anywhere." Marianne tapped her lips with her pen. "Can you remember anything else?"

"Oh, yes. I remember the tortured look on Brigitt's face when she told me everything. The tears. The fear. Knowing they were watching her. All of it. Yes, Mari, I remember a lot."

What could she say? There were no words to give comfort or understanding, so she said a heartfelt "I'm so sorry," because she understood, to a small degree. One of these men was after *her.*

She stuffed the folder into her briefcase. "There is one other thing. Brigitt wasn't at school that last day, the day she was killed. Is that right?"

His frowning gaze snapped to hers. "She was there."

"How do you know?"

"I usually took Brigitt to school on my way to work. But when I came to pick her up that morning, Helen said she took her early, that Brigitt needed extra help with a chemistry test. Where did you get the idea she wasn't at school?"

"Her best friend, Deb Engels."

Bobby crossed his arms. "She doesn't know what she's talking about. Brigitt was at school that day."

Something was terribly wrong. Either Helen had lied to Bobby, or she had lied to Marianne. In the chapel, Helen had specifically said that Brigitt was not at school, that she was at a friend's house. "Well, I guess that's it. We'll keep you posted on what we find out."

"We have to get back, buddy." Mac reached for Bobby and hugged him. "Why don't you come out to the ranch for a few days? It's been a while since you've been home. You know Helen would love to see you, too."

Bobby scrubbed his face with both hands, took in a deep breath and let it out slowly, as if he was mulling over Mac's invitation. He shrugged. "Yeah, well. Why not?"

"Stay as long as you want."

"I'll pack a few things and follow y'all up. We'll talk more when we get there." He held out a hand to Marianne. "Sorry about the attitude when you first got here."

"I didn't notice any attitude, Bobby, so no apology is necessary. Mac and I are working together on this. With this man, or men, attacking me, it's difficult to walk away. We need answers."

"Everyone does. I'll go get my things."

Marianne leaned her head against the window. Country music played softly around her. She tried to listen, to hear the words, to get her mind off the images Bobby had shown her. But she was an artist. An artist's gift was to visualize something and create it. She'd always had an overactive imagination, and it wasn't failing her tonight.

"Come here, Mari." Mac reached for her and tugged her close to him. Tears burned her eyes as she scooted into his comfort and into the pain. She let go then and silently wept. For Brigitt. For Bobby. For their lost and broken dreams.

That Bobby could love so deeply touched her. His love for Brigitt hadn't changed. He hadn't let it. Love had survived through the worst ordeal imaginable.

Without a word, Mac gently stroked her back. It felt so good to be in his capable arms. Going against everything she had come to know about love and its chances for real survival, she allowed herself to rest in the tiny sparks of a deeper relationship with Mac.

She smiled up at him and stayed beside him as they traveled the rest of the way home.

Bobby was nervous as he pulled up beside Mac's truck at the ranch. He turned off the engine. It was easier to stay inside his pickup for a bit before any of the past here could touch him. He let out a long breath, sat back, and looked around at the grounds.

It was all so familiar—and not.

He could still see Brigitt standing on the front porch, waving at him as he waited in his truck to take her to high school. Just the thought of her—her perfume filling his senses as she slid inside his truck, stopping in the middle of the seat so she would be next to him as he drove. Just the thought of her—turning her face toward him, leaning back, allowing his lips to touch hers in a brief good-morning kiss. Just the thought of her—snuggling on the way to school, laughing and saying, "I just can't get close enough to you, Bobby James."

Just the thought of her.

But the porch had been extended, the stairs widened. Hanging plants were placed in military precision around its overhang. Wicker chairs now replaced the wooden furniture of his youth.

The chapel. He turned toward it, just past the lake, and wondered what she would have worn on their wedding day. *No, Bobby, you can't see my dress! That's bad luck.*

After her death, he had given the dress to her best friend who was getting married that summer. He'd never looked at it.

"Oh, Brigitt. I miss you," he whispered to the memories of her.

The front door of the main house flew open. Helen cried, "Oh!" and rushed down the steps. Bobby hurried out of his truck as Helen opened her arms and ran into his.

"Bobby! It's so good to see you!"

"You, too, Helen."

Helen pushed him back. "Let me look at you." She brushed a curl off his forehead and laid a hand on his cheek. "I'm glad you're here, honey."

Luke came up behind them. "Bobby, about time you came home." Their arms quietly slid around each other.

"You seem healthy and fit, Luke."

"Working hard. How long you gonna stay?"

"A few days. We'll see."

"Good. I know you and Helen have a lot to talk about, so I'll catch you later. I have a horse to tend to." Luke slapped him on the back. "It's really good to have you home," he added and headed for the barn.

When Mac and Marianne joined them, Bobby patted his belly. "What time's supper? I'm starving."

"Right now," Mac answered. "Come with us, Helen. Don't tell James, but we're raiding the kitchen tonight."

The raided meal ended with dishes stacked on the dining table, cups half-filled with cold coffee, and wadded napkins on the table. Mac stood at the dining room window, looking toward Zach and Emma's cottage. Several cowboys were headed toward the lively music drifting out from their cottage.

"I see Zach and Emma still put on a show." Bobby walked around Marianne's chair and headed for the window.

"From time to time," Mac answered. "You and Helen ought to go on over, see how much Emma's improved since you last heard her sing."

"Let's do it, Helen, for a little bit." Bobby helped her with her chair. "We'll see y'all over there." Their booted footsteps scooted through the house until they reached the front door.

Then all was quiet again.

"Are visitors welcome?" Marianne glanced outside.

"Anybody can show up. Zach's on banjo. Emma's on guitar. They're quite a pair, especially when Emma sings. Usually have a card game going, too. Want to go over with me?"

"I'm not sure Mr. Grouch would want me there. He doesn't seem to like me."

"We'll crash the party then."

"I need to brush my teeth and freshen up first. I'll meet you in five at the front door."

Very close to five minutes later, Marianne walked into the den. "My Uncle Keith's middle name is Jonathan," she announced. "Keith Jonathan Longman."

"K.J.?" Mac picked up the TV remote and turned off the evening news.

"Maybe. It's something and I'll take what I can get at this point."

"Come here. I want you to see something." He took her hand and led her to the opened French doors that welcomed a soft and rosy sunset. He had just been admiring it and thought the only thing that would make it any better was her beside him.

And here she was.

"I love it here, Mac."

"It grows on you."

"I'd bet the farm you never had trouble loving it."

"It's in my blood."

"My father said the same thing about my being in criminal justice."

"And doing what? Becoming a cop?"

"Eventually. I actually went to the police academy and stayed an

163

entire week. It just wasn't for me." She lifted a shoulder. "I wanted to study art, so I have a double major."

"You obviously have a knack for investigative work."

"Because I was forced to do it or lose my dream of living at Uncle Cecil's. Leaving here was not an option."

They stood arm-in-arm for a moment and enjoyed the evening. The sunset's ebbing light washed over her face. "You are so beautiful." He hadn't planned on saying the words or flustering her.

"I, uh, thank you," she mumbled and then edged back toward the coffee table. "Now, what do we have? Georgie, George, Buddy, K.J. A beginning. Have you done a sweep of this house yet?"

Mac noted her uneasy stance, the fidgety kneading of the hem of her blouse. He made her nervous, and that was good. "They're coming tomorrow." He closed the French doors and locked them. He'd never locked them, but hearing Bobby's story had changed that. He had to protect Marianne and the other women at the ranch from the evil Bobby had described. He left the small window above the French doors open and turned around.

The room was dark except for a bit of the sunset glowing through the glass in the doors. He could feel his heart beating faster. His breath came quickly as he looked at the woman he knew he loved.

Marianne's gaze flittered around the room, landing on everything but him. "What's your favorite movie of all time, Mac?"

He laughed and took a step toward her. "I really enjoy your company, Red." With his gaze on her face, her eyes, her mouth, he took another step forward, then another.

When he looked down at her, she smiled in a slow, shy way that sent shivers of need all over him. He wanted to touch her, to hold her. The scent of fall drifted in through the open window. Cool breezes gliding over yellowed fields. Leaves falling.

Hearts falling—his, at her feet.

He said nothing more as he cupped her face with both hands. Marianne sucked in a breath. With his thumb, he caressed her cheek, her lips. He had the pleasure of seeing her close her eyes and lean into his hand.

When he stopped, she opened her eyes and searched his. "Mac."

It was all the invitation he needed. He leaned over and brushed her lips twice before he covered her mouth. Soft, warm lips answered his need. Everything in him centered on her mouth. Savoring, yielding, he knew nothing mattered but that she was here, with him.

He lifted his head. Her eyes fluttered open, and she blushed. "We'd better get on over to Zach's," he muttered as he lowered his mouth again and added, "But we have time for one more."

This time, she wrapped her arms around him and tugged him closer, taking the kiss deeper.

When he opened his eyes, he wanted to say, "I love you," more than anything, but he knew it was too soon. *Patience, patience.* "Let's get to the party."

He took her hand and led her out the front door, into an evening swathed with gentle breezes, lively music, and the sweet fellowship of old friends.

Two hours later, Mac and Marianne left Zach's and headed for the main house. His arm snaked around her, and she leaned against his shoulder.

"Tired, Mari?"

"Yes, but happy. We got up early for the trip to Bobby's and I'm exhausted. I loved the music. It was the perfect ending to a long day."

Stars twinkled. A dog barked. A horse neighed in the silence surrounding them. Moonlight draped the ranch in a soft, romantic haze, and she didn't want the night to end. Throughout the concert and the card playing, she and Mac had exchanged long glances and smiles. She thrilled to the music playing inside her, drifting over dried-up feelings and freeing them, nudging and softening solid-rock notions that couldn't survive against the approval in Mac's eyes.

As they approached the main house, she made out Bobby sitting on the steps. She was disappointed that he was interrupting her plans to park herself beside Mac on the porch's wicker loveseat, absorb the night, and talk. But when Mac shoved his brother over on the steps and sat, she walked around them and said a polite goodnight.

Bobby enjoyed the moon's handiwork on the lake. He and Brigitt had sat on this porch and dreamed their dreams together. They had been safe and loved and nurtured by it all. "Y'all have a good time?"

"Oh, yeah." Mac leaned back, rested on his elbows, and stretched out his legs. "You and Helen?"

"We did." Bobby glanced at the barn. He could clearly see Brigitt standing there, holding the harness of her horse, stroking her neck as she talked to her. She had loved riding, racing Bobby, laughing when she won. She always won. Bobby saw to it.

"It hurts to be here." He rested his elbows on his knees and held his head. "You'd think after seventeen years, it wouldn't be so painful, but it is. Dad's gone, too. I-I think I'll head home tomorrow."

"But, Bob, you—"

He waved a hand and glanced toward the chapel. "We'd planned to get married seventeen years ago last month. Too much of her is still here." He eased his head against the handrail. "I've missed coming home. I miss Dad."

"Then try to stay. Brigitt and Dad would have wanted you to come home. She's here. He's here. But that's not a bad thing, is it?"

"I don't know. Maybe. We'll see in the morning."

The front door closed behind them. "You're not thinking of leaving, are you, honey?" Helen patted Bobby's arm and sat beside him.

"Ah, Helen, shoot. I don't know what I'm going to do."

She slid her hand in his. "Then come to my house. Let's visit for a bit. And if we can't find anything to talk about, we'll stuff our faces with apple pie and ice cream."

"I've got some room left for your apple pie." He laughed and tugged her to her feet. "Wanna join us, buddy?"

Mac shook his head and stood. "Y'all go on. I'm hitting the sack."

FOURTEEN

"Good morning."

Mac smiled at the sound of her voice and yanked the cinch strap, tightened and buckled it. He hadn't slept much. His mind had been filled with pictures of her laughing last night, playing cards, blushing at him from across the room, closing her eyes and swaying to the music.

This morning, she was all he could think about, too. "You're up early this morning, Mari. Did you sleep well?"

"I did. And you?"

When he turned to her, her face glowed as she smiled. He reached out a hand, and she took it. Drawing her close, he wrapped his arms around her. He decided to be up front with her and gauge her reaction. "A night of dreaming about you kept me in bed a little longer than usual this morning."

"You, too? Although my dreams were about you." A little nervous laugh slipped out. "I've never—I mean, this is all new to me, Mac. I don't—" She shrugged and blushed.

Good reaction. "We'll figure it out as we go." *A patient man, right?*

She drew back when he reached for Pal's reins. "I think we need to put an advertisement or something in the paper to entice the other girl traumatized by those men to come forward."

He headed outside. "You could go to the Mole's Bench Press and have the editor run a special-interest story on everything that's happened to you. People around here were traumatized by Brigitt's death, and they have long memories. It might be cathartic to know someone is looking into it again. Some might even offer you valuable information."

"The special-interest story would work if our poet's the killer. If he isn't, it would announce to the killer that I'm here, to come and get me at his leisure. I'll go with the ad and see what happens."

"What would it say?"

"You see, that's my problem. I'm not sure. 'Call me if you were hurt seventeen years ago and heard a woman being hurt in the room next to yours'?"

"It's an attention-getter, that's for sure. Use the ranch's phone number, though, not yours. It'd be safer for you."

Luke walked out of the barn, holding the reins of his horse. "'Morning, Mac, Mari. We better ride, partner, and get that fence fixed."

With one finger, Mac gently lifted Marianne's chin and thoroughly kissed her. "I'll miss you this morning. We should be back by mid afternoon."

She stepped back, smiled sheepishly at Luke, and waved at them as they rode off.

She raced to the balcony of her bedroom to catch the last glimpse of Luke and Mac riding toward the horizon. They looked like two fleas crawling on a huge yellow blanket. She lifted her face to the cool breeze and sighed.

Despite her best intentions, she was falling in love with Mac.

Last night had been wonderful. A night of new-found feelings, growing expectations, and that giddy sense of 'headlong in love.' But the dark had welcomed old fears. She had awakened early, determined not to let anything happen between them that they would both regret when she left.

Then she saw Mac, and her resolve flew out the barn.

What was she going to do with him?

She walked into her bathroom, tugged the band off her hair, and rubbed her head where it had pulled her hair. Her stomach growled, reminding her it was time to eat breakfast. She checked her watch. Twenty minutes until it was served.

She couldn't say why she froze. A noise, perhaps. A feeling.

She spun around. A white cloth. A firm hand against the back of her neck. A gasp. A struggle.

And then, nothing.

Mac and Luke made it back to the ranch just as the sun went down. Mac was starving. It hadn't helped that he'd thought of James' Texas chili all day, stoking the hunger fires. Texas chili was his favorite meal, and he could hardly wait to get inside and start eating.

He and Luke headed straight into the barn where Little Bit, a squat of a man with a black mustache, black eyes, and a bald head, waited for them.

Luke dismounted. "Me 'n Little Bit 'll take care of the horses. James is gonna be fit to be tied that you're late for supper."

Mac handed the reins to Little Bit. "Thanks, buddy. Luke, come on up to the house and eat supper with me. We're almost finished with the

Laredo Oil project, and I need your input on a couple decisions."

"I'll wash up and see you in about twenty minutes."

Mac walked to the mudroom, tossed his hat on a hook, and slipped out of his boots. He could smell James' chili from here, and man, it smelled good. It literally made his mouth water. James' jalapeno cornbread was the best he'd ever tasted. And the two together? He'd be settled in hog heaven in about two minutes.

The kitchen door was ajar. In his socks, Mac pushed on it and stepped inside. Strange, that not one light was on in the kitchen. He checked his watch. After six. Helen would be in her cottage by now. "James?"

The savory smells of the chili drew him to the stove. A large pan sat over a low flame. He lifted the lid and breathed in the wonderful, hot spices. He stirred it and sniffed again before he set the lid back on the pan.

James' habit was to cook the chili all day and serve it hot. Mac considered scooping up a bowl for himself right then, but James was persnickety about his kitchen and his serving duties.

So why, then, were the lights out? And where was he?

The cellar door wasn't latched. Mac poked his head into the darkness. "You down there, James?" He wasn't sure what he heard but it was something. He groped for the switch. Light sank into the darkness below him. "James?"

Something moved. "You there, James?" Halfway down the stairs, Mac stooped and spotted him near the food storage area, sprawled on the floor, rubbing his head.

"Got me from behind, boss."

Mac hurried to him and pulled him into a sitting position. "What happened?"

James moaned and mopped his forehead with his apron. "I can't say. Someone was down here, I think, hiding, and he came up behind me and—"

"Mari!" Mac jumped up. "Hang on, James. I'll be back."

He bolted up the cellar stairs and ran down the dark hallway. There didn't seem to be a light on in the house. Where was Marianne? Mrs. Rook? The other maids? Oh, yeah. Something about a shopping trip to Childress. Did Marianne go with them?

"Mari!" He ran through the house, heard nothing, saw no one. He made himself stand still and listen, but his heart was beating too loudly in his ears to hear anything else.

Three steps at a time, and he was upstairs in seconds. He grabbed her doorknob and flung the door open. "Mari?"

He flipped on the light switch and raced to her bathroom. A single yellow rubber band lay on the floor.

The closet door was open. He looked there, under her bed, on the patio. Frantic, he raced down the hallway. "Mari!"

He called her cell phone. He heard it ringing and chased the sound to the desk in her room. Her purse sat on the floor beside the desk.

Her car. He rushed downstairs to the front window and checked her parking place. The SUV was parked next to his truck. She was still here. He called Helen. "Have you seen Mari?"

"Not since this morning. Why?"

"Did she go to Childress with the house staff?"

"No. She said she wanted to stay back."

Think, Mac! The chapel? Surely, she wouldn't have stayed out there past sunset. Maybe she fell asleep on a pew, and maybe this man hadn't found her. *Please, Lord. Please let her be safe.*

He put his boots on, bolted out the back door, and raced to his Jeep. Tires gripped the pavement as he backed up and then headed around the lake.

He slid to a stop, jumped out, ran up the steps, and opened the chapel door. It was too dark and too quiet inside. "Mari?" He checked everywhere. But she wasn't there.

He slumped against the arched doorway. "God, help me. Help me."

Find her! *Find* her! *Find* her! His heart hammered out the message as he drove back to the main house and parked in front of the barn. Luke stood in the lighted doorway.

"Have you seen Mari?"

"No." Luke took a step toward him, frowning. "What's wrong?"

Mac pulled out his cell phone and called the sheriff. "Nate, Mac McKenzie. Marianne's missing." He tried to catch his breath, but all he could think about was Marianne somewhere she didn't want to be.

"How long?"

"She was gone when Luke and I got back about thirty minutes ago."

"Is her car there?"

"Yeah."

"She's probably at one of the cottages. Have you checked Helen's? The chapel?"

"We're doing that right now. James was knocked unconscious in the basement. Someone waited for me to leave to get to Marianne."

"Check all the cottages, the buildings, the chapel. Count your vehicles. Maybe she took a ride somewhere. Lloyd and I will be there within thirty minutes. Call me if anything changes."

Mac ended the call and pressed the alarm button near the barn doors. Within minutes, every ranch hand stood with Mac and Luke, waiting for instructions.

"My guest, Marianne Glaze, is missing. Luke will pair y'all off and tell you where to look. Search everywhere you think she wouldn't be. I'll be in the main house, waiting for the sheriff. Good luck."

Three hours later, Mac and Nate met in the mudroom and shucked their boots. The strong smell of coffee greeted them when Mac opened the kitchen door. Helen had kept the coffee hot and fresh. "She's not here, Nate. We've searched everywhere. Now what?"

"We keep looking. Lloyd called for backup."

"You think she's in trouble?"

"Not necessarily. But we need to spread out. We won't stop looking until we find her."

Mac raked angry hands over his head. "This has got to stop! How are we supposed to live with these idiots on the hunt for her all the time? When is this going to *stop*?"

The expression on Nate's face said he had no idea how to answer Mac. "We keep pushing. They'll eventually make a mistake."

"They already have. They're messing with someone I care about!"

A torrent of reds and oranges swirled in front of Marianne's eyes. Stabbing pain against her skull, like a jackhammer. Her eyes rolled into pounding waves. She stilled them to stop the pain and slowly opened them. Oh! Her head hurt!

Something was over her mouth! She tried to take a breath through her stuffy nose, but the air was too thin. *I can't breathe!* She felt her blood pounding in her wrists and ankles. She couldn't move! Was she tied up? *Oh, God.* Her stomach heaved.

Frantic, she moved her head from side to side and strained into an arch, trying to catch her breath. *I'm going to die!* Then her eyes closed as her body melted into warm liquid shadows.

"Oh, no, you don't! You're finally awake, and you're gonna *stay* awake!"

Wha—?!

Rough hands shoved her onto her stomach. Her face smashed against something hard. Duct tape was ripped from her mouth. She moaned and gulped in musty, dirty air. *What is happening? Oh, God, what is happening?*

She opened her eyes but couldn't see anything. It was pitch black.

Something pushed against her back. A knee?

"The letter. Where is it?" A male voice, above her.

"I-I don't... have it."

The knee drilled into her back. The air in her lungs swooshed against the floor, and her cheek twisted against it until she could hardly bear the pain. And then the pressure increased. "P-please."

"The second you get that letter, you give it to us. If you don't, we'll kill Mac, your mother, your father, your brother, your aunt, and your cousin. Are we clear on that?"

She tried to nod but couldn't. "Yes. Yes. I'll g-give it t-to you."

"If you go to the police, we'll know. We'll kill all of them if you tell anyone what happened here today."

"Yes. O-kay."

The heaviness on her back eased until nothing touched her.

A ripping sound behind her. Tape was placed over her mouth again.

"Put the letter under the spare tire in your SUV. We'll know it's there."

And then he was gone.

On a heavy sigh, Mac rested his head in his hands. *Where are you?* His stomach ached, his head pounded, his heart hurt. "I thought you'd be safe, Mari." The ranch was his haven. Nothing like this had ever happened here. And, yet, every indicator said that whoever did this was at the ranch—or was someone who could come onto the ranch without being noticed. *I didn't protect her.* The words sliced at his soul. *I didn't protect her.*

Heart sick and so discouraged, Mac stood and shuffled toward the stairs. He didn't like being left behind, but Nate told him to stay in the house in case she came back and to contact him if she did.

Mac imagined her out in the dark, exhausted, hurt, scared. Fighting that image, he stopped at her door and gently pushed it open. The faint glow of a security light outside her window softened the room. No other lights were on. The room was gray and sad as he took in her bed, a sweater draped over a chair, her purse resting on its side on the desk where he'd placed it. Visions of her smiling at him, blushing at him, kissing him flashed through his mind.

Not this. Please, God, not this. Not when he had found the one he wanted to be with the rest of his life. "Please. *Please.*"

He left her door open and trudged down the hall. When he reached his room, he lay fully clothed on his bed. He checked his watch. *3:25.* He needed to rest his eyes for a few moments. Just for a few moments.

Mac's head popped up. "Mari?"

Moonlight draped the room in dim shadowy hues as he glanced around the absolute quiet. The digital clock on his bedside table said *3:52.* He tilted his head and listened for a few heart beats, then his head fell back into his pillow.

There. What was that?

He tensed and listened. *There.*

He bolted up and moved to the edge of the bed. What was that sound? Like a shuffle.

He sank to his knees and searched under his bed, walked to the balcony, and stepped outside. The full moon cast vague specters across the yard as a cool breeze shook the tree leaves outside his room. No one was about.

He turned around and stood in the doorway, straining to listen. Another shuffle. Could something be on top of the house? He stepped back, leaned over the rail, and searched the roof. Nothing was there and none of the branches touched the roof.

Stepping back inside, he held his breath and listened.

He walked toward his open closet doors, taking each step slowly as he strained to hear. His hand eased to the light switch, and he flipped it. Cocking his head to listen, he took a hushed step toward the rear of the closet, moved aside his clothes. He heard it again, louder, and looked up.

The attic!

He raced down the hall and into the guest room between Marianne's room and his. Frantic, he opened the double doors to the huge walk-in closet, pulled on the cord at the back. The attic stairs strained their way down, and then Mac rushed up them. He shoved against the door, ducked, and pulled the light string.

"Mari!"

She was trussed up like a turkey with green eyes wet with tears. He ripped the tape off her mouth. "Oh, Mac—" she coughed, swallowed, winced. "You found me. You found me." She coughed. "I could hear you. Everything—so loud. No one could hear me."

With his pocketknife, he cut the tape binding her hands and feet and pulled her into his arms. "Are you okay? Are you okay?"

Her arms lifted but fell back to her side. She buried her face against his shoulder and wept.

He held her as close as he could without cutting off her air, and then he rocked her. Back and forth. Back and forth. "Did he hurt you?" When she didn't answer, he stopped. *Oh, God.* "Mari, did he hurt you?"

She shook her head and wept so hard, she began to cough.

Mac gritted his teeth against the anger consuming him. This hadn't happened on some obscure road or property. This jerk had been in his house! "Come on, Mari. Let's get you out of here."

"I just came from her room, Nate. She's still asleep. She told me it was pitch black, and she didn't see anything." Mac motioned Nate toward the coffeepot. "Grab some. I've ordered a security system for the main house. They put a rush on it, and it should be here later today."

The sheriff's boots scooted on the hardwood floor and became muffled as he crossed over the rug in front of the big stone fireplace. He poured coffee into a heavy mug and sipped.

"Thought this might interest you." Nate tossed his hat on the hook near the sliding glass doors and handed Mac a folded note. "It's a copy of the one that was taped to my office door this morning."

"Not again." Mac muttered as he unfolded the note and read it out loud.

"Little Miss Muffet thought murder a fling,
Unraveling secrets of long-ago spring.
She needs to pause
From this morbid cause
Or lose her head o'er the thing."

He backhanded the note. "Now *that's* a bona fide threat!" He angrily tossed the paper at Nate. "Who *is* this guy? What does he want? Why take her to the attic and leave her? Is this some kind of game with him?"

"I don't know his motivation. Obviously, he's trying to frighten her."

"Well, this is it for me. I'm going to tell her to stop this thing. It's not worth her life. It is *not* worth her life!"

"I'm investigating this, too, Mac. I wish she would stop. But I'm not sure it's her snooping around that's causing these things to happen. I think it's her presence here. I think they're afraid she's going to find the letter and the evidence. Any news on either?"

"No. Bubbles never stepped forward with the letter when Marianne inherited."

"Did Marianne say anything about what she saw when he took her?"

"No. She said—"

"Good morning."

Both men turned around. Mac studied her face as he walked toward her. She appeared exhausted, her expression dull as she sank into his arms. "Good morning," he muttered against her hair.

She pulled back but stayed in his arms. She was trembling. But who wouldn't be afraid after what she'd been through?

"Another note? He's prolific." She turned to Nate. "I never saw him. He stayed behind me."

Nate poured another cup of coffee. "I'm wondering why he didn't kill you."

Marianne shivered as she walked out of Mac's arms and took the cup Nate handed her. "It wasn't his intent. He's trying to frighten me away. It takes a sick mind to do that to another human being." Her expression softened as she looked at something outside.

Mac followed her gaze. Two dogs were fighting over an old hat. A cowboy yanked it away from them and, laughing, threw it.

"Life is good," she said and then sipped her coffee. Her hands were shaking.

"It is."

"Sure knew his way around," Nate noted. "No one noticed him coming or going."

"So, he's one of us." Marianne nodded. "I think he's right here, watching me. Probably one of the men hunting for me last night."

Mac glanced at Nate. The sheriff had said the very same thing. Mac noticed Marianne's vacant look as she moved a strand of hair out of her eyes. All of it had to have been terrifying for her. He stretched his arm across her shoulder and tugged her close, needing to comfort and reassure her but knowing that nothing he offered her would take it all away.

Nate cleared his throat and tapped his pad with his pencil. "Anything you can tell me about him, Marianne?"

"I never saw him. But he wore cologne. Had a medium voice, not deep. A Texas accent. Beer breath. Callused hands. I don't think he was tall; his steps were quick and short."

"Good." Nate nodded as he wrote, and then turned to Mac. "Lloyd's working on the duct tape that covered her mouth. I'd like to examine her room and the attic. Dust for prints, search for physical evidence."

Mac pointed upstairs. "It's my mom's old room. Top of the stairs, turn right. It's the first door on the left. Attic stairs are in the room to the right of that room."

Nate finished his coffee, set his cup down, and left.

Marianne headed for the blue-and-hunter-green plaid sofa sitting across from the sliding glass doors, sat, and set her cup on the side table. "I like this room."

"Mari?"

It took her a moment to turn toward him. She looked like she might fall out of the chair at any moment. "Yes?"

He knelt in front of her, his eyes level with hers. She was so beautiful. "I'm sorry I didn't protect you."

She touched his arm. "It's not your job to protect me."

"Yes, it is. You're a guest in my home—"

"And you're not supposed to leave home and go to work?" She cupped his face and softly kissed his cheek. "It's not your fault, Mac, any more than it's mine for walking into my bathroom. I'd like to eat some lunch. I'm really hungry."

"What would you like?"

"A peanut butter and jelly sandwich. Maybe two of them."

"I can give you better than that. I'll have James rustle up—"

She touched his face again. "I'm craving peanut butter and jelly."

He stood and leaned over to give her a quick kiss. "I'll make the sandwiches. Do you want to join me in the kitchen?"

"I think I'll sit here by the window and enjoy the sunshine."

Marianne didn't know what to do. If one of those men was here at the ranch, then she couldn't tell Mac about what really happened in the attic. She couldn't take the chance that he might mention something to Helen or Nate or Luke—or that this person would overhear her. "We'll know it's there," the man had said about her hiding the letter, which meant that someone was watching her constantly. She had to keep all of this to herself without acting nervous or frightened. She could do it, if Mac's life and her family's lives were in danger.

How many were involved now? How many were here at the ranch? The kidnapper had said 'we' which meant more than one. Several. Many. *Oh, God.*

Her cell phone rang. "Hello?"

"Mari, can you talk?"

Patrick sounded winded. "Yes, what is it?"

"Mother was drunk last night."

Well, stop the presses. She pushed against the bridge of her nose while she sighed and waited for the punch line. "Okay."

"She started talking about some man killing someone. I played along to get more information, and she finally said he killed Brigitt."

"What?"

"Plain as day. She passed out before she could tell me who."

"She's known all this time?"

"Well, when she's drunk, she knows. I haven't approached her sober."

"Let me. Drunk or sober."

"You're coming down?"

"It's a little after twelve. I can be there by dinner, maybe stay a couple days." She glanced at Mac as he walked into the room with her sandwiches and milk. "I'll call you when I'm ready to leave. 'Bye." She stuck her phone in her purse. "I'm going to Abilene."

"I gathered. Why?" He set the plate and glass on the table next to her chair.

She stood and motioned him to lower his head. She whispered in his ear. "Patrick said Mother was drunk last night. Said she knows who killed Brigitt. Why didn't she come forward seventeen years ago? Why has she kept it a secret all these years?"

"Why are we whispering?"

"It's safer, I think. Someone could be listening."

"Not in this house."

"You don't know that."

"You're right. Are you sure you're up to the trip?"

"I have to go."

"Well, you're not going alone this time."

"You can't leave Bobby after he just came home for the first time in years."

"He has Helen and Luke, and he'll understand. We'll just be gone a couple days. I'll drive, and you can rest on the way. We both need to get away from here for a little while."

"Hopefully, no one will follow us all the way to Abilene. You can drive, but we'll take my SUV."

FIFTEEN

Mac stood beside Marianne as bells chimed a classy refrain at the huge arched doorway of her parents' Georgian-style mansion. Its white walls and bold-gray roofs made it seem cold and uninviting. Three stories overlooked meticulous grounds as well as a large gazebo near a rambling river. The circular drive afforded Mac a glance at the grandeur of the Glaze property.

Standing on the portico, waiting for someone to answer the bell, Marianne's gaze flicked from the peephole to the huge bushes flanking the wide pillared entryway. She clutched her hands together, her thumbs tapping each other.

She's nervous. And from what little she'd told him and he'd witnessed of her father, she should be. He placed a quiet hand on her back. When she looked up at him, he raised his brows, wanting to reassure her.

She sent him a quick smile, and then shrugged.

A short Hispanic woman in a gray uniform opened the huge beveled-glass door. With a pleasant expression, the woman stepped back and lowered her brown gaze. "Miss Marianne, how nice to see you. Please come in."

"Thank you, Sonja."

The maid took the small suitcase and the gym bag from Mac and led them into a parlor.

"I'd like to see Patrick, please, Sonja."

The maid angled her head and left.

Mac turned toward Marianne. Now he saw vulnerability, where seconds before he'd seen rigid control. Little licks of apprehension appeared in her eyes. She busied herself with repositioning an oil painting on the wall, although it needed no straightening. Nothing needed straightening.

With everything dressed in white, from the baby grand to the carpet to the walls and furniture, Mac felt underdressed in jeans, a T-shirt, and boots. A splash of bright red in the form of a single rose adorned the piano. Another swatch of red regally stretched toward the ceiling in a tall five-foot vase in the corner. Colorful pictures on the walls in gilded frames added linear warmth to an otherwise immaculate room.

Because he was a man at ease with himself, Mac casually tucked his hands under his arms and admired the overhead stained-glass skylight. "Impressive room," he muttered to Marianne.

"Not really," she whispered as she leaned toward him. "It has no soul." In an instant, she stood, aligned her shoulders, her eyes on the arched doorway where Sonja stood at a respectful distance.

Incredible how Marianne could change so quickly from playful to rigid. *Practiced, efficient control.*

"Miss Marianne, Mr. Patrick will be down soon. May I offer you some refreshment, miss? Sir?"

"Iced tea, please." Turning slowly, Marianne lifted her brows at Mac.

"Tea would be fine, thank you."

Sonja eased out of the doorway.

"You never let on." Mac's boots sank in the lush carpet as he headed toward the grand piano. The bench was tucked in, the keys hidden. He tugged out the seat, sat, and lifted the fallboard.

Marianne opened the curtains. Sunlight shined through a wall of perfectly clear windows. Outside, beautiful flowers lined the ruthlessly manicured yards, the warmth of the colors in complete contrast to the cold interior.

"Do you play?" She stood before the windows, twisting the diamond ring on her little finger.

His hands moved over the keys a few bars, and her eyes widened. "Chopin."

He moved to get up.

"No. Don't stop."

He was surprised to see tears in her eyes, but she quickly blinked and turned back to the window. "Do you play, Mari?"

She shook her head. "It's been a long time."

He played a few more bars, then carefully lowered the fallboard and stuffed his fingertips in his pockets as he stood. "Why?"

She lifted a shoulder, a gesture that spoke of hurt or fear. Had her music not been flawless enough? When she didn't answer him, he knew not to press her; she was under too much stress right now. He strolled to another spotlighted painting, the signature, *Barbara Glaze*, bold yet feminine. "Your mother does beautiful work."

"Did. She hasn't painted in years."

So much hurt in this house. "Reminds me of Monet's water lilies."

She turned toward him. "You know art?"

"All kinds. I enjoy the process as much as the finished product."

"You paint, too?"

"In my spare time. Which, of late, has been minimal. Are you surprised?"

"It doesn't fit the rugged cowboy image."

"Now, ma'am." Mac bowed his legs, hoisted up his jeans with his wrists, pretended to spit a wad of chewing tobacco out the side of his mouth, wiped his mouth, and ambled toward her. "I can brand with the best of 'em, rope an ornery calf, ride a buckin' bull—"

He was rewarded with a giggle. He searched her eyes, enjoying her laughter. He gazed at her mouth, then her eyes, and found no trace of wariness there. Gently, he lifted her chin with his finger.

She put a hand on his chest. "Mac."

"Hmm?" he mumbled as his lips brushed hers.

"Marianne?"

Mac groaned as Patrick entered the room and briskly walked toward them.

"Welcome home, sis." He air-kissed Marianne's cheek while Sonja walked around them holding a tray of drinks and sugar. Swiping an iced tea, he sipped it, made a face, and handed it to Marianne. "How do you drink that stuff with no sugar?"

"I'm sweet enough."

Patrick didn't even remotely resemble the quiet, wary man who had visited Marianne in the hospital. He seemed confident, self-assured, and looked Mac squarely in the eyes.

"Mac. Good to see you again," he said as he shook his hand and then motioned for Sonja.

"You're looking well, Patrick."

"I'll look better with a beer in my hand. Sonja, with a glass, please." When Sonja walked past him, he turned back to Mac. "Has Marianne been keeping you busy?"

Mac watched as Sonja walked to an intercom, pushed a button, spoke quietly, and then stood by the door.

"Hardly," Marianne answered, sipping her tea. "Is Father around, Paddy?"

"Frank's at work. Mother's—"

"Behin' you."

The woman walking toward them with hooded eyes smirked. Corn-silk wisps of hair wobbled with each faltering step. Despite the puffiness around her eyes and the overdone make-up, she was still a beautiful woman.

Drink in hand, her long, flowing dressing gown billowed about her until she stopped and rested a hand against the back of a chair. With glaring eyes on Marianne, she finished her drink and swayed.

Marianne hadn't exaggerated. Barbara Glaze was as drunk as a skunk on its way to a barn dance.

At the door, a young woman handed a tray with a single drink on it to Sonja, who turned and walked toward Patrick. She walked around Barbara, retrieved her empty glass, and presented the tray to Patrick. He plucked the single glass off her serving tray, and Sonja turned back toward the door.

Barbara stared at Patrick's drink and licked her lips. "Where's mine?"

"Mother." Marianne blushed when her gaze slid along the floor to where Mac stood. He smiled at her to reassure her, but she didn't look up at him. "Mother, I-I wanted to—"

"I see where Marianne gets her beauty."

Smudged green eyes flashed at Mac. "Da girl izz nothin' like me." She spat the words as if dirt had somehow gotten into her mouth.

Patrick stepped forward. "Marianne, may I have a word with you?"

Barbara glared at her son as she snorted and swayed. "Manners, Pat'ick?"

Marianne's face was beet red as she stared at her clutched hands.

Barbara swayed. Mac caught her and steadied her. "By all means, Patrick, have your word with Marianne. I'll visit with your mother while you're gone. Why don't we sit over here, Barbara, and enjoy the view? I'm Mac, by the way. It's a pleasure to finally meet you."

Visit? Marianne couldn't remember the last time her mother had visited with anyone. That entailed conversation, an exchange of ideas. Her mother wasn't willing or able to do either.

Mortified, she glanced over her shoulder on her way out of the room. Mac held Barbara's elbow as they walked to the sofa in front of the windows.

"Come on, sis." Patrick led Marianne upstairs to her bedroom, shut the door, took her tea, set it down, and hugged her.

"Why does she hate me, Paddy? What have I ever done to her to warrant *that?*"

"You deprived her of her punching bag for several weeks. I'm rarely here when she's vertical."

She pulled back. "I have to rescue Mac."

"He can handle her. She hasn't reached sloppy drunk yet. You'll

182

have better luck with her talking about Brigitt when she's just about to pass out."

"Mother's sick. She needs help. We shouldn't set her up like this."

"She sets herself up. Your being here or not being here has nothing whatsoever to do with her drinking." His green eyes seemed particularly dark tonight when he shrugged, as if he couldn't care less about any of it. "When she's drunk, she talks about the murder. You can't help that, now, can you?"

She did want to know about the murder. She reached for her luggage and tugged it onto her bed. "She needs professional help again, Paddy. Why isn't she in a hospital instead of out there with Mac, drinking herself into oblivion? Why hasn't Father intervened with her?"

He answered by rolling his eyes and shaking his head. The lift of his shoulders—such a *Patrick* move—told her he'd given up. She knew the feeling. How did one go about changing the lives of parents who had lost their way? Not just stumbled-and-fallen lost, but wandering-in-darkness-so-thick-that-no-amount-of-light-could-be-seen-anywhere lost.

Marianne sighed. "Mac and I are starving."

"If you leave now, you'll miss the opportunity to talk to her. She won't last much longer."

"Then I'll have Chef fix us something. Is it still Marissa?"

"Yes. Mother hasn't fired this one yet."

"I'll get Mac when our dinner's ready. He shouldn't be in there alone with her."

Patrick lifted a hand. "You and Mac eat. I'll stay with Barbara until she's ready to talk. Just be prepared."

The hallway was empty. Sonja had left for the day, and Frank hadn't made it home yet. Marianne leaned against the wall next to Mac and studied another of her mother's paintings, full of bright colors and showcased with a single spotlight.

"She's very talented," Mac said and took Marianne's hand.

She needed his touch and leaned against him with her head on his shoulder. Surprisingly, for the first time in her life, she was glad to be in this house, far away from the men wanting to hurt her.

"The last few years, Barbara's given up so much." She listened for Patrick's voice but heard nothing. "I'm going to check on her and Patrick. She might have fallen asleep by now."

"I'll come with you."

"You don't have to."

"I know."

At the entrance to the den, Marianne paused, recognizing her need for delay as an act of cowardice. She had never considered herself a brave woman, but every bit of courage she possessed was needed to walk through that door. She didn't want to see her mother like this. Before she'd left to check out Uncle Cecil's property, her mother had hidden her drinking in her bedroom, which meant she'd still possessed a measure of self-respect. But not now.

Marianne took another moment to steady herself, and then looked around the door.

Her mother lay sprawled across the love seat, head back, eyes closed, mouth open, mumbling. Marianne's stomach knotted, and she reached for the antacids in her right pocket. But the pocket was empty. She hadn't used antacids in weeks.

She tiptoed to the back of the sofa with Mac behind her.

Patrick sat up and leaned over Barbara. "Mother?" The backs of his fingers caressed her face as if he were lost in his thoughts. How could he be so loving when Barbara had all but disowned him the last few years with her acid tongue and vitriol?

Patrick gently shook her shoulder. "Mother?" he whispered. "It's Patrick."

Barbara smacked her lips and fluttered her eyes. It seemed a monumental task for her to open them. Easing back a little so she would be out of her mother's line of vision, Marianne stared at her profile. Barbara seemed so fragile.

"Mother?" Patrick put an arm around her shoulders.

Something inside Marianne ached when her mother's head fell against his shoulder, her worried eyes tearful and sad. In her left hand, she clutched an empty glass.

"Paddy." She trembled as she reached for his hand. "He killed 'er, Paddy. She'zz dead."

"I know, Mama. In the woods."

She laid her head back and closed her eyes. "Curl' dup, on rock."

"I can't see who killed her."

"Y' can't?"

Swiping at her tears, Marianne watched Patrick nudge a lock of hair off their mother's forehead. When was the last time Marianne had touched her mother? She couldn't remember. It had never come naturally. Both of them would consider it an unwelcome interruption if a

184

hug or a brush of a hand was even attempted.

"I can't see, Mama. Who killed her?"

Barbara's face crumbled as a tear slid down her pale cheek. Her head rolled away from Patrick. She sighed, long and hard. "Eddie."

What? Marianne's hand flew to her open mouth.

Patrick's eyes widened. He leaned closer and placed his ear beside Barbara's mouth. "*Eddie* killed her?" With both hands, he lifted her head, trying to get her attention. "Eddie killed Brigitt?"

Her eyes opened a fraction. "Her da'ee."

"Brigitt's *daddy* killed Brigitt?"

"Yesssss."

With her hand over her mouth, Marianne shook her head at Mac. *No, not Eddie. Helen said he was so heartbroken that—*

"I in da woods, saw 'im."

"Saw him?"

"Mmm. Saw 'im. Lay 'er down."

Marianne frowned at Mac. "That can't be right. He loved her."

"Huh?" Barbara swayed as she tried to turn around. "Ah! Da girl 'zz back!" Her gaze rested on Mac. She wobbled a smile at him just before she closed her eyes, and the sofa swallowed her whole.

Patrick shook her. "Mother? Mother?" He turned to Marianne. "She's out." His hands eased under her shoulders and knees, and he lifted her off the sofa. "Come on. I'm taking her to her room."

Marianne caught her mother's hand and the empty glass. Holding Barbara's delicate hand felt like an intrusion, so she let it go. It would have been easier not knowing, but she had to ask. "Is it this way every night, Paddy?"

"Lately." He grunted when he turned sideways to get through the door and headed down the hall toward the stairs. "Maybe tonight you can, y' know, get her ready for bed."

"She said Eddie killed Brigitt." She jogged up the stairs as he took them two at a time. "I don't believe that, Paddy. Aunt Helen said he died of a broken heart shortly after Brigitt died." She opened Barbara's bedroom door, and Patrick grunted past. "Of course, nothing would break a father's heart more than killing his own daughter."

"She knows." Barbara's troubled eyes opened as Patrick laid her on the bed. "She knows. Helen knows." Her gaze rested on Marianne. "My baby," she muttered and started crying.

"It's okay, Mother." Patrick fluffed her pillow. "Just go to sleep now. Everything's okay."

"No, izz not. He kilt 'er. She'zz dead." She closed her eyes. Her breathing evened out.

"It's done." Patrick stalked across the room and grabbed the doorknob. "Get her dressed for bed, Marianne. Mac and I will see you downstairs." He left, with the door open for Mac to follow.

But he touched her back instead.

"She's tormented." Marianne sat on her mother's bed. Tears filled her eyes again. She shook her head as if she could make them go away, make all the pain stop. "Mother," she whispered. She was aware that Mac's hand had left her back and that the door shut behind her.

"What happened back there? Who hurt you?"

Barbara's eyes fluttered open, unfocused, and then wilted shut again.

"What secrets are you keeping? And why have you kept them all these years?"

The next morning, Marianne covered her eyes as she walked into the bright kitchen, groped for the light switch, and turned it off. *Oh, dark is better.*

She opened one eye and searched for the coffee pot. It was in here somewhere. She could smell the coffee. In the haze of the kitchen's nightlight, someone sitting at the kitchen table moved. Was that a smile? Was Mac toasting her with his coffee cup and a smile? She groaned and groped along the counter.

"What's wrong, Mari?"

She wanted to whimper at the loudness of his words. A full-blown migraine had kept her from having a good night's sleep, and from the way it pounded mercilessly at the top of her head like a volcano giddy to explode, she didn't expect the morning to be any better. The medicine she'd taken for it hadn't kicked in yet.

She dropped her purse to the floor, grunted through half-closed eyes, and poured herself a cup of coffee, grateful most of it ended up in her cup. It took some effort to get the cup to her lips. Closing her eyes, she breathed in the essence of caffeine and hoped it would help chase away some of the migraine monsters. "Please remind me again why you pounded on my door so early?"

"You have a headache?" He was standing beside her and started stroking her back.

"A miserable one."

"Here, let me kiss it." *Oh, this man.* She leaned toward him as he cupped her face and kissed her right temple, her left temple, and repeated this several times.

She felt herself relaxing. "Those kisses have magic in them. I'm already feeling better."

He kissed the top of her head and muttered, "Just in case it decides to move."

One more kiss, and he reached for the pot, topped off his cup, and cleaned up her spilled coffee. "We're headed to my brother Tim's place. He owns a small ranch east of the lake."

"Okay. Why so early?" She focused on the breakfast table nestled in the bay window overlooking her mother's beautiful gardens and headed for it. Gripping a chair, she tugged it out, sat, and sipped her coffee.

"Tim has to be in Dallas around two. He has to leave at eight. You wanted to get to his home around six-thirty, so you'd have enough time to talk to him before he leaves."

"Oh, right. He might know something about Brigitt's murder." She placed her hand on top of her head. "The unrelenting claws of a migraine are toying with me this morning."

"Do you have them often?"

"Here, they're a constant." She closed her eyes.

"Stress induced."

"Call the press."

"Why do you let her get to you?"

"Well, now, Dr. McKenzie, let me tell you." She opened her eyes. "I have unresolved anger against a mother who wouldn't know a nurture if it stood up and bit her." She winced as her voice rose and took the time to lower it. "But I shouldn't let that bother me." Her fingertips gripped the top of her head. "Or take it personally, right?"

At his silence, she squinted an eye up at him.

"All little girls need their mother's love and approval."

"She approves of nothing."

"And love?"

"Don't make me laugh. I might need nurturing." She shrugged. "At times. Maybe. But certainly not from her."

"Especially from her."

"You don't give up."

"Not when I'm right."

"Being right doesn't *make* it right."

"Whatever that means."

Marianne chuckled. "I don't have the foggiest idea either."

Mac stood and placed his mug in the kitchen sink. "We'd better get going. Sure you want to come along? I can handle this alone."

"I'm coming." She gingerly stood.

Mac poured coffee into two travel mugs. "Caffeine must be working. Your eyes are brighter."

She nodded, promptly groaned, and grabbed her head. "Ohhhh. No nodding. Definitely no nodding."

"Does that mean you're going to be disagreeable all day?"

"It's a possibility." She placed her cup in the sink, picked up her purse, and plucked out her sunglasses.

"Great." He grabbed his hat, handed her a travel mug, and opened the door for her. "I'll drive."

Shivering rose bushes flanked Mac and Marianne as they stood on the landing to a large two-story home. The first thing Marianne noticed was the porch swing swaying in the gusty breeze. Hugging herself against the wind, she said, "Brrr. This wind!"

Hands in his pockets, Mac squinted up at the pewter-gray sky. "Two weeks 'til Thanksgiving. The weather's finally—"

A door opened, but Marianne couldn't see a thing past the dark screen. Someone was definitely standing there, though. She could hear the person breathing.

"We don't allow street trash in here."

Wide-eyed, Marianne gaped at Mac.

He frowned at the screen. "You better make an exception, mister, 'cause I'm comin' in."

"Says who?"

"Says me, you uncivilized vermin."

The screen door burst open. Shocked, Marianne stepped aside as a young man with short black hair bent over and ran straight into Mac's stomach, yelling like a banshee. Mac grabbed him in a headlock. The man twisted and punched Mac in the side and they both landed against a rail. She thought she heard someone snicker. Or grunt.

A hand reached out from the screen door, grabbed Marianne's sweater, and drew her inside the house. "It's safer in here." A brunette with twinkling basset-hound eyes smiled at Marianne. "I'm Arlene. And that's my husband Tim attacking Mac. Come with me. We'll get something to drink while they play warrior games."

"I'm Marianne. Is that some ritual male bonding thing?"

Straight dark hair fell like a silk scarf over one shoulder as Arlene ushered her into the kitchen. "Happens every time Mac comes down. Have a seat." She motioned her toward a dinette chair. "Would you like something to drink? Coffee? Tea? Soda? Water?"

"Coffee, thank you." One more cup might loosen the lingering migraine claws.

The front door slammed. Boots hammered the wood floors as male laughter filled the house. The two men walked in, arms over shoulders, grinning like little boys, appearing remarkably similar in the McKenzie mold.

"Be quiet, you two. You'll wake the baby. Give me a scrunch, Mac, you hunk o' good-lookin'."

"She'd sleep through a tornado, honey. You know that." Tim's eyes sparkled when he spotted Marianne. "How'd ya git so lucky, little brother?"

"She won't have much to do with me."

"Well, she's here, isn't she?"

Mac laughed. "Tim, Arlene, my friend, Marianne Glaze. Marianne, my very ornery brother, Tim, and his lovely wife, Arlene."

Tim stretched out his hand. "Marianne. Pleased to make your acquaintance." He tugged out a chair for Mac. "So why did you two veer into my neck of the woods so early this morning?"

Arlene's head appeared from behind Tim's shoulder. "Coffee, Mac?"

"Thanks." He lifted his brows at Marianne, as if to say *Show Time*. "Well, it's a long story, actually."

"Then sit, sit, and we'll work out some of what's bothering you two."

Mac straddled the chair next to Marianne.

"That's my cue." She cleared her throat and unconsciously massaged a temple.

"Any better?"

She smiled at Mac, then included Tim and Arlene. "A migraine on its last lap. Hopefully." She linked her fingers around her mug. "My cousin was Brigitt Holcomb."

"Marianne Glaze. I thought I recognized the name." He pointed at her. "You used to come out to the ranch with Lindsey when we were kids. Your mother and Helen and Lindsey's mom are sisters, right?"

"Yes. I inherited Cecil Tucker's property and have had some horrific things happen to me since, and I believe they're connected to Brigitt's murder. Mac's graciously allowed me to stay at the ranch until I can figure out what's going on. I wondered, Tim, if you remember the day she was killed?"

Tim twirled his coffee mug clockwise, then picked it up and held it at his mouth. "The day Brigitt was found?"

Bingo! He knows something. "Yes. Mac tells me you had a special tree?"

"I did." He half-halfheartedly laughed. "I'm sorry. Mac, could I talk to you outside? Would you excuse us, ladies?" He grabbed his hat and coat and walked out the back door.

Mac's chair scraped on the floor as he stood. Arlene rested her hand on his arm. "Go, Mac. I'll stay and tell Marianne."

The wind had picked up. Tim sat on a picnic table facing black clouds heavy with rain. The open field behind Tim's yard stretched for a quarter of a mile and then ended at a line of trees.

When Mac walked toward him, Tim looked up. "We need the rain. Been bone dry now for about six weeks."

Mac settled next to his brother and waited. Tim wasn't one to speak idly. He'd take his time and get it said when he was ready.

"You remember Brigitt, Mac?"

"Yeah. Everybody thought she was so pretty."

"I was fourteen when she died. She was my first love." He eased off the table, stuffed his hands in his pockets, and walked a few paces away. "Mac, what I'm about to tell you I haven't told to another soul but Arlene. Believe it or not, no one ever asked me a question about Brigitt's death until now."

"You know something?"

"I was there."

Mac frowned. "Where?"

"Where they found Brigitt."

"Did you see what happened?"

Tim looked toward the storm clouds again. "Yes."

"You *saw* it and never said a word?" *Unbelievable.* "For seventeen years, you never said a word?"

Tim's eyes flashed. "Before you start judging me, hear what I have to say. I couldn't say anything. I was sworn to secrecy."

"By whom, for crying out loud? The killer?"

Tim crossed his arms. "I wasn't in school that day. I had the flu. If you'll remember, we didn't discuss Joey after he died, and we certainly didn't discuss Brigitt."

"Who?" Mac's jaw clenched. "Who, Tim?"

His brother shook his head. "I was mostly over being sick, so I sneaked out of the house. I was in my tree that day. It was March." He closed his eyes. "The trees were full. I could get up so high that no one knew I was there. But that day, I could see the path to Cecil's house through the leaves in this one spot."

Tim frowned. "What I saw doesn't make a lick of sense, Mac, but I saw what I saw." He shuffled his feet. "Patrick Glaze was on spring break and helped me make up my mind to skip out on the nap Mom intended. We ran through the woods and practically sprinted up my tree."

"Patrick saw it, too?"

"Yeah. Helen was walking down the path that led to Tucker Spring, where all of us kids liked to play. She was acting funny, nervous. She kept turning around, looking back. Then she waved someone to come to her. It was Eddie, carrying Brigitt."

Mac jerked back, utterly shocked. *Eddie and Helen?*

Tim punched the knuckles on each hand. "Brigitt was all cut up, bruised. I thought she was dead. Eddie laid her at the base of that rock. Then he did something." Tim shook his head. "He staged her, Mac. He moved her arms, tossed one to the side, adjusted her skirt, her hair. He took a lot of time making her look as if she'd just been thrown there. Helen didn't touch her. Just Eddie. Then he stood up and looked me right in the eyes."

"He *saw* you?"

"He told Helen to go on. When she left, he came over to my tree and told us to get down. We did. He made us promise that we'd never tell a soul what we'd seen. I remember he said no one would believe us anyway, that we'd be accused of killing Brigitt."

Mac was stunned. They had lied all these years. Helen knew Eddie killed Brigitt? She was *in* on it? "You never said a word to Mom or Dad? Grampa or Gramma? No one?"

"I couldn't. I loved Eddie and Helen. He told me they had their reasons for doing it, that I had to trust him. So I did. I'm not sure Helen ever knew we knew, because she didn't treat us any differently."

"What happened after he made you and Patrick promise?"

"He let us climb back up to our perch."

"Odd."

"It wasn't too much longer that Gloria Radke and Frank Glaze came walking from the other direction—"

"Together?"

"Yeah. They were walking, talking, laughing. They didn't see Brigitt until Cecil and Nate showed up, and then they ran to where they were standing. Gloria screamed when she saw Brigitt."

Mac shook his head. "Why did Eddie and Helen do that? Were they trying to cover their tracks?"

"Not theirs, Mac. I can't believe that. She was dead when they laid her there."

"Maybe Eddie got a little heavy handed."

"Not Eddie. He wouldn't hurt Brigitt."

"Then who beat her? If they found her like that, why didn't they report it? Or take her to the hospital? Why take her out to the woods? Who were they protecting? Did they know who did that to her?"

"I don't have any answers, Mac. None of it makes sense to me and yet I remember it like it was yesterday. The coroner came—"

"Not the ambulance?"

"Cecil had already determined she was dead."

"Okay. The coroner."

"Kirk Romer took her away. A crowd was there, watching."

"Do you remember any of them?"

"Not really. It was funny, though. Eddie and Helen acted like they were seeing her for the first time. They cried and carried on. Eddie never once acknowledged me and Patrick. After Kirk Romer took Brigitt away, everyone hung out for a while. When everybody left, we came down and went home. We slipped inside the house and went right to my room. No one ever asked me a question about it."

"Well, I can guarantee you, Marianne will."

She was pacing like a panther when they walked in. "Why didn't you tell someone what you saw, Tim?"

"I liked Eddie. I figured he had a good reason for what he did. I was just a kid."

Marianne shook her head. "It doesn't make sense, except that my mother said the same thing. That Eddie had killed her."

"That's right." Tim straddled a chair. "I'd forgotten she was there. She'd found this little hidden nook and was crying. She stood when Eddie came down the path with Brigitt. I remember she covered her face with both hands. She came forward only after the police got there."

Marianne frowned. "Why was my mother hiding in the woods?"

The man sniffed and mumbled, "Stupid allergies."

His boss picked up the phone. "What?"

"They're in Abilene, talking to Tim."

He blew out smoke. "She put an ad in the Brennan paper today."

"For what?"

"Anyone who had an abusive sexual association—"

The man grunted. "Association?"

"Sixteen or seventeen years ago with several men to come forward and talk to her about it. Gave her phone number. So, she knows. You're gonna have to shut her down."

"How?"

"You've done it before. Be creative." The line went dead.

SIXTEEN

Bobby considered himself an early riser, but he wasn't usually up this early. It was a little before five. Standing on the stoop of his cottage, he glanced toward the east. Not even a hint of the sun's grandeur brushed the horizon, so he considered it a special treat that he'd get to see the sun rise over the ranch this morning. He had missed being here. The thing that surprised him the most was how much he'd missed the smells of ranch life, including this morning's dewy, wet freshness.

There were no lights on near his cottage, so he felt comfortable standing in the darkness, looking his fill. A screen door opened. His gaze followed the sound to the bunkhouse where someone was leaning against a porch post, his yawn visible in the light from the stables.

Two cottages down, Helen's door opened in a burst of light. She spotted him and waved him over. "Well, good morning!" She hugged him. "I didn't expect you up at this hour, honey."

He chuckled. "I was too hungry to sleep."

"I was hoping you'd stop by for breakfast. Biscuits are just about ready to be taken out of the oven. Come on in."

His stomach growled at the smell of fresh baking bread. He took the coffee cup Helen gave him and stared at the huge photograph hanging on the wall. Brigitt, with him at senior prom. Even now, her smile made his heart skip, maybe not as happily as it once did, but still full of love for this woman.

He had no pictures of her at his home. It simply hurt too much to look at her and remember. Every so often, he'd dig through his closet, a little desperate to see her face, and then weep when he found a photo.

But not today. He simply felt contentment. "Where did you get that picture?"

"Oh, a couple years back, I had it blown up and professionally framed. You two were so happy that night."

"I miss her, Helen. It could have happened yesterday for all the missing her I still have in my heart. Seventeen years, and I've never gotten over losing her."

Helen slid an arm around his waist. "I know, honey. I know." She patted his back. He felt a bond with Helen that he felt with no other person. She understood. She hurt, too.

"I better get those biscuits out before they burn. Bacon's ready.

194

Would you like eggs?" She reached in the fridge and pulled out a carton.

"Please." He set his cup on the table, took off his jacket.

Helen grabbed it and hung it in the closet while he washed his hands in the kitchen sink. He tugged on the blue-and-white kitchen towel draped through a drawer handle and dried his hands.

Brigitt stared at him from a picture above the sink. She was sixteen and that was his hand on her shoulder, the night of the junior Sadie Hawkins dance when he'd told her he'd wait two more years for her, and then she'd be his. "For life," he'd said, and she'd snuggled close to him.

"I remember that day." Helen stood beside him and studied the picture. "She was beyond excited about marrying you, Bobby. I thought y'all were too young to be engaged, but she didn't."

"I knew she was young, but *she* pushed for the engagement, not me. She always seemed older than her years."

Helen cracked eggs in a small iron skillet. "You were raised together. She knew what she wanted. She didn't have to push too much, as I recall."

He chuckled. "Nope, she didn't. I knew what I wanted, too." *And neither of us got it.*

As if she'd heard his thoughts, Helen quickly glanced at him as she continued cooking the eggs.

"I loved being out on the football field, knowing she was there cheering for me."

"She watched you every second. So proud of you." Helen scooped up the eggs. "Are you seeing anyone, honey?"

Bobby took a swig of his coffee and walked to the back door. It was open, and the fresh, quiet morning drew him into its softness and its peace. He decided it was good to be here again. He had missed it more than he'd known. "Aren't you cold with this door open?"

Helen laughed. "Too many hot flashes. I need the cool air. Is it too cold for you?"

"No, no. I'm fine."

"Are you avoiding my question, Bobby James?"

"I couldn't if I wanted to, could I?" He chuckled. "From time to time, I'll have a date, but there's no one special. Work is my love." He turned to her and laughed. "Although Mac says I play more than I work."

"Are you staying busy with your bands?"

"You're asking if I'm making any money, and I am."

She laughed and set their plates on the table. "That's exactly what I wanted to know. You're thirty-seven years old, honey. About time you found a woman and settled down. Now come and eat before this food gets cold."

The three-hour nap had done Bobby a world of good. He wanted to take a walk around the ranch, visit with a few people he'd known most of his life, but he'd left his jacket at Helen's. The cold front that had crept in overnight still hovered and blustered.

Just as he raised his hand to knock on Helen's door, he saw her through the window on the front door. She was talking on the phone in the back yard. He eased the door open and walked inside, intending to wave at her and let her know he was there.

But when he reached the kitchen, her words stopped him.

"He was here earlier," she said as she stooped to dig her fingers into a potted plant. "He's doing fine. He misses you."

Is she talking about me? He swatted at what felt like an icy finger racing across his neck. Who was Helen talking to?

"No. About the same. Older, but still very handsome."

Eddie's sister, in Oklahoma. No, I wouldn't be missing her. Someone else visited her this morning besides me. He tiptoed toward the door. Helen stood and walked to the next potted plant, out of his sight. He stepped to the right, so he could watch her. So he could hear her.

"He saw the picture I told you about, the big one. That's right. The Senior Prom."

She *was* talking about him. *Who is on the phone?*

"I think he still loves you."

Loves you? Who? He stopped breathing and concentrated on every word Helen spoke.

"Don't, honey. Please." She paused. "Well, maybe it's time. I can't say."

Time for what?

"We don't know that, do we? They could still be here, watching every move I make, and Bobby, too."

Who could still be here?

"We've been through this before, Brigitt. You need to—"

Bobby jerked and gasped. Everything inside him ground to a stop. He was too shocked to move, to breathe, to think. Her name had knocked the breath out of him.

Brigitt?

BRIGITT?

Oh, God. Oh, God.

He tried to take a breath, but his body wouldn't work. With shaking fingers, he grasped the counter and fell to his knees. Long unbearable moments of listening to throbbing silence passed.

"Brigitt. Honey."

Bobby gasped, stunned to the bone. His heart beat frantically, aching at the sound of her name. *Oh, dear God, what is this? What is happening?* Tears poured from his eyes. He couldn't think. He couldn't move. He couldn't breathe. Was this *real?*

"I know, honey. I know."

His lips of their own accord formed a "B," but nothing came out. Shaking, he tried again to breathe her name, but couldn't. He lifted his head, vaguely aware that Helen stood in the screen door, staring at him with wide eyes. Her jaw dropped open.

"I'll call you back, honey."

The screen door opened.

Oh, his chest. It hurt. His mind hurt. His heart hurt.

Helen stepped inside, her hand over her still-gaping mouth. "Bobby?"

He was in a tunnel. Too much pain. Black edges closing in on him. Her sweet name echoing around him.

"Bobby." Helen stared at him as if she couldn't move, as if she were waiting for him to do something, say something.

Shaking uncontrollably, he swallowed hard. He tried to raise his head but couldn't. "She's a-*live?*"

"Bobby, let me—" She touched his arm, and he jerked away and stood.

"She's *alive?*" He staggered, bent over again, and put his hands on his thighs, trying to stop the blackness from overtaking him. "She's alive?" He squeezed his eyes shut. "Helen. Answer me. Is she alive, yes or no?"

A long pause throbbed between them. Helen sighed. "Yes." She jumped when the phone rang again.

"Hello?" She looked at Bobby. "Can I call you back in a little bit, honey? Sure, I'm fine. Okay, 'bye." She disconnected the call and shut the back door.

"Why, Helen? *Why?* I saw her! She wasn't breathing! She was—" His voice hitched, and he growled at the ceiling. "She was bruised!" He shoved a chair. "Cut up! Lifeless!"

Helen took a step toward him. "Kirk drugged her. It's what she wanted."

"What she *wanted?* What she *wanted?* Says who? Says. *Who?*" He spun and smashed his palm into a wall. The room pulsated with the sound.

"Helen." Bobby took several shallow breaths that left him shaking with confusion and anger and pain. "Talk." Another unsteady breath. "Talk to me. Please. *Please.*" His forehead landed on the wall as he tried desperately to calm down so he could hear her.

"They got her again, Bobby. There were five of them. They raped her for hours, cut her face, beat her, left her for dead at five in the morning in a ditch at Cecil's house. He found her on his way to work shortly after."

Bobby shook his head against the pictures in his mind. "*Raped* her?" He turned around, gasping. "Five men?" He slid down the wall, groaning. His stomach twisted into knots so tightly, he wanted to throw up. "No." He shook his head in wide arcs over and over. "No," he sobbed, his heart broken. "No."

"Bobby."

His hands covered his face as he rocked himself, moaning, sobbing. *Brigitt. Brigitt.* "Why didn't she tell me?" He gasped, drew up his legs. "Why didn't she tell me?" His hands became fists, and he pounded his knees until spent, and then rested his face on his arms and sobbed.

Helen sank to her knees and put her hands on both his cheeks, guiding his face to hers. "Bobby. They killed her. Maybe not her body but everything she was, they took. For several hours, we talked while I tended to her cuts. She should have been in a hospital, but she wouldn't go because they would have found out. I called Cecil and Kirk. She wanted to die."

"No. I could have—we—we could have—"

"They told her they'd kill you. All day, she kept saying, 'They're going to kill Bobby. They're going to kill Bobby.'" Helen let go of his face. "She was half dead, Bobby, and could only think of you."

He swiped a frustrated hand over his face and tried to gain a measure of control. "We could have left, lived somewhere else."

"She had to make the decision that day. She wanted you to be safe."

"But that was seventeen years ago. Why didn't she call me? After a year, five years, six years, ten? Why didn't she let me know she was alive?" Tears streamed down his face. "Why didn't she give me a chance?"

Helen swiped at the tears on her face. "Shame. Guilt. Fear. You name it; she experienced it." She blew out a deep breath. "Now you know why it was a closed casket—she wasn't there. She was at Eddie's sister's home in Ada, Oklahoma. Yvonne is a nurse."

She shifted to sit on the floor. "Yvonne came to get her as soon as they could get here. After the funeral, we rushed to Ada to be with her."

"Why didn't she call me?"

"She was afraid, Bobby. The reason she died that day was still there. She couldn't even report the crime to the police because they would have investigated, and those men would have found out she was alive and that she had told someone." Helen slowly shook her head, her expression so sad. "Every way she turned, every hope she had, every thought of you, every dream—a slamming door shouted 'No' to her. She was in so much pain. Those men stripped her of all she'd held dear in her life."

His heart hurt so much for her, for his Brigitt, his love.

Helen took his hand. "She still lives in Ada, honey. She was in and out of a mental hospital for two or three years. She's finally come to grips with all of it. She's made a life for herself. A lonely life."

"Did she marry?"

"Oh, no. Wouldn't consider it. Has never dated. Those thoughts are gone."

Bobby jumped up, his heart racing. "Her address, Helen."

"Bobby—"

"*Don't*, Helen. Please." His whole body shook with excitement. "Just give me her address. Please." He held out a shaking hand to help her up. "I'm leaving right now, with or without it. I have to see her."

"But they're still out there. They could kill her this time, and you."

"I'll keep both of us safe. You can count on it."

She took his hand, and he pulled her up. Rooting through her purse, she found paper and pen, wrote down the address and handed it to him. "She gets off at four. I wrote the library's address for you, too." She patted his cheek. "She misses you."

Fresh tears welled up in his eyes. "Oh, Helen. My life. My life's been nothing, nothing."

"I'm so sorry for both of you." She brushed the tears from his cheeks.

He sucked in a breath as he fought more tears, and then turned toward the door. He spun around and grabbed Helen in a fierce hug.

"Thanks," he whispered against her ear. "I'll call you when I get there."

"Be careful, Bobby. No one can find out that she's alive. No one."

Marianne flipped a page of notes as she watched a red Corvette zoom past them on their way back to her father's home. "What Tim told us makes no sense, Mac. Unless, of course, Eddie really did kill her, and they were covering it up."

Mac shifted in his seat. "Eddie wouldn't beat her. He adored Brigitt."

"Maybe it was an accident."

"How do you accidentally beat to death your grown daughter?"

"Maybe Helen killed her."

Mac shook his head. "That makes even less sense. Change tracks, Mari. You're headed in the wrong direction."

"Why stage her on that rock?"

"So that when the authorities found her, her death would seem, I don't know, more real."

"Why make it appear more real?"

Mac tapped his thumb on the steering wheel.

Marianne looked at the river they drove over. The water level was down, with little swatches of land pushing through the water as if to catch a breath of air. Two boys stood on the bank, throwing rocks. "Maybe Brigitt didn't die from the original wounds. Maybe she died from something Eddie did."

Mac adjusted his rearview mirror. "Change directions."

"Tim and my mother said Eddie killed Brigitt. Let's say he did. He staged the death scene because the story he told wouldn't corroborate the evidence." To her right, a truck on a dirt road headed toward them, kicking up a spiraling dust cloud. "Does Helen take a vacation once or twice a year to the same place?"

"Yes. Ada, Oklahoma. Eddie's sister Yvonne lives there, and she and Helen are pretty close."

"What if Brigitt didn't die that day. Maybe she's alive and well, living comfortably in Kalamazoo."

"Without Bobby? Not possible."

"You don't know that."

"They loved each other too much."

"Maybe she realized she didn't love him, and they staged her death so she could escape. Love doesn't always survive."

"True, but for every instance you give me where love doesn't survive,

200

I can give you five where it does. Those are pretty good odds in my world."

And in my world, those odds are impossible. "Your engagement didn't survive."

"You know about that?"

"Helen mentioned you were engaged. That's all."

"Over a year ago." He shrugged. "If love had been involved, it would have survived."

"We could call Yvonne when we get to my house."

"And say what? 'Have you seen Brigitt lately?'"

"Okay, okay." Marianne closed her notebook and placed it in her briefcase. "Let's stay another day at my mom's and see if we can get her to talk, preferably when she's sober. Then we'll see what Helen has to say when we get back."

Bobby sat in his truck in front of the Ada Public Library, so excited he could hardly sit. With his heart pounding, he cracked every knuckle he had, cleaned his sweaty hands on his pants over and over, took deep breaths to calm himself. Brigitt was behind those walls!

Another glance at his watch. *4:05.* Helen said she got off at four. Would she recognize him? Should he walk up to the front door, march inside, and find her? No, he wanted their first meeting to be private, so he could hold her, and kiss her, and touch her. Feel the realness of her under his hands.

Across the deep and wide yard, he saw the library door open.

He held his breath.

Stared at the door.

It almost closed, and then opened again.

A woman stepped out.

"Oh, God, it's her! It's Brigitt!" Tears filled his eyes as he soaked up the sight of her, still slim and tall, still so beautiful. Her hand shielded her eyes against the bright Oklahoma sun. She turned left, then right. Was she looking for him? Had Helen called her? Of course, she'd called her.

Did she want to see him?

A woman walked past Bobby's truck. Brigitt seemed to focus right on his pickup, and his whole being froze. He wanted to shout at her, wave his arms, run as fast as he could toward her. And touch her. More than his next breath, he wanted to feel his arms around her.

Brigitt waved at the woman. Why didn't she look at him? If she knew he was here, why wasn't she running to him, screaming his name, her arms wide open? She looked so serious, scanning the cars lined up in front of the library. Was she searching for him? His heart stopped. Or was she looking for someone else?

She started down the walk.

Man, she was even more beautiful than he remembered, her hair still long and full but a little darker, and she looked a little older. Did he? He wished he'd lost the extra ten he'd been toting around for years.

But right now, he didn't care.

He'd just seen Brigitt!

First thing after arriving home, Marianne walked upstairs to check on her mother. She crept into her room. An odor like acidy garlic hung in the air. She wrinkled her nose in disgust.

Barbara was still asleep, her bed like a war zone with blankets spilling onto the floor, sheets wrapped around one leg, a pillow on the floor several feet from the bed. Her bedside lamp was on. It must have been on all night. Was her mother afraid of the dark? It wouldn't be a stretch to envision the alcohol demons tormenting her in her dreams.

Marianne left the room and headed to her own to take a nap.

At four o'clock, Barbara rang for her personal maid. "Sonja, pastries and coffee, please."

Since Sonja had left to help her daughter get ready for her grandbaby's first birthday party, Marianne answered the intercom. "I'll be right up."

There was no answer when she knocked. She tiptoed in and set the tray on Barbara's nightstand. Her mother was on her stomach, her face burrowed in blankets as if she couldn't stand what little light was in the room.

Staring down at her, Marianne couldn't define exactly how she felt about this woman, her mother. She didn't know her well enough to feel love for her, although she knew she should.

Pity? A measure of it.

Disgust? For the life she had chosen.

Shame? For her, and on her, because somewhere along the line, she had completely given up.

She and her mother shared absolutely nothing in common.

Marianne walked out as quietly as she had entered, without a backward glance.

With his heart in his throat, Bobby watched Brigitt get out of a two-door economy car and walk inside a small frame house. A white picket fence surrounded the neat front yard. Empty rose bushes bobbed in the breeze just above the fence.

She had loved roses.

"Oh!" She buried her nose in the dozen roses he'd given her for Valentine's Day. "I love you so much, Bobby James." Her eyes twinkled mischievously as she sniffed the roses. "And not just because of the roses."

"Don't I know that?" he whispered just before he kissed her.

He inhaled a deep breath and blew it out. "Just knock on the door, Bob," he mumbled to himself as he sat in the cool November sunshine. He glanced at her house.

Curtains opened. Brigitt stood in the bay window and looked outside. Her gaze found his, and he held his breath. Did she know him? Could she see the young man she'd loved in him?

She glanced down the street and left the window.

Maybe she didn't want to see him. She had turned her back once on everything they were. Maybe she didn't want to see him now.

But he needed answers to painful questions. "Just get out of the truck, Bob." Instead, for reasons he couldn't identify, he put the key in the ignition and started it.

Brigitt's door opened. She stood in the doorway and stared at him.

Breathless, he watched her walk toward him. He shivered when she stopped at the curb, and his body jerked when she took a step into the street. She was coming closer! He could almost touch her!

"Why don't you turn that off and come inside, Bobby?"

He turned that off and sat there. Nothing seemed to work.

She opened his door and held out her hand. Bobby stared at it, and then looked into her beautiful brown eyes; they were full of tears.

"Come inside with me, Bobby." She picked up his hand. She was shaking, too.

It was real. All of it was real.

Her hand was soft, warm.

His love. His love was here.

With tears streaming down both their faces, Brigitt held his hand tightly as they walked up the sidewalk and through the front door.

Bobby left the door open. Brigitt walked around him and shut it. As she brushed past him, they fell into each other's arms.

"Oh, Brigitt, Brigitt!" He thought he might crush her, but he couldn't let go. His mouth found her lips, and he kissed her with all the frustration, despair, and love he'd held inside for years. He couldn't seem to stop. "Brigitt." His arms tightened. "Brigitt." He kissed her until they were both breathless.

She drew back, her fingertips touching his lips. She drank him in with her eyes, then took his hand, led him into her kitchen, and sat him down. "I'm going to make us some tea now, Bobby. It's time to talk."

"Forget the stupid tea, Brigitt. Come here." He half-stood, tugged on her hand, and she landed on his lap and in his arms. "I don't want you anywhere but right here, next to me. Just stay next to me. Don't move. Ever. But talk. Tell me everything."

He felt her smile against his shoulder.

Bobby laughed and tugged Brigitt closer. "If someone had told me two days ago that I'd be in Ada, Oklahoma, talking to Brigitt Holcomb." His lips brushed hers. "Kissing Brigitt Holcomb." His arms tightened. "Holding Brigitt Holcomb, I'd have said they were crazy."

She snuggled closer. "I can't seem to get close enough to you."

He nudged a lock of hair out of her eyes, dreading the answer to the question that had to be asked. "You didn't ever marry?"

She shook her head. "I knew where you were. I never let go of loving you."

"Then why did you leave me?"

Her head burrowed into his chest. "Oh, Bobby. I didn't leave you. I saved you."

"From *you*? From what happened to you? Don't you know none of it would have mattered to me? I mean, yes, of course, everything that happened to you mattered, but we could have left the country, lived in Europe, or Africa, for heaven's sake. As long as we were together."

"You can't know what I went through that night." Her breath felt warm against his chest. "Raped continuously, beaten, and later that night, a miscarriage." She tensed and shuddered. "My face cut."

Gently, he took her face in his hands, tipped up her chin, and touched the thin scar on her cheek with his thumb. "I would have been there for you. For us."

She shook her head. "But not me. I was dead. For so long, I was broken, lost. I had nothing to give. I didn't want to live without giving to you."

His chin rested on her head. "Do you know who?"

"Georgie raped me first. Then, the others. So much of it is foggy, bits and pieces." She closed her eyes. "Absolute horror."

"Then don't talk about it, honey. Let's not—"

She pulled back. "It has to be out in the open, Bobby. You have to know everything. You have to know why I left. They promised me that night that they would get me again. And you. They said if I told, they would kill you. I didn't want us to live with that. So, I kept them from doing it in the only way I could."

He moved her hand to his mouth, kissed it, and settled it against his chest. "Why didn't you contact me later, then? Why did you let so many years go by?"

"Those men were still out there. I was so afraid for you and Mother." She shrugged, lowered her eyes. "And I was young. Hurt. Idealistic. I guess it was my punishment."

"For *what*, for crying out loud?"

"For the evil I'd had to endure. I didn't want it to touch you." She shivered and his arms tightened around her. "I was riddled with guilt that you weren't my first." She closed her eyes and sank against him. "I didn't want to give you a body that had been—had been—"

She couldn't have been more wrong. "Brigitt, none of it was your fault. None of that would have mattered to me. I'd have gladly walked through this *with* you, instead of coming in here at the end after you've been alone all this time. I'd have gladly lived with you without any pleasure at all, if I could have had *you*. Just you, and nothing else."

"But leaving you was the only way I could protect you and Mother— the only way I knew to keep all of us alive. A part of me said you would want me to leave. You had always been so strong to keep us both pure until marriage."

"I would never have faulted you, Brigitt. Never."

She looked into his eyes. "Do you still love the Lord?"

"Oh, yes. I couldn't have made it through this without Him. Do you?"

"Yes." Her forehead rested against his chin. "My faith has matured since I was eighteen, but I actually thought you'd hate me for deceiving you."

"I could never hate you."

"But if you didn't know, you couldn't. That's a little twisted, I know. But I clung to that thought, that you didn't hate me because you didn't know."

His hands held her face. "Brigitt, I love you. I always have. I always will. I was strong in the Lord because I loved *Him*. I wouldn't use that strength to judge you." He kissed her forehead. "If you had been honest with me, we could have made it through anything. We could have made it."

Her body began to shake. "Is it too late, then?"

His heart ached at the wobbly words. "Never." Abruptly, he pulled back. "Brigitt Holcomb, will you marry me? Today? This afternoon? Right now? As soon as possible?"

"Oh." Trembling hands flew to her mouth as she shook her head slowly. She threw her arms around him. "Yes!" She kissed him while she laughed. "Yes, yes, *yes!*"

The next morning, Mac's cell phone rang. "Hello?"

"Mac. It's Bobby. Can you talk?" He sounded winded.

Marianne stoked the fire in the fireplace in the Glaze's den. Patrick slung a tennis bag over his shoulder and waved at her on his way out the door.

"Yeah, Bobby. Are you okay?"

"I'm fine. I need you to fly to Ada, Oklahoma."

Where Eddie's sister Yvonne lives. "Why?"

Marianne walked to Mac and put an arm around his waist. He turned the cell on speaker phone.

"I can't tell you right now," Bobby answered. "I need you and Marianne to come to Ada as fast as you can. Sooner. Just get here. Not a word to anyone. *Anyone.*"

Marianne touched Mac's arm, and he held up a finger. "We're in Abilene, so it'll take some finagling to get the plane here. Are you in trouble, Bob?"

He laughed. "Just get here! I'll meet you when you land at the Municipal Airport. Trust me, Mac. And keep this under your hat. Don't tell a soul about your trip here. In fact, if someone from the ranch brings you the plane, *you* fly it up here. Just you. But bring Marianne."

"Will do." Mac disconnected the call.

"What's in Ada, Oklahoma, besides Eddie's sister?"

"Bobby. And he wants us there pronto."

"Then why don't we pack up everything, Mac, fly to Ada, and then return to the ranch instead of coming back here? Whoever flies your plane down here can drive my SUV to the ranch."

SEVENTEEN

Bobby waited for them at the gate, beaming like a little boy bursting at the seams to tell a tightly-held secret. Only a woman could put a smile that big on a man's face.

Marianne allowed Mac to go ahead of her. Bobby stretched out his hand to his brother and then yanked him into a fierce hug.

"What's going on, Bob? Luke said you left the ranch without a word."

Bobby motioned them toward his truck. "You'll know in a few minutes. Who brought you the plane? Did he know your destination? Hey, Marianne." He surprised her by reaching for a hug.

"Hank. And no, he doesn't know anything."

"Can you trust him?"

"I think so, Bob. He hasn't given me a reason not to. What's this all about?"

His brother shook his head with that silly grin still in place. Not much was spoken on the ten-minute drive to a small frame house, where they parked in front. "Here we are," Bobby said as he jumped out and opened Marianne's door. "Come on, come on." He jogged up the sidewalk, slipped a key into the door, and led them through the living room and into another room.

"Mac, Marianne. I'd like you to meet my fiancée."

Mac's eyes widened. "Your—"

"Fiancée?" Marianne frowned. What had happened to the broken-hearted man who just a few days ago had mourned a woman who'd been dead for seventeen years? She tried to step around Mac, but his big bulk stood squarely in the doorway, blocking her view.

"What?!" Mac laughed and threw his head back. "Are you *kidding* me?"

Agitated, Marianne shoved on his arm, but he didn't budge.

"I can't believe this!"

When he'd apparently gotten his fill, he shifted and let her go ahead of him. Inside, they both stared at a beautiful, tall woman who smiled at Bobby as if he'd just handed her a lottery check for millions.

Brigitt Holcomb. In the flesh.

So, she had been right about a cover-up.

"Mac." Brigitt extended her hand. "It's good to see you again. You're all grown up and so handsome."

"Seventeen years in a coffin hasn't harmed you any, Brigitt." He wrapped his arms around her and spun her around. "Can't wait to hear the story behind this one!"

His amusement irritated Marianne. He was just going to say, "Hey, how ya' doin'?" after Brigitt had deceived everyone?

"One of Marianne's scenarios regarding your father's part in your death scene was that you weren't actually dead. She came up with the idea after we talked to Tim." When Mac released her, he turned to Marianne. "Brigitt, this is Marianne Glaze. Marianne, Brigitt Holcomb."

Bobby beamed. "She'll be McKenzie in forty-eight hours, on November 13th. We have to wait. State law."

Marianne stared at her. Brigitt Holcomb was alive and standing in front of her as if nothing was wrong, as if she hadn't fooled all of them, as if she hadn't hurt any of her family with her lies and deception, as if she hadn't duped an entire community.

She felt herself getting too warm and unsnapped her jacket. Mac helped her take it off and laid it across a sofa table.

"Mari. You've grown up into a beautiful woman."

"Thank you. I-I don't know what to say." The faintest hint of annoyance was in her voice. It felt strange hugging this woman she'd gotten to know through the memories of other people. Words bubbled up. Bitter words of accusation. *How could you have done this? Why did you lie to everyone? Why did your mother lie to me?*

But she swallowed them down. It was naïve, if not plain silly, to think there wasn't a good reason for the deception. As much as she wanted to lash out, she would not say the words.

She would *not* be like her mother.

Mac leaned over, close to her ear. "Take off your war paint," he whispered. "Let them explain."

She lowered her gaze and whispered back, "How do you know me so well?"

Shaking her head, she turned her attention back to Brigitt. "There must be an explanation for why you lied to everyone, why your mother lied to me. I'm ready to hear it." Rigidly, she sat on a chair beside the sofa and tucked her trembling hands under her thighs.

Mac sat next to her and leaned over, but instead of rebuking her, he kissed her cheek. *Oh, this man.*

"I'll start." Bobby blew out a deep breath. "I found out just yesterday that Brigit was alive."

"How?" Marianne leaned away from Mac's nudging elbow. She'd

asked it nicely, after all.

"I overheard Helen talking to Brigitt." With loving eyes, he looked at his future wife and smiled as if to reassure her. Then his smile wilted. "Now, for the part about why the coverup."

Nodding slowly, he kept his eyes closed. "They came back for her. Five men raped her—" His voice hitched. He swallowed hard. "They beat her. Cut her. She miscarried." His words came quickly. He opened his eyes, the pain in them so obvious. "They dumped her off at the ranch. They thought she was dead. Eddie and Helen devised a plan to protect her and me and Helen, and they carried it out."

Silence pulsed in the room. Marianne squeezed her eyes shut against the horrible, vivid pictures of pure evil in her mind. She opened her eyes and looked at Brigitt. "It wasn't about deception. It was about survival."

A look of appreciation crossed Bobby's face. "Yes."

"Did I have anything to do with what happened to you, Brigitt? My mother seems to think I did."

"No. We played dolls just before I left for the mall, where they got me in the parking lot. I have so much to tell you about that night. You're going to continue investigating, aren't you?"

"Nothing could stop me now. Wait, wait." The moment hit Marianne, and her eyes filled with tears. "You found each other." She jumped up and hugged Brigitt and Bobby. "You found each other. This is incredible. This is just incredible!"

She sat again. "I have so many questions. Where have you been, Brigitt? What happened to you? Why didn't you let Bobby know you were alive?"

Glancing at Bobby, Brigitt sighed. "I didn't think I could. They killed me, on the inside. For several years, I tried to dig my way out of the grave they put me in." She tapped her heart. "Only by the grace of God these past few years have I been able to forgive those men, to keep going, knowing they're still out there. Not a day's gone by that I haven't wondered if they might find me again or kill Bobby or my mother."

Marianne laid her hand on Brigitt's arm. "Will you tell me what happened?"

"I will, Mari. Then I want you to get all of them." Her gaze shifted to Bobby. "For me, for Bobby, for the other girl. Will you do that for us?"

"The other girl?"

"I heard a girl there that first night. There may have been others. Take good notes, Mari. I have a lot to tell you."

Marianne's head popped up. "A *woman?*"

Brigitt handed her a cup of coffee. "In the room with me and Georgie. My blindfold had been removed. I asked her to help me, and she laughed at me—no, no." Brigitt shook her head. "It was more of a sneer, as if I couldn't be serious. Evil was in her eyes. I don't know any other way to describe it. Just plain evil."

Despite the heat against her hands, Marianne felt chilled. Nothing about that night made sense. She picked up her pen and started writing again. "The woman was there both times?"

"Yes. She never said a word to me, but I heard her once when they all left me alone. Her voice was coarse and angry."

"Can you tell me anything else about her?" Marianne turned toward the front door as Mac walked in with two pizza boxes. He smiled at her, and her heart took a long, slow turn.

Brigitt motioned everyone into the kitchen. "She sniffed a lot, like she had allergies or a cold. She called Georgie by his first name. He was the only one she called by name."

Mac set the boxes on the table and opened them.

Brigitt placed napkins and plates beside the boxes. "Do y'all mind if we pray first?"

When the prayer was finished, Marianne noted the little kiss between Bobby and Brigitt and the obvious adoration in their eyes. Glancing at Mac, she found his gaze on her, and her face heated.

Mac picked up a slice, set it on a plate, and handed it to Marianne. "How about we give it a rest while we eat? Then Bobby and I can take a walk and give y'all a chance to talk."

"How do you know it was Georgie, Brigitt?"

"He told me, the first time. He said he was claiming his woman."

Marianne's stomach squirmed, and she slammed her eyes shut against the vision. When Bobby and Mac left a few minutes ago for their walk, she'd actually dreaded hearing more details about that horrific night. But she gritted her teeth and managed to stay focused. "Any other names spoken?"

"K.J. and Buddy. And something else. The first time. Georgie had taken me to a room blindfolded. The door opened, and Georgie said, 'Mama, you're here.'"

"His *mother* was there?"

"Yes. She snapped at him. 'Of course, I'm here. Whose little party do you think this is?' That conversation looped in my head for years. She might have been the woman I'd seen earlier."

"She was the mastermind of the gathering?"

"That's my guess."

"Was it videotaped?"

"I don't know. I've never seen any of it on the internet."

"Anything else you can tell me?"

Brigitt shook her head. "That's about it. I've had a long time to think on everything. I've told you all I know."

"Are you planning to go to the ranch?"

"We really haven't made any plans, but it's not safe there. After all that's happened to you, it's especially prudent that we not leave here."

"What name do you use here?"

"Carolyn Carmichael."

"Nice to meet you, Carolyn," Marianne smiled and then studied her notes. "What about your second encounter with this gang?"

"It was a lot more intense. They intended to kill me."

"I've spent a lot of time searching for Brigitt Holcomb's killer, but you're alive and well, and I'm so glad."

"But Brigitt Holcomb did die that night, Mari. I'm Carolyn Carmichael now because of those vicious people. Other women died at their hands. All of those women are 'Brigitt Holcomb' to me."

"You're right. Do you want me to call you Brigitt or Carolyn?"

"Carolyn, for now. When they're caught, I might go back to Brigitt."

"Then, Carolyn, tell me about Brigitt's second confrontation with those men."

The plane rolled to a stop. Marianne disembarked and actually considered kissing the ground. The winds had been terrible on the return trip, and the plane had fought valiantly to stay in the air. Even in perfect weather conditions, she hated flying. She wondered if Mac knew she wouldn't have done this for anyone but him.

A brisk wind whipped her hair around her face as Mac's pickup pulled up beside her. She couldn't get out of this cold quickly enough. The passenger door opened. "Perfect timing," she said as she tossed her things on the floorboard and got in. "Take me away, Charles."

He chuckled, turned out of the parking lot, and headed toward home. "It's been a long day."

"I'm so ready for a nice, quiet evening with just you, Mac. Or maybe not," she muttered as her cell phone rang. "Hey, Paddy."

"Mother's in the hospital."

"What happened?" She saw Mac's head turn toward her.

"She passed out and didn't come to."

No. No. Not again. "Where is she?" Marianne groped for Mac's hand. *I can't do this again.* For as long as she could remember, her mother had been spiteful and harsh with Marianne, but after her first recovery from alcoholism, she had turned downright evil at times. Marianne had poured herself into her mother's first recuperation, but not once had Barbara expressed any sign of love or appreciation.

"St. Peter's. The next thirty-two hours will tell the tale. The doc says she's strong and should pull through." Patrick blew out a lengthy breath. "It's been a long time coming."

"I'll—I don't know—what—" She turned away from Mac. "Look, Paddy, we're headed for the ranch. I'll call you from there."

"Are you coming down?"

"I don't know."

Patrick sighed, long and hard. "Don't do this."

"Do what?"

"Leave all this to me. You know I'll need a shoulder to lean on."

"Aunt Helen may want to be there with Mother. You can use hers."

"Great. Anyone but you, right?"

Marianne closed her eyes. Her stomach tightened at the thought of having to go through this again. Of giving and giving and giving to Barbara until hardly anything was left of Marianne. "I'll call you in just a little bit, Paddy. Be available."

"Always. 'Bye."

Marianne's hand fell into her lap. "When it rains..."

Mac's fingers braided with her other hand. "Your mother?"

Nodding, she glanced out the window, so very tired after the emotional encounter with Brigitt earlier, all the traveling, and now this.

"What happened?"

Staring at nothing, she wished for a heavenly police chief who would race to her mother's rescue and make everything better. *"A description of the culprit, ma'am?"*

"A bottle."

"There must be more to it than that."

Marianne would sadly shake her head. "If there is, I don't know what

213

it is."

He would nod then, knowingly. "We'll get the perp, ma'am. You can count on it."

Mac pulled over and parked. "What happened, Mari?"

"Oh, uh." His soft voice was almost her undoing. She needed to stay strong but wasn't at all sure she could or if she wanted to. Now was not the time to sort between *need* and *want*, but God help her, she wanted to run away, change her name, and melt into a thick forest where no one could find her. All she'd wanted was a new place to live. A new life with the freedom to live on *her* terms. The old life was pulling her back with its claws again—claws with a history of maiming her and keeping her from the very freedom she was so close to having.

Both of her worlds were falling apart. She didn't know what to do about either of them.

"Mari?"

Oh. "My mother passed out. Didn't come to. She's in St. Peter's."

He tugged her close and kissed her head. She didn't move. He didn't move. They held each other and allowed the closeness to soothe and comfort.

Marianne sighed. It felt good to close off the world and hide, even for a moment. Mac's big strong arms were wrapped around her. Maybe if he squeezed her tightly enough, she wouldn't be able to leave for Abilene.

"It's late. What are you going to do?"

"I'm so tired, Mac. I just want to sleep. But first, I've got to see Nuggets. Every time I see her lately, she's chasing after a rabbit or running with a pack of dogs."

"She's happy. Do you think you're going to Abilene in the morning to see your mother?"

"I'm too tired to make decisions tonight. Let's just get to the ranch and sit in front of a fire in the den and maybe drink some hot chocolate."

Mac walked into the den. It was almost midnight, and Marianne was sound asleep on the sofa. He gently lowered himself beside her.

She bolted straight up as if a snake had crawled onto her lap. "Wha—? Is Mother all right?" She searched the den. "Father?"

"Hey." Mac stroked her arm, and she focused on his eyes. "Everything's okay." He tugged her into his arms, right where he liked to keep her. "Patrick called. Helen made it to the hospital about an hour ago and is sitting with your mom right now. She said she's staying in Abilene until Barbara wakes up. She knows it could take two or three weeks, but she's willing to stay."

"Oh. I'm so relieved." Marianne brushed a hand through her mussed hair. "I was dreaming of you." She slumped back and rested against his shoulder. "It was cold and raining and I was under the old bridge. Something was wrong. Someone was behind me, creeping up on me. I heard your voice." She looked up at him. "You shooed away all the monsters."

"With just my voice? No wielded swords or valiant steeds racing to the damsel's rescue?"

She smiled, but the green of her eyes was dull, her lids heavy. She looked up at him. "I don't want to move, but I'm so thirsty."

He gently eased her to a sitting position.

"Be right back." She walked around the coffee table and headed for the hallway. As she passed through the doorway, a quick glance over her left shoulder, toward the front door, made her pull up. It seemed like slow motion as Marianne's eyes widened, and her face lost all color. She took a step back, shaking her head.

When she pointed at the door, Mac rushed toward her. The hallway was empty. He looked back at her. She'd shifted to the doorway of the den and was using it as a shield as she peered around it.

"What?" Everything moved quickly. He grabbed her shoulders. "Mari, what is it?"

"Th-the man who caused my accident! He was standing in the window, staring right at me!"

In three steps, Mac had the front door open. He stepped out, looked around.

"He knew right where I was, Mac. He was waiting for me."

Mac unsnapped the holster on his hip, slipped out his handgun, and checked it. "Lock this door, turn off the lights, and stay low." Then he walked out and into the darkness.

When Marianne slapped at the light switch, the room fell into darkness, and she was terrified of it. *We'll know it's there. We'll know it's there.*

Her knees buckled, and she sank to the floor. She felt exposed by the open curtains, so she crawled to a hidden corner created by the sofa and the gun cabinet. With her heart pounding, she whispered a quick prayer for Mac's safety. She could hardly breathe. Fear had a mind of its own, and it was fully in charge of her.

Outside security lights cast a hazy glow in the room. Shadows jumped at her. Her heart beat hard against her chest. She could feel it in her ears, too. She tried to take a breath to calm herself, but it sputtered and shook instead.

A shout outside startled her. She held her breath and looked anxiously at the windows. Several footsteps thudded on the porch. Male voices.

A posse. She let out her breath. Mac must have made it to one of the bunkhouses.

She was too hot. Sweat rolled down her back. A quick shiver jerked her body, and she began to shake all over. *C'mon, Marianne. Hold it together.*

She was so tired of playing the 'victim' to these bullies. She just didn't know how to change the storyline. And here she sat, in the dark, hiding, feeling helpless as she waited for something to happen.

Her gun!

She'd forgotten it was on the sofa in her purse.

She stretched out on the floor, careful not to be seen, and wiggled her way to the front of the couch, felt for her purse, and tugged out her weapon.

She crawled back to her hiding spot and pulled up her legs.

Resting her gun hand on her shaking knees, she waited.

But not for long.

Heel, toe. Heel, toe. Cowboy boots, sneaking down the hall.

Marianne's heart jumped into her throat. She shuddered, so afraid she couldn't think.

The boots were getting closer. *Dear God!* She slapped a hand over her mouth to keep a whimper from coming out and tried hard to listen. She couldn't hear anything but her heartbeat. Her eyes widened as she shook like a cold wet puppy.

Soft steps now, on the carpet. He was headed straight for her!

She pushed against the wall, trying to hide behind the huge gun case. The man came into view and touched the rim of his hat. Then he winked at her as he reached for the gun holstered at his waist.

With trembling hands, she raised her weapon.

He laughed at her and tugged on his gun.

She cocked hers.

His smile wilted. "You don't know how to shoot that thang, do you, little girl?"

She fired.

With a shocked expression, the man grabbed his shoulder. He growled, gritted his teeth, and charged her. "Why, you—"

She fired again and missed. But it was enough to make him stop. He stumbled over his feet to get away from her and ran out of the room toward the kitchen.

In a matter of seconds, the front door flew open. "Marianne?"

Relief all but swallowed her. "In here, Mac." She put on the safety and dropped the gun. The lights came on as Mac came around the corner, surrounded by several cowboys. "He was just in here, Mac. He ran toward the kitchen."

"Jumbo! Curly!"

"On it, boss." The two men motioned several cowboys to go with them as they hustled down the hall.

"Who fired that shot?" Mac frowned deeply as he picked up her weapon and examined it. "Are you okay? Are you hit?"

"No." She closed her eyes, aware that she could hardly speak through the tears clogging her throat. "I-I shot him in the shoulder. But I missed the second time."

Mac punched one number. "He went out the back, Luke. Yeah, as many as possible. I'm staying with Mari." He slipped his phone into his pocket. "Come here," he whispered and hugged her.

She nestled against him. "He let me know he could get to me any time he wanted, even if I was hiding."

Mac cursed under his breath. "It was stupid of me to leave you alone."

"No, Mac." She snuggled closer, needing to feel the warmth of his body. "It was *normal* for you to leave me alone. That's what people do. They go after the bad guys and leave the vulnerable at home. But I had the upper hand this time. I wasn't the victim; he was. I-I've never shot anyone." Her whole body was shaking now. She was so cold. Tears filled her eyes. She fought hard to be brave and not weak.

Mac's arms tightened. "You did great, Mari. You're alive, and you won. You need a hot shower; it'll help with the shakes."

"Would you go upstairs with me and check the rooms?"

"Of course." He jogged past her toward the second level and turned on lights, looked into each room, and ended up at hers. "I'll camp out in your room, if you'd like. I have a cot."

"I'd love to be able to say no, but I can't. Not tonight. You know what just happened, don't you? He wants me to know that I can't hide from him. He can find me and get me even in your home."

"But he didn't. You hurt *him*. You've got to remember that."

"If he'd come in with his gun drawn, I'd be dead right now and maybe you, too."

"Boss?"

Mac looked over the rail to the downstairs area. Hank stood in the foyer with a pink envelope in his raised hand. "We found this under her windshield. It's addressed to Marianne Glaze."

Mac headed down and snatched the envelope out of his hand. "Y'all find him?"

When Hank looked down at his boots, Mac said, "Call Sheriff Nate, tell him what's going on here. Then station men around the main house and around the cottages. Let me know if anything happens."

"Sure thing, boss." He left.

Mac ran up the stairs. Marianne shook her head as tears ran down her face. "I hate those poems. We don't have to open it."

Mac took her hand and led her into her room. "Yes, we do. He'll have too much power over us if we don't." Mac opened it, slipped out the note, and read it out loud:

"Mary, Mary, quite contrary,
Almost got away.
The cloak of night
Hid you from sight
But I found you. Wanna play?"

"He'll think twice about 'finding' you again since he knows you have a gun, and you're not afraid to use it."

"Maybe. But I'd think he has something to prove enough to come back and try again." She shook her head, so very afraid. "Maybe he left some blood behind. Or we'll find him in an area hospital."

He pulled her into his arms again. "Nate will be here soon. In the meantime, I'll go get that cot while you take a hot shower."

"Not *while*, okay? *After* I take a shower. Then I'll go with you to get the cot." Against his shoulder, she said, "If I'm not safe here, Mac, I'm not safe anywhere. I'll draw a composite of him for Nate after my shower."

EIGHTEEN

The first week after she shot the prowler, Marianne was on edge. She was afraid to go outside; she was afraid to stay inside. The security system had been disabled the night she shot the man, but now, it was activated at all times. Of course, she could go home to Abilene, but Mac understood her need to wait. "I know you're not ready to see your Mother," he said, "so stay here. I want you to stay."

"And do what? I've followed every lead. They're all dead ends."

"Then swim. Paint. Play pool. Hike with me. Learn to ride. There's so much to do here. I want you to just relax."

By the time Thanksgiving Day arrived, two weeks had passed in relative peace, with no poems, no attacks, no bombs exploding, no unknown cowboys strolling through the main house. One man, incapacitated, and Marianne's troubles had stopped. But he'd never shown up at any hospital. DNA from the blood samples revealed someone who wasn't in any database. She was grateful for the respite, but it didn't stop her from jumping at the sound of a car door slamming or jerking when a dog barked behind her or gasping when something was dropped.

Her phone beeped early on Thanksgiving morning. Helen sent a text with "Happy Thanksgiving!" and a picture of Barbara, with Frank asleep on the edge of her bed, his head on his crossed arms. Marianne enlarged the picture and stared at her father.

When had the gray appeared in his hair? His stubble also held specks of gray. With his left temple propped against his folded hands, the lines in his face appeared prominent and puffy.

The fierce fighter was exhausted.

Marianne read Helen's long text and marveled at her father. He acted like a man who loved his wife, staying at the hospital, refusing to leave even when the doctor threatened to call security and throw him out. Frank had dug his heels in, without a word being spoken, with that impossible-to-refuse expression he used to denote his power and control.

Was it possible, at this stage of their unhappy life together, that he had never stopped loving her mother? Even after all the pain Barbara had caused him and that he had caused her?

A sudden sense of peace washed over Marianne. She wasn't *supposed* to be in Abilene right now. This was her father's time, to help

Barbara on the road to recovery and to heal his relationship with her.

And it was her aunt's time, to try to mend the pain of the past.

"Frank?" Helen shook his shoulder.

"Umm?"

"Come on. It's after seven in the morning." She tugged at his arm. "It's Thanksgiving. You need to go home and get some rest."

Lifting his head, Frank opened his eyes, squinted, blinked.

"Go take a shower, Glaze. You're rank."

A tiny smile appeared as he rubbed his puffy eyes. "That bad?"

"I'll sit here with Barbie until you get back."

He appeared too tired to argue as he struggled to stand. She held onto his arm while he stomped his feet as if they were asleep.

"I do stink."

"You do."

"Did you just get here?"

"Yes. I went to your house about two hours ago, showered, ate, just texted Marianne. Somewhere in there, I took a short nap."

"Where's Patrick?" He looked down at Barbara, lying still, her eyes not quite closed. Gently, he kissed her cheek twice. She didn't move.

His kindness touched Helen. She didn't remember him as a gentle man, but he clearly still loved his wife. "Patrick's holding down the fort— his words, not mine. You're lucky to have him to keep things going at your business."

"Just so he doesn't mess it all up while I'm gone." He pulled out his cell phone.

She took it, slipped it into his shirt pocket, and patted it. "Why don't you trust him a little longer? Give him a chance to prove himself."

"I've given him plenty of chances."

"With too many strings attached. He's all tangled up in them."

"Is that how you see it?"

"It's how Marianne sees it, and I suspect she's right." Grimly, Helen eyed her sister.

"No. Not with Barbara. She had all the strings attached, not me."

"Then start with Patrick and cut them, so maybe, just maybe, he'll see his way to get out from behind you."

"Stalking horses again? Which is it, strings or stalking horses?"

"Probably both. Marianne's full of these analogies. But I think she's right." She patted his arm. "Now go home." When he didn't move, she

220

tugged on his arm again. "Come on. I'll walk you out."

Across town, in his father's office, Patrick stood at the windows overlooking Abilene. *Frank's little empire.* A holiday like Thanksgiving meant nothing to Frank or Barbara. Just another work day. It would be expected of him to start work early, even today, and work late. So he would.

He scanned the skyline. In the distance, beyond the city, the flatlands spread before him. He yearned to experience some relief from the pressing feelings of despair and inadequacy standing in his father's office gave him. He would never measure up. He would never be what his father wanted.

He would never *be* his father.

St. Peter's Hospital sat to his left and somewhere in that vast assembly of buildings, his mother barely clung to life. Frank was with her, as was Aunt Helen. *Won't Mother throw a hissy fit when she realizes her sister—*

He jumped when small hands touched his waist. Gripping her wrists, he growled, "What are you doing?"

"Showing you how thankful I am." Cheryl turned him around and roughly pulled his mouth down to hers.

Marianne's phone rang. "Hello?"

"Marianne."

"Father." Their first contact since he hurt her arm in his office.

"Are you coming home?"

She inwardly groaned as she walked toward her bedroom window overlooking the ranch. "I'm hoping you and Patrick and Aunt Helen can handle things right now." *Please, please, understand.*

"Do you have *any* plans to see your mother in the near future?"

She'd resigned herself to his anger. Maybe this time, he had reason. But her rushing to Abilene could be just as damaging to Barbara as staying at the ranch. Marianne had nothing to give her right now. Others were there who did. "Maybe when she comes out of the coma, when she'll know I'm there."

"At least that's something."

"Father—" *No, don't say it. Don't start anything with him now.*

"What?"

"Nothing."

"Your mother needs love and forgiveness to get through this. I want you here only if you can offer her both."

Marianne felt like a stranger who'd wandered into an ongoing, intensely private family drama, a stranger who was expected to act the part of a loving daughter, full of concern and caring. But she didn't know how to play the part. To show up at her mother's bedside and be a devoted, affectionate daughter wasn't in her right now. It might never be. "Maybe it's best if you and Helen stay with her right now."

"I know your mother's never asked you for forgiveness, but it's a starting place for all of us, a stepping stone toward healing. At this point in her life, it's necessary. Just consider it. Please." He hung up.

It would be better for everyone if she stayed at the ranch until Christmas and let her mother's healing begin without her. She'd been there for Barbara the first time they'd gone through this and look where it had gotten them—right back where they'd started.

Marianne felt completely drained. With everything happening to her up here, she just didn't have anything left to give her mother.

One issue at a time, though. Barbara had to recover from the poison in her body. Later, maybe, they could get their relationship on a stable track, one on which it had never traveled.

Marianne was sure that compassion and caring for her mother would eventually come. But she wouldn't be duplicitous now. She had to stay away from the lies, the disguises, and the horrible masks with the glassy eyes and lopsided grins.

For heaven's sake, hadn't they all worn them long enough?

With Helen in Abilene and Mrs. Rook and the inside staff off with their families for the day, Mac made peanut butter and jelly sandwiches for Thanksgiving Dinner. Then he persuaded Marianne to watch football games and old movies with him. The ranch hands that had nowhere to go ate their dinner in the mess hall and pretty much kept to themselves.

Mac and Marianne agreed not to discuss anything negative or painful. The day was filled with shouting at a football game, snuggling on the couch with a movie, and walking for two hours with Nuggets and Daisy.

A day to be thankful, after all.

Mac received a text from Brigitt and Bobby. They were

honeymooning in the mountains of Colorado in a town called Little Texas and staying in McKenzie Cabin. All the text said was, "Enjoying the mtns, Little Texas, and being together. Happy Thanksgiving." Mac had been to Little Texas many times. The hiking trails were wonderful; the scenery, majestic; and the quiet of nature, unrivaled.

That night, Mac walked Marianne to her bedroom just as she finished reading a text. "Any change in your mother?"

She shook her head. "Helen said she's resting. She also said my father is still in love with her, something I don't quite understand. Mac, we haven't talked about anything today, but do you think the man I shot has pulled back? That he won't be bothering me anymore?"

"I think he's trying to lull us to sleep before he strikes again. We have to be diligent, Mari." When she shrugged, he touched her hair, and then slipped a strand behind her ear. "Why don't you get some rest?" He leaned forward and kissed her. "Lock your door."

"I will."

"I'll see you in the morning. Sleep tight."

Marianne couldn't sleep.

She sat on the window seat and stared at a night light illuminating the parking lot full of pickups. Aunt Helen had sent another text: "Still resting. Frank wants you here, as does Patrick. Are you coming down?"

She sent a message back: "Not right now. Maybe soon."

Her phone rang just after she sent the message. "Patrick? It's ten-thirty. Where are you?"

"At the hospital. Just got off work."

"Busy day?"

"Very."

"Keeping your head above water?"

"Barely. But I do like being at the top of the food chain."

"I'm not sure I like the sound of that. Any change in Mother?"

"Not really. I talked to a nurse. She said the coma's normal and it's healing. And that's what we want, isn't it? Normal and healing."

She accepted the sarcasm. "Are you there to stay?"

"No. Frank's snoring in a chair. I came by because he'd expect me to, and here he is, sound asleep. He won't even know I was here."

"You're there. I don't know what it says about me that I'm not."

"That the Christian can't take the heat? That's almost laughable."

Marianne said nothing.

"Then how about this one: neither of us fell far from the apple tree?"

"Umm."

Her brother was quiet for a moment. "Since when did either of them care about us?"

And there it was. Out in the open.

"This is their crisis, sis. Not ours." Count on Patrick to get the truth on the table. "Gotta go. Talk to you tomorrow."

A single tear rolled toward Barbara's temple as the door closed behind her son. She needed to go back, into the silence, into the warm soothing silence.

Where darkness cloaked the pain and quiet stilled the screams.

Marianne's phone beeped. Another text, from Aunt Helen.

Barbie woke up tonight about ten-thirty. Wanted a drink. Said she wants to be well. Wants all of you to be well. Took our first steps toward reconciliation. She's weepy, sad, scared. She wants to see you, honey. Talk to you soon. Love, Aunt Helen.

Marianne texted back: *Thanks so much for keeping me posted, Aunt Helen. Please tell her I'll see her at Christmas.*

The next couple of weeks were unusually cold, unusually quiet, and Mac was unusually busy.

Marianne was almost finished with the painting of Brigitt. It was going well, but she was restless. She'd stopped for the day, needing something to fill her time. She'd interviewed everyone on the ranch, everyone she could find that was connected to Brigitt's case. She didn't know what else to do about finding the men after her.

One thing she'd discovered about herself since coming to McKenzie Ranch was that she enjoyed the ranching lifestyle. She dressed the role, even with a cowboy hat, and tried to insert herself wherever she was welcome—to watch, to learn, to help out. She looked forward to being exhausted at night, sleeping soundly, and then sleeping in.

But there was a sense of disquiet about each day, as if—she couldn't quite put her finger on it—as if everything around her was part of a waiting script. As if all eyes were on The End but no one knew what came before it. As if it was expected that she was in danger, but nothing was happening to her. *Waiting. Waiting.*

Christmas decorations were put up. Everyone on the ranch was invited to help. It was obvious they were all accustomed to this. Cowboys laughed, Emma giggled, Mrs. Rook directed, and Mac and Marianne watched with wonder as the house was transformed into a beautiful land of gold, red, green, blue, and silver. Trees along the driveway were drenched in white lights. A well-lit nativity that told the true story of Christmas was placed near the chapel. Deer in different poses and covered in white lights stood all over the vast front lawn.

Even amongst the festivities and candy making and Christmas baking, the steady sense of expectancy surrounded Marianne. She caught herself looking over her shoulder too often. She shivered for no reason. The fear she'd walked in for a while wouldn't dissipate, despite the cheerfulness of the season enveloping all of them.

A cold front pushed through the area. One morning in mid-December, she showered, dressed, and then glanced out her window. Snow covered everything. It was a gentle snow with thick flakes falling in straight lines. Cowboys walked about. Someone drove a four-wheeler out into a field. Several riders rode straight into the barn.

Just as she turned to head downstairs, a text came in.

Hey sis. Frank fired me. We sure chose well in the parent department didn't we

Why?

The usual. Incompetent, lazy, and a new word this time. Haphazard. Whatever that means

But you're none of those! I'm so sorry. What are you going to do?

Grovel and beg. I know how. I've done it before. I'll let him simmer down and start the game in a couple days

Might be time to do something besides work for him.

Like what? Give you all the money?

I don't want his money. You can have it.

I deserve it after taking all his crap

She didn't know what to say after that last text. Maybe he'd finished unloading on her, and she could—

Her phone beeped.

No comment? You are such a coward sometimes

Maybe. But I'm not the one at home, am I?

So you're not coming? She's asking for you

Isn't Aunt Helen enough for her?

She turned off her phone and wished she could turn off all the drama as well.

As she walked past her desk, Brigitt's open file caught her eye. Her gaze fell on the name of the school nurse, a Mrs. Tomlinson, about sixty now. At the time of Brigitt's death, she lived on the other side of Brennan. Maybe she knew something. There was no mention in Brigitt's file of Cecil interviewing her.

The latest phone book revealed that Mrs. Tomlinson still lived in Brennan. Good. Marianne would go see her after breakfast. She called and then texted Mac about her plans but didn't hear back from him. He was probably in a remote area with no service. She'd try him again after she finished breakfast.

NINETEEN

By nine-thirty, she stood on the porch of a well-kept white, two-story farmhouse boasting a wide, comfortable porch. A wooden swing seemed to invite Marianne to sit for a while. Hanging around the porch were planters filled with artificial and dusty red, yellow, white, and blue flowers moving in the breeze—there was always a breeze.

She rang the doorbell. A tall thin woman with over-arched black brows, short gray hair, and a smudged apron answered the door. Her smile showed off two front teeth protruding over her bottom lip.

"Well, hello there, young lady. What can I help you with today?"

Marianne instantly liked her. "Mrs. Tomlinson?"

"Yes. Yes." The screen door squawked opened. Brown eyes squinted at her. "Are you a former student at the high school?"

"No, ma'am. I'm Marianne Glaze, a cousin to Brigitt Holcomb. I was wondering if I could ask you some questions about Brigitt, if you remember her."

"Oh, yes, child." The door swung wide, and the woman waved Marianne in. "Of course, I do. She was the light of her class, and everyone loved her." The woman indicated a sofa. "Sit, sit. Can I get you some tea? Sun tea's ready right now."

"That would be nice, thank you."

"Well, then, come with me into my kitchen and let's visit. Oh, yes, I remember Brigitt. I remember the day she died."

Bright yellows and greens greeted Marianne. Tile the color of honeysuckles lined the walls under the cabinets. Yellow walls, green plants on windowsills, and a grass green-tiled countertop finished the cozy room. In the center, green and yellow tiles covered the island where the stove top was situated. A lovely kitchen for such an old home.

Sitting in what appeared to be a built-in telephone niche in the wall was a framed picture of a young nurse with the words "First, Do No Harm" painted on the wall over her left shoulder. "Is this you, Mrs. Tomlinson?"

"Yes. All the student nurses posed next to that admonition. I've lived by it. Of course, I couldn't save every patient, but I sure tried. Then I became a teacher. In many ways, that was even more difficult."

Marianne took the tall glass of iced tea Mrs. Tomlinson offered her and followed her to a two-chair table sitting in front of a window in the kitchen. No other table was in sight. On the way to the kitchen, they'd passed what Marianne considered was meant as a dining room, but it had been turned into a computer room and library.

They sat. For ten minutes, Marianne learned about Brigitt's school activities, honors, awards, and Bobby McKenzie.

"She wanted to go to medical school after graduation," Mrs. Tomlinson added as she stared at the picture of herself as a young nurse. "Brigitt loved to come by my office and talk medicine with me. I enjoyed her enthusiasm. She loved to learn and just drank in all the information she could swallow."

Mrs. Tomlinson frowned and shook her head slowly. "That last day, I missed her at school. Maybe if she had come, she wouldn't have been killed. We closed the school the next day. Just too many heart-broken kids to deal with. We gave them a choice to stay home or come to the school and receive help. Several parents brought their children in for counseling."

"Can you recall any one boy liking Brigitt excessively, other than, of course, Bobby McKenzie?"

"Charlie Blake. He imagined himself in love with her. Of course, all the boys liked her, but Charlie got into trouble fighting boys who said anything about Brigitt, that kind of thing."

The one and only suspect with an alibi. The man and his private investigator father who'd helped the McKenzies through the years.

"He hated Bobby McKenzie. I overheard him and another boy saying that she got what she deserved. I never heard the name 'Brigitt,' but I guessed that's who they were talking about."

"What do you think they meant, 'she got what she deserved'?"

The older woman quickly shook her head. "I have no idea, dear. She was popular, pretty. Maybe one of them had issues with women. I don't know."

"Did Charlie Blake come from an abusive home?"

"Not at all, from what I could see."

"Did you tell the police?"

"Oh, yes, I did. I believe in my civic duties. But nothing ever came of it. Why this interest in Brigitt's death after so many years?" Mrs. Tomlinson burst out laughing. "That is, if I can turn the tables and ask you a question."

"Of course, you can. I'm her cousin. I just recently discovered my mother's side of the family and learned about Brigitt's death. I want to find out about her. That's all. I'm wondering, Mrs. Tomlinson, if you know the name of the boy with Charlie Blake that day?"

"I'm sorry, no. That was so long ago."

Marianne stayed another five minutes and headed back to Brennan. Charlie Blake just made the top of her list.

When she reached Mole's Bench, Marianne pulled over at the only gas station in town so she could call her father and see how her mother was doing. She touched his name on her contacts list.

He answered, "Marianne," in a gruff voice.

"How is she?"

"Resting."

"The prognosis?"

"It's bad this time." He sighed, deeply. "Too early to tell."

Marianne identified what she thought was etched in his voice. *Guilt.* "You didn't put her there."

"Yeah, Marianne, I did," he growled.

"If you did, then we all did."

"Don't give me your psychological hogwash." She shifted as if he'd raised a stiff hand to slap her. "Let me, for once, take responsibility for what I've done."

Temper flashed through her, but she kept her voice low. "You didn't make her pick up the bottle every day. You didn't hand her the glass to pour it in. You didn't force it down her throat or make her swallow. And you didn't pour the next drink for her. She did."

Marianne hugged herself with one arm, forcing herself to calm down. She didn't want to fight with him. A couple of deep breaths later, the need to comfort instead of yell at him overtook her. "I'm sorry, Father, for all of this. For both of you. For her."

"Patrick just got here. You can yell at him for a while. Patrick, here. It's Marianne."

Oh, Lord, will this stress ever end?

"Hey, sis. Are you going to yell at me?"

"Not yet. But your time's coming. Are you working for Father again?"

"Sure am." Awful cheerful this morning. "Hey, thanks for calling." He singsonged his words. "Talk to you soon. 'Bye."

In other words, he wouldn't talk to her in front of their father. A united front—his idea of loyalty.

Frustrated and annoyed with both of them, she slipped her phone into her purse and rested her forehead on the steering wheel. She had lived in relative peace with her parents for a while. That was due to her restraint, her compliance, and her determination not to rock the boat.

So why couldn't she be compliant now? Why couldn't she just pack up and go to Abilene and do what they wanted her to do?

Because rocking the boat was sometimes necessary. Sure, one of them might pitch a fit, but that's what stepping out meant. It wasn't easy. She was determined to continue to try. Not just for the sake of living life on her terms, but for the sake of being real.

She tugged out her cell phone, called Mac, and told him about her time with Mrs. Tomlinson.

"What were you thinking, going off by yourself without giving me a chance to come with you?"

"You were busy."

"You should've waited until I was un-busy and could go with you."

"Is that a word? Un-busy?" When he didn't laugh, she said, "I'm fine, Mac. Nothing happened."

"This time." For a few moments, he said nothing. "About two miles from the main house on McKenzie land is a shooting range. We can practice today, if you'd like, after I finish an important appointment."

"Practice what? Are you taking me hunting? The season's open."

"I was thinking more of a handgun so you could protect yourself. So you won't miss the next time."

Like I did the other night. "I'm willing to practice with a handgun but I want to learn to shoot a rifle, too, if you'll take me hunting."

"Okay. There's an old hunting cabin—"

There was such a long pause that Marianne thought their call had been disconnected. "Mac?"

"We'll have to postpone the shooting lesson, Mari. I'll talk to you later." And then he hung up.

Mac stood by his truck as Nate drove up in an unmarked pickup and parked next to him. Thick brush, trees of all sizes—fallen, leaning, and upright—surrounded them. Nate got out, yanked a baseball cap out of his back pocket, and slipped it on. Mac extended his hand and said, "Appreciate you coming out on such short notice."

"Sure. You mentioned a hike. Where are we headed?"

"To the key to Marianne's troubles, I'm thinking. Brigitt mentioned a musty odor and a clothesline inside. I can't believe I didn't think of this place, right here on Tucker land. Charlie Blake knew about this cabin, but I don't remember Brigitt ever going out to it. It hasn't been used in decades. Even seventeen years ago, it hadn't been used in years. Keep this under your hat, Nate. This has to remain strictly unofficial and confidential for now."

"I know how to keep a secret, Mac."

"Then let's go."

Fifteen minutes later, crouching in heavy brush, Mac studied the back of the cabin. Still in remarkably good condition, despite its years. His great-great-grandfather had been a master carpenter and built this remote hunting cabin just a year before the poker game. Then Cecil Tucker's father renovated it sometime in the '70s, but to Mac's knowledge, Cecil never used it.

"It's built like a tank and pretty rustic." he whispered. "No electricity, wood-burning stove, fireplace, lanterns, well water. I'm thinking this just might be the place where the predator gang hurt Brigitt. At the time of the investigation years ago, no one knew about the predator gang or the other girls."

Nate scanned the area. "Any reason to think it was this building?"

"It's remote. No one would see them enter the land. Brigitt mentioned a dirt path, and the driveway's dirt. It's on Tucker land. Might be the reason they've tried to scare Marianne away. C'mon. Let's check it out."

"Don't touch anything. If this is the right location, I'll need to get a forensics team out here, see if we can find any usable evidence."

Mac led the way to the front of the cabin and turned the doorknob. It was unlocked, but the door bucked when he tried to open it. He shoved hard with his left shoulder, and it grated open to dust falling off the jamb.

His first step inside yielded a creaking floor.

"Musty," he muttered and grabbed the flashlight out of his daypack. He looked around and spotted a hook high in the corner of the room. He turned around and checked the other corners. Four hooks, positioned perfectly for clotheslines that would cross in the middle of the room.

"Look up, Nate."

"Well, son of a gun."

"I never noticed those hooks," Mac said as he tugged out his pocketknife and squatted in front of the kitchen sink. With the blade, he wedged open the small door below the sink. "And the ropes are under here."

The color in Marianne's face drained as she stopped walking. "You found the crime scene?"

"I think so. It's on your land, the far side of your property, right at the border with my ranch. Nate's checked it for evidence. No reports back yet. I've stationed a concealed, rotating guard on the cabin while you're here. We'll look there first, if anything should happen to you."

"That's too much trouble, Mac. I could just go home now and—"

"No." He stopped and tugged her close. He never tired of feeling her body next to his. "I want you here with me where I can keep an eye on you. You're leaving soon enough. I've been so busy lately. Just give me these last couple days with you until then."

They started walking again, arm in arm. "Brigitt and Bobby are coming for Christmas. I've asked her to go to the cabin and get her feel for it. It's been a long time, but we need to know if we're in the right spot."

"It's asking a lot of her."

"I know. I left the decision up to her. She said she wants to help, that she'll check it out and see. If the killer or his accomplice is on this ranch, we'll have to be uber careful. I've checked all the new hires. It's been over a year since we've brought anyone on board. If he's here, he's keeping himself well hidden."

"But if he's here, then he's someone you trust, Mac."

"Yeah. Part of me is glad you'll be leaving all this behind you, even though I don't want you to go."

He stopped again, drew her into his arms, and kissed her. "I don't want you to leave, but at the very least, you'll be safe in Abilene."

"I don't want to leave either."

He nibbled at her neck. "I don't think I can go very long without seeing you. Or kissing you. Needing a kiss can be a powerful incentive to fly to Abilene." Mac smiled. "Will I get a kiss when I get there?"

"If I'm in the mood."

A corner of his mouth lifted. "And how will I be able to gauge that?"

"Well." She looked toward the sky and frowned as if deep in thought. "If I lean in."

"Lean in," he repeated.

"Lift my chin."

"Lift your chin."

"Tilt my head."

"Tilt your head."

"And close my eyes."

When she did, he thoroughly kissed her, and then rested his forehead on hers. "I'm already missing you."

TWENTY

Marianne was already wishing she hadn't come.

Maybe she should leave.

For whatever reason, she decided against it, tiptoed to the foot of her mother's bed, and watched her sleep. She hadn't wanted to feel anything for this woman or to be pulled into another of her well-spun webs. Life with her was—had been—simply too draining.

Some part of her, though, needed to see her mother awake.

Barbara looked old and unbearably sad. Her hair was flat against her head. No make-up graced her face. Even in sleep, her mouth drooped. It seemed she'd aged ten years in the past few weeks. For some reason, Mrs. Porter's words came back to Marianne: *Can't imagine being married to such a man. I pity your mother.*

Sympathy sidled up beside the festering anger in Marianne's heart. She didn't want to be sucked in again, yet she knew there was no turning back now. She was here. She wanted things to work out for her mother. But what did she expect from Barbara, and what did Barbara expect from her?

Someone had opened the curtains. The promise of sunshine had changed into overcast skies, gray and weepy. Barbara didn't like the light; she'd purposely placed heavy curtains on every window in their home to keep out the brightness.

Marianne drew back the edge of the curtain and pulled the cord.

"No, Marianne. Leave them open. Please."

She dropped her hands and tried not to wince at the sound of her mother's voice. It was different—not grating, not ugly, but gentle, without the harshness and sarcasm.

"Marianne?"

Banking the anger, she slowly turned and faced her. What she hadn't expected was a tentative smile and tenderness in her mother's eyes or a tug of concern from somewhere deep inside herself at seeing both.

She straightened her shoulders when she felt the aloofness she'd nurtured and perfected slicing through her, guiding her to the foot of her mother's bed. "Mother, how are you?"

"Better, I think." Barbara lifted a hand.

Marianne set her mouth and dropped her gaze to it. Of course, her hand was shaking. She wanted to scream at Barbara to stop it. Just stop all of it!

"You have every reason to hate me." Intense sadness crossed Barbara's face as her eyes filled with tears.

Resolved against them, Marianne lifted her chin.

"But I'm hoping we can meet somewhere," Barbara coughed, cleared her throat, "in the middle, where it's comfortable for both of us."

Marianne picked at the comforter covering her mother's bed. She didn't want to try, didn't want to meet anywhere with her mother, didn't want *comfortable*. But she surprised herself by opening her mouth and saying, "I will try, Mother. That's all I can offer right now."

"That's a good start." Barbara threw the covers off and sat up. "I'm staying in my pajamas today. It's just that kind of day." Her feet slid into her slippers as she reached for her robe. "I haven't fixed breakfast in years, but I'd like to try this morning, if you'll join me. We'll make it simple, like French toast." She smiled then.

Something clutched at Marianne's heart. She couldn't remember the last time her mother had sent her a simple thing like a smile. She honestly had no idea how to respond without being disingenuous.

"I'll get the coffee going first." Barbara stood. "Then, after breakfast, we can plan decorations and get the Christmas tree up. Your Aunt Helen left early this morning. I appreciate your encouraging her to come here." She hesitated a moment. "Would you join me in the kitchen?"

"Of course. I'll be right behind you. Oh. Do you know anyone named Bubbles?"

"Bubbles? Oh, my goodness. I haven't heard that name in years. Only one other person knows it, and he's dead. My brother, Cecil. He called me that in secret when I was being too bubbly."

"You're Bubbles?" Marianne sat on her mother's bed. "Then you have the letter."

"What letter?"

"The letter Uncle Cecil gave you to give to me when I inherited his property."

"What?" Barbara frowned at her. "I don't rememb—oh! That's right. I completely forgot about it!"

Her mother rose, moved a picture on the wall, turned a combination lock, and opened the safe. She withdrew a sealed envelope and handed it to Marianne. "I'm so sorry. I completely forgot that he gave this to me the day he left for Florida."

Marianne took the envelope and held it against her chest. She couldn't believe it. She had the letter!

"I'll leave you with it. Come to the kitchen. We'll visit and fill our faces with a good breakfast."

"Mother? Why did we stop going to the ranch?"

"Oh." A pained expression crossed her face and she sat on the edge of the bed. "I let them think it was because your father and your Aunt Gloria had walked together a couple of times. But I'd seen Helen and Eddie with Brigitt that last day, and I simply couldn't handle it. I thought my sister and her husband had killed their daughter. So." She shrugged. "We never went back."

And never talked about it with anyone.

"Come downstairs when you're ready. We'll talk more then."

Barbara left. She was really trying. The least Marianne could do was match her efforts. She went to her room and put her pajamas back on, and then sat on the bed and carefully opened the envelope.

Dear Marianne,

I hope you remember me. I'm your Uncle Cecil, and you used to come out to my house with your family when you were young. You're reading this because I am now dead. I'm sorry I never contacted you after your family stopped coming out to Mole's Bench. I thought of you often and hoped that you were living a happy life.

I have information I want you to have. It's a burden, but I have no one else to give it to. Do with it what you will—anonymously, of course. I'm not proud of what I've done, but I couldn't live with myself if I had done nothing. My time is short, so I'm giving this letter to your mother. She knows nothing about any of this.

I could no longer be an officer of the law. I live in Florida with an old college roommate who never married either.

Here are the reasons I left:

Brigitt didn't die that terrible day. (This will be a shock to you, but you can't tell anyone about this.) I was part of the deception of four family members to hide the fact that she lived. Her mother and Bobby will be killed if the 'predator gang' ever finds out she is alive. I left shortly after her memorial. Without anyone's knowledge, I came back to the Mole's Bench area several times, in disguise, and unofficially investigated. I discovered the names of the people involved with George Schroeder. They know I know who they are. I killed George Schroeder for what he did to Brigitt and made it look like he died in an auto accident. But I didn't give this evidence to the police. I had to protect my sister (your Aunt Helen) and Bobby.

All the information I found on this predator gang is in a box buried near the old bridge I showed you. The box is buried deep (about four feet) on McKenzie land just five straight paces from where you step off the bridge.

I hope you have a good and happy life on Tucker land. I always hoped that you and one of the McKenzie boys would find each other (maybe Mac), and that the land could be united again. Never forget that I always loved you and still do now.

With love,

Uncle Cecil

She re-read it. She wanted to call Mac but decided to wait until she was back at the ranch after Christmas. She hid the envelope under her mattress, and then hurried downstairs so her mother wouldn't think she didn't want to be with her.

In the kitchen, Frank stood beside Barbara with his hand on her back. Nuggets got up from her bed by the back door and nudged Marianne with her cold nose.

"Good morning, Father." She bent over and patted Nuggets' head. "And how's my sweetie this morning?" Nuggets wanted outside, so Marianne opened the back door and let her out.

Frank turned toward her, a little sheepishly. "I'm glad you're here, Marianne. I want to apologize for—"

"No need, Father. All of us, I'm sure, have a lot to apologize for, so let's agree that all is forgiven and focus on the here and now. It's a beautiful day, and it's Christmas."

Barbara smiled at her, and then looked at Frank with an expression that sought something like approval from him. "That's definitely in my favor, since I have the most to be forgiven for."

"Now, I wouldn't say that," Frank muttered and handed Barbara a cup of coffee. "It's time to move on. Together." He bent over and kissed her forehead.

She smiled and glanced at Marianne.

And the look she sent her daughter shocked Marianne: her mother was blushing like a schoolgirl.

"Well, would you look what the cat dragged in." Mac stood before the vast windows in the dining room and chuckled. "It's Greg, with Daphne and the boys."

Bobby, Brigitt, Helen and Luke got up from the dining table, looked outside, and then walked quickly to the front door with Mac. They all reached for coats on the tall rack and slipped into them as they stepped out onto the porch.

A van door opened, and four boys bounded out. Two bolted toward a horse tethered outside the barn. They backed off when the horse whinnied and stomped at them. The two younger boys stayed close to their mother as Greg walked to the trunk and tugged out luggage.

"Greg, you old skunk! What in the Sam Hill are you doing here?" Mac grabbed him in a tight embrace.

"It's Christmas." Greg grinned as he hugged Bobby and Brigitt. "And here's our resident time traveler. Welcome back, Carolyn," he whispered in Brigitt's ear. She beamed at him.

"You didn't say a word about coming home when I called the other day, buddy."

"We wanted it to be a surprise. We needed to be here, this first Christmas without Dad." Greg shrugged and blinked quickly. "The boys were so excited, they drove us nuts the whole trip. 'Are we there yet?' 'Do they still have horses?' 'Can we ride one?'" He laughed when Luke hugged Daphne. "Get your own woman, little brother. I'm not sharing mine with you."

Luke winked at Daphne. "Mom taught you better than that. Share and share alike. Especially if I don't have one."

Bobby elbowed Luke away and hugged Daphne. "Good to see you, Daphie Duck. Have a good trip?"

"Here. Make yourself useful." Greg slung a garment bag at Mac. "Nick! Mikey! Come help with the luggage!"

Both boys ran back to the van and grimaced at their uncles and aunt as heads were rubbed, hugs given, and kisses avoided.

"Where's Tim and Arlene?" Greg handed a small bag to Mikey. "They coming?"

"Due in tomorrow." Mac hefted the garment bag over his shoulder and picked up a piece of luggage. "Gives us a chance to catch up with y'all and fill you in on what's been going on around here."

"We have to leave the morning after Christmas. What about Kyle and Kevin?"

"They're staying in Granston. Said they'd be here sometime in January, when Mom gets back. Now, come on. You and Daph 'll have Mom's old room. The kids can camp out in Joey's."

"When was the last time you heard from Mom?"

"Two days ago." Mac led the way up the stairs to the porch, followed by giggling boys. "She and Aurora were in Rome, having the time of their lives. The boys don't still like hot chocolate with marshmallows, do they? They've outgrown that, right?"

"No way! We love it, Uncle Mac!"

"Well, let's get inside then, out of this cold. Catch the door for us and then y'all get to the kitchen. Chef James probably has it ready for you by now."

Piles of Christmas paper, bows, ribbons and boxes surrounded Marianne as her father snapped a picture of her standing wistfully in front of the Christmas tree. Barbara's handpicked gold ribbons, bows, and tinsel made the tree sparkle. Pulling out Christmas decorations from the attic that hadn't been used in years was almost as much fun as opening presents this morning.

Barbara hadn't lost her magic touch. The house looked beautiful and Christmas classy.

Turning her head, Marianne smiled at her father. "More pictures?"

He motioned her to the sofa. "Have a look."

She set her coffee cup on the table and took the camera as she sat. "Patrick was shocked when you gave him those golf clubs. He's been wanting to golf with you for years."

"I was too wrapped up in myself to notice. And here. *The Stalking Horse* statuette. What a look on *your* face."

"It was perfect. I can't believe you thought to have that commissioned back when I had the wreck. Oh, and there's my face when I opened Mac's gift. What a beautiful bracelet. Wait—what's this?"

He laughed. "Your mother, when the star fell over. You were out of the room. She's reaching up to put it back on the tree—"

"Like a beacon." Thoughtfully, she stared at the picture.

"What? You look as if you've seen a ghost."

She shook her head. "Why didn't I see this before? You weren't my only stalking horse, Daddy. This family is full of them. Look at mother. This is a stretch but follow me. It's like this picture."

She stood and paced. Moving helped her think. "Mother turned her back on us and hid behind her bottle. It was her stalking horse. Wherever the bottle led her, she went, and all of us followed. *You* were behind *her* holding onto her waist. I was behind *you*. Patrick was following me, holding onto nothing. He was just a shadow drifting behind the rest of us."

She placed the camera on a table and looked around. "And our guns? They were too far out of reach." As if her feet were stuck to the ground, she stretched out her arms on one side, then the other, and wiggled her hands. "None of us could reach them."

She straightened and searched her father's eyes. "We couldn't reach the guns, Daddy. Not to take aim at prey but to shoot the stalking horse."

Her father stood. "You're right, honey. I can see it. It's a turning point."

"I can see it, too."

Marianne and Frank turned toward the doorway to the hall. Barbara and Patrick stood arm in arm, watching them. Something in her mother's gaze caused Marianne to move toward her.

Barbara's eyes filled with tears. She pulled out of Patrick's arms. "I was too afraid to let go of it, too afraid to turn around and find out if all of you would still be here." A look of sheer pain fell across her face as she looked down at her hands and shook her head. "I was so afraid of losing my family. And I almost did."

The three of them couldn't get to her fast enough. "We're here, Mama."

"—love you, honey."

"—always be there—"

"—with you, Mama."

Barbara gasped and sniffed the air. "Oh, no," she laughed, brushing at tears. "The bacon! Quick, Patrick, get the pan off the burner! I'll get the spatula!"

She ran into the kitchen. "Marianne, the biscuits! There, behind you, the potholders!" Frantic, Barbara searched the counter tops, turning in a circle. "The spatula."

"Here." Frank shoved it at her.

She took up the bacon, cleaned off the spatula, and triumphantly held it above her head. "To our new stalking horse!"

"Here, here!" Patrick snatched a piece of bacon and stuffed it in his mouth.

Barbara laughed as Marianne set the biscuits on top of the stove and said, "We need a picture of our new stalking horse. Let me get the camera." She walked into the living room, picked up the camera, and just as she made it to the kitchen door, she heard...weeping?

Dear God. What happened?

She stood quietly for a moment and then peered around the door frame. The back door was closing, with Patrick on the outside of it. Her father's arms were wrapped around her mother.

Barbara was crying on his shoulder, still holding the spatula. The tie of her robe trailed on the floor as if it was lost and couldn't find its way home. "I-I just want a drink." Her mother's voice wobbled, thick with tears.

Frank rocked her a little. "I know, honey. I know." His head snuggled against her mother's as his hands roamed her back, stroking, stroking. A beautiful picture of love at its best, giving when not much was given in return.

"No, you don't know." She pulled out of his arms and faced him. "I'm trying so hard. I want to win. I want to be normal. I don't want to be drunk so that I can face life."

Marianne backed out and flattened herself against the wall.

"You'll make it, honey. I know that. Do you want to call your sponsor?"

"No. I love you, Franklin. Please forgive me for all the hurt I've caused you."

"I love you, too, sweetheart. My forgiveness has already been given, but I'll give it again and again as much as you need it, as much as you need to hear it, even if you don't return the favor."

Marianne slumped against the wall, her head back, her heart pounding. Somehow, their love for each other had survived. Marianne remembered Barbara's last journey out of alcoholism. For a long time, her mother hadn't faced her emotions. Not just sadness, rage, loneliness, confusion, and pain, but happiness as well. She'd not known how to live without anesthetizing herself to them. This time, she was facing them. Maybe she would come to realize how much she needed to face the ups and downs with feelings and not hide behind those silly masks.

Lord, I'm sorry. I haven't been empathetic enough with her. She's hurting so much.

"I forgive you, Mother," she whispered, and then walked upstairs to her room to give her parents a few minutes alone.

TWENTY-ONE

Her SUV crawled toward the main house. When it stopped, Mac opened the front door and stepped outside, his heart pounding as he savored the sight of her getting out of her vehicle. Nuggets ran like the wind toward the barn.

Lord, what a beautiful woman you've given me. His eyes locked on hers as he started down the steps. He thought his heart would jump right out of his body if he couldn't get his arms around her right then. She shut the door and took a step toward him.

Emma whooped, dashed past him, and ran into Marianne's arms. "Oh, Mari, I've *missed* you! Where have you *been?*"

"Mmm. I've missed you, too, Emma. I had to go home for Christmas and to help my mother."

"Is she okay now?"

"Yes, honey, she's recovering. And how are *you* doing? Did you have a good Christmas?"

"It was great. I got to babysit Reagan—Stella's baby—yesterday for the first time." She groaned when she heard her father yelling her name. "Coming, Daddy! See ya later."

"Alligator." Marianne looked at Mac and raised her brows.

They walked toward each other. He stopped in front of her and eased his arms around her.

"I'm here."

He tightened his hold. They held each other and rocked as the cold morning breeze brushed against his neck. "I'm so glad. I never want to be separated from you again."

She moved her head a fraction, and his mouth covered hers. All the longing and love and missing her was in the kiss. When he ended it, he placed his forehead against hers. "It's too cold out here. Let's grab your luggage and get inside where it's warm."

Her remote beeped; the trunk lifted. He pulled out two pieces of luggage, threw a strap over one shoulder and picked up the other. "Snowstorm's due in tomorrow night. Biblical proportions, they say, or at least for this area, it is. Helen said a woman phoned the ranch asking for you. Maybe it's about your ad."

"Did she leave her name?"

"Helen said she'd give you the information when you got here. She's gone for the day and will be back late tonight. Come on. There's a cozy fire in the den. Let's relax today and just look at each other. Steal a kiss or two."

"Trust me," she grinned, "there's no need to steal. Oh, did you take Brigitt to the cabin?"

"Yeah. She said years ago, she'd taken off her blindfold because they wanted to show her the mothers' pictures hanging on the clotheslines. When she walked inside the cabin, she recognized it. And she cried." He sighed. "God bless her, she cried and cried. Bobby went with us and held her, but it was still difficult to watch."

Marianne touched his arm. "I'm so sorry for her."

"I'd like to burn the cabin down, but Bobby thinks it will help her heal a little more each time she goes there. Empower her to face those demons. She-made-it-out-of-there-alive kind of thing. Anyway, we're on the right track. Now we just have to make sure you never see the inside of that place."

"I have the letter."

"You *have* it?"

"Yes. My mother is Bubbles, and what Uncle Cecil told me will surprise you."

"Can't wait to read it. But right now, let's get inside. There's a fire in the fireplace in your favorite room. I want to snuggle with you all day."

"It's no wonder he moved to Florida," Mac said as he lowered the letter. "He was deceptive about Brigitt's death, and he intended to kill the perpetrator, George."

Marianne nodded. "I guess he figured no one would find out, until he decided seven years ago to write me the letter and tell me. Did he know I wouldn't go to the authorities? Probably. He was dead already, I would surmise, so no need to tell anyone. If he gave the letter to his deputies, they would have made everything public."

"Which they will anyway once we dig up the evidence."

"Unless I keep the letter. His secret would be safe with us."

The next morning, Marianne knocked on the door to Helen's cottage. So much had happened since Brigitt's remarkable recovery from death that Marianne hadn't had a chance to talk to Helen face to face about the deception and lies. She decided it was better handled out here, where they could both get it said.

The awkwardness she felt was reflected on Helen's face when the door opened. "Hey, Aunt Helen. I wanted to talk to you, if this is a good time."

"Of course, you do, Mari." She pushed the screen door open. "Come in out of this cold. How was your Christmas?"

"A lot of ups and downs. But everyone seems to *want* healing this time." She looked around. She had expected clean and neat and homey. She hadn't expected anything to be familiar. The small rocking chair beside the sofa—she was little and someone sat beside her, reading to her. "I remember sitting in that chair."

"You used to love coming up to our rooms at the main house and playing games with Brigitt. You felt like such a big girl when you sat in the rocking chair."

The blazing fireplace beckoned to her cold hands, so Marianne shoved them toward the heat.

Helen stood with her and rubbed her hands together. "You fault me for not telling you Brigitt was alive."

"Not now." Especially since Marianne had been threatened by these same people in the same way.

"Everything I told you was the truth *except* that Brigitt was alive. I didn't think I should tell you unless she gave me permission. And she hadn't, at that time."

Marianne reached for her aunt's hands. "Had I been in your shoes, I would have done the same thing—if I had had the support team you had. Every major player was a family member. The coroner, the sheriff, the mortician, and the parents."

"Thank you for understanding." Helen hugged her. "I've missed you, Mari. Let's sit and visit a bit." She indicated a small sofa across from the fireplace. "Mac's brother Greg and his family were here for Christmas. They left this morning. Tim and Arlene and the baby were here, too, as well as Brigitt and Bobby. It was so good to see them holding hands, walking around the life they'd had years ago. I took so many pictures of them strolling around the ranch. Of course, Brigitt isn't going by the name 'Brigitt.' Geezer was beside himself when he saw her. First thing he did was show her the saddle he'd made for her graduation. It was the best Christmas he's ever had." She smiled wistfully. "She and Bobby left this morning to go visit your parents."

"I know. I wanted to give them some time together. Mother and Daddy need to see Brigitt. One thing I've learned about my family is that secrets are well kept. But I believe we're on the road to some kind of recovery now."

"So are Barbie and I."

"Thank you for helping her. It also gave me time to decide what to do about my relationship with her."

"I was happy to do it. Would you like some hot tea?"

"That would be wonderful." They both headed for the kitchen.

Helen filled a tea pot with water and set it on a lit burner. "Speaking of secrets. After Brigitt died and your family left, I never saw my sister again. Barbie wouldn't take any of my calls or answer my letters. I even went down to see her, and the maid wouldn't let me in the house. It crushed me. Then, through the years, I stopped trying."

Helen shrugged, lifted the lid of a canister, tugged out two tea bags, and placed one in each mug. "Patrick called me once when Barbie was taken to the hospital the first time. He told me the facts and then hung up. When I called him later, he told me she was better, that he'd be in touch if she was ever at death's door again, and not to call him again. I tried to contact him for a couple years, but he wouldn't take my calls. I didn't know at the time, of course, that he'd seen Eddie and me with Brigitt on that horrible day."

"It affected him deeply."

"I didn't try hard enough to help him." Helen grabbed Marianne's hand. "Or you. I'm sorry for that."

"It was difficult living there with them. I'm not sure you could've helped."

"My sister was always crabby when she came out to Mole's Bench. I suspect it had to do with my sister Gloria living there, and Barbie wondering constantly if Frank would be attracted to her again."

"What do you mean, 'again'?"

"Oh. Well. It might be better coming from your mother, but Frank dated Gloria first. They had several dates. But then he saw your mother, and it was love at first sight. He never looked back. Barbie was always uncomfortable when the two of them were in the same house or at family functions."

Jealous. No wonder she was so hurt by Frank when he kissed his secretary. "I didn't know that. It explains a lot."

"Yes. Barbara told me she saw them walking in the woods the day Brigitt was hurt. When she saw Eddie and me with Brigitt at the rock, nothing made sense to her. I regret that she saw us. We thought we'd been so careful. And now, to find out that Tim and Patrick witnessed it, too." She shook her head. "So much sadness came out of our attempt to save Brigitt's life. And mine and Bobby's."

"You did the best you could at the time."

The tea pot whistled. Helen turned it off and poured water over the tea bags. "Oh, before I forget." She picked up a small sheet of paper on the counter. "Here's the information on the woman who called for you."

Marianne dialed the number. The phone rang once.

"Hello?" A woman's voice, tentative.

"Jenny Harrison?"

"Yes?"

"This is Marianne Glaze."

"Oh." Jenny cleared her throat. "I was there, seventeen years ago."

"Do you want to talk about it?"

"Yes. Why do you want to listen to me?"

"We need to find those men and bring them to justice. It's that simple. Do you know where McKenzie Ranch is?"

"I sure do. I can be there around six, if that's a good time for you."

She hadn't bit the inside of her cheek since she was a child, nor had she chewed her baby finger in years. But Marianne was doing both tonight. The sense of 'something is about to happen' had simply engulfed her. Every sound, every spit of the fire, every door shutting had her jumping. She shivered as she walked to the window and looked outside. No one was about. The ranch looked like a ghost town.

She took several deep breaths and got to work trying to find a good book to get her mind on something else. Spotting one, she sat on the sofa and read for about a minute.

Mac walked in, poured himself a cup of coffee, lifted the pot at her.

She shook her head and tried to read. Frustrated, she re-read the first two paragraphs but couldn't concentrate. Maybe it was Jenny's phone call. Maybe it was the storm. But whatever 'it' was, it kept pulling her out of the book. "Lindsey called. Mr. Jamison brought his car into Logan's shop yesterday. Logan told her he's completely recovered from his accident."

"Good." Mac moved to the glass doors. "I hope Jenny makes it here before the storm arrives. Luke dated her a long time ago. If she's the screaming girl Brigitt heard that night, it's no wonder she never let their relationship even get to hand holding."

Mac turned from the window, punched a button, and the big screen TV came on. A bow-tied weatherman pointed to the panhandle of Texas.

"Folks, we're expecting between fifteen and twenty inches of snow tonight in a relatively short period of time. Stay off the roads unless it's an emergency. Winds are expected to reach thirty-five to forty-five miles per hour, with visibility a quarter mile or less."

Maybe there was something in the air, other than the coming storm, a sense of 'expectancy' from nature that was transferring to Marianne. She closed the book and stood. "I'm as nervous as a cat."

"I noticed." Mac muted the TV. "What's bothering you?"

"I can't pinpoint it. Maybe the storm? I don't know. Could be Jenny coming here. I want to know what happened to her, but I don't want to hear the details. It was hard enough listening to Brigitt's story. But if Jenny's the other girl, Mac, we may know the names of Georgie Schroeder's gang tonight."

"Let's hope."

"We haven't talked about what might happen to me now that I'm back at the ranch."

"Nothing's going to happen to you this evening. The blizzard will see to that. Tomorrow, I've laid out a security plan for everyone on the ranch. The cabin is being used tonight by two men. You'll be protected or someone will die trying. I won't take my eyes off you."

Thirty minutes later, Marianne slapped her notepad against the palm of her hand and peered out the front window. A tumbleweed raced across the front lawn and was captured by a truck's wheel. Luke and Mac stood on the front porch, both in heavy winter coats, talking, looking around. Marianne opened the front door and shivered as the cold slapped her body. Mac opened his jacket, wrapped her in his arms, and eyed the heavens.

"We're set, buddy," Luke said as he pulled up his collar. "As ready as we're going to be for this thing." A dog raced toward him. "Molly girl, what are you doing out here? Did you come to get me? Well, let's go home, then. It's too cold out here." Ducking his head against the wind, he ran toward his cottage with Molly right beside him.

Mac checked his watch, then the driveway. "It's getting late."

"She may not come." Marianne shivered.

"Storm sure is."

A snowflake fluttered by. Then another. "It's here, Mac. I better get indoors." Movement to her right caught her eye. "And here comes Jenny."

They walked back in. Even expecting her, Marianne jumped when the doorbell rang. Her stomach turned over, and she rested her hand on it as she glanced at Mac. He sent her a 'thumbs up' and left the room. She quickly strode to the front door and opened it.

Long blonde hair swirled around the face of a small woman in her early thirties. Graceful, slender fingers pulled strands of hair down and away from a freckled, thin face with amber eyes and soft thin lips. "I'm here to see Marianne?"

"I'm Marianne," she said, extending her hand. Her first thought was that this petite woman was probably boyish and small as a teenager, a perfect target for a predator. What horrible things did she have to endure seventeen years ago?

"I'm Jenny." She was holding an art portfolio against her chest.

"Come in, come in." Marianne led her into the den where they could shut the door and enjoy a nice fire.

"I'm really nervous about this."

"Of course, you are. Here, let's get you comfortable." She helped Jenny out of her coat and laid it across the arm of a sofa. "Would you like to warm yourself?"

"Yes. It is freezing out there." She stood before the fireplace and extended her hands as she studied the picture on the mantel of Luke, Mac and Joey smiling with a string of fish between them. Then she scanned the room, and her gaze rested on another picture of Luke.

"Whenever you're ready, you can come over here by me, and we'll get started. We don't want you to get caught in this storm." Marianne indicated a chair for her, and she sat. "I'm glad you had the courage to come here, Jenny." She placed her phone on the table between them. "I'm going to record this, if that's okay."

Jenny bobbed her head side to side, her flat hands clutched between her knees. "It's okay, I guess. What are we going to talk about, exactly?"

"Let's get this on the record." She punched the ON button. "This is Marianne Glaze, speaking with Jennifer Harrison. Jennifer, do I have your permission to record this interview?"

"Yes."

"Nothing you say will be used against you. Unless, of course, you did something illegal."

Her lips tightened, and she lifted her chin. "I did nothing but what I was forced to do. I had no choice."

"That's what I figured. I'm on your side, Jenny. Let's get started."

Marianne opened the front door and hugged a tearful Jenny. "I'm counting on these men being in custody soon, Jenny. Your identity will be kept completely confidential until they are. The sketches you brought are perfect, and you even aged each of the players. Nate is going to love this."

"Thank you." Jenny hugged her again. "You can't know how good it feels to tell someone. I've waited so long." She brushed at tears racing down her face.

"I'm grateful to know the names of these men. Hopefully, other women will come forward and testify with you. After I've spoken with Nate, he'll want to interview you."

"I'll be ready."

"And if Mac has pictures of the cabin, I'll have him send one or two to your phone. See if you recognize it."

"Okay. Well. Goodbye." Jenny stepped out into the cold icy wind and snow.

"You're sure you want to leave? You're welcome to stay."

Jenny waved. "I have an SUV. It'll get me home. 'Bye now."

Marianne watched her walk to her vehicle. The falling snow appeared like cotton balls in the night lights across the ranch. No one was out. The bunkhouse lights were ablaze as were each of the cottages.

Mac's arm eased across her shoulder, and he tugged her against his chest. "Snowing pretty hard now. And the wind's picking up."

Marianne slid her arms inside his coat as Jenny got into her SUV and started it. "I'm so glad she came, Mac." His arms felt strong and comforting and warm wrapped around her. They walked inside and shut the door.

"She knew the names of all the men, where they lived, and said she would testify against them. And two interesting facts came out. One of the men never identified himself to the others. He covered his face with a ski mask, drove a rental car to their meetings but didn't attend every time they met. And your private investigator friend from Fort Worth was in with the Schroeder gang."

"Charlie Blake?" He guided her into the den, toward the fireplace. "Are you serious?"

"Actually, I'm assuming he's the same young man that Cecil Tucker ruled out." She extended her hands to the fire. "These people killed three people, at least. The two mothers—the hanging pictures—and a girl from Vinson, Texas. Jenny said other girls were brought in besides Brigitt, that she recognized this girl from Vinson when her picture was splashed across the papers. She was found beaten to death."

"Why? Because she told her mother?"

"Jenny didn't know."

Letting out a long sigh, Marianne turned her back to the fire. "Jenny said they took her again after Brigitt died. The man in the mask was there. They called him George. This was after Georgie Schroeder died. Maybe that's why Lindsey didn't want me investigating. This George was her father."

Mac shook his head. "If she knew he was involved, she never let on. What are you going to do about it?"

"Tell Nate and let him investigate. I have no evidence it was him. If I say anything to her, she'll only deny it. It'll definitely make the divide between us even greater. Although, honestly, I don't think she'll ever bridge that chasm in this lifetime."

"You have their names? I might know some of them."

She reached for her notes and the sketches and went through them one at a time. "Oscar Wilkerson. He lived in Brennan. Buddy Haynes, his half-brother, in Sweetsville, about twenty miles from Brennan. Charlie Blake and Georgie Schroeder, of course. And Kevin Johnston, from Larramore. K.J." She looked up. "Not my Uncle Keith. And the second George, of course." She spread all the drawings on the table.

"How did she find out their identities?"

"She went to the restroom once, took off her blindfold, and peeped through the space between the hinge and the door. She vowed to remember their faces and find out their identities, and she did. It helps that she's an artist, so these composites from seventeen years ago are very accurate. And look. She aged all of them."

"They're remarkable. Why did she come forward now?"

"Her mother died two months ago." Marianne looked down at her hands, then into Mac's eyes. "She mentioned Georgie's mother, but she never saw her. She also said she saw Oscar once during the day, years ago. He tipped his hat at her and smiled as if he hadn't done a thing to her when she was younger." She jumped when his cell phone rang.

"Hello?" Mac checked his watch as he listened. "Be right there." As he rushed toward the closet, he said, "Emma's missing."

"My coat's upstairs," Marianne said, right behind him. "I'm going with you."

"You're going to your room. If something's wrong, I sure don't want you in the middle of it." He put on his coat, zipped it, and slipped into gloves. "Your room's the safest place on this ranch."

She frowned and opened her mouth to speak.

"Don't argue with me, Mari. I've got to get over to Zach's." His voice softened. "She probably got disoriented in the snow."

"But I can—"

"Go to your room. Come on." He grasped her elbow. "I'll walk you up, make sure everything's okay."

"Mac." She gently twisted out of his grip. "I'm fine. It's my bedroom, for heaven's sake. I'll be all right. You need to hurry over there and help Emma."

"With you out of harm's way, I won't be worried and distracted." He settled his hat on.

"If you need me, come get me or call me. I won't mind."

"Thanks." He shoved her toward the stairs and watched her walk up them. At the top, she turned around.

"Go, Mari! I've got to get over there. Lock your door. Keep it locked until I get back."

Marianne walked to her window. The snow was so heavy, she couldn't see the belt of trees across the yard. Actually, she couldn't see anything but swirling white. She prayed that Emma was safe by now and that Mac would be returning any minute with good news.

A thud sounded behind her. She gasped and turned toward her bathroom. The doorknob was moving!

Mrs. Rook came out, her gloved hands knitted at her waist, a pensive expression on her face. She wore a thick winter coat with a hood and winter boots. Her thin lips were covered in a dark pink color—Brigitt's lipstick! Although, not just covered. *Smeared on* would be a better description.

"Miss Glaze. How good of you to oblige me by returning to the ranch. And you locked your door. Most convenient."

"What are you doing in here?"

"Shut up." Her eyes narrowed.

Hank LeTran appeared behind Mrs. Rook. "Do what she says."

A chill ran up Marianne's spine. She took a step back. Her mind couldn't wrap itself around the obvious. "Hank, Mac's gone to—"

Mrs. Rook wagged a finger at Marianne. "We know where he is, Miss Glaze. Now."

Another man walked out of her bathroom. A balding, fat man with curly, gray hair sticking out above his ears. He held up a pair of black thermal coveralls, and Marianne stopped breathing. Her heart raced so hard, her chest hurt.

"If you would oblige me yet again, Miss Glaze, I'd appreciate it if you would put these on."

Shaking her head, she stepped back. Her legs nudged her bed. *Oh, God, help me. Help me!* She was outnumbered, had locked herself in with these people, and her purse and her gun were on the dresser across the room. *Think, Marianne, think!*

Okay. *Stall.* Maybe Mac would come up and check on her and—

"Now!"

Gulping, she grabbed at her retreating courage. "No."

Hank gritted his teeth, grasped her neck, and shoved her head between her knees. "Do it," he growled and shoved again.

She...couldn't...breathe! She felt as if an overstuffed pillow was filling her lungs. She bobbed her head, grunted, "O-kay."

Hank let her up. Clutching her throat, she coughed several times. Bald Man threw the coveralls at her, and she fell back on her bed. Taking her time, she shucked her boots, slid into the coveralls, and zipped them up.

"Your boots." Mrs. Rook lifted her chin and smiled. "We wouldn't want your little tootsies to get cold."

The men behind her chuckled.

Trembling, Marianne sat again and put them on slowly.

"Now, follow me, Miss Glaze."

"Where are we going?"

Hank slapped her. "Shut up," he said as she grabbed her cheek and fell across the bed. He seized the back of her hair and hauled her up to a standing position, then laughed and shoved her away. She stumbled back against the headboard, dizzy and disoriented, tears stinging her eyes.

Mrs. Rook smiled and turned toward the door.

"My coat."

"You won't need it, Miss Glaze," Mrs. Rook said over her shoulder.

When Hank pushed her in front of him, a sinking feeling of desperation washed over her.

"One peep and I'll break your neck," he snarled as they headed toward the stairs and the darkness below. "You're gonna die tonight. Dudn't matter to me how or where."

Oh, God. Marianne's stomach clutched tighter. *Oh, God.* She had trouble catching her next breath. She felt her stomach quivering and knew it wouldn't be long before her whole body was shaking. *No. Not this time, Marianne. Don't be weak. Not now.*

"Lock her door." Mrs. Rook sniffed. "We wouldn't want Mr. McKenzie to think she didn't obey him now, would we?"

No lights were on in the house. When they reached the foyer, Hank led them to the side door.

"That's a blind alley," Mac once told her. *"No one on the working side of the house can see you over there."*

Churning gales of snow whirled and danced, stinging her cheeks. A good three inches of snow already covered the yard. She could barely make out the main house through the thick swirling white, which meant no one could see her. *God, please help me. Please.*

Boom! A loud explosion jarred the ground under her feet! She staggered and lost her footing as one of the barns burst into flames, spewing a bright orange glow into the sky's white mantle.

Mrs. Rook didn't flinch. She turned around and smiled at Marianne. So, this was part of their plan. A diversion. *No one will notice I'm missing.*

And Emma. *Her disappearance was meant to get Mac away from me.*

Hank slammed a fist into her hair and yanked her up. He caught her before she fell again and shoved her. Gritting her teeth, Marianne hugged herself and trudged on, forcing her legs to keep moving against the fierce wind and bitter cold. Her head screamed with pain. Her whole body shivered.

But that was their intent, to make her as vulnerable as possible.

In the blinding snow, with the help of a lighted compass held by Hank, they reached the chapel. He opened the door for Mrs. Rook. Marianne stumbled inside. Her teeth chattered and her body felt like ice. She could hardly move, much less think. But it was much warmer inside; someone had turned on the furnace.

Against the door frame, Mrs. Rook kicked the snow off her boots and walked primly down the aisle, gliding out of her winter coat and tossing it onto a pew as she passed by. Regally, she angled her head at three men standing at the base of the cross.

Okay, God, I need Your help. I-I'm—

A woman stood and turned toward Marianne. Mrs. Tomlinson!

"Ah, Miss Glaze. How nice to see you again. My sister speaks very highly of your investigative skills. But I understand you're an artist as well?" She sat on one of the steps leading up to the choir loft. "You'll excuse me if I sit, dear. My feet hurt from baking Christmas pies and cookies for the nursing home the last several days."

Marianne was beginning to thaw. She needed to get alert and stay alert. She studied the three men. One sported a blond handlebar mustache. *Buddy Haynes*, according to Jenny's description. He sneezed and tugged out a wadded hanky and cleaned his nose. He was the man in the white truck, in her bedroom, at the hospital, in the den, and in so many of her nightmares.

One tall, white-headed, austere man in a long, black coat grandly lowered his head at Mrs. Rook. *Oscar Wilkerson.*

And the third man must be Charlie Blake, the driver of the black monster truck. He drew in smoke from a cigarette, pinched it with two fingers, and flicked it under the piano.

"No smoking in God's house, Mr. Blake!" Mrs. Rook shouted, frowning at him. He ignored her, and Buddy Haynes rushed to pick up the cigarette butt and stuff it in his pocket.

The fourth member, Fat Man with the curly gray hair and thick gray brows, would be K.J., with age and weight on him, very close to how Jenny had aged him.

So, the gang's all here. The same mob that had kidnapped Brigitt and the others and killed the two mothers in the photos and the girl in Vinson. These people were dangerous. *My life is hanging by a thread.*

"Miss Glaze."

When Marianne turned her head, she swayed and made herself look at Mrs. Rook.

"We haven't much time as you can see." She swept her age-spotted hand toward a corner of the room, much as a game show hostess would show off a brand-new car.

Someone, in the corner.

Marianne gasped. Jenny Harrison was stretched out on the floor with a knife in her chest! Her eyes were closed, and no blood was on her clothes. Marianne muffled a scream and fought the convulsing need to throw up. *Oh, dear God! What have I done?*

"First, do no harm," whispered Mrs. Tomlinson, who was staring at Jenny with an odd, vacant expression on her face.

"You said something, dear?" Mrs. Rook raised her brows at her sister.

Mrs. Tomlinson shook her head. "My feet hurt. I might have to get on home before the entertainment begins," she said, winking at Marianne.

Mrs. Rook tugged a book—it looked like a Bible—out of her purse and placed it on the altar. "Would you get my knife, son? Please?"

Son?

Hank circled around the men and headed toward Jenny, his boots thudding on the hardwood floor. With his hand on Jenny's shoulder, he gripped the knife, yanked it out, and cleaned it on her jeans. Oozing blood stained her blouse as he turned, walked back to Mrs. Rook, and handed her the small knife.

Marianne's stomach rolled as raw fear gripped her. She could hardly take a breath as she shivered. *Please. Please, Lord.*

"We must not dawdle." Mrs. Rook turned back to Marianne. "You've been busy, Miss Glaze, and we don't like it."

She reminded herself to remain calm and think. *Think!*

"We've positioned this piano bench here just for you, the star of our show tonight." Mrs. Rook sent her a smile that on any other day would have been lovely. "It's only fitting that you sit here at the foot of the cross. Please." Evil glinted in the housekeeper's hard, brittle eyes.

Chilled to the bone, Marianne couldn't seem to move. Two of the men flanked her and each gripped a shoulder. She shivered as the men shoved her onto the bench.

TWENTY-TWO

Swirling snow slapped Mac's face as the heavy metal bar on the barn lifted easily and then swung like a pendulum. When the huge doors opened, the flames angrily flashed. Mac covered his face and moved back from the intense heat. "There she is!"

Emma lay on her back, just inside the door, her hands and feet bound. Fire licked at a wood pile near her head. Without thinking, Mac grabbed her feet and yanked her out.

"Emma!" Zach lifted her into his arms and ran toward his house, hovering over her body. Helen ran ahead of them and opened the door.

"Who would do this to her?" Zach laid her on the sofa and fumbled with the duct tape.

Without a word, Mac pushed his hand away and sliced through the tape with his knife. Helen came in with a washcloth and gently cleaned Emma's face while Zach checked every bone on her body.

"Abe, call 9-1-1." Mac pocketed his knife. "Tell them about the fire and Emma and get an ambulance over here." Abe tugged out his cell phone and turned toward the kitchen.

"Curly, Jumbo, Grimes. Search for footprints. No one drove onto the ranch, so they walked in. The snow's a solid wall now, so we have to move fast, men. No one goes out alone. Take guns. Calhoun, Ben, Jay, Flattop. Take some men and search every barn, every building."

Ben stepped forward. "We have, boss."

"Do it again. They could still be here. Luke, Geezer, check the tack rooms, the cottages, garages. They could be anywhere. And be careful."

"Yeah, boss." Geezer nodded once at Helen as he opened the door and left.

"Why would anyone do this, Mac?" Zach closed his eyes and rocked Emma. "It's okay, honey. It's okay," he whispered. "You're all right now. Daddy's got you."

"We want to know what was in the letter, Miss Glaze."

Marianne tried not to squirm. She flinched when Hank gritted his teeth and raised his hand to slap her again.

"Answer her."

"Cecil never gave the letter to the attorney." *Please, God, help Mac find me.* She scanned the room for a possible escape.

Mrs. Rook smirked. "Don't even think it, Miss Glaze. You wouldn't stand a chance."

She wouldn't stand a chance if she stayed, either.

"Now, the letter. I know you must have found it by now. What was in it?"

She had no choice but to tell them. "The location of the evidence."

"Where?"

"Just past the step-off of the old bridge. On the McKenzie side."

Mrs. Rook smiled like Mona Lisa and blinked several times. "See, Miss Glaze? That wasn't too hard, was it? Now, tell us what you know."

"I told you all I know. I didn't dig up the evidence."

Mrs. Rook stared straight ahead at something for a long moment. "We know that." She sighed dramatically as if she was dealing with a moron. "Let's try this again. Tell us what you know *about us.*"

"I know you killed a girl's mother." The blood in her head rolled like pounding waves. She sat on the edge of the hard seat. If she stopped concentrating, she would either faint or throw up, so she focused on Mrs. Rook's eyes. "Why are you doing this, Mrs. Schroeder?"

An expression of something like respect covered her gaunt face. "You know who I am."

"Yes, but why are you doing this?"

"I don't like women, Miss Glaze."

The band of knots tightened around Marianne's stomach. "But you're a woman."

"A curse I've had to live with."

"Who hurt you, Alvina?" Marianne watched her frown, her eyes dark and brooding. "Your father, maybe? A brother? An uncle?"

The calm facade disappeared. "Shut up! Women bring nothing but degradation and shame."

"Mama—"

"Shut. UP!" Glaring at Hank, she turned to Marianne. "Eve was the first to sin, you know."

Eve? "But Adam was supposed to protect the garden."

Mrs. Rook's eyes flashed. "Eve sinned and dragged all of humanity into her evil plans. She shamed us all." She sounded like a parrot, spouting off recited words. "She shamed us ALL!"

Two candles quivered on the communion table beside Mrs. Schroeder. The stained-glass picture of a resurrected Jesus standing in clouds seemed to be balancing on her head.

"But the shame was taken care of," Marianne explained. "The Bible says that there is no condemnation for those who are in Christ Jesus. That includes women."

"Women bring shame on themselves. It is their due."

"Jesus' mother was a woman. She brought God's own Redemption into the world."

"The only woman chosen to do something of value." Mrs. Schroeder sniffed.

"Have you ever read Proverbs 31? A wife is a good thing, the Bible says."

Her lips pinched. "I read the new covenant. The old has passed away."

"Mary and Martha. One sister was busy, the other attentive. Which are you?"

"Busy." *The one Jesus didn't praise.* "Idle hands are the devil's workshop. I will have no part in pleasure. It is deceitful and vain."

"Is that what Georgie thought? That Brigitt Holcomb was to be degraded?"

Mrs. Schroeder slapped her. "Do not speak of him! He was sowing his wild oats. Anything is permissible when a young man is sowing his wild oats. Then when he is ready to marry, he is brought into the fold."

Holding her stinging jaw, Marianne opened and closed her mouth to try to ease the pain. "Did Georgie marry?"

"A wanton woman kept him from it. But she paid for her sins." She sniffed, her eyes dazed on a spot on the floor. "I saw to it."

"You killed her?" *The girl he got pregnant in Montana? How many does that make?*

Her unblinking eyes grew wider. "Georgie did. My Georgie did, and her mother. You see, Miss Glaze, redemption comes through blood."

"But only Jesus, the Lamb of God, brings redemption through blood."

"Obedience, not sacrifice. As a lamb to the slaughter." Mrs. Schroeder smiled as her gaze slowly made it up to Marianne's eyes. "Your redemption draweth nigh, Miss Glaze. Noah will kill you."

She shook her head against this woman's nonsensical ramblings. "Noah?"

Mrs. Schroeder indicated Hank. "Georgie's brother, my son, Noah Lyle Schroeder. Named after a man who allowed the world to die, except for a chosen few."

Mercy, but the woman could distort scripture!

"Now for the business at hand, Miss Glaze. Strip!" Her eyes glinted with unrestrained evil. "Your shame and degradation have caught up

258

with you, sister. Strip. *Now!"*

"You okay, Zach? I need to check on Marianne." Mac looked at Helen when Zach didn't answer him.

"Go." She flicked her head toward the door. "We're fine. I'll stay."

Mac stepped outside, lowered his head, and moved into the dense swirling snow. He edged past the burning barn and jumped back when the ceiling crashed in, spitting fire into the intense, swirling white. Biting snow nipped at his neck. He bounded up the back steps to the main house and into the mudroom, stomped the snow off his boots, and took them off. He slid out of his winter coat, hung it up, and headed inside.

Spotting a coffeepot on, he considered a cup but headed for the stairs instead.

"Mari?" He took them two at a time. "Marianne?"

He knocked on her door and listened. "Come on, Mari, don't pout. It was for your own good." He tried the doorknob. It was locked. He pounded on the door. "Mari? Come on, open the door."

When she didn't, he tugged out his keys, inserted one, and opened her door.

Darkness and an eerie quiet filled the room.

"Mari?" His gaze rested on the empty bed. A sickening feeling of dread gripped him as he strode to the bathroom and flipped on the light.

She isn't here.

He stared at her coat draped over a chair. Picking it up, he found her keys in the pocket. He tossed the coat on the bed and ran from her room, checked each bedroom, the attic, raced down the stairs. "Marianne!"

The den was empty, as was his office, the family room, the library, the living room, the media room. The pool and dressing rooms.

She's gone!

Frantic, he yanked his keys out of his pocket and slipped one into the gun cabinet. He checked the Beretta M9.

Loaded and ready, he headed outside.

"Miss Glaze, I said strip, now."

"Do what she says." Buddy Haynes leered at her, his gaze slowly gliding down her body. He twisted his handlebar mustache and sent her a slow wink.

Marianne expected him to lick his chops. Her teeth set as she made herself look into the same eyes that had haunted her. Shivering in the cold room, she plucked at a button on her shirt.

She didn't struggle when Buddy grabbed her booted foot. "Here, let me help you with these, Mizzzz Glaze."

She stared at a pew without really seeing it and tried to picture Mac smiling at her, teasing her, hugging her. She prayed he'd get to her before anything happened. She couldn't give up. But she couldn't figure out how to get out of this. *Please, Lord. Help me.*

Mac stalked around the wrap-around porch. Billowing whirlwinds of snow surrounded the house and yards, making visibility about five feet. He searched for footprints and found none. The yard lights were hazy globes through sheets of spinning snow.

It had been Marianne they were after, not Emma. He'd been stupid— *stupid!*—to leave her alone. He should have known Emma wouldn't get disoriented in the blasted snow. She'd lived here all her life and had been through worse storms than this. Stupid, stupid!

He called the two men at the cabin.

"She's not here, Mac."

He slammed a hand against the wall. "I don't know how they'd be able to get there in this weather but keep an eye out anyway."

Mac walked back outside. "Guide me, Lord, to where she is. I've done a lousy job of protecting her, but You know where she is." He stood on the side porch and considered every corner of the ranch. They had all been searched, were being re-visited by his men.

Gusts of snow-laced wind whipped at him. *Where are you, Marianne?*

His gaze settled on where the chapel would be. They would have had time to get there before the storm hit.

The gun lay cold in his hands as he ran through the blinding snow. He tripped and fell hard on his right shoulder. He grunted up and continued running through the angry wind slapping him back. With his head down, he turned and glanced behind him. The lights were no longer visible. He was blind now, groping in the white, hoping he was still headed in the right direction. He'd walked this way hundreds of times since he was a boy. *Be my eyes, Lord.*

Sensing something close by, he stopped. He reached out and felt a tree. No, a wall! He'd almost run into the chapel.

With both hands, he gripped the wall and felt his way to the front. He nudged the steps with his boot and stealthily climbed them. With the heel of a gloved hand, he cleared the snow off the small glass window in the chapel door.

Several men and a woman stood at the base of the cross with their backs to him. His breath caught when he saw Marianne sitting on a bench, facing them. Was that Mrs. Rook?

Quietly, he turned the doorknob. *Blast!* It was locked.

Feeling his way, he hurried around to the back of the chapel and blessed the day Emma had fallen from the huge oak tree in back. "I was just looking at the cross," she'd whimpered as she held her broken arm.

With spinning snow and ice in his face, Mac hugged the tree. He remembered one strategically-placed branch that led to the stained-glass window just to left of Mrs. Rook and Marianne.

He looked up and headed for it.

"Who was the woman in the picture?" Deliberately, Marianne twisted her second button in the guise of undoing it.

"What picture?" Mrs. Schroeder frowned at her.

"The picture hanging on the clothesline. Your insurance against the girls talking."

"Oh, that. You're inquisitive, aren't you, Miss Glaze? Well, since this is your final day on earth, I will tell you."

"Mrs. Schroeder." This, from Oscar. "Careful."

"I know what I'm doing! My sister and I started this little club, didn't we?" Turning back to Marianne, she cocked her head. "She was a mother with a big mouth. She went to the police after her daughter filled her in on our—" She smiled slowly. "—activities. Georgie silenced her for me, and the daughter."

"The girl he got pregnant?"

"No, Miss Glaze. We've already discussed her. Another girl."

"Where was she from?"

"Montana. Instead of keeping quiet about it, well, she paid for her sins, just like her daughter. As you are going to pay for yours, Miss Glaze. Now, hurry it up. Noah, undress her and tie her up. The fun is about to begin."

In the quiet, Noah walked to Marianne, turned her around, and tied her hands behind her. He spun her back around and reached for the third button on her blouse.

Breathless with fear, Marianne tensed as she looked up into his eyes. Evil grinned back at her.

Mrs. Schroeder pursed her lips. "If anything, I am fair, gentlemen. Each of you will have a turn."

No! Marianne's stomach muscles tightened just before she spun around and rammed Noah with her shoulder so hard that he fell back.

"Why you—!"

"Stop!" Mrs. Rook yelled as she—

The stained-glass window above her burst into thousands of tiny pieces spraying about the room. Like an avenging angel, Mac landed on his feet in a pool of shattered glass, the gun in his hand aimed right at Noah Schroeder.

"Nobody move!" Mac yelled, scanning the room. "Marianne, are you all right?"

She ran from Hank and then nodded on a sob.

Hank turned around. Mac shot him in the shoulder. Mrs. Rook screamed as she rushed toward Mac with a knife. He shot her hand, and she crumbled at the base of the cross, whimpering.

Another woman screamed and crawled on her knees toward Mrs. Rook. Mac aimed the gun at her. "Don't move!"

He waved the weapon from side to side as he eyed the other men. "Who's next? Who's next?"

No one moved.

"You." He pointed the gun at an older man. "Cut those ropes."

"Oscar."

Mac's gaze jerked to Marianne. Good. The terrified expression on her face had settled into something like relief. He shifted to Oscar. "One false move, and you're dead."

Oscar picked up the knife Mrs. Rook had dropped, cut the rope binding Marianne's hands, and turned to Mac as Marianne sank to her knees and curled into a ball, shivering.

"Are you all right, Mari?"

Her shaking fingers swept across her cheeks. "Yes."

"Oscar. Put the knife on the communion table."

Staring at Mac, Oscar opened his hand and the knife fell to the floor.

"Take off your coat and cover her." As Oscar slowly laid his coat over

Marianne, she tucked her feet up under it. "Oscar. Under the piano."

The older man straightened. His long thin face seemed comical with a gaping mouth and wide eyes. "I beg your pardon?"

"You'll be begging for more than that if you don't move *now*."

Hank shifted toward a moaning Mrs. Rook. "Another move, Hark, and your other shoulder 'll get a slug." Hank glared and froze.

"Lie down, Oscar, with your head toward me. You two." Mac waved his gun at the other men. "Here, in front of me. On the floor length-wise, feet to feet." His eyes narrowed. "Well, Charlie Blake. A small world, isn't it?" He gestured with the gun. "In the pew, on your face."

"Jenny." Sounding frantic, Marianne slipped her arms into the long coat and ran between two pews to the dark corner near the organ

"Where are you going?"

"They stabbed Jenny Harrison. Throw me a couple coats and a shirt or two. I've got to stop the bleeding."

"Oscar! Two coats and your shirt. Now!" Mac backed up and circled around Mrs. Rook and Hank, while Oscar took off his shirt, picked up the other coats, and frowned at Mac. "Take them to her, very slowly, very carefully."

Oscar inched toward Marianne.

"That's far enough. Now throw them to the right of her."

The coats landed near Jenny's head.

"Get back under the piano."

Marianne grabbed a shirt. "Jenny needs an ambulance."

"One's on the way for Emma. They can take Jenny, too."

"Is Emma all right?"

"Yes. We found her in the burning barn. She wasn't harmed, just scared."

"Noah's handiwork."

"Noah?" Mac scowled in her direction. "Who's Noah?"

Marianne pointed at Hank and Mrs. Rook. "Noah Lyle Schroeder. His mother, Mrs. Alvina Schroeder."

Mac frowned at his former housekeeper. "So, you're not Susan's aunt."

Sirens screamed outside as Mac pulled out his cell phone. "I'm calling the house, Mari, and telling them we need the ambulance up here." He punched in the numbers. "And that we've captured the Schroeder gang."

Flashing emergency lights mingled with falling snow as a kaleidoscopic cloak of peace blanketed the snow-covered yard. In her winter coat, Marianne stood with Mac on the front porch of the main house as EMTs shut the back doors on one of the ambulances. Groups of cowboys stood nearby. Geezer had his arm around Helen, which pleased Marianne no end. When she tried to smile, she yelped.

Mac touched her lip. "You're bleeding."

"A heavy-handed family, the Schroeders."

The ambulance took away Jenny and Emma, with Luke and Zach following close behind in Luke's truck. Another ambulance containing Mrs. Schroeder and Noah was being escorted off McKenzie Ranch by two sheriff's cars holding the other four gang members.

It was a night of wonders. Emma was fine, Jenny was talking and stabilized, and the Schroeder gang was in custody. Marianne nuzzled closer as Mac's arms tightened about her. "I can't believe Jenny's still alive."

"Keeping the knife in her bone actually helped. It also helped that the blade was small."

When Marianne shivered, he tugged her closer. "By the way, Hank was a lousy protector."

Mac looked down at her. "What do you mean?"

"He told me you ordered him to watch out for me, to protect me."

"I never said anything like that. I considered protecting you *my* job. Not anyone else's."

Nate walked grimly up the steps. "Been busy tonight."

"Yep." Mac released Mari and opened the front door. "So have you. Let's get some coffee and we'll fill you in on the details."

It ain't over.

The whispered words startled Marianne awake, and she gasped as she sat up in her bed, her heart pounding. She looked around. It was dark, and no one was in her room. She was alone. The ranch was sleeping. She must have been dreaming but everything was fine now. *Relax now. Everything is fine.*

Easing back into her pillow, she tried to relax her neck muscles with deep breaths, and finally did. Staring at the dark ceiling, she gave in to the sleep overtaking her.

Something pinched her cheek. Marianne tried to brush it away, but her fingers encountered something hard. Her eyes flew open.

"Well, now. You're awake, Marianne."

A ski mask covered the face of the sultry female voice just inches from her ear as a gun drilled into Marianne's face. It scraped down her jaw and then her neck. She gasped and reached up to push it away. It cocked. She stopped and raised her hands in surrender. Her ears buzzed with pure fear as her heart raced. *Who is this?*

"Get up now, nice and slow. We're going to pay Mac a visit." The gun dug into her neck. "Now." Laughter—low, slow, and wicked. "Doesn't that sound like fun?"

Keep calm. Do what she says. Breathe. Determined to keep her head, Marianne gently moved the covers off her legs and slid out. In the moonlight filtering through the lace curtains, she spotted the woman in her dresser mirror. The intruder stepped back, then jabbed the gun into Marianne's back. She flinched and twisted a fraction.

"Easy, now. We don't want anyone to get hurt yet, do we?"

She knew the voice. Where had she heard it? Her hand shook as she opened the door. The gun dug into her flesh again. She smelled a sweet fragrance and walked slowly down the hallway to Mac's door.

"Make it so quiet, Marianne, that he doesn't wake up."

Mac had no time to think. The turn of the knob. The swoosh as the door opened. Someone sprawled at the foot of his bed. He quickly turned toward the gun under his pillow.

"Don't!"

He stopped, hands frozen as he rested on his right elbow.

"One move I don't like and you're dead, Mac."

His hands slowly lifted as he turned and searched the eyes in the black ski mask. "Okay." His gaze locked onto Marianne.

"Sit, Marianne, next to him, so I can kill you both together."

What in the *world*? Who was this woman? Sitting up, Mac fluffed a pillow to divert the woman from his own pillow and the gun under it. With fear in her eyes, Marianne scooted close to him. She grabbed his hand and laced her cold, shaking fingers with his.

The woman reached over and turned on a lamp.

Mac noted the silencer on the gun pointed right at him.

"What are you doing, Cheryl?"

He turned to Marianne. "You know this woman?"

"She works for my father."

Cheryl giggled, plucked off the ski mask and tossed it happily into the air. She shook out her short blonde hair and snickered when the mask landed on Mac's knee.

"Oh." She shrugged and sat on a sofa. "I wrote a poem just for you two." She cocked her head playfully. "Are you listening?"

"We're listening, Cheryl."

Her smile changed into a pout as the gun spat at Marianne. Mac jerked. A tiny hole was in the center of the pillow next to him. Cheryl had barely missed Marianne's arm.

A totally different woman glared at them now. Evil. Ugly. "I don't like your attitude, Mari."

"I'm sorry."

"Good." Cheryl grinned like a little girl, tucked her legs beneath her, and wiggled her bottom. "Okay. Here's how it goes," she said, in a sing-song voice.

"Little Bo Peep, alone on the daze
Her mother and brother were taken awaze.
She thought it best
To let Mac rest
Beside a bloodied Glaze."

She shrugged. "Not my best work but you get the idea."

Mac noted her finger rubbing the metal trigger guard. "How did you get in here?"

"I've been in Mama's room all day. She told me to stay put if something happened to her and Noah, and to get both of you if it did. So." She giggled and shrugged as both hands flopped over. "Here I am."

"But why?"

"Why *not?*" In an instant, her teeth set; her face became stone-like and angry. "You just don't get it, do you, Marianne?"

Mac squeezed her hand, hoping she got the message: Don't talk.

Cheryl rolled her eyes and shook her head as if Marianne was stupid. "Okay. Here's the scoop. A year ago, Noah found Georgie's old diary. Georgie hated Bobby, Mac. He wrote about his plans to get back at the McKenzies because Bobby stole Brigitt from him. Mama and Noah decided to complete his plans."

Cheryl caught her reflection in the mirror and straightened her hair. "Mama's a computer genius. After you hired her, Mac, she hacked into Bonnie Milhouse's computer. She found out about the letter Marianne

266

would receive when she inherited the sheriff's property. We *wanted* her to come up here. We'd get the letter from her, and then kill her just for fun. Mama called in a tip to the police where to find Cecil's body. But ol' Bonnie spoiled our plans by placing a note in his file that said he didn't even have the letter—the day *before* Marianne came out here! Oh! Mama was so upset! You can just imagine. Our plans changed, of course. We had to find that stupid letter, instead of killing Marianne. So."

She glanced at Marianne. "We thought we could scare you away, have a little fun with you, but you just would not *scare!*"

Suddenly, her face became hard. "I'm really good with bombs, Mac. I loved watching your truck explode." Just as suddenly, her face became child-like again. "Mama didn't like it. Said too many cops would investigate what I did." Cheryl actually pouted. "Mama can think up awful, awful ways to discipline a child."

She placed a cupped hand against her mouth as if she were about to shout. But she leaned toward Mac and Marianne instead. "Cecil was killed," her words barely above mouthing them, "because he found out too much about Mama's little club. Mama believes in discipline."

She sat up straighter, fluttered her lashes at the ceiling. "Now let's see. Okay. Mama came up with this plan to not only stop you, Marianne—well, there was just so *much* she wanted to do to you. Scare you, stop you, break you. But she wanted, more than anything, to milk Mac and your daddy out of their money. She's done it before. She's really good at milking." She threw her head back and laughed. Then her head fell forward, and she was quiet for a few moments.

"So." Cheryl raised her head and giggled. "Mama hired on at McKenzie Ranch. Charlie, at I Spy. And me, with Patrick. Three of us milking like farmers!" She pulled an imaginary whistle chain. "Woot! Woot!"

Her smile wilted into a serious expression. "Patrick told me everything you were doing, Marianne. He was a real help to us."

"Did any of you kill my father?"

"No, Mac. Someone else did that."

"Do you know who?"

"No. We had nothing to do with it."

Mac pulled Marianne's hand closer. "You were the poet," he prompted. He had to keep her talking so he could figure out how to get them out of this mess.

"I'm really good at it."

"You are."

"And *you*—" A bullet shattered the mirror beside Mac. "—shot my mother and my brother!" She cocked her head, suddenly calm. Leaning back, she rested an elbow on the arm of the sofa and bobbed her head. "I have to kill you both now. Georgie and Mama said."

Was she kidding? "How old are you, Cheryl?"

"Twenty-six, Mac. How old are you?"

"Twenty-six. Do you always do what your Mama says?"

"Always." The little girl was back. "You don't know what she'd do to me if I didn't."

"Were you involved with this little gang of kidnappers, too?"

"Of course not. I was too young. The club disbanded a couple years after Brigitt died. But not for long. They just had too much fun to stop. Even then, Mama wouldn't let me be involved. Do you know where they got their girls, Mac? All over. They traveled to other states. Just all over, over, over."

"So why are you mixed up with this now? Your mother and brother are going to prison. You won't see them again for a long time."

Lifting a shoulder, she pouted. "Who says I want to?"

"Then?"

"You're as bad as she is, Mac. Why don't you just shut up and let me do what I have to do?" She sprang up, walked to the window, and pulled back the curtain.

Mac guided Marianne's hand under the pillow. She touched the gun and jerked. Their hands slid out just as Cheryl spun around.

"It's time." A hard, stone-faced Cheryl walked toward them. With a two-fisted hold on the gun, she raised it eye-level and closed one eye. "Say bye-bye, Mac. You're first."

He barked like a dog, startling her. Then he rolled off the bed. "Now, Mari!" he yelled, dodging Cheryl's aim and grabbing for her gun, but it went off just before he reached her.

"Stop it, you—!"

He was vaguely aware of Marianne falling off the bed.

"Ahh!"

"Marianne?"

Cheryl twisted against him. He grabbed her wrist. The gun fell out of her hand. "No!" she screamed and bared her teeth to bite him. Curling her arm behind her back, Mac forced her to the floor.

"My leg."

"Mari?"

"I've been shot, Mac."

"You can't do this!" Cheryl fought him as he grasped her other wrist.

He put his knee in her back, groped for a dresser drawer, yanked it open, and pulled out a set of plastic handcuffs, a birthday gift from Nate's brother when Mac turned thirteen.

"You can't *do* this! I *have* to kill you! Mama said!"

Mac quickly cuffed her hands behind her back, grabbed a blanket, and covered Marianne.

"Thank you," she said through gritted, chattering teeth.

"I need to stop the bleeding."

Cheryl wiggled, sobbing into the carpet. "The diary! Georgie wanted me to kill her! You can't stop me! You can't!"

Mac stepped over her, raced to his bathroom, grabbed a towel, and wrapped it around Marianne's leg. He stretched for his phone and dialed 9-1-1. "I need an ambulance and the police at McKenzie Ranch. I'm Mac McKenzie. We have a gunshot wound. Female. Shooter is cuffed. Yes, I'll hold." He punched the intercom button. "Ben? Ben! Wake up, buddy. It's Mac."

Cheryl squirmed and spat at Mac. "I *promised* to get her! The diary. He *told* me."

Mac pressed on Marianne's leg, and she squirmed. "I'm sorry, honey." He kissed her cheek. "I know it hurts. Please stay with me."

Cheryl growled, glared. "Georgie's diary! Don't you *see?*"

"Mac?" The intercom. "It's Ben. What's up, boss?"

Mac leaned toward Ben's voice. "I need you at the main house Now!"

"Right there."

Cheryl's feet slapped the carpet like a two-year-old in the throes of a temper tantrum. "I *have* to kill her! We're a family! He wanted me to kill her!"

"Why?" Mac rested the back of his hand against Marianne's face. "Hang in there, Mari. They'll be here soon." She squirmed, closed her eyes.

"Mama said. We're a family." Cheryl sobbed, her cheek scrunched against the carpet. "We're a family and she—"

"Yes?" Mac raised his voice to the dispatcher, cupping the phone with his hand.

"Hurt my family." Cheryl's shoulders jumped up and down as she sobbed. "We're a family. A family. The diary."

"Yes, thank you. I'll stay on the line."

Marianne smiled sleepily at him. It wouldn't be long before she was unconscious. *Not now, when we've come through so much, Lord.* "I love you, Marianne."

"I love you, Mac." Her words were slurred as her eyes slowly closed.

"Mac?" Ben, running toward his room.

"I *have* to kill her!"

The door opened. "What's going on in here?"

"A long story. Listen, an ambulance and the police are on their way." Mac gestured toward Cheryl. "Would you watch her until they get here? I have to apply pressure to Marianne's wound."

"What happened to Mari?"

"She was shot. I think the bullet went clean through her leg, maybe hit an artery. She's lost a lot of blood."

"Who's that?"

"The shooter, Cheryl Schroeder. Sister to Noah and Georgie Schroeder."

Ben stuffed his fingers into his pockets. "Thought we had all of 'em."

"Me, too."

"—have to—have to kill her—have to."

TWENTY-THREE

Helium balloons preceded Mac as he walked into Marianne's hospital room. Her quick laughter filled him.

"Who's in there?" She singsonged the words.

Lifting the balloons, he said, "Hello, beautiful." She was sitting next to the window. He quickly scanned her face and liked what he saw. She was less pale, and the circles under her eyes seemed less pronounced. Despite the tint of color in her cheeks, he could still see her lying on his bed, bleeding, hurting, drifting away from him. He honestly thought she'd stood a good chance of dying right in front of him. "How are you feeling today?"

"Better." She smiled as he bent over and kissed her. "The doctor said I could leave today with crutches. Two days is enough for me."

"And for me." He tied the balloons to the end of her bed. "Did you hear the good news? Brigitt's pregnant."

Her face brightened. "I know! Brigitt and Bobby came by this morning. They've been married six weeks, and they're already expecting. I'm so happy for them. I've had a lot of visitors today. Mrs. Porter and Tess from JoeMoe's, Brigitt and Bobby, Lindsey and Logan, Geezer and Helen—they're a couple now. Isn't that great? Jenny and Luke came by, too. I think they're building the friendship they wanted years ago. Oh, and Chef James popped in with the promise of baking me a German chocolate cake when I come back to the ranch."

"Then I better make sure I'm there when you do." Mac laughed with her. "It's been a good day, then?"

"The best. What's new with you?"

"I saw the diary." The next words he said would haunt his family forever. "George Schroeder killed my brother Joey."

"Oh, no."

"He was after Bobby and ran them off the road. Joey was killed and Bobby survived. He wrote in some detail about his feelings for Brigitt, his hate for Bobby, his plans to hurt Bobby's family."

He pulled up a chair and sat beside Marianne. "I talked to my mom this morning, and I couldn't bring myself to tell her. It'll happen. But I sure wish I could protect her and my family from knowing this."

Marianne reached for his hand. "I'm so sorry, Mac. So much tragedy caused by those horrible people."

He squeezed her hand. "Nate thinks there are more bodies. He's followed up with Montana authorities on what we know about the mothers and daughters who were killed. They're grateful for the help in solving those cold cases."

"So much to digest."

"There's more." Mac leaned forward. "I discovered that Mrs. Schroeder *is* a computer whiz. She had access to everything. I've hired a firm to check out my finances and business interests to see how much, if any, she was able to siphon off. I'd suggest your father do the same."

"He and Mom and Patrick just left to go to breakfast." She shook her head. "Did his diary mention Brigitt's death?"

"In detail. Georgie considered her his wife after he raped her. Disgusting stuff. When Bobby and Brigitt's engagement announcement came out, Georgie decided to kill her for the sin of adultery."

Mac's jaw clenched. "They had no qualms about writing down what they were doing. My father's name was never mentioned." Gently, he stroked her hair over her ear. "So, we'll continue to search for his killer."

"Did you read the entire diary?"

"Pretty brutal stuff."

"What was Cheryl talking about—George wanted her to kill me?"

"Not you specifically. Anyone who, not in his exact words, 'messed with the family.' They didn't want you exposing them. The gang wanted the letter; they wanted you stopped; and, they wanted money to flow from the McKenzie and Glaze coffers into their hands. Cheryl was the rogue, with the poems, the bomb."

"Did you find out how such a gang even got started? I mean, how do you approach someone with those wretched ideas and get them to join?"

"Mrs. Tomlinson is singing like a bird. The gang was her sister's idea, and all the men involved were cousins. Their first victims were wives of members of the commune in Montana who had ostracized the Schroeders. None of those wives were killed, just abused, punished. Later, the two mothers and daughters were killed. No one knew these men or could identify them. Then they came back here."

"Charlie Blake is a cousin?"

"Yes. Mrs. Tomlinson said the men were just 'funnin' you.' They wanted the evidence and the letter; the rest of it was just entertainment—except in the chapel. They planned to kill you that night. Oh, here. It's a copy, from the diary."

She took the note from him and unfolded it.

"Brigitt, Mari, don't be gay.

Your turn will come some day.

In shadows deep

His wish I'll keep

And blow you both away."

The paper fluttered in her hand. "They found out about Brigitt." She handed the note to him. "One thing's bothered me, Mac, that just doesn't make sense. Why in the world did they decide to have the last showdown at the chapel? Right smack dab in the middle of McKenzie land, where it would be so easy to get caught?"

"Mrs. Schroeder, the mastermind, said Georgie—and God—would be pleased to have your blood staining a holy place. She'd prepared for this night since your arrival."

"And it ended up being stained by her and her son's blood."

"They planned to leave after they found the letter and killed you." Mac shook his head. "She and Noah had stationed hidden cameras in each room of the main house, so they heard everything. That's how Charlie found you at the Tucker place, Buddy Haynes found you hiding in the den, and they got into your bedroom during the snowstorm."

"How did they know I would be at Uncle Cecil's house, that first day?"

"Mrs. Rook—Schroeder—hacked into Bonnie Milhouse's computer and set up a blind forwarding system where she saw any and all correspondence related to the Tucker place. Your call to his office that day was noted by his assistant. She saw that you were headed this way."

"And alerted the troops."

"She found out about Cecil's letter and the evidence a few months ago, after I hired her. Oh. George Radke is a cousin to Mrs. Tomlinson and Mrs. Schroeder."

Marianne's eyes widened. "So, he *was* involved."

"Probably. But there's no evidence to connect him unless someone in the Schroeder gang identifies him. Have you figured out why your uncle gave the location of the evidence to you?"

"He trusted me. He didn't want to take the chance of giving it to the wrong person."

"He didn't trust his own deputies?"

"Maybe." She lifted a shoulder. "It's the only explanation I can come up with. I've decided to give the evidence to the sheriff's department, but not the letter."

Mac stood and leaned over for a kiss. "Enough about this. When do you blow this joint, Miss Glaze?"

"About an hour. My family's taking me to Abilene."

He took her hand. He never tired of touching her. "I want you to come to the ranch to recuperate. I don't think I could stand having you three hours away from me right now. I've hired a new housekeeper, a Mrs. Thimble. She has a twelve-year-old daughter and is actually excited about having someone to take care of. Your family is welcome to stay, too, for as long as they want. We have plenty of room."

She smiled at him. "I'm not sure what my family will want to do but, yes, I'd love to stay at the ranch."

"And something else." He tugged a small, square black box out of his pocket and opened it. The ring he'd spent hours searching for sat in the box. "I know this is sudden—"

Marianne gasped and stared at the ring.

"But I'm as sure of this as I am of anything this side of Heaven." He sank to one knee. "I love you, Marianne, with every ounce of my being. But loving you isn't enough. I want you beside me as my wife, and I'm hoping you want the same dream. Will you marry me?"

"Oh!" Both hands covered her mouth as she looked into Mac's eyes. "Of course, I will." She laughed. "Yes."

He slipped the ring onto her finger, tugged her up and into his arms, and kissed her soundly.

She pulled back. "I'm a little suspicious of your motives, McKenzie. Is it me or my land you want?"

"Oh." He laughed and nuzzled her neck. "It's definitely the land."

"Well, it's a package deal, buddy boy. I come with the land."

His lips hovered over hers. "I was hoping you'd say that."

Marianne sat with Nuggets in Mac's new gazebo that faced the lake, across from the bench where she and Mac had snuggled one night. The new asphalt walking path from the house to the gazebo was a welcome addition. The path looped around the lake, ambled toward the chapel, and then disappeared into the grove of trees behind it.

"So, what are your plans now, sis?"

She continued stroking Nuggets who was asleep on her lap. "I'm getting ready, Paddy, to marry the most wonderful man I've ever known on February 7th. And to meet Mac's mother, Joan. She's due back in

274

about a week." Childish laughter raced across the expansive yards as she spotted Emma and Mrs. Thimble's daughter Miranda climbing a tree near the road. The promised warmer weather had stuck around for a few days. "What about you?"

"What about me?" In a characteristically Patrick move, his hands eased into the pockets of his slacks as he took two steps away from her. "Same 'ol same 'ol. I think the old man and I have reached an understanding of sorts. I want his money. He knows it, and in his twisted way, respects me for staying with him and working for it."

His steady gaze took in a full circle of McKenzie land. "Mac sure knows how to live. I could stand a ranch like this, with his wealth and all the perks."

"Mmm." She wanted to sigh, deeply, at his words. Patrick was so lost and didn't even know it. "And Mother?"

"We've met at a comfortable place of acceptance and, I don't know, affection."

"Is it so difficult to tell me you love her?"

"Maybe. Love and I are uncomfortable companions. I have none to give. I want none from anyone else."

"That's not true."

"Isn't it?" He sniffed and turned away.

No, Paddy, you need love more than anyone I know. "You were there when Helen and Eddie took Brigitt to the rock. You saw everything."

He lifted a shoulder and kept his gaze on the lake. "I fancied myself in love with her and was convinced she'd died because I did."

"Oh, Paddy."

"I never wanted to go back."

"Why didn't you let anyone know, especially me, after I started asking questions? That night, with Mother on the sofa. You could have told me about Eddie instead of Mother."

"I didn't want you to know I was there. Only Tim knew—well, Eddie knew but he's dead. I also thought it might help Mother to get it out, to get it said." He shook his head. "Water under the bridge now."

"You've seen Brigitt. How was it for you?"

"Difficult." He grunted. "She lived after all. Here comes Mother, on a mission, it appears. Listen, sis. Don't get in such a dither over me. I'm all right. So are you. So are Mom and Dad. So is Brigitt. All's right with the world and ain't that grand?"

If sarcasm hadn't laced his words, she would have been thrilled at them. But when she glanced into his eyes, quiet desperation looked back at her. "I love you, Paddy."

"Yeah, I know. See you later."

He ducked his head and walked off in the direction of the cottage he was using. He had the courtesy to wave at Barbara as she headed toward Marianne.

"Mother, you look well."

More than ten years had disappeared from her face since she'd entered the hospital weeks ago. Today, she wore a calf-length dress, chocolate-brown boots, a light wool sweater, and dangling gold earrings. She seemed alive and very well.

Their relationship had mended in small degrees in the days since Marianne's release from the hospital. Just this morning, her family had returned to check up on her.

"I'm good today." Barbara angled her head at Marianne. "Is your leg hurting?"

"Not much. I'm just tired of sitting around doing nothing but take, take, take. Here comes Daddy." She picked up her crutches and stood. Nuggets stretched and ambled off in the direction of the barn. "I'll give you two some time together on this beautiful day."

"No, no. He waved. I think he wants to walk with both of us to the house for lunch."

When Frank reached them, the first thing he did was kiss his wife. Marianne wanted to shake her head in astonishment. Who would have *ever* thought these two would get their act even half-way together and become a real couple again? *She* certainly hadn't. And here they were, acting like newlyweds on an extended honeymoon.

Until, of course, the next explosion.

But maybe explosions were what they needed. At least things were said, talked about, shoved out into the open. The 'pretending stage' of rehab hadn't crept up on them this time. Years ago, they'd all wanted so badly for everything to be ordinary that they'd allowed a façade of normalcy—those terrible masks—to cover up the wounds until they couldn't smell the decay anymore.

Frank offered Barbara his arm. "I'm under orders to escort the two most beautiful women on this ranch to lunch. Shall we?"

"I'll just slow y'all down." Marianne placed her crutches under her arms. "Why don't you two go on?"

"Absolutely not." Frank shook his head. "Orders are made to be followed, and Mac specifically said both of you were to come with me."

"All right." It was mildly uncomfortable being so close to her father.

Progress had been made in the last two weeks, but nothing could change his grating Type-A personality. But he tried. She tried. And somewhere in the middle, they were able to get along, for the most part, with Barbara's gentle nudges and clearing her throat when she couldn't nudge.

Hammers pounded as they walked past the skeleton of the new barn, but the sound of an engine starting drew Marianne's attention. Mac's white truck backed up and then headed down the walking path toward them.

He stopped and got out. "I felt a raindrop as I got into my pickup, so jump in if you want a ride."

They all climbed aboard and headed for the main house. When her parents got out of the truck, Mac said, "Barbara, Frank, would you excuse us? I'd like to show something to Marianne. We'll be back in just a few minutes."

He drove her out to the chapel. Just before they reached it, lightning flashed, and thunder answered. A light rain began to fall.

Mac parked the truck. "I should have thought to build a carriage entrance out here for you, so you wouldn't get wet in the rain—or snow." He leaned over and kissed her. "We'll do that as soon as we have a couple of good days of sunshine together."

He got out, opened his umbrella, and held it over her as she hobbled up the stairs and inside. "You can sure move with those crutches."

She chuckled, spotted a little book on the back table, and picked it up. "What's this?"

"My journal." Mac stood beside her as she touched the cover. "You're mentioned in it." He took it from her and fanned the yellowed pages. "I was hoping to show it to you. I was nine and apparently thought freckles, red hair, and a prissy attitude were a potent combination." He smiled and handed it back to her.

"I'll have to read this sometime." She touched the cover again, and then placed it on the table.

Mac took her crutches and leaned them against the wall. Then he slipped an arm about her back and one under her legs and lifted her.

"What are you doing?"

"Being chivalrous." He walked down to the front of the chapel, next to the podium, and set her on her foot. But he kept his arm tucked under hers, just where she wanted it.

She looked around. "Such wickedness was in this place." For a moment, she saw flying shards of colored glass, Mac freeze-framed in the center, legs bent, shoulder forward, eyes squeezed shut, crashing through the picture of Jesus' resurrection. She had never felt such relief in her life, when his gaze wildly searched, and then rested, on her. "You saved me," she whispered, "on this very spot."

He brushed a strand of hair out of her face. "I don't want you to remember that day. That's why I brought you out here. Nothing of the Schroeder gang is in here now. I want you to remember the chapel as it is now, as it will be on our wedding day. See the stained-glass window?"

A warm feeling of peace enveloped her. "It's been replaced."

"Yes. And the communion table."

The floors were spotless and shiny. The muted light of the rainy day eased through the lovely multicolored windows, making the room soft and restful. "I wish your father's killer had been found."

"It took over seventeen years to find these killers, and seven years to find Cecil's. Evil doesn't win. And besides." He kissed her neck. "We have an ace investigator in the room."

She chuckled. "No way, buddy boy. I love researching, nosing out the details, investigating. But I use all those skills in my art. No more investigating murders for me—unless, of course, evidence pops up in your father's case."

She rested a hand on his arm. "What are we going to do with Uncle Cecil's house? Have you thought about it?"

"My vote is to tear it down, but we'll do what you want with it."

"I'd like to take out some treasures first. I don't consider it a place for wishes anymore."

"You don't?"

She solemnly shook her head. "My place for wishes is right here, where you are."

He tugged her into his arms. "Listen."

A strong wind whipped against the walls and roof.

He lowered his mouth.

Lightning flashed.

His lips touched hers.

Thunder rolled.

He kissed her deeply as waves of a thick cleansing rain washed over the chapel.

She opened her eyes. "I love you, Mac."

"I love you, Marianne. Love survives." A whisper, just before he lowered his mouth again.

She wanted to say, "It does," but all she could do was nod.

Rosie Won't Stay Dead

ONE

Luke McKenzie shoved his overstuffed backpack into the bed of his pickup, secured the hard cover, and looked around the ranch. Sparse trees and vegetation surrounded him as cattle dotted the land and oil rigs slowly dipped and rose against a breeze rushing through the spring grass.

Luke loved this ranch, this part of the Texas panhandle.

But he needed to get away for a few weeks.

He hadn't slept well in a long time and leaving McKenzie Ranch and the stress since Dad's murder might help. Everywhere he looked, he saw his father, and he needed a break from the guilt and the loss.

Luke wanted to hike in the Colorado Rockies with only his golden retriever, Molly, for company and soak in the beauty that always nourished his soul. And, first thing, he wanted to hike Bear Camp Trail where he'd spend a night or two in the cave he'd discovered years ago. The trail was closed to hikers until the fifteenth of May, which meant he'd have it all to himself.

"Let's go, Molly girl. Time's a-wastin'." He laughed when his golden retriever bounded over to him and danced around his feet. He wasn't one to show his emotions much, but Luke was as excited about leaving as Molly.

Behind him, his younger brother Mac, the owner of McKenzie Ranch, came out of the main house and said, "You about to leave, buddy?"

Luke turned around, grateful Mac had seen his need for a break. But if anyone should be getting away, it was Mac. He and his wife had faced off against a gang last December that the sheriff had called 'pure reprobates.' The one week Mac and Marianne had spent on their honeymoon in February hadn't been enough of a break, Mac had told him, so they planned to get away in the fall to the family cabin in Little Texas, Colorado, that Luke was headed for today.

"Just about ready, but I hate putting more work on you by going."

"I have plenty of help. Now, go. You haven't had a vacation in two years, so have fun. Hike. Enjoy being alone. If you don't, I might have to send you back out there." Mac squeezed his shoulder. "Really, buddy. The ranch 'll survive without its foreman for a month. Take six weeks, if you need to."

"'Preciate it, bro'." When Luke opened the driver's door of his truck, Molly jumped inside the cab and barked at him. "I know, girl. We're fixin' to leave."

He turned back to Mac to say goodbye. It was harder than he thought it would be to leave the ranch, his life, his responsibilities. But he needed to get away more than he needed to stay. Maybe in the

Rocky Mountains, he'd find some peace about Dad's murder. That would be his number one goal—and maybe a little forgiveness, too, for not being there when Dad needed him.

Luke hugged his brother, then got in the truck and started it.

"Be careful and have a great time."

"I will, Mac. See you in a month." Luke backed up his truck, waved, and headed for Little Texas, Colorado, in the high country of the Rockies.

At two o'clock in the morning, Sarah Morgan loaded the last of her luggage into her car. Kansas had been unusually warm for May, and the garage was stifling hot. But if the man who'd attacked her twice six months ago was outside watching her house, she didn't want him to see her packing to leave. She would hide in here until the very last moment.

Her mother was standing in her pajamas by the door leading to the kitchen, arms crossed, a worried expression on her face.

Sarah touched her arm. "I'll be fine, Mom. I have to do this."

"I know." She gripped Sarah's hand. "Just be careful, honey. Never stop watching for him."

"I won't. Where's Dad?" She reached up and opened the kitchen door. "Dad, come on. I'm leaving."

Sarah didn't want to see worry on his face, too, but there it was as he walked down the steps and gave her a hug.

"You sure you don't want us to go with you? Help keep you safe?"

"That would defeat my purpose, Dad. Can you catch the lights, so they won't come on when I open the garage?"

Her father flipped a switch.

At least in the middle of the night, it would be easier to spot someone following her. If she suspected he was, she'd call 9-1-1 and drive straight to the nearest police station.

"Okay, then." She looked from her mother to her father. "Group hug." She felt their deep love and concern for her in the especially long, tight hug. Pulling back, she said, "I have to go. The Rockies are calling me. Oh, Mom."

Tears were rolling down her mother's face, and Sarah grabbed her in a tight hug and held her for a few seconds. She felt her father's hand on her back. "I know this is hard for you, but I'll be careful and smart. I promise."

She smiled at both of them, trying to reassure them that she'd be fine. "I love you both. I'll call you at every stop until I get to Little Texas."

Luke arrived at McKenzie Cabin a little before nine that night. He took his things inside the cabin, showered, and went to bed. He was tired, but not too tired to wake up before five and get out on Bear Camp Trail, his favorite hike.

The alarm sounded at 4:30. He'd crammed everything he needed into his backpack in Texas, and he was ready to go a few minutes before five.

He stepped outside and took a deep breath.

It was always the same on his first morning in Little Texas, Colorado. He relished the thin air, the crisp morning, and the glorious beauty of snow-capped mountains. He would never admit to anyone at McKenzie Ranch that their tough-guy foreman needed this. For him, the old saying was true: there's no place like home. He loved Texas. The panhandle was the only place he ever wanted to live, but he loved these mountains, too.

At straight-up five o'clock, he locked McKenzie Cabin and slowly made his way to his pickup as he admired the panoramic beauty around him. Molly was standing by the driver's door of his truck, her whole body wagging in anticipation. "Me, too, girl. Me, too." With a quick laugh, Luke opened the door. She jumped inside and made her way to the passenger window. He rolled it down, and she leaned out and sniffed the cool mountain air.

He drove about five minutes to the dirt road leading to Bear Camp Trail. As he passed the only cabin on this stretch, he thought the owner had one of the best views in the area.

He parked down a bit from the trail's starting point and opened his door. Molly jumped out, made a quick right turn, and passed a sign that said, "Trail Closed for the Winter." Good. He'd be alone and could hike at his own steady pace. Just too much to see to rush through this day.

Sarah tried hard not to be afraid. She'd made the trip in just under five hours, had taken everything into her parents' cabin, locked all the doors, and was sitting on the chair closest to the fireplace, ready to jump out of her skin. She took a deep breath and blew it out. No one had followed her. *He* hadn't followed her, to be more specific. Now, she just had to relax enough to enjoy being here.

Tomorrow, she decided, she'd get up early and head out to Bear Camp Trail, just around the corner from her cabin and down a bit. She would be brave and hike by herself.

But right now, she needed a nap.

She took two long naps, ate a little supper, crawled into bed, and called her parents for the third time that day. She set her alarm for four o'clock, so she could be ready to hike by five.

She awoke before the alarm, got dressed, braided her long hair, and checked her day pack. She was ready to go.

She opened the cabin door and looked outside.

It was still dark. With no streetlamps near her family's cabin, she couldn't make out specific shapes. If the killer stood beside a tree, she wouldn't see him.

But he didn't follow her here. She'd been very alert, very careful. She was as sure as she could be that he wasn't here, despite the fear she'd heard in her parents' voices every time she called them. Both of them thought she was still in danger. *"If you want to come home, honey, just call me. I'll fly out and drive you home"*—her father. *"Honey, just be careful. Keep me posted. Don't forget to lock your doors"*—her mother. Their constant worrying and hovering was a good enough reason to get away.

She needed her independence again.

She stood still and enjoyed the quiet morning, listening, watching. The longer she stood there, the more she could see; the black of night was becoming a deep gray. She narrowed her eyes, searched the area around the cabin, and took one step outside. A bull elk lying in the grass blended in with the pewter-brown colors of a tree. He turned his racked head toward her, rose to his feet, and bounded off.

She looked up. A few stars were still visible, but the sun was on its way. Her bicycle leaned against the cabin. No more treadmill or indoor cycling or stair stepping. Nodding, she turned on the flashlight. Just a few hours of hiking today. Three hours up. Three hours back.

She pulled the locked door shut. Something moved behind her. She spun around, fumbled her flashlight, and dropped it on the pavement. She swiped it up and turned it on. It didn't work.

Her heart pounded as she backed into the door and grabbed the knob—but it was locked! Frantic, she searched the yard as she imagined her attacker sneaking around the corner of the cabin and grabbing her.

A squirrel's head popped out from behind a nearby pine tree. He stared at her. When Sarah moved her hand, he hurried behind the tree.

"Okay. It was only a squirrel." She took in a deep breath and let it out. "Just a squirrel."

She'd taken to talking to herself lately. Sometimes, the words were a prayer. Other times, she needed to hear someone—herself—telling her she'd be okay again. She was determined not to let the attacks define her, but she had so many questions about that night. It had been dark. She'd been in bed. Her house had been locked up tightly. With no broken windows, how had he gotten inside without a sound?

And how had he overpowered her so quickly?

She would have been dead like his other two victims if her roommates hadn't come into the house, laughing and calling her name. When he heard them, he leaned over her and whispered, "Later, sugar plum."

The police came and left. Her parents insisted she stay with them that night. She did, but he found her there—later—five hours after the assault.

Sitting in the dark in her old bedroom, wide awake, holding pepper spray and wondering how in the world she would ever fall asleep again, she heard something. Not knowing if it was one of her parents or him, she rushed behind the bedroom door. Her whole body quaked as someone crept into her room. When she saw him, she sprayed the back of his head and continued spraying as he turned around.

And then she screamed. God help her, she screamed until she had no voice left. Her father raced into her downstairs bedroom with a rifle, but the man was gone.

The police questioned her again. She had nothing for them—not his description, his weight, or skin color. He was taller than her, but that wasn't saying much. She'd completely focused on the back of his head and the pepper spray.

The media had dubbed him the Darkslayer because he'd murdered his victims in their own bedrooms in the dark. Sarah was the only known survivor.

Most of her life, she had scolded herself for being afraid of the dark. But never again. She knew now what the dark could hide.

She didn't want to think about that night right now.

Her total focus needed to be on the bike ride. Down this street. Around the corner. About five hundred feet to the dirt road. Another half mile to the trail.

Then she'd focus on hiking for a few hours. Early, on a closed trail, so no one would bother her. She wanted to take a long nap under a tree, climb up to a great view of the mountains, and sit and enjoy her picnic. She wanted to *live*.

"Okay. It's time."

With all the courage she could muster, she hurried to her bike and rode toward the trail.

Man, it was good to be in the Rockies!

Luke breathed in deeply, held his breath, and blew it out. He looked up the trail. It was an easy, steady climb—except for the altitude. Five minutes of hiking, two minutes of catching his breath. Start and stop, start and stop for the first hour. Home was about eighteen hundred feet above sea level. Starting out at eight thousand feet and heading up was a big jump for him. But he would enjoy the pauses for catching his breath as much as he'd enjoy the hike. It was just his way.

Maybe he should have waited a couple days to acclimate to the high altitude before hiking. Most hikers would have. But he'd needed to be out here. "You doin' awright, Molly girl?"

She barked and ran ahead of him.

They came to a sign that said "Scenic Overlook" with an arrow pointing east. They climbed up to it, enjoyed the view, and then headed back down to the trail. By late morning, they'd reached the first pasture. Luke felt a couple of raindrops, looked up, and laughed. "This day's just gettin' better and better, isn't it, girl? C'mon. There's a place to settle in right over here." He headed for an outcropping of rock, sat under it, and watched the rain show. This was just what he needed.

He thought of a nap—some of the best rest he'd ever had was in high altitude. The air had cooled, and the lack of sleep from his long drive yesterday was catching up with him. He covered himself with his jacket and lay his head on his backpack.

He could already tell he was starting to relax here. Just seconds after putting his head down, his eyes felt heavy with the need to sleep. As he started to doze off, he thought how good it was to be in the mountains again. Molly curled up next to him. He draped an arm over her and drifted into sleep.

Sitting under a Ponderosa pine tree, Sarah grinned to herself. This day had been perfect. She'd done everything she wanted to do.

Picnic. *Check.*

Climbing up to a lookout point and admiring the view. *Check.*

Waking up under a tree after a solid two-hour nap. *Check.*

The rain shower was a bonus. Everything smelled sweet and fresh now. She loved how the first signs of spring had dressed up the valleys a little bit, but the mountains still wore their caps of snow. Was there any place as delightful as this?

She was alone—yes!—and so very brave. *Check and double check.*

She chuckled at herself and stuffed her things into her daypack.

Listening to the mountain stream below her had helped her to fall asleep. She stood and walked to the trail's edge. Above her, the mountains loomed, great and beautiful. Below her, the stream playfully bubbled over rocks as if it were thrilled to finally be out of the hard winter freeze. This world was exactly what she'd needed to learn to live again.

Smiling, she leaned over to better see the stream when footsteps sounded behind her. She gasped and started to turn around, but hands pushed hard against her back, forcing her over the edge.

A short, piercing scream popped the silence like a whip.

Luke jerked awake and sat up. "Did you hear that, Molly?" He rubbed his eyes and tried to shake the sleep out of his head, but the high-altitude grogginess held on. "Sounded like somebody screamed."

Molly whimpered and inched closer to him. Her whole body was shaking.

"C'mere, girl." He picked her up and stroked her side as he glanced around. "It was probably an animal. Cougars scream. Coulda been a cougar."

Molly's head snapped toward the gaping mouth of the woods that swallowed up their hiking path. She scrambled to her feet, lowered her head, and growled, low and steady.

"Or a red fox." Luke looked up. "Storm's gone. We got three hours yet to make it to the cave 'fore night gets here. So let's go—"

Like a shot, she raced through the tall grass and stopped at the opening to the woods, barking and dancing as if asking his permission to run inside.

"No, Molly. We just came from there. We need to keep go—"

She disappeared into the foliage.

"Well, great. Is 'go' the only word you understand today?" He grabbed his pack, slipped it on, reached for his water bottle and placed it in his waist pack as he sprinted toward Molly. He'd planned this day thoroughly and *running toward trouble* wasn't on his to-do list. But he knew something was wrong by Molly's behavior. He'd check it out and then get back on the trail.

He slowed down as he stepped into the quiet forest. Only in the Colorado Rockies could an afternoon rain draw such scents from the trees and brush. He wanted to stop and take a good whiff, to savor the beauty of these mountains, but Molly's persistent barking pulled him on.

He jumped over bulging roots, dodged low-hanging wet branches, and eased between pointed rocks that seemed to shoot up out of the ground. He rounded a tree-lined switchback into a narrow valley. All was silent but for the aspen leaves shivering in the breeze.

He spotted Molly and jogged toward her. She was struggling to keep her paws planted on a slippery slope as she barked at something down below.

"Okay, girl. What'd you find?" Luke grabbed her collar, tugged her back, and leaned over. About ten feet below them, a woman sprawled face-down in the tall grass, her head not five feet from the rushing mountain stream. A long blonde braid rested on top of her small daypack. Her arm lay across the small of her back, twisted in the straps of her pack.

"Well, I'll be." He'd never known a hiker who'd fallen off such a wide trail. Maybe her foot slipped on the wet incline.

Molly yelped and nudged Luke's leg several times as if to say, "Hurry! Help her!"

The woman lifted her head, rolled over, and screeched when she saw them. With the agility of an athlete, she jumped to her feet and then winced and fell to one knee, struggling against the straps of her daypack. She teetered and fell back. Her head jerked toward Luke. Her wide eyes watched him as if he was holding a bloody knife.

"Are you hurt?" Luke started the slide down and tried to keep his gaze on her, but it was difficult to plant his feet on the slick hill. He slipped and grabbed a tree. "Do you need help?"

As he continued down, she rolled to her right side. Her left foot dug into the wet grass, propelling her awkwardly through the tall thick brush bordering the stream.

"Look. I'm not going to hurt you." He reached the bottom of the ravine. "I'm trying to help you." But the terror in the woman's eyes told him to stop, to back up. So, he did.

Her gaze never left him. Her eyes were the same color as the amber-gold stone on one of his belt buckles. Her right foot touched the ground, and she sucked in a breath and reached for her ankle.

"Leaving your boot on will help support a sprain." He took a step toward her as she struggled against the straps of her small daypack. "Would you like some help with that?"

Her clothes were wet. *Dry, warm, hydrated.* The three musts in a hiking accident. "You're wet. You must be cold. Do you have a jacket?"

She didn't blink or even acknowledge she'd heard him.

Another step.

Her full lips firmed into a straight line, although she shook like a leaf. "You p-pushed me."

"No, I didn't."

Another step.

Her body shook so hard, he thought he could hear her teeth clattering. He talked to her as he would an injured horse: softly, with unwavering eye contact. "Does anything else hurt besides your ankle and your shoulder?"

Two more steps forward.

Her hand trembled as she brushed strands of blonde hair from her face and stared at him. A tiny woman, she couldn't weigh more than a large sack of feed.

"I felt you push me."

"I couldn't have. We were asleep under a ledge. Your scream woke us up."

"This trail is closed. No one else is hiking here."

"Someone is, if you were pushed."

"There is no 'if.' I was pushed."

Molly nudged her hand, and she jerked. Then she smiled for the first time and patted Molly's head as if she could sense the dog wouldn't hurt her. "Hello." She glanced at Luke as she held up the dog tag, then read it. "Molly. It says, 'McKenzie Ranch, Texas'." Another glance at Luke, as if she were afraid to take her gaze off him. "Are you a cow-herding dog, Molly?"

Good. With the woman's attention on Molly, Luke might be able to help her and then get back to the trail and his plans. "Here, let me get that strap for you."

He gave her time to get used to the idea by slipping off his pack and setting it against a tree. With his hands in the air, he approached her. "I'll just loosen this—" The woman leaned to the side, her wary gaze on him. Molly settled next to her. "—and you'll be on your way." He gently untwisted the straps and then stepped back about five feet. "There. Better?"

"Yes," she muttered. "Thank you." She rubbed her shoulder, still staring at him. "I felt hands on my back. Someone else is here if—if it wasn't you." Her arms went around Molly's neck, and she tugged her closer as if they'd known each other for a while instead of a few minutes.

"My truck's the only one parked at the trailhead. Not another place to park for at least a couple miles. 'Course, he could have hidden a bicycle somewhere. Or parked after I did. Or come off another trail."

The woman's body told him she was afraid of him. Her gaze fastened on everything but him. Her hands rubbed her lower arms and found their way to her shoulders. And, of course, her body vibrated as if she sat in ice.

"You're—you're not in cahoots with him, are you? Not part of some... some c-cowboy gang preying on women or... anything?"

"'Course not. Even if I had such inclinations, Molly wouldn't let me give in to them. It's not in her nature to stand by while someone's being hurt. *She's* the one—" Luke lowered his voice when the woman's lips pressed together as if she tried to hold back tears. "—who came to your rescue."

In profile, her chin quivered. Her gaze connected with his for a moment, and then she shut her eyes and turned away from him as if she could make him and her troubles vanish.

The trail ridge above them disappeared into thick pine and aspen trees. Nothing but dense shrubs and weeds on the way up. "We'll have to bushwhack out of here. The brush is too thick to walk in, much less carry someone."

Her head snapped up. "I can walk."

"Good." He held out a hand, moved his fingers in a come-on-give-me-your-hand gesture, and she took it. Her hand felt soft and small in his.

She took a step, sucked in a breath, and clutched his arm. "Okay. So, I can't walk."

"Yeah." Irritation gnawed at him like a burrowing tick. Just a simple trek in the mountains. That's all he'd wanted. A man and his dog enjoying the untamed mountains of Colorado—alone. Being alone had been his top priority for hiking today. And here he was, *not* alone and responsible for an injured woman. He wanted to ask her what in the world she was doing out here by herself. Every seasoned hiker knew not to hike alone. And because of her foolish decision, he was stuck with changing his plans on his first day here!

"I'm not asking you to stay."

He scooped up her sleeping bag and clipped it to his backpack. "I wouldn't leave an injured animal stranded, much less a woman. I'll have to carry you back to the trailhead."

Her jaw dropped, and she shook her head. "You can't possibly." She glanced around as if she hoped to find a trail-ready gurney with wheels leaning against a tree. "It's too far."

"And not getting any closer while we stand around and yap about it." Actually, it wasn't a bad idea to head back. Dark clouds lined the horizon. If he didn't miss his guess, snow lay thick in them—snow that hadn't been in the forecast.

"You need to get dry clothes on." He held up her daypack.

"I intended to." She took it and lifted her chin. "Turn around."

He did. "Make it quick. We'll lose light in another couple hours." Clothing rustled behind him. The woman drew in a quick breath and moaned. Must be her shoulder or her ankle. He'd have to be careful with both when he carried her out.

"I'm ready."

"Great." He clipped her pack to his. "Let's go."

He slung his backpack on and picked her up. "Arms around my neck, shift some of the weight. Better yet, straddle my waist—" She inhaled sharply. "—and I'll support your back."

A blush. The woman was blushing. Her chin eased up as her mouth pinched. "I most certainly will not."

She reminded him of his ninth grade science teacher, Mrs. Harrigan. Anyone who disrupted her class with even the slightest hint of humor was called "Mr. Hooligan" or "Miss Hooligan." She'd said it disdainfully, with the same puckered mouth and raised chin he faced at the moment. "Which part of what I said will you most certainly not?"

"I'll not...not...and you...you probably pushed me so...so you could..." Her lips pinched even more. "Put me down. I'll manage by myself." Her queen-of-the-rodeo stance probably would have worked had she not blushed all over herself again.

"Suit yourself, lady. I hope you came prepared to spend the night. That ankle will need healing time before you head back and that means no standing on it." He unclipped her pack and her sleeping bag, set them on the ground, and started walking away. He had no intentions of leaving her alone. He'd stay back. Watch her. Protect her if it came to that, but he couldn't force her to go with him.

He hadn't taken five steps when Molly stopped and looked back at her.

"All right. I'll do it."

He stopped, too, but didn't turn around. A part of him wanted to keep walking, but the stronger need to help her won out.

"I said I'd do it," she added in a louder voice.

"Then let's go. Time's a-wastin'." He walked back, attached her gear, and came as close to grumbling out loud as he possibly could without actually making a sound. The woman reminded him of a newborn colt—skittish, unable to plant her feet, and scared of everything.

Just what he needed for his vacation.

"Can't we leave your pack? I could ride piggy-back."

"No." He winced at the force of the word and made the next ones come out more gently. "We might need it. These mountains are unpredictable." As the coming storm indicated.

He settled the woman on his waist pack. Another blush crawled up her neck and face. She placed her arms to her side, but he knew she couldn't balance herself like that for long. "You're going to have to hang onto me. I have to use both hands to grab trees to get us topside. But first things first." A strand of her hair teased his chin, and he swatted at it. "I'm Luke McKenzie."

Another pinch took over her mouth as her perky little nose lifted a couple inches.

"Do you have a name?"

"Why do you want to know?"

"It's a custom in the state of my birth, actually. We exchange names in Texas, usually in a friendly manner. That way, we can communicate."

"We can communicate without names."

"Fine. I'll call you Myrtle."

She laughed. "Okay. I'm Sarah."

He looked into her eyes. Little specks of black made them interesting. "Dimples. Nice," he said. "So, Miss Sarah, I guess I can't expect a last name with that."

She raised her chin, a look with which he was becoming all too familiar. "You're perceptive, Luke McKenzie. I like that."

"Peachy," he muttered and reached for the nearest tree.

TWO

"Let's rest." Luke set Sarah on a huge boulder. "Despite the fact that you're as tiny as a mole, you're getting heavy." He checked out the trail ahead of them as he slid his pack off.

"I'm not that tiny. You're just big."

"How much do you weigh? A whopping hundred pounds?"

"Plus five."

"That's tiny. And you're what? Five foot?"

"Five-two. You?"

"Six-three."

"A foot taller. I'm impressed."

"Then you impress far too easily."

"You'd be surprised," she mumbled, unscrewing her canteen's lid. "How much farther?"

"We've been hiking an hour. It'll be long after dark before we get back."

"I brought extra rations and came prepared to spend the night if necessary."

He took out his water bottle and drank. A black squirrel sat on a branch above them, swishing its tail, staring him down. The little booger was probably wondering when they'd be getting out of here so he could scamper to his heart's content. "I'm with you on that, buddy," Luke mumbled and glanced at Sarah.

He took a moment to study her. She was small, with a long, thick braid down her back. Real blonde, like it didn't come out of a bottle. An appealing mouth with full lips and a perky nose that seemed to enjoy the air since she put it up there so often. Her body was slim and well toned. Maybe a tennis player or a swimmer. Or a hiker. It was her hair that caught his attention. Really thick and long. Not great hair for ranch life, and that made him wonder what she did for a living.

But he wasn't interested enough to ask. He just wanted to get her home so he could get home himself, rest, and try this hike again in the morning.

He turned his back to her. They were buried in a switchback where the mountains weren't visible. The sky was covered up with tall pines and aspens.

It was then that he noticed the quiet.

No birds sang. No ground squirrels popped out of hidden havens. He looked up; the black squirrel was gone. Something had caused him to leave—or the person who'd pushed Sarah was still out here.

Luke glanced around as his hand slid to the hunting knife on his belt. He held his breath and turned a slow circle, searching from tree to tree for someone watching them, crouched to strike, ready to finish what he'd started with Sarah.

Sunlight crawled across the area where he stood as more clouds separated. Luke unsnapped the knife case and eased the blade out. A spurt of wind caused the aspen leaves to quake above him.

In the quiet, he didn't move for several moments.

Then the hair on the back of his neck suddenly rose.

He squinted into the deep green shadows surrounding them. "Sarah," he spoke slowly, softly. "You're sure someone pushed you?"

She looked up, and their gazes locked. "Yes," she answered and glanced around warily.

"But why push you? Why leave you? Did he follow you down, check on you?"

"I don't know to all of your questions."

Luke sheathed his knife. "We need to get out of here. Now." He reached for his backpack and stopped, his arm in mid-air. Uneasy, he quickly glanced over his shoulder.

Molly whimpered and looked down the path with worried eyes.

Everything seemed to be on pause, waiting for something to happen.

"Get down, Sarah."

A gun fired. Bark flew off a tree a couple feet from them. Sarah yelped and swatted at her ear.

"Get down! Down, Molly!" Luke tackled Sarah by the waist and plunged them both behind the boulder as the leaves on the ground jerked and danced to more gunshots.

Sarah gasped and clutched Luke's arm. "He's back, Luke. The man who—"

Bullets stabbed the tree above them. Debris fell on their backs as they squatted. They couldn't stay in this position much longer. Luke's legs were already starting to cramp.

"Be still," he breathed into her ear. With his shoulder, he nudged her over a few inches, then they both turned around and sat. Luke drew up his legs and positioned his body protectively beside her. He opened his fanny pack holster and checked his gun. It was loaded with the safety on.

"Is that legal here?"

"Actually, yes."

They were sitting ducks. Nowhere to hide but right where they were, out in the open in this idiot's line of fire.

Unless...

He looked through the trees. It took him a few seconds to locate the brush covering the cave. This boulder was the marker he'd used to spot the hidden opening on previous hikes. Every year, he intended to explore it but had never done it. He'd been inside far enough to know that it had potential to be a deep cave.

"—and Lord, keep us safe, please," Sarah whispered. "And thank you. Amen."

Humbled by her words, Luke nodded. "Amen."

Silence enveloped them. Luke turned his head and strained to listen but heard nothing. "Do you have any idea who's after you, Sarah?"

"Maybe you're his target, and he didn't want a witness, so he pushed me out of the way."

Bullets sprayed a branch, causing it to fall across the boulder. It created a triangular opening just above Sarah's head. Luke waited a few minutes after the firing stopped, eased up, and looked through the opening, searching every bush and tree for the sniper. But the fullness of the leaves simply swallowed the gun and the person shooting it.

If the sniper changed his location in either direction, he and Sarah were dead.

Luke listened for anything that sounded like a footstep or brush being moved aside or a gun cocking. Anything that might signal where the gunman was positioned.

Sarah looked at her watch. "It's been over ten minutes since the last shot." She shifted away from him. "You're crowding me."

He waited a couple of seconds before he leaned over and said, "Would you rather he had a clear shot at you?"

"No." She scooted closer to the boulder and to Luke.

Everything was silent. Something crawled on Luke's arm, and he brushed it off. He patted Molly's head. "Have you ticked anyone off lately?"

"Why do you think this guy's after me?"

"He pushed you."

"If it's the same guy."

"You're thinking there are *two* homicidal maniacs? I've hiked this trail for years and never saw anything even remotely suspicious on it and you're saying—"

"I'm *not* saying—"

"That there could be *two* nut cases out here?"

"Maybe he's trying to scare you off."

"So he can have you all to himself?" He noted that her face suddenly went pale. "If that's his intent, he's a lousy shot."

A bullet zinged off the top of the branch angled across the boulder above them. Wood chips fell in Sarah's face, and she slapped at it.

"Just keep still, Sarah, and we'll—"

"We'll what, Luke? What if he comes closer? What if he changes positions?"

"Lower your voice."

Her body shook against him. "We can't fight a man with a gun, especially if we can't see him."

"I don't suppose you brought a cell phone with you."

"I realized I left it in my cabin when I got here and didn't want to go back and get it."

"A lot of good that does you."

"Where's yours?"

"Dead, in my truck."

"A lot of good that does you."

"Yeah, well. There was no service up here the last time I visited. Why were you hiking alone?"

"I could ask you the same question."

"I'm not a shrimp. I have Molly, and I can take care of myself."

"So can I."

"Oh, it shows." Arguing would get them nowhere. "When it's fully dark, we'll make a run for it. Let's hope he's gotten his jollies by then and moved out of here."

Time ground on. As long as Luke didn't move, no bullets sprayed at their feet. He listened and watched—wary of the hunter lying in wait for them and dreading the coming night.

At the only cabin on Bear Camp Road, Gertie Jansen slung her tattered rug over the weathered wooden rail outside her back door and ruthlessly beat it with a canoe oar.

Pausing to catch her breath, she looked toward Bear Camp Trail. The shiny red pickup was still parked a few yards below it. Did the driver honestly think he'd fooled anybody into thinking he wasn't hiking that closed trail?

She remembered the golden retriever leaning out the passenger window this morning, its ears and tongue flapping in the cool May wind, and that made her smile. She felt the same exhilaration sometimes, when the wind played in the trees and a storm threatened. She'd stand on the back porch and lift her face to the crisp, fresh wind and thrill to it wafting across her face.

But her smile disappeared when she thought about the truck's owner spending the whole day on that trail, and here was night and cold and snow on its way in, and him still out there.

"Stupid hiker," she mumbled and slapped her rug again. She didn't see many visitors until the tourists intruded around the first of June. They'd 'discovered' Little Texas in the '80s. After the townspeople realized the intruders also wanted to spend money, they made hay while the sun shined and were shed of most of them by mid-September. Gertie could bear the June-to-September rush well enough, but she'd just as soon live without the tourists herself.

Her relatives, the Jansens, were one of four Texas families who'd settled this area in the 1890s. In a hidden valley nestled high in the Colorado Rockies, Little Texas was an enclave of Texans. Everybody was very protective of the town's heritage; no one wanted to see it grow with 'outsiders.' A natural rock border prevented much growth, anyway. She would tolerate what had to be tolerated, until September.

She glanced at the truck again and shook her head. Foolish tourists didn't respect nature. As sure as she was standing here, they'd simply walked around the sign that said *Trail Closed for the Winter* and headed right into a spring snowstorm.

Well, she couldn't take care of every brainless hiker who ventured into the Colorado Rockies.

She reared back and slugged the rug again. It was as clean as she was going to get it, so she tugged it off the rail. With one last glance over her shoulder, she stepped inside her cabin and let the screen door slam shut behind her.

Something moved. Sarah squinted into the meager evening light, spotted a red fox, and breathed a sigh of relief. It scampered across a fallen log and disappeared into the foliage. "Not exactly how I wanted to spend my day."

Luke didn't say anything.

"I really appreciate your willingness to help me. I hate that this man ruined your plans, too."

"Our plans are the least of our worries."

"I know that. Still, I wanted to say thank you."

"You're welcome." Luke twisted around and looked through the opening made by the branch on top of the boulder.

"See anything?" For an hour, no movement had come from the gunman. In any other setting, with the moon shining bright around them and the cool crisp breeze nipping at their noses, it would have been a perfect night for campfires and ghost stories and hot chocolate.

"No. Do you think you can use your foot?"

"It's better. I've been off it for a while now." She gasped and looked past him.

Luke turned toward the shadows slithering across the trail and sat again. "Just a deer," he murmured. "Look, Sarah. I found a cave a few years back, but I've never been deep inside it. Right over there." He nudged her arm, but it was too dark to see where he was pointing. "We could get out of this cold wind."

"A cave? If the sniper's still here, he could trap us inside."

"We're not trapped now?"

"Not if he's gone."

"We wouldn't be trapped in there either if he's gone. At least we wouldn't be sitting ducks. We'd have a place to stay until morning, and we'd be warmer." Leaves and brush rustled in the bitter night breeze. "We'd be sitting on the other side of the entrance. That would be an advantage."

Bullets spat at them. Luke braced his back against the boulder and scooted Molly out of firing range with his foot.

Sarah struggled to think. She was absolutely freezing. The temperature had probably dropped at least twenty degrees since they'd been pinned behind the boulder.

Luke leaned toward her. "He's got to sleep. We'll wait awhile and then head inside the cave and out of this wind. Did you bring a flashlight?"

"Yes, two. Although, I dropped one. Not sure it's working."

"I brought two with extra batteries and flares."

"Flares! Why haven't you used them? We could signal someone. Some rangers!"

"And they'd find our bodies riddled with bullets when they got here. That shooter could've killed us a long time ago, but he didn't. That tells me he wants one of us alive. If we're both going to get out of this still breathing, we have to stay sharp and outsmart him."

"We could make a run for it."

"How do you think he saw us just now in this dark?"

She groaned. "Night vision goggles." She eased her head back against the boulder. In the small opening at the top of the trees, clouds floated across the bottom portion of a bright moon. It wouldn't be long before the snowstorm was here. "He's well-equipped."

"And we're not. At least, not for this. Let's get into our sleeping bags and wait until the time is right to try for the cave. You sleep. I'll keep watch."

"I can't sleep."

"Try. It might be a long night. Snow's on the way in, which might work in our favor. If he didn't come prepared for it, he might leave. At least in the cave, we'll be out of it."

THREE

No! Sarah grunted and squirmed. *His hands—all over her! She pushed against him and screamed, "Noooo!"*

"Sarah. Be quiet."

His hand pressed against her mouth. She couldn't breathe! She fought him, wildly shaking her head, kicking, thrashing. The dark. Trapped! Oh, God, help me!

"Sarah."

All over her, grabbing her, hurting her. She shoved against him, and he grunted. "A little thing like you, sugar? You couldn't budge a flea." Sweaty hands. Beer breath. The black, black dark. She jabbed his chin with the heel of her hand. He ripped her blouse. Arching her back, she fought him, kicking, clawing.

"Sarah, wake up!"

His hand tightened. She... couldn't... breathe!

"Sarah!"

Yes, she could. The hand over her mouth tightened its grip, but she could breathe. Another hand pressed against the back of her neck.

"Come *on,*" he urged. "Wake up!"

Luke's voice reached her, and she startled awake, squirming against his hand until he removed it. "Luke?" The dregs of the nightmare hung on, making the night seem darker, colder, and scarier. She shivered, and her feet dug in as she pushed back against the boulder. She took big gulps of the frigid air to even out her breathing, but her heart continued to race.

"You were dreaming."

From one nightmare to another. She shook her head and closed her eyes against the memories. *Oh, God, will this ever stop?*

She had tried so hard. The old Sarah was going to be back. She'd be brave and adventurous and enjoy nature and go with the flow of the day. She'd make her day *count.* She took a chance hiking alone, but she needed to prove to herself that she could do it, that she could be the strong woman she'd been before the attack. That she could leave the fear behind.

But it had met her here instead.

"It's been a while since he shot at us." Luke's voice sounded gruff.

He probably thought she was weak, that she couldn't hold her own out here. Let him think what he would. She knew who she was—who she used to be. She just had to figure out how to tap into that woman again.

"Let's see if we can get to the cave. Are you awake enough to move out?"

"Yes."

"Who hurt you?"

It was none of his business. The one dogged purpose of this trip had been to rediscover Sarah Ann Morgan—whatever that meant anymore. And here she was, with a man she didn't know, facing God only knew what, with a psycho firing *bullets* at them, and she was thinking about going into a cave that might end up as her grave.

"Is it him, shooting at us?"

She closed her eyes and shook her head. "Let's just leave, Luke. Now. Please."

"Look, I need to know if—"

"I don't know. It happened in Kansas. I don't know who this man is, all right?" The cold wind against her neck woke her completely, and she scooted away from Luke enough that their bodies weren't touching anymore.

"Let's try for the cave. Be quiet and roll up your bag. Stay low."

Grateful for something to do, she eased out of her sleeping bag. The shock of the cold made her want to crawl back into the warmth, but she knew they had to move quickly. She rolled up her bag and attached it to her pack. She let out the air of her pillow, rolled it up, and stuffed it into her backpack. If only she could stuff the memories away as easily as that. Then she'd hurl them into oblivion and never have to face them again.

She dug for her gloves and jacket, put them on, and then slipped on her pack.

The rustling beside her stopped. "Ready?"

She took a deep breath and made herself say, "Yes." She would not let her fear of the dark keep her from staying alive. "Just to get out of this wind."

"Shhh, Molly. Let's go." Luke took Sarah's hand. "Come on."

Bending over, they slipped into the night.

Inside a minute, they stepped around huge brush covering a small outcrop of rock. Luke led her around to the backside of it, which put them at an angle to the sniper's last position.

Luke tugged her to her knees, crawled under the brush to a cave mouth, and crouched at the opening. She was right behind him.

She looked inside the cave and shivered, not because of the cold but because of the blackness in front of her—like a vacuum ready to suck the life out of her. Squatting, she reached out to steady herself and connected with cold, rough rock.

"Bottom left pocket on my pack. Grab the fold-up walking stick and flashlight. We'll need both before we can go forward."

She was so cold, she could hardly move her fingers, even with her gloves on. But she found the pocket, fumbled with the zipper, and pulled out the walking stick and flashlight. "I think it's below freezing."

"Yeah." Luke unfolded the staff and inched inside the mouth of the cave, tapping the floor and wall and ceiling. "I can't turn on the light. He might see it. Stay low and right behind me. I was in here once. The ceiling rises in about ten feet."

She glanced over her shoulder at the shadows behind them, and bullets showered the brush. Sarah gasped as Luke tugged her inside the opening and against the cave wall. She felt the dust-up from several bullets landing in the dirt near her feet.

"Man, this guy doesn't quit. Molly, here!"

Sarah pressed against the rough wall, trying hard to control her breathing and calm her heart. "He changed positions."

"He's letting us know he's watching us every second."

"Luke, this man's a good shot. He aimed right at the tree above us and hit it. The branch and hit it. Our feet, and never hit us. He's taunting us. He's had every opportunity to kill us, so why are we still alive?"

"Maybe he likes scaring people. Maybe he came out here to hunt an elk, we scared off his prey, and he's getting back at us. Maybe we're target practice. I have no idea. But if we go in deeper, he might go find something else to practice on."

"Or follow us in here."

"Maybe, but I don't think so. At any rate, we have to decide if we're going in deeper or if we stay here. This cave might end in twenty feet, or it may go on for a mile."

She didn't know what to do, so she prayed silently for a few moments.

"Okay. Let's look at our options, Sarah. One, we stay right here, although he knows where we are and could meet us here in a few minutes. Two, head inside, wait a little while and see if he's gone, although he's shown no indication he's done with us. Three, make a run for it in the dark; are you willing to take a chance on getting shot? Four, go in deeper. That's our best option."

She shivered, so cold and hardly able to think. Kansas could be cold but not this into-the-bone cold here.

"Feel that draft, Sarah? Sometimes when there's a draft, there's another way out. It just might be large enough for us to fit through. C'mon. Let's at least go a little further inside." He turned on the flashlight. "Then we can decide."

They inched along the wall into the unknown as Luke tapped the walking stick against solid ground, wall, and ceiling. Within a short distance, they were standing.

The thought of going down into the very bowels of the earth terrified Sarah. How long would it take to get out? Would their flashlights last? Would they die? Her family would never know what happened to her. Did she have enough food, enough water? Would she ever see the light of day again?

"We need to keep moving, Sarah."

"Do we? Why don't we stop here?"

"Because he's stayed with us all afternoon and into the night. I don't think he's going to quit. We can search for another way out. If there isn't one, we'll wait him out and head back here."

"Okay. I hope you know what you're doing."

A long pause.

"I need to give you my credentials?"

"I don't know you, Luke."

"You're right. Sure." He shined the light on a creature crawling on the wall. "Every year, my family came up here for summer vacation. My brother Greg, the oldest, started caving with a church group from Estes Park years ago. He loved it. The next year, he took me along. I loved it. When we came up here, we included caving. A couple times, one of my other brothers would join us. One year, all of us went with Dad. I've probably explored fifty caves. Some, virgin. Others, crawling with people. Every cave is different. Every cave is the same."

"What's the mortality rate for cavers?"

"About three deaths a year in the U.S., mostly from drowning. It's a very safe sport."

"I'm with an experienced caver. That's comforting."

"If I don't think it's safe, we'll turn around. We're trying to save our lives here, not have an adventure. So, we're good to go?"

"Yes."

"Then stay directly behind me as much as possible." He shined the light around. "I'm only checking the space in front of me. There could be holes in the floor, so stay close."

"Maybe getting us in here was part of his plan."

"This cave isn't visible from the trail."

"You found it."

"I know what to look for. Most people don't."

She flicked one last glance over her shoulder, moved closer to Luke, and slipped a finger through a loop on his pack.

"Don't pull."

She grabbed the edge of a lower pocket on his pack.

"We'll use only one flashlight until it runs out. Be careful where you walk. It's so dark, we won't be able to tell the difference between the black of open space in front of us and the black of the cave floor. If I start to fall, let go." Luke chuckled.

She was so not in the mood for humor. "It's warmer than it was outside."

"Probably stays around fifty degrees, even at the cave's heart."

"And no wind, thank God. What about Molly? She might fall."

Luke turned around. "You've never had a dog, have you?"

It was slow going. A few steps. The tapping of the walking stick. The light scanning the walls and floor. A few steps. The tap-tap-tap of the walking stick. The light moving about.

After a while, Luke stopped so suddenly, Sarah ran into the back of his pack. "What is it?"

"Shhh." He turned around, gripped her arm. "Listen."

"I don't hear—"

The light went out. "Shhh," he whispered.

She froze. *He's behind us! Oh, God!* Her heart raced. She tried to swallow and couldn't, to speak and couldn't, to breathe and couldn't. Blackness beyond anything she had ever known surrounded them, and a madman was behind them. She imagined his hand, reaching out of the dark, grabbing her. Molly's nose nudged her leg, and she just about jumped out of her skin. Tense moments pounded along with her heavy heartbeat.

"Okay." Luke's light came back on. "Let's get your flashlight out of your pack." His hands landed on her shoulders and turned her around. "Where is it?"

"Wait a minute. What do you mean, where is it? Why did you stop? You scared me half to death!"

"I thought I heard something."

"Well, then, *tell* me. You don't have to grab me and scare the living wits out of me."

"I reacted. I thought he might be behind us."

"Then turn the light off. That'll be our signal to stop and be quiet. Great day, Luke, I'm not difficult to scare senseless in this netherworld."

"Point taken. I didn't mean to scare you. I needed to listen and figure out what was going on. Grabbing your arm was my expedited signal."

"Well, try it my way next time. A bit of restraint would be nice." A little huffy, she presented her back to him. "My flashlight's in the middle compartment." Was that a snicker behind her? Was he laughing at her?

She turned around. Yes, it was laughter. "What's so funny?"

"Not funny. Surprising. You are. Well, maybe a tad funny."

She crossed her arms, having decided to stay miffed despite his laughter. "Explain."

"I thought you were a little mouse, but you roared like a lion."

Now, she grinned. She couldn't say why his look of approval meant something to her. "I did, didn't I? A lion. I like that. You can get my flashlight now." The zipper snarled open and then closed.

"Here." He nudged her with it. "Don't turn it on. Be prepared to use it as a weapon—which I have no doubt you will."

She took it and smiled. She loved this. He thought she was a lion.

He nudged her behind him, flicked on his light, and reached toward the ceiling.

"Do you think he's behind us?"

"There's no indication of a light of any kind."

"He has the night goggles."

"You have to have some light to use them, and it's way past dark in here."

"Couldn't we be furnishing the light for him?"

"At a distance, yes, but he'd have to turn on a light to see where he's walking." His light scaled the walls and floor and stopped on a sloping area. "This looks like a good spot to eat a few bites and rest. No more than a couple minutes." Luke dug into a compartment and pulled out a baggie as he cradled the walking stick in the crook of his arm. "How's the foot?"

"It hurts a little, but I can stand it. Hold this." She handed him her flashlight and rummaged for her sandwich.

"Your shoulder?" His mouth sounded full.

"It hurts, too, but I'm tough. Little, but tough." She took two bites. "I'm starving."

"Eat only a third."

Nodding, she watched him give Molly a big bite of food and then pack the rest away. She did the same. When the man said two minutes, the man meant two minutes.

A short distance later, he stopped and leaned over. "Look. The walkway ends right here." The light trailed over the smooth, ridged ledge. "Flowing water created this. We've been walking at a downward slope since we entered the cave, the path the water would have taken. Feel how smooth this is."

On her knees, she let him guide her hand to the spot. "Where does it go?"

"Right there, see? That's the bottom of the shaft. That's what? Eight feet? Hard to tell with little depth perception." He pulled something out of his pocket, dropped it. "Yep, penny says six feet or so. Molly and I will go first and make sure it's safe. If there's a problem, Molly won't let me go down. I'll secure the rope."

"Are you leaving it here?"

"Yes. We might need to get back up. I have two more in my pack."

He tied it, yanked on it. "Here's my flashlight. Use it and put that one in my right bottom pocket." He turned around. She put it away.

He reached for Molly and placed a vest on her, slid the rope through several rings, and slipped on his gloves.

He lowered Molly first and then slid down the rope. Sarah held the light on what they thought was a landing. Within seconds, Luke grunted and stomped. Molly barked and sniffed around.

Luke's grinning face lifted toward her. "Solid rock." He slipped off his backpack. "I need to look around. It'll only take a few seconds."

Gripping the rope, Sarah watched and waited and made herself *not* look over her shoulder at the darkness pressing against her back. She made a quick mental list: she would stay brave; she would be strong; she would pray a *lot*. And she might roar like a lion.

Light shined in her eyes. "We can keep going. Drop the light." He caught it. "Come on down when you're ready."

Gritting her teeth, she scooted to the edge. "I can't hold the rope. My shoulder still hurts. Get ready to catch me." She stepped off and landed in his arms.

"Gotcha! Piece of cake." He set her on her feet.

"Thank God." She leaned against the stone wall and sank to her bottom. It was such a relief to have solid wall at her back. Just past Luke's feet, the ceiling was lower. She looked up, shined her light on the ledge they'd just come from, and imagined seeing the sniper's head and his gaze on them. But nothing was there.

She took a deep breath, grateful for the reprieve. "Listen. Is that a waterfall?"

"The river that made this cave." Luke looked under the low ceiling. "Molly and I saw another shelf below us. About three feet down. We'll take a look, see where it goes." They disappeared. A thud. Molly barked once.

"Whoa." Luke's voice sounded muffled below her. "This room is huge. What I can see is absolutely gargantuan, the size of three football fields. Not many caves like this, but I've read about 'em."

She scooted to the edge and shined her light below. Only Luke's boots were visible. "Can we keep going?"

"Yeah. It's about four feet from the bottom. Push both our packs over and join us. There's a ledge where we can catch some Zs."

The packs landed with Sarah close behind.

"Hopefully, we'll find another way out soon. Let's get to that ledge."

"I am so ready for some sleep, Luke."

FOUR

Sleep was out of the question.

Gertie Jansen glanced at her windup clock tick-tocking on her bedside table and groaned at the *1:53*. She wished to high heaven she hadn't seen that red truck parked over at the trailhead.

And because she had, she was wide awake. Easing the quilts off, she slid her old bones out of bed and her feet into her slippers. "How am I supposed to get any sleep with a hiker on the loose?"

She plucked her high-powered flashlight off the shelf, moved the stepladder to the kitchen sink and took the two steps up to the window. The flashlight clicked on. A sword of light sliced into the snowy night, landing on the red pickup now covered with seven inches of snow. The light moved past the wooden gate several yards down to a tree. What was that shape? A wheel? Two wheels?

"A bicycle," she muttered, shaking her head. "So, there's two morons over there."

Well, she couldn't do anything about it now. But come morning, she'd bundle up and get up to the phone at Alva's store and gas station and call Jim Banks at the Little Texas Search & Rescue. Sure wasn't the first time he'd have to rescue a lame-brained hiker, and it wouldn't be the last.

She stepped down, put away her light and stepladder, and headed for bed. She didn't figure on getting much sleep, if any. She was too worried about those hikers, out on a cold snowy night in the Colorado Rockies and not a single soul knowing where they were.

"Nincompoops, that's what hikers are," she mumbled and rolled onto her side, away from the ticking clock. Maybe it was time for her to buy herself a phone. That way, come morning, she could just pick it up and call Jim Banks instead of having to trudge through this heavy spring snow to Alva's store.

"Another fatality," Jim Banks mumbled to no one in particular at Search & Rescue as he slapped the paperwork on his cluttered desk. It went without saying it was senseless. Another hiker, walking right past a large sign announcing a trail was closed.

He reached for his umpteenth cup of coffee, realized it was cold too late and, without so much as a grimace, swallowed it. He dutifully set his cup on the Elvis coaster his secretary, Elva Lee, gave all the rangers to use. "I'm his namesake," she'd said the morning she had set them out. "Mama's crush on Elvis is never ending. Today's his birthday, and she bought these for all of us."

As if on cue, the thick wooden door opened and slammed shut. His secretary, Elva Lee Ward, stomped her feet. "Brrr! It's cold out there, boys!"

Jim looked up and studied her. *Well, well, well, if she wasn't losing some weight there.* She shook out her short, curly brown hair and fluffed it in the back like she always did, with those long, fake purple nails Jodee put on her about three months ago. Her typing was pretty good before that, but now she hunted and pecked like she'd never seen a keyboard before.

Her short legs were covered in thick black tights that ended in clunky, brown hiking boots with lacy pink socks peeking over the tops. Her red sweater hung clean down to her knees and had what looked like pink toilet paper wads clinging for dear life at the hem. Elva Lee called them her spring flowers.

She walked to the dual coffee pots and switched off the burner under the empty pot. "More coffee, Jim?"

He flashed her a guilty smile. "That'd be fine. 'Preciate it."

"Where did they find those two hikers?"

"Near the split between Devil's Gulch and the Branch cutoff. People today don't know how to read." He sighed. "At least one of them is still alive."

Lying in her sleeping bag in the dark, Sarah let herself imagine she was camping near a lake with the sun about to appear above the mountains; fish jumped eagerly in the mountain lake; early birds flew overhead; a deer stood nearby, watching them.

But none of that was true. They were in an underground cave system without any sign of an opening out of here.

Beside her, Molly whined.

"Come here, girl." Sarah lifted the corner of her sleeping bag, and the dog settled next to her. "Tell you what, Molly. We'll stick together, you and I. Mr. Pushy Giant here can fend for himself. He's a big ol' brute and monsters never go after the big guys, do they?"

The blackness rumbled with a deep chuckle. "I've dealt with a couple monsters in my lifetime."

"Humph. We don't believe that, do we, girl?" Sarah tugged Molly closer and burrowed her face in the dog's neck.

"Third grade. Mickey Zamora. Jumped me every day and stole the sandwich out of my lunch bag."

"Now that's scary."

"He was in fifth grade and big, and I was scrawny. I wanted my brothers to help me out, but I couldn't bring myself to tell them a bully was getting the better of me."

"What did you do?"

"I hit a mean growing spurt that summer. He never bothered me again. 'Course, it also helped that my seven brothers were all taller than me. The tallest, Mac, is six-five."

"You have seven brothers?"

"Six now. My brother Joey died when he was sixteen."

"Oh, I'm so sorry, Luke. How awful. How long ago was that?"

"Years now. About nineteen. I was nine when it happened."

"Who's the second monster?"

Luke was silent for a moment. "He murdered my father fifteen months ago."

"Murdered?" Pain wrapped around her heart at his words. She couldn't imagine that kind of wound. "Luke, oh, my goodness. What happened if, y'know, you want to talk about it?"

"My father was coming home from a cattle auction. He pulled over to the side of the road to find the radio station where my brother Kyle was being interviewed. It was dark. He was out in the middle of nowhere. A man walks right up to him and shoots him, point blank, between the eyes." He sighed. "No clues. No idea who did it. Nothing."

"I'm so sorry." They had something in common, then. They had both suffered at the hands of evil people.

The throbbing quiet surrounding her was soothed by the distant murmur of the waterfall. Molly lifted her head and rested her chin on Sarah's arm.

"Luke?"

"Umm?"

"Are you afraid down here?"

"Not afraid. Cautious."

"Does anything scare you?"

He didn't answer for a few moments. And when he did, he simply said, "Yes." Another few seconds, and he added, "Someone trying to hurt my family or someone I care about."

Although he couldn't see her, she nodded and stroked Molly's head.

"Like my dad. I wasn't there to help him."

"Would you have been able to save him?"

"He wouldn't have pulled over to find the radio station if I'd been with him. None of it would have happened."

"You think."

"I know."

"Well, if this man was intent on killing your father, he'd have found another way."

"I've thought about that. He had to have targeted Dad. When Dad pulled over, he was in the middle of nowhere. Just a spot to pull over. My father didn't see lights or hear a car drive up behind him. The man just appeared at the driver's side and shot him. My brother Kyle heard the whole thing."

"How awful for him."

"Yeah. So, you're probably right. It would've happened anyway."

"Then you can't blame yourself for his death."

The words hung between them. All was silent except for the tranquil sounds of the waterfall below them.

"Thanks for that, Sarah. I needed to hear it."

She thought he turned toward her but couldn't be sure. He didn't say anything else. "I think I'd go mad in this blackness."

"It's easy to get disoriented." His sleeping bag rustled, and she assumed he sat up. Light appeared and, in a few quick strokes, he transformed his flashlight into a lantern and set it near her feet. "Did you sleep, Sarah?"

"A little bit. Too many creepy things to worry about."

He looked over at her. "What's your last name?"

It seemed silly not to tell him. "Morgan. Sarah Ann Morgan."

"How old are you?"

In the faint light, his eyes seemed black. "Twenty-five. How old are you?"

"Twenty-eight. Twenty-nine in July."

Their gazes locked, and her heart thumped heavily. It was no secret why. Luke McKenzie was undoubtedly the most beautiful man she'd ever seen. Tall, tanned, thick black hair, incredible blue eyes, square jaw, and well-built, as if he worked hard every day.

She looked away. This trip was about pulling herself together, not falling for some gorgeous hunk she'd known only a few hours and wouldn't know much longer. She was on vacation. He was on vacation. This time together in the underworld would end, and she'd go home. As would he.

Rolling to her knees, she folded her sleeping bag.

"Where are you from, Sarah?"

"Riadon, in western Kansas. Where are you from?"

"Mole's Bench, Texas."

She snickered. "I'd be embarrassed to tell anyone I was from any place named Mole's Bench." She tightened a strap.

"Has character. Anyone pining for you back in Riadon, Kansas?"

"Pining?"

"Missing you."

The question surprised her. "That's too personal."

"Being alone with me in an underground cave system isn't? But

309

you're right. It's none of my business if you don't want it to be."

Surprised and a little disappointed that he'd given up so quickly, she tossed the bag toward her pack. As she watched him roll up his sleeping bag, she realized that she liked him. She knew from experience that some men were capable of horrible acts against someone they could dominate physically. But, like her father, others would never consider hurting a woman. She thought Luke was in the latter category. All he had done was help her, protect her, and try to keep her safe. Maybe he was someone worth getting to know.

She stood, brushed off her pants, and picked up her daypack. "What does one do in Mole's Bench, Texas?"

"Not much," he chuckled as he clipped his sleeping bag to his pack. "But if you're asking about me, I'm foreman of my brother's ranch."

"Is it a big ranch?"

"Sixty-three thousand acres, give or take." He hoisted his pack onto his shoulder and flashed the light into the center of the room below them. A thin, luminescent-green stream meandered through the rock sculptures.

"Do you think that water's drinkable, Luke?"

"I wouldn't use it to brush my teeth."

"I need a bio break."

"A what?"

"The call of nature."

"Oh. You can find a spot down there. You ready to head out?"

At Little Texas Search & Rescue, Elva Lee pushed up her bulky sleeves, set the coffee pot under the faucet, and turned on the water. She'd gotten to know Jim Banks well in the few years she'd worked at S&R as his secretary. And today, he was in one of his moods.

As the head of S&R, he took it to heart when they were unable to save someone. She'd learned a long time ago not to say anything to him when he was moody. She noticed the water pressure was low again, but now was not a good time to mention it.

His chair scraped on the hardwood floor as he stood. She moved over a little, so he could pour out his cold coffee and set the cup in the stainless-steel sink without touching her. Then he headed for the window and stood there, watching the snow falling.

She sighed. It was a disgrace what his wife, Renee, had done to him, running off like that almost a year ago now without so much as a word when she left and not a word since. How could she do that to the very best man God ever created? He seemed to have gotten his legs back under him again and was—

Jim turned around and caught her staring at him. She fumbled with turning off the water.

Scowling, he grabbed his cap and tugged his coat off one of the elk horns on the wall by his desk. "I'll be back," he muttered and slammed the door behind him.

Elva Lee didn't take it personally. Finding a victim dead was hard on Jim. She jumped as the phone rang and finished counting her scoops before she hurried across the wooden floor to catch the phone just before the voicemail picked up.

"Why, hello there, Miss Gertie. What are you doing out in this wicked weather?"

"It's business, Elva Lee. I need to speak to Jim. Is he available?"

"He just left. Let me see if I can catch him. Are you at Alva's store?"

"I am."

"Stay there. I'll have him call you in just a few minutes."

Jim put his truck in reverse and backed up. What was wrong with him lately? Elva Lee Ward had worked with him for four years, and he'd never even looked at her, and now he was noticing she'd lost weight? Oh, yeah, he'd also noticed her hair, her nails, her boots, her pink socks, and those silly flowers on her sweater.

He was just lonely.

No one could understand how much it hurt him when Renee ran out on him, leaving him with everything broken in his life. The questions had eaten him alive. Why did she leave? Where did she go? Was the baby his or another man's? Had everything they'd lived been a lie? All the teasing, the loving, the plans, the little one?

Those questions had gnawed on him for a year now, and in the midst of all that living, breathing pain, he could only see where he'd failed her.

He slammed on his brakes when his cell phone rang. "Banks."

Harriet and Henry Flagstone drove by in their like-new '69 Thunderbird. Henry waved, looked up at the thick falling snow and shook his head at Jim. Nodding in understanding, Jim waved back and listened as Elva Lee told him about Miss Gertie's phone call.

"I'll call her at Alva's." He hung up and did just that. "Hey, Alva. This is Jim Banks. Is Miss Gertie standing there, waiting on a call from me?"

"She sure is. Here ya go, Miss Gertie."

"Jim?" She told him about the two hikers who'd left a truck and a bicycle at the Bear Camp trailhead.

"I'll go on over there, check out that truck, and see if I can figure out who it belongs to. 'Preciate you letting me know, Miss Gertie."

His next call was to Elva Lee. "Get ahold of Tommy and let him know about those two hikers. We can't do much in this weather. I'll check in with you when I get to the trailhead."

He jiggled the sliding bar of the heater. It'd been gasping for breath the last couple weeks, but spring was just around the corner, and he'd put off getting it fixed. Any one of the hundreds of people who had taken his Safety First seminar through the years would be surprised that he'd let the heater go. "Now, Jim," they'd say, "don't I recall you saying that being prepared for bad weather is being prepared to stay alive?"

And his wife, Renee, would have pointed a finger at him, dipped her head, sassily raised her brows, and said something like, "Jimmy, you wouldn't want us to have to rescue you, now, would ja, honey?"

"Well, great," he mumbled against set teeth as he shook off Renee like she'd shook him off. He slammed on his brakes at the blinking red light, jerked his head both ways, and headed down the road toward Miss Gertie's dirt road.

The thick, wet snow fell in straight lines. Jim turned the wipers up and hoped to high heaven those hikers at Bear Camp Trail had had sense enough to bring warm clothes with them.

"Look." Luke shined the light down a walkway. "Another corridor. The draft is strong. I'm pretty sure we're close to the other opening."

Sarah nudged past him and gazed into the tunnel. "I didn't think we'd ever find it." Her voice wobbled. "Hours and hours of searching. Every muscle in my body hurts. Oh, thank you, Lord, for showing us the way."

Even though Luke knew she was close to falling apart, those words said more about her strength than any weakness. "Do you want to go on or stop here to eat?"

"I want out of here. I don't do well all cooped up, especially in the company of crawling things."

"Then let's away, my friend." He bowed, grandly swept a hand toward the opening, and handed her the walking stick.

Shaking her head, she flicked a thumb at him. "No way, Jose.' You first. Monsters don't go after the big guys, remember?"

FIVE

Twenty-nine years ago, Little Texas welcomed Lulu Banks into this world, kicking and screaming, and today, she was kicking and screaming to get out.

Ever since her husband Ray Baines had died in a car wreck a year ago, she'd been itching to spread her independent, red-tipped wings, *finally!,* and fly to Denver. Ray had hated big towns, so they'd never ventured past Willow Falls, thirty miles south of Little Texas, a bigger town but no less a sinkhole.

Well, Ray was gone, and, oh! she missed him! But she was itching— she told her best friend Myra Simms, *literally* itching—to get on down to Denver.

Only she couldn't drive. She had never gotten her license. *Just consider me your personal chauffeur, Lulu,* Ray had said, and she had. Working out back, fixing anything with a motor in it, Ray would wipe his hands on a work towel, grin real big, reach for his cap and say, "Come on, woman. You got your green heels on. Must be time to cruise."

She'd laugh and he'd open the driver's door and she'd slide in and wait on him to start the truck so she could listen to country music on a CD.

"High time you got your license," Myra decreed yesterday. She'd cupped her lighter, drew in a breath of smoke, and popped the lighter closed. "You can march yourself down to that driver's license office, take that test, and drive to Denver today." Her big loop earrings with the tiny turquoise beads dangled and jumped when she shook her head and gestured with fingers holding a cigarette. "No man around now to tie you down."

"But I don't know where Denver is, and I can't read a map. Besides, Ray didn't tie me down. I tied myself down, and I don't know why. Come with me, Myra? You been to Denver a lot of times, haven't cha?"

"Well, yeah, Lulu, but Fred would kill me if I went with you alone. You know how he gets when I'm out of his sight. That man is a jealous bean."

So, in front of a warm cozy fire, with the television blaring, Lulu sat in Ray's favorite recliner with her two-inch green heels on, her freshly cut-colored-and-curled hair, waiting for Myra to come pick her up to go shopping in Estes Park.

With her foot wiggling, she decided tomorrow, yessiree, tomorrow she'd get that license and shake this town lickety-split—at least for a day or two.

One minute later, she was dead.

"Rosie," a voice whispered in her ear. A finger lifted one of her green earrings as a tear fell onto her cheek. "Why won't you stay dead, Rosie?" Weeping filled the room. "Why in blue blazes won't you stay dead?"

At Search & Rescue, Jim checked his watch when Elva Lee breezed in a little after one, holding a brown paper sack from Colson's. When she kicked the door shut with her booted foot, keys on the bronze deer-head key holder above the light switch rattled.

"I want everybody to know—" She huffed as she set the sack on her desk, opened her middle desk drawer, and dropped her keys in. "—that I'm on a plateau with my diet. I hate to admit it, but I may be a little difficult to get along with. Forewarned is forearmed, all right?" She hung up her coat and scarf.

Tommy Blakesly was the first to look up. "Wuh, Elva Lee, why are you on a diet, honey? You look pretty as a peach tree as it is." He grinned at Buddy Washburn, who winked at him and said, "Does this mean you're not gonna get us any more donuts on Monday mornings?"

She glared at them. "You just laugh and joke about it. You'll see. This diet's all about eating protein and veggies and staying away from refined carbohydrates. They're the enemy—"

"Who is?" Tommy stuffed a piece of chewing gum into his mouth to hide his silly grin.

Jim was just about ready to throw the lot of them out the door.

"Why, the bad carbohydrates, Tommy. Haven't you been listening to me the last few weeks? They're the enemy. Good carbs. Bad carbs. And the bad carbs just don't sit well in some people's bodies."

"They seem to be sitting okay in yours."

Well, great. Now you've done it. Jim turned his back on Elva Lee and put his nose in his paperwork, wishing Tommy had kept his big, fat mouth shut.

He didn't have to turn around to know that the silence pumping in the room had everything to do with tears filling Elva Lee's eyes. *Lips are probably quivering about right now, too.* Jim stacked his papers, pulled out the bottom drawer of his file cabinet, yanked out a folder, and stuffed the papers into it.

She sniffed, and Jim wanted to groan.

Instead, he slammed the file cabinet drawer, turned around, cut his throat with a stiff hand, and jerked his head toward the door. He'd clearly said "Get out!" as if he'd said the words.

Tommy got the message. He took his skinny self outside, with Buddy and his pot belly following close behind.

What was Jim supposed to do now, for Pete's sake?

Elva Lee pulled out a Kleenex from the wooden box on the edge of her desk, sniffed a couple times, and sat in her squawking chair.

"Elva Lee," Jim ventured. "None of us need those donuts. You just take care of yourself now. That's what's important."

"Thank you, Jim." She neatly folded, tucked, and straightened that brown paper sack as if somebody's life depended on it. She slipped it between her desk and the file cabinet. "What did you find out about those hikers? Their truck still out there?"

Better keep his eyes off her and study the notes he'd made or he might find himself stepping outside to teach Tommy some manners. "Found the registration. Luke McKenzie out of Mole's Bench, Texas. I know the family well."

"Luke? It's been a while since he's been here."

"A couple of years. Man, we go way back. A lot of good memories growing up with that family. I placed a call to Mac, his younger brother. A woman said he was with a mare about to foal and would call me as soon as he could." He checked the wall clock. "That was an hour ago."

Elva Lee opened a bag of something and chomped on it. "I hope we find Luke alive."

"And the woman."

"A woman's with him?"

His gaze connected with hers. "If that bike's any indication," he muttered and turned back around, wondering how in the world they were going to find them in all this snow.

Grateful to be sitting, Sarah took a bite of her sandwich and leaned back against the wall of rock. They'd struggled through tight spots, squeezes, shimmied under low-hanging ceilings, and walked over loose rock for three hours before they stopped to eat. She was famished.

Closing her eyes, she enjoyed the quiet until she surprised herself with an unexpected question. "Is there anyone waiting for you back on your ranch?"

"Not on *my* ranch. Mine's two thousand acres, and I'm in the process of building my house and outbuildings right now. No one waiting for me there or anywhere." An impish grin crossed Luke's mouth. "Why do you ask?"

"Just curious."

He tore off a bite of his sandwich and tossed it to Molly. "Who hurt you?"

Sarah lowered her eyes. It was none of his business. "I don't know what you mean."

"Yeah, you do."

Turning away from him as well as the question, she stroked Molly's head. She didn't want him to know any more about her than was absolutely necessary to get out of this place.

"What do you do for a living in Riadon, Sarah?"

"I'm a glass artist."

"You mean, the long pole, bubbles, and dripping glass kind?"

"Yes." She took a bite of her sandwich, avoiding his eyes.

"Impressive. What do you do with your works?"

"I sell them in my shop."

"Umm. I'll have to come see that shop of yours some day."

"You'd be welcome, although I wouldn't think you'd take the time or trouble to come and look at glass." She couldn't tell if he was joking or serious, but she needed to thwart any expectations of a relationship outside this cave.

"No trouble." With grinning eyes that told her he knew exactly what she was thinking, he stuffed his sandwich bag into a side pocket and zipped it closed. "Let's go, Sarah. Time's a-wasting."

Jim came out of the supply room and plopped into his chair as the phone rang. It was just about quitting time.

"Search & Rescue. This is Elva Lee."

For some reason he couldn't explain, he spun around in his office chair to watch her. She covered the mouthpiece and nudged the phone at Jim. "It's Andrew Jackson, Jim. Line one."

He chuckled. His parents named both their sons after presidents. His older brother, A.J., knew everything there was to know about the seventh president. Sibling rivalry caused Jim to study up on his namesake, James Madison, the fourth president. They'd enjoyed verbal wrestling as kids, spitting facts about each president at each other to see who would win the I-know-more-than-you-do game. Usually, A.J. won.

Jim picked up the phone, leaned back in his chair, and rocked as he said, "Hey, A.J. Whatcha know good?" A long bout of silence followed his greeting. "A.J.?"

"You need to come over to Lulu's house."

Jim stopped rocking. "Why?"

Leaning forward, he rested his elbow on his desk, eased his head onto his hand, and listened, unbelievingly, as his brother, the chief of police here in Little Texas, told him their cousin was missing—or worse.

Jim squeezed his eyes shut. Took a deep breath. Blew it out.

With a hand splayed over his face, he said, "All right. Be right there." He hung up.

Without saying a word, he stood, reached for his hat and coat, and stalked out the door.

Tilted forward to keep the pack from pulling her back onto the dirt floor, Sarah waddled under the low ceiling.

Panting, she flicked her light on Luke, who was waddling, too. She wanted to laugh at the ridiculous posture but couldn't bring herself to make the effort. Her knees cramped, her back ached, and her ankle pounded a steady rhythm of pain. "Do you think he's behind us?"

"Following?"

"Yes."

"No. He may be at the other opening, waiting for us."

"I'd actually thought of that. Are you ready to rest?"

"And stretch a bit." He shined the light down the path. "Wait. It looks like the tunnel's opening up. Leave your pack on."

Another twenty feet, and the low ceiling disappeared.

"Ah, this is nice." She stood and stretched.

Luke shined the light to the right of them. "There's another room. C'mon." It was small, about the size of seven or eight stalls. "Look at that jagged fissure." It looked like a giant had stabbed the wall with a serrated knife and ripped it open, going down and to the left about three feet. It ended about chest-level on Luke. "I wonder if anyone's ever ventured inside that."

"It's big enough, but I sure wouldn't. I'd be too claustrophobic. I need to take a bio. Then, let's sleep a little. I'm exhausted."

Luke shined the light behind her. "Look. Back there. A hole large enough for all three of us to sleep."

"A cave within a cave." She turned on her light. "I'll be back."

When she returned, they both took the time to pull out their sleeping bags to rest. Molly snuggled with Sarah. In seconds, gentle snoring from Luke helped her to fall into a deep sleep.

She awoke to a hand gripping her mouth!

Her nose was stuffy, and she could hardly breathe! She tried to shake off the hand and gripped its huge wrist, feeling a warm breath as a whispered, "Shhh," sounded in her ear.

Luke. She almost relaxed but tensed again as she heard it.

Singing.

Singing? She quickly nodded. Her heart raced as Luke took her hand, squeezed it, and let it go.

317

A lustrous, rowdy song about mommy kissing Santa Claus echoed in the distance. The voice was getting louder as it headed in their direction.

What in the world? Sarah leaned forward. Molly nudged her arm. Behind her, Luke whispered a "Shhh" to Molly.

The loud tenor voice was now wishing them a Merry Christmas.

A jerking beam of light appeared. As it rounded a corner, Sarah heard a dragging sound. Her breath caught. Luke reached for her hand and squeezed it.

Across the wide expanse, into the great room, came a man. Or Sarah supposed it to be a man by the voice since she couldn't see anything but the laser-like shaft of light floating around the room.

The dragging stopped.

The singing turned to humming as the light moved behind a huge boulder. In a matter of seconds, it re-appeared. A click sounded, and a large circular light popped on. It shined on the jagged crack they'd seen earlier.

Sarah began to shake and covered her mouth in case she whimpered. Luke tightened his grip on her other hand. She clearly got the message: *be quiet.*

The flashlight bounded behind the boulder again and came out a few seconds later. Another circular light appeared. *Like stage lights.* The man moved behind the big rock, reappeared, and placed a three-rung stepladder under the crevice.

What is going on?

Molly's wet nose nudged Sarah's elbow, and she jumped. Luke patted Molly, then took Sarah's hand again and kneaded it. She was grateful for the comfort he offered.

In silence, the man disappeared into the blackness behind the lights.

The dragging began again.

It stopped.

Sarah held her breath as the man stepped into the lights and climbed up to the top rung of the ladder. He leaned into the crevice. "Hello? Anybody down there?" Then he laughed and jumped to the ground.

After a few moments, he moved into the lights again with a gunnysack draped over his shoulder. Something heavy was in it because the man struggled to get up to the top rung of the stepladder. Then he hoisted the bag onto the lip of the crevice and pushed. A woman's leg with a green high heel shoe on her foot caught on the edge of the fissure. The green shoe fell to the ground as he forced the leg into the hole. The man shoved the woman down the fissure as he

318

worked the sack off her.

Then he jumped down, picked up the shoe, laughed as he threw it into the crevice, and said, "Oh, Rosie. You're such a kidder."

He meticulously folded the sack and tucked it under his arm.

Oh, God. Sarah covered her mouth. *Oh, God.*

Suddenly lightheaded, she felt her hand slip to her lap. She'd fainted only once in her life... and knew... she was—

Jim couldn't remember a time he'd dreaded anything as much as he did walking up the sidewalk to his cousin Lulu's house. Where was she?

In the quiet, he rested his foot on the bottom step of the porch and tugged on the front of his cap, just for something to do with his hands. So many memories here. The porch swing where he and Renee had kissed for the first time. He used to smile at the memory. Now it only made him sad.

In his mind's eye, Lulu's husband, Ray, came out of the house, the screen door slamming shut behind him.

"Ray," Lulu hollered, *"you better catch that door, mister!"*

He winked at Jim. "Ain't she the cutest thing?"

Like as not when Ray spotted him walking toward their house, he would have said, "Well, cousin, you *do* remember where we live. Sit it down, friend, and fill my ear with some news."

Instead, Jim's grim-faced older brother, A.J., opened the screen door and held it with the toe of his scuffed work boot. He avoided Jim's eyes. "Come on in, then, and have a look-see. Make sure I haven't missed anything."

Jim slipped his hands into disposable gloves. He'd been a policeman for six years in Denver. Everybody in Little Texas wondered why he'd come back home after he'd hit it big in the city, but Jim wouldn't say, and nobody asked. Well, nobody asked *him.* There'd been plenty of asking going on behind his back, but he'd never told anyone outside his parents and A.J. that Renee simply didn't like living in Denver. They were trying to get pregnant, and she didn't want to bring up a child in a big city. That was enough for Jim. They'd moved back home.

His brother, A.J., had wanted Jim on the police force with him, but he had already decided to take over Search & Rescue. But when he could, he helped his brother out.

He caught the closing door as A.J. went inside first. Jim stopped on the threshold. "I smell blood."

A.J. nodded toward the chair nearby. "Ray's recliner. Got samples off already. You know Lulu liked to sit there."

Jim took two steps inside and spotted the blood. He closed his eyes and took a deep breath to fight the sudden nausea. "God help her." He looked around the room. "Don't recall Lulu ever being so neat."

"Myra said she was itching to get her license and head down to Denver, so she went on a cleaning spree. Lulu said she just had too much energy and wanted to make good use of it. They planned to go to Estes Park today, but Lulu was gone when Myra got here."

Jim listened to his brother and continued searching, wishing his cousin was here to visit with him.

"Myra said Lulu had her nails and hair done earlier down at Jodee's Salon."

Jim walked to the window overlooking the carport, touched the lace curtain, and drew it back. He remembered Lulu drawing back this curtain when Ray would pull into the carport. She'd announce, "He's here," as if Jim hadn't heard that souped-up engine himself.

"Did she get the license?" It seemed strange to see the riding mower sitting all alone in the big carport Ray built onto the house for his truck. Ray had always been good with his hands.

"No. She decided to get it tomorrow and drive to Denver where a good time was waiting on her, according to Myra."

"Alone?"

"It doesn't sound like Lulu, does it? Pipe dreams, I'm thinking."

Jim stood in the doorway to Lulu's bedroom. The bed was ruthlessly made, pillows piled high, not a speck of dust to be found on the headboard or the dresser or the chest of drawers—as if she had known they'd be in her house later looking at everything.

Ray's rifle stood in the corner where it always stood, probably loaded if the open shell box on the windowsill meant anything. His slick waders rested beside his rifle, folded over.

Jim could see Ray grinning like a 'possum when he caught himself a big one a little before dawn out at Palmer's Creek. That last trip, the summer before he died, was crystal clear to Jim, like it had happened yesterday. Gripping that bass's mouth, holding it up as if the King of all creation was watching and very proud of him.

Jim poked his head in the bathroom; nothing personal on the counter.

Voices echoed from in here.

"Get your own beer, Ray! I'm putting on my face."

"Laws, woman, don't let me interrupt you doing that. I'm partial to a woman with a face!"

Ray would laugh and Lulu would come out to the hallway and point her eyelash thing at him and try to look mad, but she ended up laughing instead.

Laughter. That's what Jim remembered most about this house.

He stepped into the kitchen and stood still, listening to days gone by. His Aunt Charlotte saying to him and Lulu, "I swanny, you two are like two peas in a pod. Now get on outside, both of you, 'fore I make use of all that energy and put you both to work." Maybe that's where Lulu got the notion to work off her excess energy.

Jim sighed, opened the back door, and looked through the snow-sprayed screen door. Footprints in the snow. "A.J."

"I saw 'em."

"Where do they go?"

"To the road. Could have been the milk man. I'm checking on his route. You know Lulu loved her whole milk and ice cream."

Standing in the cold air, nose almost touching the screen door, he studied the tree in the yard, the clothesline, the storage shed. "Why Lulu? Who would ever want to hurt her? She was so tiny, wouldn't—couldn't—hurt a fly. Just like Renee. Tiny just like Renee."

"No bigger'n a minute," A.J. mumbled behind him.

"You know what? When Buddy Washburn's wife left him out of the blue a couple years back, I felt sorry for him, but I didn't know what it felt like. I sure didn't know what to say to him. I got a little smug, figuring Renee'd never do that to me. But she did."

Jim shook his head. "And now Lulu. Same pattern. Car—or truck—gone. No sign of a struggle. Clothes packed. Her gone, but nothing making sense." He turned around and faced his brother and the truth. "Maybe Renee and the others didn't leave. Maybe there's a pattern here that's just come to light."

He looked at the old plastic lace doily sitting under the big clay frog he'd made for Lulu in third grade, now stuffed with ivy coming out its back. Leaves curled around the base, so its pink-painted toenails were hidden. "Maybe they didn't just up and leave one day." His gaze locked on his brother's. "Maybe they were all taken—or worse. Let's get out of here, meet at the station, and try to figure out what's going on."

"I'm heading to Casey's home to tell her about her sister being missing. I'll meet you in a bit."

"I'll go with you."

Sarah squirmed. Darkness surrounded her and lay heavy on her skin. She jerked when she remembered the green shoe on the woman. She tried to sit up, but arms were around her—Luke's arms. Something touched her ear. "Shhhh," he whispered.

In the pounding silence, nothing moved. Sarah couldn't stand the loneliness or the absolute quiet or the blackness anymore. She turned, pulled Luke's head down, and whispered in his ear. "Is he gone?"

A long pause, then, "Yes."

"I could have ended up like her."

"What do you mean?"

"I was traumatized, almost raped. He insisted on it being dark."

"*This* man?"

"No." She shook her head. "I don't know. A stranger. He broke into my home."

"The nightmare."

Nodding, she sniffed and made herself continue, to get it out in the open. "My roommates came home. He heard them and ran. The police came. They told me I was lucky, that he was probably the serial rapist and murderer that had beaten, molested, and killed two women the previous two nights." She shook her head and cried silently.

Luke's arms tightened around her. "He beat you?"

Leaning back against his chest, she nodded.

"I'm so sorry, Sarah."

She couldn't speak for a few heartbeats. "They never found him. I've struggled with getting my life back. That's the reason I'm here in Colorado—to try to find myself, to get over what he did to me. Twice."

"Twice?"

She nodded and told him about the second break-in.

"You think this man could be him?"

"I don't know. I didn't get a good look at him in the dark."

For the first time, the darkness didn't frighten her. Luke's arms were around her.

His head rested against hers. "You'll never get over it, but you will learn how to deal with it. Hopefully, it won't have the hold on you that it does now. You'll get stronger."

She realized she was lying back against him, in his arms, comfortably talking, without worrying that he was a man. It was... okay. Like her father. A friend.

"I know about loss, Sarah. I'm learning to live without my dad. It's not easy. I have a long way to go yet."

"I don't know what I'd do if I lost my father like that."

They were quiet for a few moments.

"This poor woman. I wonder who she was."

"I don't know. We'll report all of this to the police." He helped her up, essentially ending the conversation. He turned on his light and stood. "We'll be out of here soon."

Sarah didn't want to think about the crevice in the wall and what lay at the bottom of it. "Luke. I-I've felt God here with me, with us, ever since we came in here. Even when that monster was in here."

"It doesn't seem right that He'd be in such a place at such a time." His voice was quiet, reverent.

"But He was. He is. How do we explain that?"

"We're here. He's here."

She nodded. It was that simple.

"We've given this man plenty of lead time, Sarah. It won't be long before we're up top."

"And the sniper welcomes us to another nightmare."

"We'll find out when we get there."

SIX

Jim drove to the office. He dreaded telling Elva Lee that her best friend's sister was missing, but when he arrived, she already knew. She was crying at her desk.

He set a box of Kleenex beside her. "Here, Elva Lee."

She took one and wiped her face and then started crying again.

Jim's head hurt. He watched Elva Lee fall apart and wanted to fall apart, too, and let somebody else handle this.

He sighed. He was out at Lulu's just two days ago, having supper with her. Both of them had lost their spouses. They'd always been close, but they'd gotten closer over this last year. Lulu saw to it that Jim ate with her at least twice a week; she'd included A.J. after Penny kicked him out. Then, they'd return the favor by taking her out to eat at Penny's Bar & Grill twice a week for supper.

"Elva Lee, it's time for you to go home. You can have the day off."

"I want to stay. It's my job. I might be able to help."

She tugged three Kleenex out so quickly, he was sure they had to be connected. She pressed them over her eyes as her shoulders shook. Her nails looked like spikes growing out of the tissues. He couldn't for the life of him figure out why she'd had them put on.

"Why would anyone want to hurt Lulu, Jim?"

"I don't know, but I have to get back to the station, and I'd like to know you were at home or at your mama's or wherever you need to be." Her green eyes flicked to his, and he wanted to shake that little body of hers and make her go home, because she didn't know what he'd already figured out about the killer's fetish for small women.

"I'll stay right here and do my job." She threw the tissues into the wastebasket at her feet, reached for the ringing phone, and cleared her throat. "Search & Rescue, this is Elva Lee." She listened for a moment, and then her face crumbled. "Oh, Mama."

"Great." Jim told Tommy to get her somewhere safe and left.

Luke approached the soft glow of light emanating from above them in a maze of rock and roots. "I think I see sky and clouds."

"Thank God! I can't get out of here soon enough."

He shined his light up. "See that ledge? There, just below those roots. That's where we're headed. Ready?"

"I'm right behind you."

Luke picked up Molly and climbed to the ledge. He could hear the wind above him. He'd bet the farm it was cold and bitter. It was getting chillier the closer they climbed to the opening. "Almost there."

He crawled up through a root tunnel, shoving Molly ahead of him. "How in the world did he get the woman down this way?" He grunted as he climbed to the last level and poked his head above ground in thick brush. "Spring storm left a couple feet of snow." He shoved Molly topside and then followed her. Turning a three-sixty in the soft morning light, he said, "No one's about." He straddled the opening.

"Any sign of the killer?"

"Drag marks. A few footprints. They head up a small rise. Looks like car lights on the other side of the rise. Let's hope he didn't plan a welcoming party for us. Take my hand. I'll pull you up."

He lifted her out.

"How long were we in there?"

"Sun's rising. What time is it?"

She glanced at her watch. "A little after seven."

"Then, about thirty-six hours. Come on. We have enough light to see. Don't use a flashlight. I don't want to attract any attention."

They gave the drag marks a wide berth. When they topped the hill, twin beams from a van shone on a woman and a man standing in the parking lot. Luke and Sarah walked toward the van until Sarah placed a hand on his arm.

"Luke."

A low growl came from Molly.

"Give me those keys, Matthew Brandon Patterson. You're on restriction from driving for three days. I don't have time to teach you to drive and then you treat me like I'm the dirt under your feet."

In the bright lights, the spikes in young Patterson's hair swayed in the breeze, losing the fight to stay poised and erect and utterly cool.

Lifted brows and rolling eyes indicated Matthew Brandon Patterson was trying to decide whether to obey the woman in front of him. *His mother*, Luke guessed by his youthfulness and her tone.

"Now." For emphasis, the woman jabbed her already-extended flat hand toward the young man and pinched her lips.

Matthew Brandon Patterson held up the keys, jiggled them, and dropped them above his mother's hand. They didn't make it, though. If she'd wanted to catch them, she would have had to move her hand to the left and from the look in the gaze mercilessly piercing her son even as the keys fell, she wasn't about to.

They landed on the snow-covered road, muffled in the snow. *Oh, man, is he in for it now.*

"Pick them up." An underlying growl accompanied the words and, once again, Matthew Brandon Patterson stood still, staring at her as if he was deciding whether or not to mind her.

"Four days."

Still he didn't budge.

"Five days."

"Ah, Mom. You're being ridiculous!"

Mom didn't bat an eye. "Six."

"Okay, okay. Stop counting. Here are your stupid keys."

"Seven."

His hand disappeared in the snow. He held up the keys, shook the snow off them, and then slapped them onto Mom's hand. Even from this distance, Luke could tell that hurt Mom's hand.

"Eight."

"Jeez, Mom, you're out of control. Get a grip, okay?"

"Nine."

The young man threw up his hands and stalked around the van to the passenger side. He slammed the door.

When the woman snapped her head in Luke's direction, Luke cleared his throat and stepped back.

"Oh." She flapped a hand at him. "I only eat fifteen-year-old boys learning to drive for breakfast. You look a little too old for my taste."

Luke smiled. "Do you know my mother? I think she wrote the script you just rehearsed, and quite flawlessly, I might add."

"We've practiced it so many times, we have our lines down." The woman looked at Sarah, then Luke. "Do you need some help?"

"If you have a cell phone and would dial 9-1-1 for us, we'd sure appreciate it."

The woman's eyes widened as her gaze quickly swept over Sarah. "Are you okay? Is anyone hurt?"

Luke shifted his backpack. "We're both fine. We just need to report a crime to the police. Could we use your phone?"

"Of course." She reached into her pocket and punched the numbers. "Here," she said, shoving the phone toward Luke.

A.J. and Jim walked down the steps of Lulu's house when A.J.'s phone rang. "Hello? Well, well, about time you checked in with us, buddy. Everything okay with you?" He turned toward Jim and listened, and then he frowned, shook his head, and closed his eyes. "All right," he said quietly. "I'll send Officer Larry Traylor out to pick you up." He hung up.

"Who was that?"

"Luke McKenzie. He was in the cave near Gem's Peak Park and wants to report a murder. A woman in green high heels."

Jim cursed under his breath. "Lulu."

SEVEN

In Officer Traylor's truck, Luke was having trouble staying awake. It didn't help that Sarah's head was heavy on his shoulder, drawing him into sleep with her deep breathing.

"Here we are, folks."

The truck pulled up to a rustic brown building. A sign read "Search & Rescue, Little Texas, Colorado." A.J. and Jim stood outside on the sidewalk.

The chill of the night had turned to downright cold this morning. Luke touched Sarah's shoulder, but she didn't move. He hated waking her, but they had to get this over with before they could both grab some sleep.

"Sarah." He nudged her. Her hair had fallen over her face, and he moved it behind her ear.

Her eyes opened. She sat up and rubbed her shoulder where Luke's hand had been. "Yeah. We've got to—" Her head fell back against the seat, and then she melted against his shoulder again. "I'm so wiped out."

"One more hour and you can go to your cabin and rest." He opened the truck door. "Do you need any help getting out? Stay, Molly."

Larry turned around. "It's all right to bring her in. We have dogs in here all the time."

They went inside. A.J. and Jim greeted Luke, met Sarah, and then they all sat at a rectangular table with six chairs.

A.J. plucked a pen out of his shirt pocket. "Now, tell us what you saw in that cave."

Luke shook his head. "We actually didn't see much. Only a flashlight and the body of a woman. The man's face was in the dark the whole time."

Molly quietly slept while A.J. took the report.

After thirty minutes of questioning, Sarah rested her head on her folded arms and slept. Luke wanted to join her, but it wouldn't be too long before he'd be in bed.

Jim cleared his throat. "So, what we've got here is a diminutive man singing and humming Christmas songs, dragging a woman's body—"

"Lulu's. There." A.J. threw his arms out. "I said it out loud. It's real. She's dead. She's the only woman in this town who owns a pair of green high-heel shoes. Larry's headed to her house to see if hers are gone."

Silence throbbed. Jim sat, unmoving, and stared at the floor. An overhead fluorescent light buzzed and flickered. He started when the phone rang. A.J. picked it up, listened intently, and dropped it in its cradle with a long sigh.

"The shoes weren't there?"

A.J. frowned and shook his head at his brother. "No."

Jim stood, placed his hand on his brother's shoulder for a moment, and turned to Luke. "I don't think it's a stretch to consider that the man firing on you and Sarah might be the man who went after Lulu."

Luke had actually thought the same thing. "Would the sniper have taken the chance of bringing the body into the cave with us in there? We could have easily reached the crevice and witnessed him by the time he arrived."

Jim nodded. "Unless he's never gone far enough past there to discover that the other opening is on Bear Camp Trail. Or he figured you two had doubled back and left while he went after Lulu. Or, there are two of them." He shook his head at A.J.

"But why was he after her? What good reason could he have for killing Lulu, Jim?"

"He could have been after Sarah, and Luke fouled it up for him."

"That might explain why he pushed her over the edge instead of killing her," Luke said, nodding. "She was close to catching up with me on the trail. He wanted her alone. But why didn't he kill me and just take her?"

"We can guess that when he failed with Sarah, he went after Lulu. If Sarah hadn't screamed and caught your attention, she would've been the victim here, not Lulu."

"Me?" Sarah shivered and groggily lifted her head. "But why? I don't know anyone up here but you people."

Luke stood. "Listen, A.J., I don't think we're going to get any more this morning. Could we continue this after we've had some sleep? Sarah needs to get home."

Her head landed on her arms again. "I second that."

"That's fine." A.J. looked over at Luke. "We have two crime scenes to secure. We know exactly where you were on Bear Camp Trail. We've known about that cave entrance for a long time, but I don't think it's general knowledge around here, do you, Jim?"

"No. Do you want me on this? I could meet y'all over there."

"Yeah. We'll need help on both cases. We'd appreciate your assistance, too, Luke."

"You have it." He stood and picked up his pack. "My truck and her mountain bike are at the trailhead. Can one of you drive us over there? I'll take her home."

Sarah's head popped up again. "Us?"

"Yes, us." Luke pulled her chair back and helped her stand. "I made you a promise to get you to the hospital or your home. I intend to keep it."

"Are you staying in my cabin?"

"I hadn't intended to."

"Oh."

"Do you want me to?"

"Well, no, actually. I mean, I would appreciate *some*one staying with me, what with, you know, the sniper *and* the killer out there. The sniper may know where I live. He may have followed me to the trail."

Luke sighed. He was too tired to argue with her. But one thing was clear: surviving until they found the way out of the cave was one thing; staying with her in her cabin was another entirely. But someone needed to be with her until they could figure this thing out. "All right. I'll stay."

"It doesn't have to be you."

"Yeah, it does."

Jim stood. "Y'all sleep all day and all night, then we can meet tomorrow morning, maybe have breakfast before we do."

A.J. nodded. "Let's meet at Penny's Bar and Grill, my wife's place—my *estranged* wife's place. She fixes a mean breakfast and doesn't charge an arm and a leg for it."

Luke asked, "What time? Seven-thirty okay with everybody?"

Jim nodded. "How about we have Penny cater breakfast here at S&R? We'd be pestered to death with questions about Lulu if we ate at the restaurant."

"Sounds great." Luke picked up Sarah's pack. "Seven-thirty here. See y'all then."

Sarah fell asleep after giving Luke her keys and directions to her cabin. After picking up her bike, he drove to his home, gathered some things, and then drove to Sarah's. He unloaded her bike, opened the cabin door, turned on the light, looked around, and then went back to his truck and lifted her out. It seemed surreal, carrying a sleeping beauty into a mountain cabin with aspens shivering in the cold breeze and snow glistening in the sunshine as a heavy-racked elk trotted across the front lawn.

Luke kicked the door shut against the last thirty-six-plus hours. Sarah roused, and he set her on her feet. She fell against him, and, instinctively, he wrapped his arms around her to keep her from falling.

She gently pushed away. "I'm going to take a shower," she mumbled and turned toward the hallway.

"Good. You're rank."

"So are you, McKenzie."

He smiled and looked around. Oak paneling covered the walls. A stone fireplace dominated the small room. A cat's bed sat next to it.

Rustic, comfortable, inviting. Luke melted into a brown sofa, propped his booted feet on a matching ottoman, and prayed for an angel to start a fire in the fireplace. He listened to the shower and closed his eyes.

"Luke?"

Her voice was pulling him out of the darkness.

"Luke?"

"Umm?"

"Your turn, Luke. The shower."

He smelled her before he opened his eyes.

She stood in a white terry cloth robe tied at the waist, clean and fresh, a sweet aroma surrounding her. Her wet-spiked eyelashes framed golden eyes, her damp blonde hair brushed back from a shiny clean face. The few scratches on her face were less red now. Her robe slipped over her shoulder, and his gaze dipped to it.

At his look, she straightened her robe, took a step back, and pointed toward the bathroom. "Shower. Your bedroom. That way." She enunciated slowly, as a mother would to a headstrong child.

Weary, he rubbed his eyes and headed to a hot shower in the hopes that it would wash away the grime of the last two days.

Fifteen minutes later, he found her bedroom. She was asleep. Thick dark curtains shut out the sun. He moved a curtain aside and peered at the snow-covered yard. Outside, nothing moved. All was serene.

He dropped the curtain and flicked off a growling bear nightlight sitting on the rustic table by her bed. It was pretty dark for day time. "Good-night, Sarah."

His room was smaller with a single bed sitting below a single window. The sheets were crisp and clean, and he slid between them, too exhausted to care that his feet hung off the bottom of the bed.

Just as he drifted into sleep, a scream startled him fully awake. Another scream.

He threw off the covers and raced down the short hall into Sarah's room. In a sleepy fog, he grabbed her shoulders and gently shook her. "Sarah."

She groped for Luke. "Oh. Oh. I—I thought he was in here. I could feel him in here, hovering over my bed."

He held her hands. "I'm here. Just me." He sat on the edge of her bed. "You're safe now, in your cabin. He's not here, and you're safe."

She closed her eyes, then opened them again, but not for long. They wilted closed again, and she began to breathe deeply. He eased off the mattress.

She grabbed his wrist. "Don't go," she whispered and pulled him back down beside her.

Past exhaustion, Luke didn't think he could stay awake much longer. "I'll be in the next room. You'll be okay. Here, let me turn on the nightlight again."

"I don't want to be alone."

"And where will I sleep? In this chair?" He stood. "Look. I'll sit in here until you're asleep."

"Will you be here when I wake up?"

"No."

She rolled over and faced the wall. "I'm sorry, Luke. I wasn't quite awake. Go on back to your room. I'll be all right."

Without a backward glance, he walked out of the room, dropped onto his bed, and knew nothing as he fell headlong into sleep.

They slept all day. When Luke got up some time in the evening, Sarah was still asleep, but he saw evidence that she'd been awake. A cup with a little water in it sat on the counter beside a jar of peanut butter. He found jelly in the fridge and fixed a couple of sandwiches and enjoyed the quiet. Glancing outside, he saw nothing moving. He stayed up a while and went back to bed. He awoke at four, glanced at the clock, groaned, and rolled over.

"Sarah. Come on, Sarah. Wake up."

She lifted her head and stared into a sea of fluffy white. *Wha—?*

"You were dreaming. At least—"

Wide-eyed, she rolled off her pillow and gasped. "What are you doing?"

Luke squinted at her as if he was trying to make sense of her question.

"I said, what are you doing in here?"

"Here?"

"In my bed!"

He frowned at her and shook his head twice. "Not so loud." His patted the air several times. "You had a nightmare last night and asked me to stay—"

"I most *certainly*—"

"Did." He held up a boy scout's hand and crossed his heart. "As I live and breathe. But I didn't stay. When you screamed a few minutes ago, I ran to the rescue again. But—" He started toward the door. "The damsel doesn't need rescuing."

She closed her eyes. "Shut the door on your way—"

The door slammed.

"Nightmare, my eye!" She pulled her knees up and rested her aching head on them. "I didn't have a nightmare. He just—"

She lifted her head. She remembered. She woke up terrified. He came into her room to see if she was all right. She did ask him to stay and then changed her mind when he said he wouldn't do it.

Great day in the morning! Even half asleep, how could she have done that to herself—and to him? Thank God, he'd had the good sense to do the right thing. Angry at herself, she headed for the kitchen to fix coffee. But it was already brewing.

A door shut quietly down the hall.

Thoroughly humbled, she stepped into the hallway to make sure he heard her. "Thank you for making the coffee."

When he didn't answer, she poured herself a cup, sipped a little, and headed for the bathroom. "We need to leave in about forty-five minutes if we plan to be on time."

No answer.

She showered again, took her time dressing, and came out of her room. "Luke? Let's go."

No answer.

"Fine. I'll see you there." She headed outside. She pulled up when she spotted him standing beside his truck wearing a cowboy hat, boots, and a short winter coat. "I know that cowboy hat wasn't in your backpack. Where'd you get the clothes?"

"I went to my cabin." Holding a steaming to-go cup, he said, "Time's a-wasting, Sarah. Let's go."

She slipped inside the truck as did he. "Before we leave, Luke, I need to apologize for my attitude this morning and for last night when you came to help me. I do remember now, and I'm sorry I put you in that position."

"No problem. If that's all you've got to apologize for, then it's a good day already."

EIGHT

Pancakes, French toast, eggs, bacon, and biscuits and gravy were delivered to Search & Rescue and not the police station simply because S&R had two long tables, one for the food and one for everyone to enjoy breakfast.

Jim sipped his coffee and tried to ignore the tension between his brother A.J. and his estranged wife, Penny. When would those pea-brains get their act together and stop this nonsense of being separated? Jim watched Penny turn around and when she saw A.J. staring at her, she presented her back to him and headed for the coffee station.

Police officers Larry and Roland waltzed in, with S&R's Tommy and Buddy right behind them. Sarah and Luke popped in soon after.

"Good morning, folks." Jim waited until he had everyone's attention. "Luke, you know everybody here. Sarah, let me make introductions real quick. This is Penny Banks, owner of the best restaurant in town and my sister-in-law. Tommy and Buddy work with me at S&R. You know A.J. and Larry. You didn't meet Roland Graves last night. He's a police officer, too."

They all nodded at her. Then Penny poured coffee into cups she'd set at each place on the table.

Luke grabbed one. "Thank you, Penny."

"If everybody's ready to eat, then let's bless this food." Jim bowed his head, prayed, stood back while everyone filled up. It was a quiet group. Not much to say this morning, with police and S&R staying up late, trying to figure out what had happened to Lulu and who could have done it.

Jim caught his brother trying hard not to watch Penny. She was cross with A.J. but pleasant to everyone else. At one point, Jim nudged his brother's foot when Penny walked up behind him with a pot of coffee. But she just poured his coffee and moved on to the next person. Jim wished to high heaven those two would grow up a little bit.

The front door opened. All heads turned toward Miss Gertie as she headed toward them. Chairs scooted back as the men stood.

She flapped her hands at them. "Y'all sit, sit, and enjoy your breakfasts." She turned to Jim and A.J. "I heard about Lulu. I'm sorry for the both of you. She was a sweet woman, as was her mother, a dear friend of mine."

Jim nodded. "'Preciate it, Miss Gertie. Would you like to join us? There's plenty here."

She eyed the dishes. "Well, I just might have myself a couple of Penny's pancakes." Jim tugged a chair out for her, and she draped her little daypack over it.

But she didn't sit. "Just came from my sister's house. She tells me a couple of bona fide nincompoops are in here this morning. Been awhile since I've seen one, and I came in here to do just that." Her gaze stopped on Luke. "Luke McKenzie, don't tell me it was you." She cocked her head, a frayed ski cap with withered petunias sitting snug on the crown of it. "I thought you had more sense than that."

Luke stood, extended his hand. "Miss Gertie. Good to see you. It's been a long time, hasn't it?"

Her head fell back as she gaped up at him. "You've grown since I last saw you. How tall are you, boy?"

"Six-three."

"All you McKenzie boys are tall." She sat and reached for her coffee cup. "You know I live out on Bear Camp Road. I know two of you were up there on that trail. Who was with you?"

Luke sat just as Sarah's wiggling fingers popped up. She smiled sheepishly. "Sarah Morgan, Miss Gertie."

"You look a dern sight smarter than you acted, young lady. Don't you Texans have sense enough not to hike a closed trail with a winter storm boldly staring you in the eye?"

Luke shrugged. "Well, no, ma'am, apparently not."

Jim choked on a biscuit as a few chuckles were being stifled around the table.

"Thank you, Penny." Miss Gertie took the plate of pancakes and set it down. "Maybe this breakfast will help with the sleepless nights I had worrying over you two."

Jim thought they all needed a smile or two this morning. As everyone ate, he glanced out the window. He didn't recognize the young man sitting on the bench across the street. That wasn't unusual this time of year, when tourists began to encroach upon their last two months of winter weather in what the rest of the world called spring. The young man's gaze darted around the area—

"Jim, how long until the trails are open?"

Sarah's question brought his attention back to their table. "Another two or three weeks. Usually around May fifteenth to the twentieth. We'll remove the signs around that time. 'Course, signs don't stop some people." Jim lifted his brows. "Do they, Luke?"

Luke grinned and lifted his brows at Sarah. "Do they, Sarah?"

"Oh, right. Put it off on me."

Everyone finished eating, stood, and thanked Penny for the meal.

A.J. headed for the door. "Let's walk to the station and get your official statements on paper."

They all stepped outside, turned left, and walked past Gally's

Hardware, cattycornered to Jodee's Salon and the bank. Miss Gertie left them to go to the drugstore.

Uh-oh. Jim ducked his head and tried to hurry everyone along. He'd spotted the small, skinny frame of Miss Gertie's sister, Miss Winnie Sue Jansen, shoveling her porch. When her keen gaze spotted the group standing at the red light, she stopped shoveling, leaned her shovel against her porch wall, and moved carefully down her steps and across her yard to the hedgerow.

Thankfully, they wouldn't actually pass in front of her 1894 Victorian house, one of the first homes built here. Her property was due south of the police station. She waited for them to cross the street. *Like a hawk.*

They'd be stuck for an hour if they stopped to visit. Out of the corner of his eye, he saw her clean her hands on her apron, lean over her hedgerow, and cup her mouth to engage anyone she could catch.

He quickly checked his watch and then waved at her. Since he was bringing up the rear, he felt obliged to speak before she could open her mouth. "We can't stop today, Miss Winnie Sue. Got police business to take care of inside. Miss Gertie said to tell you she went to the drugstore and would be by your place in a little bit."

"What business?" she asked, shielding her eyes with a hand.

The group reached the front door of the police station. Seeing as how they were inches from going inside, Jim figured she might consider raising her voice, which would not be entirely acceptable to Miss Winnie Sue Jansen.

"Is it Lulu, Mr. Banks?" she asked in as genteel a voice as possible without coming anywhere remotely near a screech.

"We have to run now, Miss Winnie Sue. You take care, ma'am."

"Well, forevermore," she said just before the station door closed behind him.

Sarah sat at the table against the back wall while Luke headed for the coffee pot and poured a cup. He lifted the pot to the others.

A.J. pulled out a chair. "I'll take a cup. How long you folks expecting to be here in Little Texas?"

Luke handed A.J. a cup. "I still have almost four weeks' vacation coming so I'll stick around a bit to see what happens."

Sarah glanced at A.J. "I took six weeks off from my store, and I've been here less than a week, so I'll be here, too."

Jim straddled a chair when A.J. called the meeting to order and said, "We need to find out what's in that crevice."

"Did you learn anything, Miss Gertie? Did the Banks brothers say anything important about Lulu?"

Gertie's younger sister, Winnie Sue, sat with crossed ankles, blended knees, erect back, and a white handkerchief fisted in her thin veined hands. She wondered how her little sister could be so prim and proper every minute of every day. Winnie Sue's gaze roamed the lace-covered windows for anyone walking by before they rested on her older sister.

"They said absolutely nothing. I couldn't be too obvious, Winnie Sue. Those boys are sharp."

"Not too sharp, with three murders already, and they haven't caught on yet!" She picked up a folded fan, spread it, and quickly flapped its wings in front of her face.

Gertie put up with her prissy younger sister because she was, after all, only sixty-three and not well versed in the ways of any society other than the well-mannered kind. She watched her uncross her ankles, position them the other way, and pull on her skirt to make sure it was properly covering her ankles.

Mercy, mercy, but the woman was as tight as a purse string. "What are you saying? That I should give them a hint or two?"

"Good gracious me, no. What a preposterous thing to say. It took the third murder for us to figure it out or at least *think* we've figured it out. I'm saying if *we* can, why haven't they?"

Laws, the woman would test a saint. Did she think a pea roosted in the hollow between Gertie's ears? "I know what you're saying, and I'll try to find out what's what and let you know." *Or better yet, keep your trap shut, Gertie Jansen, because Lord knows, and most of this town, too, that Winnie Sue Jansen is a yapper of the first order.*

"And the letters. You've carefully hidden the letters, of course."

Gertie forced her eyes not to roll. "Of course."

"Where?"

"In my attic, under a loose board in the northeast corner."

"The anonymous note that said, 'You know, don't you, Rosie?'"

"It's there, too. I don't think anyone could find them even if they went up there. What are you having for supper tonight?"

"You're trying to get around me, Sister, and I won't have it."

What a trial. With the age difference, Gertie had been more of a mother to her baby sister than a sister, and the fact that her sister was sorely lacking in a sense of humor made things much more tense than they need be.

"I was just wondering if you were going to fix fried chicken." She wanted to add, *It's Friday, y'know,* because Winnie Sue Jansen *always* had fried chicken on Fridays. But Gertie didn't let her know she'd figured that out because Winnie Sue hated being considered predictable, as if it were a sin. Orderly, sensible, even prepared, but certainly not *predictable.*

"Why, yes, I am, as a matter of fact. Would you like to join me? And bring a salad. Not the green things you brought last time. Bring sweet carrot salad with raisins in it."

Ugh. Gertie hated that salad with a passion, but to get to Winnie Sue's fried chicken, she'd do it and be cheerful about it. "Consider it done. Six o'clock?" Written in stone, her time for dinner.

"As good a time as any, I'd say."

And she'd been saying that for forty years. Truth be told, Gertie was sick and tired of hearing it. It was a shame she'd never been able to marry her little sister off. Then, maybe she could endure a quiet week by herself. But her little sister demanded time together out of sheer loneliness.

"I'll pick you up at five-forty, then, Miss Gertie."

And not a minute sooner. She kissed her little sister's cheek and headed outside where most things were disorderly and illogical, and only sometimes predictable—like Lulu Baines' death.

It was no surprise at all to Gertie that someone else died. She just wished it hadn't been Lulu.

Jim needed to concentrate on his job and not on the picture of Lulu staring up at him from today's newspaper.

A.J. folded the paper. "That man down to Willow Falls, Jim. What's his name? The caver who's also a forensic investigator? He'd be our best bet to find out if Lulu's alone at the bottom of that hole." A.J. tossed the newspaper onto Jim's desk and looked out the window.

"Name's Josh Daniels."

"That's it." A.J. nodded. "I'll give him a call."

Luke sat on the corner of A.J.'s desk and cleared his throat. "The man in the cave was roughly five-foot-two or three. How tall is Daniels?"

The obvious question. "About five-eight or so." Jim picked up the newspaper and turned it over as Tommy and Buddy came into the police station. Jim had given them the day off from Search & Rescue because of Lulu's death. "You two couldn't stay away, I see."

Tommy slipped his hands into his coat pockets. His cowboy hat covered his face as he looked down. "Lulu was my friend, too."

She was everybody's friend.

"Either of y'all know Josh Daniels down Willow Falls way?"

"The caver." This, from Tommy.

"His sister married my cousin." Buddy picked up a donut, plopped it into his mouth, and chomped on it as if he hadn't eaten in three days.

"Does he still live in Willow Falls?"

"Yep," Buddy said with his mouth full. "We got his number down at the office."

"Elva Lee's gone to lunch. Would you mind getting that number for me, Buddy?"

"Sure, Jim. So long as I can take reinforcements." He stacked three donuts on a thumb. Tommy opened the door for him.

Just before the door closed on them, Jim said, "Don't get sugar gunk on that address card, Buddy." To A.J., he said, "If we call Josh and he's able to get into that crevice, we might end up tipping off the killer that we found his dumping spot. If he's still here, that is."

"He could be someone we've known all our lives."

"Yeah. I thought of that. I'd have a hard time believing that someone I know could've hurt Lulu."

A.J. crumbled the newspaper into a ball and threw it into a wastebasket.

Jim had seen his brother's temper plenty of times, but grief was driving it at the moment. Any other time, he would have engaged him in a little verbal wrestling. "But if he is local, why does he start killing our women? What would make a man do that?" Jim's phone beeped. "Buddy texted Josh's number to me."

He gave it to A.J., who called him. He put the phone on speaker.

"Josh Daniels."

"Yeah, Josh, this is A.J. Banks, police chief here in Little Texas. We have something we'd like you to investigate for us if you would."

"A cave?"

"A crevice in a cave wall that we think goes down a ways. One opening to this system is there on Bear Camp Trail. The crevice isn't too far from Gem's Peak Park."

"Heard of that cave, years ago, but I've never been down."

"We think there's a body in the crevice. Wondered if you could go down and take some pictures for us."

"A human body?"

"A murdered human body. Do you think you could meet us there and have a look-see as soon as possible?"

"I can meet you there at one o'clock today. Anyone going in with me?"

"Not with you into the crevice but, yeah, I got one. Luke McKenzie."

"A caver?"

"You could say he is."

"Are you going in, Chief?"

"No, sirree. I get claustrophobic stepping inside my shower."

338

Luke, Josh Daniels, and Moe Wiggins, a crime scene investigator on Josh's staff, headed across the grass toward the parking lot. Luke glanced over his shoulder. It had been grueling in the cave. He never wanted to go down there again.

The purpose of this trip had been to get away from the murder of his father, the sadness that still enveloped the ranch, and here, he'd walked into three murders and an entire town that was grieving. He'd get past this in the next few days and try to enjoy the rest of his trip.

The three men walked away from the entrance to the crime scene toward A.J. and Jim who were standing in the shade of a pine tree. Jim frowned at them as if he searched for news on their faces. They'd come out after two long hours with nothing good to tell anyone.

Holding baggie-wrapped camera equipment, Josh and Moe set their gear on the back seat of Josh's vehicle and slammed the door.

Luke had nothing but respect for both men, investigating the scene and then Josh going inside the crevice alone to face the horrors he'd found.

"Chief."

A.J. nodded at Josh. "What you got for me?"

"It's a long, tunnel-like cave. Goes down about thirty feet at a twenty-five-degree angle. Pretty steep. Then it splits into two passageways but at that point, the three bodies stopped their slide."

"Three?"

"All women, all dressed up, very well preserved, like he'd just put them in there. That's the norm in deep caves, being preserved so well. I got some good pics for you. Do you want me to email them to you or do you want to see them now?"

"Was Lulu one of them?"

"From the photos you gave me of her, yes. Two other women, small, dressed up. I didn't try to move them to get better pictures. I just left them *in situ* in case you call in the FBI."

"No need for that at this point. Any other evidence collected where the killer walked, moved around? Shoe size, hair samples?"

Luke looked at Moe, who didn't say anything, so Luke nodded and said, "Small tennis shoes, like a child's, a size six or seven. Got a cast of a really good one. Didn't kick up much dirt. No fingerprints, no hairs, nothing left behind."

A.J. blew out a long breath. "Got good pics of that, too?"

Josh nodded.

"Why don't y'all get yourselves cleaned up and eat some supper, and we'll meet back at the station." He looked at his watch. "Somewhere around seven-thirty. Let's keep this information hush-hush. We don't need everybody in Little Texas getting anxious until we have more information to give them. In the meantime, I'll check the photos and see what we've got."

Jim glanced at Luke. "It might be a good idea for Sarah to stay with you. There's safety in numbers."

He'd already thought of it. "She's there now, staying with my chef, Eduardo, and his wife, Yolanda, my housekeeper. I'll drive her to her cabin, get her things."

Jim turned to Josh and Moe. "Y'all can come to my house to get cleaned up and go with me to Penny's to grab some supper. Then we can head over to the meeting together."

At McKenzie Cabin, Sarah followed Luke outside as he headed toward his truck. "I don't recall anyone giving me the *option* of staying at my cabin or yours."

"It's safer for you in our cabin," he said as he opened the driver's door and slid in just as Sarah did.

"You and Jim decide something, thwack people over the head, and then expect them to just fall in line."

"Thwack? Is that a word?" He grinned, backed up the truck, and drove toward the road. "Your seatbelt."

She grunted and fastened it. "You don't *ask* if people want to do something. You just decide for them and expect them to go right along with you."

"I'm not trying to thwack you or decide for you, but when the right course of action is obvious, no discussion is necessary. You can't honestly think you'd be safer in your cabin. Three bodies, Sarah. Three. And he was so close to getting *you*. Do you really think you'd be just as safe at your cabin as at mine?"

"I didn't say that."

"That's exactly what you said." He turned onto the road to her cabin. "Thwacking, you said."

"I didn't disagree with what you wanted me to do, only with how you handled it. I need my independence. That's why I'm here, to find it and myself again. To live without looking over my shoulder every step I take. I have to do this. I don't need your help."

In silence, he turned into her driveway, parked, turned off the engine. "I'm adaptable."

She sent him a sidelong glance as she got out and shut the door. "Meaning?" The conversation wasn't moving in the direction she'd intended. Maybe his only tactic wasn't thwacking.

Luke met her at the front door. "I won't help unless you ask for help."

"Good." She looked at him as she unlocked the door. With his hands in his pockets, Luke raised his brows and smiled as she withdrew the key. "Or make decisions for me."

"Or make decisions for you," he said amiably as the door opened.

She headed for her bedroom and shut the door. Even as irritating as Luke was at times, he cared about her safety. Now that she'd rebuked him, the shield of protection he'd placed around her had crumbled. She wasn't at all sure she wanted it gone. Not *completely* gone.

Maybe that was one of his other tactics, to make her regret her rash statements and eat her words. She scooped her things out of a drawer and tossed them into a suitcase.

Well, it worked. She already regretted scolding him.

But she wouldn't take back the words.

He walked to her doorway just as her phone rang.

"Hey, Mom." She turned away from Luke and looked out the window. "I'll be staying at the McKenzie's cabin for a few days. Yes, I'm fine. What?" She couldn't speak, couldn't think. "A-are they sure?" A quick glance at Luke. "I will. I will, Mom. I love you, too. 'Bye."

"What it is? You're as white as a sheet."

"They, uh." She dropped to the edge of her bed. "Another two girls were killed in the last week. Same M.O. as the man who went after me. The Darkslayer."

"Where?"

"The first one was near Goodland in western Kansas, not fifty miles from where I live. The second, in Limon, Colorado. A man was seen leaving the scene of the crime on a motorcycle. The motorcycle is a new clue."

"Do the police think he's on his way here? That he's following you?"

Sarah's face drained of color. "I don't know. She mentioned that the FBI will probably want to interview me."

"The one who got away."

"And the one who saw absolutely nothing."

Jim's phone rang. His brother, A.J. "Yeah, A.J."

"Can you come down to the station? I'll meet you out front."

"Right now? Josh, Moe and I are about to head to Penny's for supper."

"Now, if you can. You can eat later. I'll go with you."

"All right. I'll be there in five minutes."

Jim saw A.J. sitting on top of his patrol car. He turned off his headlights as he parked. Opening the truck's door, he stood on the running board and placed his arm on top of the door as if it could somehow shield him against what A.J. had to tell him.

"Jim."

Nodding, Jim calmly said, "You found Renee."

A.J. sighed. "You always could figure things out faster than me." He touched the hood of his car. "Come on over here and sit with me."

When Jim didn't move, A.J. slid off the car and headed toward him. "Shut that door. Let's walk."

"I don't want to walk."

"Then let's drive and talk about it."

In silence, Jim regarded his brother. It was obvious he was hurting for Jim. At this moment, facing the horrible truth of Renee's death, he didn't want to feel anything for anybody but himself. But he couldn't do that to his brother. For A.J.—to help his brother deal with this—Jim would go with him. He walked to the passenger side and got in.

A.J. slid inside the car, started it, and backed up.

"I've hated her for a year for leaving me, but she didn't run off."

"Yeah." A.J. took a deep breath and let it out. "Jim, I gotta tell you something else."

"Bonnie's down there, too."

"Yeah. And Lulu."

"I gotta get out."

"I know."

"We're at City Park. Let me out."

When A.J. slowed down, Jim bolted out of the car and ran down the concrete path, away from the memories of that last night before she left—the night she died. Her eyes had filled with tears when she told him she was pregnant. They had tried for five years, and she was finally pregnant. After she disappeared, Jim thought the baby was someone else's, that he couldn't have gotten her pregnant, that she'd run off, that she'd needed another man to fulfill her dreams.

But none of it was true.

All of his accusations and blame and hate had been misplaced. She *hadn't* left him. There *was* no other man. The baby *was* his.

What kind of love had he had for Renee that he would think the worst of her so quickly? At the first sign of trouble, he'd come up with every theory on why she'd left him and all of them attacked her character. None of them involved *murder*. None of them had someone else at fault.

Bending over, he gasped for air. The cold air made his chest hurt, but he deserved it. *Did she die quickly? Did he torture her? Was she alive when he put her in that hole?*

"I don't want to do this, Lord." He stood, walked off the last of his run, and made a vow, right there and then: he would hunt down the man killing their women, and when he found him, he'd hurt him until he screamed for mercy—and then he'd make it worse.

The man took one step back behind a tree as the chief's brother ran past him. So, they had found Rosie.

He could feel the rage already boiling inside him. Red colors spiked with bright oranges and yellows swirling in front of his eyes. He ground his teeth until his jaw throbbed, and then he slammed a fist into the trunk of a tree. He whined and gasped at the pain.

He'd earned the pain.

She was getting out.

It was his fault.

It was always his fault.

He had to get her back in there.

His heart raced as he tried to think through the desperate haze.

No, not back in the hole. Somewhere else. Somewhere no one would find her.

She had to be stopped. He couldn't bear the beatings anymore, the screams, the pain.

She had to be stopped.

He stepped out from behind the tree and walked toward the lights on Edgar Drive.

"You all right, buddy?"

He jumped at the words coming from behind a tree, left of him.

The chief's brother again. Jim Banks. He was probably one of the men down in the hole today. "Sure am, sir. Just enjoying this night. It's perfect for walking, isn't it?"

Jim headed down the long driveway to his parent's ranch home, but instead of going to the main house and scaring his mother half to death at this hour, he drove to the garage. The light was on. Dad was probably inside, working on a figurine. Good memories in that garage when he was growing up, watching his father's hands work magic on a piece of wood. Jim stopped the car and got out, his steps crunching on the gravel.

He gripped the shop's door handle and opened the door. "Dad? You in here?"

His father sneezed and came out from behind some shelving. "'Course I am, son. Where else would I be at eleven-thirty at night? Come in. Come in." Tucking his handkerchief in his back pocket, he stretched out his other hand and pulled Jim into a quick hug, then held his shoulders as he looked into blue eyes mirroring his own. "What are you doing out here at this time of night? Trouble at the job?"

Jim rubbed his eyes but not before tears welled up.

Dad nodded at the refrigerator. "Grab us a soda."

Jeb—an acronym for James E. Banks—cleaned his tools and set them in a neat row on the table, then tugged on the towel in his back pocket, wiped his hands, and flapped it at the two lawn chairs sitting by the garage door. "Have a seat while I open this door."

He leaned over the miter saw workbench and felt behind the wood stack for the light switch. The double-wide garage door opened to a cool moonlit night with stars glittering in a coal-black cloudless sky. Jim handed him a soda can. They both sat, drank, and looked out at the night.

"Dad? They found Renee's body today."

With his head back, Jeb had drawn in a breath to take a swallow, but he stilled and stared at his son. "S-Say what?"

"They found Renee's body today."

"Found?" His hand was frozen mid-air.

"She was killed in our home and taken to a cave and thrown into a crevice with Bonnie Washburn."

His dad blinked at him as if he couldn't understand the words. Slowly, he lowered his hand to his lap.

"And Dad? Lulu's in there with Renee and Bonnie."

"L-Lulu?"

Jim knew this one hurt the most. Dad's sister, Melody, had only one daughter—Lulu.

Jeb sat in the darkness, obviously shaken. He glanced over at Jim. Tears filled their eyes. Jim had no idea in the world how to comfort Dad or himself. They had never been a touchy-feely kind of family, but he sure wouldn't mind a good hug about now.

"Son, I was wrong about Renee. I was wrong about her, and I'm sorry for it."

"I was wrong, too."

The night grew cold. The crisp, chilly air settled around them like an icy blanket. "And Lulu. Dear, sweet Lulu. What is going on here? Someone... someone you arrested in Denver or... or something?"

"Maybe. Maybe not."

Silence enveloped them. Jim knew this was Jeb's favorite time of the day when he could come out to his workshop to design and create his figures. His time to relax and think about his day, to plan tomorrow.

Jeb would remember this night forever, and it saddened Jim.

Gravel crunched again.

Debra appeared around the corner, smiling, carrying two small plates and two cups of steaming coffee on a tray. "Well, I thought that was you." Her smile wilted as she looked at her husband, then her son. "What is it? Something's wrong. Jim, what is it?"

Jim sighed and took the tray from his mother as he stood. "Apple pie. My favorite." He sniffed deeply. "Sure not a night for cold drinks, is it?"

He motioned Debra toward his chair and took the two cups, handed one to Jeb. "Sit down, Mama. I've got some news that won't wait on these pies."

By five o'clock the next afternoon, Police Chief A.J. Banks had rounded up a team tasked with going down in the morning and bringing up the three bodies of the women murdered in Little Texas, Colorado. Despite his best efforts to keep this news quiet, media began to arrive in the area. He held a press conference with his brother, Jim, and the staff at S&R, along with Officers Larry Traylor and Roland Graves. Briefly, he advised the press of what authorities knew up to this point and kindly asked them to respect the privacy of grieving family members.

TEN

Luke was dreading going back down in the cave this morning. He got up long before the sun rose. His routine involved jogging two to three miles at least four times a week. If he didn't run, he pumped iron and did sit-ups or followed a kick-boxing video. He looked forward to the run more than anything. Running had helped him this last year with the stress of losing his dad and the stress of his job as foreman of his family's large working ranch.

After his run and shower, he got dressed and was about to leave when a quick knock on the adjoining door was followed by the door opening. Sarah stood in her robe with her hands in its pockets, her sad expression telling him she wished he didn't have to do this.

"You're headed out?"

He grimly nodded and walked over to her.

"I've felt so useless the last couple of days. I want to help, but I don't know how."

"Your number one priority is keeping yourself safe. I ordered a security system for the cabin. It should be here tomorrow."

"You didn't have to do that."

"Yes, I did. If I thwacked you into coming here, then you need to know you're protected." Good. It brought a little smile, but it didn't last very long. "I have to go."

"Be safe."

"I will."

Fifteen minutes later, he parked at Gem's Peak Park, got out, and stood with A.J. and Jim. Reporters were standing behind the yellow tape. Every little movement made by the three men sent cameras clicking. Some of the people of Little Texas were there, too, holding up cell phones, snapping pictures, or making videos as the recovery team tasked with bringing up the bodies parked and exited their vehicles. Officer Larry Traylor drove up and joined A.J. and Jim.

Conversations ended as Luke stood with the recovery team members and then ducked under the yellow tape surrounding the area. They all headed for the hole under the tree. The crowd stood in silence as they hovered near the opening of the cave and then, one by one, disappeared underground.

Three hours later, the bodies of Lulu Baines, Bonnie Washburn, and Renee Banks were brought up. They lay side by side in bags as the recovery team stood around, making notes, talking on cell phones. Then the bodies were loaded into vehicles and driven off-site.

A.J. instructed the recovery team to clean up and meet him at the station in about an hour. Everyone but A.J. left without saying a word to those waiting around for any morsel of information. "We'll have something for you soon, folks." With that, he told them to leave the area.

They dispersed, he knew, to worry, to wait, to whisper to neighbors and friends and family about what had happened out at Gem's Peak Park.

And to wonder what kind of monster could have done this to three of their own.

Winnie Sue had her back up.

On top of all the news about the murders, the press intruding everywhere, her sister Miss Gertie too busy to come over, and no one out and about to talk to her over her fence, she had forgotten to get her library books back on time.

And, oh, won't Miss Tiger Claws like that!

Winnie Sue hugged her bag of books close to her chest as she walked across Main Street and up the sidewalk to the double doors of the library. She gritted her teeth and tugged with all her might on the right side of the double doors. She had informed the town council for years that the library door was much too large and too heavy for the ladies of Little Texas and when it got a little suction to it, when the wind kicked up, why, it was nigh onto impossible to open.

But nothing had ever been done about it.

She hated being in a cantankerous mood when she went into the library, but she was and deserved to be. She loved reading and was determined to continue to read regardless of the fact that Laura Langston sat behind the reservation desk, primed and ready to give Winnie Sue an ungraciously hard time. Most of the time, her complaints had nothing to do with Winnie Sue. "I hate the rain, Jansen. Did you do something evil to bring us this wretched rain?" or "The Simpsons' house burned down. Did you do it, Jansen?" or "Mrs. Claremore is sick, Jansen. Did you put a spell on her?"

Oh, Laura Langston was a burr in Winnie Sue's side! And she had no idea why Laura was so rude to her. She'd never once been unkind to the woman.

Not bothering to lift her eyes in any semblance of a well-mannered greeting, Winnie Sue approached the reservation desk.

She could sense Laura Langston watching her, waiting like a hawk ready to swoop. If the town council was going to do anything at all for the library, it should remove Laura Langston as librarian. The intelligent people of Little Texas who read and broadened their small worlds with the creative minds of people who wrote deserved a reprieve from the likes of Miss Sour Puss.

Very primly and very properly, eyes down, Winnie Sue quietly set her bag of books on the reservation counter and turned.

"You're one day late, Jansen."

Because of that monster, she wanted to retort, but Winnie Sue ignored her. She'd learned a long time ago that Laura Langston hated for her barbs to be dismissed. So, Winnie Sue started toward the romance section with the tip of her tongue between her clamped teeth and a deep breath easing out of her lungs. One of these days that tongue was going to jump right out of that clamp and give Laura Langston a piece of Winnie Sue's cultured and well-read mind.

"One day late, five books. A quarter, Jansen. No more books until you pay up." Her voice got louder as Winnie Sue walked away.

Heads turned. Activity stopped. Flushed, Winnie Sue hummed "Amazing Grace" ever so quietly under her breath as she walked toward the sweet haven of romance.

"This isn't a choir loft, Jansen."

Reverently, Winnie Sue slid her fingers across her favorite books. She pulled out the book she'd read many times and clutched it tightly against her bosom. She could see Bart Carpenter's large hands grabbing Lilly Tarentino's blazing bronze hair, pulling her head back as he said, "You're mine, Lilly! Now and always, you are mine!" And then his mouth devoured her.

Wistfully, Winnie Sue smoothed the cover of the book as she imagined what 'devoured' meant. She had been respectfully kissed in her younger days, once, but she didn't consider it a 'devouring' act, had no concept of *being* devoured. Certainly, if one was experiencing a 'devouring' kiss, one would know it.

She blushed as she remembered where she was and looked around, grateful no one was watching her. Then her gaze connected with Miss Grumpy Guts' quick glance as she waltzed past the end of the aisle. She rolled her eyes at Winnie Sue and shook her head.

"Never you mind," Winnie Sue whispered as she lifted her chin and walked down another row of books. She picked out four more paperbacks and, like a soldier gearing up for war, set her teeth and her feet toward the enemy and the librarian's bitter attitude.

An extended stiff hand waited for her when she set her books down. Calmly, she opened her purse, drew out a quarter, and placed it gently in the woman's claw.

Out of the corner of her eye, Winnie Sue saw a white head move. She turned and looked into the eyes of a handsome gentleman near her age. He was staring at her. She lowered her eyes, picked up her newly reserved books, pressed them close to her heart and, as she walked through the front door, she glanced at him.

The gentleman sent her smile and a wink.

Why, of all the nerve! Did he think she was some...some *trollop* who expected such...such...why the words weren't even in Winnie Sue's vocabulary! Embarrassed beyond measure, she huffed across the street and into the sanctuary of her own home where she could wonder in private if the gentleman she'd seen had ever devoured a woman and was quite certain he had, by his manners!

Laura Langston waited a mere three minutes. Without preamble, she strolled back to her library office, which occupied the enviable location of being directly across the street from Miss Winnie Sue's parlor. Laura locked the door behind her, opened her window, sat down, and smiled as the piano music began.

So, it was "Onward Christian Soldiers" first. Miss Winnie Sue absolutely tore up a piano and every time she endured a visit to the library, she waltzed home and played for a good hour. Maybe it was time to just *ask* her to play songs when she got home instead of riling her up. But riling her up was so much fun, and it produced what Laura wanted: the music.

With her elbows resting on the windowsill, she placed her chin in the palm of her hand, closed her eyes, and allowed the music to glide over her.

She sighed. Miss Winnie Sue's music was beautiful.

Ah, now. "Amazing Grace." So wonderfully played.

Perhaps by now, Miss Winnie Sue had forgiven her. Next, "Oh, For a Thousand Tongues to Sing," her absolute favorite. Laura would love to hear this song in church one day. But that would never happen.

The deaths of three innocent women lay squarely at her door. She'd been expecting him to come here. After the second death, she knew he had. Listening to this music was the only thing that assuaged some of her guilt.

But it simply wasn't enough.

A knock on the adjoining door startled Sarah, even though she'd heard Luke coming up the stairs. She'd seen him drive up and walk toward the cabin with his head down.

She opened the door. He looked so weary. "Are you okay?"

"Yeah. It was grisly, to say the least."

"What did they find?"

"The three women Josh discovered. Did you talk to the FBI today?"

"Yes. They came by and asked me a lot of questions about the Darkslayer."

Luke didn't come into her room. His gaze settled somewhere on the floor, and he rubbed his chin. "I kept thinking all day that you could have been down there with them."

Impulsively, she took his hand. "But I'm not—because of you. I haven't thanked you enough for saving my life. No telling what would have happened to me if you hadn't come along."

"If Molly hadn't."

"If you hadn't listened to your dog. If you both hadn't come to my rescue. You saved me from him."

He looked down at their joined hands. "I'm glad I met you that day, Sarah Ann Morgan," he said without looking into her eyes. It was a moment she would never forget. This hurting man gave comfort to *her*. It lasted only an instant, and he let go of her hand.

He crossed to her window, moved the curtain aside, and looked around the yard. "Have you watched any TV today?"

"No. Why?"

"The media is all over this story. A.J. wants the recovery team, S&R, his staff, and me down at his office." He checked his watch. "Listen, Sarah. We don't have any neighbors. We're secluded here. Don't open the door to anyone. Call me on my cell if you need me. Call our caretaker, Angus, if you need him. Here's his number." He gave it to her. "My chef, Eduardo, and his wife, Yolanda, are here. Let him know when you're ready for supper. He'll have it ready for you. I'm sure you've figured out that they live here year 'round. They have an apartment in the back."

"I suspected it, but I haven't actually had a tour of the house yet. Hint, hint."

"I'll give you that tour when I get back this afternoon." He headed for the door to his bedroom and stopped. "We'll try to slip in a picnic soon if we can stay out of the way of the press. Would you like that?"

"I'd love it. We both need to get outdoors and away from here."

The meeting with the recovery team, police staff, and S&R started later than Luke thought it would and ended earlier than he could have hoped for. Everyone left shortly before four. Only Luke was left, with A.J. who was writing in a notebook.

Looking out of the window blinds, Luke dreaded walking out with the chief of police to face the tall microphones swaying above reporters' heads and all the camera equipment aimed right at the station's front door. The reporters stared at the door, too, waiting for the chief of police to make a move.

"A.J., you need to get outside. They're waiting for you."

"I know. You still coming with me?"

"I am."

The door opened. Everyone shouted at once. Cameras clicked. Microphones extended toward Luke and A.J. Someone tugged on the sleeve of Luke's shirt and almost pulled him down. He jerked away and watched A.J. hold up his hands for quiet.

"Chief, Chief, do you—"

"Chief Banks, how long do you think the bodies—"

"Hey, A.J.! Do you have any idea—?"

"How were they—?"

"Were the women sexually assaulted, Chief?"

A.J. patted the air again and again for quiet. "We'll give the press a statement at six-thirty. No comment until then." Despite his words, questions continued to be thrown at him. He ducked under a flying microphone and shimmied through the mass of cameras and bodies, and both he and Luke slipped into his truck.

A.J. pulled out his cell phone, dialed Search & Rescue, and put it on speaker phone. "Elva Lee, let me speak to Jim, please."

"He's not here. He said he needed to be with Renee's sister and her family, that he'd be gone the rest of the day. You might catch him there."

He backed up his truck. "The media over at S&R?"

"Oh, yeah. They're camped out all over the parking lot, although I told them Jim wouldn't be back. They captured Tommy, and you know how Tommy likes attention, but he didn't tell them anything you didn't want told. Are you giving them a statement?"

"Yeah. You might wanna stick your head out and let them know the chief of police is giving a statement at six-thirty at the station house. That'll get 'em off your back. And lock your door. They're a pushy bunch." He shut down the phone. "Let's head over there. Maybe Jim's ready for supper, too."

"Did y'all ever consider these women might have been murdered, A.J.?"

"No, not really. Rachelle mentioned to me not two months ago that Renee would've contacted her by then, that she wouldn't have run off with someone and left Rachelle to wonder and worry. She thought Renee was too embarrassed to call her family because she'd been stupid to leave in the first place. We never really considered that she had been murdered. Not seriously considered, at any rate. Not *out loud* considered. There was absolutely no evidence to suggest it, and nothing like that had ever happened in Little Texas. She had simply driven away from her husband in her own car, which had never been found."

A.J. slowed down and leaned over just as the front door of a house opened. Jim stood with a man and a woman, hugged the woman, shook the man's hand, and walked toward his truck with his head down as he wiped his face.

A.J. pulled over to the curb and rolled down the window. "Where you headed?"

"Thought I'd stop by Penny's for supper."

"We'll meet you there."

Five o'clock was Laura Langston's favorite time of the day. It meant she could lock up the library and go home and leave all the nitwits in Little Texas behind her for an evening. She hated dealing with them all day long, listening to their stupid questions. "Could you tell me where the children's section is?" She would point up at the sign across the room that said, "Children." Some were worse than that. "What time do you close?" She'd point right in front of the patron at the sign on the counter that showed the library's hours. "Excuse me, do you have a restroom?" She'd point at the sign down the hall that said, "RESTROOMS."

But more than that, she was exhausted from the worry and stress eating away at her nerves. She crossed the street and walked by the police station with more interest than usual. The curtains were wide open. A.J. and his brother were inside.

Laura couldn't help but wonder if they'd discovered anything of importance on the murders by now.

She headed north the half-block to her home, went around to her back door, opened it, and froze.

A standard white sheet of paper sat in the middle of her kitchen table. The vase of artificial flowers that had been on the table was now sitting on the counter.

Leaning over without touching the paper, she read, "You know, don't you, Laura?" And it was signed, "Rosie." Written in simple childlike letters.

"Well, well, well. So, you found me, Rosie."

The wooden slat-backed chair she'd picked up in a garage sale scraped on the tiled floor as she tugged it away from the table. How had Rosie connected Laura to the murders? She'd changed her name and moved far away. She worked in a library, for heaven's sake, not a biochemical lab anymore.

She sat and glanced at the note again. Yes, Laura had figured it out.

352

She was sure she had no reason to be frightened for herself.

But she shuddered anyway.

Across town, Luke returned to his family's cabin around six-thirty. As he approached the front door, a crude cut-out of a red rose was stuck to the front door. He plucked it off. A piece of rolled-up tape was on the back. "Weird," he muttered. Eduardo and his wife, Yolanda, were always making crazy love-things for each other. Probably something of theirs.

He was about to go inside when he noticed his mountain bike wasn't leaning against the garage. Had Sarah taken it somewhere?

"Eduardo?"

As much as Luke wanted to be alone at the cabin, it was nice that he didn't have to cook and clean while he was here. Eduardo and Yolanda were very adept at making themselves scarce so Luke could have privacy. "Eduardo?"

The chef came out of the kitchen wiping his hands.

"Is Sarah here?"

"She insisted on going into town. I told her not to leave, but she said she needed some things, that it was a good time for her to go shopping."

On an oath, Luke grabbed his cell phone. "When did she leave?"

"About two hours ago."

"Two hours!" His heart raced as he punched in her number and tried not to glower at Eduardo for not hog-tying her to the nearest banister. Luke listened—and counted—the rings. On the fifth one, she answered.

"Where *are* you?" he bellowed as he turned his back to Eduardo.

"Luke? I'm, uh, about a half mile from your cabin."

"How can you be so stupid?" He scooped a pillow off the sofa, threw it at the curtains, and tried to shove the day's horrendous discoveries out of his mind. And here Sarah was, outside and alone! *Here, let me hand myself to you on a silver platter!*

"I wasn't being stupid. I needed some things. I'm out in broad daylight."

"And being an idiot. It's almost *dark!*" He set his teeth and paced. He knew how he sounded, but he was so angry, he could hardly restrain the need to lash out at her. But he did, although it cost him. "I want you to stay on the phone until you get here."

"I'm coming up on the turnoff."

Luke couldn't say another word. What if the killer had seen her leave? What if he had followed her, had, had—

"I'm here," she said and disconnected the phone.

Luke stalked across the room. He jerked the front door open and made sure it slammed shut behind him.

Frowning at him, Sarah slipped off his bike.

He stepped back as she bounded up the steps. "Your room," he said as she breezed past him.

"Maybe I want some privacy."

"Not this time."

Luke followed her up the stairs, opened her door, and shut it behind them. "Don't you realize the danger you're in?"

"I was in no danger. I was careful. No, hear me out." She set her backpack on a table. "I thought about the shooter. He didn't have a car or a bicycle at the trailhead. I think he was on foot. I felt relatively safe riding a bike. Also, the killer murdered his victims inside their homes. I was outside." She held up her hand. "*Also...* the man stalking us here at the cabin is on foot; no bike or car has ever been seen. And, finally, I don't appreciate your calling me stupid or an idiot."

"You forgot one. The man who almost raped and killed you in Kansas. A motorcycle can easily overtake a bike!" Luke leaned over, nose-to-nose with her. She stared wide-eyed at him. "I'll tell you this, Sarah," he said in a low, controlled voice. "You were being stupid, idiotic, and you *were* in danger. Next time you want to go on a bike ride, let me know, and I'll go with you. Use your head, and you just might stay alive."

He stormed out of the room.

"Well!" Sarah took a deep breath and stared at the door. The room throbbed with his angry words.

She sat on the bed and fell back against her pillow.

He had it all wrong. She wasn't being stupid. She was being brave.

After chastising herself for being so afraid, she'd made herself go outside and face the fear, had ridden into town, constantly looking over her shoulder as if the killer was hot on her trail. She had her pepper spray with her, with one finger on the trigger in case she had to use it quickly.

She was so proud of herself. She had faced the agonizing fear and trampled on it. Yes, she could see Luke's side. Maybe she had been a bit reckless. But she hadn't come to the mountains to sit in a cabin all day and be afraid. She loved the outdoors and desperately wanted her life back.

After stopping at the market, she'd driven to an area where the views were incredible, the wildlife abundant, and the sounds of a gushing stream all but swallowing up any man-made sounds. She'd sat on a boulder and enjoyed the peace of it all. She hadn't been followed; she'd been very careful about that.

She was determined not to let the fear win again.

She started toward the bathroom. She needed a shower.

But first, she owed Luke an explanation and maybe an apology for frightening him. She called him.

He didn't answer.

So, her shower would come first after all.

With her hair still damp, Sarah slipped into her pajamas. Her shower had turned into a bubble bath, and she'd allowed herself the luxury of taking her time. Maybe Luke was in his room now and had cooled off since his outburst. She understood his anger. He'd lost his father. She knew a little about feeling utterly helpless in the face of evil. He must have felt the same way, but more so. It was no wonder he went over the top in his reaction to her leaving. He was afraid for her.

She knocked on the door separating their rooms.

"Come in."

She did and clasped her hands.

"What do you want, Sarah?" In his tee-shirt and pajama bottoms, Luke walked across the room to his bed, tossed the covers to the side, and sat on the bed as he grabbed his cell phone.

"I want to say I'm sorry you were afraid for me. My intent was to get back a part of the life I gave up months ago. But I hurt you in the process, and I'm sorry for that."

"Apology accepted."

"And the forgiveness?"

"Given."

"I was actually proud of myself for going out alone. Yes, I was afraid, but I didn't want to let him win."

Luke finally looked at her. "He wins when you're dead."

She didn't know what to say.

"Good night, Sarah," he said and turned off the bedside lamp.

Thoroughly dismissed, she swallowed hard and groped for the doorknob.

He giggled. Rosie was back! He was so excited, he couldn't stand still. He'd seen her leave, of course, but he couldn't follow her on his bike. He had waited for her to return.

And now she was in the house, feeling safe and secure, like she had nothing to worry about with four walls around her.

355

"Morons," he whispered into the night. Did they think he'd just let them take Rosie out and do nothing about it? She had to go back in. The beatings had to stop. *She* had to be stopped.

He'd wait for a place and a time when she'd be alone, with no one around to help her. At the thought, he giggled, clapped his hands excitedly, and then slammed his head into a tree and whimpered.

"Not again." Sarah turned on the light. Her digital clock read *2:21*. She was exhausted. But every time she closed her eyes, she saw the little man laughing and singing and dragging a bag with a green shoe sticking out the bottom. It didn't help that Molly was wide awake, too, staring at the windows, whining occasionally.

If Sarah called the police, the man would be gone before they'd get here.

She crawled out of bed and headed for the bathroom. When she came back out, a floorboard creaked under her foot. She looked toward the adjoining door and listened, afraid she'd awakened Luke, but no lights came on under the door.

It was just the wind scaring her—the branches scraping across the glass, the storm howling like a persistent wolf. She slipped back into bed and pulled the covers up to her chin.

The heater came on, startling her.

A branch stabbed at the window.

Molly whined.

Spooked, Sarah flew out of her bed. She quietly opened the adjoining door and rushed into Luke's dark room. Molly followed her and stopped when she stopped. Now what?

Closing her eyes, Sarah crossed her ankles and sank to the floor near Luke's bed. *Oh, God, I don't know what to do. I'm so tired.* Molly sat beside her and nudged her hand. Needing the contact, Sarah curled her arms around her neck and tugged her close.

The branch still scraped against her window.

Molly still stared at her room with worried eyes.

Sarah didn't want to go back in there.

"Oh, Father," she whispered, clutching her hands. With her head bowed, she prayed for several moments. Nestled against Molly, she curled up on the floor, placed her arm around her, and fell promptly to sleep.

Luke woke up at his usual time, four o'clock. He'd had a peaceful night despite the stresses of yesterday. A good run this morning would help him start the day off right. He rolled over and saw Sarah snuggled with Molly on the floor. Molly lifted her head. Luke held out his hand like a traffic cop, and she lowered her head again.

God bless her, Sarah must have been terrified if she'd sleep on the floor. He accepted some of the blame for her restless night, the way he'd treated her after her trip into town.

He'd have to apologize.

He leaned over, gently picked her up, and placed her in his bed. He tugged the covers up to her chin. She didn't wake up.

He snapped his fingers at Molly and pointed to the end of his bed. She jumped up and settled at Sarah's feet. "Good girl," he whispered and patted her head.

He walked into Sarah's room and headed for the windows. Nudging the curtain aside, he noticed that from the ridge, there was a clear line of vision into this room. She'd have to keep her curtains closed all the time. But for tonight, they were switching rooms.

ELEVEN

Winnie Sue had never been so uncomfortable. As she turned off Main Street and walked the half-block to Mountain View Church, a woman in a short skirt with matching jacket and heels raced up to her, stuck a microphone in her face, and signaled a cameraman right beside her.

"Ma'am, did you know the ladies who were murdered here?"

Just past the lady reporter, cameras were positioned up and down the sidewalk leading up to the doors of Mountain View. Winnie Sue wanted to point her white-gloved finger at them and ask them why they weren't in church this fine Sunday morning instead of harassing people who chose to be.

She mumbled, "Excuse me," sidestepped the woman, and marched up the sidewalk. Pastor Clay lent her a helping hand up the steps and gently tugged her inside the door.

She sat next to her sister and considered taking off her white gloves because the air conditioner hadn't been turned on and there were so many people in church that the air was too warm and they actually had to sit close enough to smell each other's mouthwash which was entirely too snug to suit Winnie Sue considering Alvin James was sitting right next to her and he apparently hadn't used any.

She edged closer to her sister.

Miss Gertie glared at her. "Get off my lap."

"Did they accost you, Sister?"

"They who? Oh, you mean the media."

Her eyes widened. "Why, who else would I mean?" Winnie Sue touched Miss Gertie's arm and nodded toward the front. Pastor Clay had stepped up to the podium.

Shocked at having three of their own murdered, the people of Little Texas had turned out in droves at Mountain View this morning. Winnie Sue sat back to enjoy Pastor Clay's sermon, "The Total Depravity of Man," which seemed to coincide poignantly with the recent goings-on in their town.

Most of the people in church probably had no idea what 'depravity' meant, but it sure seemed like Pastor Clay was talking about their murderer having an extra dose or two of it. He ended the service with an admonition to pray for the families of Bonnie, Renee and Lulu. And as an afterthought—it seemed to Winnie Sue—Pastor Clay mentioned praying for the killer.

As the first one outside, Gertie was happy to see that the nosy reporters and all their equipment had moved on. Mountain mornings were always crisp and clear and cool. She couldn't wait to get out in it and as far away from the church crowd as possible, except, of course, for Luke McKenzie.

"Do you see him, Sister?"

"You know I don't, Winnie Sue. You've been glued to me ever since we got out here." She smiled at Harriet and Henry Flagstone inching by. "Oh, there they are."

She tracked Luke following Sarah through the crowd toward his truck. As he reached for the door, Gertie, breathing a little heavily from running, boomed, "Well, there you two are! Trying to sneak out of here, are you?"

Luke turned around and frowned at her. "We're not sneaking out, Miss Gertie. We're just headed home."

Sarah elbowed him. "Good morning, Miss Gertie. Where's your sister?"

Gertie looked around. Well, for heaven's sake. Where had Winnie Sue gone off to? "Oh, visiting, I expect. We don't get out much or invited to people's homes like we used to. So many of our friends are dead now, y'know, with me being seventy-six and my little sister being sixty-three." It grated to act like such a dimwit but, hopefully, it would get them what they wanted.

"You're welcome to come to my cabin for Sunday dinner today if you think you could stand some Mexican food. We'll be serving around one or you could come home with us now and relax a little before we eat."

Trying not to appear smug, Gertie said, "Why, Luke, that would be wonderful. Been awhile since I've had Mexican food. It's good, is it?"

"The best. You can ride with me and Sarah. Where's your sister?"

She thought she'd throttle the lot of them if anyone else asked her where Winnie Sue was again. "I'll go get her," she smiled sweetly and stalked off to where her sister was yapping away with Floyd Watson.

"Excuse me, Floyd, Winnie Sue and I have an invitation to Sunday dinner. If you'll excuse us now." She took her sister's arm and yanked her toward Luke's truck.

"Why, Miss Gertie, he was just getting to the part about—if you wouldn't *run,* I might be able to keep up with you—oh! Did you say we've been invited?"

Gertie smiled. "Mission accomplished. We're riding with Luke and Sarah. Try not to be a complete bore, Winnie Sue."

She gasped. "What's gotten into you today, Sister?"

"Nothing's—"

"My manners are nothing but proper and pleasing."

"I'm not talking about manners. I'm talking about *interesting*. Either appear intelligent and interesting or keep your trap shut. Oh, what a nice red truck, Luke. Is it this year's model?"

A few paces from the steps of Mountain View Church, Allison shielded her eyes with a flattened hand and watched the two elderly women get inside the red truck and drive away. She was sure one of the Jansen women could help her find her long-lost grandmother.

"I don't believe we've met." A tall, blonde, older woman extended her hand to Allison. "I'm Debra Banks."

"Allison McIntosh." Her stomach clenched. Anonymity was vital, and she'd given her real name to the first person who'd asked. Dolt!

"Do you live around here, Allison?"

She kept her eyes down. "No. I'm here for the funeral of my cousin, Lulu Baines."

"Your cousin! Which side of the family—?"

"The Jansens."

"Well." Debra patted her hand. "It's a small world. We lost our Renee because of that monster so I know what you're going through, dear. I'm sorry for your loss."

She wanted to mutter, "There was no loss," but she managed a smile she didn't feel, lifted her chin, and withdrew her hand.

"If you need anything while you're here, please feel free to call the church office. Chelsea will direct you to the Women's Auxiliary."

"Thank you." Allison lifted a disdainful brow as the woman left. She had no intentions of feeling free to call anyone but the elderly Jansen women.

At McKenzie Cabin, a lull in the conversation made Gertie think that now was a good time to bring up the murders of the three women. "It's strange, I suppose, for two sisters in one family to remain unmarried," she generously surmised over a pile of spicy refried beans smothered with cheese sauce, jalapenos, and black olives. "But we were never lookers, Winnie Sue and I, and never turned a man's head."

"Why, Miss Gertie." Winnie Sue leaned forward. "Don't you remember my Owen?"

Gertie glared at her sister. They weren't here to talk about their non-existent love lives; they were here to find out what Luke knew about the murders. "Well, like I said, it's unusual, I suppose, but there you are."

Winnie Sue closed her trap and stuffed it with a small bite of beef burrito.

"Where did Little Texas get its name, Miss Gertie?" Sarah asked. "It seems unusual for a mountain town in Colorado."

"Oh, it is, that. Four friends and their wives and children left Texas in early 1890 and made their way to Colorado. They happened upon the valley just below here and fell in love with it but one of the friends, Cooper Banks, wanted them to go up a mite more. He found this valley and dubbed it 'Little Texas.' Natural borders prevented the town from growing overmuch. Within a year, six or seven family friends from Texas, with their wives and children, settled here, too.

"Through the years, other Texans came to stay. We're just a little hole in the wall, actually—a well-hidden secret and we'd like to keep it that way. Almost everybody in Little Texas is kin in some way to everybody else. That's why we're all so upset about the three women who were murdered." She hoped it didn't seem suspicious to bring the conversation around to Renee, Bonnie and Lulu.

"Yes," Sarah answered. "What were the four friends' names?"

"Banks, Jansen, Washburn, and Baines. All of us kin somehow." Gertie laughed and hoped it sounded sincere, hoped someone would jump right in and start talking about the murders.

"I see. So, Jim and A.J. Banks' great-grandfather—"

"Great-great-grandfather. He was only twenty and newly married when he came here. Cooper Banks."

"Have you always lived here, Miss Gertie? You and Miss Winnie Sue?"

Frustrated, Gertie almost slammed her fork down but caught herself and managed a smile. "All our lives. In fact, your property, Luke, was originally Jansen owned." Her thumb jabbed the air behind her shoulder. "Back of there a ways was the original home site built by our grandfather, Hiram Jansen. His wife's parents owned the twenty-acre plot and culled ten acres off for Hiram and their daughter. Two homesteads on the twenty acres. Hiram's eldest son, our uncle, died without an heir. With the death of her parents, the properties were then joined into one again and passed to my father who sold it about fifty years ago to Kenneth McKenzie."

Luke nodded. "My grandfather."

"Yes, I remember him and his family visiting here, but most of his children were grown then with kids of their own. His sister, your great-aunt Doris, lived in Denver and had two sons and an adopted boy and girl. She was a nurse, and her husband, Edmond, was in real estate. They were killed in a plane crash, as I recall."

"Well, I'll be. It's a small world." Luke leaned back in his chair, patted his stomach, and grinned at Sarah, who playfully rolled her eyes at him. "That was a great dinner. Eduardo, come out here and take a bow."

The right side of the swinging doors opened, and Eduardo poked his head out.

"That meal was great. You outdid yourself."

"I'm glad you enjoyed it. Everybody ready for dessert?"

"We are. Bring it on in."

"Oh, Mr. McKenzie, I don't think I could eat another bite, sweet or not."

"Why, Miss Winnie Sue, where are your manners?" Gertie slid her practiced smile toward Luke, took the cup of coffee Yolanda offered, and kindly said, "Of course, we would love some dessert."

Eduardo reappeared with a tray. "Chocolate cake and ice cream."

Gertie muttered, "Oh, how nice." And then she smiled. Winnie Sue was allergic to chocolate and lactose intolerant. She captured the panicked look her sister sent her and nudged her knee.

"I am just too stuffed, Mr. McKenzie," Winnie Sue ventured, patted her chest, and moved her knee out of Gertie's range.

After Miss Winnie Sue stifled a second yawn, Luke offered to take the ladies home. He turned to Sarah. "Would you like to go with me, maybe take a ride?"

Surprise was in her eyes. "I'd love to get out. Let me get my sweater and my big purse. We might end up in a tourist town." She ran upstairs and was back in a couple of minutes.

"Ladies, shall we go?"

It was a quiet drive to first Miss Gertie's cabin and then Miss Winnie Sue's Victorian home. As Luke backed out of her drive, he said, "If you like tourist towns, we could drive to Estes Park and show off the mountains, maybe shop downtown."

He preferred the country with its quiet, the raw appeal of the land, the spiritual awareness he had when he was alone in it. But Estes Park had enough of nature around it that he could survive an afternoon of crowds, shoulder-to-shoulder shopping, and waiting in lines to buy a memento. "It's not uncommon for elk to cross the streets and stop traffic. We can act like tourists for a day, take a bunch of pictures, buy a few things. Estes actually has some world-class shops."

"Sounds wonderful. I miss being outdoors. Luke, thank you for putting me in your bed this morning. I just couldn't stay in that room."

"You're welcome. My windows are completely covered by trees. So, we're switching rooms permanently."

"I appreciate it." She glanced around at the beautiful scenery. "Oh, look. It's just so magnificent."

"It is. I'm sorry you have to stay inside, Sarah. I know you didn't come up here to sit in my cabin all the time."

"No, but it's necessary right now. I've enjoyed the indoor pool. I'm used to running most days or walking long distances but swimming works, too."

"We have a gym in the basement. You're welcome to use it any time. Plus, you and I could go for another hike away from Little Texas."

"That would be nice. I've thought, too, about going back home, but I just can't bring myself to leave, to admit defeat."

He slowed for a cop who'd pulled over a motorcyclist.

She gasped as they passed them.

"What is it?"

"That man. Oh, never mind. I didn't get a good look at him that night but—"

"I'll turn around."

He did, but just as they drove up, the man's helmet slipped over his face. "Could you tell if it was him?"

"Not really. Something about him... his body shape, his height. Maybe it's just the fact that he's on a motorcycle."

"Did it have a Kansas license plate?"

"I didn't see."

He made another U-turn. They drove slowly past the man and his bike. *Kansas plates.* He looked up, appeared to be tracking the truck. Luke glanced in the rearview mirror. He hadn't moved and was still turned toward them. "Let's go back to Little Texas."

"No, Luke. I don't even know if that man's the Darkslayer. He might have stared at us because he thought I was flirting with him. Oh, look." She picked up her cell phone. "That view is absolutely stunning. Let's get out."

They stood beside a rock with the mountains behind them. A woman standing near them said, "Would you like me to take your picture?"

"Oh, uh. Sure." Sarah handed her the phone.

Luke placed his arm around Sarah and rested his hand on her shoulder. *Comfortable fit.* He looked down at her, which caused her to look up at him. He smiled. She smiled. He reflexively tightened his hold. And the woman captured the shot.

"Oh, it turned out beautifully!" she gushed and handed Sarah her phone with the picture still showing.

"Thank you," she said to the woman who turned back to the man with her. Sarah turned off the camera and opened her purse.

"I didn't see it."

She dismissed him with a shrug. "It's not a very good shot."

"Let me see." He held out his hand, amused at her wary expression. What was she afraid he'd see?

363

With a grimace, she handed it to him.

He found the picture. Anyone looking at it would think the couple smiling at each other was deeply in love. He shook his head at his foolishness. "You have a nice smile."

She lifted a shoulder and took her phone. Just as it slipped into her purse, a motorcycle approached them. The same man! He slowed down, revved his engine twice, and nodded once at them. Then he sped up toward the next curve, taking it dangerously fast.

"He must like blondes." Luke knew it was a flippant response, but what were the chances that the killer of those women was right here, at this same spot, the day Sarah was here? "Come on. The elk might not wait around for us to get there."

They drove into congestion. The green lights no longer meant 'go.' Traffic cops at every corner tried to regulate all the people on foot and the long line of cars on every roadway. Luke found a spot near the library building and parked. As he rounded the truck, Sarah got out and faced the other direction. She shut the door, turned, and bumped into him. He placed a hand on her arm to settle her.

For just a moment, they stood still, frowning at each other.

"Oh, I, uh, I didn't see you." Her laugh was spontaneous, and he found himself laughing with her.

He stepped back, but a group of teens converged on them, two walking right through them. He grabbed Sarah's arm, slid his hand down to hers, and headed toward the sidewalk and the crowds.

He was pleased that she didn't resist. Maybe she felt the same way he felt, that holding hands seemed natural between them.

He wouldn't dwell on that right now. He wanted to keep her safe and try to keep his sanity as the noise of conversations, squealing kids, shuffling feet, horns honking, and traffic cop whistles ushered them into the Estes Park shopping area. To some, this was exciting. He could understand that. But to him, it was suffocating.

The snow-capped mountains stood above the fray, reminding him to get into nature as soon as he could. When he needed it, he'd look up. "Shops are this way."

"Oh, look at these!" Sarah clutched a rock cut in half with beautiful, polished colors in the middle. "Agate Bookends," according to the sign above them. "My sister, Elizabeth, is a book worm. She'll love this set."

Luke was tired of shopping. He'd picked up some gifts for the women at the ranch: a girl named Emma; his sister-in-law, Marianne; his brother's secretary, Helen; and Stella, a ranch hand's wife. He could admit he missed the ranch and its simplicities. This busy, busy, push-

and-shove, wait-and-wait-some-more world wasn't for him. "How about some taffy? There's none better anywhere, and the store's just down the street."

"I'd like that." She paid for her purchase and placed the bag in her oversized purse.

He took her hand and weaved through the people when Sarah squeezed his hand suddenly and leaned into him. "I heard him, Luke. He's here." He felt her hand trembling.

"Who?"

"The man in my home," she frantically whispered and looked around.

He searched the crowd, too, to see if someone was watching them. Was it possible he was here? It seemed too coincidental, but Sarah thought he was, and that was good enough for him.

"Let's leave, okay?"

Holding hands, they stepped outside. Crossed the street. Walked toward his truck. The same motorcycle zoomed past them. Luke still couldn't make out the numbers on the license plate. Sarah squeezed his hand as they both hurried to his truck.

Myra Simms had racked her brain every day, trying to remember anything she might've forgotten to tell A.J. and Jim about the day she and Lulu were planning to go shopping in Estes Park. That had been one of the most trying days of her life. Sometimes—rarely, really—a person found a soul mate as a best friend; Lulu was hers, despite their age difference of twenty years. She'd missed her every second of the past few days.

Myra's husband, Fred, settled into the rocking chair beside hers on their front porch. They sipped hot chocolate as night approached. "Not a soul's been by." Myra glanced over her cup at the street, blew on the still-too-hot drink, and sipped again.

"Naw, honey, they's too scared to come out now. Them murders is scaring everybody off the streets at night."

"Casey Pollard 'll be by. She never misses her exercising. I'm telling you what, that girl can fast walk."

"I don't reckon she'll be by, mother." Fred glanced at his watch. "She's fifteen minutes late already."

The familiar, steady rhythm of their rockers crunching on the wood porch was soothing. Myra leaned forward and looked past Fred, two doors on the right. "Harriet and Henry aren't sitting out either."

"I seen that." He cleaned his teeth with his tongue, smacked his lips. "It's a mite cool."

"It's not the cool that's keeping them in and you know it, Fred. Now here comes a brave soul." Myra stopped rocking and squinted into the night as she leaned forward. "Who's there?" she laughed.

"Just me, Aunt Myra."

"Joy? Honey, come on up here." Myra pursed her lips and whispered, "Something's wrong, Fred." To Joy, she said, "Come on now, honey. We got plenty of room." She lifted her brows at her husband and tilted her head. "Fred."

"I'm getting up, mother. You come on up here now and sit a spell with Myra, Joy. That supper's working its way through me already. I 'spect I need to go inside for a bit."

"You want some hot chocolate, child? I've got more in the kitchen."

Joy sat in the rocking chair. "No, no, Aunt Myra. I'm fine."

"What are you doing out and about tonight? Didn't you hear about the bodies they found at Gem's Peak Park?"

"I did, but Sonny and I had a fight. I needed to cool off and give him some time to cool off. I figured I'd make it to your house alive and well."

"With that killer loose, he shoulda come with you and not let you walk out here by yourself."

"The killer won't look in my direction. I've heard those other women were pretty and wore fancy clothes. I'm not pretty, and I don't wear fancy clothes."

"Oh, tosh."

Harriet and Henry's porch light flicked on. With her gaze on their screen door, Myra said, "What'd you and Sonny fight about?"

Joy's legs were too short for her feet to touch the floor. "Oh, same ol' thing. Leaving Texas to come up here."

Harriet's screen door opened a crack. Myra leaned forward, ever watching. "Sometimes we gotta accept the things we can't change, honey."

Harriet stuck her head out and looked at her and Joy. Myra waved. "Y'all coming out tonight, Mrs. Harriet?"

The frail woman shook her head, flapped her hand at Myra, and closed her door.

"You said some things can't change. But I could change it if I wanted to press it. I could make Sonny go back. But then he'd be hard to live with like I am now, and I don't think anything would be accomplished by it. Sonny likes having y'all close by to spoil him, so I think we'll probably stay. I'll straighten out my attitude and everything will be all right."

Myra patted her hand. "Let me tell ya something, child. Being a woman is tough. We give and give and then give s'more. It's in our nature. But in the long run, I don't think you'll regret the giving."

"I totally agree." Joy eased her head back against the slats and rocked awhile.

Myra enjoyed the peace of the cool night, the rustle of the leaves. A screen door slammed, and Myra looked toward Joy's home. Sonny stood on the porch, hands in his pockets. "Probably worried about you."

"Uh-huh." Joy stood and kissed her aunt's cheek. "I better get on back. Thanks for listening. See you tomorrow."

She waved as Joy turned right out of her driveway and headed down three doors and waved again when she reached her front door and Sonny. They both disappeared inside.

The door opened behind Myra. "Better get on in here, mother. You don't know where that killer might strike next." He held the screen door open for her.

Myra frowned and stood. "Laws, Fred, get your thinking cap on. That man's not interested in the likes of me."

TWELVE

The next morning, Jim placed his hat and coat on the elk rack. Elva Lee stood by her desk staring at him, the concern in her eyes for him obvious. It touched him deeply. "'Morning, Elva Lee."

The emerald sweater she wore made her eyes appear bottle green. "'Morning, Jim. You doing all right?"

"Getting there." She stood and poured him a cup of coffee from his clean cup—she always cleaned his cup for him—and set it on his desk.

He glanced up and smiled and took a swig of coffee and almost choked. Her fingernails were gone! Every last one of them. "What happened to your nails?"

She tucked her fingers into her palms and shrugged. "Got tired of them. Felt kinda pretentious and silly, what with everything going on. Just not important anymore."

"Looks nice. More natural."

A.J. walked in. "'Morning," he muttered and headed for the coffee pot. Jim knew his brother's brain misfired a little until he'd had several cups of caffeine in the morning. Jim joined him in the kitchen area and leaned against the counter.

"I wanted to talk to you—" A.J. grimaced as his phone rang. "Gonna be a heck of a week," he muttered just as Luke walked inside S&R and greeted them with a single nod.

"Hello?" A.J. listened for a long time without saying anything, muttered, "Thanks," and hung up. He glanced at Elva Lee, then said to Jim and Luke, "Let's go outside a minute and talk."

The three men crossed the street to a little corner park and sat on the concrete picnic table that faced S&R. Just down two blocks was the City Park. The town council was big on little resting spots for its citizens. These corner parks were at several intersections in the downtown area.

Jim took a swig of his coffee and figured Elva Lee was glued to the window, watching them.

"Jim, you know anyone named Rosie?"

He slowly shook his head. "Can't say I do. Rosemary Atkins, but everybody knows she hates to be called Rosie."

A.J. glanced at Luke. "Did this man in the cave mention 'Rosie'? Did he call Lulu 'Rosie'?"

"No, not that I—wait. Yes, he did. When Lulu's shoe came off, he threw it into the crevice and said, 'Oh, Rosie. You're such a kidder.'"

"The coroner says all three women had something written on their stomachs. 'Rosie is dead.' That's what was written on them. 'Rosie is dead'."

Jim frowned. "R-O-S-I-E?"

"Yep."

"Was Renee—were they—?" Jim couldn't get the words out.

"None of them were molested; all were fully clothed. Just the hit on the head and some bruising under their arms."

"How?"

"Crowbar. All three exactly the same area of the head. 'Rosie is dead' written on their stomachs."

Jim nodded. "He validated her death by clearly writing 'Rosie is dead' on their stomachs just in case the authorities didn't get it."

"Serials are predictable. The patterns are there."

"So, Renee was killed by someone who *thought* she was someone else." Frustrated, Jim threw out his coffee. "Rosie must be small. Miss Gertie's small. Miss Winnie Sue's small. Shoot, the whole Jansen clan is small. Let's start with them and see if they know anyone in their family, or in this area, named Rosie."

"First, let's get to my office and run a check on Rosemarys or Rosies or Roseannes or Roses around here. Heck, maybe this guy's middle name is Roseman and he's killing his mother over and over for doing that to him."

The curtain fell back as Jim stepped off the picnic table. "Elva Lee knows everybody, too."

"Computer first, then we're talking to Miss Gertie. If Rosie lived around here in the last seventy years, Miss Gertie will know."

Jim nodded at Luke. "And if this idiot is focused on Sarah because he thinks she's Rosie, then she's in more trouble than we thought."

Luke cleared his throat. "I'm about to add more to the story." He told them about Sarah's attack, the killer's return that night, the two murders that seemed to suggest the killer was on his way up here, and Sarah's thinking she saw and heard him yesterday. "Sarah doesn't want any of this to get out in case she really didn't see or hear him."

A.J. nodded. "We appreciate you telling us about this. Two men after Sarah. No wonder I haven't seen much of her the past few days. I'll contact local PD in Riadon. See what I can find out."

"And I've got to get back to the cabin and check on her. Call me if you need me for anything."

"What's this?" Sarah plucked a paper rose off the gazebo post and turned it over. Rolled-up tape was on the back.

"Probably some game Eduardo and Yolanda are playing. They're always doing something like that with each other. They haven't been married long. Still in the gooey stage."

"Gooey stage?" Sarah chuckled.

"Sticky sweet."

"The expression on your face said 'yucky'."

"Yeah, that works." Luke shook his head at her. "I've seen my brother and his wife do this stuff, too." He playfully shivered.

Smiling, Sarah leaned against a rail and crossed her arms. She really loved the quiet and beauty of this place. It was a two-story home with enough perks that the word 'cabin' fit only because of the rustic furnishings inside. "When I think of Texas, I think of cattle and oil. Is there oil on your land?"

"You're talking about McKenzie Ranch, right? Yes, there is. Lots of it. I have oil, too. Those are two separate entities, though. One is my family's ranch that my great-great-grandfather founded in the early 1880s. My ranch is brand new. I bought two-thousand acres from my brother last year."

"Oh, okay. When I think of Texas, I think of cowboys and horses."

"Yep. We have those, especially on a ranch."

Nodding thoughtfully, she shrugged, enjoying this game. "When I think of Texas, I think of big, really big."

"Yep. Everything's big in Texas. Big dreams. Big opportunities."

"When I think of Texas, I think of southern gentlemen and beautiful ladies."

He grinned. "You'll find both at McKenzie Ranch. But not on my ranch. There's only me."

She knew she was flirting with him, but it was harmless fun, something she didn't usually do. "Are you a southern gentleman?"

He took a step toward her. "You'll have to answer that one."

"Then I will. Yes, you are." Before he could react, she changed directions. "What's the name of your ranch?"

"I haven't settled on one yet."

"Hmmm. When I think of Texas, I think of miserable heat. Maybe you could name it 'The Sweating Like a Pig Ranch'."

He laughed. "I'm not sure I could get a woman to marry me and live there with a name like that."

"You won't know until you ask her." She turned toward the trees. Neither said anything for a few minutes. Luke seemed as content as she was to be quiet. "Nothing has gone as I'd planned on this trip."

"I know."

"I thought I'd be out on a trail every day, exhausted from hiking, at peace with nature, no mental stress. Instead, I'm stuck in a cabin, *not* outside, and have more stress than I've ever had."

"Then let's go for a hike, Sarah. Back of the ridge. Plenty of miles to hike."

"Oh, I'd love that!" For the first time since coming to the cabin, she was excited. "Now?"

"Sure. We'll head out when you're ready."

"I'll meet you at the back door in fifteen minutes."

They headed up the ridge with Sarah in front of Luke. In shorts, her legs showed off well-toned muscles. Her foot was sure. He'd never had a female friend that thrived on being outdoors for exercise. Working cattle or horses, sure, but not just to enjoy nature.

"This trail heads up at a pretty tough grade. Then it tees into a trail that goes on forever, connecting to other trails, so we could be out here for a month if we wanted. Once it tees, we go left. Then it's a pretty easy hike, but we'll want easy after the grade up. From there, it's mostly hiking around a mountain in a circle."

"I am so ready for this."

They hiked in silence for about thirty minutes. It was simply too difficult to hike up and talk. Grouse appeared. A ground squirrel or two popped up. A black squirrel watched them. At the tree line in a small pasture, a couple of elk rested in grass.

They finally reached the trail circling the mountain and headed left. Sarah pointed to a fallen tree nearby. "Let's sit and rest for a minute. I'm thirsty."

"There's an overlook about five minutes away. How 'bout we stop there while I take a bio break?"

She drank and put away her water. "Sounds great."

Very little dirt was kicked up by either of them; there were enough small rocks on the path to prevent that. Coming around a wide corner, a red fox scampered across the path on its way down. Sarah stopped to admire it and then continued on. "Are there any caves in this area?"

"Not that I know of."

The trail moved away from the drop-off they'd contended with since turning left. The path headed into trees. "There's the lookout." Luke pointed toward boulders above them. "If you want to wait for me, I'll go with you."

"That's okay. I'll head on up and take a look."

"Keep me in your sights. We don't know if anyone followed us."

"Okay." She headed off. After a few steps, she turned around and focused on Luke. He glanced back at her at the same time and waved, laughing. She waved back and continued up.

She was almost to the top when she stopped again and looked for him. She didn't see him, and her skin tingled.

"Come on, Luke." She took a few steps back down and looked again. He was nowhere. "Behind a tree maybe?" She moved to the right, then the left. Nowhere. She stood still, searching the trail, the area. She shivered. Something was wrong.

Then she saw him, lying face-down on the other side of the trail. "Oh, no!" She started down but realized that someone had hurt him. Someone was out here.

She froze, too scared to move.

The pepper spray!

She scrambled to get it out of her shorts pocket and turned it to the 'on' position. By now, her hands were shaking so much, she didn't know if she could press the button if her life depended on it.

She hid behind a tree. Quick breaths and her pounding heart kept her from hearing anything else. She tried to breathe deeply but couldn't. She needed to get to Luke. *Please let him be alive! Please!* Easing her head from behind her cover, she searched for any movement anywhere.

Quietly, she ran down to the next tree.

A gun cocked. She gasped and turned toward the sound, due east of her position, mid-way between the trail and the lookout.

"Put the pepper spray down."

He was hiding in thick bushes about thirty feet away. Could she make it to the next tree?

"Now."

She knew one thing for certain. If she put the spray down, she would be defenseless. It took her a moment to garner the courage to speak and when she did, she used a forceful voice. "No. If you want me, you have to come and get me." Such brave words for someone shaking like a leaf.

"I said drop the pepper spray."

"No."

He fired at her but missed. A warning shot.

Another gunshot went off, but it wasn't from this man's weapon!

Sarah looked at where she'd last seen Luke. He wasn't there.

Another gunshot from below her. Another.

Rustling in the bushes. Then a 'pop, pop, pop' from them.

Another shot, closer to her but still south of her position. Another. Another.

"Run, Sarah! Run!"

With continuous gunfire coming from below her, she raced down the mountain. She reached the trail and slipped behind a tree. Luke was now above her, scampering up the mountain, hiding behind trees as he did. He circled to the east side of the bushes with his weapon aimed right at the center of it.

He slipped in back of a tree and looked around. Using a tree as cover, too, Sarah couldn't see anything moving.

Luke started down toward her, stopping behind trees as he did.

"He's gone. For now." Luke rushed toward her, and she stepped out.

"We don't have time for anything but running. Back the way we came." He led the way. "Watch above us. He could be anywhere."

Close behind him, she huffed, "How did he get you?"

"He popped me in the back of my knees with something hard. When I fell back, he hit me on the head. I think he knocked me out for a few seconds."

"Was it a crowbar?"

"No, some sort of piping, I think."

"When I saw you face-down on the ground, I thought you were dead. I don't think I've ever been that scared in my life, including the night of the attack."

"I'm sorry for that." They reached the trail to McKenzie Cabin. "He could be anywhere by now. I'm sure he knows where we live. Now move as if your life depended on it."

Ten minutes later, they raced inside the back door. Luke slammed it and locked it. "That was stupid of us, hiking so close to the house. Next time, we'll—"

"Next time? Are you kidding? We're lucky to be alive."

"You're not thinking of leaving again, are you?"

"Of course not. I leave; he wins."

"You're a brave woman, Sarah. I admire your tenacity."

She strolled away from him to the other side of the room. This morning, her first thought was of Luke. *Feelings* for someone she hadn't known but a very short time. She'd lain in bed, excited about seeing him again after their afternoon of shopping together yesterday. Her mind told her to stop this nonsense; her heart welcomed it.

A little over a week. That's it. She'd only known him a little over a week. "Was that a line?"

He was silent for a long time. "A line?"

"Yeah, you know, what guys give girls to, you know, gain some ground." She closed her eyes. She had to put a stop to any ideas he may have about any kind of relationship with her.

"You really think—?"

When he faltered, she turned around. "No, I don't. I don't know what I think. I do know I'm going home to Kansas in a couple weeks, maybe sooner. And you're headed to Texas."

"And never the two shall meet?"

"Something like that."

"You're right."

Her breath caught as she looked up at him.

"You have roots. I have roots. They don't grow in the same area."

He was hurt and trying it hide it, but she could see it in his eyes. *Explain, Sarah.* "Luke. I'm trying so hard to regain some measure of who I am, who I was."

"So you attack my character to help you do that?"

"It was stupid. I thought I was putting distance between us, to stop anything that might be happening here. I'm sorry. I don't know what to do about anything."

He grabbed her shoulders. "Yes, you do. You just did it. You survived another attack. If you're trying to find out who you are, then start from here. Right now. You can't go back—that's gone. But he doesn't own your 'today.' He doesn't own your 'tomorrow' unless you give them to him. Don't let him steal *you*, the strong woman who's a survivor, a fighter. I see her. She's beautiful and strong."

He dropped his hands. "But whatever you decide, you're welcome to stay. I believe you're safer in this house with me. It's still not wise for you to be out and about alone."

"Thank you for making this easier for me." She touched his arm. "I need to go to my room. I'll talk to you in a little bit."

Luke watched her walk away. After everything they'd been through, she'd accused him of manipulation. The one thing he'd prided himself on his entire adult life was being genuine and treating others the way he wanted to be treated. His parents had drilled that into their boys. *Be truthful. Be kind. Do what's right.* And here the first woman he'd been drawn to in a long time was calling him a fake.

"Her problem, not mine." After a few seconds, he added, "Not true, buddy, and you know it." To get his mind off her, he called A.J. to tell him about what happened on the trail.

"Did you see him?"

"I saw a glimpse of something. He was small. That's probably why he kneed me; I'm too tall for him to hit."

"I'd like to see where this took place."

"I'll take you up there whenever you're ready." They hung up.

Luke's phone rang. "Yes, Sarah?"

"I thought you might be too angry with me to answer my call, but I had to tell you again that I'm sorry. I don't know why I said such a callous thing. I've never once thought of you as being deceptive or disingenuous. Please forgive me?"

"I already have. How 'bout a game of checkers or cards or dominoes to prove it?"

"I'd love that. We'll stay holed up here and relax a bit."

"Until A.J. calls me. He wants to see where the killer shot at us today."

Later that morning, Dr. Vince Graham, the coroner, released the bodies of the three women to the funeral home. *Cause of death: blow to the head with a blunt instrument, possibly a crowbar.* Not complicated.

"We got no murder weapon, no fingerprints, no hair samples, no body fluids, no eyewitnesses to the murder, and the only blood sample belongs to a victim."

Jim looked over at his brother.

"How are we supposed to find a murder suspect who's a male, short, wears size seven shoes, has a fondness for peanuts, and is killing 'Rosie' over and over again? No Rose of any kind in our area but Rosemary Atkins. You were right about asking Miss Gertie and Miss Winnie Sue. We'll start there and see where it takes us. Also, Luke and I hiked to the shooting site and found absolutely nothing."

"Story of our lives lately."

"Absolutely nothing to go on, and we're supposed to find a killer."

Jim listened as A.J. called Miss Winnie Sue and put the call on speaker.

"Hello?"

"Hey, Miss Winnie Sue. This is A.J. Banks."

"Why, Officer Banks. I trust you're doing well today, sir?"

Jim smiled. Miss Winnie Sue was a treasure, for sure.

"I'm fine, Miss Winnie Sue. Wondered if Jim and I could come over and ask you a few questions related to the three women."

Jim heard a gasp and thought she could very possibly be in a dead faint. She was known for her fainting spells.

"Miss Winnie Sue?"

No answer. *Great!* A.J. had gone and scared the living daylights out of her.

"Miss Winnie Sue? Are you there?"

"Oh. Yes." She swallowed hard. "Officer Banks."

Jim could just see her patting her chest and fanning herself with her white, lacy handkerchief.

"I'm sorry," she muttered. "Such a dreadful thing."

"Yes, miss. Would you feel better if we took you out to Miss Gertie's and talked to y'all together?"

"Oh my, yes. That would be much better. When may I expect you?"

"About five minutes, if that'll give you enough time."

"That would be fine. I'll expect you then."

375

With her white gloves on, Jim was sure. And all gussied up in her Sunday best. Miss Winnie Sue was never seen in pants or anything other than a nice dress and white gloves.

Sure enough, when they drove up, she walked down the steps, all prim and proper, tugging on her gloves with her purse dangling from her right elbow.

Jim hopped out and opened the front door for her.

"Oh, Mr. Banks. Would you mind if I sat in the back, sir? I have always wanted to sit in the back of a police car."

"Not at all, miss." Jim gallantly opened the back door for her.

"Thank you, sir. It's a lovely day today, isn't it?"

She didn't say another word. It took only a matter of minutes to drive up to Miss Gertie's.

Her older sister was hanging some towels on the clothesline when they drove in. Jim thought it peculiar when Miss Gertie spotted Miss Winnie Sue in the back seat of A.J.'s patrol car that she didn't even blink an eye. It wasn't every day Miss Winnie Sue Jansen rode in the back seat of a patrol car.

"Winnie Sue," Miss Gertie said with a straight face as she leaned over and picked up another towel. "You been drinking again?"

Miss Winnie Sue slipped around Jim and shook her gloved finger at Miss Gertie. "That is not funny. Not funny in the least." She touched the back of her head and patted her perfectly placed hair. "You know I never touch any alcoholic spirits."

"Not what I heard," Miss Gertie teased as she pushed a pin over the folded corner of a wet towel and slid her fingers down the towel toward the basket.

"Officer Banks has come to ask you some questions about the three murdered women."

Color slid out of Miss Gertie's face when she turned around and squinted at her sister.

"Actually, we have a lead and wanted to pick your brains, both of you. Would you like to go inside or sit out here?"

Miss Gertie flicked her gaze around the yard, then up to her porch. "I think inside would be better where we can all be comfortable."

With a lift of her chin, Miss Winnie Sue floated past Miss Gertie, through the screen door A.J. held open for her and into her sister's small cabin. Jim raised his brows at A.J. as he walked inside, too.

Jim could count on one hand the number of times he'd been in this house. The living room seemed exactly the same as his last visit. Two double-paned, over-large windows sat opposite one another. The one on the right, the north window, showcased one of the best views of snow-capped mountains he'd ever seen out a window. It had a short-backed sofa under it that didn't block any of that spectacular view. Beside it was a large fireplace. The south window showed off mostly thick trees; in front of it sat a lounge chair with a small table beside it.

To the left of the front door sat a green floral sofa with a coffee table in front it. Anyone sitting on that sofa had a perfect view of the grandeur out the north window. Above the green sofa, a rectangular window afforded a view of Miss Gertie's porch and front yard. She had a pretty good view of most of her property.

"Have a seat, A.J., Jim, and I'll get us some iced tea."

"I'll help you, Miss Gertie." Miss Winnie Sue quietly followed her sister into the kitchen.

A.J. sat on the sofa while Jim parked himself in the lounge chair.

"Man, that's one fine view." Jim took himself to the north window and looked out over the greening up of Colorado, with snow caps above all that green. Sure, they'd have more snow, but it was the wet kind that disappeared at the stroke of a sun's ray.

Gertie glared at her little sister and lugged the big container of sun tea out of her refrigerator and onto the counter.

"It's not my fault," Winnie Sue whispered as she opened the freezer top and pulled out an ice tray and twisted it. "If you'd get a telephone—"

"I don't *want* a stupid telephone!" With one hand, she grabbed three glasses and shut the cabinet door.

"Well, *if* you had one, I could have warned you."

Gertie put ice in and poured the tea. "I don't have anything to hide."

"Why, you most certainly do, Miss Gertie. We both do."

Gertie picked up the serving tray with three iced tea drinks and glared at Winnie Sue. "While we're in there, Winnie Sue Jansen, keep—"

"Your trap shut. I know, Sister. I know."

They walked into the living room. "Here we are, Jim, A.J." Smiling, Miss Gertie held the tray while each chose a glass.

"You have a great view here. I could stand here all day."

She paused in her ministrations and glanced out the window as if she'd never seen it before. "That's what everybody says, Jim."

They all moved to the small living. The two women perched on the sofa some distance apart, sipped their teas, and then rested their glasses in the palms of their hands. Both looked expectantly at A.J., who was in charge. Jim was just an observer.

"We've got a clue. Wondered if y'all have ever heard of a Rosie in these parts?"

Miss Gertie never moved a muscle.

Not so with her sister. She gasped, drew her free gloved hand to her mouth, stared wide-eyed at Miss Gertie, and sank back against the sofa.

"I take it that's a yes, Miss Winnie Sue?"

Miss Gertie recovered first. "Well, now, A.J., I don't recall ever having met a Rosie before. I've known a Rosemary, and—"

He held up a hand to stop her. "Miss Winnie Sue," he said softly and set his glass on a coaster. "Have you ever known a woman named Rosie?"

She looked sideways at her sister and frowned. "I—Officer Banks, I have never known a woman named Rosie."

He sat in the wood chair opposite her. "You sure?"

She didn't meet his gaze. "I was merely reacting to what I thought you'd said, that a woman named Rosie was the killer."

"I didn't say that."

Her hand fluttered over her chest, and then rested on her cheek. "I know, Officer Banks. I'm sorry. I don't know a woman named Rosie."

"Anyone named Roseanne—"

Both shook their heads and said, "No" and "No, sir."

"Or Rosemary."

All color drained from Miss Winnie Sue's face. But she resolutely shook it 'no,' with fingers cradling her chin as if she needed them to keep her head still so it wouldn't nod a 'yes.'

A.J. slapped his knees, which caused Miss Winnie Sue to jump and utter, "Oh, my!" He stood, Jim stood, and waited for the ladies to rise.

"That's all I had today, so I'll be on my way. If you *do* think of a Rosie, would you mind letting me know? I was hoping you two could help us out."

"We sure will, A.J., Jim, and thanks for coming by."

"Keep us posted if you hear anything, Officer Banks."

"Will do, ladies. Oh, one other thing. Do you have any idea why a man would be after our three women? Why he'd be after these three *particular* women? Any idea at all?"

Miss Gertie raised her brows, looked at her sister. "I don't, A.J. Do you, Winnie Sue?" It seemed to Jim that she did her best to put a don't-you-dare-say-a-word-about-anything look in her eyes.

"I don't." Winnie Sue shook her head. "No, Officer Banks, I don't." She lowered her gaze and then sent a sidelong glance at Gertie.

"Well, appreciate your time." A.J. nodded once and left. Jim smiled at the ladies and followed his brother.

When they reached the patrol car, Jim muttered, "I would have never thought I'd witness either of those ladies telling a lie."

"Me, either. But they sure did today."

Gertie caught the door before it could slam. She and Winnie Sue stood on the porch as A.J. backed out, waved, and drove away.

"Well, you sure messed things up, Winnie Sue!" Gertie marched to her kitchen and set her iced tea glass on the counter with a clunk.

"Me?"

"Yes, you! Almost swooning when he mentions *Rosie*. What in the world were you thinking? Don't you have an acting bone in your body, Sister?"

"Don't you 'Sister' me, Sister! I did the best I could under the circumstances!"

Gertie smacked both fists on her hips. "What circumstances? A man asks a simple question, and you fall to pieces!"

"I most certainly did not! I-I... fluttered... a little—"

Gertie snorted. "Fluttered? A little?"

A knock on the door startled them both. They held their breaths and waited.

"Miss Gertie?"

Her eyes widened as she leaned over and whispered, "It's Jim!"

Winnie Sue slapped both hands on her cheeks and gasped, then lowered her head and whispered, "Do you think he heard us?"

Gertie picked up a towel and threw it on the table as she glared at her sister and stormed out of her kitchen. "Why, Jim, bless your heart, did you forget something?"

"Yes, miss, we did. Your sister."

"My sis—oh." She laughed. "You need to take her home. Winnie Sue, your ride is here. Mercy, Jim, I totally forgot A.J. brought her."

"Yes, miss. Too much on our minds, I expect."

Winnie Sue said a meek goodbye to her sister and walked out without so much as a glance in Jim's direction.

Gertie rolled her eyes behind her sister's back and wondered just what Jim had meant by his 'too much on our minds' remark. She wondered, too, if he'd heard anything she and Winnie Sue had said.

Officer Banks draped a hand over the steering wheel and eyed Winnie Sue in the back seat. She averted her gaze.

"Miss Winnie Sue, you sure seemed edgy when I said the name 'Rosie' back there."

Good gracious, what should she say? She *had* been edgy, but she couldn't let him know she knew that. If she did, the next victim in this town would be Winnie Sue Jansen at the hands of her big sister! "Well, Officer Banks, truth be told, I knew a Rosemary once over fifty years ago now."

"What happened to her?"

"Oh." She held up her hand and admired her gloves. "She's no longer with us. A tragedy befell her a-and she's no longer with us. The only other Rosemary I know is Rosemary Atkins, but she certainly doesn't seem like a killer to me. Why, she's the president of the Women's Auxiliary at church, and I can't imagine her being a part of anything like—"

"I didn't say the killer was Rosie."

"You didn't?" She blushed. Mercy, she was no good at deception! Unconsciously, she slipped the lace handkerchief out of the sleeve of her blouse and dabbed at her upper lip.

"No, miss. I said one of the clues was a woman named Rosie."

"Oh." Miss Winnie Sue glanced at the rearview mirror, then looked down at her hands. "I see."

"I'll be frank, miss. You seem to know more than you're saying."

She cleared her throat and touched it with a gloved hand.

"Am I right?"

"Well, Officer Banks, I-I... oh, there's my house. I'm anxious to check on my tomato plants. I'm sorry I couldn't be of more help to you. I will be praying for you to have wisdom and guidance in finding this perpetrator. Now, if you'll be kind enough to open this door, I'll thank you for the ride and wish you a good day, sir."

The Banks brothers watched Miss Winnie Sue walk at a fast clip down the sidewalk to her home. She opened her outside door, walked through her screened-in porch, and opened her front door, without a key. Jim jumped out. "Miss Winnie Sue!"

She turned around as he walked toward her.

"I'm advising you to lock your doors now, miss, until this man is found. It's not safe to leave 'em open." His gaze flicked to an unopened tomato seed package—not tomato plants—sitting inside an empty window box under her first large window.

Miss Winnie Sue followed his gaze and blushed when she looked back at him. "I'll do that, Mr. Banks. You can rest assured, sir, that I will do that."

Jim walked back to his car. The world must be coming to an end soon. This was the second time today that Miss Winnie Sue Jansen skimmed the edges of the truth and almost told an out-and-out lie.

THIRTEEN

Tuesday morning brought cool showers and dreary skies, matching the mood of the people of Little Texas who opened their newspapers and found the headlines blaring that the funerals of the three women murdered in their own homes would be the next day, Wednesday, at Mountain View Church where all three women had attended. The funeral for Renee Banks would begin at nine in the morning with interment at ten-thirty. At Noon, Bonnie Washburn, with interment at one-thirty. And at three, Lulu Baines, interment at four-thirty. Mayor Terry Mason was quoted as saying, "It's going to be a long and sad day for the people of Little Texas."

Exhausted from crying, worrying over, and discussing the murders with every customer who came into her shop, Myra Simms locked the dress shop door. She'd lost her best friend, Lulu, and dear friends, the other two. She needed a break from the tears and decided a treat for lunch at Penny's restaurant next door was just the ticket.

Everyone knew A.J. came into Penny's on Tuesday. Myra wanted to see if those two birdbrains had the sense God gave a raccoon between them. Honestly. It was high time somebody did something to nudge those two back together. This separation of theirs was going on for too long now. Enough was enough.

The doorbell dinged as she walked into Penny's. Every head turned to look at her. Jim Banks' mother, Debra, sat at a small table for two. She immediately got up and pointed to a booth and waved Myra over.

"We can visit, catch up on everything," Debra said as she scooted in.

"How's Jim taking the news of Renee's death?" Myra moaned at getting off her feet for the first time that day and tried to relax.

"About as well as can be expected. You know he came to see Jeb the other night, to tell him about Renee. For the last year, he thought she had left him—we all did. That left a big hole in that boy. And now he's having to deal not only with the fact that she was murdered but with the fact that he's had some pretty awful thoughts about her."

The doorbell dinged again. Heather Ward walked in with her daughter, Elva Lee. The ladies in the booth smiled and waved them over. Debra moved closer to Myra. "Y'all come on. We'll scrunch up. How's everything at Search & Rescue today, Elva Lee?"

They slid in.

"Better yet," Myra said, "how's Jim doing this morning?"

The blush creeping clean up Elva Lee's face did not go unnoticed by Myra or anyone else at that table. She'd known for a long time—hadn't everybody?—that Elva Lee Ward was stuck on James Madison Banks. How long was it going to take that boy to sit up and notice how perfect

Elva Lee was for him? Myra hoped Jim might finally find some peace and move on now that he knew the truth about Renee.

"I don't know, Debra. He's been at A.J.'s this morning. Tommy's at work, but Buddy won't be in. He's a little under the weather today."

"Under the bottle's more like it," Myra mumbled as the other women nodded, and then shook their heads in a moment of silence.

Francie came to the table, took their orders, and left. Myra was more than ready for Penny's hot chicken noodle soup—it was always Tuesday's special. She conspiratorially leaned toward the center of the table. "I heard there's a Rosie connected with the killings," she whispered as her gaze flitted around to each woman.

Everyone at that table slowly eased forward. Myra was pleased as a pear tree to be the one enlightening them. "Rosie is dead." She over-enunciated her quiet words. "Written right there on their tummies."

"Who's Rosie?" Debra rested her arms against the table. "I don't know any Rosie." The others shrugged and shook their heads.

Francie walked up with a pot of coffee and all four women sat upright. Myra turned her cup over and patted the back of her hair while Francie silently poured everyone a cup and left. Myra lifted her hot cup of coffee, looked over her glasses, and shook her head. "No one knows who Rosie is or what the name means."

Elva Lee unfolded her napkin and put it on her lap. "Jim thinks it's a woman the killer can't touch, like his mother or something, and he's killing people who look like her."

Debra set her cup down. "Why, Elva Lee, that just doesn't make sense." She picked up the sugar container and spooned in three heaping servings. "If he wants to kill someone, he should kill *her* and not other people."

"He *thinks* he's killing her."

"And he can't tell the difference?" Debra shook her head. "Seems to me if I had a mind to kill someone, I'd certainly make sure I killed the one I intended to kill and not some stranger!"

As if to chastise the women for gossiping, A.J. and Jim Banks walked by Penny's window and into the restaurant. Jim spoke to his mother, nodded at the other women, held Elva Lee's gaze for a moment—which tickled Myra no end—and perched on a stool beside his brother who sent a general wave to his mother's table.

A silence fell across the restaurant, a reverence of sorts—like being in church—as the brothers ordered their lunch and looked around at the guilty faces behind them. When Jim looked right into Myra's eyes, she blinked rapidly and glanced toward the ceiling.

All talk ended. Their presence forbade it. When words were spoken, they were whispered. Someone loudly slurped a hot sip of coffee, and everyone turned to frown at him. Forks nudged plates but did not clink against them. Gazes darted around the room.

And not a soul asked the chief of police or his brother about the women, or the killer, or about that woman Rosie and how she fit into all this.

At S&R, Tommy and Buddy were called out on the rescue of an eight-year-old boy who slid down a ten-foot embankment and was caught in shrubbery at the base of it. His parents were frantic and couldn't reach him. It was not a difficult rescue. They were expected to be back within an hour.

Elva Lee and Jim were left alone.

Elva Lee's desk sat by the north window, facing the front door.

Jim's desk rested under a small window, facing Elva Lee.

It was difficult at best to gauge his mood, but Debra had told her privately that he was struggling with finding Renee's body, dealing with the loss, the anger, the funeral coming up.

She poured him a cup of coffee and set it on his desk. "Jim?"

"Umm?" He crossed a 't' and looked up at her.

"I just wanted you to know that I have a great pair of ears."

He rested his cheek on his fist, his gaze squarely on her, and it unnerved her.

"And sometimes my mouth shuts down when my ears are in gear."

He smiled at her.

"It's a good possibility that conditions are prime today for both to happen."

Jim leaned back in his chair. When he nodded, she wanted to touch his hand but knew she shouldn't.

"You're a good friend, Elva Lee, and I appreciate it. I'm all right, I think. Just need some time to process all this. Got a lot going on right now."

She nodded. "Well, I just wanted you to know that I'm here for you, if you need anything."

"Thank you. I appreciate it."

That night, Jim sat in the dark, alone, and stared at the picture of Renee he'd put on the mantel the day Josh Daniels had found her body. She was smiling, as usual, and her eyes, those big brown eyes, were focused right on him.

Her teeth had been perfect, her mouth small, her face heart shaped. Her long curly brown hair, hanging over her shoulders, had been full and bouncy.

He missed her. He'd missed her every second she'd been gone but he couldn't face what she'd done to him, couldn't believe their life together had been nothing but a lie.

A whole year, he'd longed to hear from her, longed to touch her, ached to find out why she'd left him. What had been the lack in him that had caused her to leave him? Had their baby been born? Was it being raised by another man?

He hadn't talked to anyone, not even A.J. or his parents, about any of that. They would have pitied him for being such a fool.

He *had* been a fool! He'd believed the worst of Renee and none of it was true. He jumped up and sent his iced tea flying.

Glass shattered all over the creeping ivy Rachelle had given Renee on her last birthday and the firewood Jim had brought in the night before. He growled and kicked the stack of firewood and when it didn't budge, he shoved it with his boot. The logs tumbled out in slow motion. Just like he felt, tumbling in slow motion and nowhere to go but down. He grabbed one and threw it into the fire. Angry sparks flew out at him.

He leaned against the fireplace, which put his face right in front of Renee's photo. He stared at her mouth, her eyes, her hair. A surge of longing hit him, and a whimper escaped his pinched lips. He gasped. Racking sobs erupted from deep within his soul.

"I'm sorry." His heart ached. His fist pounded the mantel as he gritted his teeth against the pain. "Oh, Renee. I'm. So. Sorry." He leaned on the mantel, buried his face in the crook of his arm, and shook his head, back and forth, back and forth. Then he stilled and let the grief wash over him. "I'm so sorry, honey. I'm so sorry."

Tears fell onto the brick landing where he stood. Wave after wave of sorrow and anger and regret swept over him. He cried for the loss of his love, the loss of their love, the loss of his only child.

A big hand slid across his shoulder. Lost in his anguish, Jim turned into the arms of his older brother. He and A.J. held on to each other unashamedly as Jim wept for the woman lost, the senselessness of her death, and the indescribable pain of being left behind.

Easing out of his brother's arms, Jim sniffed. With his head down, he walked into the hall, grabbed a couple of washcloths out of the linen closet, and handed one to his brother.

Wiping faces, they both stared at Renee's picture.

"Came to see how you were doing."

"You saw."

"Didn't expect anything less."

Jim took A.J.'s washcloth and put both on the mantel. "Want something to drink? Tea or juice."

"Tea. I'll turn the TV on. Game's started. Rangers are ahead."

Jim left, came back with two glasses of tea, and handed one to his brother. For the first time in a long time, Jim felt a measure of contentment. For some reason, he thought of Elva Lee. He wanted to tell her about tonight. He wanted to tell her that he was going to be okay now.

Easing into a chair opposite A.J., he took a good-sized guzzle as the commercial ended and the baseball game came back on.

"You let her go."

Several seconds ticked by as Jim stared unseeingly at the screen. "I did."

A.J. lifted his glass.

Jim leaned over, clicked his glass against A.J.'s, and turned up the volume on the TV.

Sarah was curled up on the sofa closest to the roaring fire in the den, grateful for the thick woolen socks that kept her feet warm. She tried to read a mystery book, but it was difficult to stay in it with the wind kicking up and noises creeping around the windows and the house creaking in the blustery weather. "I sure wish we could steal some warm May weather from Kansas and bring it up here, Luke. I'm ready for winter to become a distant memory."

"Won't be like that until the middle of June."

She groaned. "Are you going to any of the funerals?"

He looked up. "I thought I would. Are you?"

"I don't know these people. I'd feel like I was intruding."

"Then I won't go. It's going to be an all-day event." He popped the newspaper and folded it. "That's too long to leave you by yourself."

"Won't Eduardo and Yolanda be here?"

"No. They've lived here all their lives. They'll be at the funerals."

Through the dark trees, the lighted clock on the bank said *11:36* as Casey Pollard jogged down the empty town square, headed west. She crossed the street to the City Park. It had been horrible the last few days, what with losing her sister, Lulu, and dealing with everyone coming to the house, bringing food and hugs and tears and... she was just so very tired of it all. And she was angry. This man comes to their town and *kills* her sister! Tonight, when she'd thought about running, she remembered what A.J. had said earlier today at the grocery store: "No running, Casey. Not after dark."

It felt good to be running at night for a change, even with all this wind. Her husband, Will, had taken the day off, and they'd both worked hard on fixing some things around the house. When he fell asleep on the sofa watching the baseball game and all the kids were asleep, too, she figured she'd get in a short run.

Not once, in all the years she'd been running, had she ever experienced fear in Little Texas.

But tonight, she sure did.

But what were the chances that this lunatic would be in her path? Small town, sure, but he could be anywhere. She did think about turning around. A little farther and she would.

Her gaze darted into the row of trees along the sidewalk. Up ahead, around a corner, the brush was close to the sidewalk. She edged over to the right and avoided it and breathed a sigh of relief as she—

Her hair was caught! Something was pulling her back, dragging her into the dark shrubs!

Pain gripped her temples. She grabbed her head to stop the agony, but she couldn't.

"Stop it, Rosie." Next to her ear, smelly breath hissed.

Rosie! The killer! "I'm not... Rosie." Her face contorted as she gritted her teeth against the ripping pain. "I'm. Not. Rosie!"

He yanked on her hair. Casey almost fainted.

"Shut up, Rosie. You got out, didn't you? You got out *again!*" He yanked her hair. Casey barely hung on to consciousness. "You're going right back in there, y'hear me? Right back in there!"

Casey knew she was dead if she didn't do something. "Let me go."

The killer stopped, and the screeching pain yielded. "What'd ju say, Rosie?"

"I said, let me go." She didn't have the strength to grab her hair. "I'm not Rosie, you fool. I'm Casey. You can't kill the wrong person, can you?" She looked up and couldn't see anything in the dark surrounding them.

The man jerked her to her feet and what she could only describe as a scuffle occurred behind her.

"Let her go." A deeper voice, more mature.

"No, it's Rosie. I have to—"

"It's not Rosie! Rosie's dead!"

"No, she isn't. She got out!"

"Let her go. NOW!"

"No!"

Casey tried to see who was behind her, but a crushing weight slammed into her head, and she knew nothing.

"And it's a home run!"

Will Pollard stirred enough to watch through narrowed eyes as the batter ran around the bases. "Honey? Could you get me a beer?"

"With the score four to two—"

"Honey? Casey?" Will sat up, threw the pillow he was hugging onto the sofa, and looked over his shoulder toward the lighted kitchen. He clicked the TV off and listened. "Casey?"

He stumbled into the kitchen and pulled out a beer, popped the top, and drank. He took another swig and listened. She didn't go out running, did she, after A.J. told her not to?

He headed for the basement. "Casey?"

No answer.

He checked their bathroom. Ran out the back door. "Casey?"

Rushing back inside, he plucked the keys off the hook by the garage door and cursed. He grabbed his phone, punched in the numbers, and waited. "Mom, Casey's out running. I've got to go find her. Okay. Thanks."

Will hustled inside his truck and started it as the garage door lifted. He backed out. His mother was running down the sidewalk.

"Be right back," he yelled as she waved and walked inside the house.

He knew Casey's route. If she was out running, he was going to let her have it, in spades. Running in the dark with a killer on a murder spree!

He was frantic after twenty minutes. He drove by the police station, but no one was there. He headed over to Search & Rescue.

Lights were on. He ran inside. A.J. and Jim both jumped up when he crashed inside.

"Casey's missing!"

Larry's hands shook as he reached for his radio. He fumbled it. It crashed beside Casey's body, and he swiped it up as if he could take back the clattering sounds. "A.J.? Uh, I-I found her, A.J. In the shrubs, just north of the curve in the walking path on the west side of the park. We need an ambulance. She's in bad shape."

FOURTEEN

The news spread like wildfire that the killer almost succeeded in snuffing out the life of Casey Pollard. Jim called Luke early in the morning to let him know to be alert, that the killer was spiraling out of control. He hadn't succeeded with Casey or with Sarah the day before on her hike, so he might be more desperate to get Sarah.

The funerals began at nine in the morning with Renee's. Surprisingly, Jim felt sadness, not torment, at seeing Renee's closed casket at the front of the church. She was at peace; he was at peace.

By the interment at ten-thirty, snow clouds hovered. A chilly breeze glided over and around the tombstones. Long winter coat hems lifted in the blustery air; scarves floated above shoulders as if they wanted to fly away from all the sadness while mourners' hands held hats securely on their heads.

Myra Simms was clinging to Jim's arm. Fred stood to the side, hands in his pockets, head down, his long black coat flapping in the wind. Myra pulled away from Jim and took Fred's hand. He led her away to their car.

All during the funeral and the interment, Jim had caught Penny looking at A.J. with something like regret in her eyes. He supposed that death made people re-evaluate their lives. That's what she seemed to be doing, standing by her car, watching A.J. again. Hopefully, something good with those two would come out of all this.

She got inside her car and slowly drove off.

Jim was alone now, standing over the grave of his wife with his head down. His new black suit felt awkward on him—it was tight in the wrong places and way too thick. The black tie he'd bought to go with it danced on his shoulder in the cool breeze.

Renee's family had left right after the graveside service ended.

A.J. came and stood beside him. He heaved a sigh. Neither said a word for several moments. "You know she's in a better place."

Jim tilted his head back and stared up at the gray-layered clouds. "I had nothing to do with her going away." He sent his brother a sidelong glance and lifted his brows. "'And the truth will set you free.'"

A.J. smiled at him. Like Jim, he was probably remembering Mrs. Musselman's scripture-of-the-week for the kids in Sunday school and how she'd have them stand up and quote it and put a star by the names of those who'd learned it. Jim memorized his scripture every week because he wanted those multi-colored stickers beside his name. Because he wanted to shine. Because he wanted Mrs. Musselman's praise for a job well done.

Looking around at the huge array of flowers surrounding Renee's grave and feeling peace right now, he'd like to tell Mrs. Musselman that her diligence had paid off. "Wasn't she something?"

"Mrs. Musselman. Man, she was tough. But also kind. Such a sweet woman."

Nodding thoughtfully, Jim said, "The truth," as he squatted, picked up a clod of dirt, and bounced it in his hand. He stared at it, then squeezed his hand and sprinkled the dirt on top of her shiny mahogany casket. "Good-bye, Renee. I will always love you."

The two of them walked back to A.J.'s patrol car.

A.J. slid in. "There's a community-wide dinner at eleven at Mountain View Church. It's for all three funerals. Plenty of food. Let's head over there and get something to eat."

Jim nodded. "Sounds good. I'm starving."

At Bonnie Washburn's funeral and interment, her husband Buddy was not among the mourners. He'd been too drunk to come to his own wife's funeral.

Miss Gertie and Miss Winnie Sue stood with the family. Howard Jansen, their brother, was Bonnie Washburn's grandfather.

"Hold on, Jim," A.J. said as he leaned over and studied a young woman he'd never seen. "Who's that?"

Jim's gaze swept the faces. "Where?"

"The small woman, right there beside Will Pollard, looking at us and making an effort not to. Who is she?"

"I don't know. Never seen her before."

"Sure seems interested in my patrol car. Maybe we need to take a closer look-see."

"Not at a funeral. We'll keep an eye on her when she leaves."

But she slipped away during the long prayer closing out the interment service.

Jim and A.J. went over to the station to check in.

Both dreaded the final funeral at three o'clock. It was packed. Everybody had loved Lulu. After the interment, A.J. and Jim, weary from this emotional day, headed to their offices to check in.

"Do you see any straight edges, Luke? I'm missing two pieces over here." Sarah checked the time. "The funerals should be over by now. I'm so sorry for all the hurt in this town." She was grateful Luke had stayed back with her. She looked outside. "What a beautiful snow. It's getting thicker."

She folded her arms on the card table holding their one-thousand-piece puzzle and leaned toward Luke as she scanned the pieces. "I saw that. You took my straight edge."

When he pulled his hand out of her reach, he said, with a nonchalant expression, "What do I get for finding this one?"

"Absolutely nothing. Now let me see it."

"For a price." He raised his brows and smiled.

"Extortion from such a fine, upstanding Texas cowboy?"

"Yes, ma'am."

"All right. What do you want?"

"Hot chocolate."

"Me, too."

She plucked the puzzle piece out of his hand and stood. "What's that?" Leaning over to see better, she pointed at something outside. "That red in the snow over there."

Frowning, Luke scooted around the card table and opened the sliding glass door. "A rose?" He picked it up, blew the snow off it, and sniffed it as he looked around. "In this weather? Why is a rose on my patio?"

"Maybe Eduardo gave some to Yolanda."

"And what? One of them got away?"

"Okay, smarty pants. You come up with an answer."

"I don't have one." He glanced up at Sarah's window and shook his head. "No footprints so it was here before the snow started about thirty minutes ago." One more quick look around. "Snow's not deep enough yet to cover anything up."

"Maybe someone dropped it from a window?"

"But that would mean someone was in the house. No one could have gotten in here without one of us hearing. Eduardo and Yolanda left before nine." Luke checked his watch. "Eight hours ago."

"So, it couldn't have been them. I'm cold. Let's go inside."

Luke followed her inside the house and shut the sliding door. "Why would someone walk to this cabin and place a perfectly beautiful rose on the patio in this cold? No one here has a family member who was killed."

"Maybe it's a custom in Mexico. Maybe it's for Eduardo and Yolanda. Are they related to anyone murdered?"

"Not that I know of." His gaze held Sarah's. "It might have something to do with the Rosie connected to the murders."

Sarah nodded slowly. She was surprised and pleased when her heart rate didn't spike. "He could have stood behind the garage and thrown it. No one sees him, and he leaves no footprints on this side. Let's check it out."

They both walked to the other side of the garage, but there were no prints anywhere. They searched around the corner of the house closest to the patio. Nothing. "So, what's the purpose of this rose?"

"It's for you, Sarah. To acknowledge that you're Rosie and that you're here." He checked the security system. It was set. Then he tugged out his phone. "I'm calling A.J."

Luke turned to the sliding glass door and watched the snow fall. "Hey, A.J. I hate to bother you today." He told him about the rose. "The security system is on at all times. Sarah and I checked it; it was on. I don't see how he could have gotten into this house. We have to disengage it to go outside the front door."

"Did you and Sarah go anywhere today?"

"To Alva's store, just down the road. But I'm sure I reset the system when we left."

"Does Sarah's bedroom overlook the patio?"

"Her old room did. We switched rooms."

"He could've slipped upstairs, dropped the rose, and left while you were gone. Have you checked her room?"

"No." Luke covered the mouthpiece. "Sarah, A.J. wants us to check your bedroom. Hold on, A.J." They walked upstairs and opened the door.

Sarah gasped. Red rose petals dotted the comforter covering her bed. "He was in here."

Luke nodded toward Sarah's bed. "He was inside this house, A.J. Rose petals are all over her bed. You need to come over here."

"On my way." He hung up.

Sarah hugged herself. "He knows that this is now my room, not yours, Luke."

Sarah couldn't sleep with Molly whining and staring at the open window. She looked out and saw only trees in the soft glow of the nightlight at the corner of the house. A chill crawled up her back. Something didn't feel right.

"It's your imagination," she whispered to herself.

She wanted to believe it, but she couldn't.

Something wasn't right.

Molly was still staring at the window.

Then she barked.

Sarah made herself walk calmly to her bed and fluffed the pillow. Then she quickly opened the drawer, tugged out the flashlight, and turned it on. She rushed to the window and searched the trees with the light.

She stopped.

Something...

Was that a pair of eyes surrounded by green?

They blinked.

"Oh, God!" Beside her, Molly barked several times. Sarah dropped the flashlight, lunged for the curtains, and drew them together. Her heart pounded. She had looked into his eyes!

The adjoining door opened. Luke rushed in. "What is it?"

"He was here!" She couldn't breathe. She was shaking so hard that when she picked up the flashlight, she fumbled it. Angry at herself, she plucked it off the carpet, opened the curtains, and shined it on the spot where he'd sat. He was gone, of course. "Right there. He'd completely covered himself in green and was sitting right there, staring at me."

"Then don't open the curtains."

"I thought, with the trees, that—"

"I know." He wrapped his arms around her. "I'm sorry, Sarah." He tightened his hold.

"*Did* you reset the system when we went to Alva's store?"

"I guess I didn't. I know I pushed the right buttons, but maybe I didn't hit ENTER or something."

She pulled out of his arms. "I prefer thinking that than thinking he was able to breach your system."

The next day, Thursday, promised to be beautiful. Snow glistened with the promise of spring in the sun's rays. Elva Lee opened the door to Search & Rescue, thumped her boots against the door jamb, and slammed the door shut. "I'm here to tell y'all, I am glad today's Thursday and yesterday's over with." She hung her coat on a fuzzy pink hangar and set it inside the coat closet.

She fluttered a hand at the room in general. "Now, don't get me wrong. I loved Lulu and I'm gonna miss her like crazy but I'm glad those funerals are over with. It gives all of us a chance to get on with living. Anybody know how Jim's doing? I haven't talked to him since before the funerals. Tommy, how's Buddy doing? Has he crawled out of that hole he dug Tuesday night?"

Without waiting for his answer, she picked up the empty coffee pot, filled it with water, and raised her brows at Tommy as she reached inside the cupboard and pulled out the red coffee can. She yanked off the lid and took out the scoop.

"He sure feels like a fool for missing the funeral."

"Well, he should. Two, three. Missing his own wife's funeral—four—because of his drinking. Five, six. Jim had the same thing—seven, eight—happen to him and—nine, ten—he was there *and* at the hospital with Casey and Will, *and—*"

The door swooshed open, and their boss stepped in.

"'Morning, Jim." Elva Lee dropped the scooper into the can and pressed the lid on it.

"'Morning. You losing some weight there, Miss Elva Lee?"

She felt her smile slide across two states. He noticed! "Yes, I am, Mr. Jim Banks. I've lost twenty-five pounds already." She shrugged and turned on the coffee pot. "'Course, I'm sure some of that at first had to do with stress and water weight."

Water weight? What in the world was water weight? Jim sat and rifled through some of the papers on his desk.

Search & Rescue was gearing up for the summer months when people tried to pull foolish stunts against unyielding natural laws. Nature lived by the rules even if the tourists didn't. They unwittingly proved over and over again that nature held the upper hand when they didn't use the brains God gave them.

The sun slanted morning rays across his desk. His cell phone rang. "Hey, A.J."

"Our little miss's name is Allison McIntosh."

"How'd you find her?"

"At Penny's. Just waltzed in, spotted me, and clipped out of there as fast as her legs could carry her. But I caught up to her. Her brother has a rap sheet."

"Doing what?"

"Petty theft, twice. Jail time, less than a year."

"What's his name, and where does he live?" Jim's pen was poised to write.

"Brian McIntosh. Last known, Pueblo, Colorado. No permanent address. Her other brother is spotless. Name of Robert McIntosh, an accountant out Denver way. He's in Arizona this week as part of a team auditing a company in Phoenix."

"Interesting. What would Brian's connection be to our women?" Out of the corner of his eye, Jim saw Elva Lee's head turn toward him.

"Don't know that either. She didn't have anything else to tell me. And just for your information, I stopped by Luke's last night. Apparently, our killer dropped rose petals on Sarah's bed and then tossed a rose out her window. We didn't find a single print. A rose for Rosie. If he's the killer, he sure has a talent for B&E without making a sound."

"Any prints on the crowbar you found with Casey?"

"No. Lulu's blood was on it, though, as was Casey's."

Winnie Sue tentatively answered the phone because she didn't recognize the number on her caller ID. No one called her before nine in the morning, ever. "Hello?"

"Miss Winnie Sue Jansen?"

She hesitated, as she didn't recognize the voice either. "Yes, who's calling?"

"You don't know me. I'm looking for my grandmother, Rosie Jansen." *Rosie Jansen!* "I wondered if I could come by and talk to you and your sister Gertie for a little bit sometime today."

The girl at the funeral. Miss Gertie had noticed her and had pointed out that the little woman standing beside one of the Pollards was the spitting image of herself at twenty-five. "Were you at the funeral yesterday?"

"Yes, ma'am, I was."

"I saw you there." Winnie Sue edged toward the front window and regretted watching Trace Simms walk by without being able to visit with him. Owning Gally's Hardware afforded a wealth of information passing between Mr. Simms's ears and Winnie Sue liked to avail herself of that knowledge as much as possible.

"Would it be convenient for me to come by today or tonight? Maybe we could go to your sister's house and talk or go out to eat somewhere. Maybe dinner?"

Winnie Sue re-crossed her ankles and smoothed her skirt. What in the world would Miss Gertie want her to do? Since the subject had never come up, she simply didn't know. "And what is your name, miss?"

"Allison McIntosh. I'm looking forward to talking to you, Miss Jansen. I hope you can give me information on Rosie Jansen. What time shall I come by?"

Mercy me. "Seven would be fine." *That gives me all day to prepare myself.* "Do you know where I live, Miss McIntosh?"

"Yes, I do. I'll see you at seven." And then she hung up.

"Forevermore!" Winnie Sue cradled the phone and heard the dial tone buzzing. Carefully, as if her life depended on it, she set the phone down and wished her sister wasn't such a tightwad and would get herself a phone.

There was no way to warn her that a McIntosh granddaughter neither of them knew even existed was coming to visit.

Sarah and Luke stopped by the police station after lunch. A.J. was sitting at his desk, holding a bag with the rose inside, studying the contents as if a clue might squeeze through the bag's zipper and jump onto his desk.

"Afternoon, you two. Wanted to update you on what I found—or didn't find, in this case. No prints or any evidence of the killer being in your cabin, Luke, or in your room, Sarah." A.J. lifted the bag. "This rose isn't much help, but it might point us in the direction of our next victim."

That would be me. Sarah felt the blood drain from her face, leaving her cold. But she refused to be afraid. She would be a lion—strong and brave and wise and maybe even send out a growl or two. But she would not be afraid.

"Uh, possible victim." A.J. glanced at her, a little sheepishly.

"So, it *was* him in my room."

"I believe it was."

A phone rang behind A.J. and someone answered, "LTPD."

Sarah glanced outside as Molly barked from the bed of Luke's truck. A man was patting her and laughing with her. He walked off, turned, and waved at Molly when she barked at him. She watched him until he turned a corner.

Luke poured himself a cup of coffee. "A.J., why is this man so hard to find? He's small, has a fetish for peanuts, and must be strong, maybe a bodybuilder or an athlete."

"It's tough sometimes. We'll keep looking until he snags himself on a mistake. You have a gun, Sarah?"

"Yes."

"We also have guns at the cabin." Luke turned to her. "Do you know how to shoot?"

"I had lessons years ago. But shooting another human might be a little challenging for me."

"Not if your life is at stake."

FIFTEEN

Allison pulled up to Winnie Sue Jansen's property and parked.

She considered herself a tough woman. She was mostly kind but tended toward quarrelsome and sometimes sulking when under pressure. It wasn't difficult to understand why. A messed-up father meant a messed-up daughter and a messed-up family.

As he'd explained—she groaned. Explained? Ha! As he'd *beat into them* so many times— his little witch of a mother was the source of all his troubles, and theirs. And there were many.

Marek Riley McIntosh had resented just about everything in his life. His parents had given him a strange name with no nickname in sight except 'Mary' so he called himself 'Butch' to compensate for the name.

At the top of his list of resentments—again, a mild word for virulent hate—were his two brothers who were both well over six feet tall. Marek, at five-foot-three, had never fit in. One of his brothers in particular teased and bullied him, pulling on his arms, and shouting, "Grow! Grow, little munchkin! Are you off to see the Wizard? You're not even tall enough to get on the rides at the fair!"

Both his parents died in an airplane crash when he was twenty-one. It was then, as he sifted through their papers, that he found his original birth certificate and his adoption papers.

His focus of hate now rested squarely on his birth mother.

And eventually on his oldest son.

Her father never let Brian forget that he was inadequate because of his short stature. He beat him senseless, pulled on his arms and legs, screaming, "Grow! Grow, you little toad! You're going to amount to nothing if you don't grow!"

Their useless mother had stood by, quietly fretting—as did Allison and Robbie—while Brian curled up into a ball and wept. They weren't even allowed to comfort him.

Allison had asked both her brothers if they knew their grandmother's address. Robbie said a definite no. Brian told her to look for someone in her seventies or eighties with the name Jansen or a maiden name of Jansen. After asking at the post office, Allison was told that "Miss Gertie will know who you're looking for."

A curtain moved at Winnie Sue Jansen's house. She was probably wondering why Allison was sitting in her car, staring at the front door. Allison squared her shoulders, walked up the steps, rang the doorbell, and listened to the melting snow dripping from the corners of the house.

The door opened.

"Winnie Sue Jansen?"

"Yes?"

"I'm Allison McIntosh. I believe I may be related to you." She extended her hand. Winnie Sue simply stared at her and turned white as a snowbank as she slowly melted toward the floor.

Allison caught her. "Miss Jansen? Are you all right? Miss Jansen?" She couldn't explain the genuine fear gripping her for this old woman she didn't know. She weighed almost nothing and was a good two or three inches shorter than Allison's five foot two.

She carried the woman to a sofa and sat beside her, stroking her arm. "Miss Jansen? Are you all right?"

The woman finally opened her eyes. "What happened?" she whispered.

"You fainted. Are you all right?"

"Oh, my goodness." She tried to sit up, fluttered a hand in front of her face, and smacked her lips in a very unladylike fashion.

Allison smiled. She didn't think she'd ever heard "Oh, my goodness" in her life. "May I get you some water?"

"Yes, please."

Allison patted her small spotted hand. "I'll be right back. Will you be okay while I'm gone?"

A weak smile, a flicker of a nod, and Allison scampered down a hallway.

The kitchen was delightful with colors of bright yellow and cherry-red. A low-sitting island in the center was perfect for Winnie Sue's height, with hanging pans above it that she could reach. Flowerpots stretched along the windowsills.

Allison opened a cabinet door and found a glass with cherries painted on them. Everything was pristine and in order. The woman who lived here must be very special. She smiled at the sentimental thought, filled the glass, and hurried back to her.

Winnie Sue was sitting up, pale as a ghost but wearing a wan smile. "I'm so sorry, dear one," she said as she took the offered glass and sipped.

Allison fell in love with her right then.

"You're so pale, ma'am. Is there any medicine or anything I can get you?"

"Miss."

"Excuse me?"

"It's 'miss' not 'ma'am'." The older woman patted her hand. "I'm fine. Coming out of a good spin takes a moment." She smiled. "You have the same height and coloring as Miss Gertie and me. Light brown hair, big brown eyes, thin lips, a heart-shaped face. You're very pretty."

"Thank you. Are you feeling all right?"

She touched Allison's hand again. "If I could sit here for a moment, dear, and catch my breath."

She took her time sipping water and taking deep breaths. "I am much better, Allison. Maybe we should go to my sister's home now."

Allison helped her up.

Winnie Sue straightened like a pin rod and slipped on the white gloves sitting on her white purse. "If you're ready, then, dear."

Resting on Allison's arm, she walked carefully out the door.

It was a cloudy evening, although it wasn't late—not even six o'clock. Snow was on the way again, and it was cold. Luke thought he and Sarah shouldn't be outside too much longer. A few more minutes on the porch swing, and they'd head inside.

"The news coverage about the murders has been constant back home. My mother's worried." Sarah welcomed Molly with open arms and scooted over to allow her room to sit between her and Luke.

"You've spoiled Molly rotten."

"And proud of it, I am. It's such a pretty night. I wish we could take a walk down your road and just enjoy it."

"Me, too." Holding hands while doing it would be nice, too.

Molly's head jerked up. Around the corner, the sliding glass door opened. She jumped up and raced toward it. *Eduardo or Yolanda.*

"My mom's worried. Thinks I should come home, get away from all this. She's probably right. Leaving would solve all my problems."

"The Darkslayer could be back in Kansas." Luke was a selfish man and wanted her here with him. He liked her. He didn't consider it unreasonable that he didn't want her to go home. He'd spent more time with her than with any other woman he'd ever dated.

She touched his arm. "Luke? Were you listening?"

He nodded. "You said your mother was worried sick and wanted you to come home."

"After that."

"Okay. You caught me. I was thinking I didn't want you to go."

She searched his eyes. "I'm not ready to leave. There's just too much I want to see, and no other place I'd rather be."

Darkness pressed in around them. A twig snapped. Sarah gasped and jerked back.

Luke spun around, searching behind them. He unsnapped his gun holster and tugged out his weapon. "Come on." He eased off the swing, his gaze circling around the front yard, the side yard. He nudged her in front of him, pushed her toward the front door, and opened it.

Hustling inside, they both breathed a sigh of relief when the lock clicked, and the security system was set.

The man watched her rush inside. "Now, Rosie, you know you can't run away from me." He gritted his teeth as he slammed his head against the smooth bark of an aspen and whimpered.

"He was out there." Anger sliced through Sarah. Breathless with it, she spun around and looked into Luke's eyes. "I was wrong. I've got to get out of here. He's waiting for me to make a mistake. I have to go home as soon as possible." She sidestepped Luke and ran toward the stairs.

Early evening was Gertie's favorite time of the day. She loved sitting on her porch, listening to her knitting needles clicking away as the cold crispness of night settled in. Snow was on the way. An elk strolled past the cabin, glanced at Gertie, and lay in the cushion of green grass in the same spot he'd chosen the night before.

"Hello, old friend," she muttered without looking up from her knitting and smiled at the easiness between them.

In the distance, a car came down her gravel lane and crept toward her cabin. The elk jumped up and bounded across the yard, head erect and rack simply magnificent.

Gertie set aside her knitting and stood, wrapped a hand around a gnarly post, and felt the blood drain from her face as the woman at the funeral and her sister exited the little blue car.

The young woman reached her steps. Gertie stepped back.

Neither of them spoke or took their gazes off the other.

Winnie Sue, being graced with all kinds of good manners, moved forward and waved a gloved hand first at her sister, then Allison. "Miss Gertie Jansen, Miss Allison McIntosh."

Gertie had never been speechless a day in her life, unless it was the time a doctor had spoken the word 'pregnant' and 'home for unwed mothers' after the brutal rape. That news would have made a magpie speechless. But she wouldn't think of that time. She *never* thought of that time, over fifty years ago now. She'd buried it deep within her so that it wouldn't have the power to crush her.

And now she faced the offspring of that rape, with not a clue what should or should not be said in such a situation.

Winnie Sue ventured, "Allison's come all the way from Portland,

Oregon, Miss Gertie."

Allison turned to her. "You call your sister 'Miss Gertie'?"

Winnie Sue patted Allison's upper arm. "Yes, dear one, out of respect. She's considerably older than me and helped raise me."

"I *did* raise you, Winnie Sue, and you know it." Laws, she didn't want to fight with Winnie Sue first thing after meeting Allison.

"You're nothing like your sister."

Winnie Sue gasped.

Gertie frowned.

"But what could I expect from a woman who gave my father away as if he were nothing? You're Rosie Jansen, aren't you?"

Gertie smirked. The best course of action would be to ignore the little whippersnapper's sarcasm. "Portland, you say?"

Allison looked as if she might scream, but she didn't. She glared up at Gertie. "Yes, my father moved from Denver when I was fifteen."

"Oh, dear," Winnie Sue patted again, "that must have been so difficult at such a young age. To lose all your friends and... and..." She floundered when she glanced up at her sister and connected with the fierce glare she was sending her way.

With her unyielding gaze on Gertie, Allison said, "You're quite right, Aunt Winnie Sue."

Aunt Winnie Sue? Gertie ground her teeth while Winnie Sue smiled and patted Allison's arm again.

"It was hard to leave everything I knew and move to a strange town."

It was hard to give the baby away. Gertie crossed her arms and pursed her lips.

"Well." Winnie Sue touched Allison's arm. "I'm sure you made friends very quickly, my dear."

Allison continued to pout and glare at Gertie.

Winnie Sue looked from one to the other. "I need to check on the roses I planted last year on the other side of Miss Gertie's cabin and see if there are any buds on them yet, for roses have to be tended to and my sister is not the tending-to-roses type."

"Turn on the outside lights."

"I know, Sister."

Winnie Sue stared at both of them for an uncomfortable moment, sidestepped Allison, and teetered along the thin path beside the cabin.

The roses were eager for attention, but she couldn't tend to them tonight, with snow coming in. She stepped into the basement, turned on the light, and looked for the pruning gloves she'd given her sister last year.

"You're never too old to learn to garden, Sister," she'd said to Miss Gertie who, quite disgusted, had rolled her eyes, shook her head, and stalked off. Winnie Sue slipped out of her white gloves, placed them in her purse, set her purse on a table. She yanked the work gloves from under a pair of metal thingies. They hadn't been cleaned since she'd used them.

"You're going to have roses whether you like it or not, Sister," she muttered as she brushed off the gloves. She'd be back in the next few days and tend to the roses. Right now, she needed to keep herself busy for a few more minutes to give the two on the porch enough time to settle in with each other.

She jumped when she heard it.

"Forevermore," she whispered. Then she heard it again.

Laughter.

Well, her plan had worked. Pleased as punch, she nodded once as she smiled rather smugly. She turned off the light, tugged on her white gloves, picked up her purse, marched around the house and found her sister and Allison sitting on the porch steps with smiles on their faces.

Allison flapped a hand at Miss Gertie. "And then the goat lunged for his suit jacket, grabbed a mouthful and yanked—"

Head back with laughter, Miss Gertie slapped her knee.

"He led my brother around the yard with him yelling, 'Stop it! Help!'"

Winnie Sue stood in front of the giggling pair, not sure what she should do, if anything. She wanted them to tell the story from the beginning, but it didn't look like the appropriate time to suggest it.

"Come on up, Sister. Sit with me and our kin." Miss Gertie nudged Allison's knee and grinned ear-to-ear at her.

"I believe I'll sit in a chair, Miss Gertie, if you don't mind."

"Suit yourself."

Allison and Miss Gertie looked at each other and burst out laughing again.

"And what, pray tell, is so funny?" Winnie Sue was on the verge of being miffed.

"The story she just told." Miss Gertie slapped her knees and stood. "Let's go inside and have some iced tea and visit for a spell."

Winnie Sue was beginning to feel a little left out. Then, Allison wrapped her hand around her arm and walked in with her.

"Your gloves are so pretty, Aunt Winnie Sue."

She smiled at Allison.

Having a new member of the family around was surely going to be a very pleasurable experience.

When Sarah passed him the bowl of mashed potatoes, Luke's fingers brushed the tips of her hand. He glanced at her, hoping for a playful response, but she lifted her chin slightly and kept her gaze on the bowl.

The thought of her leaving—even if it was for the best—left him unsettled. He thought something good was happening between them. Maybe she didn't think so. But he didn't want her to walk away from it or from him. Not yet. He could keep her safe if she'd just trust him to do it.

She picked up the bowl of bacon-laced green beans, scooped up a spoonful, dumped them next to the mashed potatoes on her plate, and passed them on to Luke.

He grinned and tried his best this time to completely cover her hand as he took the bowl.

Her golden eyes flashed. Man, she was a beautiful woman, even when she was annoyed. She probably didn't realize it, but her dimples deepened when she pursed her lips like that and glared at him.

She'd been doing plenty of that since they'd run inside the house an hour earlier.

He sat back.

He'd have to let her go.

But he wouldn't let their friendship go. Four hours wasn't a long drive, and he was willing to drive it. They could stay in contact through e-mail and phone calls and texts. It was workable.

"I need to pack so I'll be going back to my cabin in the mor—"

"The heck you will!" Luke threw the spoon back into the green beans and glared at her.

She set her roll down. "Heck has nothing to do with it. And yes, I will."

"You can't be that dense."

"I am *not* dense. I'm merely—"

"*Being* dense!"

She scooted her chair back. "Obviously, you're not in the frame of mind to discuss this civilly."

"And you're not in the frame of mind to listen to reason!"

She stood. *"Reason?* I've yet to hear *reason."*

He stood. "You want reason, then I'll give you reason. You just had the life scared out of you at *this...very...cabin,* and you expect me to let you go to your cabin *alone?* God didn't give you the sense He gave—"

"Apparent—"

"Exactly!" Point scored, Luke threw his napkin down and stormed out of the room.

Sarah sat in a huff, not sure what to do with the napkin she found in her hands. "Well."

"For what it's worth, Sarah, I think Luke's right."

She looked at Yolanda and then Eduardo. "Of course, he is. He gets my dander up in the worst way when all he has to do is *ask* me but, no, he has to lay down the law as if I'm a nitwit."

"Not a nitwit. As if you're someone he cares for deeply." When she looked up at Eduardo, he raised his brows, pursed his lips, and nodded.

Sarah pushed back her chair and stood. "Thank you for the—" She burst into tears and sank into the chair again. "I'm so tired of being afraid to do *anything,* even admitting to liking Luke. I know it's too fast, and I don't know what to do. I don't even know him."

Yolanda put her arm around Sarah as Eduardo left the room.

"You can't help who you love, Sarah. If it's your time and the man is right, then go for it and enjoy it. I've known this family for years. You couldn't have picked a finer man than Luke McKenzie, and I think you know it."

"My parents will think I'm absolutely nuts when I announce I have feelings for someone I haven't even known two weeks."

"Maybe not. They were there once, caught up in new love. You've spent time with Luke in difficult situations. You've gotten to know him quickly and well."

Sarah nodded. "It's too early to talk about *love.*" She searched Yolanda's eyes. "Isn't it? I don't want to go back to Kansas and lose what we're discovering here, but I don't want to leave my life in Kansas either. It just seems hopeless."

"If you care for each other, you'll find a way."

"I don't know if Luke even likes me. He's bossy and domineering and—so gentle and kind and giving. Oh, I'm so confused."

Yolanda smiled and lifted a brow. "I think it's safe to say he feels the same way about you. Maybe you two should talk and get everything out in the open."

Nodding, Sarah stood. "Please don't say anything to Luke about this. I'm sorry about ruining dinner. Please make my apologies to Eduardo. I don't—maybe if—I'm sorry." She ran from the room.

Sarah found the quiet and solitude of her room oppressive. She was afraid to turn on the lights. The killer had been in this room, so he knew it was hers.

She dressed for bed and slipped under the covers. She heard the twig snap again and again. The killer had stood within inches of her, watching her, watching Luke, waiting. What if Luke had gone inside for just a minute? What would have happened?

Thinking about the killer took her to that night in her apartment. She shuddered as she remembered the power in the man's hands. If her roommates hadn't come back—but they had.

Sarah would never forget how small and weak and impotent she'd felt against the utter dominance of that man.

She never wanted a man to have that kind of power over her ever again, even if her heart gave its permission.

Even if that man was Luke McKenzie with all his wonderful attributes and good intentions.

Luke simmered for another thirty minutes. He'd never once had a temper problem. Even with Dad's murder, he'd held it together. Cried, of course. Threw things. Worked extra hours until he was exhausted. Rode hard with his horse, Pepper, until they were both ready to head for home. But none of his frustration and anger had involved another person. What was he doing with Sarah? His temper frightened *him,* so he couldn't imagine how it affected her. He was just so afraid her carelessness would end up with the killer getting what he wanted.

He sighed.

He loved her. He knew it now.

God help him, he loved a woman he hadn't known two weeks.

He'd always figured that when love hit him, it would be quick and hard. And, man, it was.

He loved her.

And he'd do whatever it took to keep her safe.

When all was quiet in Sarah's room, he opened the adjoining door and found her asleep with a book on her chest and the lamp still on. He set the book on the table, left the light on, and gently touched her cheek. "I love you, Sarah."

She mumbled, "Luke," and turned on her side.

He left the adjoining door open and prayed they'd have a chance to talk first thing in the morning.

Sitting alone at his desk at eleven o'clock on Thursday night, one day after the funerals, Jim's phone rang. *A.J.*

"Casey's awake."

"I'll meet you at the hospital." Jim grabbed his coat and hat.

A few minutes later, they stood at the foot of Casey's bed with Will on one side and Dr. Vern on the other. A beeping monitor, two hovering nurses, and soft lights surrounded them.

"Casey?"

Her bandaged head rolled toward Jim's voice. Her eyes fluttered open.

"Hey, Casey. Glad you're back." Her lips moved and her mouth twitched, but Jim couldn't make out what she said. "Casey, we need some information. Can you answer a couple of questions for us?"

"Yessss." Her eyes drooped closed, and she stilled.

Jim waited, looked at A.J., at Will, back at Casey. Her eyes trembled open.

"Can you describe him?"

She tried to shake her head, and her frown deepened. Drool had accumulated in the corner of her mouth. Her eyes seemed sunken and dark. "No. Behin' me."

Jim leaned closer. "He was behind you?"

"Yes. Two." She winced, sucked in a breath.

Jim waited until the lines between her brows eased a little. He took her hand. "Two, Casey?"

"Men."

A.J. bent over. "Honey, there were *two* of them?"

"Two."

A.J. sent Jim a so-you-were-right look. "Any details about them you can tell me?"

"Strong. Pulled my hair. Called me Rosie." She swallowed and flinched, and her face softened so much that Jim thought she had fallen back to sleep.

Will turned to Dr. Vern. "Can she have ice?"

He nodded. One of the nurses left and came back with a cup of shaved ice and a spoon. Will thanked her. "Casey, honey, would you like some ice to wet your whistle?"

She opened her eyes and her mouth. Will spooned in some ice. She moved it around, swallowed.

"Anything else you can remember that might help us catch these men?"

"One voice deep, one voice young." Will slipped more ice into her mouth. "He stopped him."

"Who?"

Her eyes wilted closed. "Deep stopped... young."

"Anything else?"

She coughed, gritted her teeth. "He said I got out. Rosie got out."

Jim nodded. "Did he say he was going to take you back?"

"Yessss. He was mad, so mad."

"Did anything about these men seem familiar to you? Their voices?"

Casey tried to shake her head and cringed.

"Okay, Casey, we're going to let you rest now. If you remember anything else, tell Will to call us, all right?"

She blinked a couple times as she pinched her lips and tried to swallow. "K."

Jim and A.J. thanked Will and the doctor and left. Walking across the parking lot, A.J. pulled up the collar of his coat. "Why didn't Sarah and Luke see two men, Jim?" His breath frosted and disappeared as he spoke.

"Maybe they did. One was the shooter. The second was in the cave. I'm not sure I go with that theory, though. The shooter had plenty of time to leave, find Lulu, and get her to the cave."

"Only one set of prints at Lulu's, too." They stopped at A.J.'s patrol car. "Although it's hard to tell in that amount of snow."

Jim nodded.

"Could be Allison McIntosh's two brothers. Whoever the killers are, they're as clean as polished grits. Haven't left behind any prints or anything. No mistakes. We even have an eyewitness, and she can't tell us a blasted thing about either of them. Oh. And, uh." A.J. cleared his throat. "Penny and I are back together."

"Yeah?" It didn't surprise Jim. He'd seen Penny looking over her shoulder at A.J. at every funeral with a look that said she was sorry. "So, you're out of the doghouse and back in the house? About time." His keys jingled as he pulled them out of his jeans. The night was cold, hazy, and starless. Jim stuffed his hands in his coat pockets. Probably more snow on the way in. He could smell it in the air.

"She called me this afternoon and asked me over. We talked. Everything's good, for now." He reached for the handle of his truck.

"That's great, buddy." Jim's vehicle beeped. "Have a good one."

"Oh, I intend to." A.J. laughed and got in his truck.

"Yeah," Jim muttered as he walked toward his empty pickup on his way to his empty house.

SIXTEEN

Jim swatted at his ringing cell phone and groaned as it fell to the floor next to the digital clock reading *3:10* on Friday morning. He rolled over and groped on the floor until he found it.

"Jim? You there?"

"Yeah, A.J." He thought about jettisoning himself back onto the bed, but he needed to be alert and slid to the floor. "Whatcha got?"

"Another body."

"Where?"

"That new family. The Martins. Just moved here about three weeks ago. The husband came home from partying and found his wife Joy on the living room floor. M.O.'s changed. The killer left the body and didn't pack anything or take a car."

"Versatile guy. We found his dumping place so no reason for him to do that other stuff." Jim rubbed his eyes. "Joy Martin's small, isn't she, Larry?"

"Little over five foot. Kin to Myra Simms. Her niece. I'm headed over now."

"I'll meet you there."

With gloved hands, Jim lifted Joy Martin's blouse. Red letters spilled out of the band of her pants. He knew what was written there, but he tugged them down to expose all the letters. *Rosie is dead.*

"What kind of monster are we dealing with here, Jim?"

"Only one set of prints outside."

"Maybe his friend didn't come along this time, or maybe he was the lookout."

"But why choose Joy Martin?"

A.J. squatted beside him. "Other than her size, I don't know. We'll run all the vics through the computer and try to find something they had in common, other than their height. We'll keep trying to find Brian McIntosh and see if he has an alibi. He's the only person of interest we have in this case. And not much of one."

"And bring Allison McIntosh in. See what she knows about her brother."

"Her door was unlocked." A.J. leaned against a cold flagless pole concreted into the Martins' front yard and crossed his arms. "Sonny Martin said she always left the door open for him."

"Not anymore." *Stupid, stupid, stupid!* Sometimes people invited trouble to waltz right in and have its way with them. Jim shoved his cup toward A.J., pivoted, and walked inside the house where he found the husband sitting spread-legged on his bedroom floor, his back against his bed, and his blood-shot eyes focused on absolutely nothing.

"She didn't want to come." It was more a dazed mumble than speaking to anyone in particular.

Sonny Martin's calm appearance belied the horror Jim had seen in his eyes when they'd first arrived.

Moments after finding his wife murdered on their salmon-colored carpet, he'd collapsed into incoherent sobbing. The 9-1-1 operator had trouble understanding him. When he said "Myra Simms," they put it all together. He'd been able to confirm his address.

Jim had heard the man's wailing, but the halo-like pool of black blood around Joy Martin's head had stopped him from seeking out the husband. Her petite hands were neatly folded over her stomach, legs tied together, and eyes taped shut.

Jim prayed recognizable prints would be on the tape. "She didn't want to go to the party, Mr. Martin?"

"Colorado. She didn't want to come to Colorado."

Jim could certainly relate to the backwash of guilt the man would carry with him the rest of his life. Why had he dragged his wife to Colorado? Why hadn't he stayed home tonight? Why hadn't he come home earlier? Why hadn't he taken her with him? She'd still be alive if he had—or so they always thought.

Jim joined A.J. outside. "He scrawled 'Rosie is dead' on her stomach in much larger letters. He tried to make her look suitably dead this time. He expected her husband and the police to verify for him, to make it official, that Rosie was absolutely dead this time."

A door slammed behind them. The coroner, Vince Graham, exited a burgundy van.

"Good. Vince is here. I'm headed home." Jim shook Vince's hand and headed for his truck. He searched the horizon for any sign of Friday morning, but it was still too early. He might sneak in an hour or so of sleep before he had to be at work—if he could get these visions of Renee lying in blood, too, out of his mind.

Sarah opened her eyes to sunlight shining around her curtains—the best way to wake up. She remembered her last thought before she fell asleep: it's time to leave Little Texas.

A litany of other thoughts bombarded her. A killer was after her. She was making herself too available to him. Being here was not fun. She was too stressed. Too afraid. And, most importantly, she had to get off this man's radar.

She needed to get out while she still could.

Come tomorrow morning, she would leave Little Texas. That meant, of course, that she would be leaving Luke, too. She didn't know how to process that part of her plans. She didn't want to leave him. She wanted to know if these feelings she had for him were real. The best way to find out was to spend time with each other.

Time, unfortunately, was running out.

She glanced at the clock on her phone. She needed to get up. After not eating dinner last night, she was starving. She showered, dressed, and went downstairs.

Luke sat at the dining table. When Sarah walked into the room, he studied her for a moment and then plucked a coffee mug off the serving tray. "'Morning."

"'Morning." She poured her coffee and his.

"Thanks. I'm sorry for yelling at you last night."

"I understand why you did, Luke. You're afraid for me."

He nodded. "Were you able to sleep?"

"A little."

"I know I said I'd wait for you to ask me to help you, but I'm going back on that. I'm *asking* you to let me go with you to your cabin."

"Of course, you can. I want you to go with me. I'm leaving in the morning for home."

"I know."

"I am so ready to get this behind me. But not you. Just this stuff."

"Not me?"

When she shook her head, he was grateful that something shone in her eyes when he stood and walked toward her. *Friendship? Maybe the beginnings of love?*

"No, not you."

His arms went around her. He held her gently and caressed her back. It felt so good to feel her in his arms. "I'll look forward to making the trip to Kansas if I know you're at the end of it."

"I will be."

"Maybe Mac will let me borrow his plane. Make the trip about forty-five minutes."

She pulled back and grinned up at him. "He owns a plane?"

Nodding, Luke looked into her eyes, then down at her mouth. He needed the kiss he saw in her eyes. Gently, he lowered his head and touched her lips with his. "Is this a good memory?" he whispered against her mouth.

"Yes, but I need a little more than that to—"

He tightened his arms and deepened the kiss until she finally relaxed and let them both savor this moment.

On her way to Search & Rescue, Elva Lee slowed down as she approached the town square on Ridge Road. The trees in the middle of the square obscured the words of the sign hanging from the courthouse until she turned left onto Edgar Drive.

TOWN MEETING FRIDAY (TONIGHT) 7:00
Concerning Our Women

On her left, Norman Poindexter shuffled with his walker to the corner of Edgar Drive and Ridge Road and lifted a hand at Elva Lee.

She slowed down. "Lookin' good there, Mr. Norman! How's that new hip?"

"Needs a little oil this morning. You hear about that Martin woman?"

Elva Lee slammed on her brakes, looked in her rearview mirror, found no one behind her, and stuck her head out the window. "Joy Martin?"

"Yep. Found her dead this morning around three."

Elva Lee gasped. "Oh, no. Myra." She covered her mouth. Luke and Sarah stopped behind Mr. Norman just as he finished talking.

Huffing and puffing, they jogged in place, and then stopped. Luke touched his shoulder. "Excuse me, sir, what did you say?"

Norman pointed a gnarly finger toward the road. "I was telling Elva Lee there that that Martin woman—"

"Joy, Mr. Norman," Elva Lee said. "Did y'all hear about Joy Martin?"

Sarah and Luke high-stepped to loosen any muscles tempted to tighten up on them. Elva Lee had run track in high school and understood that need not to seize.

"Not until this second," Sarah answered and turned back to Mr. Norman.

"Yep. This morning around three. A.J., Larry, Roland, and Jim were there at the crime scene, looking things over."

"Joy was at home?" Elva Lee leaned further out her window. "He left her body there?"

"Yep. Apparently same fella who killed our other three women." Mr. Norman looked longingly at his bench which was another four feet in front of him. "Better watch your step there, Elva Lee. He likes his women short." He glanced at Sarah. "You, too, missy."

"I will," Elva Lee said. "Have you heard how Myra's doing?"

"I don't know but Imogene's over there with her right now."

"I'll give her a call when I get to work. You take care now, Mr.

410

Norman. Luke, Sarah, I'll probably see y'all later." She waved and continued on around the town square until she hit Ridge again.

She slowed down. A sign on Myra's shop door said: CLOSED DUE TO DEATH IN FAMILY. Elva Lee headed north to Barrett's Auto Repair. When she parked around back, she pulled out her cell phone and dialed Jim's number.

"Banks."

"Jim, it's me, Elva Lee. I just heard about Joy Martin. What happened?"

"Found her at her home. Crowbar again. Same perp. The mayor's called a town meeting tonight at seven."

"I just saw the sign on my way to Barrett's."

"What are you doing there?"

"My car's missing a little. Barrett's going to look at it."

"How're you getting to work?"

"Well, that's why I'm calling you." She laughed. "I may be a little late. I might see someone here who could take me, or I can wait around until they get it fixed. Or, if you need me right now, I can start walking. It's not far."

"I'll come and get you. Are you there right now?"

"Yes."

"I'll see you in a few minutes." He hung up.

Elva Lee looked at the phone, a little confused. Jim had never offered to do anything for her. Why, she'd never even ridden in his truck. She dropped her phone in her purse. Just at the thought of riding with him, her heart jumped. Giddiness swept over her. "It's just a ride," she mumbled, chastising her crazy heart.

"Elva Lee?"

Oh. "Hmmm?" She internally shook herself. "Uh, yes, Barrett?"

"We'll have your car ready for you during lunch."

She thanked him and turned back around.

Jim was getting out of his truck. Oh! She didn't know how to act! *Like this is an every-day situation. Be cool.* Her heart laughed at her silly thoughts and beat harder.

Walking quickly, Jim reached them, nodded once at Barrett. "How's that baby doing?"

Barrett grinned from ear-to-ear. "She's the prettiest thing God ever made, plain and simple. You ought to come by and see her. Katherine would love to show her off to you."

"Just might do that." He turned to Elva Lee. He stared at her a moment. "You ready to go?"

"Yes," she murmured. He stepped back and ushered her to lead the way with a sweep of his arm. It was a strange feeling walking with Jim

411

Banks to his truck, knowing she'd be sitting near him, watching him do something as simple as driving. Her heart fluttered at the thought.

"You take care of that baby now, Barrett. Say hey to Katherine for me."

"Will do."

Jim's arm brushed Elva Lee's when he grabbed the door handle. She smiled up at him and slipped inside the truck. No way could the words "Thank you" get past her tight throat. The door slammed. In the driver's side mirror, she watched him and wondered why he was grinning like a possum as he walked up to his door.

They rode in silence. But what did she expect? This wasn't a date. It was an expression of friendship. Hmmm. Friendship? Were she and Jim friends now because he'd offered her a ride?

"I appreciate everything you do at S&R to keep things going."

She glowed all over. "It's my job. I love helping people."

"It shows." He nodded several times thoughtfully, and then he looked out the window. He slowed down as he approached the stop sign in the town square. "Sarah and Luke are up early today."

Elva Lee nodded. "I saw them a few minutes ago at the square when Mr. Norman told me about Joy Martin. How awful for Sonny and for Myra. Bless their hearts. Lulu and now Joy."

Luke ran in place, waiting for the white "WALK" sign to appear so he and Sarah could run across Ridge Road on their way back to the cabin. A casually dressed man put a key in the glass door of Gally's Hardware store, opened it, flipped over the "CLOSED" sign, and turned on the lights.

Sarah paced behind Luke and waved at Jim and Elva Lee as they drove by. "I'd fly home if I could, but I can't leave my car here and you know it!"

Luke turned around. "You expect me to just let you go, on a road trip, by yourself, all the way to Kansas? Why don't you just put a blinking sign in your back window and have it say, 'Okay, here I am. Come and get me'?"

She followed him across the street. "Now, that's just brilliant, Luke." She sidestepped an open manhole and bumped into him. "I need some room here."

Luke ran ahead, jumped the curb, turned right, took another left, and ran in place until a scowling Sarah caught up with him. "My legs are shorter than yours!"

She'd been grumpy all morning. He didn't know why. He'd like to think it had something to do with leaving him tomorrow.

412

Waiting for her, he jogged a circle and smiled at her. At the lift of her chin as she jogged past him, he figured it was going to be a long day. "We need to talk, Sarah."

She ignored him and kept running.

Another fifteen minutes, they jogged up the driveway to McKenzie Cabin. Luke stopped at the back door, but Sarah kept running, right up the rise behind the cabin to the top. She jogged in place, then high stepped, and walked up and down the backbone of the ridge. She picked a flower, sniffed it, threw it to the wind, and disappeared down the other side.

Luke raced up and over the ridge and caught up with her. "What are you *doing?*"

Sarah jerked around and glared. "*Now* what's wrong?"

Luke flapped his hand at her. "Four women—count 'em—four." Dramatically, he swatted at his fingers as he ticked off the numbers. "Dead. And you're up here, *alone*, picking wildflowers where no one can see you. You can't be so careless!"

"I'll be as careless as I want." She frowned at him and then started laughing.

Luke threw up his hands. "It's not funny. You *have* to be more careful."

"I was just thinking how pretty these Indian paintbrushes are up here and how much I'd like to pick them."

"He was at the cabin. Maybe *up here* is his favorite place to hide. No one can see him *up here* which means no one can see you *up here*. You only have one more day to endure this."

"I know. I'll try to be more careful."

"Good." He scooped up a flower and handed it to her.

Smiling, she sniffed it and tucked it behind her ear.

"You have a beautiful smile." And with those words, he took her arm and guided her down the rise.

A white sheet fluttered on a clothesline as Allison parked her car under a nice shade tree. When she opened the door, she smelled bacon—crispy bacon—and bread baking. She couldn't remember the last time she'd smelled fresh bread.

"Wuh, hey there." Her smiling grandmother came out on the porch, wiping her hands on a smudged apron swatting the tops of her boots. Gram held the screen door open for her. Allison decided this morning to call her 'Gram.'

"This is a nice surprise. Come on in and make yourself at home. Biscuits and gravy and bacon sound all right to you for breakfast?"

413

Allison walked inside the small cabin. "Throw in a cup of coffee, and I'll help you wash the dishes." She followed her grandmother past the living room/dining room and into the small kitchen. Everything was small.

"What brings you out here so early this morning?"

The oven door wheezed as it opened. Gram pulled out a pan of big fluffy biscuits and slammed the door shut with her knee. "Have a seat there, girl. I'll get you that coffee. Black?"

"Is it strong?"

"Not for me."

"Then black." Allison opened her purse and drew out a yellow packet of pictures. "I wanted you to see your son, Gram."

"That's what I called my grandmother." She set the bacon on the table next to the biscuits, a bowl of gravy, two canning jars of jelly, and a bottle of honey. She set a cup of black coffee beside each plate and sat down.

Before Allison could blink, Gram bowed her head and said, "For these and all other blessings, I thank thee, Lord Jesus." She looked at Allison and patted her hand. "I consider you one of those blessings."

"Thank you, Gram."

She waved a hand at her. "Help yourself, child."

Allison buttered a biscuit. "Have you ever seen a photo of your son?" She took a bite of heaven. "Mmm, this is great."

Gram took her time buttering a biscuit. "No, I haven't. In those days, over fifty years ago now, we weren't allowed to even look at the baby at the place we stayed."

"We?"

"Winnie Sue and I. We went together. She was only thirteen, and by then, our parents were dead." She set the knife on her plate. "At the girls' home, they thought it best for the mother not to see the baby so she wouldn't get attached—or be hurt. But the hurt came anyway. It came with a vengeance."

"I'm sorry, Gram." Her father had been so wrong about his mother. "Would you like to see his picture?"

Gram's hand shook as she held an almost-burnt piece of bacon half-way to her mouth. "Maybe after we eat."

When Allison frowned, her grandmother patted her hand. "After we eat, okay, honey?"

Allison crunched on bacon, sipped her coffee, and jellied her biscuit. As she watched her grandmother in her comfortable little world, she couldn't forget the horrors her son had brought on their family.

Anger, warm at first, hummed. "He hated you."

Her grandmother jerked and slowly put down her biscuit.

"He hated my brother, Brian." Her hands fisted as she gritted her teeth against the shakes. "Hate was everywhere."

"I know." Her grandmother whispered the words.

But they reached Allison. She sat up straight and took a deep breath. "Allison."

Gray eyes the color of melted steel gazed into Allison's eyes.

"Let's look at your pictures, if you've a mind to show me."

"How do you know about everything, Gram?"

"Your father wrote to me many years ago. There was no return address. I couldn't answer any of his accusations, but I wanted to. Lord knows, I wanted to. I read and wept over that letter so many times. I never told anyone about it, not even Winnie Sue. He told me he hated me. He asked me why I didn't want him. Did I give him to such a tall family because I hated him? And *why* had I hated him? All those questions went unanswered because he didn't give me a chance to answer them. They've haunted me for years."

Allison looked at the ring on her right hand. "This was my father's. I've worn it to remind me how much I hated him." She slipped it off and handed it to Gram. "I don't want it anymore. I want you to have it, to remind you of what I'm about to tell you.

"My father found out he was adopted when he was twenty-one. He'd been adopted into a family of tall brothers and at five-three, he never fit in. His second oldest brother teased him, called him 'Runt,' beat him any chance he could, taunted and bullied him. None of my father's family ever checked his brother's behavior."

She shook her head. "My father hated being short. He could see the disparity between how people treated him and how they treated his taller siblings. He hated himself for it.

"When he found his birth certificate, Rosie Jansen was identified as his birth mother. No father was listed. A picture was paperclipped to it. On the back of it was written: 'Baby's mother, Rosie Jansen, Little Texas, Colorado.' Rosie was standing beside a car. It was obvious she was very tiny. The next year, my father married my mother, who was five two. They had two sons and a daughter, me."

"I remember the nurse at the girls' home taking that photo."

Nodding, Allison clasped her hands around her knees and rocked. "Something happened to my father when my oldest brother, Brian, was six. Brian was small for his age. My father started beating him, screaming things like, 'Rosie did it, Rosie did it,' and 'It's Rosie's fault. It's Rosie's fault.'

"He'd yank on Brian's arms and say, 'I'm gonna pull Rosie right out of you, boy'." Allison rubbed a spot on her forehead until it hurt. "The beatings, Gram. They never stopped until Brian was almost unconscious. No one stopped my father. No one.

"When I was in middle school, we had a project to do. We were to talk to one of our grandparents about their history, like an interview. My father threw that picture of you at me like a Frisbee and yelled, "There's your grandmother. Go find *her!*" But I didn't. I sent the picture to Brian, who was on the streets at that time in Pueblo, Colorado." She abruptly stood. "Can we walk, Gram?"

The old woman took her hand, and they walked outside and down the steps. "Brian is the sweetest man I know. But he's confused. He fights the demons like I do, but I don't think he can control what he does when the demons get too big."

"What demons?"

"Anger. Ugly anger. I'm in baby steps on how to control it and deal with my father's intense hate—along with my feelings of helplessness growing up. Abandonment. Low self esteem. You name it; we all experienced it."

"God help me, I tried to do the best thing for the baby."

Absently, Allison picked up a stick and threw it. "I wish someone had told my father he was okay, no matter how tall or short, that he could do or be anything he wanted. But because no one told *him*, no one told Brian or Robbie or me.

"My mother stood by and let my father destroy her. She died when I was eleven. By then, the damage had been done. Brian had already run away from home. Robbie was withdrawn but did well in school—learning was his escape. My father was a bitter, vicious man. He died of a heart attack three years ago when I was twenty."

"Hate kills." Gram took his ring and studied it, then clutched it tightly. "I don't want this."

Allison grabbed the ring and threw it as hard as she could. "My brother Robbie would say 'good riddance' and I will, too."

"Tell me about Robbie."

Allison's face softened. "Robbie's my lifeline. He's gentle, like Brian. He's been there for me so many times, especially after our father's death. He's a salesman for a pharmaceutical company. He defied the odds and became a success, despite my father."

"And you, Allison?"

"I'm a writer. Romance, believe it or not. I haven't been published, but I'm working on it. It's therapeutic for me to have two people come together against all odds and make it."

Gram patted her hand. "You'll be all right, Allison. I know you will. I have one question for you. Why are you here in Little Texas?"

Allison looked past her to the mountains beyond. "I've always wanted to meet you. I thought the time was right to do it. Plus, I needed to tell you about Brian."

Their gazes met. "And now you have. Let's go inside and finish our breakfasts."

SEVENTEEN

"Would you come to Texas with me?" Luke pulled up to and parked at the high school gym about six-forty-five and lifted a hand in greeting as Jim, Elva Lee, and Myra walked by. He'd come up with the idea of introducing Sarah to Texas as he was dressing for tonight's town meeting here at the gym.

"Something's between us. I don't want us to walk away from it. Come to my ranch and stay for the rest of your vacation."

Luke framed her face with both hands. He held her eyes another moment, then lowered his mouth to gently kiss her. "I want you to see where I live, where I work, get to know my family, me. We have two more weeks to spend time together. I'd prefer doing it where no wackos are trying to kill us."

She smiled at him as his thumbs rubbed her cheeks. "Luke. I would love to go to Texas—"

He kissed her quickly.

Something hit the hood of the truck, and they both jumped. A.J. shook his finger at them. "Better get out of that vehicle, son, before I cite you for taking liberties with that young woman."

Luke grinned and waved as A.J. walked on. "If it's okay with you, Sarah, let's skip this town meeting. No reason for us to be here. We can leave early in the morning as planned."

"Sure. I need to pack. I want to see your Texas, Luke, but, uh, this doesn't mean that, you know, I mean, I feel strongly that we need to wait for, y'know, for anything that might be, uh." She blinked at his frowning eyes. Surely, she didn't have to spell it out for him.

He laughed and pulled her closer to his side. "I feel the same way. Not until marriage."

"Well, I'm certainly not suggesting that we get married."

"Let's not worry about the future, Sarah. Plenty going on in the here and now. Let's go to your cabin and get your things."

Five minutes later, when Luke slipped the key into the lock of Sarah's cabin, something crunched under foot. He yanked the key out of the door, turned on the key-ring flashlight, stepped back, and shined it on the landing. "Peanuts. He was here. Get behind me."

She did.

His skin tingled with anticipation as he tugged his weapon out of his holster. "Do you have something that I can cover the doorknob with?"

She pulled her hand up into her sleeve and opened the door.

Leading with his gun, Luke flicked on the light, swept the room.

Surprisingly, nothing was out of place in the living room or kitchen. But in the hallway in front of Sarah's bedroom, a single rose lay on the floor.

Sarah backed up to the front door, locked it, and hugged herself.

Luke walked over to the rose. "Looks like he placed it in front of the room I was using." He grabbed a washcloth from the bathroom, covered the knob, and opened it. Nothing was out of place. On the bed was an outfit—a blouse, pants, shoes, socks, underwear, a winter hat, all lined up as if someone lay there. As if Sarah lay there.

Gingerly, he lifted the blouse. "She is dead" was written on a white sheet of paper. Luke ground his teeth, so angry. He picked up a shoe and threw it as hard as he could against the wall.

"Luke?"

When he reached Sarah, he grabbed her in a tight hug. "We're out of here now, before daylight."

She nodded against his chest as he called Jim.

"Jim, Sarah had a break-in at her cabin."

"Is she okay?"

"Shaken up, but okay." Luke told Jim about the rose and the clothes.

"He's escalating. He wants her. I'll call A.J., then we're on our way over."

Luke hung up. It was freezing in the cabin. He unzipped his jacket and held it open as Sarah walked into his arms. He held her tightly without saying anything. He wanted to grab her and leave. Drive to where this jerk couldn't find her. *My ranch.* He owned two thousand acres. No way this psycho would get close to Sarah with the fortress he'd build against him.

His phone rang. "Yeah, A.J."

"Just got word that a man attempted to rape a woman in Estes Park. An eyewitness saw him leave the victim's home, jump on a motorcycle with a Kansas license plate, and roar out of town. The police haven't been able to find him. Because of the string of murders from Riadon, Kansas toward Estes Park, they believe there might be a connection with the Darkslayer."

Luke could hardly breathe.

"Luke?"

"I heard you. Do they have him in custody?"

"No. As to Sarah's break in, I'm on my way. Stay there."

Luke became aware of cold penetrating one spot on his shirt. Sarah was crying, quietly. "Did you hear A.J.?"

"Yes."

Still hugging her, he noticed the curtains were open. He wondered if the killer was standing in the trees, watching them, wanting her, calculating when he could get his hands on her and kill 'Rosie.' "We're leaving tonight," he mumbled to the man outside, daring him to come close to her again. "As soon as we can get packed and the cabins closed up."

She nodded as pink touched the trees just before swirling red lights pulled into her driveway.

A.J. approached Luke, patting the air with both hands as if he was trying to calm Luke before he said something. "I know you don't want to hear this, but I'm asking you and Sarah to stick around one more day. We might be able to catch this guy if she'd be willing to—"

"She's not going to be your bait."

"Yeah, 'bait' is a strong word. I wasn't thinking of her walking in cold somewhere. We'd have the place staked out, inside and out."

"No." Luke leaned into Sarah's bedroom. "Are you about ready, Sarah? We need to be going."

"I have to question her again, Luke."

"Fine. Then do it here and forget this other."

Sarah stepped out of the bedroom, her face pale, her eyes red.

"Sarah." She turned toward Luke. "A.J. wants to ask you something." Her gaze moved to A.J.

"I need to question you again, early tomorrow morning. Will you be available then?"

"We're planning to leave tonight. You can ask me whatever you'd like right now."

"Would you—?" A.J. glanced at Luke and then placed his attention back on Sarah. "Would you stay another day—"

"No. I said no." Luke held out his hand to Sarah.

She took it. "No to what?"

"You being the killer's bait."

Her eyes widened. "Bait?"

A.J. shook his head. "I wouldn't say 'bait.' You wouldn't be in any danger. We'd have every inch of you protected."

"No." Luke drew her against his side. "Question her now. Then we're packing and leaving as soon as we can get everything done."

The chief huffed out a long sigh. "Let's sit at the table."

For the next hour, A.J. interviewed her. Then he stood and pushed in his chair. "All right. We're finished. I appreciate your time. Y'all are free to leave. Be careful on your trip out of here." He shook both their hands. "Hopefully, your next visit to Little Texas will be a lot less eventful."

"Thanks, A.J. I'm sorry we have to leave like this." Luke lifted his brows at Sarah. She nodded. "We need to go."

As they drove off, Luke glanced in the rearview mirror. A.J. stood on

420

the porch and watched them leave.

"We really aren't going to stick around and help A.J. catch him?"

Luke grunted. "Absolutely not. We're leaving as soon as possible. He'll have to figure out another way to get him."

Although the doors and windows were locked, Luke acted on the uneasy feeling he had and hurried down the hallway to the kitchen. It was dark. He almost turned around to go to the den when he heard a whimper.

His heart stopped. "Sarah?"

He found her curled up in a shivering ball under the table. He tensed, scanned the huge kitchen, found nothing out of place, and squatted beside her.

"Sarah?" She twitched when he touched her shoulder.

"The w-windows."

Luke looked over his shoulder. Open windows spanned the walls around the kitchen. A small night light shined above the sink.

"He's out there, Luke. I saw him."

He quickly turned off the night light. The kitchen was suddenly dark. "The moon's bright tonight. He's not there now. Look."

She did. "He won't show himself again."

"I won't let him hurt you."

She rested her head against his shoulder. "I know you won't."

As they walked out of the kitchen, the man stepped to the sliding glass doors, hands in his pockets.

"Rosie," he whispered, his face ragged with grief and despair, his breath fogging the door.

Shoulders slumped, he turned and climbed up to the ridge above the house where he had a clear view of her bedroom.

EIGHTEEN

Saturday morning's overcast skies couldn't deter Gertie from her mission. She had to talk to A.J. Banks and his brother Jim if he had a mind to listen, too.

Dressed for the cold, she sipped one last gulp of coffee and headed out the front door.

And there sat Miss Allison McIntosh for the second day in a row, looking pleased as a pea hen. "Well now, another good morning to you, Allison. What brings you by so early?" Her breath frosted on this cold, sunless May morning.

"I need to tell you the truth about Brian."

Gertie locked her front door, pulled on the knob, and slipped the key in her coat pocket. "And what would that truth be?" She slipped into her gloves as she walked down the steps toward Allison.

The young woman stepped in front of her. "Gram, I think Brian is killing these women."

"Do you, Allison? That's quite an accusation from a sister to a brother and just yesterday you telling me how sweet he is." Gertie edged around her and continued walking. "I have to get on into town. You're welcome to walk with me."

"Gram, wait up. I know how this sounds."

"Accusing a brother of murder?"

She shrugged. "I mean, I know it sounds terrible."

"That it does." Gertie sniffed as she tugged on the ends of her cap and stuffed some rebellious hair back under it.

"But what if it's true and I *don't* tell anyone? What if he's out there killing these women he thinks is Rosie? My father told him to kill you, to rid us of you." Allison brushed her hair over her shoulder. "Because of the picture of you, we all knew Rosie Jansen lived in Little Texas. After I read the news accounts of the bodies with "Rosie" on their stomachs, I came here to warn you that Brian would be after you. To kill you."

"Then I've been warned, and I thank you for coming to tell me. Brian can come on and kill me if he wants to. I'm ready to meet my Maker. Not too anxious, mind you, but ready. Now, I've got to get into town. You'd best be talking to our police chief about what you've told me. So, I'll leave you now and wish you a happy day."

"I can drive you into town."

"I like to walk. But thank you for the offer." With that, Gertie headed up the long driveway to Bear Camp Road. Allison slowly drove by and waved at her.

A quiet stretch of the road gave her a chance to watch ten or twelve elk lying in the grass, eyeing her. When she reached the highway, the blare of a horn announced Tommy Blakesly passing by. He lifted his hand and waved through the gun rack across the back of his truck window.

It had taken her years to train her friends not to stop to pick her up. They had learned that she needed to walk and enjoyed it, no matter the weather. She'd told them many times that she lived a quiet life out in the country because she wanted to. The perks that went with it included these nice long walks into town.

In the brittle cold, a squirrel scampered part way down a pine tree, spotted Gertie, flicked his head and tail a time or two, and ran right back up. Circling overhead, a blue bird landed on a branch and studied Gertie as she crossed a small bridge.

She looked up as a truck took the curve ahead of her.

A chill arrowed up her spine.

The truck slowed down, let out a young man, and drove off. The young man carried a backpack on his shoulder. He scaled a rock embankment opposite her. High above her, he sat and looked down at her. He didn't just look. He stared with an expression of wonder and sadness and yearning.

He looked like her brother when he was in his mid-twenties. He neither smiled nor frowned but stared at her with big brown eyes.

Slowly, deliberately, Gertie nodded once. The man's eyes filled with tears, and he rubbed them with the heels of his hand. Still, he stared as if he expected her to offer him something. He abruptly stood and turned to leave but he pivoted and faced Gertie again. Then, he disappeared into the trees.

Flushed with wonder, Gertie stared at the last spot she'd seen him. Who was he? Was he one of Allison's brothers? Robbie or Brian? Or a cousin? Was he the killer?

Absently, she waved as another car honked at her. She decided in a split-hair's second that that young man was no killer. Not the man who had gazed into her eyes as if she could answer all the questions he had.

Besides, if he was the killer, why didn't he kill her right then and there?

A vehicle honked and pulled up beside her.

"Miss Gertie, you're up and at 'em early this morning." Jim Banks leaned over and opened the passenger door. "Can I haul you some place this morning?"

Gertie obliged the man and hoisted herself up onto the seat. "You're just the man I'm walking to see, you and your brother. Take me to his office, would you now? I have business with you and the chief of police this morning."

"Sounds serious."

"It is, that. How's your daddy doing these days? Don't see much of him and Debra. They doing all right?"

"Staying busy. Saw them a few days ago and then, of course, at the funerals."

"I'm sorry for your loss, Jim."

"Thank you, Miss Gertie. Here we are." He pulled up to the police station. Gertie helped herself out and walked inside. A.J. was talking to the dispatcher.

"A.J. Banks, I'd like to talk to you this morning, sir, if I may."

His face radiated with the smile he gave her, and she assumed the rumors were true that Penny had opened their door and said he could come home.

"How are you doing today, Miss Gertie, and up and into town so early, too?"

"It's not so early. I need a private place I can visit with you and Jim for a spell."

"All right." He led her into his office and pulled out a chair for her. Yep, a might cheerful today he was, so he and Penny must be getting along all right.

She yanked off her wool cap and pulled off her gloves. "Is there a coffee pot on somewhere?"

"Yes, ma'am. Black?"

When she nodded, Jim said, "I'll get it." He came back with two and handed one to her.

"All you need's an apron, Jim."

He shoved a cup at his brother. "You wanna wear this, A.J.?"

"A might touchy today, little brother." A.J. grinned at Gertie. "Do you want me to take notes or is this a social visit?"

"You know me better than that. I wouldn't bother you at your work if it was social. This is about the murders."

His grin disappeared. "I'll record this, Miss Gertie." His gaze flicked to Jim's as he opened the throw-up-green metal cabinet and took a recorder out, plugged it in, and searched for the record button.

He pushed it. "All right. You can begin. Identify yourself, please."

"I'm Gertrude Jansen. Years ago, I was the victim of a rape and went to a home for unwed mothers. One of the nurses wanted to adopt the baby. I used the name 'Rosie Jansen' there and that's the name that was put on the birth certificate." She let the words take root.

"Rosie. You're Rosie," A.J. whispered.

With rapt attention, A.J. and Jim listened to the story of a woman giving up her son for adoption and hearing not a word from that child until the letter she'd received years ago.

"I'd like to see that letter, Miss Gertie."

She took it out of her pocket, unfolded it, and handed it to A.J. She gave the chief and Jim a moment to read it. When they finished it and looked up, she told them of Allison's visit, her accusations against her father and her brother Brian. Of seeing one of the boys this very morning.

"Do you know where Allison McIntosh is staying?"

"I do." She told him. "She's been to my house a couple times."

"Miss Gertie, that day I visited with you and Miss Winnie Sue, why didn't you tell me then?"

She shook her head. "I don't know exactly. The name 'Rosie' brought back terrible memories. We—Winnie Sue and I—went to a home, lived there for seven months, had the baby, and left. Allison told me her brother Brian was behind the killings. I thought you ought to know."

"We appreciate you coming in and letting us in on this." A.J. looked at Jim. "We'll get a psychological profile drawn up on Brian, Robert, and Allison McIntosh. Their father died a while back?"

"Yes. A heart attack."

"And the, uh, the baby's father?"

"I never knew him or his name." She let that information sink in, too. After the attack, she and her sister were a little fearful of men and dating or socializing with them.

"I need to speak with Allison. Hopefully, she'll have a picture of her brother, Brian." A.J. threw out his hand. "Thank you for this, Miss Gertie. We'll work up a plan to get this young man, alive. I know it took a lot for you to come in and talk to us."

She put her hand in his. "Not as much as you think, once I decided to do it."

"Can I take you somewhere?"

"Thank you, Jim. I can walk to my sister's house. She'll be surprised to see me. But a little surprise at her age is a welcome thing," she chuckled, "so long as it doesn't kill her."

Twenty-eight pounds in three months!

Elva Lee grinned like a cat waiting to pounce on a mouse as she stepped out of Jodee's Salon, itching to tell someone her good news, that she had reached her goal!

Her Lighter and Brighter weight loss group met at seven-thirty in the morning on Saturdays at Jodee's before she opened at nine. Elva Lee had won the prize, a gift certificate to Myra's Dress Shop, for losing the most in the past three months. She thought she'd walk over to Myra's but remembered she was closed because of Joy's death. Would her sister Irma have it open for Myra?

Elva Lee had an hour before she had to be at work at ten. Search & Rescue closed at two on Saturdays until the season opened. Elva Lee wouldn't have time to shop today after work because she planned to see Myra and Fred and that visit would take a while.

"Girl, just look at you!" Irma fluttered a hand at Elva Lee as the door dinged behind her and shut. "How *much* have you lost?"

Beaming, Elva Lee answered, "My goal was twenty-eight pounds, and I met that goal today." She hugged Irma as they both laughed.

"Well, twenty-eight pounds on your little frame is a lot! If you're gonna get that man to sit up and take notice, you're gonna have to get out of those baggy clothes. They don't show you off. Haven't you treated yourself to any new clothes yet, hon?"

'That man' being Jim, of course.

Elva Lee shook her head. "I wanted to keep wearing big clothes, so nobody would know until my big reveal."

"Your *little* reveal, right?" Irma laughed at her joke as did Elva Lee. "Well, an eight's way too big for you now. Come on." Irma set off toward the petites and pulled out a dress. "This is *you*, girl. Come back here and try this on. Let's work on knocking Jim's socks off the next time he sees you."

Irma pulled the curtain across the dressing room doorway. "I saw you two at the high school gym. Did he take you?"

"Yes, but it's only because my car's in the shop. Barrett found something wrong with it and told me he'd have it ready for me some time today. Jim was just being a gentleman."

"Well, it don't matter *how* you get him alone, just so you make hay while the sun shines."

Elva Lee stepped out, shy and self-conscious. The dress fit her perfectly and showed off the curves that had been hidden under the fat she'd thrown away. She tugged at the waist. "Do you think it's too long?"

"It's just a couple inches below your knees. It's stunning on you. Turn around. You just have to treat Jim to that dress. Here, let me clip those tags. You keep it on and wear it back to work."

"That'd be a little obvious, wouldn't it?"

"Now you're getting the picture. Obvious is good!" She laughed as she took the tags to the cash register. "How about some chocolate boots? Go over there and check out a pair. And since you met your goal, I'm gonna give that dress and the boots to you for half price, kind of as a celebration."

"Oh, that's so sweet, Irma, but I have a gift certificate for losing the most weight."

"Then you keep that for another time. This purchase is on me."

"Thank you. How are Myra and Fred doing?"

A little bit of the sunshine fell from Irma's face. "As well as can be expected. Myra loved Joy and so did Fred. It's a crying shame what happened to her. Sonny's like a ship without a rudder, just drifting on through. You pray for him, Elva Lee, and keep yourself safe, y'hear? You being so little now, you'd better be careful."

"I will. Have arrangements been made for Joy?"

"When her body's released, they're flying her home to Texas for burial. Myra and Fred will be going. Sometime next week, I think."

"I'm so sorry for them."

"It's a tragedy, all around." Then Irma smiled at her and shooed her off to work. "I'll call you tonight. I just have to find out what Jim said about your dress."

Well, he couldn't say a single word, not a single word.

He could only stare.

What had Elva Lee been doing during her lunch hour? And where had all that weight gone? She was just a little thing now, and she'd come back looking like a Saturday-night date, all flushed and rosy and shy. And those green eyes. When did they get so big?

His gaze caught hers, and he couldn't seem to let her go. He hadn't been flustered by a woman since he was fourteen and Katie Washburn was sixteen and she'd pranced by him wearing a short skirt that barely covered her and a halter top fit to tongue-tie a gossip.

Elva Lee blushed and looked toward her computer screen while Jim threw his pen down, yanked his cap off his elk horn, announced, "I'll be back," and slammed the door behind him.

But Elva Lee only grinned as she scampered to the ladies restroom to the full-length mirror and stared at herself in her new dress. Jim Banks had noticed her, really noticed her, and by golly, that man was going to keep right on noticing her if she had to buy every petite dress Myra had.

With newfound confidence, Elva Lee pranced back to her desk and waited for Jim to come back. She'd be ready for him this time.

The phone rang. "Search & Rescue, this is Elva Lee."

"It's Jim. I'm leaving for the day but wanted to know if Barrett called yet about your car."

Disappointment ripped through her. "No, not yet. He said it'd be around two when it was ready."

"Well, when he calls, let me know, and I'll take you out there to get it."

She swallowed down the excitement of seeing him again and tried to sound normal. "All right, Jim, I will."

"I'll wait to hear from you then." And he hung up. The dial tone buzzed as Elva Lee hugged the phone for a moment before she hung it up.

A little before one, Barrett called to tell her the car was ready. Before she left to get it, she needed to check on supplies and went back to the storage room.

"Elva Lee?"

Jim! Why had he come back? "In here, boss. Did you forget something?"

Breezily, she walked out.

"Where, uh, where'd you get that dress?" Jim cleared the frog from his throat, but it jumped right back in. He felt like an absolute fool for standing and gawking and not knowing what to do with himself. It was only Elva Lee, after all.

In her pretty green and brown dress, she walked around her desk, reached under it, and pulled out her purse without even looking at him. "At Myra's."

"Umm." Was she doing that just to get under his skin? Prancing around like that? Ignoring him? Looking so good a man could forget to breathe? "Barrett just called me. Said your car was ready."

"Yes, he called me, too." Elva Lee turned toward him.

"He, uh, said he got your car done earlier than expected. Did you want to go ahead and get it?"

"That'd be fine, Jim." She picked up her purse.

Without a word, he opened the door for her.

Elva Lee turned off the lights as she walked outside to the passenger side of his truck. He opened the door for her, touched her elbow to help her up, and set his teeth against that dress flowing all over her legs. He slammed her door.

Then he slammed the driver's door, jabbed the key into the ignition, started the truck, and yanked it into gear. But he couldn't back up. Two women strolled by, behind his truck.

Elva Lee crossed her legs, turned around, and waved at them.

Jim tried to swallow and made himself concentrate on the ladies, too. They waved at him. He waved at them and then glared into the rearview mirror.

Elva Lee watched them push their baby carriages, surrounded by their other kids, toward the City Park. "It's a pretty day for a stroll in the park," she said and turned those big green eyes on him.

Jim grunted. For some reason, he was mad at Elva Lee. He didn't want to notice her, didn't want to have these feelings come to the surface. He'd struggled with them for months and had prayed and prayed that God would take them away.

But He hadn't. So, what was he supposed to do now?

They drove down Deer Meadows to Ridge and hung a left. Two more blocks and she'd be out of his truck.

What was happening to him? This was Elva Lee. His good friend.

Barrett's shop. *Finally*.

He drove around back and stopped as Barrett ambled toward his truck and opened the door for her.

"Right on time." He winked at her. "Man, Elva Lee, that's a pretty dress. You been losing some weight there?" He turned to Jim. "Thanks for bringing her."

But before the door could even shut, Jim took off.

Across town, Luke was pumped to be on the road. He tossed in the last of his stuff and secured his truck's hard cover. He hadn't intended to sleep in so late. He and Sarah had eaten a late breakfast out, packed up everything, and were finally ready to go. Not exactly how he'd planned it.

"All right." He gave Sarah a quick kiss and glanced at his watch. "Just talked to my brother, Mac. Told him we were about on our way. Do you have everything?" He took one last glance around the yard, grabbed his shades out of the glove compartment, and shoved it closed.

Sarah looked under the front passenger seat, then the floorboard in back. "My purse. I thought I had it with me. It must be in the hall bathroom. Did you lock the front door?"

"Yeah." Luke yanked the keys out of the ignition and held them up. "Kiss."

She playfully lifted a brow. "And if I say no?"

"You won't." His hand snaked around her neck and drew her to his mouth. He took his time, his sweet, sweet time.

She laughed and held out a hand. "Keys."

Handing them to her, he said, "Let's hustle, Sarah. Time's a-wasting."

"Be right back." She jogged to the house, opened the door, and smiled over her shoulder at Luke before she disappeared inside.

Luke rolled down the back windows and turned on the radio. Reception was pitiful in the mountains, but Little Texas had its own FM station of Golden Oldies. Marty Robbins crooned out, "My woman, my

429

woman, my wife."

Luke tapped his thumbs on the steering wheel to the beat as he gripped it with both hands and thought of his woman becoming his wife. *Rushing it a little bit, aren't you, buddy?* He smiled. *Absolutely not.* He checked his watch and stuck his head out the window. "Sarah, come *on!* Time's a-wasting!"

Molly barked at him from the truck bed. He tapped the window separating them and grinned at her. As he did, his gaze caught the vision behind him. He slid out of the truck, folded his arms on the cold wall of the truck bed, and admired the mountain splendor of white-topped peaks.

In the back of his mind, he was aware of Molly barking.

When Carrie Underwood started a song, he glanced toward the house. The door swayed a little in the gusty wind and he thought of saloon doors swinging in a deserted ghost town with tumbleweeds rolling down the middle of a dusty road.

Despite the fact it had only been five or six minutes, he stalked toward the house. Molly joined him. "Sarah, let's go."

He moved into the dark hallway. His heart pounded faster at the deafening silence. "Sarah?"

No movement. No answer. No sound.

"Sarah?"

He ran to the bathroom and flipped the light switch. Her purse was sitting on the lavatory. His heart hammered, and his breath hitched as he stepped into the hallway, glanced both ways, and raced toward the kitchen.

The back door slammed against the wall as he moved stealthily through the kitchen, jerking his head as he looked around the room. Molly barked at the back door.

"Sarah! Come *on*. We need... to..." The back door had been locked! He'd locked it himself and checked it. The only way it could have been opened was from the inside. "Sarah!"

He ran outside, his head snapping in every direction. "Sarah! Saraaaaah!"

A short piercing scream—or was it a bird screeching?—bounced off the mountain and splayed in an echo across the open air. Was it in front of him? Behind him?

God, no, please!

He had her! The killer had Sarah!

Blood raged like a madman through his body as he scanned the looming ridge, the gazebo area, the path down to the stream below the cabin, the pool house. He could have gone anywhere with her.

Luke darted down the path to the stream. Wild with fear, he pulled out his cell phone. Ran back up toward the house. Raced down the path past the gazebo. His gaze darted in every direction. His heart jerked his body with each pounding step as he punched in A.J.'s number. Desperately, he searched the trees where the killer had stood that night.

"A.J. Ban—"

"He's got her, A.J.! He's got her!" Almost delirious, Luke started up the ridge, stopped to catch his breath.

"Who's got who, Luke?"

"Sarah! The killer's got Sarah! At McKenzie Cabin. Hurry!"

Breathless, his head pounding like a jackhammer, Luke grunted as he reached the top of the ridge, bent over to catch his breath, and searched in every direction. Then he headed down to the house to scour the area below it where the path led to the pool house.

"God in heaven." A.J. spun around to face Larry and Roland on his way out the door. "The killer's got Sarah. McKenzie Cabin. Get out there." At their dazed looks, he shouted, "NOW!"

A.J. called his brother. "Jim. McKenzie Cabin. Killer's got Sarah."

"On my way. Call the mayor. Sound the alarm."

They'd just discussed it last night at the town meeting. A.J. punched the mayor's numbers. "Carol, sound the alarm. The killer's got Sarah Morgan, and we need *help!*"

"I'll... I... I'll let you talk to—"

"Then do it. We don't have time to chat!"

In two seconds, the mayor came on the phone. "A.J.?"

"Sound the alarm, Terry. The killer took Sarah Morgan out at the McKenzie's cabin. I'm on my way out there. Sound the alarm!"

"Okay. But who's gonna be there to talk to the people?"

"*You* are. We need help at McKenzie Cabin, at the cave site. Josh. Call Josh Daniels in Willow Falls, the caver. Terry, we picked out leaders for this kind of thing. We'll have something figured out by the time they get there."

He'd reached the driveway to the cabin and punched it.

A.J. slung gravel as he skidded to a stop and didn't wait to get his hat on or close his car door. He raced through the open door, into the cabin, weapon poised and ready to fire.

Jim swerved to miss a tree as he slammed on his brakes, barely missing his brother's patrol car. He ran toward a frantically waving Luke in back. "What happened, man?"

"He got her. W-we were in the truck, ready to leave, when she went back inside to get her purse. He must have been hiding inside. Maybe he took her purse, so she'd have to go back in and get it. I don't know. They went out the kitchen door and left before I realized she was taking too long. Five or six minutes. That's it. God help me, I should have gone with her."

Jim scanned the back yard. "Any sign of which way they went?"

"No." Luke pointed and walked toward a path. "This leads to the stream. They could have gone up, but I think that would have been too tough with him carrying her." Suddenly, Luke lowered his head, rubbed his eyes. "Oh, God, don't let her be hurt. Jim, we gotta *do* something!" Molly nudged his leg, and he patted her head.

"A.J.'s called the mayor. We have a system set up for such emergencies. This guy is probably close to the edge at this point." Out of the corner of his eye, Jim saw a movement in the house. "Wait." He stuck out his arm, hushed Luke, and pulled out his firearm. He backed around a tree just as A.J. walked out the glass door. Jim shook his head and put his weapon back in the holster.

"What have you got, Jim?"

"Luke was out front in his truck when Sarah went inside to get her purse and didn't come out. She's not here. Couldn't have been more than five or six minutes from the time she entered the house and she went missing."

Two doors slammed. A.J. took a step back to look around the corner of the cabin. Larry and Roland held their holstered revolvers against their sides as they ran toward him.

"Okay, men, two at a time. Luke and Jim, head up to the ridge, look for signs, clues Sarah may have had the presence of mind to leave if she was conscious. Larry and Roland, go down this path, weapons drawn, follow procedures. I'm staying here and checking every inch of this house, the attic, the basement. Meet back here in fifteen minutes. I have everyone's cell phone numbers. Go!"

NINETEEN

With her tongue, Elva Lee shoved the carrot pieces to the inside of her cheek and answered the phone. "Search & Rescue, this is Elva Lee." She pushed the receiver up above her nose and hurriedly chewed and swallowed.

"Hello, Elva Lee. This is Miss Winnie Sue Jansen. We just heard from Carol down at the mayor's office that Sarah Morgan is missing. Is that true?"

"What do you mean 'missing'?"

"Well, Carol said the killer had Sarah, that he took her from McKenzie Cabin just a few minutes ago."

"I have to call Tommy and Buddy and send them out to the cabin. There's the alarm. I need to be at that meeting. Are you coming?"

"Why, yes, of course. Jim's parents, Jeb and Debra, are scheduled to pick me up. Miss Gertie's here so she'll come with me. We'll see you there."

Elva Lee called Tommy and Buddy, and then Jim.

"You stay at the office for now, Elva Lee, and search for information on Robbie or Brian. A.J. has Greta doing the same thing at the station. Let me know the second you find anything. Oh, and would you call Marilyn and Scott Morgan in Kansas and let them know their daughter, Sarah, is in trouble? Here's the number."

At Myra's Dress Shop, Irma cringed when she heard the alarm. She looked across the square. Mr. Norman fumbled to his feet and shuffled toward his home. She threw Myra's store money in the bank bag, locked it in the safe, picked up her keys, ran out the door, locked it, and raced to her car.

Penny hurried out of the restaurant next door, gritting her teeth as she tried to undo the knot in back of her soiled white apron. "Are you going to the meeting, Irma?"

"Yes, I'm an alternate leader. My George is a Team Leader, and I don't know if he'll be there or not. Do you need a ride?"

Pulling the apron off her shoulders, she nodded. "If you don't mind. I know A.J. will be there. Can my server—I mean, Francie—can she come, too?"

"Of course. You have any customers in there, Penny?"

"The last one just left."

"Did you turn off your grill?" At Penny's blank look, Irma said, "Run, girl! Get your purse, too. Catch the lights behind you."

Francie scampered out the door Penny held open for her. "I turned off the grill!"

Penny stopped and shook her head.

"Your door, Penny, honey," Irma shouted from the car. "Lock your door. Then jump in, both of you."

Penny's hands visibly shook as she followed Irma's instructions.

Fred and Myra's son, Trace, from the hardware store next door, watched as Francie eased into the back seat of Irma's flaming red, totally-rebuilt '67 Mustang. Penny sat in the front. "Y'all heading over to the high school gym?" he yelled from the doorway of Gally's Hardware.

"Yes. Is your daddy coming?"

Trace nodded. "Fred's a team leader. He won't leave Mama behind by herself, so Myra will be there, too."

"You keeping the store open?"

"Yeah." He looked around the town square. "If this is a search and rescue, people might need some things, so we'll stay open. Y'all be careful now."

All three women nodded and waved as Irma backed up and headed out.

"Wonder what's going on," Penny mumbled as Irma turned north and lead-footed the gas pedal.

Allison McIntosh flinched. A piercing alarm seemed to be right outside her car windows. She drove slowly around the town square as people scurried about, stopped to talk for a moment, then waved and jumped into their cars. Every single one of them headed north on Ridge.

She frowned as she drove up to Jodee's Salon, but Jodee was just coming out, nails wet apparently because she held her fingers up as if she hoped the breeze would dry them.

"We're closed, honey!"

Why were they all in such a hurry? What was that alarm? She opened her mouth to ask, but Jodee was already inside her car and backing up. Allison drove the full square. It had turned into a ghost square in mere minutes.

Annoyed, she headed down Main Street. The library was across the street from Miss Winnie Sue's house. A sign boasted "Spelunker's Club Meeting" tomorrow night. It might be interesting to see what a caver's meeting was like. Maybe the library had a book on caving. She pulled in and parked and was grateful the door was not locked.

The library was empty but for the woman behind the reservation desk. Allison walked to the counter and expected a friendly yet hushed greeting. But the woman behind the counter was efficiently ignoring her and continued to work on her computer. Allison rested her arm on the counter and drummed four long fingernails impatiently, with her head cocked.

She lustily sighed. The woman still ignored her.

"Excuse me?"

The librarian didn't bat an eye. Her fingers clicked away as if she had nothing better to do than to ignore a library patron. Finally, she popped one key particularly loud and turned toward Allison, brows raised, and offered not a word.

"I'm visiting here in Little Texas for a few weeks and wondered if I could get a library card."

"Identification?" The librarian's lips barely moved.

"Yes." Allison reached into her purse and drew out her wallet.

The woman slapped a white card on the counter and turned back to her computer.

Irritated, Allison filled out the card and slid it over the counter toward the woman.

She picked it up and set it beside the computer, punched some keys, and glanced back at the card. "Name?"

"Allison McIntosh."

The woman gasped. Her hand flew to her mouth as her face paled. Wearing this shocked expression, she stared at Allison as if she were an alien with two heads. Then the woman looked down at the card, picked it up, studied it, looked at Allison again, and promptly hurried out the front door of the library.

What was that all about? *Did that woman know me?* Allison frowned at the door. She hadn't looked familiar. *Strange.* "Hello? Is anyone here?"

The water fountain gurgled behind her, and she jumped.

A head appeared around a corner. A short frumpy woman was attached to it. She came into full view and looked at Allison as if she were a chicken dressed for Sunday dinner. What was it with these people, reacting to her that way? Was something on her face?

A replica of a pile of gray cow dung roosted on top of this woman's head. Her mouth rounded into a perfect O as if helping a customer was as foreign to her as eating grass.

Irritated, Allison said curtly, "Can you help me here?"

"Why, where's Laura?"

"She's sick, I think. She left the building in a hurry."

"Her ulcer must be acting up. How can I help you today?"

"I filled out this card." Allison pointed to the one beside the computer. "I wanted to get a library card."

The old woman twisted her plump freckled hands at her waist as her worried gaze looked at the computer, then at Allison, then back at the computer. "I'm the archivist. I've never been trained to do this. Maybe if you could come back in an hour or so, Laura will be feeling better by then."

"What time do you close?"

"Eight o'clock. Sharp."

"Thank you." Allison left the library, thinking the librarian had to be the rudest person she'd ever dealt with. She backed out of her parking spot and headed north on Ridge to see where most of the people of Little Texas had taken themselves to earlier.

Within fifteen minutes of the alarm sounding, most of the people of Little Texas were standing inside the gym, two blocks down from Barrett's Auto Repair, waiting for instructions from Mayor Terry.

He picked up the bull horn and spoke into it. "Thank you, everyone, for responding so quickly to the Little Texas Emergency Alarm. Team leaders, find your reference points. If you don't remember your reference points, Team One stands in front of Section One. Team Two, Section Two, and so on. There should be ten teams. If you don't remember what team you're on, Team Leaders, hold up your cards. Folks, find your Team Leader now. Quickly, quickly."

Josh Daniels jogged in, searched the room, and ran toward the mayor who was pointing someone toward a man holding up a K-P sign above his head.

Terry shook his hand. "Josh, good to see you."

"I was at Penny's restaurant, Mayor. Came as quickly as I could."

"Just stand by. We'll get everyone's attention, and you can talk to the group searching around the Gem's Peak Park cave area." Terry held up his hands. "Okay, folks, listen up! Sarah Morgan was taken from the McKenzie's cabin about twenty minutes ago. Based on the evidence, we believe she was taken by the killer of the other women."

A widespread gasp and mumblings ensued.

"Time is our enemy. Remember the things we discussed at our town meeting. Your Team Leaders have your stations. Get to them and good luck."

Josh Daniels and five team members squatted next to the crevice where the three bodies had been found. It had been sealed with a thick, blue plastic covering. It was still in place. Two-man teams searched the area, in and around trees and brush.

Jim Banks' twenty-member team met him at McKenzie Cabin and scoured the area east of it for a quarter mile. Will Pollard and twenty-two others searched north of the ridge above the cabin and beyond. Tommy and Buddy's team of twenty explored the stream area below the cabin and circled around for a quarter mile.

Allison took Miss Gertie and Penny around town, posting flyers of Sarah Morgan at all major intersections, churches, grocery markets, the library, Barrett's Auto Repair, Gally's Hardware, Penny's diner.

Officers Larry and Roland went door-to-door along McKenzie Road, asking if anyone had seen anything.

Miss Winnie Sue stayed in the gym with seven other senior ladies and helped serve hot drinks to returning team members.

After five hours of exhaustive searching, all teams stood in the gym, tired, thirsty, hungry, discouraged, and with absolutely nothing to report. No one had seen or heard a thing.

The media showed up in droves. Reporters were not allowed inside, but they dogged weary searchers, asking unanswerable questions, pointedly reminding everyone that one of their own was not being recovered in anything like a timely manner.

Miss Winnie Sue supervised seating the team members at tables loaded with food and drinks. Pastor Clay thanked the Lord for the food and the people's generosity in lending a helping hand.

He asked for Sarah's safe return.

Then everyone ate quietly as they pondered where Sarah Morgan could be and why there had not been even a trace of a clue as to where he'd taken her.

Elva Lee had given Sarah's mother, Marilyn Morgan, perfect directions. Marilyn turned her rental car into the McKenzie driveway and parked behind a red truck, grateful she'd left Scott at the gym and her daughter Elizabeth and the family cat with Jodee's sixteen-year-old daughter Paige.

From the moment her family had arrived in Little Texas, its people could not have been kinder. She was surprised Jodee remembered meeting her on their last visit here.

"Why, of course, I remember you, Marilyn. It was two years ago at the rodeo. I had done your nails earlier in the day, and you went to the rodeo that night. You wore a yellow cowboy hat and rode Bullheaded the mechanical bull and lasted ten seconds as I recall." Jodee had made her sit beside Miss Winnie Sue, and they fussed over her.

She knew she couldn't hold it together if they did, so she asked if anyone had directions to the McKenzie cabin. She needed to see Luke McKenzie. She desperately needed that connection with Sarah.

And here she sat, in front of the cabin where her baby had last been seen. Marilyn made herself get out of the rental car. The front door of the cabin opened. A tall, utterly handsome young man with coal-black hair and, she could see even from this distance, stark blue but weary eyes walked toward her.

"Marilyn?"

Before she realized it, their arms were around each other. She was sobbing against him as if he was an old friend. She felt herself being led into the cabin through the front door and seated at a kitchen table.

A chrome napkin holder sat in the middle of the breakfast table. She fumbled for a napkin and yanked it out. "I'm so sorry. I hadn't intended—"

"That's all right, Marilyn. Here, would you like some ice water or something else to drink?"

She thought she'd die if she had to concentrate on getting something to her mouth. "No, no, I'm fine. You're exactly as she described." Another bout of crying, and she dabbed her face and blew her nose.

His eyes clouded, and he abruptly stood, left the room, came back with a box of Kleenex and set it on the table between them. "There, that should take care of both of us for a while."

"Tell me what happened."

He frowned as he stared out the windows. "We were ready to leave, everything was packed. She forgot her purse and went inside to get it. After a few minutes, I thought, I hoped, she was dawdling so I came in. She was gone. The back door was wide open."

"It had been locked?"

"Yes. I ran outside, screaming her name, ran everywhere. She was gone, vanished. He had such a slim start that I thought we'd have found them by now. And here I sit, doing absolutely nothing. A.J. said I should stay at the cabin in case she comes back."

Marilyn yanked another Kleenex out and pressed it against her eyes as a sob caught her unawares. "She—she's in love with you."

Luke stared at her. "I hoped she was, but she hadn't told me. She'd been hurt by the Darkslayer and didn't think she could ever—" He shook his head and searched her eyes.

"She's a strong young woman, Luke. Not many women can go through that experience and come out of it as determined as she is to let it go. But it catches her sometimes, when—" She sniffed and blew her nose. "—when she doesn't expect it to."

She looked outside. "The littlest things frighten her about people. She told me she should've been scared to death of you because of your size but she wasn't. She trusted you from the moment you helped her with her twisted straps."

Marilyn looked around the kitchen. "She loves to cook." She brushed her cheeks with a tissue. "Are they sure it's not the Darkslayer who took her?"

"They don't know, for sure. But evidence points to the killer who's stalking small women here in Little Texas." He abruptly stood and walked to the sliding glass doors. "I'm afraid of what he's doing to her. Or planning to do. Or-or—"

She got up, walked over to him, and touched his arm. "Keep praying. It's our best shot at getting her back alive and safe."

Scott appeared with A.J. Banks in the back yard. "Let me introduce you to my husband, Scott. Sarah's father."

Luke opened the glass door and stepped outside. "Mr. Morgan? I'm Luke McKenzie, Sarah's friend. I'm sorry we're meeting—"

Marilyn watched her husband reach for Luke and hug him. His shock of white hair stood out against Luke's black hair. Scott was a much smaller man but his arms easily enveloped Luke.

Her husband pulled away, reached for Marilyn, and folded her into his comfort. They both wept and rocked and unashamedly held onto each other.

"Luke brought tissues," Marilyn said as they moved toward the back door.

Scott patted Luke's back. "Let's go inside, son, out of this cold wind, and you can catch us up. A.J., will you join us?"

"In a few minutes. Luke, do you have a private room I could use?"

Luke called his brother, Mac, and told him about Sarah.

"I can fly there, buddy. Be there in a couple of hours at the most."

"Stay home for now. We have plenty of help. I'll keep you posted, then you can give updates to the rest of the family."

"Will do. If you change your mind, call me."

"Pray, bro.' Just keep praying."

"We all are."

Luke couldn't sleep. He had to get outside. He quietly tiptoed through the house and opened the sliding glass doors. He ran full-throttle up to the ridge and sat in the Indian paintbrushes Sarah had admired. The house was dark except for the light in the kitchen.

It began to snow, a light snow at first. He didn't care for himself.

But he worried about Sarah being out in it.

TWENTY

Gertie couldn't sleep. Gentle folds of Winnie Sue's long blue gown wafted around her legs as she paced the kitchen in her sister's fuzzy house shoes, rubbing her arms as if she were chilled. But she wasn't cold. She was worried sick.

It had always been there at the back of her mind—the rape, the overwhelming anger, the doctor's grim face when he said a pregnancy had resulted, the decision to leave, the decision to give the baby away.

Winnie Sue and she had hoped and prayed that he'd have a better life than the one they could give him.

No one knew when she and Winnie Sue had left. An ailing aunt had sent for them, a worn-out excuse that no one questioned because they were well-respected in Little Texas.

But something had happened the night they gave the baby away. A part of Gertie had died. She withdrew inside herself—the part that could give and receive affection and love unconditionally. She had become a cold woman. Oh, caring, certainly. She'd give the shirt off her back to help someone. But touching, hugging, loving had been stripped from her when she'd allowed them to take the baby away.

A part of Winnie Sue had died, too. She'd become rigid and orderly, as if she could protect herself from anything bad ever touching her if she presented herself properly and lived by a strict code and schedule—if she could control her life.

And now his seed was here, doing far worse than his grandfather had done. How was a soul to bear it? Gertie picked up her coffee, glanced outside at the moon-cloaked night.

And looked into the somber face of the young man with the backpack!

She gasped, dropped her cup, and cringed as coffee drenched Winnie Sue's house slippers and gown. She slapped her hand over her mouth and tried to squelch the whimpering scream as she tiptoed out of the mess. She looked back up. He was gone. She looked at the back door. It was locked.

She patted her chest, so like Winnie Sue, as her heart pounded like it was drilling a hole in her bones.

"Miss Gertie, what happened?" A sleepy Winnie Sue, hand over her mouth, looked down at the floor. "Are you all right?"

Gertie's heart settled down as she turned toward the broom closet. "Yes. I'll get the broom. I'm sorry I woke you. I just had myself a little fright." She glanced over her shoulder at the window. "I'll get this, Sister. You go on back to bed now."

"What do you mean 'a little fright'? Are you in any pain?"

"Oh, no, no, no. I'm fine."

The coffee smeared on the floor as she swept up the cup pieces. Winnie Sue opened the broom closet, picked up the trash basket and a mop, and presented them to Gertie. "Is there more coffee?"

Gertie swept the pieces onto the dustpan and shook them into the basket. "There is, but it's three o'clock in the morning. You shouldn't be drinking coffee at this time of night."

"Don't tell me what I should and should not be doing at three o'clock in the morning, Miss Gertie. I'm perfectly capable at sixty-three years of age to determine what I should and should not be doing at three o'clock in the morning."

Gertie gaped, plain and simple. Winnie Sue Jansen had never talked back to her big sister like that. "Suit yourself," she muttered as she wiped up the coffee with a mop. "Pour me a cup if you don't mind. I don't think either of us is going to get any more sleep tonight."

Winnie Sue put the broom and mop away. "More? I haven't slept at all."

"Me neither. The third shift of searchers is due in at seven o'clock. We'd better be ready. They're going to be tired, cold, and hungry."

As she quietly shut the closet door, Winnie Sue said, "Who do you think is behind this, Miss Gertie?"

"I'm not sure. But I think it's Jansen blood."

"It's that monster's blood, not Jansen blood!"

Not once in the past fifty years had Winnie Sue referred to the rape or the perpetrator or the baby they'd given away. Gertie was more than a little surprised at the passion of her words.

Winnie Sue fussed over pouring the coffee, puttered over the percolator's insides as she dumped the grounds and cleaned out the strainer. She carefully avoided her sister's eyes as she handed her a cup of coffee and turned toward the napkin holder, shimmied two out, and handed one to Gertie.

Their eyes connected.

Gertie smiled.

With her gaze flickering between the coffee cup near her mouth and Gertie's eyes, Winnie Sue smiled and blushed.

Lord o' mercy, she blushed at her own sister.

Gertie reached out a hand. Winnie Sue hesitated, then she took it and squeezed. "You are a treasure to me."

It was apparent her sister didn't quite know how to act. But somehow, she found—in her vast repertoire of good manners—a proper response. "And you are to me, Sister."

Whether or not the young man watched them, Gertie didn't know. She was not so much afraid of *him* as she was the fact that someone could stand outside her sister's home and watch her.

She and Winnie Sue sat at the kitchen table, the special moment gone but still on their minds. They sipped and considered and worried over Sarah Morgan and wondered if she could possibly still be alive.

The next morning, Elva Lee was up before the sun. Too afraid to stay in her own home, she'd spent the night with her parents. By five-thirty, she was showered, dressed in her new size two jeans, and ready to go to the high school gym to help with serving a light pastry breakfast to the searchers.

She stepped over the rolled-up morning newspaper, saw the word "Joy," slipped off the rubber band, and spread it out. The headlines stated that Joy Martin would be flown home to Texas on Monday.

Elva Lee slipped the rubber band back on and threw the paper behind her onto the front porch.

The morning was bitter cold. A light snow dusted everything. She was scraping the snow-covered ice off her windshield when Jim Banks' truck pulled up behind her car.

Smiling, she raised her ice scraper in a wave.

And froze.

He certainly looked none too happy to see her. She took a step back at the fierce anger on his face as he slammed his truck door and marched over to her.

"Why didn't you tell me you weren't going to be home last night?"

At the vehemence and anger and, yes, concern in his words, Elva Lee's mouth dropped open. She took another step back. When her widened eyes blinked, her mind simply drifted out her ears like wind through a tunnel. "I—"

He pointed a stiff arm down the street and jabbed a pointed finger at absolutely nothing. "Didn't you think I'd go by your place and check on you?"

No, the thought had never entered her mind. "Well, Jim, to tell—"

He grabbed her shoulders, and she had to tilt her head back to find his eyes.

"You scared me half to death, Elva Lee! I thought..." He tightened his grip and gave her a little shake. "I thought he..." He closed his eyes and lifted his head toward the heavens. "Elva Lee, don't..."

She didn't—couldn't—and braced herself as he sputtered, "Ah, great," and lifted her—lifted her!—off her feet and kissed the absolute wits out of her.

After the initial shock of discovering Jim Banks' mouth on hers, she poured herself into the kiss. Where there was anger, she soothed.

Frustration, she cooed. Weariness, she encouraged.

With no embarrassment or shame, Jim lowered her to the ground as if it was the most natural thing in the world for him to be kissing Elva Lee Ward at dawn on Faircrest Drive and lifting her plumb off her feet in the process.

He searched her eyes as his mouth lowered again, gentle this time, soft. When he let her go, he rested his forehead on hers and sighed. "Next time, let me know where you are."

She could only nod, barely able to hold back the bulging whimper clogging her throat.

He grabbed the ice scraper and attacked her windshield. He finished all her windows and handed her the scraper as his gaze locked on hers.

Her heart stopped. She had a vague sense of his face lowering to hers, of her chin lifting to meet his mouth.

"Been wanting to do this for a while," he said and kissed her again, a long and lazy kiss that caused her knees to buckle.

His strong arms gathered her up as he grinned at her. "Can you stand, Elva Lee?"

She nodded. He set her against her car and turned on his heel toward his truck. Leaning on the open door, he said, "I'll see you at noon," and, with a satisfied nod, he hopped into his truck and left.

She couldn't move. Thinking was out of the question. As morning light arrived in her parents' neighborhood, Elva Lee stared, unmoving, at the spot behind her car where his truck had been parked.

And smiled.

Winnie Sue was in her element. At seven o'clock on this sad but beautiful Saturday morning, coffee needed to be made again. A new batch of searchers came in; stomachs were empty and needed to be filled.

Busy about her work, it was then that she noticed the straight-backed gentlemen of elderly years standing near the back wall, down from the serving table, staring at her.

She fumbled the cup of steaming coffee she was handing to Eduardo. He smiled, nonetheless, shook the coffee off his hand, and thanked her for her kindness.

The man at the library! The one who had stared and *winked* at her! Why, Winnie Sue had never had a man stare at her before and thought him far too bold to be doing so.

Certainly, she was nothing worth staring at, and she shouldn't even be considering whether she was or was not, with Sarah missing. But a hand fluttered to her neck anyway, and her fingers stroked across her lips.

She must have something on her face. She mumbled an "Excuse me, Penny, Irma," and made her way to the ladies' room and checked, but nothing seemed inappropriately placed on her face. He must have mistaken her for someone else.

Satisfied, she returned to the beverage serving table.

The gentleman was no longer against the wall.

He was waiting in line for a cup of coffee, with his gaze boldly on Winnie Sue.

Well, forevermore! She would simply pour his coffee and send that old man on his way.

Will Pollard handed her his empty coffee cup. "Good morning, Miss Winnie Sue."

She smiled and poured his coffee. "How is Casey doing, Mr. Pollard, after that vicious attack in the park?"

"Better. She's at home now," he said, thanked her, and left.

The old goose was still staring at Winnie Sue.

Determined to ignore him and not blush, she smiled warmly as Tommy Blakesly took a cup from her. "Miss Winnie Sue, you're an angel. Thank you for the coffee."

Buddy Washburn mumbled, "Got anything to go in that, Miss Winnie Sue?" At her disapproving look, he looked a tad remorseful and thanked her anyway.

Then the gentleman stood in front of her. "A refill, if you please." His base voice seemed to reverberate through every bone Winnie Sue owned as she kept her eyes on his large hand. "Young lady."

Young lady, indeed!

"I haven't had the pleasure of making your acquaintance, ma'am."

Winnie Sue couldn't bring herself to meet his eyes. "Miss."

"Beg your pardon?" He cocked an ear and raised his brows.

Her eyes down, she whispered, "It's 'Miss' and no, I don't believe we have met, sir."

His stuck out a large, thick hand. "Name's Carl Jefferson."

Winnie Sue was beside herself with embarrassment. She took his hand, shook it, and couldn't get a word past her dry throat.

He leaned forward and smiled. "And whose hand do I have the pleasure of holding, miss?"

Blushing and trying very hard not to, she said in a low voice, "Winnie Sue Jansen, Mr. Jefferson." Very graciously and with as little discomfort to him as possible, she eased her hand out of his and looked behind him at a smiling Keith Liboski.

"A pleasure, Miss Winnie Sue Jansen." Carl Jefferson tipped a non-existent hat, smiled, thanked her for the drink, and went to stand in his spot against the back wall.

"Miss Winnie Sue, I do believe you have an admirer."

"It would seem so, Mr. Liboski." She gave him a cup of coffee and glanced over at Mr. Jefferson.

He saluted her with his cup and smiled.

She frowned and wiped her hands on her apron. "Forevermore."

The mayor blew a whistle to gather all the teams together and begin the day's business. Mr. Jefferson stayed where he was and watched them, *and her*, and she wondered why he was in Little Texas and just what that old man was about.

It wasn't a long walk from Gertie's house to the McKenzie's cabin, and she'd enjoyed the crisp early morning and the quiet. She was glad to see A.J.'s patrol car parked in front. It was seven-thirty, and she wondered if he'd been here all night. She knocked.

A disheveled Luke opened the door, squinting against the cold breeze. "Come in, Miss Gertie, and have some fresh-made coffee. We were just talking about you."

"We were?" She walked down the hallway to the kitchen. A.J. and Jim rose from their chairs.

She flapped her gloved hands at them. "Sit, boys. No account of getting out of those warm chairs this early in the day. Any news?"

Luke shook his head. He looked the worse for wear as he poured her coffee and gestured for her to sit beside him.

Will Pollard's father, Truman, a psychologist who helped the police out from time to time, continued where he'd obviously left off when Gertie knocked.

"He's a hermit, a recluse, likes to hole up where no one can find him. Hence, the pit where he dumped the bodies. He's meticulous. Driven. He hasn't killed Luke because he's on a mission to kill Rosie. He won't kill indiscriminately. That's why Luke is still alive, although he could have killed him and taken Sarah—or 'Rosie' as he believes she is."

Gertie set her purse on the table and got out of her winter things. "I think you're talking about my kin, Truman. I also think I know how to get that gopher to come out of his hole."

"Now, Miss Gertie."

"Don't you 'now Miss Gertie' me, A.J. Banks. I know what I'm about. That boy believes he's killing *me,* but when he sees a woman that looks like me, he thinks Rosie isn't dead, that she got out. So he kills again. In his damaged mind, he's obeying his father and doing what he was told to do. This is totally beyond his control now. That being said, I'm willing to use myself as bait to get him to come after me. Provided, of course," she nodded at A.J., at Jim, "that you boys are ready to get him when he does. I've got some living to do yet."

A.J. glanced over at Jim, who raised his brows and cocked his head. "Well, Miss Gertie."

"I can tell by that look that you're not buying what I've said, A.J. You've got a psychologist fellow here—no offense, Truman—who's gonna tell you about someone he doesn't know. I don't know him either, but I think I know more about him than anyone here."

She walked in front of A.J. and Truman. "I don't mean to be disrespectful of your job, Truman, but I've got a stake here. I intend to use whatever advantage I have to get him to set Sarah loose if he hasn't killed her already and maybe save himself in the running."

A.J. picked up a pencil and let it fall back to the table, picked it up, let it fall. "All right, Miss Gertie. Let's hear this plan of yours."

Raw, hammering pain radiated from the crown of her head into her neck. She moaned and tried to move her arms, but every part of her body screamed out in torment.

Sarah struggled to open her eyes and keep them open. Complete blackness engulfed her. Sharp points of pain dug into her left shoulder and arm. Unable to keep her eyes open, she drifted along black corridors of agony. Where was she? Was she in the cave?

She remembered being groggy, and a voice saying, "There ya go, Rosie. Dead and buried. Finally!" Then he'd shoved her, and she'd fallen a good distance onto dirt and into sudden, excruciating pain.

She tried to turn on her side, but spasms of unbearable anguish racked her left foot and shoulder. She cried out and made herself be still. Even without moving, pain stabbed her body, radiating in every direction. "Help me," she whispered and then drifted away.

A cameraman entered the gym, followed by several other people. In minutes, he said, "On my mark, five, four, three, two, one." A red light came on and the anchorwoman for Channel 11 News smiled into the camera.

"This is Toni Pruett, live from the Little Texas high school gym in Little Texas, Colorado, where hundreds of volunteers are still searching today for twenty-five-year-old Sarah Ann Morgan, who was abducted from the home of Luke McKenzie yesterday morning.

"Many volunteers help to make things flow smoothly in a search and rescue. One of those volunteers is with me today: Rosie Jansen. Miss Jansen, how many people are here today helping with food preparation and serving?"

Gertie looked at the camera. "Approximately thirty."

"And you, Miss Jansen, have helped several times through the years with such efforts?"

"Oh, yes," she laughed, "many times. I was born here in Little Texas, and my mother would say, "Rosie, someone needs our help." I remember the rescue of a man and his wife right behind our cabin there on Bear Camp Road. He had a broken leg, and she had a broken collar bone. So, yes, my sister and I have helped on many rescues."

"Do you still have hope, Miss Jansen, that Sarah Morgan will be found alive?"

Gertie focused on the camera. "Of course, that's our hope. My mother used to say to me, 'Rosie, if you need to find someone, stay with it until they're safe.'"

"We also have with us today A.J. Banks, chief of police here in Little Texas. Chief, what are your plans today?"

A.J. shifted his feet. "Same as yesterday, Toni. We have team leaders in constant contact with command control, scanning the area where she was last seen as well as other areas in and around Little Texas. We couldn't do this without the help of people like Rosie Jansen and the other volunteers."

"How many searchers do you have, Chief?"

"Around two hundred fifty."

"Do you think she'll be found alive?"

"None of us would be out here working this hard if we didn't."

Toni Pruett smiled into the camera. "This is Toni Pruett with Rosie Jansen and Chief A.J. Banks in Little Texas. Back to you in the studio." She stared at the camera until the red light went off and then turned to Gertie. "I sure hope this works."

"Me, too. I sounded like an absolute dingbat, tooting my own horn like that. A.J., thanks."

"Nothing to it, Miss Gertie. I think the talk of the town will be why in the world we called you Rosie."

Within minutes of the interview, Jim Banks walked into the gym and scanned the room. Elva Lee's heart skipped a beat when he spotted her talking to Penny.

She couldn't breathe as he walked toward her, eyes intent, teeth set. He edged behind the serving table, wrapped an arm about her waist, pulled her up to his mouth, and kissed her thoroughly.

Penny's mouth dropped open. Irma giggled. Miss Winnie Sue Jansen blushed and glanced back at Carl Jefferson who nodded and smiled at her.

The whole room quieted.

Jim stepped back. Both he and Elva Lee blushed. He bent over, kissed her again. "One for the road," he muttered, and then turned to Miss Gertie. "Are you ready to leave, Miss Gertie?" He headed out with her but sent one last glance over his shoulder at Elva Lee.

Irma grinned and hugged Elva Lee. "It was that dress we picked out, girl!"

Penny smiled. "It's about time that man opened his eyes."

And, in general, Little Texas had something to smile about. News traveled fast. Everyone felt heart-warmed about Elva Lee and Jim, especially with the prospects getting better of finding Sarah—well, no one could say the d-word yet. It was almost as if they were afraid it would come true if anyone said it out loud.

TWENTY-ONE

Holed up in a tiny closet inside Miss Gertie's house, Officer Larry Traylor smelled musty shoes and stinky socks and just plain 'old' around him. He figured her grandfather had stuffed an old pair of well-used socks in a corner, and no one had ever discovered them.

Something crawled on his arm. He wanted to swat at it but couldn't. Not when a murderer might be sneaking into Miss Gertie's cabin right now and hear him. He wasn't ashamed to say that he was terrified. He'd never even fired his gun, much less pointed it at a human being with that intent. He hoped he'd be able to aim and shoot when he needed to without dropping it.

In Miss Gertie's basement, Officer Roland Graves peeked over the rickety worktable, grateful he wasn't allergic to dust. For crying out loud, the floor was made of *dirt*. If he so much as breathed on the lopsided table next to him, it would crumble at his feet. His knees and his back ached—neither liked being in a constant bend. But A.J. said he had to be ready to fire his weapon. And he couldn't be ready sitting on the floor, knotted up like a pretzel.

A.J. looked through a slit in the wall of Miss Gertie's old worn-out barn, searching the house and grounds for any activity. His fingers cramped on his weapon, so he set it on a dusty crate near his foot and sat on an old bench where he could keep his eye on the cabin.

It had been an hour since the interview. Channel 11 said they would run it three more times today. It was a long shot that the killer had access to a T.V., much less that he was watching the news.

At McKenzie Cabin, Sarah's mother, Marilyn, glanced at Luke. He was asleep at the kitchen table with his head on his arms. She fixed peanut butter and jelly sandwiches while Scott watched the TV for any news of Sarah.

She closed her eyes as exhaustion pressed in on every cell in her body. She'd lain wide awake all night, not even a little drowsy, the hurt and worry too deep for sleep.

She was rinsing her plate when a knife fell off it and dropped into the sink. Molly barked at the intruding sound.

Luke jerked awake. "Wha—?" He looked around the room and sighed. He rubbed his eyes and glanced outside. Sadness sat heavy on his heart as the afternoon sun waned and still no news of Sarah.

He wearily stood. "Marilyn, I think I'll take a walk outside, see if I can, you know, see anything. Come on, Molly."

He needed to be outside, where Sarah had last been.

Two days. And another night approaching.

Did she have any water? Was he giving her food? Was she tied up? Was she alone?

A surge of desperation seized him. He ran like a madman up the ridge, welcoming the raw pain in his chest and legs as he topped it, spun around, and groaned like an animal in pain.

He could see for miles and wondered if his gaze skimmed over the man's hiding place.

"SARAH!" he yelled as loudly as he could. He turned in a circle and looked down at the cabin nestled comfortably in tall trees, the pool house below the cabin, the gazebo, the path leading down to the stream.

He couldn't for the life of him figure out how the killer had made off with her so quickly. Luke had long legs that ate up distance in a hurry. Stubby little legs couldn't cover much ground even if the guy was fast, especially if he was carrying someone his own size.

He hadn't had that much of a start on Luke, considering how fast Luke had run. "So why didn't I catch up with him?"

How was the man able to outdistance him?

A bike? Impossible in this terrain.

A dirt bike? No, he hadn't heard anything, and they were loud, and he couldn't have carried someone limp on it.

Luke searched through the trees. Thick brush was everywhere. How had he made it through the brush?

He turned around. The man couldn't have gone in front of the cabin. "I would have seen him."

Luke looked toward the stream. Too much underbrush.

He glanced past the gazebo. Same problem—underbrush with a single path through it toward nothing but more trees and brush. So how had the killer done it? How had he—?

Luke's body and mind froze. He stood on the ridge, stunned to the bone. Of course!

She was still here. She was still here!

Luke stumbled over himself getting down the slope, gained his feet, and made it the rest of the way down. She's still here!

Why hadn't he thought of that earlier?

Frantic, he walked around the house, hunched over, searching the ground for a storm cellar or a root cellar. There had to be some sort of an underground room on the property. This was old property, dating back to the 1890s. People built root cellars back then. It was accepted practice for preserving foods, for protection.

He pulled out his cell phone and punched in Mac's number.

"Mac, it's Luke. Do you have the original plans to this property?"

"The original plans? My architect can get them. Why?"

"I need to know if there's a storm cellar on this property, a root cellar of some kind. Probably where the original house or cabin was built in the 1890s. I think Sarah might be in it."

"Okay. I'll call Calvin and get him to email it to you. You can print it off in the downstairs office."

Luke told him he'd keep him posted and disconnected the call. He kept searching the ground. He could hear Marilyn yelling upstairs, "Scott? Scott! Luke's onto something. Go outside and help him."

In minutes, Sarah's father was rushing outside.

Luke bent over, scraping old leaves and mulch away from the gazebo with his foot.

A little out of breath, Scott said, "What are we searching for?"

Luke's gaze was riveted on the ground. "A root cellar, a storm cellar, an underground room. He couldn't have outrun me, Scott. My legs are much longer than his, and he was carrying Sarah." Luke looked up. "She's still here. I can *feel* it! She's still here. Come on."

Luke raced to the garage and pulled down two rakes and handed one to Scott. Both started working on the yard.

"Look for an indentation or an opening. You start here. I need to go inside and get into my email. Mac's architect is sending me the original plans. Marilyn can watch for his email for me."

He took Marilyn to the office and opened his email. "Come get me when it gets here. Then we'll print it off." He thanked her and rushed back outside. "Scott, I'll search over here. We'll increase in five-foot increments until we hear from Calvin, the architect."

They worked in silence for twenty minutes until Marilyn hollered at him that the email had arrived. They printed the blueprints.

Nodding, Scott quietly studied them for a few moments. "You're right, Luke. Isn't that the root cellar right there?"

"It is."

"Give me a minute to figure this out. Do you have Calvin's number? I need his input."

Luke gave it to him.

"Okay," Scott said as he joined Luke outside a few minutes later.

"Calvin thinks we're going to have some difficulty finding it. The easiest way to do this is for him to talk us through it. Calvin?" He put the phone on speaker. "We can both hear you now."

They listened to the architect for a few moments as Luke led Scott down the path toward the stream. "It's exactly 310.78 feet from the west end of the property, going east. That means you have to find the west end of the property first. Look for a large boulder. That's where you start."

Sarah awoke to complete darkness.

Her head hurt. Her left arm and shoulder hurt. Her left ankle hurt. She was chilled but so grateful she'd started the day off in warm clothes.

She had the presence of mind to know that tape covered her mouth and secured her wrists. Dusty. Dirty. Old. She was underground. A cave? *Oh, God, no. Please.*

She tried to move and screamed from the pain radiating up her left arm. *It must be broken.* With swollen, stiff fingers, she tugged the duct tape off her mouth. "Hello? Is anyone here?"

She was alone; she could sense it. She chewed on the strips holding her wrists together. Her left arm dangled unnaturally when she held up her hands. Pain seared through her arm and shoulder as she continued to nibble at the tape. Sweat dripped into her eyes, burning them.

Gasping for air, her head fell back against the dirt surface. She was so tired, she wanted to close her eyes again and escape into the darkness.

But she couldn't go back to sleep. She had to get out before he came back. *Sit up, Sarah. Sit up! Stay awake!*

She struggled into a sitting position and gently patted her lower leg. Everything felt normal until she touched her ankle. It was hot, swollen, and incredibly tender. It didn't feel like her foot. *Oh, Lord, please help me. Too much is wrong with my body. I don't know if I can do this.*

Because she couldn't pull against her left hand without causing more pain, she had to gnaw through the tape on both sides of her hands. She rested. She nibbled. She breathed. She rested. She chewed. She gasped for air.

After what seemed like an hour or more, her hands finally broke free. She screamed at the throbbing pain radiating through the left side of her upper body and wept uncontrollably for a few minutes.

"Okay, Sarah." She tried to maneuver to her good knee and shrieked. Moaning, she whispered, "Get on your right side, Sarah. Come on."

She tucked her left hand into the waistband of her pants to secure it and then scooted on her bottom, using her right arm as an antenna to figure out where she was and what could help her escape. Time dragged by. She screamed as her foot dragged on the dirt floor, throbbing in pain. Gritting her teeth, she reached out again and touched something. Wood. A rung! He had left an upright ladder for her.

But why?

Of course, it was for his convenience in getting down, not for her to get out. But where was she? She would have to climb the ladder to find out.

Okay. She'd head up backwards.

She reached for a higher rung, tugged her bottom up to the first rung, and wept. Everything hurt too much. She couldn't do this.

It's just a matter of time now. Luke's words, at the cave.

"I can't, Luke. I can't."

You roared like a lion.

I didn't, didn't I? A lion. I like that.

"A lion. A lion." She hoisted herself to the second rung using her right arm and leg. She kept herself from falling forward by digging into the ground with her right foot. "And I thought the dark was my worst enemy. That's nothing compared to this."

Her left hand wriggled out of her pants and sent stabbing pain all over her body. She cried out as she lifted her useless, broken arm and stuffed her left hand back into the band of her pants. "Father?" She sobbed. "Help me. Please help me get out of here."

She rested for a while. She thought she might have fallen asleep, draped over the ladder rungs.

Then she pushed with her right foot on the bottom step, and she eased herself up to the next run. She couldn't tell how tall the ladder was, but her strength was ebbing. "I can't do this...much longer, Lord. You know I can't."

My grace is sufficient for you, for my strength is made perfect in weakness. "Perfect... strength," she muttered. "The lion has perfect strength."

She reached for the next rung and slowly hoisted herself up. Her swollen left foot grazed the ladder. Oh! She sucked in a breath and set her teeth against the crushing pain. Suddenly nauseous, she thought she might throw up. "Perfect strength, Sarah. Perfect strength."

She stopped and rested.

Time crawled by.

Another rung. She rested.

Then another. And another until she was dripping wet with sweat. Every muscle in her body was shaking. The air was getting thinner.

Her chest was hurting.

Everything hurt.

"Luke, find me." She wept, hard. "Father, help him find me."

Time meant nothing. Once, she thought she'd stayed in one position for more than an hour. Another time, she'd rested so long that her muscles seized up. She tried to shift her working foot, but it wouldn't obey her.

Just relax. Rest a moment.

Perfect strength. Perfect strength.

She closed her eyes and listened to time ticking away. Then she reached for another rung and touched something hard. She was at the top! She felt wood, like a trap door. "Oh, Father, we did it!"

She wanted to cry, but she didn't have the energy. No light shined around the small door, but she pushed against it anyway. It didn't move. Okay. Okay.

"Get your back against it."

She heaved herself up one more rung and stooped over. With her back, she shoved hard against the wood.

It didn't budge. *Come on, Sarah. Push!*

She did. Nothing happened.

"It's too heavy for me." Was there something on top that prevented her from lifting it? "Come on. Try again."

She took a deep breath, marshaled every bit of strength she had, and pushed as hard as she could against the door.

It shifted, letting in some light.

Her whole body was shaking uncontrollably.

She was dripping wet. In horrible pain. Nauseous. Weak.

"Don't fall, Sarah." She looked up. Dirt fell into her eyes. She blinked furiously and wiped her eyes with her wet shoulder. Shoving again, the door lifted a little more. She pressed as hard as she could against it, shoved back with her head, and the door gently fell open.

Sunlight!

Little white dots danced. She closed her eyes and grabbed a clump of grass and weeds. Whimpering, she shoved with her foot and tugged herself up, an inch at a time.

With one last push of her right foot, her body passed the door. She fell to her back in tall weeds.

She saw Indian paintbrushes before the encroaching blackness made them disappear.

Miss Gertie had been in her cabin about an hour and a half, A.J. guessed, as he looked at his watch in the dimly lit barn.

454

If the killer was waiting on her to settle in before he made his move, A.J. sure wished he'd make up his mind to do it. His allergy to hay was kicking in, and he needed to sneeze something fierce.

Gravel popped. A.J. looked out the slit in the barn wall. A late model white SUV crept down the lane toward Miss Gertie's house. A young man sat at the wheel. His gaze darted around Miss Gertie's yard as he parked and slowly opened the driver's door.

He was a short fellow who wore his blondish-brown hair a little long and pulled back in a stub of a ponytail. A.J. thought he spotted a dangling earring in his left ear.

As the man crept up the wood steps, a board creaked.

Gertie had been primed as to how to get the man into her house.

She'd heard the car pull up, stood at the closet door and told Larry to get ready, that someone had just driven up.

He whispered, "Okay, Miss Gertie, just keep your head, all right?"

She nodded. "I will. Just be ready for anything."

She walked to the edge of the living room as she held onto a well-worn dish towel as if her life depended on it.

Her mouth was dry. Fear did that to a person.

The young man stood on her porch and looked around the yard. He raised a knuckled fist and knocked three times on the wood frame of her front door.

She swallowed hard. This was it.

She made herself move one foot forward, then the other, again and again, until she stood in front of the door.

The man rubbed his knuckle and looked right at her as she smiled at him, opened the screen door, and looked into the face of a killer.

Within fifteen minutes, Luke and Scott found the general area of the root cellar but no sign of a break in the ground where a door had been lifted.

Luke rubbed his burning eyes and looked around his feet. "Let's spread out about fifteen feet, Scott. Yell if you see anything."

But after another twenty minutes of searching, Luke threw out his hands. "Something's wrong. It's not here. There has to be another one." He called Calvin back. When he answered, Luke said, "We need to check for newer blueprints. Hiram Jansen's wife's parents lived in this area, on this very property."

"I'll do a search right now."

"I'll wait for your call. Thanks." Luke hung up.

"He's looking for them, Scott. On the same online site where he found the first set."

It didn't take long for him to find them.

Luke put the phone on speaker. Calvin said, "You're right, Luke. Another one was built up above the ridge. Pretty much right smack in the middle of that original pasture."

Luke's heart pounded hard like a fist fight rolling down a flight of stairs. "Come on, Scott." He heard Calvin say, "I'll give you the parameters—" but he didn't wait for them. He raced up the ridge with Scott somewhere behind him and headed toward the field of Indian paintbrushes. As he got closer to the center, he spotted something in the tall weeds. "I see her! I see her!"

He ran as fast as he could and landed on his knees beside her. "Sarah? Sarah?" He reached for her but stopped. "Don't touch her. She's—Oh, God." He gasped as tears flooded his eyes. "She's broken. Look at her arm, her foot, her face. She's broken. Bruised. Where did the blood come from?" He gently moved her matted hair aside that covered a gash on her forehead.

He touched her neck and then stilled as he struggled to feel a pulse. "She's alive. Call 9-1-1, Scott. Get an ambulance over here!"

But Scott's hands were shaking too much.

"I got it." Luke called A.J., told him the location, answered some questions, and hung up. "Ambulance is on its way."

Behind them, Marilyn stifled a scream when she saw Sarah. Her frantic gaze searched Luke's face. "Is she—?"

"She's alive." Luke touched Sarah's cheek. "Sarah, can you hear me? Sarah?"

Scott knelt beside her. "They're on their way, honey. No more than a couple minutes. The ambulance has been on call since yesterday." He stroked her face. "Sarah, honey? It's Dad. You're all right now. Stay with us, honey. Stay with us."

Luke's phone rang. "Yeah, A.J." He listened and said, "That's good news, man. Thanks for telling us. Yes, she's still alive. I hear the sirens now. Talk to you in a bit."

Leaning over Sarah, he said, "The police just arrested the Darkslayer. He's in custody, sweetheart." His heart ached for her. "Sarah," he whispered, "I love you. Please stay with me."

Sirens screeched loudly outside the cabin. Two EMTs raced up the ridge and over to them. Luke, Scott and Marilyn backed off and let them try to save Sarah.

"She did it all by herself," Luke said as he hugged Marilyn. "With a broken arm and a broken foot, she crawled out of that hole by herself."

"She's amazing."

In the bright sunlight, the EMTs gently and competently prepared Sarah for transport to the hospital.

Scott said, "How did the killer find this cellar?"

"Probably the same way the architect did. Blueprints were online. Did you hear me tell Sarah that the police have captured the Darkslayer?"

"That's great news," Scott said as he watched the EMTs work. "Now, they need to concentrate on finding the Little Texas killer."

Nodding, Luke said, "One down. One to go."

TWENTY-TWO

A shout of joy rose from the bleachers at the gym when Mayor Terry Mason announced that Sarah Morgan had been found alive. Winnie Sue hugged several of the women as team members straggled in, exhausted and ready for the evening meal. But when they heard the news, discouraged expressions changed into happy ones.

"How is she, Mayor?"

"EMTs are working on her right now to take her to the hospital. That's all we know at this point, Miss Winnie Sue. She's unresponsive but her vitals are strong." A collective sigh flew across the crowd. "Chief Banks believes she was unconscious when she was thrown ten feet down into a root cellar that he believes was used by the killer as a hiding place. Bones were broken. She sustained other injuries but, folks, we have a lot to be grateful for tonight."

"Where was this root cellar?"

He told them everything Luke had told him. "Sarah managed, with at least a broken arm and a broken foot, to get herself up a ladder and out of that root cellar by herself. Now, that's one very brave and very strong woman, folks."

Winnie Sue was decidedly uncomfortable when Carl Jefferson entered the high school gym during the announcement and stood right behind her. Lord o' mercy, what was a good Christian woman to think about such boldness?

"—pray for her recovery, and Search & Rescue wants me to pass along a great big thank you for all your help! Give yourselves a hand, folks!"

Elva Lee's mother, Heather, leaned over her daughter. "Would you like to stay with us again tonight, honey, seeing as that man hasn't been caught yet? You're more than welcome, you know that."

Elva Lee smiled at her. "Maybe one more night, Mama. This time, I think I'll let Jim know where I am."

Myra's sister, Irma, heard her. "A good shaking up was good for him. Look where it got you." She nudged Elva Lee with her shoulder, and they both laughed.

Winnie Sue cast what she hoped was a surreptitious glance over her shoulder and discovered that Carl Jefferson was leaning toward her.

She gulped. The whiskers on his mouth tickled her ear as he said, "May I have the pleasure of taking you home, Miss Jansen?"

She backed away from his mouth as hot as an August house-a-fire and feared she might be close to swooning. But she gathered her wits about her and glanced over the crowd for her sister. "Oh, my," she whispered. "I can't seem to locate my sister, Mr. Jefferson. She's staying at my home this evening."

"I'd be more than happy to take both of you home."

"No, no. That's not the point, sir," Winnie Sue said as she shook her head. "I don't see my sister anywhere."

With every ounce of courage she possessed, Gertie grinned at the man cupping his hands around his eyes and peering through her screen door.

"Howdy, young man. What can I do for you?" Bold as brass, she pushed the screen door open. She tried not to react to the slight bulge in the nice blue shirt he had loosely tucked into his dress pants. "Are you lost, then?"

"Are you Rosie? You can't be Rosie. You don't look like the picture."

A chill raced from her neck clean down to her toes. She stepped back and made herself look surprised. "Why, how'd you know my name, young fellow? Did you see my picture there on the TV?" She thought she was doing a fine job of acting addle-brained as A.J. had suggested.

"So, you *are* Rosie. I couldn't find you." He pulled a paper rose from his pocket and stuck it to the glass in her screen door. Then his hand moved so quickly, Gertie couldn't react. In a second, he had a gun in his hand, and it was pointed right at her. "I couldn't find you. You're old. Nothing like the picture."

"Why, no call for a gun. Nobody's gonna hurt you here." She backed up as he stepped inside with a glint of something way past anger in his eyes, past being human.

"Rosie, Rosie. You can't know how long I've searched for you, how long I've needed to see you." Tears filled the young man's eyes, but he quickly sobered—too quickly—and bared his teeth. "How long I've needed to kill you." A deeper voice. "I've tried. I've tried and tried to kill you."

He shook the gun at the sofa. "Sit down, Rosie. I want you sitting down."

Gertie obliged him and sat primly, as if Winnie Sue was watching.

"Feel my heart, Rosie." He leaned over with the tip of the weapon square between her eyes. "Feel my heart, how excited I am to see you."

Her trembling hand touched his chest. "Yes," she whispered. "I can feel it, Brian."

"Don't call me that!" In an instant, his voice was higher. "DON'T CALL ME THAT!"

The young man sat on the coffee table and hugged his head with both hands, the gun pointed straight at the ceiling.

"He never could do it." The young man wept and wiped his eyes with the back of the hand holding the gun. "He'd just sit in the corner and curl up like a cat. And take it, and take it, and TAKE IT! Over and over and over and over and over and over, again and again, he'd just TAKE IT!"

His whole body shook. The man jerked up and lunged toward the north window, gasping for air.

"But *you* didn't, did you, Robbie?"

He spun around with noxious hate in his eyes and quick-stepped to the sofa. "How do you know my name?" He snarled as the barrel of the gun slapped her forehead.

She'd seen it coming and leaned away as he hit her, but still the stars came, the gripping pain. A drop of blood ran down her temple. "Allison told me, Robbie. She's my friend."

"NO!" He jumped up and down like a fit-throwing two-year-old. "She doesn't understand! You're in Brian! I'm going to kill you."

He sat on the table again, suddenly quiet. "He said you were in Brian, that you had to come out of him. I-I was a little boy. I didn't know how to do it then." He glared at her. "But I do now." The deeper voice was back. *A split personality.* "Oh, Rosie." He laughed as if they were at a dinner party and he was telling an old story among friends. "You're finally going to die today."

Officer Larry could hardly breathe. If he took a good breath, Robbie might hear him. He covered his mouth and breathed into his hand as his heart galloped. The confession had to come first and then he could step out. A.J. had been very clear about it.

"Robbie, don't."

Gertie hadn't heard a car. Nor had she heard the librarian, Laura Langston, walking up her steps. She opened the screen door and stepped inside, glanced over at Gertie, and then placed her attention on Robbie.

"Who are you?" Robbie swung the gun and aimed it at the woman. "I *said,* who *are* you?"

"You were my quiet child. Always acquiescing, always in the shadows, hiding, afraid. But you don't look afraid now, Robbie."

Gertie agreed. He looked evil, depraved, insane. His eyes were gripped in the blank look of madness.

"I'm your mother, Robbie."

It was pathetic watching his face scrunch up like a little boy who didn't want to cry but couldn't help himself. Big gasping gulps filled the air as his wrist pushed away the moisture on his face. With the gun in his hand, he stared at this woman who was his mother. His bottom lip quivered.

A young boy's voice said, "No, my mother's dead. He said she was dead."

"Well, I'm not, Robbie. I'm alive."

Robbie's eyes glinted, and he growled. He squinted at his mother and, in a grand sweep, pointed the gun at Gertie. "Did you do this?" He flicked his head toward Laura. "Did you put her up to this?"

Gertie's mouth had gone completely dry. "No, Robbie. It *is* your mother. She's the librarian here in Little Texas." Keep it smooth and easy, A.J. had said. Don't upset him. "I've known her for many a year."

"Robbie, I came here where Rosie lived because I knew you would eventually find her. You were always so inquisitive. I wanted to be here, in Little Texas, to give you answers if you needed them. I've been here since I left you."

Angry eyes bored into Laura as Robbie raised a straight arm with the gun pointed right at her face. One side of his mouth lifted. His head dipped. He looked down the barrel at her.

Utter silence filled the room.

Gertie could not get a breath. Robbie smirked, and his gun arm swayed. Then he made little circles with the gun, outlining Laura's face. He stopped and reversed the path of the circles. His eyes closed as his right eye began to twitch.

"You're dead, Mommy." Quick as a snap, Robbie sneered, squeezed the trigger, and the gun popped. Wide-eyed, Laura stared at her son, swayed, and fell to the floor.

Robbie spun toward the large window and stood there, so still.

In a flash, Gertie thought of the note she'd left on Laura's kitchen table and regretted leaving it. Lying on the floor, Laura looked at her, sent her a "thumbs up," and then closed her eyes. The bullet hadn't even touched her.

The closet door opened a bit. Gertie slowly shook her head at Larry and winked, the signal not to come out of the closet. She mouthed, "She's alive." Larry nodded. She knew he was sending A.J. a quiet text right now, as instructed.

A.J. put away his phone. So, Laura Langston was unharmed. Good for her for faking being shot. That might come in handy later.

In the waning light outside, A.J. bent over, scurried across the front yard, and squatted at Gertie's steps. She had purposely left the door open so he could hear everything.

Slowly, slowly, he crept up the steps, hoping Larry wouldn't get antsy and jump out of the closet and get himself killed.

Roland backed away from the cabin, craning to see what was happening above him. A.J. caught his attention and shook his head. Roland disappeared under the overhanging porch. A.J. lifted his head enough to see that Robbie was standing at the north window, looking out. A.J. bent over and headed under the rectangular window above the sofa. He could get off a good shot from here if he had to. He decided to move to the south window and watch through the tall potted plant he'd stationed there after the interview.

The signal for Larry to exit the closet and capture Robbie was a shot fired in the air. A.J.'s safety was off. His finger rested against the trigger. Now, all he could do was watch and wait.

Robbie hit Miss Gertie, and A.J. cringed.

Robbie pointed his gun at his mother on the floor. "You're gonna die just like *her,* Rosie!" He swung around and slapped Gertie again.

The blood on his hand caught his attention.

Panting, he brought his hand close to his face as he stared at the red streaks. He wiped his hand on Gertie's shoulder. She wanted to cry over the loss of this precious young man who was her blood, to weep over the injustices done to a child unable to fight against the terror in his own home.

The pain in her head was raw and unforgiving. When Robbie grabbed her hair and yanked her head back, she groaned and opened her eyes.

"Now that's better." Robbie spoke in a deeper voice. He shoved her away, backed up, and sat on the windowsill. The gun dangled from his right hand. "You don't know what happened, do you, Rosie?" Still, the deep voice of an older man.

With her head buzzing, Gertie didn't know if he wanted her to answer him, so she said nothing.

"Well, you're gonna listen to all of it!" The child was back. "You're gonna know what you did to me! What you did to your own flesh and blood." At the word 'blood,' a dazed look crossed Robbie's face. He held his hand up in front of his face again. "It's all gone," he whispered in awe.

"Robbie, I-I didn't know you."

Wildly, he shook the gun at her. "Don't call me 'Robbie,' Rosie! I'm not yours!" He jumped up and down. "I'm not yours!"

Gertie figured she'd better keep her mouth shut. Robbie was past being able to be soothed, past understanding. Her head ached. Her stomach was queasy. She reckoned it didn't really matter that much, seeing as how she wasn't going to be alive to have to deal with any of it.

"Are you listening to me?"

When had he moved? He was so close, she could feel his breath on her face. "Your eyes are so much like your sister's."

"Robbie?"

He stiffened as his head jerked toward the front door. Allison stood on the other side of the screen door.

"Robbie?"

Shaking, he rubbed his eyes, tilted his head to one side, and looked again. The little boy was back. "Allison?"

The screen door opened, squawking as if to warn her off. Her face was pale as she looked at the gun in his hand. "Robbie?"

Then she saw the woman near the television and gasped, "Oh, my God, Robbie!" and started to crouch beside her.

"No, Ally, NO! You can't be here!" He wildly waved the gun at her. "Get back. Rosie's not dead yet." He looked at Gertie, then at their mother sprawled in a heap, and started to sob. "GO, Ally! Rosie—"

"Robbie, stop it! Why did you do this?"

Wide-eyed, his glazed eyes stared at his mother. "Mother's dead now, Allison. Mother's dead."

"Mother?" Allison shook her head, glanced at Gertie. "Gram?"

Robbie screamed, jumped up and down as he pointed the gun at Allison. "Don't call her Gram! She's Rosie! Rosie hurt all of us."

"Robbie."

At the sound of his voice, Robbie jerked as if he'd been shot. He slowly turned toward the kitchen, his breathing quick and shallow, his eyes glassy. Tormented, he closed his eyes and shook his head and looked again at the man standing in the back door with a gun in the hand that rested casually against his pant leg.

Robbie swayed, wiped his forehead with his gun hand and, with a wan smile, took a step toward him.

Gertie knew it was his brother, Brian, just as she'd known somehow that it was Brian in the truck and Brian at Winnie Sue's window. Instinctively, she wanted to warn him, shield him, but there was no shielding anyone tonight.

He made no move to use his weapon as he stepped into the dining area. "Robbie," he said gently, quietly, soothingly. "I'm here. Everything's going to be okay now."

Gertie couldn't believe the transformation. From a raging bull to a little boy and back again, from black eyes filled with anger to brown eyes filled with obvious love.

"I tried, Brian. I tried to kill her, but she wouldn't stay dead." Robbie gasped and held his breath as tears streamed down his face. "Rosie won't stay dead, Brian."

Carefully, Brian took two more steps toward his brother, stopped at the open closet door, turned and looked into the eyes of a policeman. Their gazes connected for a second, then Brian kicked the door shut with his boot.

Robbie jumped and swung the gun up. Seeing only his big brother, he whimpered and lowered his arm.

Allison eased down beside Gertie Jansen and grabbed her hand.

Brian took another step toward his brother. "I know you tried." He wanted to wrap his arms around his little brother and soothe him and tell him that the world wasn't a bad place, that all fathers didn't abuse and beat their sons. He was very much afraid it was too late for Robbie to hear any words of truth.

Brian glanced at the woman lying on the floor and recognized her from pictures. He hoped Robbie didn't notice the pulse throbbing in their mother's throat or the lack of blood on her. He took another step toward him.

Robbie snarled as the shadows of evil crawled back into his face. He pointed the gun at Gertie. "She won't stay DEAD!"

Robbie swung his straightened arm at Brian, the gun cocked, his hand shaking. "Don't come any closer. It's Rosie. It's Rosie!" Frantic again, he pointed the gun at Gertie, then at Brian, then Gertie.

"I know, but I didn't come to see her. I came to see you."

"Me?" His face softened. A little smile tipped up the corner of his mouth. "You came to see me?"

Brian cursed himself for leaving his brother and sister when he was younger. He'd had no choice but to get out. But at what price? He'd abandoned Robbie and Ally just as their worthless mother had and left them to deal with their father alone.

He'd just been a kid himself at fourteen and didn't know the first thing about saving his siblings from the man. He knew now that he shouldn't have been put in the position of having to choose between *them* and *living*. He'd actually thought that if he left, then the abuse would end, since he was his father's favorite target. He didn't know, one way or another, what had happened after he left.

But he knew now, with his father's madness in Robbie's eyes, that the violence hadn't stopped. "Yes, just you, Robbie." He was almost there, just another six feet.

Robbie took one step back, his straightened arm swinging from Brian to Rosie, back and forth, as if he couldn't decide which one needed his attention. "Allison?"

464

"Robbie, I'm right here. I'm always here for you, Robbie."

"I—" Frozen like a deer caught in a truck's headlights, Robbie stared unseeingly at his brother's slow approach, then flicked his gaze to the old woman. "Allison?"

"I'm here, Robbie."

One more step, and Brian would be close enough to touch him. "It's okay, Robbie. I'm here just for you, buddy."

But Robbie shook his head and stepped back with a pathetic sob. "I can't, Brian." The hand holding the gun on Brian shook uncontrollably. "Too much... the pain... too much."

For a moment, his pleading gaze met Allison's, then rolled to Brian's, then slashed to their grandmother as the change ripped through him. In a split second, his arm straightened as he pointed the gun at Gertie Jansen.

Brian lunged and cried, "NO!" Allison screamed as she shielded Gertie with her body, and, smiling, Robbie's gaze flicked to Allison's just as he turned the gun toward his own head and fired.

Glass shattered. Robbie slumped to the floor.

Allison screamed. With her hands violently shaking over her face, she screamed and screamed and screamed.

Larry jumped out of the closet, arms straight, gun at eye level.

A.J. opened the screen door. "Drop your weapon, Officer. Mr. McIntosh?" A.J. held out his hand, with his other hand holding a gun aimed right at Brian. "Your weapon, son?"

He handed it to A.J., then turned and bolted out the back door.

"Let him go!" A.J. yelled at Larry. "Just let him go. Miss Gertie? You all right?"

She couldn't say. She touched Robbie's cheek. It was still warm, still tear-streaked. He looked like an angel lying on her floor, his face relaxed, his eyes closed, his mouth soft as if he dreamed of cotton candy fields.

She wished she could have given him—all of them—anything but the life they'd lived.

"We need an ambulance at Gertie Jansen's cabin immediately. Two victims. One gunshot wound."

Allison looked up. "Wounds? You mean my brother's still alive?"

"Yes, as is your mother," Gertie whispered, still stroking Robbie's cheek. "A.J. shot him through the window. Robbie just grazed his head."

"I thought he—oh, Gram—I thought he killed himself."

Gertie shook her head, so grateful he hadn't. "Maybe now, he can get the help he needs. I'm willing to do whatever it takes to get him help. I just wish Brian hadn't run away."

"Stop fussing over me, Winnie Sue. I'm fine. Really." But truth be told, Gertie's head was pounding ruthlessly.

"But it's my fault. If we'd only told the truth—"

"And what? Have Robbie hurt you instead of me? That's ridiculous."

"But you wouldn't have been—"

"No, Winnie Sue." Tears gathered in Gertie's eyes. Must be all the trauma to her head. She never cried. Unless, of course, someone hurt her little sister. "I would never have done that to you. The truth is that I took care of the baby. I did my best by him."

Winnie Sue placed her hand on Gertie's arm. "And by me."

"You were only a child, barely thirteen. I wanted to kill that man. I wanted him to die for what he did to you that night. I'm ashamed to say it, but it's true. It took me a long time to forgive him, but I did."

Winnie Sue nodded. "I don't know if I ever told you—" She slipped a hankie out of her sleeve and dabbed at eyes spilling over with heavy tears. Her bottom lip trembled. "How much... it meant to me... that you were with me during the darkest hours of my life."

"I loved you. You were my baby sister. Family sticks together."

"But you took all the blame, all the shame."

"Shame? There was no shame. None of it was your fault. All the fault belonged to that monster!"

"But now A.J. and Jim know. They think *you're* the one—"

"They'll never check out my story. Rosie Jansen never existed. All will be well. You'll see." Gertie looked over at her and took her hand. "You are dear to me, Sister."

"You've proven that to me so many times."

"Well, then."

"I bought you something." Winnie Sue handed her the small box that had been sitting on the kitchen table all day.

Gertie lifted her brows. "What's this?"

"Just a little something to help me sleep at night."

Gertie opened the box and looked at a shiny white cell phone. She lifted it out of the box. "Well, I'll be."

"I have one, too. It's easy to use. Here, Sister, let me show you how it works."

The next morning, Brian stepped stealthily over the gravel and crossed to the grassy borders of Gertie's driveway. He headed up to the familiar, perfectly flat tree stump and shooed away the ground squirrel sitting on top. "Mine, little fellow."

He glanced down through the trees at her cabin as he sat. The early-morning light lay atop the mountains like a halo.

He couldn't count the number of times he'd come here to wait for her, to watch her, to be a part of her life. To remember.

Not long after he'd run away from home, he'd written a letter to 'Rosie Jansen, Little Texas, Colorado.' Accusing words from an angry and withdrawn fourteen-year-old struggling with life.

But she'd written him back, signing the letter, 'Gertie.'

He'd read that letter so many times, he'd memorized it. He wrote her again, on the streets, tired, hungry, and weary of life.

Another letter addressed to "Brian McIntosh, General Delivery, Pueblo, Colorado," arrived, and she'd asked him to come to Little Texas and stay with her. It took him months to answer that letter. But when he did, he told her everything about his family—his father, his mother's death, and his own torment.

She'd written him again, with another invitation to come to Little Texas—and her. And then the letters flowed between them; so many, he couldn't count. He'd even sent her the one picture he had of his parents. She'd told him about his father's ugly letter to her, how it had crushed her not being able to answer his hurtful questions.

Brian glanced at her cabin.

His father had been totally wrong about his mother.

Through the years, she had, quite simply, nourished Brian's soul.

He only wished Robbie could have had her love during those horrible years of living with their father. Brian was sure it would have made a difference for him, too. At least now, he would get the help he so desperately needed.

Her screen door screeched a rusty *'Good day.'* His grandmother stepped out, coffee steaming from her cup as she scanned her yards. She walked to the corner of her porch and faced the coming sun. Full of her, Brian watched, holding his breath.

Gertie knew he was there, behind her, sitting on a tree stump. It thrilled her that he had come here after last night's horrors. Did he blame her for what happened? Was it at all possible that Brian would let her love him and not just in her letters to him?

A yearning deep inside her had been born last night when Robbie was shot. After the rape, she'd become a woman unable to draw people into her heart. But she wanted a chance to prove that she could do just that, with Brian—even if he wasn't her grandson.

It was a shame that Brian's mother left Little Texas last night without a word to her children. Gertie shook her head at the thought as she went back inside, picked up the basket of wet things, and headed outside to the clothesline.

Brian moved to the right, the better to see her.

She stretched up to the line, pinched a corner of the towel over the wire, slipped a clothes pin on it, slid her hand across to the other side, pinned it. Her fingertips glided down the length of it.

Next, she popped a wadded sheet, tucked the corners, pinned it. Then she hung another towel, a pillowcase, a fitted sheet.

Life here breathed a sense of permanency. The line itself, the pins snug over it, knowing what would happen next, how she'd fold, pin, touch each piece, pause to look at the mountains, begin again.

When she finished, she eased her two fists onto her hips, faced the mountains, and didn't move a muscle for a good two minutes.

Then she picked up her basket and walked inside. Always, it was the same ritual. And always, it soothed him to watch her.

For an hour, Gertie watched him. He picked up a pebble, tossed it, kept an eye on it as it rolled a few feet. Then his gaze would fix on her cabin as he frowned like a little boy unable to gauge whether his mother was happy or unhappy with him.

He picked up another one, tossed it, glanced at her home the same way he'd looked at her at Winnie Sue's house, sad but expectant, as if he'd bust a gut if he couldn't say what was on his mind.

Biscuits were ready, as was the bacon, white gravy, scrambled eggs, coffee, and preserves. Gertie wiped her hands on her apron, walked back to the front door, and peered up. He had a stick in his hand now, scribbling in the dirt. What was traveling through his mind? She figured it was high time she found out.

Brian couldn't explain why he stood and headed down the hill toward her house. He wanted to stop at every step but couldn't. He needed something. *From her.* Or maybe he needed to give her something. He didn't know.

Almost to her yard, the screen door opened. "Hello, Brian."

He pulled back as she stepped out. Tears stung his eyes.

She took a step toward him. "You're welcome to come in and have some breakfast with me."

His feet seemed concreted to the dirt. Weariness swept over him. His heart pounded a heavy beat, and his throat tightened. Bone-tired in his soul, he flicked a glance at her again, this woman he'd never actually met. This woman his father had hated.

This woman he loved.

"Biscuits and gravy, bacon, fresh-made coffee. Blackberry jam I made myself."

For some reason he couldn't explain, Brian glanced over his shoulder, his heart swelling as he stared at the stump he'd just left. Years of pain and abuse had taken a part of his soul from him.

But now, the words of a psalm entered his mind: "He restoreth my soul." Brian no longer stood in the shadow of the father who had taught him to hate himself, because *she* had taught him about acceptance and love.

"Come in, son, if you've a mind to. Stay as long as you'd like."

The screen door groaned open, and he glanced toward the cabin. She held the door open for him, a look on her face that spoke of expectancy, joy, and sorrow all at once. She smiled and nodded at him, as if telling him he could do it. He could come to her, and she would wait until he did.

But it took more than he could manage to take that first step. Tears overflowed. A little sob escaped from behind his hand as he tried to hide his face and his shame.

The screen door slammed.

He looked up.

She was coming toward him. Tears fell down her face as she walked down the steps with a sure foot.

Brian stepped back—and still she came. He sobbed. Tried to stop but couldn't. Then she was in front of him. All the years of hate and pain and grief washed over him as she held out her hand.

For a moment, he simply stared at it through his watery gaze.

Then he looked into her eyes. For the first time in his life, what he needed, what he'd yearned for and never had, stood before him.

He reached out. Almost touched her. And then, before he knew it, she was tugging him toward her cabin. Not a word was spoken as they walked up the steps. She reached to open the door, but he nudged her hand away and opened it for her. She looked up and smiled at him.

When they walked inside, she headed for the north window so they could admire the glorious view of her world. He stood there, soaking in the vision he'd seen so many times while she went into the kitchen and fixed their plates.

"Here, Brian. Sit, now, son. Let's enjoy this bounty the Lord's given us today. And after we do, we'll visit with my sister, Winnie Sue. She wants to tell you a story."

Luke heard her car coming up his driveway. August was a terrible time of the year for Sarah to see the panhandle for the first time. It was hot and dry and miserable. He'd stayed at her parents' home for over five weeks while she healed from her injuries, and it had been a month since he'd seen her. That was a month too long.

He rushed to the front door in time to see her get out of her car. Man alive, the sight of her made his heart go wild.

He whooped, ran out the door, jumped over the steps, scooped her up, and spun her in a circle. Laughing, he stopped and kissed her like a madman. "I've been waiting all day for that. One more." He took it slower and deeper. "Just what I needed." He was pleased when she melted against him and pulled his head down so she could enjoy another long kiss.

"I've missed you so much."

Words he needed to hear. "I've missed you more. How did your arm and foot make the trip?"

"An occasional twinge of pain but that's it. Almost one hundred percent healed." She turned around. "Your house is beautiful. And big. I've always loved log cabins. Where's Molly?"

"She's at my brother's ranch. She goes there every day. We'll see her later."

"Good. What's the construction?"

"A surprise." He walked with her to the skeleton of a small building in the back. "A shop for a glass maker, just in case, y'know, one happened to be here and needed—umph!"

She'd grabbed him in a tight hug. "Oh, Luke! I love it! Thank you for this. You're so thoughtful."

"Well." He was embarrassed. Her reaction was exactly what he'd hoped for. "I wanted you to have your special place to work when you're here."

"It's perfect. Thank you."

"Come on. Let's get you out of this sun." He led her into the barn where a mist promptly cooled them off.

"A misting system in a barn?"

"It's for my horse, Pepper. He was restless earlier today, so I turned him out for just a few minutes. It's too hot for him to be out long. The mist is above his stall and at both ends of this aisle." He flipped a switch, and the barn lit up.

Sarah looked over at him. "It was in the darkest blackness that I first realized I loved you."

"The cave."

She nodded. "You held me after we saw Robbie." She reached for his hand. "And when I was in the cellar, I was terrified at first. It was worse than any nightmare I'd ever imagined. But God helped me out of there, and you found me. I'm not afraid of the dark anymore."

"And you taught me about forgiving myself for my Dad's death. We've come a long way, Sarah." He drew her close. "I knew I loved you the moment I saw you."

"That's a bunch of hooey. You thought I was a brat."

"Any direction I head after that remark will get me in trouble." He led her past some trees and stopped. In the far distance, his brother Mac's two-story, ten-thousand-square-foot log cabin sat in a wide valley. The chapel his family built in the 1880s was situated down from the house at the edge of some trees, with a gazebo sitting near the huge lake in front of the chapel.

Luke gestured toward Mac's property. "Did you notice the lake?"

"Oh, yes. It's lovely."

"Mac's house?" He picked her up.

"Magnificent." Laughing, her arms encircled his neck.

"The chapel?" He lowered his mouth and kissed her.

"It's beautiful," she whispered against his mouth.

"It's functional."

"Is it?"

"Church services on Sunday, Bible studies, funerals."

"We don't like funerals."

Luke shook his head and kissed her again. "Weddings."

She gasped playfully. "Not weddings, *too*?"

"Yep."

"Any while I'm here?"

"Yours, if you'll have me."

"Is that a proposal, Mr. McKenzie?"

"Yes."

She grinned up at him.

"Is that a yes, Miss Morgan?"

"Yes!"

He war-whooped and swung her around and around. "I love you, Sarah." He kissed her again.

"I love you, Luke. You, uh, you didn't name your ranch 'The Sweating Like a Pig Ranch,' did you?"

"You've already said 'yes,' so it's too late to change it."

Grinning, he carried her toward the house. "We've been invited to the main house for dinner with Mac and Marianne. They're excited about meeting you. Marianne's pregnant with their first baby. It's due in November."

"I'm looking forward to meeting them. Do you want me to call my parents and tell them to come on down to Texas?"

"Yes." An impatient man, he stopped. "When?" He caught her scent and nuzzled her neck. He was, quite simply, totally lost in her.

"Well, time's a-wastin', McKenzie. How about Friday, four days from now?"

"Don't you want a big wedding with all the trimmings?"

"No. I just want you. Now tell me what you really named your ranch."

"The L & S Ranch."

"Oh!" She hugged him warmly. "I'm a ranch!"

Laughing, he opened his front door. "I'll carry you over the threshold when you're my wife and not a second sooner." He set her down and led her inside. "Welcome home, Sarah."

All of Little Texas was gearing up for the wedding of Miss Winnie Sue Jansen and Mr. Carlton Mitchell Jefferson. The week before, Jim and Elva Lee had tied the knot, and many were thinking something suspicious could be thriving in their drinking water, especially with the news that Penny and A.J. Banks was expecting their first child in the spring.

Miss Winnie Sue's wedding dress arrived at Myra's Dress Shop. It had come in two days before the wedding and, of course, the bride had to try it on, friends had to fuss over it, and the hang of it had to be just so.

"Miss Winnie Sue, I declare," said her friend Myra as she tugged on the lace sleeves and straightened the floor-length white chiffon folds. "You are a beautiful bride."

The wedding day finally arrived. Gertie was beside herself with joy at having her new teeth firmly in her mouth and having Carl Jefferson take her sister off her hands. And him a younger man, at that. Three years younger than Winnie Sue.

Gertie laughed as she remembered the angst her little sister went through after discovering their age difference.

"Why, people will think I'm desperate."

"Well, truth be told—"

"I am *not* desperate to be married, Miss Gertie, but," her eyes grew soft, "I am so desperate to marry this particular man. We have two new grandbabies and another on the way." Winnie Sue sighed wistfully. "Oh, Miss Gertie, he is a dear, isn't he?"

Gertie couldn't help but snicker. The woman was a goner. But he was worse, unashamedly singing her praises everywhere and truly believing the sun rose and set in his Winnie Sue.

And Gertie supposed it did.

For when the newlyweds came out of the church beaming and blushing with flowers falling around them and Mrs. Jefferson's white veil pulled back so that everyone had a clear shot of her husband devouring her right there on the steps of Mountain View Church, her smile was as bright as any sun Gertie Jansen had ever seen.

Brian sat on his stump and admired the yellow ribbon of light outlining the mountains. There was no other place he'd rather be than right here, watching the sun rise.

Aunt Gertie opened the screen door and waved at him.

He stood and headed down to her as the door slammed shut behind her.

"I didn't hear you get up, son."

Brian nodded. "I tried extra hard to be quiet this morning."

"Well, you were." She glanced toward the mountains for a long moment or two. "Breakfast is ready."

"Good. I'm starving." He walked up the steps. "After we eat, I thought I'd chop some more wood. We sure go through the firewood."

"It's been cold at night, and you like your fireplace."

"Especially when you sit with me and tell me stories about my family." He joined her at the edge of the porch and draped an arm around her shoulders. She settled close to him, and together, they admired the morning's glory.

"Oh, your cousins Walter and Mike called. They want to hire you again for another project. A renovation near the bank. Said your carpenter skills are the best. And, God help us, your grandmother called. She says it's time to prune the roses."

"Oh, no." He chuckled. "Not the roses again."

"She's determined that we learn how to tend to them. Well, we better get this breakfast eaten so we'll have the strength to face them." She grinned up at him.

He grinned back and opened the door for her. "After you."

Deception at Fairfield Ranch

ONE

Her heart pounded so fast, she could hardly breathe, but she'd said it. She'd finally said it. And the devil take Kyle McKenzie for all the misery he'd put her through!

"Margot, did you mean—" Kyle looked as if he'd just been sucker-punched. "You're saying you wanted them to *kill* her?"

Margot shivered and stepped deeper into the dark walk-in closet, wishing it would swallow her up and spit her out somewhere else. Anywhere else.

"Is that what you meant?"

Gritting her teeth, she covered her ears.

"Margot?"

Squeezed her eyes shut.

"Margot?"

Stop it! Stop it!

"You wanted them to kill April?"

Yes! Yes! That's exactly what I meant!

His words hissed at her from where he stood like a sentry blocking her escape. She wanted to run from him, from the words, from the truth, from their life. She wanted to screech at him that it was all *his* fault, that he'd sacrificed everything when he'd let their daughter live. None of this was supposed to happen. She wasn't supposed to be a mother. She wasn't supposed to love her daughter.

She wasn't the kind of woman who could.

"Margot?"

Her hands shook as she cupped her elbows and fought the need to rock herself. Like a living thing, his words slithered over the carpet toward her feet. *Kill her? Kill her?* They pricked at her heels on their way up her legs. She took a frenzied step away from them, tightened her jaw, and willed nothing to matter anymore.

"Margot." A whisper this time, imploring. He took a soft carpeted step toward her.

She spun around, unable to bear his pity or his compassion or his need to comfort what couldn't be comforted. "I hate you for letting her live."

Kyle jerked as if she'd slapped him. His eyes widened. His jaw dropped.

She wanted to sneer at him, to yell, "You should have known. You should have *known!*"

"You hate me?"

This time, she smirked. The power of letting him go, of letting it all go, surged through her. It hadn't been so very difficult after all. "Are you surprised, Kyle?" She brushed past him. "You really didn't know?"

He followed her into the bedroom like a puppy. "But I thought—"

She pivoted as anger sliced through her. "*You* thought! *You* thought! It's always been about *you!* Did you ask me what *I* wanted, what *I* thought? No! You just shoved and shoved—" She gasped, pressed her fingers against her mouth, and turned her back to him.

"But God blessed us with a—"

"Oh, that's rich." She threw up her arms. "By all means, bring God in on your side. Use him for leverage. You always have." She slapped the closet door so hard, it slammed against the wall.

"*Bring* God in? But we've—"

"No, *you* have. God's always been your thing, not mine." She grunted. "At least you could have picked a god who could give your kid a *complete* small bowel. Pretty pathetic, huh, Kyle? Your God making a kid without the proper plumbing?"

Kyle collapsed onto the edge of the bed, his head in his hands, his mind in a fog. Where had all this hatred come from? He watched Margot stalk out of the closet, a suitcase rolling behind her with a travel tote perched on top.

"I played the part of the dutiful wife, going to church with you in this sad excuse for a town." The luggage smacked the bed. "It was a waste of my time." She leaned over him. "But the dutiful wife keeps her mouth shut, doesn't she? You don't *ask* her opinion. You just *decide!* Or—" she whispered, her breath brushing the area just below his ear. "If she can't hear or talk—" she shrugged innocently, "—all the better now, isn't it?"

"You were unconscious. I couldn't ask you." He clearly remembered those anxious days and nights a year ago, pacing, praying, wondering who would die first, his wife or his baby.

The doctors *had* given him a choice about April. Her life would be tough, they'd said. She would have to fight for it. He'd chosen to give her a chance, assuming her mother would want the same for her.

But it was obvious—now—that he'd been dead wrong.

Margot yanked open a dresser drawer. It plunged to the floor, spilling her clothes. He took a step toward her, but she glared at him and gritted her teeth. "Don't."

Kyle stepped back. Her eyes. He'd never seen such an evil look. Two years ago, his mother had tried to warn him. *"I'll support you, son, in your decision to marry her, but something isn't right. She's not... I think she's... your dad's only been gone five months. Give yourself some time to heal before you jump into this."*

But he had jumped—and he'd been falling ever since.

Margot fell to her knees, scooped up the scattered clothes in quick, jerky movements, and tossed them into her luggage. The air pulsed with her anger.

Kyle stood helplessly by, his gaze glued to a spot of bright red in her bag. "What—?" He cleared his parched throat, his voice suddenly raspy. "What are you doing?"

She jerked another drawer out, dumped its contents into her luggage, and tossed it on top of the other drawer, the scraping thud like a slamming door.

"Margot, what are you doing?"

She turned around, raised her brows. "Who, me? Are you talking to little ol' me?"

"Cut it out."

She threw a hairbrush at her bag. "The only thing that should have been *cut out* was when you decided your daughter would have a miserable life and me right along with her!"

Kyle slammed his hands into his pockets, dropped his head, and sighed. For just an instant, he saw himself in the same position two years ago, standing in February's bitter cold, looking down at his father's coffin, remembering so clearly the total emptiness he had felt at that moment. And, he had to admit, almost every moment since.

Shaking off the memory, he watched Margot slam around their bedroom. "I only let her live. That's all."

"That's *all?*" Margot disappeared into the bathroom and came out with her hands full of bottles. "That's *all?* Well, then, let's examine her life and mine, shall we?" She blew her bangs out of her eyes. "What kind of a life has she had?" The bottles landed next to the luggage and rolled off the bed.

"She's survived."

Margot grunted and glared. "Is that what you call it?"

Granted, April wasn't like other children. She couldn't eat or drink or crawl or sit up by herself. ER visits were the norm, infections from where the feeding tube attached to her body. At least he didn't have to drive the forty-five minutes to the Houston hospital for care. St. Michael's here in Granston was an excellent medical center.

The toughest part was her pain. His baby couldn't tell him where it hurt, and it broke his heart. At those times, he'd gather her into his arms and rock her and sing to her and love her completely.

But mentally and emotionally, she was like any normal little girl, her eyes wide and eager when she spotted a kitten, or afraid when her cousins' little dachshund BeeBee charged at her, or delighted when Kyle sneaked up behind her and asked, "Where's my April? Where's my little angel?" When his head popped into view, she would giggle and bounce at him, and his world would be complete with the wonder of her.

There were bad days. Lately, there seemed to be more of them. But mostly, her days were good. He made himself open his mouth and say the words. He had to hear them, had to believe they were true, had to believe he'd made the right decision. "She's had so many good days."

"What would you know about her days? You're never here."

"She's our baby. I wanted to give her a chance."

"Oh, well, just shoot me. There's that nasty word again. *I! I* wanted. Not *we.*"

Anger slapped him in the face like a blast of cold water. He moved to block her path. "Do you think I *wanted* her to be in pain? To have to be fed through some *tube?*"

Glaring, she walked around him.

"To have to endure surgery after surgery, waiting for the day she has to have a transplant or die? Do you think I wanted this for *you?* Tying yourself to this house and... and..." Embarrassment made him fight the sudden, stinging tears. His voice lowered to a whisper. "Knowing I couldn't fix it for her or for you?"

She stopped and stared at him. She looked shocked. Didn't she know how much all of this had hurt him? Surely, she didn't think his facade of being strong meant anything other than what it was—his feeble attempt at normalcy? "Margot, honey."

She seemed very close to baring her teeth. "Don't *honey* me." Angrily, she zipped the luggage. "Her first year was on me." She smirked and lifted her eyebrows, her shoulders. "You wanted her? You got her." She zipped the tote bag. "With my blessings."

Her hands were shaking.

He leaped at the vulnerability. "You can't mean that." *Please, God.* He took a step in her direction.

Her eyes narrowed. "I despise you."

The look on her face as much as the words stopped him cold. He didn't know his heart could physically hurt like this.

She settled the tote on top of her luggage. "She's going to die, you know." She stormed past him, pulling her luggage behind her.

For the life of him, he couldn't make his feet work, or his mouth, or his hands reach out and stop her. If his brain hadn't made his heart beat, it would've stopped the second she walked out the door.

Her luggage chugged down the stairs like a giant timepiece ticking away the seconds before an explosion.

His chest ached. He could hardly breathe, waiting for something to stop her. He held his breath. And listened. And hoped.

The chugging stopped as the wheels moved across the carpet. He stared at a picture of a smiling Margot on the nightstand and listened to what sounded like a closet door slamming and quick steps stabbing the tiled hallway floor. Then silence.

The front door opened. He tensed, waiting for it to slam.

They had had their problems. He'd known for a long time that Margot wasn't happy, but he didn't know how to fix it. And he'd tried. God knew he had tried. But how did a man make things right when the mountain on top of him was so unbearably heavy?

He'd suggested counseling with their pastor. She had refused.

He'd suggested a weekend away. "Without April?" she'd replied, and the familiar guilt consumed him.

Countless times, he'd reached for her in the middle of the night, only to have her shove him away in disgust as if he were a filthy dog.

But not once had he ever considered that she would walk out. How, in all that was right, did a mother justify leaving a daughter who needed her so much?

The front door slammed.

He tensed and looked toward the nursery. When April whimpered, he strode down the hallway, thankful she was awake because he desperately needed to hold her.

He walked to her crib and eased his hands under all thirteen pounds of her. This was his life, his love. This precious baby was his gift from the very heart of God.

"Da-da." Her brown eyes seemed enormous in her tiny face.

His heart ached with an incredibly boundless love. "There's my girl," he crooned, lifted her, and nuzzled her neck.

He couldn't stop the tears, any more than he could make her mother come back home and love them both enough to stay.

Kyle could hardly think. He managed to call his secretary and tell her he was taking the day off for a long weekend, as well as Monday and Tuesday.

His next call was to his mother. He told her everything.

"You'll need a nurse to care for April," Joan announced. "Do you remember Natalie Palmer, the dancer? *Swan Lake* a few Christmases ago? Long blonde hair, blue eyes, slim, about five-six. She's also an R.N., has a couple other degrees. The Palmers of Crayton Cove."

One of the wealthiest families in Texas. "Just what I need. Some rich woman who can't decide what she's going to be when she grows up. She won't do it, Mom."

"She's in my Bible study group on Tuesdays. I'll call her and set up an appointment for you to visit with her sometime today, maybe even this morning."

His financial manager phoned. "Your joint checking account was cleaned out yesterday just before closing."

His head. Someone screamed inside his head. Kyle squeezed his eyes shut and found his voice. "How much?"

"Four hundred eighty-three thousand."

Kyle leaned against the kitchen counter. His hand spanned his forehead, and his fingers dug into his temples. "Close everything. Anything that has her name on it." He paused, added, "Now, everything," and quietly hung up.

His phone dinged with a text message. *Natalie will meet with you this morning at her home at your convenience. I'll be at your house in about thirty minutes to stay with April. Love you. Mom.*

Kyle decided to stop at Maudie's Coffee Shop on his way to Natalie Palmer's home. He'd been stopping by Maudie's before work for years. Most mornings, he'd sit with his good friend, Grayson, who met him there on his way to work, too.

It was long past their usual meeting time, so the visit would have to wait until tomorrow.

But today, instead of going to work, he'd leave everything in his brother Kevin's capable hands and maybe sit in a quiet corner at Maudie's and try to figure out what had just happened with Margot.

He wrote his mother a reply text, and then the doorbell rang.

He glanced at April sitting in her highchair. "I'll be right back, sweetheart." He hit SEND, made his way to the front door, and opened it to a lanky man dressed in western clothes, sporting a white hat and a grim expression.

"Kyle McKenzie?"

The cowboy reached behind his back and came out with a white envelope. It took a moment for it to register what the man held.

No.

Kyle stepped back and looked into the man's eyes, hoping to see something other than the truth there.

"Sir, are you Kyle McKenzie?"

When he nodded, his head wobbled like an anvil teetering on his shoulders.

"Consider yourself served." The process server quickly handed him the envelope and left.

Kyle stood in the open door, letting in the sweltering southeast Texas heat, and stared at the envelope. He opened it, took out the papers, and read the black words, "In the Matter of the Marriage of..."

He slapped the papers against his hand, blew out a long breath, and eased back against the door. A car drove by and, even from a distance of fifty yards, he could hear the slurping sounds of the hot, sticky asphalt as it did. Into his line of vision came a stout pair of legs wrapped in support hose walking down the sidewalk toward his gate.

"Kyle? Honey?"

His gaze made the journey up to Mrs. Wilson's eyes. His neighbor frowned at him, a hand lifted in a cautious wave. He made himself come out of the mush, flutter the papers at her.

She cupped a hand around her mouth. "Is April all right?"

Shaking with sprouting anger, Kyle swallowed hard and bit out, "She's fine, Mrs. Wilson." *She's going to die, you know.* "She's doing just fine. I have to go inside now."

He stopped Mrs. Wilson's forward advance by stepping back and gently closing the door. Nausea swept over him. "Oh, God," he whispered. "Please help me."

By all means, bring God in on your side, Kyle. Use Him for leverage. You always have.

He felt the papers in his hand. How could she do this? Whatever happened to talking things out? Whatever happened to loving each other?

She's going to die, you know. She's going to die.

"No!" He crumpled the papers into a fist and slammed them into the door. His daughter was dying, his family was being ripped apart, and there was no way he could fix it.

Margot stood in front of the dressing room mirror in the beautiful red suit. The dowdy housewife of the handsome and rich Kyle McKenzie had simply vanished. No one would recognize her now. She hadn't dolled herself up like this in a long time, with her hair no longer in a ponytail but flowing across her shoulders, bouncy and full. Her eyes were lined; her lashes thick with black mascara; the brown eye shadow looked perfect with her coloring.

She puckered her bright red lips at herself and smiled.

And the jewels! Her ears sparkled; her neck sparkled; her wrists sparkled; her fingers sparkled. Everything about her sparkled. She laughed. She felt so *alive!*

She paid for everything in cash. With long confident strides, she walked through the mall like a glittering model in her four-inch heels.

People stared. Let them look. She looked great, and she knew it.

She drove to the seedy motel and got out. The scarred maroon door slammed shut behind her. She hated staying in a room that smelled of stale cigarette smoke, and everything was old and used. Gordon thought no one would look for her at this nasty, roadside dump.

"How much?" He yelled from the restroom.

"How much what?" Dropping her boxes, she tossed her purse on the bed and braced herself for the coming confrontation. "I told you we have enough. Almost three million five, baby. It's our biggest haul ever." She expected a flash of temper from him, and it happened when his hand slammed into the wall.

"I *told* you it wasn't enough! We need *more!*"

"Then you marry him. I'm done." She fell onto the old mattress and rolled out of the sagging middle and onto her side, away from Gordon. Guilt gnawed at her, and still he wasn't satisfied. He'd been satisfied in the past. Why not now, when she'd given up everything?

She wanted her baby. It didn't matter that April was sick or that she might die or that she herself hadn't had a life outside that suffocating house for two years. She wanted her baby. And Kyle. *Oh, God, I miss her so much. I miss him. Please forgive me. Please, please forgive me.*

She heard a click just as Gordon stalked around the end of the bed toward her. She gasped and stared wide-eyed at the gun muzzled with a silencer in his hand. She dug her heels into the bedspread and frantically crawled on her hands and feet toward the back wall. "No, Gordon," she wailed, wildly shaking her head. "Don't! Please!"

Gordon backhanded her, hard. "*My* way, baby. You didn't do it *my* way. You *know* I can't have that! This is *your* fault!" His expression softened as he leveled the gun at her. "All the world's an ice cream cone, remember?" he whispered to her. "It's our job to grab it and run before it melts. But, baby, yours is all gone." And then he fired.

Her body slumped as if an exhausted sleep had overcome her.

Except, her eyes were still open. Gordon cupped his hand over them and stepped back. She made a pretty little picture, lying on the bed, dressed up in her fancy red outfit. It was a good color on her.

He leaned over and whispered, "Thanks, love, for everything." He plucked off the glittering jewelry and muttered, "Nice."

He grabbed his overnight bag, stuffed the gun and jewelry inside, and headed for the restroom and the open window. He'd already planned his escape, and it was foolproof.

The pity of it wasn't that she was dead, but that he had tired of her after she'd had that blasted brat. The baby had ruined everything between them. Now the brat was alive, and Margot was dead. Where was the justice in that? That disgusting kid had killed her mother as surely as if she'd fired the gun herself.

It was really *her* fault, and she would pay for it.

It wouldn't be too long before he'd need more money. He could blow through three point four mil in no time.

But why wait until he was depleted?

That wasn't managing his money well. He'd come back very soon and see what the little cripple could fetch for him.

He shimmied through the restroom window. Racing into the woods, he headed for the car he'd bought earlier that day. He opened the door, looked over his shoulder, and slipped inside. Now, for the fun part. He plucked the bag out from under the seat and started his transformation.

Five minutes later, he smiled into the mirror, tugged on the gray hairpiece, and playfully wiggled his white brows. "Why, hello, Grandpa. Whatcha say we vanish again, ol' boy?"

He chuckled. No one would ever find Gordon Jesser.

Taking his time, he pulled out onto the two-lane road, careful not to do anything that would draw attention to an old man out for a drive on such a fine, sunny morning.

TWO

Natalie Palmer walked into her mother's office with a spring in her step. "Good morning, Mother. Will you join me for breakfast?"

Regally, Regina Palmer stood, closed her leather briefcase, and arched a brow. "Ernestine served me hours ago, dear. I must go now. Several stops today. The Library Council could use your help this morning."

Not again. "I'm sorry, Mother. I have an appointment in a few minutes." With Joan's son, Kyle McKenzie. This morning was perfect for meeting with him about his daughter, April, since she had no other plans for the day.

"Excuse me, Miss Natalie," the maid Celeste said as she stepped into the room. "Mr. Kyle McKenzie is here to see you."

"What business do you have with this man, Natalie Grace?"

Natalie turned too quickly toward her grandmother's accusing voice. With practiced ease, she closed her mouth and straightened her back in a manner that would please her. Standing just inside another door, her grandmother silently stared at her, mouth pursed, back rigid—clear indications of disapproval.

Natalie opened her mouth to respond but her mother said, "McKenzies? Do we know any McKenzies?"

"Yes. His mother's in my Bible study on Tuesd—"

"McKenzie Engineering. Ranching. Oil," her grandmother stated, her gaze squarely on Natalie. "The patriarch, Gerald McKenzie, was murdered two years ago."

Natalie's eyes widened. *Murdered?*

Her grandmother smiled in triumph. "Kyle McKenzie owns Fairfield Ranch, his maternal grandfather's prosperous ranch, oil rights intact. Why is he here, Natalie Grace?"

She resisted a long-suffering sigh. "I have business with him." She turned to the maid. "Refreshments would be nice, Celeste." She dismissed her with a smile and looked at her grandmother. "I'm not going to discuss this right now."

"Don't you dismiss *me*, child. I asked you a question."

"I am not a child. Please excuse me. I need to see to my guest."

She'd learned long ago to be concise and make a hasty-yet-dignified retreat when dealing with her grandmother—although her tennis shoes making little squeaking sounds as she quickly walked away wasn't dignified. She was sure they announced her arrival to Mr. McKenzie as she reached the doorway of the parlor. She clasped her hands and took a deep breath. Satisfied she was ready, she took the last two steps into the room.

And almost stumbled.

Good gracious, but the man was gorgeous.

Easily six-four. Sky-blue eyes framed by curly black lashes. Rugged. Square jaw. Short, black hair trimmed neatly. A man's man. But a touch of something she couldn't readily identify resided in his eyes. Sadness? Exhaustion? Anxiety? Probably a little of all three, considering his wife's desertion.

His shirt and slacks seemed smoothed to perfection, a nice complement to his outdoorsy tan and lean muscles. When she held out her hand, his vague attempt at a smile failed miserably in conveying any warmth at all. The little wrinkles beside his eyes merely blinked and disappeared. His handshake was firm, however. His stance, stiff.

All business. Good. If she had seen anything resembling flirtatious behavior, she would have turned the man down flat. "Mr. McKenzie, how nice to meet you."

"Miss Palmer. A pleasure."

His hand in hers was overly warm. It appeared he was as nervous as she was. "Please." She indicated he should sit. He waited for her to take a seat first. Manners were always a plus.

He set his cowboy hat on the sofa beside him as he sat and then leaned toward her. "I understand my mother spoke to you about my daughter."

She kept her gaze firmly on his eyes. "Yes."

"I need a pediatric nurse to come into my home and take care of her. She has—"

"You cannot be serious, Natalie Grace."

Natalie wanted to hang her head at the staccato words behind her. She turned instead. Her grandmother stood in the doorway, frowning at Kyle McKenzie. Natalie rose and turned to her guest, who now

486

stood. "Mr. McKenzie, Lenore Carsdale, my mother's mother."

Her grandmother ever-so-slightly inclined her head at Kyle, more, it seemed, in condescension than greeting.

"Mr. McKenzie." Her grandmother's hands rested on top of her cane. Her piercing gray eyes narrowed at the man. She slowly lifted her chin as if she were about to make a decree. "What you ask of my granddaughter is absolutely unthinkable. Her position in this community, in this *state*, will not allow it."

"Mrs. Carsdale, I'm merely—"

"Grandmother, this is not the time—"

"You're quite right, my dear, this is *not*—"

"Grandmother!"

Good breeding finally re-visited Lenore Carsdale, and she haughtily looked at Natalie. "We will continue this in private." She nodded once at their guest and left the room.

Natalie wanted to crawl into a hole. Clasping her hands, she turned to Kyle and hoped he wouldn't notice the blush heating her neck. "Please forgive her behavior."

He held up his hand and took a step toward the door. "I didn't think this would work," he offered. "I'm sorry to have bothered you."

"But I haven't given you my answer. May I have the day to think about it? I'll get back with you this afternoon around four o'clock if that's convenient."

Another step toward the door. "I'll look forward to your call."

"I wasn't thinking of calling." Amazing, how quickly hope could spring into someone's eyes. But there it was, looking right at her. "Are you a praying man, Mr. McKenzie?"

"More from desperation lately than anything else. You?"

Nodding, she said, "I'm so grateful He's willing to listen to me in desperate times, too." He joined her as she indicated they should walk toward the front door. He opened the door for her, and she caught a hint of aftershave and looked up at him. "I look forward to meeting April at four or so, if she's awake."

"Thank you." He looked relieved. "I'll see you then." He nodded once at her and left.

She watched him slip his white cowboy hat on and walk briskly to his truck. She slowly shut the door behind him.

Direction, finally. It had been three months since she'd involved herself in a project that was truly meaningful to her—other than, of course, volunteering in pediatrics at the hospital. She loved children. Taking care of a child like April was perfect for her.

She glanced at the door leading to the hallway where she'd last seen her grandmother. She then considered the door hidden under the stairs that opened to an elevator to the upstairs rooms and walked toward it.

In her room, she changed her clothes. A trip to the beach house— with warm sand under her feet and warm water nudging her toes and a little advice from her cousin—should help her decide what to do about Kyle McKenzie and his daughter. Although, she felt in her heart that she had already made the decision.

The sound of a car pulling into his driveway had Kyle moving aside the lace curtains covering the parlor windows. Margot had insisted on lace. "So I can see the world out there," she'd said when she put them up. Heavier curtains hung at opposite ends of the windows. They were never closed.

"Two men dressed in suits are walking toward my house," Kyle spoke into his phone. "They look like police." He'd dealt with detectives the first year after his father's murder. They had a certain air about them, a certain walk of authority. A swagger.

"Find out. I'll hold while you do," his attorney said.

The doorbell rang. His mother, Joan, looked up from where she sat in the parlor. "Do you want me to get it?"

He shook his head, walked to the front door, and opened it. Two grim-faced men stood before him.

One stepped forward. "Kyle McKenzie?"

"Yes?"

"I'm Detective Phillips. This is Detective Mancini. May we come in, please?"

His heart jumped. *Kevin's been hurt.* "Is it Kevin? Is he all right?"

"Kevin, Mr. McKenzie?"

"Is this about my father's murder?" He motioned them toward the den.

When they arrived there, Detective Phillips turned around. "Sir, there's no good way to say this. Your wife, Margot McKenzie, was found shot to death not thirty minutes ago."

Kyle jolted as if the detective had slugged him. His heart stumbled. His breathing stopped. Everything around him faded away as he tried to focus on the detective, tried to make sense of his words. *Wife. Shot. Death.* He tried to move his head from side-to-side, but it wouldn't cooperate. He was aware that his mother had gasped. He turned and stared at her. Had she heard the same words? Margot, shot? *Shot?*

"On my way." Barry's voice. His attorney's voice on his Bluetooth. In his ear. "Don't say anything! I'm on my way. Five minutes."

A wave of pure cold—like he was encased in ice—washed over him. His whole body shuddered. "Is she—?"

Dead. She's dead. He'd said dead, hadn't he? *Oh, God, he'd said dead.* In an instant, the ice melted, and he began to shake.

His mother's perfume. Her warm arms around his waist. Soft words, but he couldn't make them out.

His brother Kevin appeared in the doorway and quickly strode toward Kyle. "What's going on?" Kevin placed a firm hand on Kyle's shoulder. "What's wrong? Why are the police here?"

In a daze, Kyle looked at him and sat on the sofa.

"Is April okay? Kyle, is April okay?"

He blinked at Kevin. Nothing was real. *Oh, God, Margot.* "She was shot."

"April?"

"Margot. Someone shot Margot."

The white sack in Kevin's hand fell to the floor. "Shot? As in, a gun? Is she okay?"

One of the detectives stepped toward Kevin. "And you are?"

"I'd think that was obvious since we're identical twins." Kevin squeezed Kyle's shoulder. "Is she alive?"

"He's Kevin McKenzie." This gentle answer, from his mother.

Nausea swirled as Kyle shook his head.

"Mr. McKenzie, where were you the last hour?"

The last hour? "I was at Crayton's Cove visiting Natalie Palmer."

"You drove past the Plaza Motel?"

"The, uh, oh, yes. It's on the way."

The two detectives looked at each other. "Your wife was killed at the Plaza Hotel."

"At the Plaza Hotel? She wouldn't have stayed there. You must be mistaken. She wouldn't have stayed there." Heat coursed through his body. "Are you sure it was my wife who was shot?"

"We found divorce papers on Mrs. McKenzie that were filed yesterday. When were you served, sir?"

Kyle rubbed his right temple. "This morning."

"Must have made you pretty angry?"

Kevin glared at the detective. "Let's call Barry, Kyle. You don't have to answer any questions."

"He's on his way." Kyle's head wobbled. "But I have nothing to hide."

"Mr. McKenzie, do you own a gun?"

"I'm telling you to wait for Barry, bro'."

"Why were you visiting Miss Palmer, sir? Did your wife know?"

Kyle looked into the detective's accusing eyes. He dropped his head and pressed the heels of his hands into his eyes. "Help me, Lord," he whispered and waited.

For what, he didn't know.

Natalie drew her hair into a ponytail, picked up a visor, her purse and her keys, and hurried downstairs. She didn't want another confrontation with her grandmother. Her 'annoyingly perky side'—her grandmother's words—had slipped out after her meeting with Kyle McKenzie, demanding that all the restraints, expectations, and pretenses of being a Palmer be left behind for one day. A ride to Galveston Island should clear her head. She was as certain as she could be that she would help the McKenzie family.

"As I expected. You're sneaking out of here without settling this."

So the confrontation wasn't going to wait. She spun to face her grandmother. "The beach house should help resolve it."

"Running away never settles a thing."

"Praying does." She touched her grandmother's arm. "I really must go, Nana. I'll see you tonight."

It had slipped out, the old name. She hadn't used it in years, but she felt free and probably a little too perky for the first time in a long time and the name she'd called her grandmother until she was eleven years old blurted out. She walked past her.

"So God is in on this, too, is He?"

Natalie whirled around. "He's always in. He could be with y—"

Her grandmother held up a hand. "Church is enough for me. I won't sully God's name by talking about him on every street corner."

Walking backwards, Natalie smiled. "'Bye, Nana." She spun around, waving as she left. This time, calling her 'Nana' had been deliberate. Her grandmother visibly tensed when she'd said it.

Natalie could remember laughing and playing with her parents and her grandparents when she was much younger. It was a shame that the coldness of propriety had taken over her family. The laughter, the happiness they'd once enjoyed languished under the strain of rigid control, rigid rules, and rigid expectations.

Everything changed after her father died. But she wouldn't think about that right now. She slipped into her Jaguar and started out for Galveston Island.

The detective grimly pulled out a small notebook, flipped pages. "When did you last see your wife, Mr. McKenzie?"

Kyle shook his head. "Before she, uh, left. Around six-thirty." His stomach cramped into a tight knot, but he made himself say the words. "We had a, uh, a, uh, a talk this morning. She was, we were—" He lost his train of thought. What was he talking about?

"A talk, Mr. McKenzie?"

Talk? Oh, yes. He tried to nod but his head was too heavy to move.

"A talk, Mr. McKenzie?"

Kevin squeezed his shoulder. "Kyle."

"This morning. She said..." *She said she despised me, that she hated me. That*—what had she said? Something about leverage. He tried to focus on the detective, but his vision blurred. *Tears.* He was crying. He was crying because Margot was dead. "She, uh, said she didn't want to—"

"Didn't want to what, Mr. McKenzie?"

"I don't know. She—"

"I'd like to speak with my client, gentlemen," Barry announced as he rushed into the room, breathing heavily. "Are you okay?"

Kyle nodded.

"Barry Harrison," his attorney said as he shook both detectives' hands. "Mr. McKenzie's attorney. I was on the phone with him when you two arrived. Have you read him his rights?"

"Your client's not under arrest, Mr. Harrison. We'd just like to ask him some questions regarding his whereabouts this morning and his relationship with Mrs. McKenzie."

"I can tell you where he was. Talking to a nurse about his daughter and on the phone with me until about five minutes ago."

Detective Phillips looked at Kyle. "Mr. McKenzie, would you mind if we asked you some questions, sir?" He lifted his brows and looked at Barry. "In the presence of your attorney, of course."

"No, no, not at all." A handkerchief came into his line of vision. Kyle took it from Barry and wiped his eyes. "Where is she?" He looked up at the detective. "Are you sure it's Margot?"

"Yes." He consulted his notes. "Sir, why were you divorcing?"

"She—"

Barry touched his arm.

"She what, sir?"

Kyle rested his head against his fingers and tried to think. "I don't know. I don't know why my wife filed for divorce." He thought of their wedding day. She'd been so beautiful standing outside among all the flowers—a garden wedding is what she'd called it. Flowers were everywhere. Smiling up at him a little shyly, Margot was everything he'd ever wanted in life. He had found his love. They would begin the family he'd wanted for years. And when she became pregnant a month later with April, he'd been thrilled. Fairfield Ranch represented a new beginning, where their beautiful life had begun together.

"That made you pretty angry, Mr. McKenzie?"

What?

Barry conspicuously stepped between Phillips and Kyle. "What a stupid question. If you're going to ask my client questions, then ask intelligent ones."

Phillips squinted at Barry. "Do you own a firearm, Mr. McKenzie?"

he asked, without taking his gaze off Barry.

"Yes. My father passed away a couple years ago, and I inherited it. It's registered in my name, but I've never used it."

"Then you would have no objection to our examining it?"

"No, none whatsoever. Wait." Kyle glanced up. "You're not insinuating that *I* killed my wife?" He stood. "I loved her! I wouldn't have hurt her for any reason!"

Barry touched his shoulder. "Calm down, Kyle. They have to ask."

"Did you and Mrs. McKenzie quarrel today, Mr. McKenzie?"

"We had words." *What would you know about her days? You're never here.*

"Angry words?"

"Some. She announced she was leaving me and April, our daughter."

"How did you react to being served with the divorce papers?" Phillips glanced at Barry and raised his brows in an obvious, silent challenge.

"Stunned. I had no idea she wanted a divorce. I was absolutely stunned." Heartbroken, shattered.

"What did you do?"

"I, uh, I cried."

The detective wrote down his answer. "Why were you visiting Natalie Palmer this past hour?"

Barry opened his mouth.

Phillips frowned at Barry. "Mr. McKenzie, would you answer the question, sir?"

"Yes. My daughter is ill. She needs a nurse to take care of her. I asked Miss Palmer if she would be that nurse."

"The Palmers of Crayton's Cove?"

Yeah, those Palmers. "The same."

"How long have you known Ms. Palmer?"

"I met her this morning for the first time."

"And she said yes to the nursing job?"

Kyle could hear the astonishment in Phillips' voice, and he couldn't agree with him more. It was crazy to think she'd do it. "She's one of my mother's friends. A Registered Nurse. She said she'd give me her answer this afternoon." Kyle looked at the detective. "Did she, did you find identification on her? On Margot, my wife?"

"Her purse was found near her. The ID matches."

Dazed, Kyle squeezed his eyes closed, trying to remember. "She was wearing a, uh, a pink blouse, with little gold earrings. Auburn hair. Dark auburn hair."

"Mr. McKenzie, it's not necessary—"

"Is it Margot?"

"The victim was wearing a red suit."

"A red suit?" Margot didn't own a red suit.

"But if this picture is of your wife—" He indicated the framed portrait above the fireplace. "—then the victim in the motel—"

"Her name is Margot." Kyle gritted his teeth against the sudden spurt of anger. "What's being done to catch this guy?"

Phillips finished writing, glanced at Kevin. "And you, sir? Where were you in the last hour?"

Kevin looked at Kyle, then the detective. "I was in my office all morning. Tons of witnesses. For lunch, I walked to a deli, ordered a ham and cheese sandwich." He held up his hand, but nothing was in it, then he looked down at his feet, picked up the sack, and lifted it. "I came here for lunch, to check on my brother after I heard Margot left him."

"How well did you know Mrs. McKenzie?"

"We weren't close at all."

"Why is that?"

"I don't know. She wasn't an easy person to get to know."

"Do you know anyone who would want to kill her?"

"No." Shaking his head, Kevin added, "No one."

Phillips turned to Kyle. "Any friends she was close to that she would have confided in?"

"Margot wasn't social. To my knowledge, she had no close friends."

"Why is that, Mr. McKenzie?"

"I don't know."

"Was she a member of any clubs?"

"No."

"Church?"

"Westside. But she didn't attend regularly this past year."

"Any businesses she was involved in?"

"None." Unless stealing the money out of their joint bank account was considered a business.

"Did you notice her chatting on the net or spending time e-mailing a particular person? Porn sites? Social sites? Dating sites? Anything like that?"

"I never saw her use the computer."

"Were there times she was late getting home, and you suspected she was involved with someone else?"

Kyle shook his head. "No. Never." She was always at home.

"Do you have any idea who would want to hurt her?"

"No. Not at all."

"May we have her cell phone?"

"Yes, of course." He looked around. "Wasn't it in her purse?"

The detective didn't answer him.

"If you think of anything else." Phillips handed him a card.

Kyle nodded, stared at the card. "Am I allowed to go to her now? To see her?"

"Are you sure you want to do that?"

He frowned deeply. "She was my wife. I want to see my wife."

Phillips nodded at Mancini, who pulled out his phone, stepped away from them, made a call, and spoke quietly. After disconnecting the call, he turned around and dipped his head once at Phillips.

"I'll take you to her." Phillips slipped his small notebook into a pocket.

Kevin stepped forward. "I'm driving, buddy. Are you coming, Barry?"

"Wouldn't miss it."

THREE

Just shy of an hour later, Natalie could hear nothing but gentle waves lapping at the beach house. Standing on the vast deck overlooking the Gulf, she savored the feel of the saltwater breeze on her face. She didn't resent the sounds of a distant boat drawing near or the squeal of a woman as her skis upended just before she did a belly flop. It was all part of the experience.

She let out a long, contented sigh. She remembered a sunny day, so long ago, and her father's patience as he taught her how to water ski.

"Lean back when you feel the pull of the line in your hands, all right, honey? You'll want to go with the pull, but resist it, okay? Lean back and push your bottom forward, to keep it in line with your body. Like this."

Patiently, her daddy held out his arms, his hands together as if he held the handle of a ski rope. He leaned back. "See how I'm straightening my body and making it look like a long slanted line?"

Even now, Natalie stifled a giggle. Her daddy had looked so silly that day.

"You have to lean back, almost like you're going to fall over backwards, but you don't." But he did and sprawled on top of the ottoman. Natalie burst out laughing.

"Oh," he grinned as he tried to scramble up. "You think that was funny, huh?"

She remembered the look on his face and smiled.

She squealed when her daddy lunged for her, tickling her as she shrieked and giggled. "Da... deeeee!"

She couldn't even talk, she was laughing so hard.

Natalie's smile widened. Oh, how her daddy could make her laugh. She looked past the deck and into the sunshiny day garnished with steam and heat on the Gulf of Mexico.

Her phone rang. *Andrea. Good.* "Hey. How are you? Are you sleeping any better?"

"I'm *starting* to sleep better. Still all the lights on at night, but it helps me get to sleep and stay asleep with Jason not here. How are you?"

Natalie resisted sighing. Any problem she had couldn't compare with the loss of the love of Andrea's life. Jason and Andrea recognized the 'soul mate' status of their hearts within an hour of meeting. Married just four months later, they had been living the 'happily ever after' until Jason's tragic wreck almost ten months ago. "I'm fine. Is it getting any better for you?"

A long pause. "I miss him so much, but yes, I'm learning to live without him. I'm stronger."

"I'm so glad to hear that. How's Tinker Bella?"

Andrea sighed. "She keeps thinking Daddy will be home any day now. She cried the other night because she's having trouble remembering what he looked like. I've read that that's normal. A man from our church has stepped in as a grandfather figure, and they've grown really close. Bella loves him. But enough about me. How are you? And Kath? Have you heard from her? She was out of the country the last I heard."

The three best friends had met in elementary school, remained glued to each other from that time through college, and now rarely spent time together. Phone calls, emails, texts—lots of them—kept them up-to-date. Each kept saying they needed to get together, but with Kath traveling and Andrea focused on her marriage and her daughter the last five years, getting together just hadn't happened.

The three remained as different now as they were as children. *Ready, Willing, and Able,* their mothers had called them. Andrea, the *ready* romantic. Life had spread out a path of love just for her, and she'd thrived until recently. Kath, the *willing* adventurer. Her wealth had provided a magnanimous feast of world-wide discoveries, and as a writer, she could create her own worlds. She thrived, but alone.

Natalie, the *able* thinker. An eccentric grandmother and a sometimes-moldable mother had seen to it that she'd expanded her world with knowledge and travel and degrees, and nursing children was her niche for thriving. "Kath's traveling Europe. I'm not sure when she'll be home. But you know her; one of us will find out when she rings the doorbell."

"I miss her. I miss you."

"Me, too, Andrea. We need to get together when she gets back.

Let's plan on that."

"Y'all will probably have to come to Dallas with Bella in school. So, what's new in your life?"

Here goes. "I think I'm about to start a new adventure." She told her about April and Kyle McKenzie's situation.

"The hired help, huh?"

"Yes."

"What's the father like?"

A loaded question. "Well, if I'm truthful, he's absolutely gorgeous and wealthy and—"

Hands gripped her shoulders, then a rough beard nuzzled her face. "Are you talking about *me?*"

Natalie swallowed down a shriek and laughed instead. "Da-vid!"

He turned the grab into a hug. "Gotcha, cuz. Who's on the phone?"

Natalie jerked away from him, laughing, and spoke into the phone. "Andrea, I'm sorry. My very rude cousin, David, just tried to scare me—"

Her very rude cousin David leaned into the phone, laughing. "I *did* scare her, Andrea. She just won't admit it."

Natalie playfully nudged him with her shoulder and walked a couple steps away. "Yes, he is. Listen, I'll call you back the second I can get rid of David. Okay." She laughed. "Love you too." And hung up.

Fingers dug into her ribs. "Get rid of me, huh?"

She gasped and spun around, laughing as she launched herself into David's open arms. "David, you old skunk. Since when are you up and at 'em by noon?"

He squeezed her, released her, and chucked her nose. "I live to see you, even at noon."

She swatted at his hand and walked to the rail, resting her hands on it. "I'm glad you came by. I needed someone with me today."

"Just someone?" he teased, standing beside her and squinting into the sunny day. "Any ol' body would have done?"

"Oh, stop it. You know what I meant. How did you know I was here?"

"You drove by my little shack, and I couldn't resist coming over here and needling you about whatever's bothering you. You know you only come out here when something's wrong." He crossed his arms, put his back to the water, and leaned against the rail. "So, how is everything? How's our dear grandmother doing?"

She ignored the sarcasm and answered him honestly. "She called you. That's why you're up at noon."

He shrugged and nodded. "So, what's troubling you?"

As only children, she and David considered themselves more siblings than first cousins. Their mothers had been not only sisters, but best friends, until David's mother died a year ago. The families had spent a lot of time together growing up. Just three years separated Natalie and David, and she loved him like a big brother. "I just need to talk."

"Take off your shoes then, and let's walk, if we have to talk. Do I have to listen, too? Or can I just grunt from time to time?"

Laughing, she threw off her flip-flops, shoved him, and dashed down the stairs.

"You know you can't outrun me."

"Just watch me!" From three steps up, she jumped into the sand and then raced toward the water.

David growled and raced after her.

She gloried in the water washing over her feet, the sand between her toes.

After a few minutes of chasing her, David yelled, "All right, all right! You win. I didn't come over here to watch you outrun me. I just ate breakfast. I'm going to throw up all over your back if you don't stop."

Grinning, she did, turned around, and wiggled her eyebrows.

He grasped his knees and bent over.

She didn't trust him. He was up to something.

Cautiously, she sauntered toward him as her stomach jiggled from trying to stop the giggles. "You're just getting old. Out of shape. I told you I could—"

He sprinted toward her. She squealed as he grabbed her around the waist and ran with her toward the water.

"No, David, don't!"

"But it's so hot, cuz. And I deserve a prize for winning."

"You didn't win. You tricked me!" She kicked and squirmed. "You cheated."

"Did not. You just didn't consider all the possibilities." He set her on her feet in the water and held out his hand. She slapped it and glared at him playfully.

"You let your defenses down. Now come on." He held out his hand again, waiting while she considered it with a little grin. "Let's walk and get this talk over with."

Taking his hand, she squinted one eye up at him. He reminded her of a young Robert Redford, except David was about three inches taller. David Zachary's sun-bleached hair and tanned skin were a testament to the lazy days spent at the Zachary beach house, writing and making gifted music.

But as the sole heir to the Zachary fortune, his father demanded more from him than 'a guitar pick and a tab book.' A year ago, in the midst of the unbearable loss of his mother, David simply couldn't meet his father's demands.

His passion wasn't the world of business but the world of music, and, according to his father, the two didn't mix. They'd hit an impasse shortly after his mother's death, and neither was willing to give an inch.

"Any gigs lately?"

"Some. My father came to the Cherry Tree last weekend. I almost dropped my teeth when he walked in and sat down, front and center." He shrugged. "He was there to intimidate me."

"Did he?"

He lifted his brows. "What do you think?"

She shook her head. "Maybe Uncle Gil just wanted to hear you play."

She could feel her daddy's eyes on her. He always sneaked up behind her and closed his eyes when she played the piano, acting like she was some great pianist, some world-famous pianist, when she was just a little girl learning simple songs. She tried to keep playing just because he'd want her to, but she stopped, put her hands in her lap, and turned around. "Daddy. I'm not ready for anyone to hear me yet."

He kept his eyes closed, his chin lifted as if he could breathe in Heaven with her music. "It's beautiful, honey. You're so talented."

No, I'm not, Daddy, she wanted to say but he'd only tell her, yes, she was, so she just shrugged and placed her fingers lightly on the keys.

"Play for me, Natalie. Daddy loves to hear you play."

She sighed. "All right, but I don't have to play this one, do I? I don't know it very well."

"Play anything you want, sweetheart. Everything you play is beautiful to me."

"—the fights we've had? Get real."

Natalie swallowed down the lump in her throat. Why was she thinking of her father so much lately? Why was she remembering so many little things he'd done, things they'd done together? "I'm sorry, David. What did you say?"

"I said, Gil comes to a gig, and I'm supposed to think everything's okay? After all the fights we've had?" He dug a shell out of the sand, rinsed it, and handed it to her. "You know Gil Zachary doesn't do anything that isn't calculated to undermine the enemy."

"Are you the enemy?"

"Anyone's the enemy who doesn't do exactly what my father wants. And that includes his only child."

"Forgive him."

"Works for me. But it doesn't change a thing. Believe me, it's easier living without him and his demands."

"Oh, David. Having a father is so much better than not having a father."

He put his arm around her shoulders. "I know you're right. I just don't know how to make it work with him." He walked into the water to mid-calf and tugged her along. "But we didn't come out here to talk about me. What's up with you? Are you going to take the baby-sitting gig?"

Frowning, she shaded her eyes and looked into his. "Are you against me, too?"

"Of course not. She was persuasive, but I want to hear your side of it. Are you going to take it?"

"Yes."

"Why?"

"Because I believe I'm supposed to help April and, in a round-about way, her father."

"He's being divorced."

She could feel his gaze on her, so she looked directly at him. "I have no interest in the man. Just the baby." At his grunt, she backhanded his shoulder. "I'm not kidding. In fact, I hope he and his wife get back together."

"You're serious about this."

"I am." She studied the shell he'd given her for a moment. "You know how much I love children. This is exactly what I wanted to do with my degree. Specialized, individual, *personal* help."

"But?"

"I'll be staying there during the week and I'm afraid of what the neighbors might think, a single woman and a man just separated from his wife in the same house. Alone and together."

"They'll think what they want to think."

"I know. But I don't want to appear—you know."

"Then take Aunt Essie with you."

She stopped, opened her mouth to say something, and then shut it. "What a great idea. David. What an absolutely wonderful idea! That would solve everything, and Aunt Essie would feel useful again. She would love that." She kissed his cheek. "You're a jewel."

"So we're done talking?" He playfully shivered.

At her nod, he spun her around and headed the other way, taking her with him. "In that case, come to my house and listen to the song I've been working on all morning. I need an objective opinion."

"Like I know anything about writing music."

"You'll know if you like it. That's all I need from you."

"I like all your stuff."

"I'm brilliant. What can I say?"

She nudged his shoulder, caught him off-balance, and raced toward the beach house. She looked over her shoulder as he floundered in the water and then started after her. She ran harder. He was close behind her when she raced up the stairs to the deck.

It felt so good to be on the beach again with David.

Gasping for air, he bent over when he reached the deck. "You were on the phone with Andrea earlier. Is that the Andrea from high school that I've never met?"

Natalie nodded. "If you'd stayed in this country during your teen years, you might have met my wonderful best friend."

"The Andrea with only one picture in your yearbook with the funny face?"

"The funny expression. Her face is perfect."

"Yeah, yeah. So you've said. She lives in Dallas, right?"

"Yes. She lost her husband in a car wreck about ten months ago." She reached for the sprayer. With a few squirts, her feet were clean. "I stopped at the Cheesecake Palace and bought your favorite."

He squinted one eye at her. "With strawberries?"

"Yep. Wash off your feet before you come in."

He grasped the hose and sprayed the glass door just as she slid it shut. She opened it a crack. "You're slow today, David."

"Just watch me devour that cheesecake," he said as he opened the door. "You didn't want any, did you, cuz?"

FOUR

Aunt Essie flapped a brown-spotted, chubby hand at Natalie. "Yes, yes, I see what you mean. Flee the appearance of evil and all that, you know, dear." She popped the top off the flour container and reached for a measuring cup.

Natalie bit the inside of her mouth to keep from laughing.

Her great-aunt was adorable, all five-feet-two-inches of her. She'd always reminded Natalie of Aunt Pittypat in *Gone with the Wind*, so full of energy and fuss. Aunt Essie could talk up a storm and flutter about, which drew the ire of her older sister, Lenore. Almost sixteen years separated the women, and everyone in the family knew that her grandmother considered her a childish embarrassment.

But Natalie loved being with Aunt Essie. Her husband, Henry, died over five years ago, and she was all alone.

Natalie couldn't say yes to Mr. McKenzie unless her aunt agreed to her proposal.

"I'm at loose ends anyway." Aunt Essie bobbed her gray curly head at Natalie and smiled. A measuring cup full of brown sugar followed the flour dumped into the big bowl. "But you know that now, don't you, child? Else why would you be asking me to join you in this little caper?" Her chin dropped onto her chest and—there it was—her famous sputtering, high-pitched giggle. It was contagious, and Natalie laughed right along with her.

She placed a hand on her aunt's arm. "No, Aunt Essie. I want you to come with me and bring some happiness back into that house. His wife left him and filed for divorce, and he has a very sick little baby who needs us."

It was just the right thing to say.

Aunt Essie's eyes filled with tears. "Poor child." She slipped two fingers up the sleeve of her blouse and withdrew a small lace hankie and patted her eyes. A child, any child, sick or well, could easily capture Aunt Essie's heart. "Poor, poor man. Of course, we'll help him, dear." She patted Natalie's arm. "Oh, my, yes. Yes, we will. When do you think we'll be moving in?"

"Probably Monday."

"Well, now. I have much to do by then. I wonder." She tapped two plump fingers against her mouth. "I wonder if Mr. McKenzie would like some help in the kitchen, dear. Do you think he would like some good home cooking?"

Natalie threw her arms around her aunt. "Oh, Aunt Essie, I love you so much. You are such a treasure to me." She squeezed her aunt hard and then took her hands. "What man wouldn't want to have a great cook in the house? He probably has a cook, but you could make the desserts and maybe give her a break from time to time."

Natalie smiled. "I think Mr. McKenzie's going to get a whole lot more than he bargained for."

Aunt Essie's face crinkled into a well-used smile. "We'll see to it, dear. Maybe we could make him a cinnamon roll cake for tonight?"

"That would be wonderful." Natalie checked her watch. "I need to get to his home by four o'clock to give him our answer. It's three-fifteen, just enough time to run home, freshen up, and meet him there."

Natalie turned off the Jaguar's engine and sat in the quiet in front of Kyle McKenzie's home. The heat pressed against the car windows, quickly consuming any lingering cold from the air conditioning.

The McKenzie home was beautiful. Its white antebellum architecture included two stories, tall pillars in front and on the sides, a wide wrap-around porch, and stunning green lawns with flower beds along the brick walkway to the front porch. A large swing at the northeast corner could easily sit four people.

May was typically fair but not this week. Both the ninety-five-plus-degree heat and the overbearing humidity hovered like a sauna over southeast Texas.

With a quick decisive nod, Natalie opened the car door and walked to the gate. She unlatched it as her gaze wandered across beautiful grounds that would soon be very familiar to her.

A spring wreath on the door welcomed her, but as she reached the landing, a little piece of paper taped below it caught her attention. Her name was on it.

She opened it.

Natalie—St. Michael's hospital—April.

She gasped and raced back to her car, tossing her purse in with the note. Strapping herself in, she started the engine, her wheels peeling on the pavement as she hurried to St. Michael's, praying all the way that April was all right.

She rushed toward the bright lights of the Emergency Room entrance. The huge sliding glass doors opened, and she heard, "Code Blue, 427, Code Blue, 427," as she stepped inside the ER. She had done this as an eleven-year-old when her daddy was dying. She remembered the nightmare she'd had several times.

She stood rooted to the shiny floor, frantically searching through the mist. A nurse came out of the fog and walked by her in slow motion, her gaze straight ahead, her long legs taking her toward another door. The steady pounding of her own heart was the only sound she heard. "Daddy?"

Someone touched her arm.

"Natalie? Your father's not down here. He's in ICU on the third floor. Is your Aunt Essie with you?"

"She's parking the car."

"Come on, then. I'll take you there."

"He's alive?"

"Yes. I think he's waiting for you."

Waiting for me so he can die.

She didn't want to go. He'd die if she went. It would be all her fault. No, Daddy, don't die. Don't die!

"Good. You got my note."

Kyle McKenzie's voice.

She turned toward him and away from the memory. "Yes. How is April?"

"A line infection. Diarrhea. Typical of her condition, but it never gets easy to go through this. Her doctor, Lynette Weisbrod, just left."

Natalie stood beside him to better see April. "Is she out of danger?" The residual effects of the foggy dream clung to Natalie. Unconsciously, she chafed her arms as if she was chilled and as she did, her shoulder grazed Kyle's. As nonchalantly as possible, she moved to her right and turned her face away from him.

"Lynette wants to keep her tonight." He took a deep breath and blew it out. "Something's wrong."

The fog left. "What do you mean?"

"I don't know. They said they wanted to run some tests on her when she stabilized."

"Did Dr. Weisbrod say why?"

"I wouldn't be surprised if her liver's failing." He took a sip of coffee from a Styrofoam cup and glanced at Natalie. "I'm not sure if you've had much experience with Short Bowel Syndrome but continued use of the TPN—the feeding tube—sometimes causes liver damage. But April needs the nutrients. So." His words drifted off as he looked into April's room.

"A catch 22."

"Yes. She has to be fed, but this feeding system can actually cause problems for her liver."

"Kyle?"

Natalie turned around. Three men walking toward them looked incredibly like Kyle. Very tall, wiry, virile men, all wearing cowboy hats and boots, looking essentially too big for the hallway. The same clear blue eyes, the same black hair, and the same thick, curly eyelashes. Whoa. McKenzie men were—no other word for it—*beautiful*. But there was no doubt that Kyle was the most handsome of the bunch.

He pointed to each man. "Natalie, my brothers: Mac, the baby; Luke, next to Mac; and Bobby, second eldest. Natalie Palmer."

His brothers are here because of a routine hospital visit? "Nice to meet you. I'm a pediatric nurse and, if I'm not mistaken, your brother has hired me to take care of April."

Footsteps sounded behind her. She turned, and her eyes widened. She looked at Kyle, back at the man who had just walked up, to Kyle again. "You're twins."

Kyle nodded. "Natalie Palmer, my brother Kevin."

"Nice to meet you, Kevin."

A quick smile, and he said, "A pleasure, ma'am. I'm sorry. I don't mean to be rude, but would you excuse us for just a minute?"

"Certainly."

The brothers inclined their heads or touched their hats at her as they walked toward the sliding glass doors. While they stood outside April's room, Kyle stepped inside. The brothers stood in a circle, whispering, nodding, shaking heads, shuffling feet.

Shelley, a pediatric nurse, walked over to Natalie with her gaze on April's bed. "She's resting now. Would you like some coffee?"

As a volunteer at the hospital for several years, Natalie knew most of the nursing staff. "I'd love some. Thank you, Shelley." Natalie studied April. She seemed so tiny in the hospital bed. She didn't look like a twelve-month-old. Because she couldn't eat, her growth had been inhibited. She looked too frail to live.

Kyle stepped out of the room. "She's beautiful, isn't she?"

"Yes."

From behind the glass wall, a nurse adjusted something on April's monitor, checked her IV, and gently stroked her head.

"If God would allow me, I would gladly take all this from her, bear her pain for her."

Natalie looked up at him. "I'm sure you would. Any parent would."

"No," he said, shaking his head. "Not any parent."

Natalie had nothing to say to that. She was hoping he would bring up her employment, but maybe this wasn't a good time. "Well, I'll leave you with your family."

"I'm not thinking. You're here to discuss caring for April. Or was there something else you wanted to talk to me about?"

Something else? "I want to take the position. If you approve, my Aunt Essie will be joining me. She's wonderful in the kitchen and would be a chaperone of sorts and an extra pair of hands."

"That sounds great. My cook's daughter is having her first baby, and Lettie left four days ago to help her. She'll be gone for at least six weeks. I've been grabbing breakfast on my way to work, and I come home at lunch and make myself a sandwich, just to see April. I'd only need a dinner meal, although we could do take out, too."

"My aunt wants to make you a cinnamon roll cake for tonight. We could bring it by later."

"I'd like that. Thank you. For everything."

She nodded and then quietly walked down the hallway toward the exit.

"Natalie?"

She turned around. "Yes?"

With quick steps, he made his way to her. "I need to tell you something. You'll probably hear it on the news. My w—"

"Kyle?" One of his brothers. "The doctor wants to speak to you. He's in April's room."

Kyle nodded and looked back at Natalie. "Call me if you need to ask me anything."

"All right." She smiled and left.

Thirty minutes later, Natalie inserted the key and opened Aunt Essie's front door. She had learned a long time ago that she was not to knock. "Like a stranger? Unthinkable," her aunt told her once.

"Aunt Essie?"

"In here!"

She headed for the kitchen.

"I'm making the cinnamon roll cake, dear. But my hands are already in this dough, and I forgot to take off my rings." Aunt Essie wiggled her fingers at Natalie. "Would you mind?"

Natalie twisted the ring set off, turned on the water, rinsed them, and set them on the window ledge. "I was just at the hospital with Kyle and several brothers."

Aunt Essie's head lifted. "The hospital?"

"April was in some distress, but Kyle indicated it was a normal occurrence, that she would be fine. I told you about her condition." Natalie leaned over and sniffed the dough. "I didn't stay long; his family was with him. This smells scrumptious. When I take this to Kyle's home tonight, I'll find out the latest about April—what? What was that?"

Natalie lunged to turn up the radio. *"—was found dead at the Plaza Motel."* She gasped and stared at the radio. *"Repeating, Margot McKenzie, estranged wife of McKenzie Engineering CEO Kyle McKenzie, was found shot to death at the Plaza Motel this morning. We'll have more details as they become available."*

"Oh, no." She stared wide-eyed at Aunt Essie, then at the radio as if it would laugh at her and say it was all a horrible joke.

Both women stood in stunned silence.

Natalie was vaguely aware that a steady stream of water flowed from the faucet, but she couldn't seem to move her feet to get over to it and turn it off.

She remembered, years ago, when her father died.

"Brent Allen Palmer, native son of Crayton's Cove, died today at St. Michael's Hospital. Mr. Palmer was critically injured in a car accident three days—"

"Turn that radio off, Clarence."

Natalie's mother held a handkerchief to her mouth and looked at Natalie, sitting across the wide seat of the limousine from her. "How could they do that? We haven't even notified your grandmother yet." Her words were muffled by her handkerchief. She sobbed and looked at Natalie and then pressed it with both hands against her face.

Every sniffle, every sob, every tear drove Natalie deeper into the blame. She couldn't remember anything about the accident, but she felt that she had somehow caused her father's death.

"Dear me." Aunt Essie washed her hands and dried them. "What's happened, Natalie? Mr. McKenzie's wife was murdered?"

Natalie pulled herself out of the stupor and shook her head. No wonder all of his family came in to support him. "He started to tell me about this, but one of April's doctors called for Kyle. What should we do, Aunt Essie? Call him?"

"We're not his friends, dear." She dropped into a chair. "We're his hired help. It's not our place to get involved."

She was right. How many times had Natalie stopped a discussion with her mother or her grandmother when one of the staff entered the room? "I'm not accustomed to being in a position where I can't help."

Aunt Essie sniffed. "Our poor April, without a mother now. Did our boy... did our Mr. McKenzie have anything to do with this?"

Kyle, a killer? "No, of course not. I'll take them the cake and maybe find out what's going on."

Just before seven that night, Natalie drove up Kyle's street. Several trucks and vehicles lined both sides of the street in front of the McKenzie home, and she had to park some distance away. His brothers, probably, and more family and friends.

She picked up the cinnamon roll cake and approached Kyle's home. Tall leafy trees filled the expansive yard. Blooming flowers in all kinds of colors surrounded the front of the house.

Another car pulled in opposite the line of parked cars. An old man sat in the banged-up car and rotated his white head toward the house. But his gaze landed on Natalie. He stared at her without any sign of recognition or greeting or warmth.

Something about him made her uncomfortable. With a stoic expression, his eyes tracked her as she walked slowly down the sidewalk. His head never moved. His expression never changed. She tried not to look at him, but every time she did, his focus was on her. Probably an old friend, grief-stricken and dreading going inside.

But whoever he was, he gave her the creeps.

She rang the doorbell. One of Kyle's sisters-in-law greeted her— Marianne McKenzie—and took the cake. Natalie politely refused the sincere invitation to come in. "How is April?"

"Kyle's with her at the hospital. She's better and will probably be home in the morning."

Natalie thanked her and wished them all a good night.

Calmly, she turned around. The old man's head was still turned toward her, his gaze glued to her again as she headed toward her car. When she drove past him, he still sat in his car, but his attention was now on Kyle's home.

Kyle's phone beeped. *I'm here.* He looked at the large clock on the wall that read *2:55.* Mrs. Naugitt was right on time, as usual.

The chair beside April's hospital bed was uncomfortable, to say the least. He was simply too large for it, but he'd snoozed a little here and there. He was exhausted and tried to work out the stubborn kinks that had settled in hours before.

He was always the one to stay with April when she had to go to the hospital. Margot never came. He hadn't minded, though. He knew her days were full of taking care of their baby, and this was a time when she could catch her breath a little.

But never again.

Nothing would ever be the same again.

Wearily, he stood and leaned over April. She was over the worst of it, so he could leave now. "I love you, angel," he whispered and kissed her. "Mrs. Naugitt's coming to see you, so I'm going. I'll be back in a few hours to take you home, okay?" He straightened and stretched thoroughly.

Behind him, the door opened on a swoosh of air and let in the soft night lights of the hospital corridor. Mrs. Naugitt smiled at him. "You go on, hon. I'll take over now. Get yourself a little sleep."

"I appreciate your coming. I don't know what we'd have done this past year without you." He was grateful the retired nurse had wanted to keep up her medical skills by helping his family. Margot had complained about many things, but Mrs. Naugitt was not one of them.

"Kyle, I'm so sorry about Margot."

He nodded. "I appreciate that."

"Do they have any idea what happened?"

"Not yet."

"Well. I know you're going to need extra help. Let me know if I can lend a hand."

"I've hired a full-time pediatrics nurse to care for April. But I'll let her know you've offered to help. Thank you." He gently squeezed April's foot and left.

Kyle grumbled and shut off his alarm. *What a night.* His body ached as if an eighteen-wheeler had rumbled over it, backed up, and made sure every inch had received its fair share of torture. Rolling over, he glanced at Margot's pillow and groaned.

His first morning to wake up without her.

He'd had trouble getting to sleep, even at 3:30 in the morning, because he couldn't for the life of him understand why she'd chosen such a sleazy place to spend the night. She had a lot of money. Why stay where known drug users and vagrants hung out? Did someone break into her room? Did a strung-out druggie push his way in? Knowing Margot, she'd have fought him. Is that why he killed her because she wouldn't give him any money? The only problem with that theory is that the detectives said there was no sign of a struggle.

Then, knowing Margot, why hadn't she fought back?

So many questions with no answers.

Kyle rubbed his eyes, which made them hurt more. "Get up, get up." He groaned as he made his weary body get out of bed. He needed to shower and dress, so he could pick up April at seven o'clock and bring her home. The hot shower relaxed him a little. When he opened the door to his empty bedroom, he remembered their fight. Her words. *I despise you.*

Then she left him.

He was served with divorce papers.

She was murdered.

Just yesterday. One day, and his world had fallen apart.

At the hospital, he parked and tried to avoid a news reporter apparently waiting for him to arrive. "Did your daughter get ill because of her mother's murder, Mr. McKenzie?" God help him, but he wanted to shove her microphone out of his face and growl at her. Instead, he walked inside and tried to ignore the stares and pitying looks from staff as he walked toward the office. A man sitting nearby stared at him as he walked by. Short blonde hair, thick blonde brows, slim, expensive suit, shiny dress shoes, and the bluest eyes. He dipped his head once at Kyle and actually smirked, as if he knew something about Kyle that no one else had discovered.

Who was he? Another reporter?

Someone said, "Good morning, Mr. McKenzie," and held the office door open for him. He thanked her and walked inside. He turned around, but the blonde man was gone. Kyle looked out the glass windows. The man was nowhere in sight.

"May I help you, Mr. McKenzie?"

"Yes. Good morning. I'm here to take April home."

The secretary smiled and said, "Everything's ready for you. Just sign these papers." He did. "Dr. Weisbrod would like you to come in on Tuesday so she can discuss test results with you. Around three?"

"That's fine." He nodded and left. Lynette usually texted him results. Why would he need to come in?

Opening April's door, he studied her while she slept—but not for long. She opened her eyes and smiled at him and made his world complete.

"She rested very well." Mrs. Naugitt gathered up her things. "A man came by and stuck his head in. Said he was a friend of yours and just wanted to check on April."

A friend? Kyle frowned at her. "Did he leave a name?"

"No. It was a quick visit."

"Describe him."

"A very nice suit, thin, blonde hair, and the prettiest blue eyes. He said he was glad that she was doing better and left."

"Thank you." Kyle had no idea who the man was, but he was obviously the well-dressed man Kyle had seen in the lobby. Maybe he was a friend of Kevin's. Or a reporter snooping around.

Mrs. Naugitt left then.

Kyle scooped his baby girl into his arms. "Are you ready to go home, sweetheart? Hmm? Your aunts and uncles and cousins are waiting for the party to get there."

A nurse opened the door. "I'll walk you down, Mr. McKenzie."

Nodding at her, he carefully positioned April into the curve of his arm to avoid the tube in her chest and kissed her forehead. "I love you, sweetheart." Saying it was never enough. Now, he felt the overwhelming need to be both mother and father to her and wondered how in the world he would ever be able to manage.

FIVE

Kyle didn't have time to think about Margot. As soon as a thought crept in, one of his brothers managed to distract him. All morning, the McKenzie men entertained him with card games, dominoes, and quiet talks around the dining table about his options for the future.

Kevin went with Kyle to make funeral arrangements for Margot's graveside service, a private family gathering set for ten o'clock Monday. On their way home, Kyle called Natalie. He was sure she'd heard by now about Margot's death, and he dreaded her response to it. "Natalie, it's Kyle McKenzie. How are you?"

"I'm fine. More importantly, how are you?"

"You've heard about my wife, Margot. You must have questions. I'd like to meet with you and Aunt Essie to discuss the answers with you. I don't know much myself, but if you'd like to step back from taking this—"

"Excuse me, Mr. McKenzie. But my aunt and I would like to come to your home and care for April. Nothing has changed."

Her response was surreal and difficult to believe. "You've checked up on me."

Kevin turned his head and looked at Kyle.

"Well, yes. I've talked to friends and also had a background check done."

"That was quick."

"It helps to have friends in high places."

He could hear a bit of a smile in her voice. "Did I pass?"

"'Squeaky clean' were his exact words."

"'Squeaky clean'?"

Kevin winked at his brother. "Thank you, Mom," he whispered.

Kyle nodded. She had preached 'the future' to her eight sons constantly. Her favorite mantra was, "Don't get involved in anything your grandfather would disapprove of. You wouldn't want to disappoint Papa Kenneth, would you?" And, of course, none of them did. Kenneth McKenzie was the backbone of the McKenzie family until his death when Kyle was nineteen. "I appreciate your willingness to help us, Natalie. It may be rocky at times as they search for her killer."

"I'm not fragile, Mr. McKen—"

"Please, call me Kyle."

"All right. I don't know if my aunt will be able to, but I will. What time would you like us to arrive at your home?"

"The service is set for ten o'clock on Monday. My brothers will be leaving shortly after to go home. April naps around three o'clock. If you could come early afternoon, say by one, Mrs. Naugitt can take you through her routine."

"That sounds great. We'll see you at one on Monday."

It was late. No one was in Kyle's bedroom to shoo away the ghosts or the memories or the realization that Margot was really gone.

In the dark, he squinted at the bedside clock that said *1:43*, so tired he couldn't muster up the energy to get off the bed and undress. His bones felt absolutely formless; his chest, heavy with pain; his heart, empty.

It had been two unbelievably difficult days, even with his family here. Maybe because they were here. If he'd been alone, he'd have punched a hole in something, thrown things, yelled.

The house was as quiet as a tomb. He heard Margot say, "I hate you for letting her live." He glanced over at the closet. In his mind, he re-played her stomping around the room, throwing bottles, glaring at him, shouting, gritting her teeth. So much anger and hate.

He glanced at her picture on the table next to his bed. His gaze rested on the Bible beside her picture. He reached for it, but a miserable kind of guilt and emptiness prevented him from opening it.

A man's voice. "I've always liked the sound of your laughter, Margot."

Kyle slowly lifted his head, slamming his eyes shut against the memory.

Her husky response. "Have you?" And then she chuckled as if the man had said something foolish.

The memory had haunted him all day.

He clearly recalled the day, some months after they'd married. He'd come home late and heard Margot laughing. He'd been suspicious, or he wouldn't have calmly walked to the phone, carefully lifted the receiver, and listened to a man telling her he had always liked the sound of her laughter.

Kyle silently replaced the receiver, stalked to the front door, and slammed it. "Margot?"

She came out of the bedroom, scowled at him from the loft outside their bedroom, the laughter gone.

"Who was that on the phone?"

She tugged on the hem of her maternity blouse. "What phone?"

"Just now. Who were you talking to?"

A shoulder lifted. "Who says I was talking to anyone?"

"I do. I heard you."

"You couldn't have. You just walked in." She lifted her brows as she walked back into their bedroom.

He'd guessed that she used the house phone instead of her cell because there wouldn't be a record of the call.

He never brought up the subject again. Had she run off with this man, and then he killed her? That's the only explanation that made any sense.

He knew so little about his wife—but not for want of trying. Every door he'd opened, she'd slammed shut. He'd loved her from the moment he'd met her, but he honestly didn't think she'd loved him back. Or if she ever had, it hadn't lasted past getting pregnant.

Kyle fell back against the comforter and closed his eyes. He could smell the vanilla-scented candles on the bedside table, but for the life of him, he couldn't remember the last time Margot had lit them.

His life was in shambles. It *had* been for a long time.

He could clearly pinpoint the second the edges had begun to unravel.

Two years ago.

February 11th.

Nine-thirty-seven p.m.

"My interview, Dad. It's on the radio." Kyle switched the phone to his other ear and paced around his bedroom. "KWBE, AM. Quick."

"I'm pulling over, son. I'm in the middle of nowhere. Hold on." A long pause. "There. I found it."

They listened together on their cell phones. Kyle imagined his father's proud smile as he heard his son being interviewed as an up-and-coming executive at McKenzie Engineering. A commercial came on. "Okay. This next part's about the—"

A thud. Another thud. "What was that, Dad?"

His father grunted. "Some jerk—what do you want? Who are you?"

"Nobody, Mr. McKenzie. And neither are you."

A gasp. A sound like a spitting whisper. A moan. Then nothing but the sound of Kyle's voice on the radio.

"Dad, what happened? Dad?" Frantic, he raced to the phone on his desk while he held his cell phone, screaming, "Dad? Dad?" He managed to punch in 9-1-1.

His father had been shot between the eyes.

If Kyle hadn't called him.

If Dad hadn't pulled over to listen.

If he hadn't been in that one spot, at that particular moment.

And Margot.

Kyle had only to think her name to feel the blame.

She had to have been miserable. No other explanation made sense. She had to have felt hopeless, weary, desperate.

But how had she gotten to that place where hope no longer thrived, and joy died under the trampling feet of despair?

And how much of it was his fault?

Saturday morning sunlight warmed his back. With his eyes closed and his head back, the heat soothed him. He rested for a while and almost drifted into sleep when he jerked awake. Someone had placed a hot cup of coffee on the table next to his chair.

He picked it up and sipped. Sitting in the flowered nook overlooking the Cupid fountain, a wedding present given by an aunt two years ago, he squelched the urge to knock the little grin off Cupid's face, especially since the last two years had been nothing but a dismal failure in the love department.

Bacon scents filled the air. Mac's wife Marianne was talking to someone behind him in the kitchen. The screen door opened. "Morning, Kyle."

Without turning around, he said, "Thanks for the coffee, Marianne."

"You're welcome. Breakfast will be ready in about five minutes," she said and then the door closed.

He'd checked in with his secretary earlier and let her know he'd be taking off not just Monday and Tuesday but the entire week.

After constantly worrying over April the last two days, he could set aside some of his anger. Margot's life hadn't been easy.

He'd never intended that.

The first time he'd met her, she'd come to the single adult group at church. She seemed a little nervous, like a butterfly among bees, which plucked every protective string his male heart had. She was beautiful. Dark auburn hair—from a bottle, he found out later—and rich brown eyes. All the men were fascinated with her. But she'd chosen Kyle to go out with later that week.

He'd felt like a king.

He stared at her flowers lining the path to the gazebo. He recalled her childlike joy as she walked around the empty yards, planning and designing her flowers. She worked for weeks, preparing the soil, coordinating colors, planting, nurturing, fussing. She seemed eager to get her hands dirty, waving off his suggestion to hire a gardener. *"Oh, no, Kyle. This is something I enjoy doing. Really."*

Gardening was Margot's gift. She created beautiful flower arrangements. But this last year, he had rarely seen her tending to anything but April.

The mornings before work, his quick kiss good-bye barely made contact on her or the baby before he grabbed his keys and left.

He couldn't wait to get out of the house.

He'd stop at Maudie's Coffee Shop and get a pastry with coffee or drive through a fast-food restaurant and gulp down a breakfast sandwich.

At the office, he was successful, admired, sought after for answers to difficult problems. People could count on him to make things right.

But not at home. There, he was a failure, and Margot constantly let him know it. Not by words so much as by her looks, her coldness, her accusing glares. And, certainly, their lack of intimacy. They hadn't made love in months. The strain of raising a handicapped child, he'd assured himself. When April was better, things would be different.

When April was better.

She's going to die, you know.

"No, Margot. *You* died." Abruptly, he swiped up a bunch of flowers and threw them as hard as he could across the yard. Of course, they defiantly fluttered to the grass not four feet from where he stood.

"A lot of good that'll do you."

He turned around.

Kevin stood by the fountain, arms crossed, mouth set. "You need one of those bats made out of foam rubber."

"Did you bring one?"

Kevin was staring at him. He was probably going through his list of appropriate things to say at such a time and figured he was coming up short.

"You look tired."

"I haven't slept."

"I'm so sorry."

"I know."

"Have the police contacted you about anything?"

"Not today."

A long pause. "Would you like me to pray with you?"

Kyle tried not to smirk. He wasn't exactly in a let's-get-spiritual frame of mind. He couldn't ever remember a time in his life that he didn't want to pray. Even when his father's murder had knocked his world off its foundation, he'd continued the connection.

But not now. He didn't know how to put words together to make sense of anything Margot had done. "I don't think He wants to hear what I have to say today."

"Kyle."

"Yeah, yeah, I know, Kev." With both hands, he squeezed the back of his neck and leaned back. "I'm just, I don't know, just trying to make it through one day at a time, all right?"

Kevin nodded. "The girls told me to come and get you. Breakfast is ready."

"Good. My coffee's cold."

The house phone rang as Kyle walked toward the coffee pot.

Marianne answered it. Grimly, she held out the receiver. "Kyle, it's the police."

He took it. "Hello? Yes. Yes, of course." He hung up. "Detectives

Phillips and Mancini want to come by the house in about two hours. They suggested all the McKenzies be in this meeting. Marianne, would you be in charge of the kids while they're here?"

"Of course," she answered. "Is there news about Margot?"

"I don't know." Kyle lifted the coffee pot. "But it's important enough that they want all of us together."

Kevin nodded. "Call Barry. He'll want to be here."

After breakfast, Kyle walked with April to the den's sliding glass doors and opened them. He turned so she could watch her older cousins running through the rotating lawn sprinklers, giggling and clapping their hands, chasing one another. Kevin's children were playing in the sprinklers. Four-year-old Mikey sneaked up behind two-year-old Ramon and tickled his ribs. They both screamed when their big brother, Jeremy, loomed above them like a monster with his arms high, his hands like claws. Ramon squealed and ran into his mother's arms; Lila laughed and rocked him. Kyle had always wanted what Kevin had—a family that loved each other.

He watched all his brothers and their wives, seated in a circle around the children. Mac held his sleeping five-month-old baby girl on his chest. His wife, Marianne, reached over, stroked his arm, and slid her hand down to his. He gripped it and held it as he smiled at her. *Had he and Margot ever touched each other like that?*

His brother, Bobby, and his wife each held an eight-month-old twin girl, obviously relaxed with each other. Bobby leaned over, holding a baby, and kissed his wife. Luke and his wife, Sarah, hadn't been married but a few months; they laughed at lot together. Kyle had never had that indefinable ease with Margot. Everything had been a fight.

He looked down at April. She was smiling, and his heart swelled.

"April's here!" Marianne laughed when Sarah stood at the same time she did. "I'm ready to fight for her," Marianne said as she sent her sister-in-law a 'double-dog-dare-ya' look. "First one to the wall wins!" Marianne leaped over a lawn chair.

"No fair!" Sarah laughed. "You got a head start!"

"Yeah, and I'm going to win, too!"

"I get next dibs on her." Sarah sat back down next to Luke.

Marianne walked to the door and beamed at April. "Did our little girl wake up?" She gently took her from Kyle. "Hello, sweet angel." Marianne turned around and said, "Hey, guys! Look who's here! April's awake."

The kids stopped and waved at April, then started chasing one another again. Mac, Luke, and Bobby waved from their lawn chairs, and Kyle thought how blessed he was to have four of his six brothers and their families here.

Marianne settled April in a car seat beside her. From this direction, Kyle could only see April's little hands, popping up as if she were reaching for a butterfly.

She's going to die, you know.

Biting back a heavy sigh, Kyle crossed his arms and watched the children play. His mother walked up beside him and looked outside.

"For the life of me, I cannot understand how a woman could plan something that would involve leaving her baby behind."

He slipped his arm around her shoulders. "Margot didn't leave us last Friday, Mom. She was never here. I just didn't know it." He glanced down at her. "I should have known, don't you think?"

"Don't blame yourself."

"There's no one else to blame." Desperate to get outside, he tugged her through the sliding glass doors. "Come on. Let's join the party."

"I can only stay another five minutes. I have an appointment." She laughed as she accepted the running, wet hugs of her grandkids.

"You have no regard, I'm to understand, for the position of your family, then? You will do this thing against our express wishes? Your mother's and mine? Am I to understand that as well?"

It always amused Natalie that when her grandmother wanted to make a point, she would speak in a language far better suited for the nineteenth century than the twenty-first.

"Grandmother, all you need to understand is that I want to do this."

"And your *wants* are certainly more important than ours."

Natalie held up a hand. The woman could make a nun at least

want to *consider* saying something uncharitable. "I didn't say that. You were talking about understanding and I'm trying to make sure you do."

"You will be implicated in this sordid and unsavory drama as a third party, as a *paramour*. Mark my words."

"Grandmother, please."

"The man's wife was murdered on Thursday. Are you so sure that you can walk into his home and know that he wasn't the one who killed her?"

"I've talked to several friends who gave him a glowing recommendation. Jake Fletcher did a quick background check for me. Mr. McKenzie is 'squeaky clean.' Jake's words." She stopped packing and turned to her grandmother. "This won't be a forever thing. I know I'm supposed to do this. Please allow me to walk my own path without this opposition."

"Such a grand speech, young lady. It's a shame it's a self-centered one." On a deep sigh, her grandmother lowered herself into a chair and suddenly looked as old as she was. No amount of make-up or cosmetic surgery could cover it. "Just like your Uncle Abbott, leaving his wife and kids to go off on some harebrained venture that ended up embarrassing the entire family. It took us—"

"Years to overcome the humiliation. I've heard the story many times, especially when *I'm* starting a new venture. Now, if you'll excuse me, I need to keep packing."

"Very well. When this thing falls apart around your feet, don't expect me to help you pick up the pieces."

"I would never ask that of you." She lifted one side of her mouth. "I know how you hate menial labor."

"Impertinent child."

So much like you.

"Go, then, and have your way."

As you would.

"You will live to regret this."

"My only regret is your disapproval."

"Well, that is something I *never* wanted you to have!" And then she left.

"This is something I want you to have, Natalie."

Another memory! Why was she remembering her father so much lately?

They were outside, playing tea party, and her daddy asked her about her dreams.

"I don't have any."

He leaned over, plucked at her heart, and set something imaginary on his hand. He lifted his hand and studied it as if it were a glittering diamond. Lifting an imaginary lid, he peered inside and gasped. "What? No dreams?"

She shook her head and lowered her eyes.

"Then we'll have to put one here in the secret place—a place where dreams stay alive. Tell me a dream you have, Natalie."

"Like at night, when I sleep?"

"No, when you're awake."

"What?"

"Like a wish. Tell me one of your wishes."

"Oh." Her shoulder lifted. "I don't know."

He lowered his hand, his eyes suddenly serious. "You have to have dreams, Natalie. They don't come from here—" he pointed to his head, "—but from here." He tapped his chest. "You can't dream, sweetheart, without engaging your heart. You have to set your heart free to dream."

She scrunched her nose and frowned at him.

"Okay. If you turn the key to your heart, it starts to dream. Like this." He closed his eyes as if he were about to blow out birthday candles. Then he opened them and plucked at the air just above her heart. With his pinkie, he opened the lid of the imaginary box on his hand and dropped what he'd plucked from the air inside. "There. Your first dream."

"What is it?"

"I can't tell you. But someday, when this dream comes true, you'll know you found your treasure."

"My treasure?"

"The dream I have for you."

"I have one."

"You do?"

He seemed pleased when she nodded, smiling. She wanted to

grow up and marry someone just like her daddy. But she didn't tell him that dream. She told him she wanted a Barbie doll.

"Good, good."

Solemnly, she plucked her dream out of the air and carefully put it in the beautiful box and closed the lid.

Her father beamed. "You have two dreams now." He laughed and raised the imaginary box into the air. "Engaging your heart is fun, isn't it, Natalie?" With a flourish, he put the secret place back inside her heart.

And then, in a matter of months, he was gone.

As were her dreams. For dreams surely couldn't live inside a little girl's broken heart.

SIX

The same two detectives, Phillips and Mancini, stood on the front porch when Kyle opened the door. Phillips held a briefcase.

"Mr. McKenzie, we have new information we'd like to discuss with you."

Kyle stepped back. "Of course. My brothers are here, so they'll join us, as well as my attorney, Barry Harrison. Let's go to the den again."

Kevin was pacing by the fireplace and stopped when they entered. Mac, Luke, and Bobby introduced themselves to the detectives. His attorney, Barry, lifted a yellow legal pad in greeting and kept his seat next to a small sofa.

Phillips placed his briefcase on a table. "It might be best if all of you sat down. This might take a few minutes. You'll have questions, I'm sure."

"All right." Kevin sat beside Kyle. Luke, Bobby, and Mac eased onto a large sofa, completing the half circle facing the detectives.

Phillips chuckled as he looked at Kyle and Kevin. "It's strange seeing you two side by side. Y'all are sure identical."

Kevin turned and looked at Kyle. Kyle raised his brows. So, this was going to be a friendly exchange today?

Phillips didn't expect an answer apparently because he opened the briefcase and tugged out some papers. "Mr. McKenzie—Kyle—do you know a man named Marlin Candles?" The detective's gaze never left the papers.

Candles. Candles. "No," Kyle answered. "I can't say I do."

Phillips nodded thoughtfully, still looking through the papers.

"Should I?" Marlin Candles. Something was familiar about his name.

"He handles some of your accounts with Granger and Grimes."

"They're my accountants, but I don't recognize his name."

"Ah, here it is." Phillips read for a moment. "Seven months before you met Margot Springs, he was hired on at Granger and Grimes."

"That was right after I inherited my grandfather's ranch, Fairfield."

"Yes. A month after. And within six months, Candles was promoted to handle some of your accounts with supervision."

"Okay." All of his accounts were rather substantial, worth millions. He seemed to recall someone from Granger and Grimes informing him of this change but didn't think anything else of it. He trusted them, as had his grandfather.

"Yes. Apparently, Candles is brilliant. 'Very, very good,' they said. 'Thorough'." Phillips lifted his brows at Kyle. "We found out yesterday that Mr. Candles was legally married to Margot Springs."

What? "Was?" Kyle frowned, trying to understand what he meant. "Before she married me?"

"No. While." Detective Phillips slowly shook his head. "*While* she was married to you."

"While?" Shocked, Kyle looked at Kevin, his brothers. "*While* she was married to me? But that can't be. That would be—"

"Bigamy." Barry nodded grimly.

Phillips' gaze locked on Barry's. "Yes, sir, it would. And the name he used on the first marriage certificate three years ago was not Candles. It was Jesser. Gordon Jesser. Several law enforcement agencies know Gordon Jesser."

"Know him? Why?"

"I'll get to that in a minute, Kyle." Phillips flipped a page, read a little. Then he looked at Kevin, then Kyle, and the other brothers as if he dreaded saying more. "There was a match for the bullet found in Margot Springs."

Kyle leaned forward.

"It matched the bullet that killed your father, Gerald McKenzie, over two years ago."

Kyle jerked. He felt as if a wrecking ball had just slammed into his chest. He couldn't breathe or think for a few moments. Then he was suddenly so angry that he stood and stepped toward the detectives. "You're saying the woman I loved killed *my father?*"

His brothers wore the same shocked expressions. One by one, they rose to their feet. They stood around Phillips, stunned into silence. Then they all began to talk at once.

"What are—?!"

"Are you saying—"

"—his name again?"

"What's being done to find—"

"—me get my hands on—"

Barry raised his hands and patted the air around them. "Guys, calm down. Let the man get everything said."

Phillips and Mancini presented a united but smaller front against the six-foot-four average of the McKenzie brothers. No one sat, but they did quiet down.

"Gordon Jesser is a known con man. One of the best out there. A predator. Has an extensive rap sheet, including murder. Everything he does is based on deception. He's been known to take two or three years to set up a con. Kyle was his mark; your father's death was revenge but also the catalyst for his con."

"Revenge for what?" Mac stepped forward. "Our father wouldn't have been connected to this man for any reason."

Phillips nodded. "Most of his victims have no idea Jesser is entangled in their affairs. We cross-checked Jesser and his aliases with your father. We found a possible motive for revenge *and* to set up the con."

"All right. What?" This, from Kevin.

"Twenty-five years ago, Lamar Jesser was caught rustling cattle off McKenzie Ranch and was sent to prison. He escaped after three years, was shot and killed in a hostage situation. He was a grifter who trained his son to run different cons. Gordon Jesser is his son."

Kyle quickly glanced at his brothers. "Wait. Are you telling us our father was killed because of something that happened twenty-five years ago that wasn't his *fault*?"

Phillips nodded again. "We suspect Gordon Jesser never forgot the man who sent his father to prison. You inherited your grandfather's very lucrative ranch in July, almost three years ago. At that time, you became their mark."

"Their? Margot and Jesser?"

"Yes."

"But why kill Dad? He didn't have anything to do with *any* of this."

"Cons like Jesser and his wife are pros. They try to make sure they're successful in every respect. Killing your father helped make you vulnerable to their con. We suspect this because Margot made her move on you within two weeks of his death."

Kyle inwardly groaned. Phillips had nailed it. Kyle had felt lost after his dad's murder and so alive from Margot's attention.

"Let's look at the timeline, as far as we can figure it at this point." Phillips nodded at Kyle. "July, you inherit Fairfield Ranch. August, Jesser is working at your accounting firm. Glowing references. February, six months later, three things happen: he's handling some of your accounts, he kills your father, and you meet Margot Springs. Five months later, in July, you're married to Jesser's accomplice. The con is now a full go—a year, almost to the day, after you inherited Fairfield Ranch. Almost a year for Jesser to be established in the accounting firm."

Phillips seemed to let that sink in for a few seconds. "Like we said, Jesser takes his time setting up the con. Twenty-one months later, the scam ends, and Jesser's accomplice is dead."

"But what was the scam? I married his wife. It was part of their plan. There's got to be more to it than that."

"Since he had access to your money, we suspect he stole from you. Money is usually the motive for a scam."

Barry leaned forward. "You need to set up an independent audit *today* to find out just how much they took."

Kyle slowly nodded.

Phillips slipped the papers back into his briefcase and closed it. "Jesser is dangerous. He's been known to re-visit a mark. He threatens, extorts, kills. You need to be cautious and keep your family safe. Hire a security expert. He'll be able to tell you how to stay safe. Right now, *our* top priority is to locate Jesser."

"He shouldn't be too difficult to find." Luke, his quiet brother. "The motel owner saw him, could identify him."

"Our sketch artist has done just that, but Gordon Jesser is a master chameleon. He never showed himself to the motel owner as Gordon Jesser but as Clarence Dewberry."

Mac scowled. "A chameleon?"

"A master of disguises. He can become anyone, any nationality, either sex. He can completely vanish with a new persona and identity. That's how he's evaded the police for so many years, and that's how he'll evade you—until he strikes again."

Phillips picked up his briefcase. "We can't stress that aspect enough. He could be anyone you meet. Think of him as a predator in disguise. He's about five-foot-ten, slim, charming, athletic, and brilliant."

He glanced at Mancini. "I spoke with a detective who told me they had Jesser in their sights a few years ago. They watched him go inside a small, two-story building. Police surrounded it, searched inside, and found four women who lived there, all with proper IDs. They interviewed them; one left. No one else was in the building."

Kevin said, "He was the woman who got away."

"Yes. Jesser had vanished in plain sight. That was the one mistake he made: the police discovered he was a chameleon, that that was how he'd been able to outsmart us at every turn. That's all we have right now. Any questions?"

Mac said, "Do you have any idea where he is?"

"None whatsoever. We'll let you know when we discover more information." The detectives left.

In a daze, Kyle dropped onto the sofa. *They killed Dad. Margot killed Dad. She lived with me, I loved her, and she killed Dad.* Kyle was so angry, he wanted to punch something.

Mac said, "He could be anyone. A pastor, a police officer, an old man."

Luke frowned. "A woman."

"How am I going to protect April against someone I don't know is a threat?" A sickening thought entered Kyle's mind. "Oh, no."

Barry looked at him. "What?"

"If Margot was married to Jesser, then—" His gaze locked on Barry. "April may not be mine."

Silence answered him.

Barry shook his head. "Okay. Look. If she isn't yours, it would usually open up legal possibilities for the father, but no court in the land would grant Jesser custody. Plus, he's a wanted man, a murderer; he wouldn't come out of hiding to get her. Third, he won't take her for leverage; she wouldn't live very long in his care."

"The *threat* of taking her would be enough for me to give him everything I own."

"First, call Lynette Weisbrod today and ask her to set up paternity tests. Second, talk to a security expert. Third, order an audit of your accounts at Granger and Grimes and find out just how much Jesser took." Barry made notes on the yellow pad. "I'll work the marriage end, see if there was a previous divorce or annulment. First and foremost, you have to keep April safe." He left.

Kyle stood beside his brothers, all wearing similar expressions of anger, frustration, and sadness. No one spoke. There was simply too much hurt in the room.

"One thing, Kyle," Mac said quietly. "Jesser could have chosen me, or Luke, or you. The three single McKenzies at the time. It just happened to be you."

Yeah, but if I'd listened to Mom's warnings about Margot, none of this would have happened. But I wouldn't have April, either. "Thanks, buddy. Right now, we have to get to Mom and let her know what the police said before she sees it on the news."

That night, Kyle excused himself from the family gathering and went to bed. Tomorrow was Sunday. He longed to hear something that would help ease the guilt of not recognizing that the woman he met at a church party was capable not only of stealing from him, but of murdering his father.

In the morning, Kyle dragged himself out of bed around six after another restless night. He showered, dressed, and went downstairs. Of course, his family was up. They greeted him with coffee and breakfast. He took the coffee but not the food.

He needed to get away.

"I'm taking a ride to the park. Just need some time to think."

Kevin argued with him about going alone, but he stood firm. Everything was caving in on him, and he didn't think he could stand another second in the house. Margot was everywhere. She had touched everything in his home. Besides, he was tired of being civil. He needed to get away, so he could vent a little and not hurt or frighten anyone with the anger overwhelming him.

Ten minutes later, he parked and got out. He looked up at the quiet overcast sky and strolled down a wide path. His mind was a jumble of questions, and he couldn't find any answers to them that made sense—only more questions.

Thunder cracked right above him. He ducked instinctively and then looked up just as hard rain pelted the park. He dug his keys out and ran to the far corner of the parking lot, hustled inside his truck, and glared at the umbrella sitting on the seat beside him. He angrily slung water off his hands.

The storm hit with a vengeance, which perfectly matched his foul mood. Quarter-sized raindrops pounded everything in sight. Trees floundered against the force of the wind. A woman walked in front his truck, bravely fighting the wind to keep her umbrella in one piece. He looked closer. Was it a woman? Or was it Jesser, following him? She got in her car and didn't leave.

Backing out of the parking space, Kyle's tires spun then hydroplaned as he turned too quickly. Jerking the wheel, he straightened it just in time to avoid hitting the woman's parked car. He pulled over and took a moment to calm himself. It wouldn't do April any good if he got himself killed.

But calm never came.

The frenzied rain smacked his windshield.

Wind lashed out at his truck in angry swipes.

He pressed the heel of his hand hard against his chest as he lowered his forehead to the steering wheel.

Everything hurt so much.

He wanted to run away from all of it, to escape to a place where nothing hurt, where his little girl was well, where his father was still alive, where the woman he had loved was his wife and not a murderer who'd stolen his father and his money.

Kyle closed his eyes and took deep breaths for several moments. The woman still sat in her car. Was she watching him? Was she Jesser? He couldn't see. Her windows were fogged.

He looked around. He wouldn't be leaving anytime soon, so he turned on the radio. Good Shepherd's service came in clearly, despite the storm.

"It is for freedom that Christ has set us free."

The words from the worship leader taunted him.

When Kyle thought of freedom, visions of flying angels and floating bubbles and dogs enjoying the wind as they hung out a car window came to mind. What did, "It is for freedom," mean?

Freedom from pain? That was a laugh. Pain followed him everywhere he went because April was ill, and he couldn't do anything to help her.

Guilt? It was in everything he did. He was guilty of choosing a wife for all the wrong reasons. Of putting his father in the wrong place at the wrong time. Of not knowing who his wife was.

Freedom from anger? He failed there, too.

He turned off the radio. The windows had clouded.

She's going to die, you know.

He closed his eyes, eased his head back, and listened to the storm raging around him as his truck shimmied in the terrific wind.

But he wasn't afraid.

He was simply too bone tired to care.

Kyle woke up. It was dark.

He glanced at his phone. *8:42.*

How could he have slept that long in his truck?

He backed out and drove for home. The storm was long gone. The pavement shined in the streetlights. Puddles were everywhere. A man walked down the sidewalk in a shopping area, stopped, and turned as Kyle drove toward him. As he passed him, the man continued to stare.

Was it Jesser? Was he waiting for Kyle's truck to drive by? The detectives said Jesser was about five-foot-ten and thin. But this man looked much taller. It wasn't him.

But another man stood in the doorway of a store, watching him, too. His body type fit. Was he Jesser?

Frustrated, Kyle drove home to face his family and to gear up for saying good riddance to Margot in the morning.

"It's funeral day," Gordon sing-songed as he adjusted the hump on his back and tightened the straps. It was risky, but he couldn't resist the chance to see Margot's other family fawning over her, weeping for a woman who had detested them. It was just too absurdly funny to miss. He would go to the funeral today, not that he owed her anything.

He just wanted to watch. Then he'd leave this scummy little anthill of a town with all his money intact.

Maybe. Maybe not.

He looked in the mirror. An elderly, feeble man looked back at him. It had taken him close to two hours to get every detail perfect, every line and wrinkle and puffy spot. When he grinned at himself, his face cracked like a porcelain pot. He admired first one side, then the other. "Excellent, if I do say so myself."

The final touch: his teeth. He slipped on the dentures and smiled. Now he had gray, chipped, and lopsided teeth.

He tugged on the wig. It was secure.

He patted the eyebrows. Like glue.

Picking up his hat and cane, he did a little song-and-dance twirl and chuckled to himself. "Show time, old chap." He slipped into character, leaned over, smacked his lips, and shuffled his way toward the door, leaning heavily on his cane.

No one would think this wobbly old man would hurt a fly, much less kill. Absolutely no one at all.

Kyle stood over Margot's grave. The day was hot and humid already. He had asked his brothers not to attend this fiasco, but they had insisted on supporting him, as had his mother.

A small gathering ushered Margot Springs Jesser into eternal life. Closing his eyes, Kyle decided, then and there, as the words 'dust to dust' were coming out of his pastor's mouth, that he would shed no more tears for her.

It surprised him how easily he could shut the door on this chapter in his life just four days after her death. Any regrets he harbored centered around his poor judgment and how effortlessly he'd been taken in by the Jessers. He was determined that the regrets would not hold him in the past—which meant, of course, that he would have to forgive both of them. Margot was easy; he was magnanimously forgiving someone who could no longer hurt him.

But Jesser. Now that was a different story.

He glanced at Margot's coffin and could well imagine that were she alive and able to watch this spectacle, she—and Jesser—would have enjoyed seeing their mark standing over her grave, pretending to grieve for a woman he had never known.

He had never known.

His pastor finished his prayer with an "Amen" and "God bless you all," then reached over to shake Kyle's hand. He also spoke a few words to his brothers and then left.

Kyle took in a long breath and discovered only a deep sense of relief remained. It was over. Healing could begin. He nodded at his mother. She smiled quickly, took his arm, and they walked away.

An old man stood beside a nearby grave, leaning on his cane with both hands. Kyle had noticed him glancing over at Margot's small group of mourners several times. When he did, he almost fell over. He must be visiting the grave of his wife.

Kyle looked up as they strolled past him and pitied him as he struggled to slip big sunshades over his glasses. The old man said something to him, and he stopped.

"Excuse me, sir?"

"I said, young fella, did your wife pass on?"

Kyle's jaw clenched. "No. She was someone I didn't even know."

The old man cocked an ear. "How's that now?"

"Nothing."

"Well, maybe so. I'm sorry for your loss, then, young fella."

Kyle turned to look at the mound of dirt ready to be thrust on top of Margot's casket. "It was no loss," he answered, "but thank you for the sentiment."

The old man turned back to his grave. He said something to the headstone. When he wiped his nose with a hankie, an unusual marking on the back of his hand caught his eye: a tattoo of a poised-to-strike snake.

He glanced back at the old man a few seconds later. He was laughing about something, shaking his head, and looking remarkably happy.

Aunt Essie, bless her heart, fixed a big lunch for all the McKenzies: roasted chicken, sweet potato casserole, fruit salad, green beans, cream gravy, dinner rolls, and pecan pie. Her face was a little red from either the exertion or the excitement of having eager stomachs to fill. Natalie guessed it was a little of both.

"To Aunt Essie," Kyle stood at the head of the huge table and raised his glass of iced tea. Everyone followed suit. "You have created a delicious masterpiece. Thank you!"

"Hear, hear," his family members chorused, and all sat down to enjoy it.

Aunt Essie acknowledged their praise with a blush and escaped to the kitchen with Natalie. She grinned from ear to ear. "I'm overwhelmed. Let's just hope, my dear, that it's tasty to them."

"I know it is." Natalie hugged her. "You've set everything out for them, so let's slip up to our rooms and enjoy some quiet time. We can check on April and say our goodbyes to his brothers when they leave later. But right now, I'm exhausted."

"Me, too." Aunt Essie giggled. "But oh, my dear, it feels so good to be useful again!"

SEVEN

The next day, Tuesday, Lynette Weisbrod came into the room and smiled at Kyle. At that moment, he knew something was wrong. He dreaded the word he figured she would say; it was the thing he feared the most.

"She needs a transplant within the next few weeks."

And there it was. For several moments, he stared at her, then anger gripped him. *Not this soon.* He'd thought they'd have more time.

"The reconstruction surgery at birth hasn't lived up to what we wanted. She needs a new liver within eight to twelve weeks at the outside. A small bowel would be a bonus."

She's going to die, you know.

"Will she be strong enough to handle the surgeries?"

Lynette blinked several times at him as if she were trying to choose the right words. "I hope so. I think so."

"Thank you," he said and left.

The rain had started after he'd arrived at the hospital. Weeping skies—a perfect metaphor. He hurried to his pickup and got inside. He was sopping wet, but he didn't care. His baby was dying.

Ten minutes later, he drove straight into the garage, scrambled out of his truck, and shoved the kitchen door open, expecting to find someone inside. But no one was there. He stood for a moment in the silence and waited impatiently for the first sound of her. Then he heard a tiny giggle, and Natalie's low-pitched voice. "I'll huff, and I'll puff, and I'll—"

His heart soared at his daughter's laughter. "April?" He took quick steps down the hall. "April?"

Natalie smiled and tapped April's nose. "Daddy's home! Did you hear him? Daddy's home."

Dripping wet with an anxious expression on his face, Kyle strode across the room with his gaze on April.

Natalie's heartbeat quickened. Something was wrong.

"Here, Kyle," she said as she stood and handed him April. "Let me get you a towel."

April giggled when Kyle burrowed into her neck and gave her kisses, careful, Natalie noted, to keep his kisses away from the feeding catheter that entered her upper chest.

"Daddy loves you, April."

He seemed frantic, desperate. Backing out of the room, she watched him struggle to smile at April. His eyes were brimming with tears. Something was horribly wrong.

When she returned with a towel, he handed April to her and took the towel without looking at her. Wiping his face and neck, he draped it over his shoulder and reached for his daughter. "Daddy's wet, huh, sweetheart? It's raining outside and all I could think about was getting back here to you." He quickly turned and headed toward the stairs.

Aunt Essie stood in the other doorway, her face anxious. "Oh, my goodness," she whispered as Natalie walked toward her.

"The test results," Natalie said as Kyle hurried up the stairs. "He must have received the test results, and they weren't good."

Aunt Essie's fingers touched her mouth as she blinked back tears. "What could it mean? Is she in any danger of, of—?"

"It could be any number of things. We'll just have to wait until he tells us. Come on, now. Mr. McKenzie probably needs to eat his lunch. I'll help you set the table."

Carrying April, Kyle cleared his throat when he walked into the dining room a few minutes later. The table was set for three, with lighted candles on either side of a fresh arrangement of colorful flowers. Margot's flowers. The sight of them made him sick.

Aunt Essie clutched the back of a dining chair, blinking back tears. Natalie was next to her, watching him intently.

Knowing he had to get the words out, he looked down at April. "Our little girl needs a liver transplant." He swallowed hard, blinking quickly, and kept his gaze on her. "Lynette says she has eight to twelve weeks to get it. She's on a waiting list."

He kissed the top of her head twice and then smiled at Aunt Essie. "Thank you for the dinner and the nice flower arrangement. If you don't mind, I'd like to go up and change my clothes. If you want to go ahead and eat—"

"We'll all eat together when you're ready, Mr. McKenzie, unless you'd prefer to eat alone."

"No," his gaze flicked to Natalie, "no, I wouldn't. Thank you."

Aunt Essie walked around the table toward him and held out her arms. "May I?"

He kissed April before he handed her to Aunt Essie.

"There, there now, sweet girl. Everything's going to be all right. You'll see. Now come with me, little angel, and let's see what's cooking for supper tonight, all right?"

When Aunt Essie turned her back, Kyle looked at Natalie and found her eyes full of tears. She ducked her head and turned away from him.

His cell phone rang. He kept his gaze on Natalie for another moment, then turned and strode into the den to talk to his secretary.

Later that night, Natalie stood at her bedroom window as the rain fell, no longer in raging white sheets buffeted by an angry wind, but steadily now, as if the storm had exhausted itself by expelling all its rage and could only muster up a simple offering of tears. Late spring in southeast Texas always meant fierce rainstorms, sometimes gentle rains, and tornadoes, rarely.

She sighed. She needed to talk to someone, but Aunt Essie was asleep. Her best friend, Kath, was still out of the country, although Natalie had called her earlier and left her a message. Her cousin, David, tolerated her ramblings, but at least he listened and sometimes intently. He might be awake right now, but this was his time to work on his music. Her mother would cut her off after the first sentence and say something like, "It'll all work out, dear." Her grandmother? Out of the question. "Oh, grow up. You made your bed, now sleep in it without complaining" would be her response.

She wished her father were here. She could see him so clearly, sitting on the sofa in his library with a book in his hands. She remembered the time she'd stepped on a nail, and he'd scooped her up and taken her to the emergency room to get a tetanus shot. When they'd returned home, she'd gone straight to bed, but she couldn't sleep. Instead, she'd limped down the hallway to her daddy's library and stood in the doorway, watching him read.

When he looked up and saw her, his face lit up as he smiled broadly at her. "Are you okay, sweetheart?" He stood, tossed the book on a table, and walked toward her.

Even now, she felt the same anticipation as she had those years ago, waiting for his arms to surround her and lift her up to his heart.

"Is your foot hurting, honey?"

She nodded as her face burrowed into his neck.

"Well, now, does your foot like to read books, too?"

She giggled and kept her eyes closed. Her daddy shifted her and held her tight with one arm while he pulled a children's book off the bookshelf.

"Ah, here's one called 'The Shoemaker's Gift.' Do you think your foot would like this one?"

She found herself smiling at the memory.

She was wide awake and decided to get dressed and enjoy the fresh scent of rain from Kyle's huge front porch swing. In a matter of minutes, she was walking down the stairs as a grandfather's clock chimed twice.

She unlocked the front door, stepped outside, breathed in the rain's sweet fragrance, and walked to the edge of the porch. Everything was fresh and clean and a dark shade of green. Hugging herself, she took in a deep breath.

"Natalie."

She gasped, spun around, and found Kyle sitting on the swing at the other end of the porch. She couldn't see his face clearly in the shadows. "Oh, I'm sorry. I didn't see you there."

"I couldn't sleep."

"I couldn't either." Feeling awkward, she waited a few moments before she said, "Well, if you'll excuse me."

"It's beautiful out here, isn't it?"

"Yes." She looked out over the wet yard. "I love the rain."

He was leaning forward with his elbows on his knees, his hands clutched, and his head down. "It's cleansing."

She understood his meaning. They all needed cleansing after the last few days of deception, scams, and betrayal at the deepest level.

The warm humid night wrapped itself around them. She was just about to go back inside when he said, "I'd like to talk to you, if you have a minute." They both knew she had a lot of minutes at this hour of the morning.

"We haven't had time to find out about each other or talk about April and what the next few weeks might look like."

Nodding, her gaze wandered to the streetlamp's soft light, streaked with straight lines of rain. Resting her hip against the wooden porch railing, she wasn't at all sure if this was the right thing to do, but she surprised herself by replying, "All right."

"There's plenty of room over here."

She could see there was when he moved far to the right, leaving an expanse of swing wide enough for four people. He patted it once. "I promise I won't bite."

There was a smile in his voice.

She hesitated another second, straightened her back, and put purpose in her steps. "Thank you." She sat as far away from him as possible. She was grateful he wasn't in his pajamas either.

The swing began to lazily move. Natalie didn't know which of them was moving it, but the warmth and fragrance of the wet night seemed to cast a comforting arm around her.

"Any progress with your grandmother?"

What? Oh. "No."

"She still disapproves of your helping April."

Disapproves was putting it mildly. "She deems it beneath me."

"Do you?"

"I wouldn't be here if I did."

"Family means well."

"Yes, sometimes."

Kyle smiled. "I'm trying hard not to worry about April, but somehow the trying isn't enough to let me sleep." Turning toward her, he said, "Why couldn't you sleep?"

"Oh, pretty much life in general."

"Your grandmother."

She touched her temple. "That's part of it."

"Mitch Worthington?"

She looked up, surprised he even knew Mitch's name. "How did you—?"

"I saw the note on the fridge for you to call him, and I asked Aunt Essie."

"Oh."

"Is he a boyfriend?"

Mercy, no. "Just a friend. And I use the term loosely."

"But he wants more."

"Yes."

"And you don't."

She smiled, uncomfortable with his insight. "No, I don't."

"What else?"

She figured the one area she needed to be open with him about was April, so she sighed and said, "April, of course."

"But you knew going into this—"

"No, no. It's not her condition. It's—" Her voice lowered. It took another moment or two before she could say the words. "It's my heart."

"She's easy to love."

Nodding, she blinked back the sudden tears. She waited until she thought her voice wouldn't wobble with emotion and said, "I thought I could do this—" The words faded away as she struggled against tears.

"Without falling in love with her?"

She nodded quickly and whispered, "Yes."

"Sometimes we find love in the most unexpected places."

"Yes." She wiped the tears off her face.

Clouds parted, and a full moon shed its light on the dripping night. Kyle looked at her. "I understand you're a dancer."

"Yes."

"I have a gym downstairs. You're welcome to use it. It has hardwood floors, mirrors, plenty of room, and the sound system extends to the basement, if you want to practice to music."

She smiled. She had discovered the gym in her ramblings and was going to ask him if she could use it. "Thank you. I appreciate that."

"How long have you danced?"

"Since I was three."

"So young?"

"My grandmother was determined that I be a successful dancer."

"And are you?"

"Somewhat. But I don't have the talent or the drive to be a Sensation. What I would love to do is teach."

"Are you going to open your own studio here in Granston?"

"I've thought about it. The time is coming soon when I'll retire."

"At the ripe old age of—?"

"Twenty-eight. In the next year, probably."

"You're four years younger than me. That seems young to consider retiring."

"If I were serious about dancing, I could dance for several more years, but I'd really like to teach." She paused and pursed her lips. "I was wondering if you would mind if I put a *barre* in the gym. At my expense, of course. When I leave, I'll take it down and repair any damage to your walls."

"I'm good with my hands. I'll install it for you."

"Thank you."

"By the way, I'm headed back to work in the morning. Lynette wanted me to know that April will be getting weaker until she has the transplant. If you notice anything, call me, and we'll decide if she needs to go to the hospital. It's one day at a time now."

"Yes."

"But there's something else you need to know." He told her everything the detectives had told him and his brothers about Gordon and Margot Jesser. "Don't let anyone in the house that I haven't approved. If anything needs repairing, I'll let you know. If we're not expecting anyone, don't answer the door. I spoke with a security expert tonight, and we're getting set up with a maximum-security system tomorrow."

"I'm so sorry, Kyle, for all your family."

"Yeah. It hurts, especially since I was the one who allowed them in." He stood. "If this causes you to want to leave, I understand."

"No, no. We're here for the duration."

Nodding, Kyle walked a couple steps away. For a moment, he seemed lost in his thoughts again. "Well." He turned and smiled at her. "I guess I'm ready to go in now. Was there anything else you wanted to talk about?"

"No, no. I'm fine. Good night."

"Good night."

As the door shut, Natalie glanced around. Was Jesser hiding somewhere, watching her? At the thought, she rushed inside and quickly locked the door.

Kyle hadn't been to Maudie's in days. He got up a little early on Wednesday, dressed, and headed that way at five-thirty. Outside the coffee shop, he bought a Granston newspaper, folded it, and saw Grayson as he was walking out.

"Hey, buddy." They hugged. "You just caught me." Grayson glanced at his watch and opened the door. "I'd rather spend a couple minutes with you than get to work early."

Grayson walked back inside. He was about ten years older than Kyle. He wore thick glasses which made his brown eyes like small dots, a black goatee, long black hair that he pulled back with a rubber band. He looked more like a hippie than a businessman. But he was his own boss, so he could call the shots on the dress code.

"You're sure going through the ringer, aren't you, buddy? I've been keeping up with you in print and online."

Kyle nodded. "It's been rough. Let me order, and I'll sit with you for a few minutes and catch you up."

"I'll get us a table by a window."

Maudie's face lit up when she saw Kyle. "Oh, my goodness, hon, what in the world is happening with you? Are you awright?"

"I'm really doing well, Maudie. How are you?"

"We've been busy. The usual?"

"Yes, the usual." He made small talk with her as she worked on his drink, and then he headed over to Grayson.

"So what happened with Margot, man?"

Kyle shook his head and took a couple sips of coffee. "I was taken. I'm ashamed to say it, but I just found out yesterday that I was the mark for a scam by this couple who bilked me out of a lot of money."

Grayson's eyes widened. "Are you serious? What kind of scam?"

"The stealing-my-money kind."

"Do the police know who?"

"They do. They're looking for him since he apparently killed his partner in crime, Margot."

They talked for a few more minutes. Kyle needed to leave. "I've got a lot of catching up to do at work." He scooted back his chair and stood. "How's Gloria doing?"

"Better. The surgery went well, and her ankle's healing." Grayson stood. "I should go, too. Houston traffic is miserable about now. Keep me posted. Call me if you need to talk. I'll be praying for you, buddy."

"Thanks. I need it. Tell Gloria I'm glad that ankle's better."

Kyle was the first one at work. In the dark quiet greeting him a little after six o'clock on this Wednesday morning, he picked up his messages and wrote instructions for Vera: "If Dr. Weisbrod or Natalie calls, put them through immediately."

He shut the door to his office and set his double espresso on his desk. He was glad he took time off to deal with everything, but his overflowing inbox was daunting. He needed to get focused on work, to keep his mind occupied.

He worked steadily for over two hours before he heard the sounds of people arriving. A door closed. Kevin laughed. A phone rang. It was just as well. He had reached an impasse on the Montgomery project and needed input from Kevin and John Greene, a long-time friend from college with a master's degree in engineering.

A knock on the door had him muttering, "Come in."

"When did you get here?" Kevin walked in and slid into one of two leather chairs in front of Kyle's desk.

"Couple hours ago."

"Long night?"

"Frustrating night. Jesser. Margot. Dad. April. Security. Losses. All of it."

"Yeah. Me, too. What's next for April?"

Kyle slipped the papers he was holding into a file folder. "The reconstruction surgery at birth hasn't lived up to expectations and Lynette says she needs a small bowel transplant as well as a new liver. We have eight to twelve weeks to get them."

A wall of silence surrounded them, cocooning them from the rest of the world. Kyle had experienced this many times with his brother.

Their world. Their connection. He didn't bother to look at Kevin. His brother wasn't one to jump in with platitudes. He'd sit and think on the right response and then give it.

The silence continued until Kevin said, "How many times have the doctors said she wouldn't make it through the night? She'll be just fine. You're blessed to have found Natalie Palmer. She's great with April."

"I *am* blessed." Kyle thought of last night, pleased at the first steps they'd taken toward friendship. He nodded toward the papers on his desk. "But right now, I'm blessedly ignorant of the Montgomery project and need some help with it."

"Figured you would. Now?"

Kyle checked his watch. "That would be great."

"I'll get John and be back in a few."

Kyle called Natalie. When she answered, he immediately relaxed. "Good morning. How's everything with you today?"

Her laughter managed to brighten his day. "April's being a silly willy right now, that's how my day is going. I slipped and fell on the floor and landed right on my bottom. And what did she do? She giggled at me! Ah-ah. There she goes again! Giggling over there."

Kyle could hear her. Had this ever happened? He couldn't remember one time that Margot had called to tell him something happy about April. "Put me on speaker phone."

"Okay. You're on, Daddy."

"Hey, funny face. Are you laughing at Miss Natalie?"

Another giggle.

"I hear you, stinker."

He also heard kisses. "Is somebody giving you kisses?"

"I am!" Natalie laughed and continued.

More giggles from April. This was just great. Made his day.

"All right, my little angel. I'm going to talk to Daddy right now. Do you want to look outside?"

April loved sitting in front of the dining room window, looking out at all the flowers. After a few seconds, Natalie came back on the phone. "So, how is your day going?"

"Productive. I have meetings this morning and might not make it home for lunch. If I can, I'll call before I come. Is April doing okay?"

"It comes and goes. She was a little grumpy earlier. She's about due for a nap."

"Good. I've got to run. Just wanted to check on y'all."

"We're fine. I'll keep you posted if anything changes."

EIGHT

The last person Natalie expected to find standing on the McKenzie's front porch that afternoon was her grandmother. Wearing a navy blue suit with a small yellow angel on her lapel, she lifted her chin at Natalie and pursed her lips.

"Grandmother, I wasn't expecting you."

"And why should you? Did I or anyone you know tell you I was coming?"

"No."

"Then you couldn't have been expecting me now, could you?"

So, this wasn't a social visit. If she knew her grandmother, and she did, it would be a manipulative session geared to get her home and away from the ignominious Kyle McKenzie. She stepped back. "Please, come in."

Nana stepped inside and sniffed as Natalie led her into a small sitting room.

"To what do I owe the honor of this visit?" Good gracious, she was beginning to sound just like her grandmother.

"Must I have an agenda when I visit my only granddaughter?"

When Nana settled into a chair, Natalie sat and tilted her head. "Yes."

"Very well, then. Mitch Worthington called Palmer House asking for you. You know he's been interested in you for some time, Natalie Grace. It's time you stopped this foolishness and let the man pursue you all the way to the altar. You could do far worse." Her eyes censoriously roamed around the room, implying, of course, that Kyle McKenzie was definitely far worse.

Calmly she said, "If the reason for your visit is to tell me about Mitch Worthington, I've already spoken with him. How's mother?"

"She's fine. She misses you."

"And do you?"

"I have learned that life is full of disappointments."

Mercy, the woman was infuriating. "Isn't it? Mr. McKenzie found out yesterday that April will have to have a liver transplant if she is going to live."

For the first time in recent memory, her grandmother faltered. She seemed to be searching for the right words and came up short several times before the words, "I see," stumbled out.

Natalie stood. "If that's—"

"What is her life expectancy?"

"Twelve weeks, maximum."

"And if she gets the liver?"

She sat again. "A liver and a small bowel. If she gets them both, she stands a good chance at a normal life."

"Then that is what we need to pray for."

Pray? Since when did her grandmother pray?

"I see I've surprised you."

"No." Natalie looked up. "Yes. I don't see you as a praying person."

"Sometimes we are driven to our knees by circumstances we cannot control."

"My being here drives you to your knees?"

"Your being here is a disgrace, but I'm not on my knees about it." Her grandmother stood. "We're having a small dinner party Thursday night and would be honored if you and Esther would join us."

Ah, so that's the reason for the visit. "I would love to. Are you setting me up with Mitch Worthington?"

"I'm setting you up to join us at six for hors d'oeuvres."

Without another word, her grandmother left.

Kyle's secretary, Vera, buzzed him. "I'm sorry to bother you, Mr. McKenzie, but your new accountant is on the phone. He says it's important. Line three."

"Thanks." *Now what?* He punched the button. "Yeah, Charles. What did you find?"

"A well-hidden joint savings account. It was opened two years ago. It quickly grew to a little over three million. All of it was legally withdrawn by your wife."

"When?"

"The same day she cleaned out your checking account."

The motive for the scam.

For some reason, Kyle thought of Margot's red suit.

And Dad. *Oh, God.* He abruptly stood. If they wanted money, why didn't they just come into his home and demand it? To save Dad's life, he would have given them anything—everything—and kept quiet about it.

But, Kyle realized, it wasn't just about the money.

He sank back into his chair. It was about an eye for an eye—a life for a life. *My dad for his dad.* If he'd offered the Jessers twenty million not to kill Dad, Jesser wouldn't have taken it.

Kyle bit down on the sudden anger. "Anything else?"

When Charles said, "Not at this time," Kyle thanked him, hung up, called his attorney, Barry, and filled him in.

"Tell me you want to go after Granger and Grimes. Safeguards should've been in place to prevent this. They're negligent and liable."

"They were scammed just as I was, but taking the money was perfectly legal. Her name was on the account."

"But there shouldn't have even been an account."

"The money's gone, Barry. She's gone. Let the police take care of Jesser. After the audit, I'll have Charles inform Granger and Grimes of his findings."

"They probably already know, with the police over there this past week," Barry added, with resignation in his voice. "Do you want me to call the police or will you?"

"I will. Charles can provide the details."

Just before noon on the next day, Thursday, Natalie answered the door and laughed. Her cousin, David, pushed his sunglasses up to his forehead and grinned at her.

"I can't believe this! What are you doing here, David? Did Galveston Island flood?"

"She's so funny," he said dryly and hugged her.

Natalie motioned him inside. "Let's go to the kitchen." She led him down the hallway and told him to sit while she retrieved the iced tea pitcher from the fridge. "Would you like some tea?"

"Sun tea?"

"Of course." She took two glasses out and filled them with ice. "Why are you here, David?" She poured the tea and took the glasses to the breakfast nook and sat at the table.

"Murder, mayhem, and damsels in distress. Although," he squinted at her and tilted his head, "you don't look like you're in any kind of distress, cuz."

"Well, I thought I heard your voice!" Aunt Essie exclaimed. "David Michael, give me a hug, you good-looking boy." He stood and hugged her. "Tell me what you're doing these days."

"You know good and well what I'm doing, Aunt Essie, because nothing is ever a secret in this family. The question is: what are *y'all* doing? You've both walked into a hornet's nest here. Dual lives. Murder. Scandal."

"And a little girl who lost her mother." Natalie frowned at him. "You've obviously been talking to Grandmother."

"Guilty. Actually, *she* did all the talking. Did McKenzie kill her?"

"Oh, David, of course not. Gordon Jesser's fingerprints are all over everything. Aunt Essie, would you like some tea?"

"I wouldn't. I'll just sit here with you two and listen."

David smiled at her. "I read that Jesser crawled out the motel's restroom window and escaped through the trees. Tire marks indicate he'd stashed a getaway car. Gone in broad daylight."

She shrugged. "Probably in disguise. The detective told Kyle that he's a chameleon, a master of disguises."

David sipped his tea. "It intrigues me how two people could plot to do this, that the woman would stay for almost two years, have a baby, take care of her baby, and walk out without a backward glance. How do people do that? And then, of course, that the legal husband would murder her right when they were free to go anywhere they wanted and live high on the hog."

"I don't care why she did it or why he did it." Natalie got up, opened the warming oven, and took out a plate of cinnamon rolls. "Here. Stuff your mouth and stop asking so many questions." She placed them on the table, along with napkins.

"But how did she do it? How did she keep up the facade for so long? Twenty-one months. That's a long time."

"Money."

"Gotta be more to it than that. I guess we won't know until they find Jesser and he's in a talking mood."

"I don't care, David. If he never talks, that's fine with me. Those two people hurt this family and if I could, I'd... well, I don't know what I'd do." She turned around and gasped. "Ky—Mr. McKenzie, I didn't see you there."

"I just arrived. For lunch."

He stayed where he was, leaning against the doorjamb, arms crossed, his gaze on David. She couldn't read what was in his eyes, but something was wrong. He fairly simmered with something.

"Where's April?" Kyle glanced at her, then David.

"Upstairs, asleep." He had probably heard more than just the last few remarks. She blessed the doorbell's ringing at that particular moment. "Excuse me. Oh, Mr. McKenzie, this is my cousin, David." He stood. "David Zachary, Kyle McKenzie. I'll just—"

Aunt Essie walked past her, flapping a hand. "You stay put, dear. I'll get the door."

"All right." Natalie ventured a look at Kyle as Aunt Essie left the room. "I'll bet you're hungry. Let me—"

He bounced off the doorjamb and extended his hand. "David, was it?"

"David Zachary," he said and shook his hand. "Good to meet you. I'm, uh, sorry to hear about your... your... situation." He flicked a glance at Natalie, and she rolled her eyes.

"Thank you. Do you live around here, David?"

"On Galveston Island."

"Ah. Those Zacharys. That's a nice home you have."

"My father built it, Mr. McKenzie," said a voice behind Natalie, and she tensed.

"Actually," David added, "I don't live in *that* house. I live in a little shack on the beach."

Natalie turned as her grandmother inched her way into the kitchen. Visiting two days in a row? But the look on Nana's face told Natalie this visit wasn't going to be pleasant. Their gazes connected. Nana's chin lowered a degree as her eyebrow lifted in a what-did-I-tell-you? look. Her gaze slithered back to Kyle.

"When I was a small girl," she added, heading for a chair. "But I clearly remember watching those men building it. Natalie, my dear, how are you today? And David, Esther. I see we have almost the entire family over here."

Trying to defuse, defuse, defuse, Natalie answered a bit too cheerfully, "I'm fine, Grandmother. Would you like a glass of tea?"

"And what brings you out of your hole, David?"

"My desire to see you, Grandmother." He kissed the top of her head. "And other interesting things that are going on."

"Interesting? I'd hardly call them—"

Natalie placed a hand on her shoulder and squeezed a warning.

"Well, be that as it may, how are you, Mr. McKenzie? I'm sorry for your loss, although I would hardly consider losing an adulterous—"

Natalie squeezed again.

"Stop it, Natalie. Surely, I can say my piece in these trying times."

Aunt Essie set Kyle's plate on the table as Natalie leaned toward Nana's ear and whispered, "Not in this house, Grandmother. You forget yourself."

"As have you."

Nana glared, Natalie stared, and David, ever the peacemaker, said, "Well, Mr. McKenzie, since my family is here to entertain you today, I thought I'd do my part. I saw a couple of swings out back, sitting comfortably under a huge oak. Maybe you and I could enjoy a quiet lunch outside and leave the ladies to entertain themselves."

Natalie sent him a 'thank you' look. "Let me fix you a plate, David."

After the men left, she whirled on her grandmother. "How dare you come into this house—"

She stabbed the floor with her cane. "How dare *I*? What about you? Do you know what people are saying, now that his wife has been found murdered? They're saying that you're a part of this, that you're the one who broke up this family. That he *killed* her because—"

"Grandmother, no one is saying any such foolish thing. I will not discuss Mr. McKenzie's business with you. I know nothing, anyway. If you want answers, then direct your questions at him."

She lifted her chin. "I intend to."

"Not in this house."

"Then where, pray tell? In the gutter, where he's—?"

"Stop it! Stop it!"

Natalie looked at Aunt Essie, not believing her ears. Aunt Essie never raised her voice, and even now, the words were more firmly spoken than yelled.

"Enough sadness is in this home without you adding to it."

"I have a right to—"

"Not here, you don't, Sister. You parked your rights at the door when you entered this house. Now, I shall be more than happy to walk you to your car, if you've concluded your condolences."

"Condolences? Such an old-fashioned word for stupidity and poor judgment. The man had an adulterous relationship with a scam artist and a thief." She grunted. "Condolences, indeed. The only condolences offered will be to *us*, make no mistake about it."

As her grandmother turned to leave, Natalie said, "I'll not be attending your dinner party tonight, Grandmother, under the circumstances. Please give my regrets to Mitch."

She turned around and sent a long, scathing look at Natalie. "And yet you stay in *this* house, knowing full well that that Jesser man killed Mr. McKenzie's father as well. The McKenzie name will continue to be sullied, yet you refuse to—"

"What? What did you say?"

Her grandmother relished triumphant looks, and she sent her best one to Natalie. "Ah, I see you haven't heard the latest in this continuing and vulgar drama. Gordon Jesser killed Gerald McKenzie, as well as his wife, Margot. It was on the radio just now."

Natalie looked outside. David and Kyle were swinging slowly as they talked. How in the world could Kyle deal with so much heartache and still be cordial to his guests? "No," she whispered, "I hadn't heard. How do they know this?"

"The ballistics reports from both bodies. Margot Springs Jesser married Kyle McKenzie just five months later."

"When he was at his most vulnerable."

"Yes. The police think it was for revenge. Mr. McKenzie caught Gordon Jesser's father, Lamar, rustling cattle off his ranch twenty-five years before. Lamar was arrested but killed after a prison escape." Lenore sniffed and glanced outside. "And yet, you continue to associate yourself with such a man."

"The man responsible is Gordon Jesser, not Kyle McKenzie." She whipped around, fighting the urge to be drawn into sudden despair. "I'll stay here until I know I'm to leave."

"Well, if *this* doesn't bring you to your senses, nothing will." Nana glared and held out her hand to Aunt Essie. She took it and walked with her sister outside.

Natalie sank into a chair. She sat quietly for a moment, grateful that she had some time to compose herself. Another quick glance outside revealed David and Kyle headed her way. The door opened at the same instant April's waking-up cries could be heard on the monitor.

"I'll get her," Kyle offered and left Natalie and David alone in the kitchen.

Natalie leaned over and whispered, "Did he say anything to you?"

David frowned at her. "About what?"

That afternoon, Kyle sat in his office and stared out his window. He enjoyed working in the offices of McKenzie Engineering, but get him on an outside project, and he thrived. He loved spending time at his ranch. It was just ten minutes away by air. Maybe it was time to spend a weekend away and get his head on right.

Vera buzzed him. "Dr. Weisbrod is on line two, Mr. McKenzie."

"Thank you." He quickly punched the blinking light. "Lynette?"

"The paternity results are in, Kyle."

His heartbeat soared. His stomach tightened. "And?"

"She's not yours. There is no match. I'm so sorry."

He couldn't breathe. The air simply disappeared from the room. He gasped then, and his teeth gritted in anger, disbelief. He lowered his head into his hand. "Don't tell me that, Lynette."

"The tests are ninety-nine percent—"

Just under his skin, something clawed. He recognized it as rage about the time he noticed his hand was shaking. He curled it into a tight fist. He wanted to punch Gordon Jesser in the face and watch him fall. "Now what? *Now* what?"

"That's a legal question. Maybe you should—"

He couldn't think. "Thanks, Lynette. I'll talk to you soon. Will this stay completely confidential?"

"Of course."

He stabbed another line, punched in the numbers. "Is Barry in?

Kyle McKenzie. It's urgent." He paused, listened to music while the anger pulsed. A voice sputtered at him. Kyle gritted his teeth and in a low, controlled voice said, "I need to talk to him *now*." A few seconds passed. The music stopped.

"Kyle, what is it, buddy?"

"She's not mine, Barry. She's not mine. The tests... Jesser is her biological father."

"All right. Listen. Jesser's a criminal. He's wanted for murder. He won't just show up and say, 'I'm taking April.' And no court would grant him custody. I'd think he'd be more interested in taking *you*, buddy. You're the one with the money." He paused. "She's very ill. If he takes her, she'll die. He probably knows that. I'd take a good, hard look at how to protect *you*."

"I hadn't thought of that angle."

"Either way, take precautions."

"You're right. I'll let you know what plans I make." He slowly hung up the phone, lowered his head, and closed his eyes. "I don't know what I'd do if I ever lost April, Lord."

He sucked in a breath and lifted his head.

And in the way of the Unexplained, he opened his eyes and focused on the small picture on the cadenza across the room. His father had placed it there. Kyle, Dad, and Grandpa Jared stood arm-in-arm, grinning, their cowboy hats almost touching. In the background, a bold, black ranch entrance declared, "Fairfield Ranch." His grandfather's ranch—now Kyle's.

Looking now into his father's eyes, Kyle could almost hear him saying, "Trust the Lord, son. No matter what."

Words to live by.

And then it hit Kyle like a brick. The ranch!

It was suddenly clear what he should do. Turn McKenzie Engineering over to Kevin. He had proven his leadership skills the past couple years. Kyle would run the ranch. He and April would live there, and Aunt Essie and Natalie could fly in on Sunday nights and leave on Friday afternoons. Opal, a registered nurse, lived at the ranch; she could oversee April's care on the weekends.

By air, they were ten to twelve minutes from the Granston hospital. The ranch had a landing strip; Kyle was a pilot, as well as one of the ranch hands. McKenzie Industries owned three planes; one would stay at the ranch, as well as one of the two helicopters, until April had the transplants.

"Yes." He began to pace. This just might work if he could convince Aunt Essie and Natalie to join him there. Jesser would have a harder time getting to April and getting away with her. "Or getting to me."

There would be too many eyes at the ranch and too much surveillance equipment focused on every area around the main house, all entrances, the outbuildings for Jesser to get inside.

Kyle looked at the picture again. *Yes. This just might work.*

NINE

Kyle slowly rode toward the old tree.

Even in all this heat, his horse, Handful, was eager to reach it. It was Kyle's favorite spot on Fairfield Ranch. He and Handful had done this several times in the six weeks since moving to the ranch. The old tree was atop a rise that overlooked a wide, deep pasture.

Tucked into the rolling landscape and thick woods of southeast Texas, Fairfield Ranch stretched comfortably across the countryside. Cattle sprawled under huge shade trees or stood still as statues in ponds, as weary of the blistering heat as the humans. In any direction, oil rigs bobbed.

Fairfield Ranch wasn't huge, but it was prime, rich land.

It always pleased Kyle to get away from his responsibilities and come here to think. He and Kevin, his Grandpa Jared and his father and brothers had sat under this same shade tree many times and enjoyed the quiet of the rambling land before they headed for one of the many trails on the ranch.

Kyle missed Kevin. He'd only made it out here twice since Kyle had decided to make this his permanent home. The workload at McKenzie Engineering was just too heavy to leave right now.

It was a hot, steamy day. Kyle lifted his work hat, wiped his forehead with the back of his hand, and settled it low on his head, covering his eyes and neck from the glaring sun.

Life had finally settled down. Once the media learned of Margot's double life and her murder, it had been a circus trying to keep them off his land and out of his face when he traveled into one of the nearby towns—especially when the media discovered that his father had been murdered by Jesser, too.

Tabloids had relentlessly called. People from Hollywood asked him for the rights to his story. They'd hounded Kevin, too. Publishers called, wanting to splash the lurid details across newspapers and books. So much of what they'd already written wasn't the truth. He had no desire for further publicity and despite his reticence to talk to any of them, the newsworthiness of the story had finally died down.

But Jesser was still out there, spending Kyle's money. A man like

Jesser would never be satisfied with almost three-and-a-half million dollars. He would want more.

He'd either scam a new mark or come here. Dark anger swept over Kyle just at the thought of Jesser touching April.

He had to stay ready for anything.

A state-of-the-art alarm system had been installed at the main house. Video alarms had been mounted at all entrances. A security expert had briefed all the staff and ranch hands on how to stay safe. Everyone was on alert. Kyle constantly kept one eye over his shoulder, the other in front of him, and prayed Jesser wouldn't hit him on his blind side.

Something moved down by the creek. Of course, his first thought was of Jesser. But he wouldn't be this far into his land. He'd stay closer to the house, closer to an exit.

Whatever it was had just disappeared into the trees covering the walking path. Up ahead, a fence was down and, like bees to honey, cattle crossed the pasture and the walking path toward the thickly shaded creek.

Probably nothing to worry about, but he needed to check it out. He tugged out his rifle, pushed it back in, and then urged Handful in the direction of the creek. "Come on, boy. Let's have a look."

Natalie was accustomed to the quiet and aloneness of the walking path by now. No droning lawnmowers, no traffic, no honking cars, no barking dogs. It was a good mile from any ranch entrance, and she felt safe here. Occasionally, an airplane flew overhead, but it was too far in the distance to hear. The only noise was the wind rustling the leaves of the trees lining the path, the gravel growling under her boots with every step, and the occasional moo of a cow.

In the six weeks she had been coming to Fairfield Ranch, she had discovered that ranching was an uncomplicated life with few pretensions and many simple joys. She'd discovered that early morning skies had grayish-lavender beginnings, just before tentacles of light effortlessly reached for the horizon and pulled the sun up.

She'd also found out, through experience, that boots were incredibly comfortable and, with time, felt like a part of her feet. And she'd learned firsthand that a cowboy hat was not for looks. It was part of the armor used against the belligerently hot and persistent sunshine.

Under a shade tree, she stopped to wipe the sweat off her forehead, so it wouldn't drip into her eyes. It was a terrible time of day to be walking in a Texas July, mid-afternoon, when the heat and humidity were at their worst.

How did the ranch hands, or Kyle, stand to work in this heat day after day?

Kyle.

She rarely spent time alone with him. He had completely immersed himself in the duties of his ranch and when they happened to pass one another, a solemn but polite distance passed between them. It had crept into their budding friendship when they'd first moved to the ranch.

And it was probably for the best.

He had healing to go through, and she had skimmed the dangerous edge of believing that she actually belonged at Fairfield Ranch.

But she didn't. This arrangement wasn't going to last. She would be returning home soon. April's health was much worse. It wouldn't be long before she was in the hospital.

Every day was filled with a quiet desperation, knowing her time in their lives was short. Each morning, Natalie wondered, "Is this the day we lose April?" Hopefully, a donor would save her life. It was so difficult to know how to pray because April couldn't live without someone else's body parts, but a precious baby would have to die to help their little girl.

Sighing, she took a Kleenex out of her pocket and wiped her neck. Standing in the shade didn't help one bit. The hot air was like a sauna. There was no other way to describe it.

A squirrel scampered up the backside of a tree, and she pitied it. *All that fur.*

Natalie looked around her. Walking this path had become a sanctuary for her, a place where she could plan her day and retreat from responsibilities. Up ahead, the large wooden bridge was her indicator to start back, but she wasn't ready yet. She sat on the bridge, dangled her booted feet over the sluggish water, leaned her head against a post, and closed her eyes.

She was exhausted. She hadn't had a good night's sleep in a week. Maybe that was part of the reason it was a struggle dealing with April today.

Another nightmare had jolted her awake last night, as it had every night this past week.

She was in the car with her father. She wasn't a little girl anymore, but a grown woman.

Her father looked the same.

He glanced at her and laughed.

She screamed, "Daddy!"

A flash of light, a horrible crashing sound.

Then nothing but absolute quiet.

Over and over, night after night, the same nightmare. What did it mean? Was it actually a memory? Why did he laugh at her? And what had she seen that made her scream?

The pain was old, as was the blame.

And, oh, the longing to be free of it was overwhelming.

She noticed the time and groaned as she scrambled to her feet and crossed the bridge. April would be awake soon. She checked her beeper. She hadn't missed any messages from Aunt Essie.

After walking a couple hundred feet, she stopped abruptly as she rounded the bend and gasped. Several cows were practically jogging toward her! She stepped back and quickly looked around. Not another soul was in sight. She slipped behind a tree. Some of the cattle slowed to a stop and spread across her shaded path. Others meandered down to the creek.

She stood stock still, hoping they would move off her path, but they didn't. "Well, this is just great." She slapped her hands on her hips. *Now* what was she supposed to do?

Biting her lip, she looked around her. She could go neither to the right nor the left without running into an animal or the creek. She picked up a stick. She would just have to get them to move off her path. She'd seen the ranch hands scatter cattle by simply walking toward them. So she would, too.

She took several cautious steps and stopped. Why weren't they moving? She waved the stick at them. Not a one looked at her or moving a muscle. She clapped her hands. They totally ignored her. She flapped her hands at them. One cow lazily turned its bulky head just enough for a big brown eye to blink at her, but the cow didn't budge. "Shoo!" she said, backhanding the air at them. "Shoo, now! Shoo!" She clapped her hands again. Nothing happened.

Maybe if she threw something at them. She collected several pebbles and tossed one at a cow. When several cows turned their heads, Natalie gulped and took a cautious step back.

And heard laughter.

Gasping, she spun around. Down the path, Kyle sat astride Handful, laughing as he gripped his saddle horn.

Oh! She was so embarrassed! She dropped the pebbles and wiped her hands on her shorts. She saw Kyle lower his head to cover his laughter, but it didn't work. She wasn't blind, was she? His shoulders were still bobbing!

Kyle tried to stifle the chuckles. It was apparent Miss Stoic was having difficulty biting down on a hissy fit. Just in case he hadn't seen her first glare, she glared at him again and marched toward the creek as he slid out of the saddle and left Handful to wander.

Finally, some emotion. He had begun to believe her devoid of it. For weeks now, they had all lived under the cloud of apprehension that Jesser would try to take or hurt April. Kyle assumed Natalie's indifference to him personally was the result of her fear of Jesser or her disappointment at Kyle's stupidity in being taken in by Margot.

Either way, he had been careful to keep the distance she obviously needed, making sure he seldom spent time alone with her.

It had been a couple of weeks now since he'd come to the conclusion that she didn't like him; she'd made it perfectly clear by her aloofness and her businesslike demeanor.

He felt just the opposite about her.

He enjoyed seeing her play with April when she didn't know he was watching. She'd sing her a silly song or read to her in cartoon-like voices, acting out the words. At those times, her defenses were down, her reserve gone. At the end of his work day, he looked forward to seeing his little angel enjoy the stories.

He appreciated Natalie's willingness to play with April. So much of April's life was dull or dealing with pain. It was nice to see Natalie's playful side, although it was never directed at him.

Cocking a hip, he dipped his head at the cattle. "They can't ignore the invitation."

His words made absolutely no sense at all. What invitation?

"It's the fence."

He was near her now, a few feet down.

"What invitation?"

"The, uh, fence." He covered his laugh with a cough and looked relaxed as the corners of his mouth kept twitching. "Cattle can't refuse the invitation from a downed fence."

"Oh." Her face heated with embarrassment. It had probably been comical for him to ride up on her trying to shoo cattle off her walking path with a stick and a pebble.

A giggle gurgled.

She tried to swallow it but couldn't.

Another giggle. She covered her mouth and met his crinkled eyes. It struck her that this was the first time she'd ever seen him laugh out loud. Not the forced kind of laughter that praised April for something she'd done, but a from-the-gut kind of joy that transformed his face, easing the lines of strain from past weeks.

Before she knew it, they were both laughing. She rubbed her eyes. He rubbed his eyes. Struggling for composure, she turned her back on him and noticed that the cows were off her path and in the creek. She gasped, spun around to see if Kyle had noticed, and sputtered when she saw his shoulders bobbing up and down, his face covered by his hat.

She snickered and fanned her face. "Oh, my," she ventured, wiping her eyes. "That was too funny. I looked ridiculous, didn't I?"

"Yes," he nodded solemnly, "you did."

"You'll have to show me sometime how to get cows to move."

He pointedly looked around her at the path the cows had vacated. "Apparently, now is not a good time."

They laughed again. Natalie felt a touch of the friendship they'd discovered weeks before. Edging toward the path, she said, "This is our secret, right? You won't tell any of the hands about this or the women, right?"

With another chuckle, he glanced over his shoulder. "I don't know, Natalie. This would sure make a good—"

"Kyle. Please?"

He looked at her. "All right. It'll be our secret."

Feeling suddenly hot, she quickly nodded, pressed her lips together, and looked down at her hands.

"You do that when you get nervous."

"What?"

With his finger, he drew circles in the air. "That thing with your mouth. Like you've just put on lipstick or something."

She pressed her lips together.

"There." He adjusted his cowboy hat. "You do that when you're unsure of yourself or embarrassed or nervous."

"Do I?"

"And—" He dipped his head at her hands.

They were clutching each other, her left thumb urgently rubbing her right thumb.

"Why are you nervous, Natalie?"

She threw her hands to her sides. "I'm not."

"You are." He took a step toward her. "And I'm wondering why."

She would have backed away from him, but she had nowhere to go. Instead, she pulled out the best line of defense she had. She crossed her arms, lifted her chin, and pursed her lips. Her good friend Oscarella had stopped the most aggressive of men.

He smiled. "There. That's better."

Better?

"I recognize you now. The scared rabbit wasn't you."

"Oh, yes, it was." She winced at the honest words and shook her head in disgust.

"Aren't we all scared sometimes?"

"You?" She took a step around him. "You look life in the eyes and dare it to stop you."

"You do, too, Natalie."

"Mine's just an act."

"So's mine."

"You're a better actor then."

"You're not bad yourself."

"We're a couple of fakes?"

"Everybody is."

Another step away from him. "I haven't felt like such a fake out here." Part of it was because her grandmother wasn't around to censor her at every step. It must be difficult for Nana right now, not being able to control Natalie's life or surprise her with a visit.

"Same here." He shifted his feet, looked out over the land.

"I've even allowed myself to get comfortable." And wouldn't Nana love that? "Maybe Jesser won't be coming back."

Kyle shook his head. "I don't believe that. We have to stay ready."

"I am ready. But I feel secure out here."

"We're not safe anywhere, as long as Jesser's out there."

Squinting into the hot sun, Natalie nodded and looked over at the horse, at the path, back at the horse, and felt every drop of sweat clinging to her body. It was just too hot to be out here, and April might be awake by now.

"I'm heading back to the main house. Would you like a ride?"

"I—" She glanced at her watch. She needed to get back. "Would you mind?"

"Not at all," he said. "Front or back?"

"I don't know. Which is the most comfortable for you?"

"Either way. It's up to you."

She considered a moment and said, "In the back."

"The back it is, then." He clucked at Handful and the horse trotted over. Kyle hoisted himself up and held out a hand. Natalie hesitated only a fraction before she took it and allowed him to swing her up behind him.

"Ready?"

She nodded. "Yes." And instantly regretted her hasty decision. He was far too close. She moved back so her knees wouldn't touch him at all. She didn't know where to put her hands and rested them on her legs.

Then he started off.

She squealed as she almost slid off the horse. In a flash, Kyle turned around, grasped her arm, and yanked her back on. Their eyes connected, and they both sputtered a laugh.

After she was settled again, he plucked her crooked hat off and settled it on her head. "Are you ready now?"

"I know how to ride in the saddle. Back here is a different story."

"If you put your arms around my waist, you won't fall off."

She wiped her hands on her legs. She could do this. It wasn't as if it meant anything. Carefully, she slipped her hands loosely around his waist and felt herself blush.

"You can move closer, Natalie. I promise I won't bite."

The same words he'd spoken the night they had talked on his porch. She scooted closer and tried to keep her back straight. If she leaned forward even a little, she'd be resting on his back. He sat tall in the saddle, and she couldn't see over his shoulder. With the added strain of sitting up straight, her back started hurting.

"You can't sit that way much longer."

She relaxed a little, barely touching his back.

"That's better."

Another few minutes and her hat was cockeyed, her cheek resting on his warm back as she listened to the steady beat of the horse's hooves. The heat was overwhelming. Lack of sleep quickly caught up with her, and she closed her gritty eyes. She told herself she was resting them for just a moment.

For just a tiny, tiny...

Kyle smiled. She was asleep. Her hands weren't rigid anymore, and her head lolled comfortably against his back. Not the moves of a person who disliked him.

The scared rabbit wasn't you.

Oh, yes, it was.

Scared? Natalie? She exuded anything but fear. Yet, fear would certainly explain the calculated distance she had kept between them. Maybe another day, they would talk about it. Today, they had laughed together. It was a small beginning to a friendship again. Maybe this time, the friendship would stick.

Her hands were no longer around his waist but were resting on her legs. She felt totally limp. He leaned forward, so she would be a little more comfortable.

And in the shade of the tall, towering trees next to the lazy creek, he slowly, and as gently as possible, made his way back home.

TEN

Kath Michaels spotted the two-headed rider coming toward her as she slammed her car door and quickly scanned the wide expanse of green yards and gently sloping land blanketed with tall trees. East Texas reminded her of Scotland in parts with its wide open, green pastures and thick, lush trees, although the weather couldn't be more different. Tuscany, too, minus the Tuscan Cypress trees. She was so glad to be back on American soil now. She had missed her best friend, Natalie.

Her interest returned to the man riding toward her, and in the way of a woman, she patted her hair to take some of the wind out it as she moved to a strategic spot in the shade to watch his approach.

He's perfect. She tilted her head and smiled as she studied him. *A perfect counterpart to Victoria Chandler.* The prim and proper heroine of her next novel won't know what hit her.

Unbelievably, the closer he got, the better he looked. Classically rugged, virile, big. Incredible eyes—blue?—frowned at her from under a cowboy hat, completing the appealing image of a man at ease with himself and his world.

"Oh, Victoria," she murmured, "have I found your match or what?"

Natalie's head bobbed out from behind the man. "Well, well, well," Kath mumbled, pleased. "Do my eyes deceive me?"

With a hand from the man, Natalie slid off the horse and ran toward her, an unmistakable look about her that said she was not only content but happy. Kath couldn't remember a time in her life that her friend had looked so radiant and carefree.

"I don't believe this!"

Amazed at the exuberant welcome, Kath hugged her tightly. When Natalie pulled back and looked at her, Kath did as well and studied her friend's face. What she found there pleased her no end.

"Why didn't you tell me you were home?"

"And spoil my surprise?"

"You're so dark. Did you stay in the sun the entire time you were in Europe?"

"Mostly." Glancing past Natalie, she raised her brows approvingly at the man who was silently watching them. Maybe he was the reason she looked so happy. And who could blame her? He was gorgeous. Add a little brooding around the eyes and mouth, and he would be the perfect distraction that Victoria would, no doubt, disdain initially. And to think Kath had come very close to pairing Victoria with a city slicker from New York who was defying his family and heading west to dig for gold. Oh, no. The Yummy Cowboy with the beautiful eyes was a much better match. "Who's the hunk?" she whispered for Natalie's ears only.

"Oh, uh."

A blush worked its way up her best friend's face as she turned toward the man and raised her voice. "Kathryn Michaels. Kyle McKenzie, the owner of Fairfield Ranch."

Kath was pleased as punch when she noted the obvious trouble Natalie had looking directly at Kyle McKenzie, the owner of Fairfield Ranch. Delighted, she raised a single brow and casually cocked her head. "Mr. McKenzie."

He tugged on the rim of his hat. "A pleasure, ma'am. And welcome." With one more look at Natalie, he led his horse into the barn.

"Whoa." Kath watched him ride away. "What a gorgeous man. He'd make a great—"

"Kath—"

"Love interest—"

"Kath—"

"For Victoria. Wait, wait. I'm having a moment here."

Natalie rolled her eyes and tugged on her arm. "Have your moments inside. This heat is unbearable."

Tearing her gaze away, she slyly looked at Natalie. "So that's the reason you live out here in the boonies."

"You know better than that."

"I suppose I do, having known you since you were five years old. Let's see. Back then, you kicked the boys. In junior high, you slapped them. In high school, you snubbed them. What are you doing with this one?"

"Nothing."

"Nothing?"

"Nothing."

"Not even—?"

"Nothing."

Rolling her eyes, Kath shook her head. "You're hopeless."

"No, just smart."

"So Oscarella came out here with you."

Natalie smiled as they walked toward the house. "I use my alter ego from time to time, but today, I gave her a break."

"Good. She doesn't fit you anymore."

At Natalie's indication, Kath opened the front door and stepped into the foyer as her gaze roamed approvingly around the big room beyond it. "Nice," she murmured at her first glimpse of beautiful knotty pine walls stretching toward a cathedral-like ceiling. Red and yellow pillows flanked two rather large hunter-green leather sofas in one of two conversation areas.

Another appraising step inside the vast room revealed tall and curtainless windows, a well-positioned loft that would take advantage of the sun's morning light, and a wide wall of glass overlooking an extensive and green valley.

"I like it." Kath turned around, nodding. "This helps explain why in the world you would come to the ends of the earth to baby-sit a little girl."

"This house had nothing to do with it."

"How long have you been living here? Gram wasn't sure."

"Six weeks. I stay five days, fly home on the weekends." Kath allowed her to take her arm. "There's someone else here who would like to see you."

"Aunt Essie. Gram told me she was staying with you as some sort of a chaperone." Kath grinned. "Don't tell me that gorgeous man is an uncontrollable rake?"

"Certainly not. Your writer's imagination is working overtime."

Kath stopped. "Surely there's something between the two of you by now, Natalie. You've lived in this house for six weeks. Sparks should be flying by now."

"Only in your books. There's nothing between us but friendship and respect. Welcome to the real world."

"The real world has romance."

"Not here. So how was Europe?"

"What's wrong with him?"

"Nothing. How was Europe?"

"Then what's wrong with you?"

"Nothing. Besides, his wife—"

"Was murdered. I know." Kath stepped around what looked like a milk churn with a beautiful arrangement of daisies hanging their heads shyly as if watching them walk by. "But Gram said she really wasn't his wife."

"He didn't know that until after she was killed."

"Did they ever catch the killer?" Hmmm. How would Victoria handle a murder in her world?

"No, which is the main reason we're here—protection for April. Not that he's tried anything yet, but Kyle is convinced he will. Come on, let's go see Aunt Essie."

"Try what, exactly?"

"Now you can use your imagination. It could be any number of things. He's called a chameleon, someone who can become anyone, male or female or nationality."

"That's scary."

"It is. Sometimes at night when I can't sleep, I imagine him sneaking inside this house dressed like a clown, kidnapping April—"

"Talk about an imagination."

"Well, Kyle thinks anything is possible, especially with Jesser's lust for money. But enough of this. Let's go see Aunt Essie."

As they walked into the kitchen, her aunt was shaking her hands free of water. She plucked a dishcloth off the counter and turned around. Her mouth dropped. "Why, Kathryn Michaels. Welcome home, dear. However did you find us out here?"

Kath stepped into her warm hug. "Easy, when the whole countryside knows where your destination is. This place is huge."

"Dorothy told me you made it home yesterday. Did you enjoy Europe, dear?"

"I had a wonderful time. So many beautiful old buildings. Some of the most magnificent were the churches." She eyed Natalie playfully. "How can you not worship God in such beautiful places?"

"Worship?" Natalie gasped, wide-eyed. "Kath. Oh, Kath, did you?"

A little embarrassed, she nodded. "Yes."

Natalie squealed and hugged her. "You did it?"

"I did it."

"After all this time?"

"Yeah, well, some of us are more stubborn and strong-willed but you whittled the stubborn off me down through the years."

"And then I wasn't even there when it happened."

Kath pulled back and looked into the eyes of her best friend. "I wanted to call you, but I thought you'd like to hear it in person."

"I'm so happy for you. When?"

"Two weeks ago."

Aunt Essie slipped her apron over her head, folded and patted it. "Happy about what, dear?"

Natalie beamed at her aunt. "May I present my sister in the Lord to you, Aunt Essie? Miss Kathryn Eileen Michaels."

"Oh, how wonderful, Kathryn. Tell us all about it."

They were gathered around the kitchen table an hour later, laughing and talking, when Kyle walked into the mudroom. Kath could see him from her vantage point, taking off his boots, his eyes on Natalie. For an instant, Kath's gaze connected with his, and she lifted a knowing brow.

Nodding once, he grinned at her, glanced at Natalie, looked back at Kath, and winked. She couldn't help but smile at his impertinence. *Oh, yes, Victoria. You're going to love this man utterly and completely, once you get past your pre-conceived notions that all cowboys are uncouth, marauding despoilers of all that is good and decent. Yes, yes, yes, Victoria! Are you in for the time of your life!*

She almost chuckled as she envisioned Victoria prissily dismissing him. Hmmm. What name would fit? Adam. No, no, no. Something more romantic. Roman. Yes, Roman... Delaney. Roman Delaney. Okay, now, where had she left Victoria?

Oh, yes, prissily dismissing the rugged, gorgeous, persistent Roman Delaney. But, of course, he won't be put off. When he wants something, he goes after it. Ruthlessly determined. And despite her best—

"Oh, Kyle." Aunt Essie immediately stood when he opened the door. "This is our dear friend, Kathryn Michaels."

Kath watched Natalie lift her chin, press her lips together, and primly cross her arms on the table—all the bells and whistles that told Kath she was attempting to send a message that she wasn't interested in him which, of course, told Kath she was.

Victoria would respond in exactly the same manner. Now, wasn't that interesting?

Kyle smiled. "We met outside, Aunt Essie."

Oh, yes, his eyes were definitely blue. "My friends tell me you're a hard taskmaster and unbearably cruel, Mr. McKenzie."

Natalie gasped and playfully slapped her arm. "Kath! We did not." Kath noted that Natalie's gaze didn't quite make it up to Kyle's when she said, "My friend has a wicked sense of humor. She's a writer, which explains her inclination toward fiction."

"Well, Miss Palmer, what *did* you tell her about your employer?"

Kath had to smile. Still no eye contact, and the slightest hint of a blush creeping up to and past Natalie's words as they tumbled out. "That you're a wonderful father."

He turned to the sink to wash his hands. "I hope that's more the truth than the other." He dried his hands, opened the oven door. "Do you plan to stay with us awhile, Ms. Michaels?"

Oh, yes, *now* she did. "Kath. And, yes, if I can coax an invitation from you, I'd like to visit a few days."

"Then," he turned and saluted them all with a carrot cake in his hands, "consider the invitation issued. Do you ride?"

"Yes, quite well." She deliberately eyed the cake. "I'm hoping for another invitation to join you in devouring that scrumptious-looking carrot cake."

He opened the cupboard door. "Dig out four forks, and I'll retrieve four plates."

"I will," she answered with a wink at Natalie, "although I'm not *that* hungry."

Laughter filled the kitchen. Kath thought it was good to be with her best friend at Fairfield Ranch, especially when that best friend showed remarkably good progress in taking the first faltering steps toward falling in love. And with such a hunk.

She couldn't have written it better herself.

Kath's heart broke a little when big brown eyes blinked at her from a tiny, thin face. She held out her hand and gently took April's. "Hi, April. I'm Kath. You sure are a pretty girl."

April seemed to be drinking her in and a tiny smile lifted the corners of her mouth, even as her eyes slowly closed. Kath blinked back tears and looked helplessly at Natalie. When she looked back at April, she was sound asleep. Kath pulled the lightweight blanket out from under April's feet and placed it gently on her, stroking her tummy as she did.

"She sleeps a lot now," whispered Natalie.

"How can you bear it? She's so tiny and sweet. And those eyes. So big and trusting."

"Let's step out into the hall." They did. "She's getting weaker. We're all praying that God will give her new parts, but that means another child has to die first." She sighed. "It's hard to know what to pray for. It won't be long until she's in the hospital for good."

Kath held Natalie's gaze a moment and, unable to bear seeing the truth there, looked away.

Natalie turned on the monitor. As they walked out of the room, she showed Kath her pager. "We all wear them now, even the cowboys, in case April, or anyone for that matter, needs help and no one's around. There's a landing strip about two miles north of the house. One of the hands is a pilot, as is Kyle."

"You called him Kyle."

Natalie rolled her eyes. "It takes about twelve minutes to get to the Granston hospital or twenty-two minutes to the Houston hospital. If she needs to get to Houston, Kyle has a helicopter at the landing strip."

They linked arms going down the stairs. "And this Jesser who murdered her mother? Why would he come back for her?"

"Ransom. She's his biological daughter, but Kyle is her father. This is all very hush-hush. No one can know. The Jessers scammed almost three point five million dollars from Kyle."

"But what's to stop him from getting her? You're leaving her right now, and no one's—"

"Eight tough cowboys and five tough women: Aunt Essie, Bonnie,

574

Janet, Opal, me."

"And me."

Natalie smiled at her.

"Who's Bonnie?"

"The foreman."

"A woman foreman? I bet that goes over real well with the men."

"Actually, they all like her. She was raised on a ranch with six brothers, so she understands men—and other animals."

Kath studied Natalie a moment. Her friend was more relaxed, more playful. Her romantic heart told her it was because of Kyle McKenzie. She wondered, however, if Natalie even realized she was falling in love with him. "Who's Janet?"

"Kyle's secretary."

"Opal?"

"A Registered Nurse and the head housekeeper. Since the nursing doesn't keep her busy, the house does."

"All this and maid service, too. I'm impressed."

"Why don't I show you around 'all this'? I never thought I'd enjoy living on a ranch, Kath, but I do. We'll go for a ride, see some things of interest."

"Just things?"

When Natalie looked at her, Kath raised her eyebrows twice with a sly smile on her face.

Natalie shook her head. "He'll be in for dinner. You can see him then. In the meantime, let's ride. After dinner, we could go for a swim, or you can join me in the gym."

"Ballet practice?"

"Yes."

"Ballet sounds great."

"Maybe some exercise will take your mind off this other nonsense."

Never. Not when her friend—her impassive, usually unaffected and very composed friend—grew nervous at the mere mention of a certain man's name.

ELEVEN

Regina Palmer was flattered. The man was obviously flirting with her. He had to be at least ten years younger than her forty-eight, much better suited for her daughter, Natalie, than herself, but she wasn't one to let numbers stand in her way. She gave him a welcoming smile, and he glided in her direction. *So predictable.* He was medium height, dark, and handsome. His confidence reminded her of Brent, the first time they had met on the beach near her family's home.

Galveston Island. Thirty years ago.

She smiled as she remembered Brent Palmer strolling past her, his hands in his white shorts' pockets, eyes intent, jaw clenched, obviously thinking on something because he had simply nodded curtly at her and kept walking. Then, as if suddenly noticing he had snubbed a beautiful woman, he stopped, slowly turned around, and swaggered—there was no other name for that walk—toward her.

He stopped in front of her and seemed to study every inch of her face with something like awe. "Do I know you?"

"I don't think so." She looked into his eyes and found them enchanting.

"That has to change." He took her hands and kissed them. It was silly, really, to get flustered over such an old trick, but it had worked for her eighteen-year-old heart. They were married four months later.

The swagger of the younger man was much like Brent's, although he didn't possess Brent's easy confidence, and his tactic, unlike Brent's, appeared tedious and worn out. It might have worked, however, had sincerity ruled his actions instead of intent.

"You're a beautiful woman," he said as he retrieved a glass of champagne from a passing tray.

"I know."

His attempt at nonchalance almost amused her, but it missed the mark enough to bore her. As she turned away from him, he touched her arm, with just enough pressure in his fingertips to rile her.

"Get your hand off me, squirt."

He did and saluted her with his drink and a smile. "Have it your way, sweetheart."

"I always do."

He bowed slightly, turned around, and walked out the patio doors to the lighted terrace. Relieved, Regina made her way around the room, spoke briefly to friends, sought out her hostess and told her she was leaving.

"So soon, dear? Surely—"

"Really, Sophie, I must go. A headache, you know." Regina air-kissed her, wiggled her fingers in good-bye, and left.

The night was warm and sticky. She heard a car start up and recognized it as her BMW. Within seconds, it whipped around a corner and a smiling valet stopped, bounded out, and held the door for her. She fumbled in her bag for a ten and handed it to him as she slid in. "Thank you."

The top was down. On a sultry night in southeast Texas, it was absurd to ride in a convertible with fabric above one's head instead of the stars. Regina felt wildly restless tonight and took the curve out of the driveway a bit too fast.

To her right, something moved in front of her car.

She slammed on her brakes. In the glow of the car lights stood the man she had snubbed, his hands in his pockets, a strange smile on his face.

Two steps placed him in-between her headlights. "Hello, Beautiful."

She gripped the wheel, snapped it to the left.

He sneered as if he were amused. In a flash, a gun appeared in his hand, pointed right at her.

The sound of her stammering gasp bumped against the utter stillness of the night. She was terrified, beyond anything she'd ever felt in her life.

Staring at her with a lazy smirk on his face, he walked to her side, leaned over, and whispered, "Don't move so much as an inch, Beautiful. Do you understand?"

Wide-eyed, Regina nodded, her breathing ragged as she shivered in the sweltering heat. She stared at the gun and realized it had a silencer on it. If he shot her, no one would hear, and no one would come to her rescue.

"I'm going to walk behind the car. If it so much as twitters, I'll take great pleasure in shooting you in the back of the head. Understand?"

He looked like pure evil. Numb, unable to think, Regina nodded.

"Here I go-o," he sang the words as if this was a game and she, a willing partner. "'Round the mulberry bush. Do you know what a mulberry bush is, Beautiful?"

She shook her head.

"No?"

He had reached the other side and she shuddered, hugging herself as he reached for the door handle. She hated that tears were filling her eyes. "What do you want?"

"You." He slid in, slammed the door. His voice sounded soothing, as if he were talking to a child. "Just you, Beautiful. I have all night." The gun glinted in the waning light as he signaled her to get moving. "And, apparently, my dear, so do you."

Regina felt as if her life had just ended.

"So, are you going to tell me what happened to you and Jorge?" Natalie sat on the steps of the porch and leaned her head back, into the moon's light. She needed this time with Kath tonight. She felt restless and couldn't pinpoint why.

Kath leaned against the other side of the steps. "Nothing happened. I broke up with him before I went to Europe. I just didn't tell you."

"Why not?"

"Because you'd worry about me, thinking my heart was broken. It wasn't right with Jorge. I chickened out and called him just before I left."

"You called him?" So like her to just get it over with.

"I couldn't deal with the whining any longer." Kath looked at her and rolled her eyes. "That man could whine."

Chuckling, Natalie sighed. Kath was such a strong woman, it'd take an even stronger man to catch her heart. "So now what?"

"I would never listen to you before when you talked to me about dating God's way. But I'm ready to listen now."

She smiled. "It's simple. You don't let the physical guide you. It's a spiritual connection, not a physical one."

"You make it sound easy."

"It's not easy." *Not at all.* "It can be very difficult at times."

"Ah-ha! So, you *are* attracted to Kyle McKenzie."

"I'd like to be friends with him, and I've made that very difficult for us. I had a glimpse of what friendship would mean with him, and I turned my back on it. There was too much going on, with April being sick, his wife leaving him, then being killed, the speculation."

"About—?"

"The media hinted that Kyle might have had something to do with Margot's murder—"

"Who could blame them?"

"—although the forensic evidence didn't even place him at the crime scene. And, of course, it stopped when they discovered that the bullet in Margot matched the bullet in Kyle's father. Jesser had murdered both of them."

"But why?"

"Two reasons, actually. Revenge and money. When Jesser was a young teen, his father was sent to prison for rustling cattle on McKenzie Ranch in the Texas panhandle—Kyle's father's ranch. His brother, Mac, now owns it. The elder Jesser escaped from prison and was shot to death. Jesser never forgot the man who'd sent his father to prison. The second motive was money. Lots of money. When Kyle inherited this very profitable ranch, Margot married him, which gave her and Jesser an open door to his money."

"Any idea where Jesser is now?"

"No. But I feel him sometimes. I think he actually knows where we are and is watching us."

"There's that imagination again."

"Maybe. We can only hope he's in Monaco, enjoying the fast life."

"Who? Jesser?"

Natalie spun around at the sound of Kyle's voice. He was standing in the doorway. She turned away from him, hoping he hadn't seen what was in her eyes. She wasn't sure she could identify what it was herself, but it sure felt like longing. *Longing,* of all things! What in the world was she doing *longing* for Kyle McKenzie? Definitely not in her job description.

Glancing over her shoulder again, she saw him wink at Kath, then look at her. Oh! The man was insufferable, flirting with Kath behind her back.

"I need to check on April. Excuse me." Natalie jumped up and brushed past him as she walked inside.

A chill ran up Natalie's back. It was dark, but she'd taken a walk many times in the dark and had never felt an ounce of fear. Touching the back of her neck, she turned around. A couple of cowboys were rocking on a porch, but she couldn't make out their words. The barn door was open, but it was black inside, and no one was about.

She shook off the panicked feeling as she walked toward the path. She and Kath had talked this afternoon about Gordon Jesser, and Natalie was spooked, that's all. Kath was intent on making him the villain in her next book.

"I think he'd be perfect," Kath said, smiling wickedly as she picked over the spread of fruits and pastries, "and name him Jessie. Victoria will detest him on sight."

"Victoria?"

"The heroine." She bit into a strawberry. "And, of course, Roman will ride to her rescue. Tell me more about Jesser. Have you ever seen him?"

"No, but the police showed us a picture of him." Natalie looked over her shoulder and lowered her voice. "Kath, this isn't appropriate, designing a character after Margot's murderer."

"Oh, all right." She popped a grape into her mouth. Her eyes glazed over as she stared at the pendulum of a grandfather's clock. Typical of her. She was in her head, writing a scene or something.

Kath looked at Natalie. "But it seems to me that a man like that wouldn't stop with three million five, Natalie. He'd want more and wouldn't stop until he got it. Until he got all of it."

"You're scaring me."

"Not anything you haven't thought of before."

"Yes, but you make it sound as if he absolutely will when I've been lulled into thinking maybe he won't."

"The man is evil. He killed his own wife. You're too smart to think he'd stop with such a paltry take. Not when he could have ten times that amount. He isn't finished. And since you've entered the picture,

he might switch his target to your mother. Regina's a lot richer than Kyle McKenzie."

"Natalie!" The front door swung open, bringing her out of the memory. Wide-eyed, Kath ran down the stairs, carrying Natalie's purse. Kyle was right behind her. "Your mother's been hurt."

Her world spun. "What?"

"Some jerk hurt her."

She gasped and stared at Kath. "What?"

"Some guy at a party. Your grandmother wasn't specific."

"She's hurt? But what—?"

"I don't have the details. She's not in the hospital so she's—"

Behind her, Kyle said, "Let's go. I'm flying you home."

Aunt Essie appeared behind him, wringing her hands.

Natalie felt her purse strap slipping onto her shoulder, and Kath's hands pushing her as they walked to Kyle's truck. "But—"

"Don't worry about April. I'll stay and help take care of her. If you have any instructions, you can call me when you're in the air."

"But, but what happened?"

"I don't know. You and Aunt Essie need to go, all right?"

Natalie couldn't seem to move. Everything was happening too quickly.

Kath said, "Go! Kyle?"

He stopped, turned around, and held out his hand to her.

Natalie stared at it. He nudged it toward her once, and unable to resist, her palm touched it. He squeezed it, led her to his truck, and opened the front passenger door for Aunt Essie. Then he opened the back passenger door for Natalie. She slid in, and they sped off. "Is there any way I can find out what's going on?"

"Did you bring your cell phone?"

"Uh."

He nodded at her shoulder. "Your purse."

"Yes, of course." Rummaging through it, she found it, dialed, and tried to listen to Nana as they boarded the plane. When Kyle climbed inside, she was putting her phone in her purse.

"We're ready to go. Buckle up, you two. Do you need help, Aunt Essie?"

"No, I'm buckled in."

"I'll get us in the air, then you can fill us in on what happened."

A couple minutes later, Kyle turned to Natalie. "What did you find out about your mother?"

"Physically, she's fine, but some man forced his way into her car at gun point and played some mental games with her. Nana said they didn't know much more than that."

"Then she'll be all right, dear?"

"I think so, Aunt Essie. No one knew this man at the Trenton's party. He just presumed himself into the house and went after my mother. Mother told Nana the man had flirted with her. She rebuffed him and he got even. 'Male knee-jerk reaction,' she called it. Mother said she'd never seen him before tonight."

"A random act of violence, then."

"Maybe."

"Got even—how?"

"I don't know. Nana didn't want to go into any details. She's going to call the police after we get there."

"Why wait?"

"I have no idea. It doesn't make sense." Then, out of the blue, Natalie said, "I'm sorry for my behavior when I left the porch."

Without hesitation, he said, "You're forgiven. You thought I was flirting with Kath."

She was surprised he'd noticed.

"For the record, I was teasing Kath." He glanced at her and held her eyes. "I was flirting with you."

Well.

Okay.

She looked away, and then glanced at him again. He was grinning at her. "I don't understand," she said and pressed her lips together.

"Then, Natalie, you understand far too little."

He seemed content to let the subject drop. They traveled in silence until he announced, "We'll be landing in just a few minutes."

The plane taxied to a stop. Natalie unfastened her seat belt and reached for her purse. "You left April."

Kyle efficiently shut off instruments. "She's in good hands."

"When are you going back?"

"When are *you* going back?"

"I may be here a few days."

"Then I'll head back in the morning."

Aunt Essie touched Kyle's arm. "And, my dears, I think I'll stay here this time. You have a chef on the ranch and plenty of chaperones, Kyle. I believe my place is here now."

"I appreciate everything you've done for my family, Aunt Essie. I hope you'll come out again soon, just to see all of us."

"I'm sure I will."

Kyle helped her down. She carefully walked toward an idling cab.

Kyle held out his hand for Natalie. Without hesitation, she took it, tempted to hold on even after she stepped onto solid ground, but she didn't. She followed him toward their ride.

TWELVE

"He didn't hurt me, not physically at any rate." Regina pulled the throw over her shoulders and took a deep breath as she reached for Natalie's hand. The cold in her bones was slowly leaving. "He hit on me at the party. I was flattered." She closed her eyes tightly. "Embarrassed now that it had been so easy to be flattered."

"Any woman would have been, Mother."

She nodded and addressed her comments to the two officers. "He was beautiful. Dark, slim, not tall. But there was something about him that kept me from believing he was genuinely interested in *me.* Everything he did seemed contrived, but not in a flirtatious way. It seemed more—" Her fingertips touched her forehead. "—more evil. I know I'm not making sense. Flirting can be fun and harmless. I didn't think he was fun or harmless at the party. There was a, uh, a *feeling* about him that something wasn't right."

One officer stopped writing. "It's called woman's intuition. If it could be bottled, it'd make my job a whole lot easier."

Grateful, Regina smiled at him. "At one point, he had one hand on my neck, pushing me back against the door. H-he traced the line of my jaw with his gun. All I could think was that it didn't feel like what I expected."

"What, Mrs. Palmer?"

"The gun. It wasn't cold."

"How could it be, in this heat?" Natalie ventured.

"I-I know. It was silly of me. He said one thing, though, that didn't make any sense. It was while he had me trapped against the door. He said, 'I'll be back in April.' Why would he tell me something like that?"

"April?" Kyle's face paled. He looked at Natalie, then Regina. "It was Jesser. Medium height, blonde—"

"He was dark. Black hair."

"He disguised himself, then. It was Jesser."

"Excuse me." The officer stepped into the hall. In a few minutes, he came back inside. "Detectives Mancini and Phillips are on their way here, ma'am."

Regina nodded and called Celeste for tea.

Just as the maid entered with the tray, Detectives Mancini and Phillips arrived. The police officers spoke quietly with them and then left.

Officer Phillips nodded at Kyle and said, "Mr. McKenzie." He turned to Regina. "The height works but not the coloring. It would be easy to change that, though. A tan, hair dye. Did he have a mustache, Mrs. Palmer?"

"Yes." She squeezed her eyes shut. "The man was thin, not overly tall, attractive."

"It could've been Jesser. We have a photograph of him." He reached for his phone, texted for a few seconds, and slipped the phone into his pocket. "We should have the photo in a few."

Regina sat up. "One more thing. Tattooed on his left hand was a coiled snake with its head reared. I hadn't noticed it at the party probably because he kept his hand in his pocket. But outside, in my car, h-he—" She shuddered, remembering that hand on her shoulder.

"I've seen that tattoo." Kyle frowned.

"Where?"

He shook his head at Regina and stared at the floor.

"Can you remember where, Kyle?"

"No. But it was recently. I thought at the time it seemed out of place." He looked up. "At Margot's funeral. An old man. He was standing at a grave near us. He asked me if I had lost my wife. On his left hand was a coiled snake, ready to strike."

Regina nodded. "Yes."

"And maybe you have two men who went to the same tattoo artist." At the sound of her mother's voice, Regina looked across the room where Lenore sat with her hands gripping her cane and an I'll-tolerate-this-not-a-moment-longer look on her face.

Lenore stood and made her way into the half-circle around Regina's bed. "Similar tattoos, one on the hand of an old man, and one on the hand of a young man, do not necessarily mean you're dealing with a master of disguises. Detective, I would appreciate it if you would bring good sense back to the discussion."

"We're analyzing the evidence, considering all the possibilities."

"It's also possible this man who did harm to my daughter flew in from Mars. Will you consider that as well?"

"Not if the evidence doesn't corroborate it."

"This incident was unfortunate, but it in no way connects us to that monster who killed Mrs. McKenzie."

"Mrs. Jesser."

"Whoever she was. The only connection is my granddaughter caring for her daughter. Will you please keep your rambling speculations away from the press and save us the indignity of injurious conjecturing?"

"If I understood you correctly, Mrs. Carsdale, you're suggesting I withhold facts from the press."

"Not at all, Detective. *You* misunderstand *me*. I was merely—"

"I think what my mother is saying is that the evidence doesn't say that both men were Jesser. Until it does, would you confine any news releases to strictly the facts?" Regina smiled sweetly at the detective.

Her mother nodded once. "Precisely."

"Of course, ma'am. I always do."

"Then we understand each other. I am retiring for the evening. You'll be all right, Regina?"

"Yes, Mama. Good night."

The detective's phone beeped. He turned his phone to Regina. "Is this the man?"

She took the phone. "Oh, yes, that's him. He had darker hair, darker skin, but that's him. That's the man who accosted me."

"May I?" Kyle reached for the phone. "He looks vaguely familiar. But I can't remember where I've seen him." He passed the phone to the detective.

"Did you notice if he had a car at the party, Mrs. Palmer?"

"No, I didn't. He was on foot when I saw him after I left."

"Did he have an accomplice? Someone at the affair that he stood beside, talked to at length, anyone he seemed to know?"

Regina squeezed her eyes shut, thinking back. Most of the faces belonged to friends, acquaintances, people introduced to her as friends of friends. The first time she'd seen him, he'd strolled over to her. And then she'd left. "I didn't see anyone. I'm sorry."

"And you left him on foot at the corner of Mason and Naples?"

"Yes, and when I drove off, I looked in the rearview mirror and saw him standing on the corner. He had the audacity to smile and wave

586

goodbye to me."

The detective closed his notebook and slipped it into his pocket. "We'll search that area, see if anyone recognizes him. Probably had a car stashed close by and is resting comfortably in a hole somewhere. Take appropriate precautions. Jesser is a cold-blooded murderer, unpredictable, and able to disguise himself. I wouldn't put it past him to finish what he started tonight, ma'am."

Regina swallowed hard and looked warily at Natalie.

"Let me know if you remember anything else. Stay low for a few days. We'll keep you posted." He and the other detective left.

Suddenly weary, Regina fluffed the sofa pillow at her back. "Show Kyle to his room upstairs, Natalie. I'm going to try to sleep."

"Mother, are you sure you're—"

"Yes, yes. Now, go, dear. Kyle, thank you for bringing her home. You are welcome here as long as you wish to stay."

"Thank you, Mrs. Palmer."

She flapped a hand at him. "Regina. For heaven's sake, we've been through enough to call each other by our first names, Kyle." She didn't miss his hand reaching for Natalie's elbow.

"Mother, if you need anything—"

"I shall rouse the National Guard. Good-night, kids."

"Sleep well."

"I'm sure I won't but I will try, just for you."

Kyle followed Natalie upstairs, waited as she opened a door, and stepped into pure luxury, a room obviously meant for a visiting head of state. "I forgot my crown."

"It is rather pretentious, isn't it? My mother insisted you have this suite. She believes in rewarding heroic gestures and you have gone above and beyond the call of duty by bringing me here tonight."

"Not really. You needed to come home. I had the means to get you here. I'll be leaving in the morning. Are you staying?"

"I don't know. Do you have to rush off?"

"No. What about noon? Would that give you enough time to decide?" He took a step toward her.

She faltered, straightened her back, lifted her chin. "Yes, thank

you."

He watched her defenses spring up like a geyser. "Why are you nervous?"

"What makes you think—?"

"Your hands."

Her hands were clutched at her waist, one thumb kneading the other. She quickly dropped them. "I'm concerned about my mother, that's all. If you need anything, dial one-four. Georgia will help you. Thank you, Kyle. I appreciate all you've done."

"You're welcome. Where's your room?"

"Just next door." She smiled. "And, no, it's not as elaborate as this."

His gaze slid to the adjoining door and noticed it was latched. Deliberately, he avoided her eyes. It was simply too tempting tonight to throw caution out the door and begin something that they both might regret. "Good-night, Natalie. Sleep tight."

"You, too. Thanks."

She seemed hesitant to leave. *So she was tempted, too.* All the more reason to be rational and strong. He smiled at her and then walked to the bed and turned down the covers, giving her a chance to leave. When he turned around, she was gone.

Good. He sucked in a deep breath and blew it out. He would take this slowly. He just hoped Natalie, in the meantime, wouldn't slam the door on 'more than friends' just because she was a little uncomfortable with the idea of it.

A piercing scream shattered the night's quiet. Kyle threw his covers off, reached for the robe that had been provided as a courtesy, and was struggling into it when he opened the door and almost collided with Natalie in the hallway.

"My mother," she said frantically and raced down the hall.

They found Regina sitting up in her bed, holding her head with both hands, breathing raggedly. "I'm sorry, kids. It was a nightmare. It seemed so real. I'm okay now. Go on back to bed."

Kyle stayed at the foot of the bed while Natalie sat beside her mother and touched her arm. "Are you sure, Mother? I could stay with

you."

"Yes, I'm sure. But I remember something that man said. Just before he left, he said, 'Daughters are gifts, aren't they, Regina?' I didn't notice at the time that he knew my name. I hadn't told him. He called me 'Beautiful' when we first met, and I know I never told him my name."

"Of course, he knew your name. You were his target," Kyle offered. "The only reason he was at that party was because of you, or—oh, God."

"What?"

"It could have been a reference to April. Maybe this was all a ruse to get us here and leave April at the ranch." He tugged out his cell phone and called Bonnie as he walked out into the hallway. "Bonnie, I'm sorry to wake you but you need to know that Jesser may try for April while I'm gone."

"I've already thought of that. We have four armed cowboys sleeping in four of the bedrooms, two upstairs, two downstairs. I'm in April's room. Baldy is sleeping on a mat in the foyer. The security system is set. We're on high alert here. And, no, you didn't wake me. I was up with April."

"Is she all right?"

"She's fine. How's Natalie's mom?"

"A little spooked but okay. Thanks for everything. I'll see you in the morning."

Kyle walked back in and told them about his phone call to Bonnie. "There could have been a threat to April in all this, but I don't think so. Jesser would have made his move by now. He might have been alluding to Natalie. I wouldn't put it past him to try to get money out of you, Regina. You have a lot more to offer than I do."

Natalie glanced at him. "You're suggesting *I'm* his next victim?"

"It makes sense. You might be safer here in your mother's home."

She stood and turned toward him. She was beautiful in a floor-length pale blue robe, her blonde hair mussed a little around her face, her eyes regarding him with obvious frustration. "What if you're wrong? What if it isn't Jesser and this man's statement means nothing? I'm not giving up what I think I'm supposed to do just to sit around and wait for something to happen that may not."

She looked from Kyle to her mother. "Look. I'll stay for another day, Mother, and make sure you're all right. Then I'm going back to the ranch to look after April. In the meantime, I'm off to bed, unless you want me to stay with you. I'd be happy to."

Regina smiled as she sank back into her covers. "I'm fine. Shut my door on your way out, dears. And pray I won't have any more nightmares."

Natalie closed the door quietly and walked with Kyle down the hallway. "Do you know when you'll be leaving now?"

"I'll probably be gone before you get up in the morning."

They stopped at her door. "All right. I should be home—" she flinched, embarrassed, but quickly recovered, "in about two days. I'll drive up." She looked down at her hands. "Thank you."

"I'm glad to be of some help."

It took every ounce of courage she had to look up, into his eyes. And what met her there frightened her. It wasn't difficult to see warmth in his eyes. They were intent, focused on her.

Embarrassed, she looked down and made herself say the words that needed to be said. "Well. Good night, then."

She shut her door and leaned against it. Their friendship had changed tonight. That thrilled her, amazed her, humbled her. But mostly, it frightened her. For someone who had run away from relationships her entire life, she wasn't sure she knew how to do this. She wasn't even sure what 'this' was. She hoped she wouldn't get cold feet and withdraw from what she supposed to do, even—or especially—if it meant falling in love with Kyle McKenzie.

THIRTEEN

Natalie didn't need to look at the clock to know it was a little before six. Early morning light crept through the elegant sheers and colored her mother's room a soft gray. She had fallen asleep on the chaise lounge near her mother's bed after the second nightmare.

She walked to the windows, moved the sheers aside, and feasted on the parade of colors announcing the sun would arrive soon.

Flowers were already beginning to open in welcome. At precisely five-forty-five, underground sprinklers sprang to life in mushroom formations. Easing the glass door open, she stepped out into the dawn as birds chirped.

She closed her eyes and breathed in the morning as contentment closed itself around her. The long night behind her was forgotten.

Glancing at the balcony of Kyle's room, she wondered if he was awake yet. As if her thoughts had conjured him up, his glass door opened, and he stepped out. He was dressed in the same clothes, holding his cowboy hat in his hand, his hair wet and neatly combed.

The distance was not great between them, and Natalie caught herself wanting him to look her way, for their gazes to connect, for him to smile at her.

She moved.

He glanced over.

And it happened.

She could hardly breathe. It was remarkable what was happening to her. It felt as if an invisible rubber band was between them, contracting, pulling them closer. If she allowed herself, she could actually see his eyes more clearly, smell his aftershave, feel his arms around her.

With his gaze on her, he put on his cowboy hat and touched the rim of his hat in a salute. Then he turned and left.

Relief, sadness, and confusion hit her. With one more glance at the beautiful yards, she picked up the book she'd found about four o'clock this morning, went inside, and sat on the chaise lounge. She turned on the little book light and tried to concentrate on the words, but after three paragraphs, she started over.

"You always did like to read."

The book landed in her lap as she smiled at her mother. "Did I?"

"Oh, yes. Your father spent your first four years reading everything in sight to you. He could make all the story characters come alive. He used different voices, different pitches, growling and singing and whispering the words so that it all seemed very real to you."

"Where were you?"

"Nearby. Listening. You didn't like me to read to you because I couldn't do the voices. Only your daddy would do."

Natalie nodded. "I've been dreaming a lot about him lately, remembering the things he did with me."

"He was a good father."

"I remember everything being different when he was alive."

"Different?"

She shrugged. "It's hard to put into words. Everything seemed happier back then. We all seemed happier."

Her mother sighed. "I suppose we were. Death is so permanent. It took me a long time to realize that. When your father died, I expected him to come home every day around six and yell, "Regina Cantina, I'm home.""

Natalie smiled. "He said that, didn't he? I'd forgotten."

"Every day. It was hard for me to let him go. I suppose I moped around here for months—years, really—expecting him to be in the next room or outside barbecuing or in the garage puttering with his tools or in the bathroom, shaving. I missed him so much. He made me feel as if I were the most important person God ever created."

"I'll bet you were, to him."

Her mother shook her head. "Not when you were born. That man fell instantly in love with his baby. He'd bundle you up and take you to speaking engagements, business meetings, church, grocery shopping." She smiled. "People teased him and called him crazy. He took it in stride and laughed with them, knowing they were right. He *was* crazy... about you."

Then why did he die?

Natalie squirmed at the thought. For years, she'd been too afraid of hurting her mother to ask a simple question. "Mother, what happened the day of the accident? Did the police ever find out what caused it?"

"No, dear. Your father slammed into an eighteen-wheeler. It was no one's fault."

Natalie sat up. "How can you say that? It was my fault. It was clearly my fault."

"What are you talking about?"

"It was my fault." She sprang to her feet. "Everyone knows that. *I* caused the accident."

She heard her mother throw off the covers behind her. "*Your* fault? Where did you get such an idea? The police said it must have been something in the brake mechanism that caused the car to be unable to stop. No one blames you, sweetheart. No one."

"You did."

"I *never* did!"

"On the way home from the hospital when Daddy died. You were crying. You blamed me."

Her mother stood. "That's not true. I never once thought of you being to blame."

Natalie crossed her arms. "Grandmother thinks it was my fault."

"She's never said anything like that to me. And if she believed that, you know she would have said something by now."

Natalie threw her hands up. "Then why did she become so cold? Why is she so exacting about everything? Why is it that nothing I ever do pleases her?"

"Or me? Is that what you think, honey? That nothing you do pleases me either?"

Natalie walked to the windows and looked out, seeing nothing. A quiet desperation raced through her, an old familiar feeling. "After Daddy died, everything changed. I assumed it was because you blamed me for his death."

"Maybe my tears and the depression I suffered added to your guilt, I don't know. But I tried, sweetheart, to meet your needs. I was suffering so. I knew you were, too."

At her pause, Natalie wanted to turn around but couldn't. "Then why did life become so cold? Why did you and Nana change toward me?"

"We were all struggling, honey." Regina sat on the edge of the bed, closed her eyes, and rubbed her temple. "Something happened the day your father died. I saw your face. I saw the tears you held back. I felt resentment building in you, but I couldn't do anything about it. I simply could not reach you. Mama and I tried for weeks to get you to talk about it. But you withdrew from us, a little every day."

"You're saying *I* changed?"

Her mother looked up. "We sent you to a psychiatrist. Joel Broker. You called him 'Dr. Joel.' Do you remember?"

"He played games with me. Board games."

"He said it would help you to trust him."

"I remember thinking he might die if I was around him too much."

"You said the same thing about the puppy we bought you. Freckles. In the box. Remember?"

Oh, yes, she remembered Freckles. "I wanted him, but I didn't want him to die because of me."

At that moment, Natalie realized that a pattern had begun in her life after her father's death: she wouldn't allow people to get close to her for fear that somehow, she would hurt them.

She thought of the men who had been interested in her the last few years. She'd methodically rejected them, not from a desire to do the right thing but because she was afraid of not just hurting *them,* but in being hurt *by* them when they left.

"Mother, I may not remember what happened in the car that day, but I do know that I had something to do with the accident. And the three days it took Daddy to die..." Natalie tried to swallow down the sudden tears. "I remember thinking my heart was broken." She brushed away tears. "That it would never heal. It was something I'd heard you say, and I figured mine was broken, too. And the secret place..." Her voice had drifted into a whisper as she struggled to get the words past her tight throat.

"What, Natalie? What about the secret place?"

She made herself say the words. "That it was lost to me forever, because Daddy was the only one who knew where to find it in my heart. When he died, I thought all my dreams died with him."

The lump in her throat was almost too big to speak around. Swallowing hard, she took a deep breath and let it out. "I'm realizing right now that I've blamed myself for all of it. I've pushed myself away from any kind of a healthy relationship with anyone." She looked at her mother as tears streamed down her face. "Especially you and Nana."

"Oh, Natalie, I'm so sorry." She stood. "Please forgive me for not knowing what you were going through. It was never your fault. It was my fault, for not driving you."

"Mother—"

She held up a hand. "I had a headache, and your father volunteered to take you to your dance lesson." Her mother's face softened as she smiled gently. "He said, 'I'll take her, Cantina. Just turn off the lights, stick your head under a pillow, and I'll be back in a jif.'" She sighed deeply. "It wasn't your fault or mine. It was just an accident."

Natalie wanted to believe her. "Accidents do happen. And sometimes little girls are careless, and they cause accidents—"

"No—"

"*Even*—" She closed her eyes, lowered her voice. "Even if they don't mean to." She paused a moment. "Mother, my faith is strong. I believe it was Daddy's time to go home. But I'd like to remember what happened that day, so I can finally put this to rest, no matter what the truth."

Her mother nodded solemnly, blinked at brimming tears. "I love you, Natalie. I may not have shown it as well as your father did, but I love you with all my heart." She touched her face and smiled. "Maybe now, we can regain some of what we had when your father was still alive."

Natalie went into her arms and held her tight. "I want that so much."

After a few moments, Regina pulled back. "When are you going back to the ranch?"

"In the morning. I'd like to spend the day with you and Nana. I'm going to talk with her about what you and I discussed. One thing I'm not going to do is think about Gordon Jesser."

"He's certainly not going to get much of my attention today. That, I can promise you."

Tormenting Regina had been more fun than Gordon could have

imagined. The woman was simply dripping with fear. He had felt her trembling, had seen little sweat beads just above her top lip, had heard the little gasps as he moved closer to her.

And then, to do nothing.

That had to have been pure genius.

He had simply left her, totally terrified. He would have loved to have been a cell flying through her body, experiencing the deafening pounding of her heart, riding the wave of fear that jolted through her body.

But he'd have to content himself with having merely watched, felt, and heard how the terror had affected her.

She had wept, silently shuddering as the tears ran down her face. That was the best part. The crying was by far the best part.

Was she thinking about him right now, terrified he'd come back and finish what he'd started? It was exhilarating, actually, to know that he could put that kind of fear inside someone. He shouldn't have killed Margot so quickly. He should have taken his time and let her truly experience her own death in a deeper way, from the inside out.

Next time, he'd take his time.

What he had to decide now was whether it would be Regina, to give him—and her—the satisfaction of finishing his business with her.

Or Natalie.

Or Kyle.

Or April.

He smiled. *So many choices.*

Of course, money was his primary focus.

But he wouldn't deprive himself of the pleasure of coming back for them, one at a time, making sure, of course, that each fully experienced the true and beautiful meaning of death.

Gravel popped as Natalie's car crawled to a stop. Kyle's head appeared from under the lighted hood of his truck. He smiled and waved at her, then yanked a rag from his back pocket and wiped his hands. "I could have flown you home."

"I know." She opened the door. "But I wanted my car here. How is April?"

His face darkened. "About the same. She misses you."

"I miss her. That's why I'm back so early."

"I only left yesterday morning. I could've stayed and brought you back."

"I had some unfinished business to take care of with my mother and grandmother."

"I'm glad you're back. I hardly had time to miss you, but I somehow managed to."

She looked up, met his gaze, and saw truth behind the teasing. Her heart pounded as if to say, 'Get on with it. Say something encouraging.' So she did. "It's mutual. It's good to be back." She smiled at him over her shoulder as she walked up the stairs and into the main house.

Natalie walked up to April's room. Opal, the Registered Nurse, was singing to her as they rocked. Her little head slowly turned and when she saw Natalie, she lifted a tiny hand and opened and closed her fist. "Na-tee."

Her heart simply melted. She reached for the baby and held her. "How's my girl, huh? How's my April?" She nuzzled her neck and kissed her face. "Are you all right, sweetheart? Natalie's praying for you." She looked around the room. "Where's Kath?"

"She went into town about an hour ago. Said she had some shopping to do." Opal patted April's back. "Is Essie here?"

"No. She decided to stay in Granston for now."

"That's a shame. I really like that old girl." Opal left then.

With nurse's eyes, Natalie looked at her little angel. Her coloring was more sallow. The smudges around her eyes were darker. She seemed too lethargic. Natalie closed her eyes and held April close, hoping time would stand still and the disease would stop marching forward. *I'm not ready for this, Lord. Please.*

She had to let Kyle know. She left the room with a sense of urgency, knowing her words were going to crush him.

His boots thudded on the hardwood floors as he walked from the kitchen toward her, smiling.

"Oh, there you are. I was hoping you'd—" He frowned when he saw her face. "What is it? What's wrong?" He lovingly touched April's face and smiled at her.

"Kyle." Natalie shook her head, avoiding his eyes. "It's time to take April to the hospital."

"But she's doing fine. She hasn't... she's not..." His face contorted with pain. "No."

Neither said a word as she took the last step down the stairs and into his arms. In a matter of seconds, their world had turned upside-down.

Natalie pulled away and started back up the stairs. "I'll get her ready and call Kath."

"I'll call Lynette Weisbrod and then my mother. I know she'd like to be there."

FOURTEEN

Day four. Kyle stared at April while she slept. She looked smaller in the hospital bed, hooked up to thin lines of liquids giving her nourishment and medicine for the pain. *Let me, Lord. Let me take her place.*

Beside him, Natalie looked up and smiled weakly. They were both tired. The television quietly droned behind him, and occasionally, April would focus on a cartoon character and smile, but for the most part, she slept. And lost weight.

Kyle nudged Natalie's elbow. "Mom's on her way. You need a break."

"We both do."

A few minutes later, his mother walked into the room, and he hugged her. She had been a lifesaver the past four days.

"Any sign of a donor?"

"No. Lynette told me she's been contacted four times, but none were compatible."

"Y'all go on home. I'll stay with her for a while."

Natalie smiled a thank you while Kyle leaned over and kissed April. "I love you, sweetheart. Daddy will be back soon. Grammie's here, okay?" He stood and took Natalie's arm. "We'll see you around six, Mom."

Outside, the skies brooded. The wind had picked up, and the air was thick with humidity and the scent of rain. "We need the moisture," he said as he and Natalie walked to the truck.

He opened her door. "Do you want to eat out or go home?"

"Yes," she mumbled, got in, and closed her eyes as her head fell back against the headrest.

In silence, he drove them to Granston. Somehow, he ended up in front of Palmer House. When the truck stopped, Natalie jerked awake, looked around.

"We're here."

She looked up at her mother's home. "I must have fallen asleep."

"You needed it."

Closing her eyes, she groped for the door handle. "Call me the second you hear anything."

"I will. Get some sleep."

She nodded. "You, too."

He put the truck in drive. "I'll be back for you at five-forty-five."

She shut the door and waved as he pulled away. Her legs felt like lead as she walked to the house. She didn't know a body could hurt this much from pure worry. Her head buzzed, her shoulders ached, her stomach growled. One of the gardeners stood on the landscaped island in the middle of the large, brick, circular driveway, clipping the hedges. He lifted his head and nodded once at her with a somber expression.

In all her years of living with her parents, she'd never seen a gardener do that. He was black headed, dark skinned, but something about his eyes said he didn't belong here. Natalie thought he must have fallen on hard times. Ignoring him, she continued walking up the long steps toward the front door.

Celeste opened the door before she could knock and smiled at her. "Refreshments, miss?"

She trudged inside. "Thank you, Celeste. But right now, I just need some sleep."

"I'll turn down your bed then."

"Thank you. Do you know the gardener outside working on the circular island?"

"No, miss. He's new. Mrs. Pattison hired him yesterday."

"Were his references thoroughly checked?"

"I'm sure they were. I will advise Mrs. Pattison that you'd like to speak with her. Oh, miss. You have mail. It came today."

Natalie absently took the envelope from her and would have ignored it but for the return address—McCarthen School of Dance where she'd studied when she was fifteen and sixteen. What in the world could they be writing about?

As she plodded up the stairs, she read the letter and gasped. They wanted her to teach! She would start the middle of September and teach until May first of the following year.

Despite the weariness, she shook with excitement. This was a dream come true! To have an offer from McCarthen, with its solid reputation and... oh, no. She couldn't accept it. Not with April so ill.

But maybe she would be out of danger by then.

And Kyle. Could she leave their budding relationship and go to Dallas for almost nine months? Her best friend, Andrea, lived in Dallas and would open her home to her. She would love to have Natalie stay with her and her little daughter, Bella. She and Natalie had been best friends for years, and she'd visited them several times since Andrea's husband, Jason, died. So, where to stay in Dallas wasn't an issue.

But she was getting ahead of herself. She hadn't even accepted the invitation.

Folding the letter, she wearily shut her bedroom door behind her. She couldn't think right now; she was simply too tired. After she slept a bit, she would consider the letter.

Someone shouted at her. She couldn't pull herself out of the tunnel. It was warm, and she couldn't see. The light had disappeared.

"Miss Natalie, wake up! You have a phone call!"

Shaking her head, Natalie forced her heavy eyes open and gasped when she saw Celeste looming over her. "What is it?"

"You have a phone call, Miss Natalie. It's Mr. Kyle, and he says it's urgent."

"Oh, no!" In one fluid motion, she sat up and reached for the phone with shaking hands. "Kyle? Is April—?"

"They have a donor. I'll be there in ten minutes."

"Thank God!" She tossed her phone and ran to the bathroom, washed her face, brushed her teeth, refreshed her make-up, changed her clothes, picked up the overnight bag she kept ready, and ran down the stairs. As she walked outside, Kyle was pulling up to the curb. He leaned over and opened her door.

"Good timing," he said as she got in, a huge smile on his face. "It's a match, Natalie." He reached for her and pulled her into a hug. "It's a miracle."

Nodding, she slowly pulled away. In his exuberance, he had yanked her beside him. Trying not to be too obvious, she edged over to her side of the truck. "Now her body needs to accept it. A small bowel, too?"

"Yes." Smiling, he reached for her hand and squeezed. "We have a chance. A real chance for April to have a normal life."

"When?"

He released her hand and started the truck. "As soon as possible." He glanced at her. "Our little girl is going to make it. I know it. She's going to make it."

"And some precious baby lost her life to make that happen. Let's pray for the family of the donor, that God will give them peace and comfort."

On the way to the hospital, Natalie thought of the letter. If April lived and thrived, she would have plenty of time to accept the position in Dallas.

Her stomach sank at the thought of telling Kyle she was leaving. She already missed him, and April, and the ranch. In her mind, her place in their lives had already shifted. She didn't want to leave, but with April better, she would be out of a job.

The quiet pounded against Natalie's ears. Whispers occasionally broke the silence in the family waiting room. A group of three from Kyle's church stood in the corner, nodding, murmuring, glancing toward the door expectantly.

The waiting was almost unbearable. An hour went by, then two, three, four, five. Lunch came and went. By midafternoon, hunger set in, and everyone left for the cafeteria except Natalie and Kyle. Neither spoke.

Natalie left to get some exercise. She paced down the halls, ran up and down the stairs, walked back to the waiting room, then Kyle left to do the same. Every time someone appeared in the doorway to the waiting room, Kyle, Natalie, Kyle's twin brother Kevin, Joan, and several church members looked toward the door, hoping to hear something about April.

A nurse came in and turned on the TV. With the volume muted, a soap opera over-dramatized a man stalking one of the female characters. Without seeing it, Natalie stared at the TV, then glanced at Kyle with a how-much-longer-will-it-take look. For the umpteenth time, she checked her watch and sighed.

Kyle squirmed on the hard plastic chairs. "I need to get up. Would you like some coffee?"

"I'll go with you."

As she led the way out the door, a doctor rounded a corner toward them. "Kyle, the surgeon."

Before he reached them, he said, "She looks good. The surgeries went very well, extremely well."

Natalie grabbed Kyle's hand and squeezed it. He let go and put his arm around her waist, tugging her close.

"We're very pleased at this point. Now it's a waiting game to see if her body will reject or accept her new organs."

The doctor stayed another minute, answering their questions. When he walked away, Kyle spun Natalie into his arms and held her tightly.

She'd never felt such peace in her life.

She didn't know if it was April's good news or the fact that she was in Kyle's arms where she felt she belonged.

FIFTEEN

Stepping off the back porch, Natalie followed the path to the gazebo. There was nothing quite as perfect as early morning, when the world was still asleep and promises of things yet to come were whispers on the air.

Sipping her coffee, she considered the progress April had made the past three weeks. She was alert, wide-eyed, saying more words, and so very adorable. She had gained weight, too, despite wrinkling her nose at her first taste of food. She was eating much better now, and her new organs were working properly. She would soon be out of the hospital—

"You didn't hear me pull up."

She jumped and laughed at herself. "Good morning, Kyle. It's such a fine morning that I had to come out here and enjoy it." She scooted over and patted the seat beside her. "Have you had breakfast?"

He sat down. "No, have you?"

She shook her head. "Why don't I treat you to breakfast this morning? I have some things I'd like to talk over with you."

"Yeah? What things?"

She had dreaded this moment. April was better now. When she got out of the hospital, she and Kyle were going back to the ranch. He said he thought ranch life would be good for her, with the animals and the routine and the people there who loved her and were trained to protect her against Jesser. Natalie agreed with him, although he had no idea that she didn't intend to go back with him. But nothing had ever been said between them that indicated they were a couple—or even headed in that direction. Just a look or two, a hug or two, and wishful thinking on her part.

It was time for her to move on. It was time to go to Dallas. "I received a letter three weeks ago." This was more difficult than she'd thought it would be. For some reason, she felt she was letting him down, letting them both down.

"A letter?" he prompted.

She wrapped her hands around her cup and took a sip, avoiding his eyes. "An invitation for me to teach ballet."

"Teach?"

"At a school I attended when I was fifteen and sixteen." The next words she spoke would seal everything, but she suddenly didn't want to say them. She closed her eyes.

"Where is this school?"

Hearing the hurt in his voice, she almost doubted herself. But resolve rose within her. She kept her eyes closed and said, "Dallas."

Dallas? It wasn't far. "Are you going to take it?" He'd already seen the answer in her eyes.

"Yes. Yes, I am."

Why? He squeezed his eyes shut. *She's leaving.* He quickly shook his head to free it from the incoming fog. *She's leaving.* He couldn't quite get his mind around it. She'd be going away soon. It was September. It wouldn't be long before she left.

"When?"

"In about a week. School starts the fifteenth."

"Why?"

"What do you mean?"

"Why are you leaving? Why are you taking this position?"

"I'm at loose ends now that April is better."

She hadn't talked to him. She'd known for three weeks and hadn't said a word to him about it. "You're sure about this?" Why now, when April was healing and growing stronger? When he could finally get on with his life? He'd thought that life would include her.

Had he been wrong? Had he been the only one thinking this relationship was developing into something more?

"As sure as I can be."

What could he say? She had already made the decision. She had already left his world.

He had been a fool. Again.

Struggling with temper and hurt, he abruptly stood. He had to get away. "I need to get to the hospital. Did you plan to go with me?"

She stood, too. "Of course, I'm going with you. Aren't we going to get breakfast on the way?"

Uncomfortable, he shifted his feet. "Look, Natalie, I think I'll just go by myself this morning. I need to do some thinking, spend some time alone with April. Why don't you just stay at your home and get some things done, all right?"

He didn't wait for her answer.

He turned and walked as quickly as he could toward his truck.

"Kyle?"

He drove away. Contrary to the way they had handled things in the past, they wouldn't be able to support and comfort each other through this. He was in too much pain to even consider talking to her about it.

Instead of spending the last week together, Kyle obviously, pointedly, avoided her.

When Natalie arrived at the hospital to see April, he would find some excuse to leave. When she called, he wouldn't pick up, and she'd leave a message that he never returned. She thought it was a childish and immature way to treat a friend who was just doing what she thought was right. And it hurt that he'd rejected her when they could have spent this time together, growing more into a relationship that might or might not continue while she was in Dallas. They could have worked out some of those details.

The night before she left, Aunt Essie came into her room. "Is there anything I can help you with, dear?"

Natalie smiled at her and tucked a folded nightgown into her luggage. "No, I'm just about done here."

"It'll be cooler in a month or so."

"Hmmm." She folded a lightweight sweater and placed it on top of the gown.

"Have you heard from Kyle?"

"No, and I don't think I will. I've left him several messages. I think he's avoiding me."

"I wonder why."

The luggage clicked shut. Natalie pulled it off the bed and placed it by the door. "That, I cannot answer. The man's being childish. I didn't expect such stupid behavior from him."

"Childish or hurting?"

Natalie stopped. "What do you mean?"

"I mean, my dear, that Kyle's gone through a lot of hurt in the last few years. Maybe you should give him a break on this one. His father died, his wife totally betrayed him for two years and then died, his daughter's been at death's door since she was born. Maybe he's avoiding you because the hurt is too deep."

"But we haven't... he hasn't... our relationship isn't—"

"None of that has anything to do with hurt, dear. Do yourself a favor and go see him. Say good-bye. Talk to him. You'll regret it if you don't."

She placed a kiss on Aunt Essie's soft cheek. "Thank you." She picked up her keys and left.

A few minutes later, she slowed to a stop, turned off the car lights, and looked toward his house. Everything was dark in the front, but a light was on at the back of the house.

Kyle was sitting on his picnic table, under the security light, with his elbows on his knees and a book in his hands. She had missed him so much. She had missed her friend. "Hello."

His head snapped up. For one second, their gazes locked. Then just as quickly, his head lowered to the book in his hands. That one movement told her volumes. She almost turned around and left, but Aunt Essie was right. She needed to say good-bye to someone who had been a good friend to her.

"I wanted to stop by and... and say good-bye."

"Then say it."

She took a step toward him, and he jumped off the table and headed for the screened-in porch. She thought he was going to walk inside, but as he reached for the screen door, he said, "Would you like something to drink?"

"Yes, thank you."

With his back to her, he said, "Sweet tea?"

"Yes."

When he disappeared inside, she walked across the yard and sat on the picnic table. She needed to be totally honest with him. She shook her head, appalled at her thoughts. No, she couldn't. She wouldn't. Besides, what would she say to him? That she thought she was growing to love him? That she didn't want to go to Dallas because she didn't want to leave *him?* That maybe if she stayed, they would have a chance to....

She stood and started pacing. No. A thousand times no. She just needed to say good-bye. That's all. Besides, what was the use of bringing it all up when she was leaving?

She sat again and watched the door, struggling against waves of emotion.

Kyle came out holding two glasses. Wordlessly, he thrust one at her and turned his back on her, walking a few paces away.

The cold glass felt good against her warm hands. "Why is it *you* get to pout when things change? When you knew you were supposed to go to the ranch, did I pout and make you feel guilty? No. I went with you—"

He spun around. "Are you suggesting I go with you to Dallas?"

"No. I'm suggesting you shouldn't pout and avoid me just because I'm moving. I don't think I deserve such treatment and... and..." Her voice trailed off as her breath lodged in her throat.

He looked up at the night sky and sighed. "You're right. You don't." It wasn't difficult to see the regret etched on his face when he looked at her. "I apologize."

Aunt Essie was right. He was hurting. "I'm sorry, too, Kyle. I didn't handle things very well."

He walked toward her and sat a good two feet away. "I don't want you to go."

Oh, God, why does this have to be so difficult? Why did I have to go and fall in love with him? "I don't want to go either."

"I thought we were getting closer."

"We were." She shook her head. "Are."

"So, I didn't imagine it?"

"No." *So I didn't imagine it either.*

"Now what?"

"We say good-bye. That's why I'm here. I didn't want to go without saying good-bye to one of the best friends—"

He snorted.

She looked at him. "One of the best friends I've ever had."

"Well, good-bye then." He eased off the table. "I hope you have a wonderful life in Dallas."

Natalie stood and faced him. "I really do mean it, Kyle. You're the best friend I've ever had, outside of Kath, who is a woman."

"Yeah, I noticed that."

Trying to break the tension, she nudged his arm and smiled. "You know what I mean."

He slid his hands into his pockets. "I want you to be happy and do what you think you're supposed to do."

"If I email you, will you email me back?"

He nodded. "I will. Do you think you'll be here for the holidays?"

Thanksgiving and Christmas. So far away. "Probably. I don't know yet."

In the soft light, his gaze was intent on hers, and she had trouble breathing. "Kyle..."

Someone moved and suddenly, they were in each other's arms, holding on tightly. She wished their relationship had developed into something more meaningful than just 'really good friends' by now.

"I'm going to miss you, Natalie."

She wasn't sure she could talk around the lump in her throat. "I already miss you. And April."

The seconds ticked by as they quietly held each other.

Natalie didn't know who pulled back first, but the hug ended, and she stood before him, not ready to leave but knowing she needed to go. "You'll write me?"

"Yes."

"And call?"

"Yes."

"And video call, for April. She'll be able to see me." Were there tears in his eyes? She'd never meant to hurt him.

"You'd better go."

"I'll talk to you soon, Kyle."

"Call me when you get there."

Nodding, she pressed her lips together to stop the tears. Somehow, her feet moved toward the gate. She looked back once and waved and heard the gate close behind her as she ran to her car.

SIXTEEN

The back door opened and shut. Sitting on the tree swing, Natalie heard the dry grass rustling behind her as Andrea walked toward her. It was a nightly ritual, swinging together and talking. "Is Bella asleep?" Andrea never wavered on keeping her four-year-old on a strict schedule. "She'll be healthier, knowing what to expect," she'd told her.

"She fought it, but she's out now." Andrea sat, and the swing moved at the urging of her long legs.

The last two months had flown by at times, and at other times, had crawled by. Andrea and her daughter, Bella, had opened their home to her, and she had loved living with them.

Pulling her sweater tighter around her, Natalie held her hot tea with her cold hands, enjoying the stars in the cool night. In the house behind them, Jonathan Casey's puppy cried at the back door. His mother, Bobbie, opened the door and said something to Bowzer. The door shut. The night returned to quiet.

"I've loved staying here with you and Bella. You've made me feel like I'm a part of your family." Silence hummed between them as the swing rocked and creaked.

"You're going back."

Natalie looked at her. It was too dark to see if Andrea was crying but it sounded as if her voice had hitched. She didn't want her to cry. This wasn't an easy decision for her, and it probably wouldn't be permanent. But she had missed Kyle more than she ever thought she would. The phone calls were wonderful. The texting, constant. But she missed April and Kyle. The growing feelings for Kyle would not be prayed away or willed away or reasoned away and she had finally determined last night that maybe they shouldn't be shoved aside as if they were a nuisance.

"Just for the holidays." Which, she knew, would be hard on Andrea.

Her best friend sighed and took a breath as if she was going to say something, but she didn't for a moment or two. "I've never understood why you came up here in the first place."

"I've always wanted to teach."

"It was more than that. You were running away from someone or something. Has something changed? Do you think you can go back now?"

"I don't know." The swing moved again. "I just know I want to go home."

Andrea dreaded being alone again. Having another adult in the house had made it easier to deal with life without Jason. With Natalie here, she didn't have to face an empty house—there was someone to talk to, someone to listen to her and share the mundane things of life with.

Her family lived in Florida. They had left the day after Jason's funeral. When the door had shut and Andrea faced the emptiness of her home for the first time, she honestly thought she would go crazy trying to live without him.

She squeezed her eyes shut as she remembered that horrible day—although the day had started out beautifully.

They'd made love in the wee hours of the morning, took a giggling shower together, and as they dressed, Bella came into their bedroom and asked why the television wasn't working.

"Probably the cable, honey." Jason squatted to Bella's level, but he kept his eyes on Andrea. "It'll likely be back on soon. But let's go check it out, all right?" He stood, slowly winked and grinned at Andrea as they left the room.

The rest of the morning was a haze of memories now.

Jason—kissing her good-bye, heading for work.

Jason—waving as he backed out.

Jason—knowing she'd be watching him, tossing the "I love you" sign out the window as he disappeared around the corner.

Forty-five minutes later, two police officers stood at her front door.

The female officer had a wary, apologetic look on her face as she asked Andrea if she was Mrs. James Borden.

Numb, she'd nodded.

"Mrs. Andrea Borden?"

Andrea gripped the doorknob, frozen in fear, staring unseeingly at them.

"Ma'am?"

The words were fuzzy, as if mosquitoes buzzed in her head.

"Andrea?" One of them touched her arm. "Would you like to sit down?"

The female officer's hands were gentle on her arm and back as they led her to a chair. When she was settled into it, the woman squatted and looked her squarely in the eyes. "Ma'am, there's no easy way to say this. There's been an accident."

More than a year later, Natalie called and told her about the job offer in Dallas. She was thrilled to have her old friend come live with them.

"Andrea." Natalie's voice drew her back to the here and now. "The studio will be closed the Wednesday before Thanksgiving until January third, and I'm going home for the holidays. I've missed my family." She laughed. "My cousin, David, called me yesterday and told me that, yes, I am coming home for the holidays or he'd come up here and drag me home."

Andrea had known something was wrong. Last night and tonight, Natalie had been restless and wouldn't look her in the eyes. "Why did you come to Dallas?"

"I told you, I wanted to—"

"No, the real reason. It has something to do with Kyle McKenzie, doesn't it?" Which was a no-brainer. Every morning, Natalie checked her email first thing. Andrea had witnessed many times a winsome smile on her face as she read them or talked to him on the phone, but she couldn't for the life of her figure out why she had left him. She had never once offered an explanation.

"It was easier handling things at a distance."

"What things?"

Everything. "Nothing. It seems silly now."

"What seems silly? Coming to Dallas or the reason you came?"

"Why don't you come home with me, Andrea? I would love for you to meet April, Kyle, David, and see Mother and Grandmother again. What do you say? Come home with me for the holidays."

"I would love to. But I think you're sidetracking me."

"No, I'm not."

Andrea raised her brows in a look that said she didn't believe her.

"All right. It's simple, really. We weren't in a place where we could grow the relationship—April was at death's door. But she's doing very well now. The last two months, I've discovered I love him, and I think he loves me. This separation was the best thing that could have happened to us." She stood.

Andrea stood, too, and took her hand. "Let's go inside and visit over some hot chocolate. I want details, now that you're talking. I think it's time we opened the Kyle McKenzie can of worms and get this thing totally out in the open."

"Well, if my granddaughter is coming home for the holidays, then I want to treat her to a trip to Maui." Lenore raised her brows at Regina. "It's lovely this time of year. A month or so there would do us all a bit of good, I'm sure. The Four Seasons, of course."

Regina sighed. "Mama, you cannot be serious. Natalie doesn't want to go to Maui. She wants to see April and Kyle and, hopefully, you and me. Now, please, dear, no more talk of flights. I want to spend the season here at home. Maybe Maui in the spring."

"I've already booked the fare. We're due to leave Monday."

"Then you and Natalie go. I'm not spending the season away from home. Or Reginald. We have plans next weekend."

"You're *not* still seeing that man! Haven't I *told* you—"

"It's none of your business whom I'm dating, dear." Regina picked up her jeweled purse and strode to the door as the doorbell rang. "I'm off with Reginald Allen Rockwall, the third, for an evening at the theater. Please don't wait up, Mama."

Lenore slammed her cane into the carpet. Her plans would not be thwarted by her short-sighted daughter or her willful granddaughter! They would all go to Maui and have a wonderful time. There would be no other choice in the matter.

She punched a button to summon her chauffeur. If Regina didn't have the sense to stop this nonsense with Reginald Rockwall, then she would have to take matters into her own hands. It was time to find out a little more about the Rockwalls and use whatever she found to persuade Mr. Rockwall to leave her daughter alone.

And Natalie. Surely, she wasn't seriously thinking of starting things up again with Kyle McKenzie. She had spent over two months away from him, two precious months that Lenore had used to douse the embers still glowing from their recent scandal. Besides, Jonathan McCarthen had agreed to hire Natalie at her behest, involving no small amount of financial wizardry on her part. Natalie simply could not walk away from McCarthen. The money involved was a small fortune.

And now, for her to come home to That Man again was unthinkable! The trip to Maui, however, should settle most of this. Unless, of course, Natalie decided not to go.

Lenore sniffed. Another plan would have to be devised then.

The elevator door opened. "Thank you, Clarence," she managed as he helped her inside.

"It's a lovely night, isn't it, Mrs. Carsdale?"

"Is it?" she answered with her eyes closed as she leaned on her cane. "I hadn't noticed."

The flight from Dallas to Houston had been delightful. Natalie had slept while Andrea and Bella sat beside a cowboy named Tex who owned a ranch in west Texas. He seemed to think it his duty to entertain them with hilarious stories of life on the range. He seemed so clichéd: big and tall, holding a cowboy hat, loud and funny.

He had been wonderful.

Regina Palmer had sent their baby plane to pick up all three of them in Houston. The short flight to Granston was the only part of the trip that Andrea had actually hated. At the Granston airport, the plane taxied to a stop.

Natalie looked at her. "You look green around the gills."

"I am green around the gills."

Leaning over, Natalie squinted at her. "You really are sick, aren't you? Do you need a barf bag?"

"No." She held up a brown bag. "I've been clutching this to my chest since we left. We've become very close."

"Can you find your legs?"

"Are they still attached?"

Natalie laughed. "Yes, everything's in place. Try to stand."

She did, wobbled, and moaned as she fell back into her seat.

Natalie pointed a finger at her. "Stay. I'll get the pilot to help you to the terminal. Then David can get you into the car."

"David's here?"

"Always. He never lets me fly into town without meeting my plane. I'll be right back." In a few minutes, Regina's pilot easily picked her up and carried her down the stairs to a waiting wheelchair.

"Thank you so much." Andrea kept her eyes closed. Natalie pushed her into the waiting area. Everything around her was swimming. "Bella?"

"She's with Mother's very patient flight attendant behind us."

It seemed as if only seconds had passed before Andrea heard a deep male voice. She'd missed that, the sound of a man's voice. She'd missed Jason.

"Andrea?"

A little nudge, and she opened her eyes and thought she had died and gone to heaven. Standing behind Natalie was a man with long, golden hair and dark golden skin. Beautiful blue eyes. He was tall, like her. She gulped and closed her eyes. "Yes, I'm still alive."

"Andrea, this is David. David, this is Andrea. Are y'all ready to get out of here? She's dizzy, David, and too wobbly to walk."

"Then I'm your man." He slid his arms under her legs and lifted her as if she were a feather.

His arms tightened around her. "I've got you, Andrea." His voice was right beside her ear. *Oh, help.* "Just hold on. We'll get you out of here. Inner ear trouble?"

What? Oh, the dizziness. "I have a little known condition. It comes and goes. But when it's visiting, I don't drive or ride my bicycle or," she shrugged, "fly in airplanes." She looked up to smile at him at the same moment he looked down at her. She blushed at the closeness.

Man-oh-man, he could get into real trouble here.

David knew everything about Andrea, except that she was utterly beautiful. Natalie had neglected to tell him. Not a stitch of make-up on and she could have been plastered on the front of any magazine, even as green as she was. A wobbly smile lit up her face.

"A Rolls-Royce? Am I looking at a classic Rolls-Royce?"

He laughed as he helped her inside. "My grandmother's. She insists on us riding in it. She insists on a lot of things." He glanced over at Natalie as the door closed. "Have you heard the latest?"

"No. Do I want to hear?"

"You, Andrea, and Bella are on your way to Maui this afternoon."

"You're kidding."

"Would I kid about that?"

"Are you coming?"

"No way. The holidays at the ranch every year, remember? That's my idea of the season."

"There's no way I'm going to Maui then. What is she up to?"

"I don't know, but I think—" he raised his brows and ever-so-slightly nodded at Andrea, "I think I'll stick around for the fireworks."

"Nana, I am *not* going to Maui for the holidays."

"Don't call me that insufferable name. It has no dignity." Her head slowly turned toward Natalie. "Dignity, child, is everything."

Why was she being so pushy about going to Maui? "Maybe to you but not to me."

Her grandmother sniffed. "Apparently."

"Andrea is too sick to fly anywhere right now."

"Then you come with me."

"Why this sudden desire to go to Maui? We never go to the Islands for Christmas."

"Can't an old woman want to see her home one last time before she dies?"

"You were there last summer, and it's not your home. It was your mother's home when she was married to her fourth and last husband, and you're not anywhere near death's door. You're too ornery to die." Although the thought of strangling her right now was a tad tempting.

Natalie headed for the stairs. David had carried Andrea upstairs ten minutes before. "I need to check on Andrea. I'm sorry to disappoint you, but—"

"Then don't."

Natalie turned around. Her grandmother was trying very hard to look dignified in the face of defeat. Natalie knew what this was all about. She didn't want her to see Kyle or April, and she was trying to preserve the *dignity* of the family. The thought softened her growing resentment. "I'm sorry, truly I am, but I don't want to go to the Islands for Christmas. Maybe in the spring?"

"That's what your mother proposed. In the spring. Well, I don't want to go in the spring. I want to go now."

"Then go and take Aunt Essie with you."

"Esther? You've got to be jesting, child. Your Aunt Essie is about as interesting as a book of used matches."

Natalie smiled at her and turned to walk up the stairs.

"You're going to see him, aren't you?"

Slowly, she pivoted and sought her grandmother's gray eyes. Why did it have to be a battle? Everything Natalie had wanted in her life had been a battle. Dancing, school, adventures, trips, Kyle and April. Except teaching in Dallas. That had not been a battle. "Yes, I am." She lifted her chin.

In a mirror movement, Nana lifted her chin. "He may be rich, but his name is sullied."

"Why do you think that?"

"His wife, the scam artist. Do you want to be associated with someone who doesn't have sense enough to know when he's being scammed of millions of dollars?"

It was always about money. "What about his heart? His heart was deeply bruised."

"All the more reason not to ally yourself with such a man. He lacks the—"

"It doesn't matter to me."

"It should."

"I love you, Grandmother," Natalie whispered as she turned and, with as much dignity as she could muster, walked up the stairs.

She found Bella holding a doll, sitting in a bright red beanbag in front of a big-screen television, watching a cartoon. Andrea was lying on the bed with her eyes closed and David, bless his heart, was standing with his hands in his pockets, head down, staring at her.

Natalie dragged him across the room and whispered, "She's

beautiful, isn't she?"

He nodded. "You never said a word."

"Would it have made a difference?"

"No." He shrugged. "Well, okay, yes. I'm a man, and she's a gorgeous woman. But it wasn't difficult at all seeing the woman beneath the beauty." He paused a moment. "Like a soul mate."

Oh, brother. "David, don't get carried away. You've just met her, and she's been through a lot."

"I know. I do pay attention when you talk to me. Is she a dancer, too?"

"She's an Olympic swimmer."

"No kidding?"

"Never medaled but came close."

"How old is she?"

"Twenty-six."

"And I'm twenty-eight. How's she doing these days?"

"You'll have to ask her, David. Now that there's an interest in Andrea the Woman instead of Andrea the Best Friend of Your Cousin, you'll have to get your information from her. Oh." She turned around as little arms tightened around her leg. "Hey, Bella. Are you hungry, sweetheart?"

David had known many beautiful women over the years, women who knew about his wealth and wanted that more than they had wanted the man. But Andrea hadn't seemed impressed with the wealth, except when she'd seen the Rolls-Royce. That had been more like a playful curiosity, not the greed monster he'd seen so many times in the eyes of the women he'd dated.

No, he thought as he watched her sleep, this woman was special. And if he could, he would get to know her outside the clutches of wealth and prestige. He knew just the place to do that, if Natalie would be willing to go with them.

He'd take her to his world—Galveston Island. After the holidays.

SEVENTEEN

Natalie pulled up to Kyle's home, parked, and studied the house, soaking in the sight of the things that were now familiar to her. A child's swing set, off to the side of the house, had been added, where April could spread her wings and fly. "Oh, April, your daddy loves you so much," she whispered, and her heart swelled with pride.

Love had chosen well for her.

She got out and stood still. They had come a long way since that night when she'd decided, standing right here, that she was meant to be in this place, helping this man's little girl.

Little had she known that she would grow to love them both.

The weather had been hot and sticky then. Now, a brisk, cool wind reminded her that winter was just around the corner. She strolled to the gate and grasped a balled post. The curtains were open, and the living room light was on. It was only nine-something and Kyle didn't go to bed until eleven or so. No other lights were on in the house, so April must be in bed.

At that moment, Kyle walked into the living room and retrieved something from the coffee table. A book. He flipped through the pages and read a little bit. He looked so good with his dress shirt bloused above pleated dress pants, his sleeves rolled up, his hair a little mussed. Quite unlike the rigid man she'd first met.

Suddenly, his head jerked up, as if, her heart told her, he'd sensed she was there. He walked to the window and looked out. She froze and watched him absently drop whatever he'd been reading and turn from the window.

The front door opened.

He stepped out.

Her heart pounded.

With his gaze on her, he stepped off the landing and walked down the path toward her. She drank in the sight of him.

And then he was there, in front of her, with only the gate between them. She could hardly breathe.

He whispered her name, opened the gate, and they stepped into each other's arms, holding so tightly that they seemed like one being. He moved his head and found her mouth and kissed her, a long, passionate kiss that shook her to her toes.

He pulled back, looked into her eyes, and then kissed her again. "You're here."

"I'm here."

"I missed you."

"I missed you, too."

With an arm around her waist, he led her inside the house. "Why didn't you let me know you were coming?"

"I wanted it to be a surprise."

"Well, it was. Come here." He tugged her beside him as he sat. "How long will you be here?"

"Until January second. I start back teaching on the third."

"What are your plans for the holidays?"

"I was hoping you'd come with us to our family ranch outside San Angelo for Thanksgiving. The ranch isn't as large as yours, but there are cattle and a few hands."

"What does your grandmother think of that plan?"

"I haven't told her."

"Why don't you talk to her, and I'll check with April's doctors and see if they'll let her get that far from Houston. Lynette said it would take about six months before she would get the 'all clear'."

"Is your nurse, Connie, still with you?"

"She left yesterday to spend the holidays with family. It'll just be me and April."

"I can't wait to see her. I appreciate all the pictures you texted me. She looks so healthy."

He smiled. "She's doing really well. You mentioned in your last email that you thought David and Andrea might hit it off. When are you getting them together?"

"I already have. She came home with me." She laughed. "And, boy, is David hooked. You should see him. He's like a little kid in a candy store. She's beautiful, you know. Auburn hair, big brown eyes, athletic, lean. You may have trouble yourself when you see her."

He leaned forward and took her face in his hands. "Let's get something straight right now, Natalie Grace Palmer." His eyes flicked to her mouth, to her eyes. "There's only one woman I'm interested in," he leaned forward and kissed her, "and I'm looking at her right now. Are we clear on that?"

"Crystal," she said, laughing as he tugged her closer.

"So, how is Mr. McKenzie, cuz?"

As Natalie closed the front door of Palmer House that night, she spun around. "He's fine. Great." She glanced around the foyer and conspiratorially lowered her voice. "I love him, but that's a huge secret. I haven't said the words to him yet."

He leaned forward, too, and whispered, "And he loves you?"

"I think so, but like I said, the actual words haven't been spoken. It's not the right time. I want to get to know him better." She set her purse on the hall table. "Oh, David, I never thought it would happen to me, but I love him so much."

"So why wait? Why draw out the inevitable?"

"You mean marriage?" She took his hand and tugged him down the hall. "You always were impulsive."

He shrugged. "When it's right and you know it, go for it."

"It's not that simple and *you* know it. There are other things to consider." She pulled him into the library. "Grandmother wouldn't want to see Kyle come into this family."

"Then do it her way."

"If she could get to know him, see him with April, then she'd know what a wonderful man he is."

"And wish you both every happiness?" He snorted. "We *are* talking about the same person here? Grandmother? Matriarch? Dictator?"

"Maybe she could be persuaded to change her mind."

"Ha! Since when?"

"There's a first time for everything."

"Well, now that you've gone off the deep end, I'm going to bed. Wake me when you start making sense again."

"David."

He turned back around, lifted his brows.

"It's that hopeless, then?"

His expression softened as he walked toward her. "Not hopeless.

Inconceivable." He kissed her on the forehead. "I'm going to bed."

"Mum's the word, all right?"

He nodded and zipped his mouth. "My lips are sealed. Good night."

Andrea woke to the smell of fresh-brewed coffee. She identified the bundle curled up at her back as her daughter, Bella, and gently lifted the covers and crawled out of bed so as not to wake her.

A clock on the bedside table read 5:16. Her stomach growled. No wonder. She had slept through the afternoon and night, and she was starving. She showered, dressed, and tiptoed down the stairs, following the wonderful scent of coffee.

"Oh," she said as she stepped into the kitchen and found David, dressed only in rumpled shorts, pouring himself a cup of coffee.

He turned around. "Good morning. Would you like a cup?"

"Uh…" Andrea glanced over her shoulder into the dark hall. She hadn't seen a man dressed so casually since Jason died. It was obvious that David availed himself of the beach. He was muscular and tanned—all over. "Yes, please."

He poured her a cup of coffee, set it on the table, pointed at the chair. "Sit, please. I'll be right back."

She did and in a few minutes, he appeared again, fully dressed, with sandals on. "Oh, I'm sorry. You didn't have to get dressed on my account."

"I could see you were uncomfortable." Opening the oven door, he pulled out a long dish covered with foil, placed it on the table between them, and sat down opposite her. "I suspect you thought you'd have the kitchen to yourself at this hour. I don't usually get up at the crack of dawn, but it was too quiet."

"Too quiet?"

"I live at the beach. The waves are anything but quiet." He placed a cinnamon roll on a plate and handed it to her.

The beach. Water. She hadn't been near water since Jason passed away. She bit into the cinnamon roll. "Umm. This is delicious."

"It's been proven that Aunt Essie has magic in her fingers."

Andrea pinched off a bit of the roll, sopped up the icing on the plate, and shoved it in her mouth. "What kind of music do you play?"

"Any kind. Depends upon the gig. No rap, though, or hip hop."

"What do you do in the band?"

"Lead guitar, bass guitar, drums, sax, write the songs, sing."

"Wow. I'm impressed."

"Not everyone is."

"Your father." She licked her fingers and wrinkled her nose at him. "Natalie's told me about you."

"You know about my beach bum lifestyle." With a wry smile, he toasted her with his coffee.

"I know nothing of the sort."

He lifted his brows. "You don't?"

"Natalie's told me you're brilliant, funny, creative, athletic—"

"Okay, okay. What about you? You're a world-class swimmer?"

She finished her cinnamon roll. "*Was* a world-class swimmer. Not anymore." She hadn't been to the pool in months.

"What do you do for a living?"

"I don't work. Jason had prepared for a day he might not be here, and I'm being very careful with it. My focus is on my daughter. That's all." With her napkin, she wiped crumbs into her hand.

"Sounds like we're in similar boats."

Water, again. She hadn't been boating since Jason died. "Do you own a boat?"

David nodded. "Sure. Several. What kind were you thinking of?"

"I wasn't. Just curious."

"I love to be on the water—or in it."

"Me, too." But she hadn't been near water—well, for heaven's sake!—*since Jason died*.

"Maybe while you're here, we could go sailing."

A memory flashed—sailing with Jason and Bella, the salty breeze, the boat cutting through the waves, her hand in the water pushing against the force. But she hadn't been sailing—she wouldn't even finish the thought. Had she done *anything* since Jason died?

Maybe a little sailing would open the world to her again and to Bella. Had she kept Bella from living too? "When?" She could see the surprise in David's eyes at her abrupt answer.

"When do you want to go?"

"Go where?" A sleepy Natalie shuffled into the kitchen, dressed in a bathrobe with matching slippers, and squinted at David. "Where's the coffee? I can smell it, but I can't see it."

David poured her a cup. "Wake up, sleepyhead. We're planning the day."

She squinted one eye at the black windows. "Is it day?"

"It's a sailing day. What do you think?"

"Sounds great, but I have to be back by five. Kyle and I have plans for dinner. Is Bella going sailing, too?"

"Of course. She loves to sail. We used to—" Andrea's gaze flicked to David and then dropped to her hands. "Jason used to take us out." Abruptly, she stood and walked to the sink. She felt someone behind her—David—and didn't know what to do. She missed Jason so much this morning.

"Tell me about sailing with Jason, Andrea."

David's voice was quiet, soothing.

His hands touched her shoulders. She didn't jump or pull away. Ever-so-gently, he turned her around. "Where was it? Did you have a lake near your home?"

She shook her head. "The ocean."

"Did you dock your boat there?"

"Yes." She glanced at Natalie. "Bella loves to sail."

"Do *you*?"

Gently, without pulling, he led her back to the table and sat her in her chair. He lifted the carafe of coffee and topped off their cups.

Andrea smiled at him. "Yes. I love water, sailing, swimming. Well, I did before." She stopped the sentence. It wasn't fair to them to have to listen to her tales of woe since Jason died. Jason was gone. She was not. Bella was not. "I still do. So." She made the effort to smile at Natalie. "Are you coming with us?"

Two hours later, Andrea buckled into her life jacket and helped Bella with hers.

"Mommy, is Daddy coming with us?"

She hadn't asked for Jason in a month. Andrea tucked a strand of hair over Bella's ear. "No, sweetheart. Daddy's in heaven. He won't be sailing with us, but David will, and Natalie."

"Hey, anybody know a good sailor on board?" David yelled from the front of the boat. "I need some help up here." When he turned

624

around, his eyes widened when he spotted Bella. "Boy, howdy, would you look at those muscles! Are you a strong girl, Bella?"

Natalie smiled at Andrea as a laughing Bella jogged toward David. "He's great with kids."

In her element, Andrea nodded and lay back as the boat gently moved. She closed her eyes. "God, thank you for the water. Thank you for good memories."

Natalie touched her arm. "And thank you for good friends."

"No, I will not go to the ranch if *that man* is going to be there!"

Regina Palmer could battle with the best of them, Natalie thought, sitting on the window seat, watching her mother and grandmother duke it out. Although, if she knew her mother, her grandmother would be put in her place kindly, without a scene. Nana's intimidating ways didn't seem to affect her mother at all.

"You *will* be going to the ranch with the rest of us, Mama."

Her grandmother's answer was to purse her lips and glare.

Natalie stood. "Actually, I won't be going to the ranch this year. Dr. Weisbrod says that April can't be very far from the hospital. Kyle mentioned his ranch is about twelve minutes by air to the Granston hospital, and she agreed that that was as far away as she wanted April to be. So, we'll be spending Thanksgiving at Fairfield Ranch. You're all invited to spend the holiday with us. The ranch is huge and can accommodate everyone."

"Well!" Her grandmother's cane stabbed the carpet. "I will certainly not be going *there!*" She turned to leave.

"You will be going, Mama. Unless, of course, you want Marjorie Rockwall to become the new president of the Women's Auxiliary. As outgoing president, if I recommend her, she *would*, of course, become—"

"You wouldn't."

Regina smiled pleasantly. "Wouldn't I?"

"So." Nana frowned, deeply. "It has come to this. That man," she pointed her cane at Natalie, "has brought extortion into this family."

"No, Mama. You did, a long time ago. I've learned well, haven't I? Now, don't you think it's time you let Natalie live her life as she wishes? And let her bring the man she loves to our home for the holidays?"

Nana lifted her chin and left the room.

"I never said I loved him, Mother."

"You don't have to."

"It's that obvious?"

"Love usually is, sweetheart."

Natalie looked at the door her grandmother had just walked through. "Why can't life be simple anymore?"

"Your grandmother has no intentions of ever letting anything *simple* come into this family." She touched her daughter's arm. "Sometimes, I think you don't think I care about you, but I do. Maybe I'm going overboard not to be like your grandmother and not interfere in your life, but make no mistake, dear. I care about everything you do because I love you. By the way, I'm very fond of Kyle."

"You can't know how much that means to me."

"You're mistaken. Your grandmother wouldn't give her approval for me to marry Brent Palmer either. So, yes, my dear, I know how much it means to you." She picked up her purse. "I really must be going. I have plans."

"Reginald Rockwall?"

"No, dear, I broke off with him last night. He was simply too boring. I'm going out with girlfriends tonight. Please confirm with Kyle that we would all love to spend the holiday with him."

"Thank you, Mother." Natalie kissed Regina's cheek.

"You're very welcome. I'll see you after six."

David poked his head into the room after Regina left. "Is the coast clear?"

"Yes. It's not my mother we have to worry about."

"You're the worry-wart, Nat, not me."

"So are you ready to leave Wednesday morning for Kyle's ranch?"

"Yes. Is Grandmother going?"

"It appears she is."

"Well, then, we're all set for a good time, aren't we?"

EIGHTEEN

Gil Zachary slammed the proposal on his desk. His fist followed. He cursed and stood before the windows encasing his penthouse office, but he was too angry to just stand, so he began to pace.

When would his son come to his senses? How long was David going to bum it on the Island when he had all these business responsibilities facing him? Why couldn't he see that if he was going be a man, he had to—well, Gil thought, that was the problem, wasn't it? '*Had to*' never set well with David.

Or Gil either, for that matter.

Gil's fierce expression softened a little as he thought of David as a little boy, determined to have his own way. He remembered thinking many times that David would make a great executive because he took the bull by the horns, tossed it around a few times, and made it kneel before him. *Just like me*, he chuckled.

But if he and David were so much alike, why couldn't he make David understand the necessity of taking over the helm of Zachary World, Inc.? He was made for it and David loved it—or had until they'd butted heads over David's blasted music. He couldn't do both. Why couldn't he see that? A CEO did *not* play in a band!

Gil would not dispute the fact that David was talented. He'd heard him play and sing many times, and he recognized giftedness when it was staring him down behind a microphone. But there came a time in a man's life when he had to stop playing and start working. Why couldn't David see that?

Gil stopped pacing when the intercom buzzed. "Yes?"

"It's Ms. Palmer, Mr. Zachary. Line three."

Two days before Thanksgiving. Regina had waited just a tad late this year to invite him to the ranch, although he wouldn't have accepted anyway. He didn't like being with those people, his wife's family. Thanksgiving was no different than any other day and he could well spend it alone. He had last year, hadn't he, when it was the toughest, when Cheryl had died just a month before? When he and David had quarreled, and David had stormed off to the Island?

Let them offer their charity to someone who needed it. He certainly didn't. He yanked up the phone, punched the light. "Yes?"

"Uncle Gil? It's Natalie. How *are* you?"

Natalie. What a surprise. Regina didn't have the guts to call him this year? "Natalie. I'm fine. How are you?"

"I'm wanting you to spend Thanksgiving with us this year, Uncle Gil. No, now wait. Please don't say no. It's easy to say no. It's difficult to say yes and to come on out."

"I have pressing things that need to—"

"Uncle Gil, it's Thanksgiving. Come spend some time with your family. We all want you there." She paused. "Please?"

No one could ever accuse him of being heartless. "Well—"

"Great! Oh, I'm so looking forward to seeing you! I'll text you directions to the ranch where we'll be staying. Bring clothes for several days. You know we like to make a long weekend of it."

"But—"

"I have a friend visiting from Dallas, and she and her daughter will be there, too. And don't forget your swimsuit! He has an indoor pool. We'll be leaving Wednesday morning. Would you like to ride with us?"

Steamrolled. That's what she had done. "No, I'll ride up by myself. What ranch is this?"

"Fairfield Ranch. I'll explain everything when you get there. I'm so glad you're coming! Have a safe trip!"

He slowly placed the phone into the cradle. What had just happened? How had that girl finagled him into a Thanksgiving weekend? David would be there. Maybe they could get this thing settled between them, if he was willing to grow up a little bit, that is.

Taking responsibility was a man's lot in life. Maybe now David would take that bull by the horns again. Gil sighed. He could only hope.

At Palmer House, Ernestine brought another bowl of eggs and a plate of sausage into the dining room. David grinned at her around a bite of toast and declared, "I'm so glad you agreed to come with us to Kyle McKenzie's ranch, Ernestine. We'll be leaving in about two hours."

"'Course I'm comin' with y'all. How else would y'all eat?"

628

"You sure look nice today."

It was an old game between him and the family cook. He hid a mischievous smile behind his fork of sausage as she grumbled and frowned at him and placed a basket of biscuits on the table.

"Nice, indeed. I'm an old woman as wide as a haystack."

"Well, then, when are you going to run off and marry me? I been waitin' all these years for you to say yes."

"Yes, *sir*, be more like it, Mr. David. You full of the mischief this mornin'." She looked at Andrea, who looked down at the sausage link in her hand. "Uh-huh, you full of the mischief this mornin', Mr. David." She wiped her hands on her apron and eyed Andrea. "Reckon I have to keep my eye on you and that pretty girl with the brown eyes. Don't want no carryin' on at this ranch. Miss Lenore, she'd have a fit if she knew you had notions about this young thing." Laughing, Ernestine walked into the kitchen.

David's face grew hot. He could see Natalie's shoulders bouncing up and down as she struggled to hide her giggles behind her napkin. She caught Aunt Essie's eye and winked.

Aunt Essie giggled, and the whole table erupted into laughter.

"I hear you folks laughin' at Ernestine," came from the kitchen.

David was the first to recover. "We aren't laughing at you, Ernestine." He grinned and wiped his eyes with his napkin.

"Yes, sir, I believe you are, Mr. David."

Aunt Essie giggled, and Andrea giggled into her napkin as her gaze flicked to David's.

Man-oh-man, the woman was even more beautiful when she laughed. How in the world was he going to make it through a long weekend with those puppy-dog eyes looking at him? And that mouth—full lips that begged to be kissed?

"David, are you all right?"

He looked up. Natalie's question had settled everyone around the table and all eyes were on him. "You betcha. Soon as I can get Ernestine to say yes!"

Everyone laughed again. He scooted his chair back, picked up his plate, and left the dining room, purposefully avoiding Andrea's eyes.

Man-oh-man-oh-man, was he in trouble here or what?

Kyle drove up to Palmer House and parked beside David and several piles of luggage behind an SUV. It appeared David was in charge of the packing and the beauty watching him load the truck must be Andrea. Yes, she was beautiful, but not sad as he had expected. She was laughing at something David had just said, and her smile was enough to light up a city. The little girl beside her must be Bella.

April squirmed in her car seat. "Na-tee?"

"Yes, sweetheart, she's here. Let's go say hello." Kyle got out of the truck and waved at Natalie. It took him a few moments to unbuckle April's seat belt. He kissed her as he lifted her out of the truck.

"Well, there's my girl!" A smiling Natalie appeared from behind him, leaned over, and smooched April's neck as she took her out of Kyle's arms. "How's my angel this morning, huh? You sure look pretty today in your little pink outfit."

"Well, I certainly know who rates around here."

Natalie pouted at April. "Oh, no, is Daddy going to fuss? Is Daddy going to pitch a *fit?*" April giggled, and Natalie turned toward Kyle with a sweet smile as she fluttered her eyelashes.

"Cute," he muttered and wrapped his arms around them.

"Let's go say hello to Bella. How 'bout that, April?" Natalie walked toward Andrea. "Is Joan riding with us, Kyle?"

He shook his head. "Mom wanted to drive herself up. Aunt Essie and Ernestine are riding with her. I suspect they'll get there before any of us. My cook, Lettie, is already there. Oh! I almost forgot. Come here, sweetheart."

He took April out of her arms. "We have a surprise. Remember, April? Let's show Natalie your surprise. Ready?"

Gently, he sat her on the pavement and held both of her hands up. "Look, Natalie!"

April giggled and took a wobbly step, then another, so obviously proud of herself that Kyle wanted to burst. "See? April's walking!"

Natalie clapped her hands and bent over, her splayed hands ready to catch her if she fell. "Oh, what a big girl! Just look at you, Miss April! Such a big girl!" She scooped her into her arms, twirling her around and around. "Come on, let's go show the others!"

Lenore watched the banter from the upper windows and grunted. Her entire family was going down the gully. Regina dating Reginald Rockwall, of all people. Natalie interested in the likes of Kyle McKenzie. David and Andrea—well, need she say more? At least Gil Zachary would be on her side. The man was like her: driven, intolerant of mistakes, a person of few words, and ruthless at times.

Yes, she nodded as she left the window. This weekend was shaping up to be a circus side-show.

She had known from the moment her daughter, Cheryl, had died that Gil had his eye on Regina. But she'd wondered why he hadn't done anything about it. It would be a good match. The Zachary and Palmer estates would combine into a powerhouse of wealth, prestige, and domination. Maybe this weekend, things would progress in that arena. She would have to see to it herself, she supposed.

She pushed a button to summon Clarence to pick up her luggage, so they could get on the road.

The weekend was going to be memorable, at the very least.

"We're here." David bounded out of the SUV to the rear, opened the hatch, and announced, "You're all responsible for your own luggage." Andrea was right beside him. "Unless," he said to her, "you're too dizzy, of course."

"No," she smiled, "I'm fine. I can handle it." She looked up and tried to take in the absolutely huge ranch house sitting like a mountain on this green, rolling land. Two-story, it had to have at least six or seven thousand square feet. Several outbuildings spread out in a giant U around the perimeter of the property; one of them, she guessed, was a pool house with glass windows. A red-and-white barn perched quite a distance from the house, next to white fences.

A smaller residence sat back of the house to the left, but, still, it was at least three thousand square feet. A guest house, maybe.

Andrea hadn't realized that there were cowboys who lived here and obviously worked the ranch year-round. Several of them rode by on beautiful horses and tipped their hats at her. One young cowboy turned in his saddle and grinned at her as if she were a prize-winning cow. She lifted her chin, turned her back, and heard raucous laughter behind her.

With his hands fisted, jaw popping, David glared at the men as if he could barely contain his anger. She took a step toward him. "David."

"Who was that man?" he growled at no one in particular.

Kyle glared at Evan Grant. "I'll take care of it."

"No, Kyle, please." Andrea touched his arm. "It was nothing. Don't spoil Thanksgiving over something so minor. Please?"

Kyle glanced at Natalie, who nodded and said, "It was just an innocent appraisal. She gets it everywhere we go. Now, come on, everybody. Let's get the luggage inside."

David's gaze flicked to Andrea's. His eyes softened as she felt a hot blush creeping over her face.

She had dealt with this kind of thing her entire life, and it shamed her. She tried to dress as conservatively as possible and not draw attention to herself, but even though she wore no make-up and wore unsexy clothes, men still leered at her. It felt wonderful, however, to have a champion. Jason had rarely noticed the looks of other men. He had been proud of her, but he wasn't that aware of what was happening around him.

David apparently was. It made her feel special again.

She picked up her luggage and followed Natalie inside.

The main house was rustic in an elegant sort of way. Woodsy, but the accessories were fine and expensive. Natalie cuddled April as she led Andrea upstairs to the room she and Bella would share. It had a high pinnacled ceiling, throw rugs, a king-sized bed, and a view that took in the gorgeous green land and beautiful trees. "I love it."

"There isn't a room in the house that doesn't have a beautiful view. We have time to have fun before dinner. Walk. Swim in the indoor pool. Ride. There are plenty of gentle horses. Or explore. I'm sure David would be happy to do anything with you and Bella."

"Do you think Jesser knows where we are?"

Natalie sighed and glanced outside. "I feel him watching us all the time. I keep remembering what the detective said, that he 'vanished in plain sight.' It's the not knowing who we're looking for that frightens me. Security cameras are all around the house, at the gates, the entrances. If someone intrudes, an alarm sounds, and they contact us."

Andrea nodded. "We're out in the middle of nowhere. I hope we're safe."

"I do, too."

Kyle had seen his mother's car parked in front when they'd driven up, so he went straight to the kitchen. "I thought you'd be in here." Dressed in a lacy apron, Joan was peeling potatoes beside Ernestine and Aunt Essie and his cook, Lettie.

His mother smiled and offered her cheek for his kiss. "You know I love to cook. Oh, Kevin called. They're coming early tomorrow, around eleven. Where's April?"

"Natalie has her. I think they're planning to go horseback riding or swimming."

"Why aren't you with them?"

"She wanted time with April, and I wanted to come see my mom. I haven't talked to you in a few days."

She lifted a shoulder. "I've been busy."

"As usual. Is there a man in your life?"

"What an impertinent question from my impertinent son. Of course not. What would I do with a man in my life?" At his grunt, she added, "Don't answer that. I've been content since your father died. Missing him, but content."

"I'd like to see you meet someone who sweeps you off your feet, someone who would go with you to the theater and maybe have a love of cooking. You know, someone to *share* your life with."

"I don't need anyone like that. I have my sons, my grandkids. That's enough."

"No, it's not." He reached for a cherry tomato.

"Shoo." Joan flapped her hands at him. "Out of my—" she looked at Kyle's cook, Lettie, as she came out of the huge walk-in pantry. "Sorry, Lettie. Out of *her* kitchen, mister."

He laughed at her and then walked down the hallway. He spotted a large white SUV pulling up to the house. Regina was driving, with Lenore beside her. He felt tension grip his shoulders. How could he reach Natalie's grandmother? What would help her see that he meant no harm for her granddaughter or her family?

Maybe if she could see him for who he was, she wouldn't resent the excess baggage he brought into his relationship with Natalie. But he wondered how he could do that as he watched the chauffeur open her door.

"Uncle Gil! You made it!" Natalie raced down the steps and into her obviously-astounded uncle's arms. Pulling back, she said, "I'm so glad you're here. Come on, I'll show you your room." She scowled at his briefcase. "What's this?"

"Work. I, uh, it was hard to get away without making myself some promises."

She picked it up and nodded. "All right. We'll make sure you have some down time to work." She looked up and saw David standing at the front door, glowering at her. Oh, if looks could kill. She'd thought it would be better for both of them if neither knew the other was coming. But now she had second thoughts as the two men silently regarded each other. They reminded her of two cowpokes facing off in the middle of a town.

She quickly appointed herself sheriff and stepped between them. "Look who's here, David. Your father was able to make it this year."

Great. Not even a twitch. She looked from one to the other. "He'll, uh, have the room next to yours, if that's..." She glanced at Gil. "You can just..." *Oh, no, did I make a mistake here?* "I was thinking of putting him..." To heck with it. They could sort out their own problems. She walked up the steps to the front porch.

"I thought you were going to show me my room."

She turned around. "Yes. Of course." A quick flick at David and whoa, was he angry. She tried to put a little lilt in her voice as she said, "If you'll just follow me, Uncle Gil. David, were you and Andrea—?"

David spun on his heel and stomped down the hall.

Okay. She walked inside and saw Kyle in the front den. "Kyle. This is David's father, Gil Zachary. Uncle Gil, my friend, Kyle McKenzie."

The men shook hands. Natalie smiled at Kyle just as the back door slammed.

"Gracious me. What was that?" Aunt Essie poked her head out of the library. When she saw Gil, her frown transformed into a big smile. "Why, Gil Zachary. What a nice surprise." She hugged him and said, "I see you've met Mr. McKenzie."

Joan McKenzie came down the hall from the kitchen, wiping her hands on her apron. "Natalie, what's gotten into David? He was certainly—oh, hello."

"Joan McKenzie, Gil Zachary. Joan is Kyle's mother, Uncle Gil. She's helping Ernestine and Lettie in the kitchen. Gil is David's father, Joan."

"It's a pleasure, Mr. Zachary. Have you seen Andrea? There's a little munchkin in the kitchen who insists it's time for cookies."

Kyle said, "I'll help you look for her."

Natalie was finally alone with Gil. "We *are* going to make it to your room, Uncle Gil. Right this way."

David was furious. Natalie had crossed the line! At the very *least*, she should have told him his father was coming. Of all the idiotic, stupid things she could have pulled. He threw a rock as hard as he could at the lake. It skipped four times and disappeared under water. He scooped up a handful of rocks and slung them at the water.

He couldn't pull this off. If Andrea wasn't here, he'd just ignore his father. But if he did, she would think he was a sulking brat, and his father would appear as the perfect father because Gil Zachary could pull off 'charming' when he wanted to.

Why had he come? Did he figure they'd gone long enough without speaking to one another? Or, more likely, it would be another attempt to force David to do what his father wanted: the business world and no music, which wasn't even a consideration for David. He would not give up his music. Period.

"David!"

He turned around, mesmerized by the enchanting woman running toward him, long auburn hair flowing like wings behind her, her laughing eyes beguiling as she waved at him. He imagined her opening her arms as he enfolded her in his and kissed her.

"David?"

"Uh, yeah. What's up?"

"Your father's here. I didn't know if you knew."

It was already starting. Should he pretend or let her know now that it wasn't a happy reunion? "Yeah, I saw him. Are you up for a swim?"

"I'm always up for a swim. Bella's in the kitchen being spoiled by Kyle's mother, Joan, and Ernestine, and Natalie's with your dad."

"What do you mean, 'with my dad'?" *Keep the edge off, buddy. She'll suspect something.*

"You know, showing him his room, visiting. So, c'mon, let's go swimming."

NINETEEN

"A toast to our first day at Fairfield Ranch!" Natalie held up her glass of sparkling apple cider and everyone sitting around the huge oval dining table followed suit. The late lunch had been wonderful, and now dessert was about to be served.

"Don't you have anything stronger than this?"

Everybody looked at Gil and continued to hold their glasses up for the toast. Natalie didn't miss a beat. "I'm sure Kyle does, Uncle Gil, but first—" she raised her glass even higher, "to a wonderful Thanksgiving weekend! Cheers!"

"Cheers!" the group echoed and drank.

While the others began to chatter, Natalie watched Kyle nod imperceptibly at Sally, the maid, and then he leaned toward Gil. "What would you like to drink, Gil?"

"Bourbon. Neat."

Sally smiled at Kyle and silently left the room.

"I see you haven't changed, Gil."

He turned around and stood. "Lenore. Good to see you again."

Her grandmother nodded at him as she stood in the doorway, both hands on her cane, her gaze roaming around the table before it rested on Andrea. When she and Regina had arrived, Nana had gone upstairs to rest and had missed lunch.

"And who are you?"

Natalie stood. "Grandmother, you'll remember Andrea, my friend from school. This is her daughter, Bella. My grandmother, Lenore Carsdale."

Bella appeared as if she were about to cry. Andrea hugged her, smiled wanly at Grandmother, and said, "Nice to see you again, Mrs. Carsdale."

"Both quite the beauties," Nana pronounced as her gaze slithered to the next victim.

Joan stood. "My name is Joan McKenzie, Mrs. Carsdale. It's a pleasure to meet you. Welcome."

"Ah, Mr. McKenzie's mother. Yes, I can see the resemblance." She looked around at the others and slowly walked to the one empty chair.

"Where is your mother, Natalie?"

"In the kitchen with Ernestine. Kyle's cook, Lettie, is here as well."

"And the baby?"

"She's napping."

Kyle stood and pulled out Nana's chair. She nodded at him and sat, with his help. Then she glanced at Natalie and only the most perceptive could have seen the venom aimed at her through such smiling, amiable eyes. *Kyle McKenzie, beside me? Unthinkable.*

Natalie smiled back and cleared her throat. It was going to be a long night.

David was completely ignoring his father.

Gil was totally engrossed with his drink.

Andrea seemed nervous, sitting beside an obviously edgy David.

David made the effort to be attentive but with a scowl on his face.

Nana spoke to no one even when Kyle made overtures. Each time, she simply nodded once and looked away.

Kyle sent Natalie longing looks and, invariably, they were intercepted by her grandmother.

Kyle's mother, Joan, talked mostly to Bella, who sat next to her, but kept glancing at Kyle and Nana, obviously wondering what was going on.

And Regina glided into the room, full of apologies and laughter and announced that the swing band they had hired for tomorrow night should be arriving around seven but could only stay three hours, and wouldn't that just be a *perfect* ending to a *perfect* Thanksgiving Day?

"Well, God help us all," Nana spoke softly as she stirred her coffee without looking up.

After desserts, everyone left the main house for outdoor activities. Joan walked downstairs to the library to get a book. As she opened the door, she saw something move in a far corner of the room, in a reading nook surrounded by shelves of books.

Uneasy, she stepped into the room.

"Who's there?"

"It's me. Joan."

"Come in. I was just leaving." Gil appeared from behind a

bookcase. He had a glass of wine in one hand and a cigar in another. "You're Kyle's mother. Joan, is it?"

"Yes, and you're David's father, Gil?" Joan noted that he was in remarkably good shape for someone around her age, she'd guess. His light brown hair was thick and stylish, his hazel eyes serious. A square jaw and firm mouth seemed to correlate Natalie's assessment of him: strong-willed, somewhat intense. She'd told Joan all about the problems David had had with his father. She'd also mentioned that Gil had a dry sense of humor.

Nodding, he said, "I saw you laughing with your son earlier, near the barn."

"We're very comfortable with each other."

He lifted his brows, a wry smile touching his mouth. "Meaning?"

"We have an easy relationship."

He squinted at her and appeared amused. He seemed to take his time lifting the glass of wine to his lips, tasting it. "You're aware of the rift between my son, David, and me."

"Yes."

"And, I'm sure, the blame has been placed squarely on my shoulders."

"Blame? No. Just a father who hasn't learned to let go. One who probably had a father much like you who wouldn't let you go, either."

Gil tilted his head. "Pretty close to the truth. So, the apple didn't fall far from the tree. Well." He tipped a non-existent hat. "Miss Joan, I'm off to take a nap."

"I noticed your son's obvious pain at lunch earlier."

His brows knit. "Pain? I saw nothing but anger and rudeness."

"You see what you expect to see."

He looked into his glass and swirled its contents. "A philosopher."

"No, just a mother of eight sons, originally."

"Originally?"

"I lost my Joey in a car wreck when he was sixteen."

"I'm so sorry," Gil said quietly. "Someone I might learn from," he added, then lifted his glass in a salute and left.

Joan walked to the corner he had just left. She enjoyed the sweet scent of his cigar and wondered at a man who couldn't read the pain on his own son's face.

639

Across and down the hall, Gil found he couldn't sleep after all. Her words taunted him. *You see what you expect to see.*

He didn't, not really. Gil knew how to succeed in business, and it certainly didn't involve a CEO who played the guitar, who wrote music and played in dives until three in the morning. One did not succeed in business doing that. He didn't see in David what he wanted to see. He saw what was there and judged him lacking.

Pain? If anyone was in pain, it was Gil. His son had virtually thrown everything Gil had worked for in his face and turned his back on all of it. And *David* was the one who was in pain?

Frustrated, Gil paced his room.

What had Joan said? That his father had probably been just like Gil, someone who wouldn't let go. That was certainly true. Gil's father had forced him to set aside his dreams of becoming an architect. He had wanted to build more than anything. He still did. And his son wanted to make music.

Why hadn't he seen the similarities before now?

Gil had ended up just like his father.

How well he remembered the man. Totally unyielding, a tyrant, unforgiving. When Gil was twenty-two, his father had a stroke, and Gil had taken over the family's business ventures and had acted responsibly, even though it had cost him his dreams. Many times, he had wondered if his father had ever loved him.

Gil *knew* he loved David. Without question. And he was tired of the separation, of not seeing his son, of not being involved in his life. He didn't want to end up as his father had, alone and separated from his son, estranged from every member of his family because he couldn't let go of the control.

Gil wanted to know his son again.

The little boy who had been so inquisitive, so eager to learn, so full of life and energy. And music. His love of music had been evident at the age of two when he'd dance to any melody. By three, they'd discovered he had perfect pitch. By four, he was playing the "drums" on anything with a flat surface and mimicking the guitar. He had been born with a passion for music.

The thought struck Gil as if someone had slapped him: David had been given a passion—for music.

Oh, David. I'm so sorry.

After a while, Gil was finally able to nap. When he closed his eyes, he dreamed of a lost little boy who wandered around a dark forest, listening to his father's frantic voice calling out to him. Just as the sun came up, they found one another. But Gil was the little boy. And somehow, David had become the father.

"Grandmother means well, Kyle." Natalie snuggled closer to him on the love seat and stared at the fireplace. "She loves me and thinks our relationship could lead to embarrassment for our—"

"So, I am not safe here. You dare speak of me behind my back?"

Startled, Kyle looked over his shoulder and found Natalie's grandmother standing ten feet inside the den, glowering at him and Natalie.

He stood abruptly. "Mrs.—"

Natalie stood as well. "Grandmother—"

"No! I did as you asked. I came here to his home, against my better judgment, and now I find you sitting there, discussing me with him as if I am excess baggage and not your grandmother, not your blood. Is he your blood?"

"I'm sorry, Grandmother—"

"No." Kyle took a step toward Lenore. She raised her chin and squinted old eyes at him. "We did nothing wrong, now or in the past."

"Don't speak to me of wrongs *or* the past. You've dragged her into this mess you've made of your life, and you expect me to *listen* to your explanations? If you cared at all for her, you would leave her alone—"

"Nana, stop!"

Kyle placed a hand on her arm. "Let her finish."

Lenore's back straightened as her chin rose. Piercing gray eyes regarded him. "If you cared for my granddaughter, as you indicate, you would leave her alone and never look back. She would then have opportunity to make a better choice."

"What makes me a poor choice?"

"Your first wife, for starters."

"She wasn't my wife. She was a scam artist."

"I rest my case."

"You've never been deceived, then, Mrs. Carsdale? No one's ever torn your heart in two or ripped it to shreds by being disloyal to you or cheating you of the truth? No one's ever lied to you or stolen from you or committed horrible crimes against you?"

Lenore drew in a deep breath and scowled at him, her face flushed, her eyes wary. And the most telling sign: she couldn't seem to find a word to speak.

Clearly, he had hit a nerve.

"I see you have. Then you and I have something in common. We've been hurt by someone we loved. It's that simple. None of us can escape the pain when someone we care about betrays us. But I've let it go and forgiven her."

He put his arm around Natalie. "My home is open to you, Mrs. Carsdale. I would like you to stay until Sunday when everyone plans to leave. I will respect you and whatever decision you make."

Kyle could see she was visibly shaking, yet she lifted her chin and tightened her mouth as she did. Respect for her mounted as she kept her gaze solidly on him and seemed to be trying to control her temper.

"My granddaughter and I have made peace with each other. I have no desire to cause a wedge between you two, Mr. McKenzie, or between you and me. Let's all hope that you will not betray Natalie as you have been betrayed." She looked at Natalie, then at Kyle. "We are at peace with one another. Good day."

In silence, she walked out of the room. Kyle watched her leave and felt nothing but pity for her.

"How did you know?"

"I didn't. I was winging it."

"I would never have imagined my grandmother capable of being hurt by anyone. It suggests vulnerability, and I've rarely seen that in her. How about that walk?"

He nodded and headed toward the front door. Natalie plucked a lightweight jacket off the rack by the door. "It has to be a short walk. Everybody's meeting in here to play "Out" in an hour."

"'Out'? What is 'Out'?"

She grinned. "It's like solitaire. Build on aces all the way to kings, but it's fast and furious. Teams are made up of two people. David and I love to play. We brought the cards for it."

"I don't like that look in your eyes."

"Don't worry. You and I are going to be partners."

"Well, I do like the sound of *that*."

"Ace! Ace! Here!" Natalie snatched the card out of Kyle's hand and slapped it on an open spot on the table.

"Two? Two?"

"No! Keep dealing! There! A four!"

"Mine was first!" David covered his four of clubs with a flat hand.

Andrea counted three cards and turned them over. "David, your four of diamonds! On the three of diamonds! Good! A queen of hearts! Do you see a—?"

"Got it!" He grunted as he reached across the table and slapped it on a jack of hearts.

"Five more," Joan whispered to Gil who nodded and frowned at the stacks of cards.

Hands slapped cards on the table. Arms stretched across bodies. David yelled, "No! You can't do that!" and Kyle yelled, "I just did, buddy!"

"A king of spades!" Natalie pointed frantically at the card in Kyle's hand. "There's a queen!" He slammed the king on top of the queen of spades. "Out!" she screeched as everyone groaned, stopped playing, and counted their cards.

Natalie high-fived Kyle and laughed as Gil whispered to Joan, who was standing beside Kyle. "This was too fast for me."

"You did just fine."

"No, this is a game for young folks. How about a walk? I'm stuffed and it's not even Thanksgiving yet."

"All right, Gil. That would be nice."

"Don't accuse me of being *nice*—"

"I wasn't. I said the *walk* would be nice."

"But not me?"

"You said it." Shaking her head, she turned around, plucked a flashlight off a shelf beside the back door and their coats off the coat rack. With her mouth twitching, she announced, "If you'll excuse us, this not-so-nice man and I are going to take a very *nice* walk and be back in an hour."

"An hour? Who said anything about an *hour*? My legs are killing me after riding earlier. If I last thirty *min—*"

They left.

Beside Natalie, Andrea leaned over and asked David, "Is he always cantankerous?"

David stared at the door. "I don't know. I'm not around him that much."

Natalie separated the cards. "We've lost two players. Does anyone want another round?"

Kyle shook his head. "I think another walk sounds like a great idea. Maybe a long, drawn-out one this time. Andrea? David? Y'all want to join us?"

"No. We'll have the place to ourselves if y'all leave, other than the people sleeping. Maybe I can talk Andrea into playing chess with me."

Gravely, Andrea shook her head. "You don't want to do that, David."

He grinned. "I don't?"

"Oh, no. I'm unbeatable at chess."

"Ah. A challenge. I can't resist a challenge."

"Don't say I didn't warn you."

"Hey, you two." Natalie grabbed her coat and a flashlight. "Listen for April, okay? The monitor's on the table." She walked out with Kyle as David and Andrea sat at the chess table.

It was cold out, but not so much that she'd be uncomfortable. There was no darkness like the night far away from any towns. "I've missed being at your ranch, Kyle. Look how bright the stars are." She was grateful when he flicked on the flashlight and took her hand. They walked in silence for a while. She loved the quiet, the coolness, and the time alone with him.

"Your grandmother retired early."

"Yes. She usually does, as do Aunt Essie and Ernestine, although I can't imagine any of them sleeping through that card game." Gil and Joan's light glowed a good distance ahead of them. "What do you think about your mother and Gil?"

"At this point, I don't think there is a 'my mother and Gil.' I think they're enjoying themselves. That's all."

"Would you mind if this grew into something?"

"Not if Gil is good for her."

"That's your only pre-requisite?"

"And if the law isn't looking for him. Other than that, it's between the two of them."

Her shoulder nudged his playfully. "What a concept, letting adults decide for themselves."

"Your grandmother means well."

"Meaning well can make someone's life miserable." She noticed Joan's light went out. "Do you think something's wrong?"

Kyle cupped a hand around his mouth and yelled, "You two all right?"

"Yes! Gil's sitting on a stump to rest!" Joan yelled back and yelped as if she'd been pinched.

"I am not! I have a rock in my shoe!"

"That's just an excuse. He's pooping out!"

"Am not!"

Kyle squeezed Natalie's hand and lowered his voice as he heard them laughing. "I've never seen my mother have so much fun with someone. Usually, she chooses stuffy, reserved men."

"Uncle Gil can be hard-headed but not stuffy. He's got a great sense of humor. Maybe they're a perfect match."

"I don't know. We'll see."

With a quick glance at David, Andrea triumphantly moved her queen and giggled. "Checkmate."

Frowning, his gaze roamed over the board. "You beat me."

With a pinched grin, she raised her brows, cocked her head. "Told ya so."

"Oh, you did, did you?"

At the glint in his eye, Andrea's smile disappeared as she scooted her chair back. "You wouldn't listen. You're not a great listener, David."

His hands smacked the table and chess pieces fell over and onto the floor as he stood and challenged, "I'm not?"

Suppressing a smile, she shook her head slowly and stood. "No, you're not. You might consider—"

David took a step around the table.

Andrea counter-stepped. "—taking interpersonal skills training—"

Suddenly she was running through the house, screeching, with David close behind her. "You're a sore loser!" she threw over her shoulder.

"You cheated!"

"I did not!" She raced for the back door, flung it open, and felt David's hand on her arm. Twisting away, she laughed and raced outside. "I need my coat, David."

"Then get it."

"Will you let me by?"

"Sure."

"You're fibbing!"

"Am I?"

She ran around to the back of the house and discovered an opening in the shrubbery under the dining room window and slipped behind it. She was breathing so hard, she was afraid he'd hear her.

David ran around the corner. "You think you can hide from me, eh, little girl?"

Andrea giggled and covered her mouth, holding her breath as David jogged by, singing, "Andrea? Come out, come out, wherever you are."

A rustling behind her caused her to gasp, but before she could turn around, an iron hand clamped over her nose and mouth. She couldn't breathe! She wanted to scream for David, but she couldn't breathe! Her chest was on fire! She needed air! She struggled against the clamp on her mouth, but it only tightened. *Oh, God, help—*

When she fell limp in his hands, Gordon Jesser let her fall, gently, quietly, to the ground. He felt for the gun in his pocket, released the safety, and peered through the brush, waiting for David to come back.

"How are your legs, Gil?" Joan's shoulder bumped into his arm.

"They hurt, but I'm surviving."

"A survivor. You're so tough."

"I live a life of sacrifice."

She smiled. Gil Zachary was fun. She hadn't teased like this in a long, long time. "You don't ride often?"

"'Often' is the key word here. 'Never' would be more accurate."

"Never? As in not even once?"

"Your grasp of the English language astounds me, Joanie."

Joanie. Gerry's pet name. She had missed it. She punched Gil's arm. "But this is Texas. Surely you know someone who owns a horse, who likes to ride."

"*I* own horses and I don't like to ride."

"Why not?"

"I'm allergic to them."

She snickered. "What? You get around them and start choking up?"

"Something like that."

"That's pathetic."

"I never said I was proud to be allergic to horses."

"But you seem fine right now."

"It shows up in different ways."

"Like?"

"Unmentionable ways."

"Oh." Her eyes widened. "Oh!"

"No, not that way, but different, nonetheless."

"Oh."

"Do you realize you say 'oh' a lot?"

"Oh?"

He nudged her with his shoulder.

She laughed and said, "Bully."

"I'm a weenie." He held out his elbow and nudged her. "Take my arm, Joanie. I'm freezing out here."

She found she could and did. "Complain, complain."

"Now you're talking."

"You two are walking so slow, we caught up with you."

Kyle's voice startled Joan. She hadn't even heard them coming up behind her. "This ol' coot is having trouble keeping up with me."

"Ol' coot, is it? I was 'survivor' a second ago."

Laughing, she slapped his arm and squeezed it.

"We're taking a long walk," Kyle said, "maybe a couple hours. Are y'all heading back?"

Joan looked up at Gil. "What do you think, ol' coot? Can you handle fifteen more minutes? Then we'll turn back."

"I can if you can."

"I can." She looked at Kyle as they walked past. "Y'all be careful. It's wild out here. You never know when you might trip over a monster."

"Right, Mom. You'll protect her, won't you, Gil?"

He patted Joan's hand and squeezed it. "Now I'm 'protector.' Will wonders never cease?"

TWENTY

"Andrea, it's not funny anymore. Come on out. I concede." David's eyes had adjusted to the night, and he didn't see her anywhere. Where could she be?

He walked to the barn. The doors were latched. He checked behind brush, around the corner. She couldn't be over here. She wasn't that far ahead of him. He would have seen her if she'd gone this way.

He grinned. *The cars. Of course.* She was hiding behind the row of cars. He jogged over to them. "Andrea, come on. You win. I won't chase you anymore." Squatting, he looked under all the cars at once. "Come on, honey. This is spooking me." He checked the beds of three trucks. "It's not funny anymore, Andrea. I mean it."

Where was she? A chill sprang up his back as a terrifying thought entered his mind. She was hurt. She had tripped over something and hit her head. "Andrea!" He started running. "Andreeeaaaa!"

Racing to the side of the house, he saw the bushes. "Andrea!" He leaned over but the bushes were too wide for him to see anything behind them. She wouldn't have gone back there anyway. "Come on, Andrea! I'm going back inside. You'll be out here by yourself." Panic had him plunging both hands through his hair. Where *was* she?

He was near the dining room window when he heard a sliding click. Only one thing made that sound. *A gun.* He whirled around and faced a man holding a gun aimed right at David's heart. "What—"

"Shut up! *I'm* in charge here, not you."

Without moving a muscle, David glanced around the yard. "Where is she?" Swallowing hard, he rubbed his hands on his jeans. "Where *is* she?" *Oh, God, don't let her be dead.*

The man stepped back and nodded at the bushes. "Back there. Get her and bring her inside."

David scrambled behind the bushes and saw her. "Oh, no," he whispered, crouching beside her, his shaking fingers touching the side of her neck. Squeezing his eyes shut, he tried to stop his own heartbeat from pounding so loud, but he couldn't. It seemed an eternity before he felt her pulse, and relief washed over him.

"Pick her up!"

"Shhh, Andrea," David whispered as she stirred.

When her eyes slowly opened, she gasped and grabbed his shirt. "David! There's someone—!"

Her hands were shaking. Leaning over, he whispered, "I know, sweetheart. Can you stand?"

She pulled herself closer to him as she spotted Jesser. "He has a gun. He has a gun."

"Andrea, be calm," he whispered. "We *have* to stay calm. Now, stand up and hold onto my arm, honey, okay?"

She nodded and, with his help, stood.

With the gun, the man indicated the back door. "Inside. And don't try anything heroic." He took a step back. David noted the good deal of distance between them as he helped Andrea up the steps to the mudroom.

"Take off your boots and shoes."

Leaning into the walls, they both did. The concrete felt cool under David's feet. He looked around, trying to think of something he could do. Grab the door as the gunman came through it? Tackle him?

"Inside. Quietly. We wouldn't want to wake up any of the women and children, would we?"

The man waved them into the living room. "David, grab the phone and yank the wires out of the wall. Good, now pull two chairs over here, two feet apart. Good. Now, Andrea, you sit here and David, there."

"Who are you? Why are you doing this?"

Jesser nodded. "An inquisitive mind. Gil must be proud, even though you haven't spoken a civil word to him in a year."

The man knew too much. David's stomach churned. How did he know so much about his family? He studied the man's long black hair, his medium frame, his dark skin. "Do I know you?"

The man laughed. "Oh, that's rich. Don't you know who your friends are, David?"

"A friend wouldn't be doing this."

"Does the name Gordon Jesser mean anything to you?"

David felt the blood drain right out of his face. The man who had killed Margot and Gerald McKenzie. His mind raced with the possibilities of why he was here. April? Kyle? *Natalie?*

"I see it does. How nice to be remembered." Jesser pulled up a chair across from them and set it against the wall. "Now, we'll just wait for the others to get back."

"Why? What do you want?"

"That's a fair question, David, but I'm not going to answer it right now, because if I've calculated correctly, I'd have to answer it three times." Jesser smiled as the gun touched the fingers on his left hand, one at a time. "Let's see. Once for you. Once for Joan and Gil—that's two. And once for Kyle and Natalie. That's three."

With his eyes on Andrea, Jesser scratched his temple with the barrel of the gun. David's jaw tightened at the leering look in his eyes.

"You have to be the most beautiful woman I've ever seen."

Andrea felt sick to her stomach and closed her eyes. This was the man Natalie had told her about, the man who had killed his scam partner, Margot. *Oh, God, please protect us. Please keep Bella safe. Warn the others somehow, Lord. Help us. Help us!*

"I bet you're used to ogling, aren't you, Andrea?"

Wary, she said nothing, and just watched him.

"Aren't you, girl?"

The smile on his face had turned to a sneer. Out of the corner of her eyes, she saw David look at her, and she found the courage to answer. "Yes," she whispered and lowered her eyes.

"Do you like to be ogled, Andrea?"

She took a shallow breath and shook her head. "No."

Jesser cocked an ear. "What's that?"

Her bottom lip quivered. "No."

"You mean you don't like men to notice you, a pretty thing like you? I thought women liked to be noticed."

How did she answer that? The shaking in her hands had crawled inside her stomach, and she felt nauseous. "I think I'm going to be sick."

"Well, throw up on David. He'll catch it."

David leaned forward. "Look. There's a bucket in the mudroom. Could I get it for her?"

Jesser licked his lips. "Yeah," he said as he waved him toward the door. "But don't try anything or she's dead. I'll give you five seconds. One."

David jumped up.

"Two."

Opened the door.

"Three."

Grabbed the bucket.

"Four."

Raced toward his chair.

"Five," Gordon said at the exact moment David sat down. "Put it between you two."

The room was spinning. Andrea put her hand on her stomach and swallowed, but the queasiness wouldn't go away. She tried to swallow again, made a little gasping sound, leaned over, and fell out of her chair.

David must have reached out to put his hand on her back, because Jesser said, "Don't, David. She's a big girl. She can handle this."

No, I can't. Her head was spinning, her stomach was churning, and she was absolutely terrified for Bella. Did he know she was upstairs? Nausea coursed through her as she glanced at Jesser.

"Are you okay, Andrea?"

He almost sounded like a concerned father. "Yes," she swallowed. "I think so. Just dizzy."

She was more frightened than she'd ever been in her life. Her whole body was shaking now. She tried, desperately, to make it stop but she couldn't. Tears filled her eyes as she squeezed them shut. *Oh, God, help me get control. Please.* She kept her eyes closed and continued praying.

Slowly, her face relaxed.

Her body stopped trembling.

She sighed, deeply, and opened her eyes.

Nothing had changed. Jesser was still holding a gun on them, but she felt strength unlike anything she'd ever experienced. She pushed off the floor and sat in her chair again.

"What is your life like in Granston, Joanie?"

652

Too busy. Lonely. "Oh, I don't work, per se, but I volunteer a lot. The hospital, women's organizations, the orphanage, that sort of thing."

"I can add 'modest' to your many favorable attributes."

With a laugh, she said, "By all means, Gil, add whatever you think makes me look good."

"Your looking good needs no supplementation."

Charmed, she did laugh. "Was that a compliment? I do believe that was a compliment."

Gil was silent.

"I also believe I've just embarrassed you."

"The truth needs no supplementation either."

He fascinated her. Smiling, she said, "Tell me about your life in Granston, Gil."

"I *do* work, too much actually. Some might consider me a workaholic, but I've got a lot on my plate."

"Where do you like to vacation?"

"Anywhere I can scuba dive. I love the ocean, uncovering secrets, finding treasures."

"Treasures?"

"Sea shells, unbelievably beautiful plants, a world unlike what we experience here above water, full of bold colors, odd-looking creatures, sunken ships."

"You make it sound so romantic. When I think of being in the ocean, I think of sharks seeking me out for dinner. Do you go snorkeling often?"

"Scuba diving. And, yes, three or four times a year. What do you consider a wonderful vacation?"

"Hawaii. And snorkeling is about all I've done there, besides, of course, swimming and surfing."

"I've been to Hawaii many times. It's one of my favorite places on earth. When did your husband die?"

She almost choked. Where had *that* question come from? She wasn't sure she wanted to go in that direction but answered him anyway. "In February, it'll be three years."

"Cheryl died a year ago."

Sadness draped his words, and because of it, they lapsed into silence for a few steps. "Are you about ready to start back, Gil?"

"Are you?"

"Yes. I think my body's asking me why in the world I'm torturing it today with riding and now walking." She laughed as he expertly spun her in the opposite direction.

"I believe that was a square dance move."

He chuckled. "It was. We have a great caller in Burl Hanson. The club meets every third Thursday of the month."

She didn't mind when his arm remained comfortably around her shoulder. "I used to square dance in college. I haven't done it since."

"It's like riding a bike. You never forget. Maybe I can jog that memory of yours at our next meeting."

"I'd like that. Did you just ask me out on a date?"

"It was merely a suggestion."

"Then call me when we get back to Granston and let's make it an official date."

The anger sizzled through David like a lit fuse. When Jesser leaned toward Andrea with a smug smile and said, "Little lady, I want your cell phone," it took everything in him not to lean over and grind a fist in his face. It made David sick to see fear in Andrea's eyes as she nodded at Jesser. "It's in my purse, in my bedroom."

David glanced at her, but his eyes didn't linger. He didn't want Jesser to see the hope in his eyes that Andrea might have a chance to call 9-1-1.

"A little eager to get it, aren't you, sweetheart?"

David felt as if he were looking into pure evil when Jesser's gaze flicked to his. "I tell you what, Andrea." He made a point of keeping his eyes on David's while he held up his watch. Another long moment, and he glanced at his watch. "I'll give you five seconds—"

"My bedroom's upstairs. It'll take longer than that."

He seemed to consider it, then smiled. "All righty. Since you've been a little under the weather, I'll give you twenty-five seconds to go get your purse. If you're not back by then, you know what'll happen to our friend here. Ready?" Like a father encouraging a daughter, Jesser smiled warmly at her. "One."

Studying his watch, he stopped counting after the first ten seconds.

Andrea raced down the upstairs hallway, then David heard nothing. He squirmed, his hands wet with perspiration. He closed his eyes and took a deep breath. *Hurry, Andrea!* Unconsciously, he kept up the count when Jesser stopped. Craning his neck toward the upstairs loft, David breathed a sigh of relief when he heard Andrea's quick steps down the hall, down the stairs, into the dining room.

Breathless, she plopped into her chair with two seconds to spare.

"My, my, but you two are swift of foot. Throw me your purse, Andrea." While he caught it and rifled through it, David tossed a quick wink at Andrea.

Looking at Andrea's phone, Jesser said, "David? Do you have a cell phone?" Before he could answer, Jesser said, "I know what you're thinking. Let's see if I'm right, shall we? You're thinking, 'If I say yes, then Jesser's got my cell phone and I won't be able to use it. If I say no, then maybe I can get to it and use it without Jesser's knowledge.' Am I right?"

When David didn't answer, Jesser leaned forward and very quietly said, "Am I right, David?"

What could he do but answer him? He nodded, wanting more than anything to ram the gun into his pompous face.

"Let me help you decide then, David. If your cell phone rings, Andrea is dead. There, now." He grinned from ear to ear. "Did that help you decide to tell me the truth?"

"Yes." *Jerk.*

"All right. I'll ask you again. Do you have a cell phone, David?"

His jaw tightened. He had never felt more helpless than he did at this moment. "Yes."

"Where is it?"

"In my bedroom."

"I'll give you five—"

"My room's at the top of the stairs, all the way at the end."

"How about ten, David? Do you think you can make it in ten?"

"Twenty, for sure."

Jesser playfully shrugged. "I'm a reasonable man. I'll give you twenty seconds. One."

David raced up the stairs, hurried down the hall to his room, picked up the phone, and ran back down. He knew he had no time to do anything else. Without breathing heavily, he handed Jesser the phone and sat.

"Three seconds before time was up, David. Very good."

Shuffling footsteps and muffled voices sounded outside the front door. Jesser's head popped up, his face like flint. He waved his gun frantically at David and Andrea. "One word, one movement, and one of you is dead." His voice sounded like grating sand when he whispered through gritted teeth.

Jesser slipped into the hallway and peered around the doorjamb, the gun leveled at David and Andrea. His gaze slid to the front door, and they all waited with bated breaths for the door to open.

"I've so enjoyed our walk, Gil. I have to be honest and tell you that I haven't enjoyed a man's company this much in a very long time. Thank you."

"It's been my pleasure, Joanie. And, likewise, I've thoroughly enjoyed being with you. You're a breath of fresh air."

Joan noticed the porch swing moving. "Would you like to sit for a few minutes? It's out of the breeze."

"Sure." He chuckled. "Anything to get off these feet. It's quiet here, isn't it? Peaceful. I like it."

Andrea hated anyone else walking into this insanity, but the odds of four against one were better than two against one. She placed a hand over her stomach and felt as if she was going to be sick.

Jesser sneered at her. "If you throw up," he whispered, "you'd better be quiet. I'd hate to have to kill David because you made too much noise."

She wanted to suggest that a gun discharging would probably be louder than she would be, but she didn't. Nodding quickly, she glanced at the door expectantly. Whoever was outside wasn't making a sound. Either they were kissing or hugging or sitting on the front porch swing as she and David had this afternoon.

Jesser held the gun on them while he crept to the window and moved the curtain. He tiptoed back to his chair. "David, does your father have a cell phone?"

So it was Gil and Joan outside.

David gritted his teeth. "Yes."

"Call him. Tell him you're having a problem with the, uh, the toilet, that you couldn't reach Kyle or Natalie."

"My father knows nothing about plumbing. Besides, we haven't talked in a year. He'd think it strange that I call him in the first place, much less about a toilet."

"Okay, okay." Jesser rubbed his chin, frowning. "Andrea, call him," he reached for the phone and handed it to her, "and tell him he had an urgent call from his—David, does he have a brother?"

So, he didn't know everything about them, Andrea thought.

"No," David answered, "he's an only child."

"Are either of his parents alive?"

"No."

"Who would call him here with something urgent?"

"I don't know, Jesser. My father and I haven't—"

"Yeah, yeah, you aren't talking. Okay. Andrea. Call him and tell him Bella's sick, that you couldn't reach Kyle, and David's truck won't start. That you need to get her to the doctor—yeah, that's it." He nodded quickly. "That'll work. Make it convincing, little lady, or your friend dies."

"All right." She looked at the phone. "What's his number, David?"

"I don't know."

Jesser yanked the phone out of Andrea's hand and cursed at her. "Fine. We'll go to plan B. Go to the door, Andrea, and tease them about being outside in the cold. Tell them you've made hot chocolate for all the walkers."

Andrea swallowed, nodded, and made herself stand. Her legs were wobbly, but she gritted her teeth and made it to the door. Putting a hand on the doorknob, she took a deep breath, and opened it. "H-Hello? Who's out there?"

"It's Gil and Joanie. We're sitting on the porch. Is that Andrea?"

She stepped outside and chafed her arms in the cold breeze. "Yes. I, uh, have some hot chocolate on in the kitchen, on the stove, and, uh, thought you might like to have some." She looked toward Jesser, who was standing behind David's chair with the gun resting against

David's temple. "Won't you come in and have some?"

With a concerned look on her face, Joan stood. "Andrea, are you feeling all right? You look a little pale." As a mother would, she touched her face. "No fever. Are you not feeling well, honey?"

"I was a little queasy, but I'm fine now. Oh," she smiled wanly, "I washed my hands before I, uh, before I made the hot chocolate."

"Well," Joan laughed, "we're all talked out, aren't we, Gil? Come on." She reached back and took his hand. "That was very sweet of you to do this, Andrea." Joan followed her inside, and then gasped. "What in the world?"

Andrea said. "Just don't—"

Gil shut the door and turned around. He stopped dead in his tracks when he saw Jesser holding the gun against David's head. Gil's face turned as white as a sheet, and he took an urgent step toward Jesser. "What are you doing? What do you want? I'll give you anything you want, just don't hurt him."

Andrea placed a hand on his arm. "Please, Mr. Zachary—"

"Shut up, Gil, unless you want to see David with a bullet in his head." Jesser took a step back and indicated the rest of the dining room chairs. "Gil, grab two chairs and put them two feet apart, here, behind David and Andrea."

Andrea nudged him. "Please."

"Now, Gil!" Jesser cocked the gun. "Get the chairs *now!*"

A pale Gil jerked, looked back at Joan, walked to the chairs, picked up two, and woodenly sat them behind the other two chairs.

Andrea felt as if she had no form. Blackness swept over parts of the room. She watched everyone disappear into it except Joan. When Joan turned toward her, she screamed Andrea's name then disappeared into the blackness and silence.

Blessed, blessed silence.

TWENTY-ONE

Essie was on a ship, tossing in a violent storm. She rolled from one side of the ship to the other, reaching out, trying to grab onto anything that was bolted down. Waves swept over her as the wind and rain slashed at her body, slamming her against a metal pipe. A pain shot through her leg. She whimpered, sat up, and reached for her leg.

Just as she did, she heard a man's voice say, "Pick her up, Gil."

What? She rubbed the muscle cramp in her leg and listened. The man said something else. She couldn't make it out. Was this some kind of a parlor game? He sounded much too serious for a game. No, she thought as she strained to listen. Something was dreadfully wrong.

She slid off the bed and into her slippers as the man yelled, "Now!"

"Oh, dear Lord," she whispered as she crept to her bedroom door and ever-so-quietly opened the door a sliver. Through the banister poles, she saw a man holding a gun on David, Andrea, Joan and Gil. She didn't recognize the man, but she'd bet her bottom dollar it was Gordon Jesser. She watched in horror as the man put the gun to Joan's head and told Gil to pick up Andrea.

"Is something wrong with your hearing, Gil? I said pick her up now!"

As Gil walked toward Andrea, the man said, "Bring her over here and put her next to the china cabinet. That way, I can keep my eye on her."

Gil did and felt for a pulse.

"Is she alive?"

"Yes, she must have fainted."

"Then she'll come to in a minute or so. Joan, she's in your charge. Take care of her. One misstep, and David is dead, got that?"

"Yes." Joan sat beside Andrea and held her limp hand.

"Gil, let me introduce myself. My name is Gordon Jesser—"

Essie gasped. *Oh, dear Lord, it is him!* She wanted badly to panic a little more, but she couldn't. She had to keep her head. Where were Kyle and Natalie? They weren't in the house. Oh, yes, she'd heard them say they were going for a walk. *Think! Think!* What could she do to warn them?

The phone. Call the police! As carefully as possible, she turned the knob and shut the door. Rushing quietly to the phone, she lifted the receiver. Not a sound. Of course, he cut the lines.

"Do you have a cell phone, Joan, Gil?" Jesser's voice.

Straining to hear, there was silence for a moment or two, then Jesser said, "Good, good. We're getting quite a collection of cell phones here, aren't we, folks? Put it on the table, Gil, with the others. Neatly. In a row, touching. There, that looks good. Now, we all sit and wait for the star attractions, Kyle and Natalie. It's just not a party without them, is it, kids?"

Essie walked to the window and looked out. They were coming! They couldn't be more than three hundred yards from the house! The light was bouncing with each step they took.

She grasped her hands and wrung them. How could she warn them? What could she do?

Oh, God, help me think of something!

The light! She was upstairs, on the corner, across from the living room where Jesser had everyone captive. She would have to place something along the base of her door so Jesser wouldn't be able to see the light. If she signaled Kyle, maybe he would come to her window. *Please, Lord, let him see the light and come to my window.*

With her foot, she quietly shoved the circular rug by her vanity table next to the door. She made certain no light could be seen. Then she turned the light on, then off. On, off. On, off.

She paused and continued to pray. Then, on, off—three times. Pause. On, off—three times. Pause. On, off—

"I am absolutely freezing out here, Kyle. The wind's picked up, and the temperature's dropped." Natalie snuggled closer under his arm. There was strength in them and in his upper body, even though he was lean. "I'm glad we're going back. Well, would you look at that."

"What?"

She pointed. "Look at the house. That light has a short."

Kyle was quiet for a moment. "It's not a short—it isn't random. It's almost like a signal. Watch. Three on, then a break. See? Three on, a break."

"But what could it mean?"

"Maybe David and Andrea are playing a game or something."

"In this wind?" Natalie shook her head. "It doesn't make sense." She watched the light. "You know what, Kyle? I think that's Aunt Essie's room. The far corner there." Then she stopped and gasped. "Oh, no. Jesser's here! I know it! Turn off the flashlight!"

He did. "How do you know?"

"One day, Aunt Essie and I came up with a plan to turn the porch light—any light, really—on and off over and over if Jesser was in the house, so it would warn anyone coming up to the house." She stared at the light. "He's here, Kyle. I know it. That signal is from Aunt Essie."

"That means everyone inside the house is in trouble."

She grabbed his arm. "The children! Oh, Kyle, April and Bella!"

"But how did Aunt Essie get away?"

"She was getting ready for bed when we started the card game. Maybe he just left her in there to sleep. There's no way for anyone upstairs to escape anyway."

"Come on." He took her hand. "We'll go to her window and throw a rock at it."

"It could be a trap."

"A better trap would be using someone on the first floor, not the second. Hopefully, she'll be watching for us. Come on."

David watched as Andrea moaned, fluttered her lashes, and looked at Joan. "What happened?"

Joan leaned over, "You fainted, Andrea. Just stay calm, honey."

She gasped. "Bella? Is Bella... is Natalie...?"

Joan stroked her arm. "They're all right. Kyle and Natalie are outside walking, remember? Bella's asleep upstairs."

David heard Jesser curse and watched him walk back to the dining room after he'd looked out the front window. He reminded David of a sleek, great cat with evil in its eyes, stalking a deer who had miraculously outwitted him.

"Where are they?" he thundered. "Why aren't they here?"

Gil said, "They told us they wanted to take a long walk."

"Take off your shoes and socks, Gil. Joan, get yours off."

Joan slipped out of her shoes, and Gil groaned as he slowly bent over.

"David, slap your father. I don't want to hurt my hands."

Confused, David frowned as he looked at Jesser, at his father.

"I said slap Gil, David. He needs to be disciplined for disobeying me. Now, do it."

"I can't."

Jesser pointed the gun at Gil's head and smiled smugly. "Now can you do it, buddy?"

"All right." With apology in his eyes, David wiped his sweaty hands on his jeans and took a moment before he turned and slapped his father across the face.

"Harder."

David gritted his teeth and avoided his father's eyes. The *whack* sounded loud in the quiet room.

"Better, better, but you can make it harder, can't you, David? From what I understand, you've probably wanted to smack him real good for ignoring you this last year, haven't you?"

No, no, not like this. Hurt him? Never. "No."

"Excuse me?"

David looked at his hands.

He felt utterly helpless to stop this madness. "Yes," he said and looked into his father's eyes with an apology in his own.

"Good, good. I'd like to see blood this time. Can you do that for me, David? Can you give me some blood this time?"

He deliberately aimed for his father's mouth and nose. *Dad, I'm so sorry.* Blood trickled out of Gil's nose and into his open mouth as he leaned back in his chair, his head against the wall.

"Good job. That was much better. Now, Gil, take off your shirt and clean yourself up."

When Gil didn't move, David began to unbutton his shirt.

"What a good son you are, David. You make a father proud, doesn't he, Gil?"

"Yes, he does." Gil worked first one arm, then the other out of his shirt, leaving his undershirt on.

David swiped it out of his hands and wiped his father's face. He wanted, desperately, to smack the smile off Jesser's face. His father moaned. Their eyes connected. "I'm sorry," he mouthed, and his father blinked twice. Tears came to David's eyes. He mouthed, "I'm sorry," again, folded his father's shirt, and wiped his eyes.

"Ah, we're having a tender moment here between father and son. That's what life is all about, isn't it, chicks? So many lessons to learn, so little time. Sit, David." Tapping the gun against his mouth, Jesser turned toward Andrea and Joan. "How's our little beauty doing?"

Andrea pressed her lips together. "I'm fine."

"You're awake. Good. Get in your seats, girls. No slacking off because you're females. Which reminds me, where's Regina? Did she go beddy-bye?"

"Yes," David answered, his hands fisting.

"Oh, but I wanted to see her again. She and I had an intimate moment at a party last summer. She'll be so disappointed she didn't get to see me again." He nodded at David. "Go upstairs and see if you can rouse our Regina Cantina. She'll be thrilled. Really, she will."

Kyle motioned Natalie to be quiet as they crept under Aunt Essie's window and looked up. The lights were still going on and off. Kyle found a little pebble and tossed it at her top window. The light remained on as Aunt Essie's head appeared in the window. She waved at them frantically.

"It *is* a signal!" Natalie waved to her aunt.

Aunt Essie unlocked the window and raised it without a sound, then lifted the storm window. "Oh, my dears!" she hoarsely whispered. "I prayed and prayed that—never mind. Gordon Jesser is here! He has a gun. He's in the living room, and he has Gil, Joan, David, and Andrea in there. He's threatening to *kill* them if they don't do what he wants."

With his heart racing, Kyle whispered, "Is April still asleep?"

"I haven't seen or heard either of the children."

Relieved, he asked, "Do you know if he's alone?"

"I think he is."

"Hang on, Aunt Essie. I'm going to get a ladder." He remembered seeing one leaning against the west wall near the back door. He retrieved it and positioned it under her window.

Climbing up quickly, he tossed his cell phone to Natalie. "I can't get a good signal yet, so keep trying 9-1-1." He reached the top. "Aunt Essie, where are they positioned in the room?"

She tapped her bottom lip. "Okay. Let's see. There are four chairs against the south wall, two in front, two in back. Jesser is against the north wall, where the china cabinet is. He's sitting in a chair, holding a gun on them. Andrea fainted. David's without a shirt and had to slap Gil, so he's a little out of it. Oh, Kyle, what are we going to do?"

Kyle pushed on the storm window until it was fully up. Carefully and quietly, he and Natalie climbed inside. Kyle shut the curtains. We'll leave the window open in case we have to make a quick exit. Who's next door?"

"Natalie's mother, Regina."

"I know I advised y'all to lock your doors, but did I give you a key to your doors?"

Both women shook their heads.

"Great. Now what?"

"Yes," Natalie whispered into the phone. "I have an emergency. There's a man here at Fairfield Ranch, 21567 Cattleman Road. He has a gun. He's holding thirteen people hostage, including two children. He's alone. Please hurry. Yes, I'll stay on the line."

"We can either try to do something or wait on the police."

Natalie nodded at him and spoke into the phone. "Yes. He's slim, five-ten. Aunt Essie, what's he wearing? Here, you tell her."

As Aunt Essie described him to the dispatcher, Kyle leaned into Natalie's ear. "I vote for doing something now. No telling—"

Loud knocking startled them. They all held their breaths and stared at the adjoining door.

"Aunt Regina? It's David. Can you open the door, please?"

"Oh, no." Natalie mouthed. "He wants to see my mother."

"Aunt Regina? It's David. Can you open the door, please?"

"David?" Regina's voice sounded muffled. "What do you want? I'm not dressed."

"There's someone here who wants to see you. He says he's an old friend."

"Here?" There was a long pause. "What's his name?"

"Gordon Jesser."

"What?"

"Aunt Regina, he has a gun to Gil's head, and he's going to kill him if you don't come down."

"A note!" Kyle whispered. "Slip a note under the door. Where's some paper?"

"Yes, ma'am, I'm still holding." Aunt Essie opened her desk drawer and pulled out a sheet of paper. She handed it and a pen to Kyle. "Yes, they're in the dining room, on the north side of the house."

In bold letters, he wrote, "Open this door," and shoved the paper under the door, sliding it back and forth so she would see it.

In a matter of seconds, the lock clicked. "Thank God." Natalie quickly opened the door. "Mom, Jesser's here."

In her long pajamas, Regina hugged Natalie. "What are we going to do? Does he really have a gun on Gil?"

"Yes. If he wants you downstairs, you have to go, so we can have a chance to get to Kyle's room. He has a weapon in there. The police are on their way, but it'll take twenty minutes at least for them to get here. Just do what he wants, okay?"

Regina nodded quickly, kissed and hugged her daughter again. "I love you. Always remember that."

"Mom, nothing's going to happen."

"Aunt Regina?" David's voice was muffled behind the door. "Jesser says if you don't come out right now, that he's going to shoot me in the back."

"I love you, Natalie," she whispered and ran and opened the door.

Kyle was grateful Regina had the presence of mind to shut her door. Listening intently, he waited several heartbeats to make sure she was downstairs before he moved. "Aunt Essie, get back in bed. If Jesser checks on you, pretend to sleep like the dead but whatever you do, don't wake up. If he thinks you're a deep sleeper, all the better."

"I love you, Aunt Essie," Natalie hugged her. "If this works out, just remember it was you who saved the day."

"Nonsense," Aunt Essie whispered. "I love you, Natalie, and you, Kyle. Take care. Yes," she frowned into the phone as she waved good-bye to them, "I'm still here."

Andrea felt sick to her stomach again. Regina walked down the stairs, obviously frightened but trying hard not to show it by lifting her chin as Jesser walked toward her.

"Well, hello, Beautiful." Jesser held out his hand as if he and Regina were at a gala ball and she was the long-awaited debutante. When she didn't take his hand, he snapped his fingers and pointed the gun at her. She took his hand.

"I have really missed you, Beautiful. Have you missed me?"

"No," she answered too quickly, and Andrea felt for her as Jesser yanked her against his chest and put the gun under her chin. In a quiet voice, he said, "I don't think I heard you right, Regina Cantina. I said, 'Did you miss me?' and *you* saaaaid?"

"Yes."

"Ah, now, that's better. The truth is always best, isn't it?"

"Yes." Her voice seemed as stiff as her back appeared.

"Beautiful, don't you remember what a good time we had last summer?" He traced her chin with the gun and lowered his voice, as if, Andrea thought, he was speaking to the woman of his dreams. "You hated to see me leave, didn't you, sugar?"

With her eyes closed, she answered, "Yes."

Jesser laughed out loud. "You are priceless, Regina. Really. Now, go sit down like a good little girl, and let's all wait for Kyle and Natalie to get back. Joanie, how *are* you, dear?"

"Fine."

"Good, good. And Gil, does that boo-boo your son gave you hurt very much?"

"No."

"Character." Jesser proudly smiled and winked at Regina as she sat in the chair David provided. "That's what I like to see in the children of today. Character. It's learned from facing difficult situations and coming out a winner. Wouldn't you agree?"

No one answered. Andrea noticed that everyone stared at him with varying expressions of uncertainty.

He slammed a fist into the wall, making a dent. "I *said,* children, 'Wouldn't you *agree?*'"

"Yes," they all answered in unison.

He immediately calmed and smiled at them, a smile usually given amongst friends. "You all must be wondering why I'm here tonight."

No one acknowledged him.

"Aren't you?"

"Yes."

"Then, since you're so curious, I'll tell you. Regina, my beautiful, I've selected you as my adventure capitalist. Money, money, money. There is so much I want to see in this world. After I kill everyone here, you and I can travel together." He tapped his chin with his gun. "I was thinking it would be a nice touch to have Natalie holding April when I kill them."

Regina quickly stood. "No!"

Jesser pointed the gun at her. "Or you. It could be you instead. I'd hate that, really. I'd hoped you'd go with me after your investment tonight. But if you die, Natalie could go with me just as well."

Regina sank to her chair, crying silently, visibly shaking.

"Mommy?"

Andrea jerked. *Oh, God, no, not Bella.* She was standing at the top of the stairs, rubbing her eyes. "Yes, sweetheart?"

"What was that noise?"

"Nothing, sweetheart. Go on back to bed."

"Mommy, I'm scared."

Andrea turned to Jesser and lowered her voice. "May I put her back to bed, please, Mr. Jesser?"

"Certainly, dear. How long do you think it will take you?"

"Sometimes I have to sing to her to get her back to sleep."

"One minute, then?"

"Whatever you give me."

"I'm proud of your attitude, Andrea. Let's make it two minutes. I'll warn you when you have ten seconds left, and you'd better be back down here, or—" Jesser placed the tip of the gun on his chin as his gaze roamed around the room. "Let's see. Who would I like to kill if Andrea doesn't make it back on time?"

Gil looked up at that particular moment, and Jesser said, "Joanie. I'd like to kill Joanie if you're not back on time."

As Andrea walked past him, Gil lowered his head and closed his eyes.

TWENTY-TWO

Kyle jimmied the stubborn lock as quietly as possible. "One more room, and we'll be to my room."

With her mouth next to his ear, Natalie whispered, "The police should be here soon, shouldn't they?"

"I don't know." The lock clicked. He quietly opened the door.

And there stood Lenore Carsdale. "It certainly took you long enough to get in here," she whispered as she tugged them both inside. "There's a lunatic holding everyone hostage downstairs."

Kyle nodded. "That's why we're sneaking into your room. Why didn't you unlock the door?"

"Because I didn't know who was trying to get in."

"We have to get into my room."

She held up a key. "Here. This should make it easier for you." She placed it in Kyle's hand, curled his hand closed, and patted it. "Good luck. Hopefully, you will save the day and the lives of all downstairs. Let's pray that Jesser won't get his hands on the children."

"That won't happen on my watch," he whispered.

Natalie hugged her quickly. "I love you."

"And I, you, my dear."

Kyle looked at her bed. "Get back under the covers. If Jesser comes in here, sleep like the dead. Don't wake up for any reason."

She nodded.

Kyle inserted the key and turned it. The door opened. He quickly, stealthily, headed for the gun under his pillow.

"Ten, nine, eight—"

Andrea raced down the upstairs hallway, her chest aching from the stress of leaving Bella, knowing what she was about to face.

"Seven, six, five—"

Down the stairs.

"Four, three, two. Very good, Andrea. Because of your attention to detail, Joanie will live a few more minutes at the very least. And now that you're back, we'd like for you to sing for us, wouldn't we, kids?"

668

"Yes," everyone said.

He grinned like an excited two-year-old. "Good, good. Such obedient children. Now," he clapped twice, "pay attention, kids. You may start when you're ready, Andrea. But sing very quietly. We wouldn't want to wake those sleeping."

She placed a hand over her quivering stomach. She sought David's eyes. He nodded slightly, offering her hope. Fortified, she took a deep breath and began to sing. "Jesus loves the little children, all the children of the world; red and yellow, black and white, they are precious in His sight; Jesus loves the little children of the world."

"You have a lovely voice." Jesser looked at the others. "Let's all join her in that song. Andrea, lead us as if we're a choir. Oh, yes, that would be wonderful. In whisper-quiet tones, kids."

With as straight a face as she could muster, she willed herself not to faint. Nausea swam through every cell she owned. She raised her arms, lifted her face to heaven, and began to sing.

The noise was just what Kyle needed.

He quickly checked his gun and grabbed Natalie's hand. "Just passing through," he whispered to Lenore as they scurried through her room. "Remember, like the dead."

He opened Aunt Essie's door. "Passing through. We have the gun." He walked quickly and quietly to the window. "Natalie, I'm going outside."

"I'm going with you."

He turned around. "Not this time. I need to move quickly and quietly. I'd feel a lot better if you were up here with Aunt Essie, just in case. Crawl under her bed. Jesser won't think to look for you there." He leaned forward and kissed her quickly. "Take care of April. Hopefully, I'll see you in a few minutes."

With that, he crawled out the window, down the ladder, and headed for the back porch.

"—black and white, they are precious in His sight; Jesus loves the little children of the world."

Jesser clapped as he held the gun toward the ceiling. "Good, children, good! My, we do have lovely voices, don't we?" He glanced over at the front door. "David, check to see if they're coming. I'm getting rather anxious."

Reluctantly, David stood, walked across the room to the window, and peered out. "No, I don't see anything." He thought about grabbing the doorknob and rushing outside. But he knew someone would die if he did.

"No sign of a flashlight?"

"No."

"Then I think it's time for us to play some parlor games."

David caught Andrea's eye as he walked back to his chair and sat, willing her to be brave. He was so angry that he couldn't do a blasted thing to stop this idiot.

He looked up and found Jesser's smirking eyes on him. "Andrea, dear," he said, without taking his eyes off David, "would you stand, please? I think we would be particularly pleased—" At that moment, a wail came from upstairs. "Was that April?"

No one answered him.

"Once again, children, was that April?"

Everyone said, "Yes."

Like a child in a schoolroom, Joan raised her hand. "I think so. I could go check if you want."

"Would you, Joanie? And bring her down here, please. Let's see. I'll have to kill David if you're not back soon. Two minutes, dear?"

With her legs shaking so violently she thought they would surely fall off, Joan stood, said, "Yes," and walked up the stairs.

"I think, since the men have their shirts off, that Andrea—"

Joan shut the door behind her. "Hello, precious. Are you awake?" She lifted April up and over the bed rail, and almost screamed when a hand touched her back. She quickly turned and saw Lenore, dressed in a long flowing nightgown, standing behind her.

"Are you all right, Joan?"

"Yes," she said as she held April closer. "That man is crazy. I don't know what he wants. Is he going to kidnap April or kill us all or both?"

"I don't know why he would hurt Natalie. She's an innocent bystander in all this."

"Innocence has absolutely no bearing with Gordon Jesser." Behind her, the adjoining door opened.

Essie walked in and held the door as it shut quietly. "Is April all right? When she cried out, I thought for sure Jesser had her."

"He wants to see her."

Essie covered her mouth as she gasped. "No! You can't take her down there."

"I have to, or he'll kill David."

"Kyle has a gun," Lenore whispered. "He's probably close to being inside the house by now. God forgive me, but I hope he puts that man out of commission permanently."

Kyle eased the back door open and stepped inside the mudroom. As quietly as he could, he slipped out of his tennis shoes, left on his socks, and took off his coat. He needed to be free of anything that might prevent him from moving quickly. Carefully, he turned the kitchen doorknob.

The door opened without a sound. He looked around the room as he quietly let out the shaky breath he was holding. *Please, God, help me do this right.*

His heart pounded so hard, he could feel it drumming in his teeth. Stealthily, he took one step inside the kitchen, slid his other foot in, and stood in the dark and the quiet, listening for Jesser's voice down the hall.

"I think, since the men have their shirts off, that Andrea should take her shirt off, too." Another long pause. "What do you men think, huh? Is that a great idea or what?"

That voice. Where have I heard that voice? Kyle moved several feet away from the mudroom, toward the door leading into the hall. Another ten feet, and he'd be at the dining room door.

"Please, Mr. Jesser, don't make me do that."

Andrea. By her voice, she must be near Jesser, possibly even next to him. Kyle slid a few more feet, almost to the doorway, and tried to control his breathing. His heart was racing. His hands were sweating and shaking.

"Ah, now, there's my little girl, April. Are all of you aware that this precious baby is my daughter?"

April! Kyle's hand fisted, his stomach clenched, his teeth bared as he thought of Jesser touching his baby. *Calm down. Calm down.*

"I can see all of you very well, but if one of you makes a move, I'll have to end first April's life and then Joan's."

No! Frantic, Kyle stepped into the hall.

"—and no one would like me to do that, right?"

Kyle made himself take a deep breath. He tried to think. Jesser kept talking as Kyle slid across the wooden floor.

"Then, come here, Joanie, and let me have a look at her." A long pause. "No, I don't want to hold her. You keep her, Joan."

His mother! And April! Near Jesser, by the door. *Think, think!*

"There! You see? She knows her daddy."

Kyle gritted his teeth so hard, his jaw hurt.

Not a sound came from the other room.

"She has her mother's eyes, doesn't she, Joanie?"

Okay. He was getting closer. Down this hallway. A board groaned under his foot and he stopped, frantically listening for any sound from Jesser. He could hardly get a breath past the angry lump in his throat, and his heart hurt from sheer panic. He couldn't afford to make any mistakes now. Too many of the people he loved—

"You didn't like her, did you, Grammie?"

Eight more feet.

"All right. Take her away, Joanie. I've decided to kill someone."

Oh, God!

"You're all going to die tonight but I've decided that Gil, yes, it's going to be you. First in line. Would you stand, please?"

Kyle heard a chair scrape on the floor.

"No!" *David's voice.*

A gunshot.

A scream. Two more screams.

"Mommy?" Bella's voice, upstairs, *"Mommy?"*

"What is it? What in the world is happenin' in here?" *Ernestine, the cook.*

Alert, his ear cocked, Kyle slid toward the door.

"What are you doin' with that gun in your hand? Give me that—" *Ernestine.*

"Bella, go!" *Andrea.* "Turn around and—" *Andrea must be running toward the stairs.*

"I didn't give you permission to leave, Andrea! Stop or I'll shoot!"

Another shot. Screams.

"Stop that!" *Ernestine.*

Chairs scraped, fell against the floor. People were running.

Gunshots. Screams.

Kyle leaned into the doorway, both hands clutching his firearm. Jesser was not two feet in front of him.

Ernestine gasped when she saw Kyle's gun.

Jesser whirled around. Kyle fired his weapon—at Grayson! His friend from the coffee shop!

Another scream as Grayson ducked and raised his weapon.

"Kyle!" *Natalie.*

A gunshot!

Searing pain. Splintering into every part of his body.

"Kyyyyyyle!"

Natalie.

He opened his eyes long enough to see the triumph on Grayson's face. Kyle pointed his gun at his friend. He squeezed the trigger and fired. Grayson sank to the floor.

Natalie's voice, near his ear. "Kyle? Kyle? You're all right. Somebody get me a clean cloth!" She lifted his head.

"Here, here!"

Something soft covering his face.

"The bullet grazed the side of your head, Kyle. There's a lot of blood loss but you're okay. You're okay. Hang in there."

He summoned every ounce of strength he had. "Grayson."

"Grayson?"

"I shot... my friend... from Maudie's."

"He wasn't here. You shot Jesser."

"Jesser?"

"He's dead. It's over, Kyle. It's all over. Jesser is dead."

In the swirling haze, Kyle couldn't think straight. He had shot a friend. He had shot Grayson. Why was Grayson at his ranch?

Natalie stared at the spinning red lights as the ambulance carrying the man she loved drove down the long driveway away from her. An arm wrapped around her shoulder, and she turned into her mother's hug.

"You did very well, sweetheart."

Staring at the lights as they disappeared around the bend, Natalie shook her head. "Kyle did very well, Mother. I only went along for the ride."

"You screamed and distracted Jesser. It probably saved Kyle's life."

"At least he had the presence of mind to shoot Jesser."

A police officer standing on the steps looked over at them and said, "Ma'am, Mr. McKenzie didn't shoot Jesser. The bullet entry was in the back."

Baffled, Natalie blinked several times. "In the back? But none of us had a gun."

"Lenore Carsdale did. She shot Gordon Jesser from the balcony."

"What?" Natalie gasped, as did her mother, and both stared at the officer as if he'd grown wings. "What did you say?"

"Lenore Carsdale is the shooter here, not Kyle McKenzie." The officer took a step back and revealed her grandmother standing behind him in her long nightgown and robe with an I-told-you-so smile on her face. Aunt Essie stood beside her, looking a little lost.

"You shot Jesser, Grandmother?"

She nodded and leaned on her cane. "You know I'm always packing, Natalie Grace. When the shooting started, I walked out of my room and braced against the banister." She lifted her chin. "When I saw Jesser aim his weapon at Kyle, instinct took over, and I shot him."

The officer said, "If all of you have some place to sit this out, please do. The investigators are still working the crime scene."

Natalie said, "Let's go around back, through the kitchen, to the den. We'll put the kids back to bed. It's going to be a long night."

Lenore walked down the steps.

Natalie shook her head in wonder at her, neither of them moving as Regina walked around her mother, took Aunt Essie's arm, and headed to the mudroom.

"So." Natalie crossed her arms and lifted her chin.

"So." Nana raised her brows and lifted her chin.

"You saved Kyle's life."

Joan was walking down the steps holding a sleeping April. Natalie was itching to get her hands on April, but it would have to wait.

"It's what I intended."

"Are you going to expect him to owe you his life after this?"

"I'll expect much more than that. I'll expect him to take very good care of my granddaughter for the rest of her life. And you, him."

Natalie felt the sting of tears. Would the wonders of this night never end? "Oh, Grandmother." She hugged her and pulled back. "Thank you."

"You are too much like me, you know."

"That's why we get along so well, isn't it?"

"When will you be returning to Dallas?"

"I'm not sure I will be."

"What?"

"Nana—"

"You will *not* walk away from your responsibilities, Natalie Grace! Palmers do not shirk their duties! Too much money is involv—" Her grandmother's eyes widened.

"What money?"

Lenore put up a hand, glared at her, and shuffled toward Joan and the others.

"Grandmother!"

An officer called her name, and she turned around. He asked her a couple of questions, and then she hurried to the back of the house.

What had she meant? Too much money for what?

Natalie stopped. Oh, no. She wouldn't.

Of course she would.

A large donation for a job offer?

"To get me away from Kyle." *Oh, Grandmother.*

Right now, she didn't have time to deal with this. She needed to get to her room, change her clothes, and get to the hospital.

David was seething. Pacing back and forth in the barn, he wanted to hit something, mangle something, kick something. He had never been this consumed with anger.

He had sat there and done nothing to protect his father or Andrea! He'd slapped his father! Three times! And that idiot, Jesser, had leered at Andrea, insulted her, ogled her, almost undressed her, and David had sat not two feet away from her and done nothing to protect her!

He should have jumped Jesser.

Or startled him somehow and taken his gun.

Or gotten a message to Gil and devised a plan.

Or moved to tackle him when he returned from looking out the window. Anything!

But he had sat there, in front of Andrea and his father and the others and done absolutely nothing.

How could he live with himself now? How could he ever look Andrea in the eyes again?

He had totally failed her, this gentle woman who wouldn't hurt a fly, who had denigrated herself and called the dog, "Mr. Jesser." This beautiful woman had already captured a good portion of his heart, and he had done *nothing* to help her.

How could she ever look at him again?

Andrea's head jerked toward the barn where a light shone under the barn doors. A shadow passed by. Maybe David was inside. She had looked everywhere for him.

She was so restless. She had lain beside Bella until she fell asleep and then watched her and listened to her deep breathing as it filled her room. "Thank you, God, for sparing all our lives," she'd whispered as her daughter slept.

The images of the night kept swirling in her mind. Everywhere she looked, that monster was sneering at her, or laughing at Gil's pain, or humiliating Regina, or threatening Kyle's little girl.

"And I did nothing to stop him."

For almost an hour, she'd been the closest person to him and just sat there. Just sat there! Over and over, she thought: *I should have grabbed something and hit him over the head. Or, at the very least, tripped him when he walked right past me.*

But she had been too afraid to do anything, so afraid that someone would die because she'd done something stupid.

What kind of a person did nothing? A gutless one.

She had to apologize to David. She didn't want this between them. She wanted, more than anything, for him to know that if it had entered her mind to do something, she would have. Fear for them all had frozen her to her chair.

Gentle knocking. David stalked to the barn doors, lifted the bar, and let one of the doors ease open. Andrea stepped inside, a blush rising from her neck and covering her face.

Searching her face, he noted that she wasn't looking him in the eyes. She must be disgusted with him. "What is it?"

She seemed too pale. "David, I came in here to say that I'm so sorry I let us all down."

What? No. Not Andrea. She had done nothing wrong. He threw up his hands. "What are you *talking* about?"

"I was the closest to him and I could have done something. I should have—"

"No. *I'm* to blame. I did absolutely nothing to protect you or anyone else." Frustrated, he started pacing. "I just sat there and let that *lunatic*—" He punched the air. "I just sat there and did nothing!"

He kept his back to her, his breathing labored. In the quiet that followed, with the scent of hay around them, David's voice seemed utterly small, even to himself. "I'm so sorry I didn't stop him."

Andrea ran to him and threw her arms around his back and hugged him. "David, don't. You were my hero tonight. No, don't pull away. Listen to me. Every time Jesser made you do something, I saw the pleading in your eyes for me to understand. And I *did* understand, David. You did what you had to do for all of us to survive."

Letting go of him, she walked in front of him. "It's the loss of control that we're blaming ourselves for. I felt that when Jason died. Somehow, it was my fault. I should have stopped him from going to work that day. If he'd left just two minutes later, he'd still be alive. If I had taken longer fixing his breakfast, he wouldn't be dead. If, if, if!"

Gently, she touched his arm. "We had nothing to do with this tonight, David. I see that now, through your pain. Jesser deserves the blame for the helplessness we felt. *Jesser's* to blame, David. Not you. Not me."

She looked so angelic with her big, brown eyes imploring him to believe her. She whispered again, "It's Jesser's fault, David. Not ours."

Slowly, gently, he lifted his hand and cupped her chin. His throat was tight with emotion, his heart filled with something he couldn't readily identify, but he knew this woman standing before him was the reason he felt more alive than he ever had in his life.

"Andrea," he murmured, "you are so beautiful to me, inside and out." He searched her eyes for something belonging to him, and he found it. "I'm in grave danger." He wanted to smile at the puzzled look on her face. "I'm in grave danger of falling deeply in love with you."

He half expected her to move away, but she didn't.

Instead, she moved closer and touched his face with cool, gentle fingers. "I'm in grave danger, David, of falling just as deeply in love with you."

She smiled.

He smiled.

Gordon Jesser had not won, after all.

Gil dug his keys out of his jeans pocket and walked toward his SUV. As he did, David and Andrea strolled out of the barn together, arm in arm, smiling at each other. When David looked up and spotted him, his step faltered. He said something to Andrea, and she nodded and continued on toward the back of the house as David walked toward his father.

Gil took a few steps toward him.

"Where you headed, Dad?"

"Natalie and Joan left for the hospital a little bit ago. I thought I'd go check on Kyle and maybe bring Joanie back here when she's ready to leave."

"You probably need a doctor."

Gil laughed. "I look ridiculous, don't I? But I don't need a hospital. I just want to see how Kyle is doing, get some closure with Joan about this mess."

"Would you like some company?"

"I would, but don't you want to get some sleep?"

"I can sleep anytime."

Pleased, Gil opened his door. "Hop aboard then. I just bought this SUV last week. She rides better than a luxury car. You remember Norm Elliott, the salesman at the Ford place?"

Both doors slammed shut at the same time.

"Yeah. Sammy Elliott's grandpa, right?"

Gil started the truck, backed out. "One and the same. He sold this thing to me. At first, I thought he was crazy telling me I should buy it."

"Dad, I'm so sorry I slapped you tonight."

Gil stopped the truck, shoved it into PARK, and reached for him. "Davey—" Tears filled his eyes. *Oh, God, my son is still alive. Thank you. Thank you.*

"I didn't have a choice, Dad. I wanted you to know I'm sorry."

"And I'm sorry I ever gave you a reason to enjoy doing it."

David pulled back. "I didn't enjoy it."

"I know that." Gil chuckled. "It was a joke. We used to like a good joke between us."

"When I hear a good joke, I'll let you know."

Gil laughed, reached over, and clutched David's shoulder. "I've missed you, son." He blinked back tears. "I've missed you more than I can ever say."

"Me, too, Dad, but I didn't want to admit it. A pride thing."

"You come by it honestly. I know all about that pride thing. I enjoyed hearing you at the Cherry Tree last summer. You've made yourself into a fine musician." Man, what those words would have meant to Gil coming from his own father about his dream to build. It wasn't difficult to see that they meant as much to David. "I'm glad you stayed with the music. You've been given a great talent. You knew better than I did what you needed to do with it."

Gil cleared his throat, wanting to say the next words to his son so he would remember them, with clarity, for a lifetime. "I'm so proud of

you."

David's eyes filled with tears, and when he lowered his head to wipe them away, he laughed. Gil looked at him and laughed, too.

"I've always been told that Zachary men don't cry, Dad."

"They do tonight."

Natalie leaned over Kyle and kissed his left temple. He was asleep. The bullet had grazed the side of his head, and when he fell to his back after being shot, his head hit the hard wooden floor. He'd lost a lot of blood, and the pain medications he needed had knocked him out.

But he was alive and well and had already complained to the doctor about being in the hospital on Thanksgiving Day. The doctor said he could leave in the morning if everything looked good.

Natalie leaned over Kyle, stroking his jaw with her finger. "Kyle McKenzie, I have something I want you to know. The hour is late. You're asleep, and I'm exhausted from worrying about you. But the time has come for me to say this."

She rested her head on his shoulder and whispered, "I love you. I think it started the first time I saw you with April, at a time I had no right to begin to love you. Something stirred within me that this was where I was supposed to be, helping you and April."

She lifted her head and drew circles on his chest. "How does one explain something like that and have it make sense?" She shook her head. "Life is strange, and God knows we've had so many twists and turns in our short life together, but this I know. I love you and I love your daughter, and I hope someday you can love me, too. I want us to be a family. I feel in my heart that we already are."

She lay her head on his chest and listened to his heartbeat. It was beating a little too fast. She looked up at the drip. It was fine. She looked at the monitor. Everything seemed in good order.

Then she looked at Kyle. His eyes were open.

"Natalie. I am so in love with you."

She gasped and covered her mouth.

"Will you marry me and be my first and only wife?"

She stood up and leaned over him, so full of love she thought she

680

just might float away. "Yes," she whispered. She kissed his cheek.

"That was nice, but this time, could you aim for my mou—?"

She did and thoroughly kissed him.

"And be the mother of our angel?"

"Oh, yes."

"And live with us out on the ranch?"

"I wouldn't want to live anywhere else."

"And be grateful for all the babies God gives us?"

"Unbelievably grateful."

"Then let's get this done as soon as we can. Are you going back to Dallas?"

"Dallas? What's in Dallas?"

He smiled. "What about your grandmother? Her approval won't be easy to get."

"I already have it. She gave it to me tonight just before I came to the hospital. Did anyone tell you who shot Gordon Jesser?"

"I did. That, I remember. I aimed and fired, and he fell."

"No." She shook her head solemnly. "It wasn't you. My grandmother shot him in the back."

"What?"

"When the shooting started, she left her room and shot Jesser in the back with her own gun."

"I owe her my life."

"All she wants is for you to take good care of me and for me to take good care of you."

TWENTY-FOUR

Bright sunlight welcomed Thanksgiving Day as Natalie walked behind a nurse wheeling Kyle to his truck parked at the curb. The nurse opened the truck door and took Kyle's hand to help him get inside. Then, she stepped back and wished him well just before the door shut.

Natalie waved and walked around to the driver's side, got in, and started the truck. "You're hurting."

"I can handle it. No pain meds today. They make me too sleepy."

"You look like a sheik with your head wrapped up like that."

He winced as he reached for the seat belt. "I keep thinking about Jesser making himself out to be my friend, Grayson. He came here as Grayson to make sure I knew he'd fooled me for two years."

"Probably. You trusted him, Kyle. You did nothing wrong."

"I'll be more cautious."

"Don't give him that power. Stay trusting. The Jessers of this world win too often as it is. Here. Let me get your seat belt." Brushing his hand aside, she reached for the seat belt, tugged it across his chest and almost had it clicked in when she gasped.

"What is it?"

Stunned, she shook her head. "We were singing. My father and I." She looked in the back seat. "That day. We were singing. We always sang when we went somewhere together. I got in the car first. My father wasn't there. Then he got in, buckled up, and we left."

Her hands gripped the steering wheel. "I was eleven. I was sitting in the back. I was small for my age, and he didn't want me in the front seat. He started singing, "The Wheels on the Bus," and I told him I didn't want to sing that song because I wasn't a baby, and then a big orange school bus drove by. He was so excited that he turned around and laughed at me. A big truck pulled out in front of us. I screamed, "Daddy!" She looked at Kyle. "He couldn't stop."

Kyle stroked her arm as she stared out the window.

"We were happy, singing a silly song."

"It was no one's fault. It was just an accident."

"And I have to believe that that day, my father was supposed to go

682

home."

They sat in silence for a few moments. Kyle said, "I was on the phone with my father when he was murdered. I heard Jesser call him a 'nobody' and then shoot him. I blamed myself for asking Dad to listen to my stupid interview on the radio while he was driving out in the middle of nowhere."

"It wasn't stupid. It was important. It was life. Your father, my father. They were living their lives. Their deaths were not our fault."

"That's freeing."

"It is for freedom that Christ has set us free."

He looked at her. "Your worship leader said those words the first Sunday after Margot died. I listened to Good Shepherd's service on the radio."

"I was at that service. *It is for freedom.*" She shook her head. "How many times have I mulled over those four words. Today, I understand one tiny part of what they mean. Forgiveness is freeing."

He nodded. "For both of us. Let's get to the ranch and our families. All of us could have died last night, but no one did but Jesser. It's a day to celebrate second chances for both our families."

She smiled. "Second chances. I feel that way about you."

"I especially do about you. I'm making the right choice this time. And," he checked his watch, "the Cowboys have a second chance today against—I don't remember who they're playing. The game 'll be starting soon."

"Then we better get out to the ranch."

There were far more trucks parked in front than there were yesterday. Kyle recognized his brother Mac's truck. And Bobby's. Luke's. Tim's. Greg's. What was going on?

The front door of the main house opened. Mac and his wife, Marianne, walked out and hurried toward him. Mac helped him out of his truck. "Are you okay, buddy? Mom conference-called all of us last night and told us what happened. We all decided to bring our meals here and spend Thanksgiving together. You should see the dining room. It is stuffed to the gills with food. How are you, buddy?"

Marianne hugged him and whispered, "We heard how brave you

were last night, Kyle. Are you okay?"

Before he could answer their questions, his other brothers came outside, surrounding him with more questions and hugs and back poundings. Bobby, holding one of his twins, said, "We just got here, bro'. Wanted to spend Thanksgiving with you and—"

"You awright, Kyle?" His brother, Tim, and his wife, Arlene—who was very pregnant and holding their little girl—gave him hugs.

"I'm fine. Everybody, this is my fiancé, Natalie."

"Your fiancé?"

"That didn't take long, bud—"

"Congratulations, you two—"

"It's a fine day for congratulations," Luke said as he and his wife, Sarah, joined in with well wishes.

Greg, his oldest brother, and his wife, Daphne, laughed at their children as they converged on Kyle and asked if he could take off his bandage so they could 'see the bullet hole.' "Did it go through your brain, Uncle Kyle?"

As Kyle made his way toward the front porch, his entourage followed along with him. Everyone was laughing, loud, and happy— perfect for Thanksgiving.

His mother stood on the porch, watching her children and their families. Kyle stopped when everyone went inside the house. "This is a true Thanksgiving, isn't it, Mom? If it weren't for Jesser, all the family wouldn't be here."

She nodded. "I'm so grateful everyone's alive and we're all together and that Jesser is gone. Oh, look. Kevin's finally here."

The Thanksgiving meal was over, and the football game on. It was a good thing that all Kyle's brothers and their wives supported the same team—the Dallas Cowboys. It was loud enough in the den—with all the shouting, fist throwing, grumbling over bad plays, and hoorays— without arguing over which team was the best.

Natalie slipped outside. She walked to a corral and watched a colt running and jumping playfully. She smiled at him, absorbing the quiet around her as she looked across the beauty of the ranch and the cattle on a distant rise.

A car door shut behind her. She turned and beamed when her best friend's head popped up at the end of the long row of cars.

"Hey, girl. You look surprised. I told you I'd be here Thanksgiving Day." Laughing, Kath studied Natalie as she walked toward her and then held her tightly in her arms. "Are you all right? Were you hurt?"

"Not physically." Natalie pulled away, so her friend could see her eyes. Eyes were important to Kath. "I'm fine, as you can see."

Like a mother, Kath held Natalie's face and looked her over. "Yes, I can see you are. And Kyle?"

"On the mend. He's inside, watching football with his six brothers and their wives and kids."

"Ah, modern medicine."

"What do you mean?"

"My next book is set in 1870's America. I wish I could go there and see it firsthand, so I wouldn't have to do this painstaking research about all the primitive things Victoria has to deal with." She sighed. "She has a very tough life and doesn't even know it." Kath touched her shoulder. "Are you really okay?"

"Kyle asked me to marry him, and I said yes."

"Oh!" Tears appeared in Kath's eyes as she reached for Natalie. "I'm so happy for you. I *knew* he was the right one for you, but I was so afraid you wouldn't see it. Congratulations, my dear friend." She pulled back. "When's the big day?"

"Valentine's Day. A small, intimate wedding with family and close friends here at Fairfield Ranch."

"It'll be so much fun planning your wedding. You'll make a beautiful bride. Let's go all out on it."

"I'd love to. You and Andrea will make beautiful maids-of-honor."

"We will do our best, just for you."

"Andrea's here, you know."

"Oh! I can't wait to see her. Is she okay?"

"Traumatized, but she has someone who's very interested in helping her get over it."

"Oh, really? A love interest?"

"I'll let her tell you. I think they're out walking right now." She took Kath's hand. "We're all finally together, the three of us. I didn't tell her you were coming because I wanted it to be a surprise."

"What fun! I better get inside then and say hey to that handsome man of yours. If you see Andrea, send her my way." She plucked her luggage out and started toward the house.

Natalie turned back to the corral. David and Andrea came out from behind the barn, walking hand-in-hand as Bella ran toward the playful colt. She turned around, walking backwards, and said, "Can I pet him, Mommy? Can I, can I? Oh, please?"

Natalie smiled. Life goes on.

She thought of that long-ago day when her daddy gave her a dream—an 'unexpected treasure' he had called it.

"You have to have dreams, Natalie. They don't come from here—" he pointed to his head, *"—but from here." He tapped his chest. "You can't dream, sweetheart, without engaging your heart. You have to set your heart free to dream."*

It is for freedom.

"I found the treasure, Daddy," she whispered as she looked over her shoulder toward the house where April and Kyle were. "There were *two* unexpected treasures." She lifted her face toward Heaven and smiled. "But you know that now, don't you?"

She glanced over at David as he lifted a squirming Bella up and over the fence, so she could touch the colt's nose. But when the skittish colt jumped back, Bella squealed, the colt scampered away, and Bella rolled, sobbing, into David's arms.

Natalie remembered a time when her daddy had held her while she tried to pet a colt. She knew Bella would try again when the colt came back to her, as she herself had done so many years ago, when her daddy's gentle, strong hands lifted her up again to give her a second chance.

"Natalie!"

She spun toward Kyle's voice. He was standing on the porch, looking relaxed and happy. She couldn't get to him quickly enough and hurried into his hug. "Oh, I needed this."

"Me, too." His arms tightened around her.

"Thank you, Lord," she whispered, "for keeping all of us safe."

"Amen to that." Kyle stepped off the porch and took her with him. "Let's head for the walking path and find a bench. I want nothing more than you sitting beside me for a while."

"Is the football game over?"

"No, but it'll wait. I just want you right now. Look." He nodded toward Kath and Andrea, laughing and hugging near the back of the house. They both waved exuberantly at Kyle and Natalie, and they waved back.

"They're part of my family, Kyle. I'm so thankful that all our loved ones are together today." Natalie smiled up at him. "I haven't had dessert. Why don't we go inside and have some before your brothers devour everything? Then we'll snuggle while we finish the game."

From Tamara:

I hope you enjoyed getting to know the McKenzie brothers! If you did, would you please post a review on the review site of your choice. And thank you!

Come join me in East Texas for my cozy mystery series, the Sophie O'Brion Mysteries. Sophie is a little quirky, funny, and loves writing mysteries but not living them!. Book 1 in this new series is "The Vacant House" and it is available now.

If you enjoy a good romance, join me in Chapel Lane for "Love, Again," a story of two hurting people who somehow find friendship and possibly more, until trust is needed and neither is able to give it. Will they be able to let go of their painful pasts and find love again?

Made in the USA
Monee, IL
07 March 2025

13633707R00402